The Best Team Ever

Λ Novel of Λmerica, Chicago, and the 1907 Cubs

The Best Team Ever

A Novel of America, Chicago, and the 1907 Cubs

By Alan Alop and Doc Noel

© 2008

Mill City Press

Bascom Hill Publishing Group
212 3rd Avenue North, Suite 570
Minneapolis, MN 55401
612.455.2293
www.bascomhillpublishing.com
www.1907cubs.com

ISBN - 1-935098-02-0
ISBN - 978-1-935098-02-7
LCCN - 2008927942

Book sales for North America and international:
Itasca Books, 3501 Highway 100 South, Suite 220
Minneapolis, MN 55416
Phone: 952.345.4488 (toll free 1.800.901.3480)
Fax: 952.920.0541; email to orders@itascabooks.com

Cover Design by Brent Meyers
Typeset by Tiffany Laschinger

Printed in the United States of America

Alan Alop dedicates this book to the memory of his daughter, Rebecca Lynn Alop, a beautiful and remarkable child.

Doc Noel dedicates this book to the memory of his son, Benjamin Daniel, who played catch often with his Dad, and more catch is always better for fathers and sons.

Foreword

In the early years of the 20th century Chicago was a young city aiming to take its place among the great cosmopolitan centers of the world. This emerging metropolis had all the temperament, growing pains, and blemishes of adolescence. It was less a melting pot than a mosaic of disparate cultures on the brink of degenerating into strife, despair, crime and corruption.

Struggling through this confusion and tumult was a common drive for a fresh start and a better future. Along with all the problems, new opportunities were emerging based on a positive "can do" attitude of accomplishment and achievement by means of honest hard work. Chicago was beginning to assert its own bold new identity.

At this time America was fully embracing its passionate obsession with baseball. More than a sport or pastime, baseball was developing into a unifying force for the city, and later for the nation.

Chicago was treated to its one and only City World Series in 1906, with the White Sox (the "Hitless Wonders") upsetting the Cubs. Despite superior talent the Cubs did not prevail.

The Cubs learned their lesson, and they went on to provide Chicagoans an example of renewal and hope. The 1907 Chicago Cubs meshed into an unstoppable juggernaut that roared on to the World Championship. Overcoming intense personal differences, this collection of remarkable individuals pulled together as a team -- the best team that ever played the game, far and away above their competition. They set a standard that has never been matched.

These Cubs won the right way, with talent, hard work, toughness, and unwavering dedication. Powerful leadership tolerated nothing less than all-out effort, squeezing every measure of resolve from every player in every contest.

Gallant heroes of this legendary team earned the respect and admiration of all layers of Chicago society and captured the imagination of Chicago's youth. Any baseball fan remembers the phrase "Tinker to Evers to Chance." The 1907 Chicago Cubs, by their fierce pride in uncompromising excellence, inspired an entire city to greatness.

This truly magical congruence of the times, the team and the city is properly memorialized in *The Best Team Ever*, so the inspiration of the 1907 Chicago Cubs remains always woven through the fabric of Chicago history.

Robert W. Fioretti
Second Ward Alderman
City of Chicago
January 14, 2008

"I was still just a kid trying to cope with one of the most amazing teams of all time… [T]hey taught me as much baseball in a short, painful time as any opponent I ever met."

Ty Cobb, referring to the 1907 Chicago Cubs

"This [1907] Chicago team [is] considered by many the greatest team that ever took the field… "

Alfred H. Spink, The National Game (1911)

From the Journal of Kid Durbin

Today I journeyed from my home in Lamar, Missouri, to Chicago, to begin the greatest adventure of my young life. I found myself on Randolph Street in the Loop, excited, bewildered, and chilled to the bone by an icy wind off Lake Michigan. I was searching for the Masonic Temple Building, where I had an appointment with Charles Webb Murphy, the president of the Chicago Cubs. I approached a well-dressed colored man, an elderly fellow with sad, drooping eyes and perfect teeth, and asked for directions. His reply was like a message from God. "Jes' look to the sky, mister." I looked up and saw the tallest building in the world! Right on the corner of Randolph and State, it shot straight up more than twenty stories!

Crossing State Street was a chore. At first I wasn't sure I could do it on my own, me a small-town boy. Rivers of traffic ran up and down the broad avenue, flooding it with dozens of streetcars. Automobiles tooting their horns bumped crazily over the tracks, bearing down on horse-drawn buggies, wagons, bicycles, and pushcarts. And so many people! All the men with great overcoats and black bowler hats, and women hiking the hems of their skirts to avoid the garbage and horse apples. Patches of ice coated the cobblestones. I paused to figure out the rhythm of the traffic and scooted across, narrowly avoiding the creaking wooden wheels of a large water wagon. On the other side, a dead horse lay in a heap near the gutter and I noticed, for the first time, a number of unshaven men in tattered clothes and ragged coats. Some begging, some wandering about, two of them sporting half-legs. One scruffy man in a threadbare overcoat gazed at me and asked, "A nickel so I may have lunch, sir?" I gave him the nickel. Hell, I was feeling prosperous with a job offer waiting for me and a double eagle in my pocket. Seeing me part with the nickel, two guttersnipes extended their little hands but I turned a blind eye. You cannot help every beggar.

I had a pretty good notion of what was going to happen at the Cubs office. It was likely that I would be offered a two-year contract to pitch for the Chicago Nationals. Why me? Why now? The Cubs had won the National League pennant in 1906, running away with it by winning 116 games and losing only 36. Knowledgeable baseball men predicted the Cubs would easily beat the "hitless wonders"—their hated local rival Chicago White Sox—in the 1906 World's Championship Series. But things don't always play out the way folks expect. The White Sox nailed the Cubs hides to the wall of South Side Park. So here I was, just four months after the Cubs' inglorious defeat in six games. Even though the Cubs owned a fabulous stable of pitchers, they wanted more left handers. My south paw might be just what the doctor ordered. Of course I had never pitched an inning in the Major Leagues. But that's how it works—you pitch in the Western Association and earn your opportunity to advance.

I entered an elevator car on the north side of the Masonic Temple Building. Polished marble floors and chromium appointments. My first time in an Otis elevator! I read about them in newspapers. The elevator operator, an old fellow about fifty, wore a green and blue velvet uniform with a yellow hat that did not match. Without looking at me he asked, "Which floor, sir?" and I told him, "Eleventh floor, please." My stomach lurched as we shot up the shaft. Jerking to a halt and clanking the door open, he loudly and boldly exclaimed, "Eleven!" After I got out, his yellow hat bid me goodbye through the brass bars, gliding down the shaft like a canary in a cage.

Before I entered the Cubs offices in room 1115, something my mother told me crossed my mind. She said I would have my "One Day," an unforgettable day when my life would change forever. A few steps from the Cubs office I figured this could well be it. My mother's One Day came in July 1877. She and my father lived on a small farm then, about seven miles north of Lamar. They grew corn and wheat and kept some chickens, pigs, and a couple of cows. On a Tuesday (ironing day) in July 1877, she awoke to a strange sound. She said it sounded like "God was humming." The horizon to the west was dark, like a line of storms was approaching. Only it wasn't a nasty storm coming in. It was a giant cloud of full-

winged grasshoppers. Turned out that swarm of pests stretched a mile into the sky, fifty miles across, and extended back west some one hundred miles. It took two days before those critters moved on to our Illinois neighbors to the east. The hungry grasshoppers pretty much devoured all the crops on my parents' farm and took some hefty chunks out of the farm tools, leather animal harnesses, and the wooden house. My mother tried to cover her vegetable garden with muslin cloth but the hoppers just devoured it. At times those critters covered the fields entirely, maybe three to five layers deep. "The ground breathed and moved up and down like it was alive," she said. Some got into the house and munched away at the curtains, clothing, and food. No matter how many you scrunched or burned, more took their place. Later my folks learned that these were Rocky Mountain locusts, first cousins to the ones in the Bible.

These insects, in a way, pushed my family off the land. It was the final straw. My folks sold the farm and headed for a new life in Lamar, where my mother taught school and my father went to work as a railroad conductor. Mom also taught me. She made me read the classics and spent a lot of time teaching me how to write. Bucky Gunderson, a Protestant and the son of an undertaker, loved baseball and taught me the game. I later pitched and played outfield on a team sponsored by the Lamar Grange Association. Which is how I ended up playing in the Western League. So I guess I owe my career in professional baseball to a swarm of locusts, and the writing of this journal to my mom's love of literature.

The Cubs office impressed me, with its richly crafted mahogany walls, landscape paintings, and a thick dark rug. Two brass cuspidors—shaped like tiger heads—bookended the big leather couch on which I waited. But I was too nervous to spit. I was early, so I sat there and worried that maybe something could have changed from when I had last spoken to the Cubs. After thirty minutes, a smiling and motherly secretary named Miss Clannon led me into President Murphy's office. He sat at a grand teak desk in front of a window that framed the whole west side of the city. A stout man with a combed mustache, he had a pinkish complexion and short brown hair. He also had what my mother used to call a "patrician" air about him, but I would call it a "smug" look. That was simply the way God made Mr. Murphy's face. He just couldn't help *looking like he knew better than you. He came out from behind his desk to shake my hand and exchange greetings. Mr. Murphy had a way with words and knew how to make a nervous youngster like me comfortable. In a moment or two I began to enjoy our meeting.*

Noticing my gaze over that vast city expanse, Mr. Murphy noted, "You can see our ballpark from here, Durbin," and he pointed it out. There, about two miles to the west and a little south, lay the West Side Grounds, the sun reflecting off the upper deck. After a bit more chitchat, Mr. Murphy laid it on thick.

"Blaine," he stated, "we received a series of reports about you from our Midwestern representative, Mr. Charlie Bastian." When he said "Bastian," he made it into three syllables when two might have done just fine. "Mr. Bastian was enthusiastic about your professional abilities and your potential," he continued. "We think you still need some polish, but that's where we come in. With our professional assistance you could help our club reach the next level. Even though we have an able squad of pitchers, our club could use another left-hander. You are a very lucky young man, because not only can you be playing in the Big Leagues in 1907, but you can play for the team that will win the championship of the world." He said all of this in a firm, resonant voice. He meant it. And I had no reason to doubt him.

He finished with a question that answered itself. "Are you interested in pitching for our Chicago club?"

Now of course Mr. Murphy knew I wanted to be a Cub. I was sitting in his office on a frigid January day, hundreds of miles from my home. He knew that I would rather pitch for Chicago than do anything else in the world, let alone return to Joplin in the Western League. The only unresolved issue was money, and that was not a problem because Joplin was only paying me eighty-five dollars a month. Mr. Murphy probably knew that I would play for the Cubs for free.

I told him, "Mr. Murphy, I am eager to help your ballclub. It would be an honor to pitch for this team." I did not exaggerate.

Mr. Murphy gleamed. He shuffled a few documents.

"Good… I am tendering you a two-year professional contract— what our lawyers have labeled 'Articles of Agreement.' Your salary will

be $1,750, payable in six monthly installments commencing in April. The salary will increase to $1,900 in 1908. Unlike most other ballclubs, we will assume the cost of your uniforms, other than your footwear. You will also receive a per diem."

I was gratified to hear these terms. The money was more than I expected. While I did not know what a per diem was, I figured if they wanted to give me one, I would take it. I could go to the library later and find out what it meant. I signed the contract "Blaine A. Durbin." Mr. Murphy seemed like a right nice fellow. He told me if I ever needed help I should call on him. I exited those offices happier than a flatworm in a hump of fresh cow dung. The elevator man in the yellow hat came to take me back down, but it could not be done. Floating on air like a feather in the ether—that's how I felt. Twenty years old and a pitcher for the Chicago Cubs!

The putrid stench of the Union Stockyards drifted north over shabby immigrant homes in the Back of the Yards to the Loop, where it settled and mixed with the stink of City Hall. Two First Ward aldermen, Bathhouse John Coughlin and Hinky Dink Kenna, ran a criminal conspiracy called City Council, composed of seventy saloon keepers, gambling house proprietors, and undertakers. About sixty of them, in the vernacular of the time, were boodlers. They took bribes. Boodle fueled, among other things, a huge and thriving red light district. But calling the Levee a red light district does not do it justice. One thousand whorehouses and half as many saloons lined Clark, Dearborn, and Wabash, from Polk Street south to 22nd. Men and women lost their money and sometimes their lives in dance halls, opium dens, bordellos, burlesque theatres, and gambling establishments. Penny peepshows catered to boys under fifteen. "Low dives" offered whiskey at a nickel a shot and a woman for a quarter. Many a patron was robbed with his pants down.

Large numbers of prostitutes came to the Levee in different ways. Many arrived voluntarily, as pimps found that they could recruit women from the ranks of low-paid sweatshop and factory workers. Some young women chose the life of the Levee over the drudgery of menial work and crushing poverty, often without fully understanding the consequences. Others were deceived by men paid to lure women into sexual relationships and then abandon them in the Levee. Procurers literally snatched a great number of women and girls off the streets and held them as slave sex-laborers. Forced opiate injections kept those that resisted under control. Residents of the Levee called the dazed prostitute-addicts "air-walkers." To sell newspapers, the press gave this horror a name, "white slavery." Editors massaged the story, stretching it into accounts of international syndicates run by Jews, trading in white women from Russia and Europe, and kidnapping American women for the enjoyment of Arabian caliphs. Journalistic exaggerations clouded the issue, but it is clear that criminals regularly forced huge numbers of females of all colors and nationalities into prostitution. It occurred every day. The chairman of the congressional White Slave Traffic Committee described the rescue, in just a two-month period in 1907, of 278 girls *under the age of fifteen* from the Levee. In 1911, the Chicago Vice Commission reported that Levee whores sold more than twenty-seven million acts of prostitution each year. Postal authorities deemed the 310-page commission report obscene, banning it from the U.S. mails. May Churchill Sharpe, a longtime denizen of the Levee, believed that "Rome at its worst had nothing on Chicago during those lurid days." This place of open, unblushing corruption and lewdness was literally the largest brothel in the world.

More than 7,300 licensed taverns dotted Chicago's landscape, and another thousand sold alcohol illegally, evading the one-thousand-dollar license fee. Saloons served as a focal point, a social base in the everyday life of most men in Chicago. Each day, half the adult male population visited a saloon for camaraderie, beer and whiskey. The many Midwest beer breweries expanded their sales by aggressively financing the establishment of new saloons. In return for a mere two hundred dollars, anyone could open a new saloon in Chicago, with the breweries providing all necessary fixtures, furniture, inventory, the license fee and monthly rent. In return, the new saloon keeper signed a contract to exclusively sell the beer of his sponsoring brewery. Each barrel of beer included a "tax" for the set-up and rental expenses. Fully 80 percent of the saloons in Chicago paid the piper in this manner. The breweries, many with German names like Peter Schlitz, Gottfried, Schoenhofen, K.G. Schmidt, and Bielfieldt, competed fiercely by opening more spigots, scouring the streets and neighborhoods of the city for new watering holes. The result was catastrophic. The typical Chicago male consumed more than 110 gallons of beer annually, four times the national average. The intense competition among rival saloons created incentives for these small businesses to offer their customers extras, and while sometimes that meant free food and larger drinks, frequently it meant gambling or prostitution in the back rooms.

Chicago grew from two separate waves of newcomers. A steady flow of young men and women from family farms and sleepy towns of America poured into the Windy City, attracted to the largest metropolis of the Midwest like moths to a flame. They came for the excitement that could not be found in the drab flat lands or the dusty streets of small communities. Chicago offered economic and social opportunities unavailable at home.

Immigrants constituted the other wave of new Chicagoans. Many viewed the influx of foreigners as "a succession of rough and hairy invading tribes." Cheap fares on crowded ocean-going vessels, like twelve dollars from Italy to New York, allowed the poor of Europe to make it to the New Land. Syndicated columnist William Allen White spoke for many Americans when he described the incoming tide of immigrants as "the very scum of European civilization."

The Irish arrived first, settling in a wide swath across the South Side. Then came the Germans, mainly to the North Side, soon followed by the Italians. In the next waves came the Jews, the Poles, the Czechs, the Bohemians, and the Scandinavians. Each group formed a new bottom rung on the economic ladder. They came to work. But they arrived in such great numbers, peaking in 1907, that they glutted the labor markets, driving wages down. The budding labor movement had yet to make a difference. The average worker earned wages of thirteen dollars for a week averaging fifty-nine hours. In meat packing plants, steel mills, retail shops, mail-order houses, shoe factories, and on the railroads, the new Americans worked hard and earned enough to gather their hopes and devise new dreams. Rather than attending school, their children toiled for pennies an hour to add to the family incomes.

The immigrants filled up the dilapidated tenements and vermin-ridden slums on the Near West Side, Plymouth Court and Clark Street just south of the Loop, and on the South Side. They died like flies from a wide assortment of terrible diseases, the worst being tuberculosis—called the white plague—which constituted more than 20 percent of the death rate. The newspapers blamed the wretched living conditions of the immigrants on nasty foreign cultures and dirty imported habits. Once the newcomers lived in Chicago for a decade or more, they turned up their noses at the next wave of immigrants, either out of fear that the newly arrived might threaten their jobs, or simply out of snobbery. The numerous ethnic groups did not mix—they remained separate, warring populations. No melting pot in Chicago.

African-Americans suffered the greatest hardships under the stifling blanket of an uncompromising, pervasive racism. White Americans simply refused to acknowledge the humanity of their black brothers. Numerous books, like *The Negro, A Menace to American Civilization*, by Robert W. Shufeldt, reflected and spurred a Negrophobia that swept the nation. Jim Crow laws proliferated around 1890, with the establishment of separate passenger train cars, waiting rooms, and public washrooms. Next came the exclusion of blacks from white-owned restaurants and saloons, separate entrances to factories and theaters, and rules prohibiting black barbers from scissoring the hair of white women and children. In 1892, an African-American shoemaker, Homer Plessy, was jailed for attempting to ride in a railroad car reserved for whites. When he sued, the United States Supreme Court upheld the separate but equal standard. But three years later the Court allowed a Georgia school district to provide a high school for white students and no high school for the black students. "Separate but equal" became simply, "separate." An American apartheid excluded blacks from educational and employment opportunities, relegating them to the fringes of white society. The lynching rope and other forms of physical intimidation kept them "in their place."

On the night of October 16, 1901, President Theodore Roosevelt invited Negro leader Booker T. Washington to dinner with the First Family in the White House. This breach of apartheid—at the highest level of government—stirred a storm of controversy. An editorial in the *Memphis Scimitar* blared a typical response:

> *The most damnable outrage which has ever been perpetrated by any citizen of the United States was committed yesterday by the President, when he invited a nigger to dine with him at the White House.*

Other newspapers headlined the story with "Roosevelt Dines a Darkey" and "Our Coon-Flavored President." Senator Benjamin "Pitchfork Ben" Tillman of South Carolina made the press seem moderate:

> *The action of President Roosevelt in entertaining that nigger will necessitate our killing a thousand niggers in the South before they will learn their place again.*

Threatening mail flooded the White House and the Tuskegee Institute, where Mr. Washington presided. Roosevelt was a remarkably tough, fearless man. One year before his dinner with Mr. Washington, on a hunting trip, he had leaped off his horse onto a cougar that had been cornered by his hounds, and knifed the cougar to death. But despite his toughness and independence, Roosevelt did not buck the public backlash to his dinner with the black man. He stepped back, coming to accept the view that blacks did not merit social equality with whites. Mr. Washington also came to have doubts about the wisdom of his White House visit. Another fifty years would pass before things began to change.

The hue of a person's skin also infected relations among some immigrant communities. Fair-skinned Northern European immigrants treated the darker-skinned Italian immigrants as "less than white." The *Washington Post* defended the practice:

> *The Italians... remain isolated from the rest of any community in which they happen to dwell. They seldom learn to speak our tongue, they have no respect for our laws or our form of government, they are always foreigners.*

Lynch mobs targeted Italians too, including the 1891 mass lynching of eleven in New Orleans, six of whom had just been acquitted of murdering the chief of police. Led by a white lawyer, the mob overran the jail, shooting some of the defendants and hanging the others. Teddy Roosevelt, then thirty-three years old and serving as a U.S. Civil Service Commissioner in Washington, described the New Orleans lynching as a "rather good thing." He gloated over these remarks at a gathering that included, in Roosevelt's words, "various dago diplomats." The *New York Times* ranted at "these sneaking and cowardly Sicilians" and described the New Orleans lynchers as "a very respectable mob." The Premier of Italy disagreed: "Only savages refuse to respect the inviolability of prisoners and distrust the justice of their own courts."

Many forms of danger lurked on the avenues of urban America, especially Chicago. Railroad companies refused to elevate their street-level grade crossings in the city, so trains and streetcars crisscrossed Chicago's avenues without the benefit of even a crossing gate. Consequently, on average, one Chicagoan lost his life every day beneath the wheels of a train, while others suffered crippling injuries. Great numbers of men with amputated limbs walked and crawled the streets. In 1894 a visitor from England, W.T. Stead, lamented Chicago's "multitude of mutilated people" and pressed for gates and railroad bridges.

A shady Irishman, Mickey Finn, exemplifies the dark side of Chicago and the times. In 1893, the year of the World's Fair, he earned a living as a "lush worker," mugging and robbing drunks in the Levee District. Graduating to the job of bartender at a dive on Custom House Street, he received his walking papers after gouging out the eye of an unruly customer. He tried pickpocketing with some success and became a fence for small-time thieves. But Finn gained everlasting renown with the opening, in 1896, of his Lone Star Saloon and Palm Garden on Dearborn near Harrison. A Chicago police inspector described the saloon as "a low dive, a hangout for colored and white people of the lowest type." Finn sat down with Hinky Dink Kenna and Bathhouse Coughlin to arrange for protection against any police interference. Then he hired a string of prostitutes to work the Lone Star, and taught them the art of pickpocketing the sober and rolling the drunks.

For a while Finn was content to share the proceeds with the whores, but then he met Dr. Artemus Hall. Dr. Hall, a black man who practiced voodoo and other occult arts, dealt in love potions, magic charms, cocaine, morphine, and other assorted commodities. He sold Finn a large brown bottle of chloral hydrate, a white crystal powder that put a person into a semi-conscious state of immobility. Finn put up signs in his establishment urging patrons to "Try a Mickey Finn Special." His bartenders pushed the cocktail, and it delighted Mickey to hear the order that would cost the victim dearly. Eventually, Mickey slipped the drug into the drink of any customer who exhibited a sign of prosperity. The slumbering victim was dragged to an "operating room," laid on a table, and stripped of all clothing. Finn oversaw these duties garbed in a clean white apron and a derby hat donned for the occasion. Finn and his employees took everything of value, including clothing and shoes, replacing them with rags. The victim woke up in the alley behind the saloon in a confused state that lasted for days. Mickey did not, however, kill these victims. "I am a Christian man, you know," he explained.

Another Christian gentleman, forty-four-year-old Rev. William A. Sunday, trudged up and down the Levee streets, preaching that God would exact merciless vengeance from the dissolute men and loose women of the district. His shouts pierced the cold gray mists and were heard inside the saloons and whorehouses. "Sinners and fornicators! You will die miserable deaths," he screamed. "Your tongues will swell up in your throats like cucumbers and Satan will drink the blood that vents from your ears. Then you will sink into everlasting fire, into the den of demons." As a younger man, Billy Sunday played center field for an early version of the Chicago Cubs, the Chicago White Stockings, piloted by legendary manager Adrian "Cap" Anson. Sunday quit baseball at age twenty-eight, after stealing eighty-four bases in one year, preferring to fight for Jesus in Chicago and small towns across the Midwest. He had a unique, athletic preaching style, leaping onto tables, thumping his chest, and sliding across the stage like a ballplayer sliding into home plate. Later he blossomed into one of the first evangelists to gain a national reputation, bringing in large amounts of money and maintaining cordial relationships with presidents. But Rev. Sunday could make little headway against the city of sin—a popular song later called Chicago the "town that Billy Sunday could not shut down."

Many Chicagoans believed the world would end on January 1, 1900. One month later, the earth still intact and Chicago still a raucous, dangerous town, sisters Ada and Minna Everleigh established the grandest house of prostitution ever known to Chicago, the Everleigh Club at 2131 South Dearborn. The sisters Everleigh, middle-class daughters of a Kentucky lawyer, had no experience either as prostitutes or as proprietors of a bordello. They simply desired an investment that would be profitable. The Everleigh sisters did not, like many of their competitors, use criminal means to staff their establishment. They paid their prostitutes more than any other house, and, as a consequence, always maintained a very attractive staff.

The Everleigh Club welcomed only wealthy men of Caucasian persuasion. Twin brownstone mansions housed the enterprise, complete with walnut and mahogany paneling, oriental rugs, twelve themed parlors for large orgies, a sumptuous dining room, and over forty-five richly appointed bedrooms. The Everleigh Club did not admit customers without appropriate references, and no man who spent less than fifty dollars in a night could ever return. The Club admitted Illinois legislators and Chicago aldermen without charge. The fee for the services of a woman ranged from fifty to five hundred dollars, but the cost of wine and epicurean victuals could exceed this. Diners feasted on caviar and lobster in a room designed to look like a Pullman dining car. Gold spittoons, marble statuary, impressionist paintings, and the best French wines graced the Everleigh mansion, as did Chicago politicians, bankers, the sons of new money, and upper-class visitors from around the world. Every banker and hotel bellboy in Chicago knew the Club's telephone number, Calumet 412. Minna Everleigh gave specific advice to her employees. "You have the whole night before you, and one fifty-dollar client is more desirable than five ten-dollar ones. Less wear and tear." Minna understood her customers. "It's not the ladies they like best, really. They like cards, they like dice, horse racing best. If it wasn't unmanly to admit it, they'd rather most of the time gamble than screw." An orchestra played and an artificial waterfall bubbled in the Club's main drawing room. Only three blocks away, in grimy Bed Bug Row, prostitutes sold their services for a quarter.

Women could not vote in early twentieth century America, save those who lived in Wyoming, Utah, Colorado, and Idaho. But women's suffrage groups had hit upon a two-pronged strategy to gain the vote, an approach that ultimately succeeded. They would strive to attract women of wealth and influence, so that they could not be attacked as fringe fanatics. And they rebuilt their movement to attract the middle class, mainly by focusing solely on the right to vote rather than subsidiary, "radical" issues like divorce laws and feminist biblical interpretations. If they could overcome the indifference and inertia of many women themselves, they could move to the next level. Still, in 1907 while suffragists marched to get the vote in Chicago and elsewhere—and were frequently spat upon for their efforts—most men continued to resist the logic of female suffrage.

British author Rudyard Kipling breezed through Chicago in 1886, dismissing it as "inhabited by savages." Directed to the finest hotel in the city, the Palmer House, he described it as "a gilded and mirrored rabbit warren… crammed with people talking about money and spitting about everywhere." In 1904, Lincoln Steffens, the American muckraker, judged Chicago in equally harsh tones:

> *First in violence, deepest in dirt; loud, lawless, unlovely, ill-smelling, irreverent, new; an overgrown gawk of a village, the "tough" among cities, a spectacle to the nation.*

Easterners derided smelly, meat-packing Chicago as "Porkopolis," but Chicagoans, as Carl Sandburg wrote, took pride in being the "hog butcher… to the nation." While New York City in 1896 enacted an ordinance against public expectoration and enforced it with more than 2,500 arrests, Chicago let its population spit. "You expect them to spit in their pockets?" asked an alderman. Chicago remained a frontier town of pickpockets, crooked politicians, workingmen, gangsters, whores, tramps, gamblers, and corporate thieves. A city that reversed the flow of the Chicago River in 1900 to carry city wastes to the Mississippi rather than Lake Michigan, Chicagoans contributed their end to making the grand old river run muddy and brown.

Big change ripped across America, fast and formidable. The march away from an agrarian small-town nation toward an urban society accelerated. Teddy Roosevelt, who slept with a loaded gun next to his bed, occupied the White House. A rash, vigorous executive and hero of the Spanish-American War, Roosevelt convinced Americans that they could change the world overnight. Thousands spent the decade digging through the Isthmus of Panama to link two oceans. Automobiles of all shapes and manufacture gradually replaced horse-drawn vehicles on the cobblestone streets of every great city. The Wright brothers invented powered, heavier-than-air flight in 1903, although most of their countrymen didn't learn of it until 1908. Electric lights slowly replaced gas lamps. Indeed, America's fascination with electricity produced strange manifestations. Like the fictional Dr. Frankenstein, U.S. physicians experimented with electrical currents in efforts to revive corpses. Galvanizing belts sent electricity through the scrotums of impotent men in the hope of stimulating an erection. And, at Thomas Edison's incessant urging, electric chairs began to jolt men to death. The first attempt, in New York in 1890, was botched—the condemned man began to burn and survived the initial seventeen seconds of juice.

Employers, pressured from labor unions and civic reform organizations, reduced weekly working hours. As the number of hours in a working week began to fall, leisure activities increased. Cultural attitudes began to shift. Across the nation the old tethers of society eroded. Community, manners, customs, traditional courtship systems, and religion were displaced in part by great public entertainments, vaudeville, daily newspapers, nickel movies, politics, stage magic, the circus, new forms of music, alcoholic beverages, drugs and professional sports.

Baseball in particular took hold in America in the early twentieth century. Every small town and large factory boasted a team to play "the national game." Two professional baseball leagues struck pay dirt in the greatest cities of America, which now vied for team franchises to enhance their reputation. Men who had grown up in rural America and played the game in their youth streamed into baseball "parks," green oases in otherwise barren industrial landscapes. In these dilapidated wooden ballparks men found an escape from routine lives and unrewarding work. They connected with a game that had changed little since the time they played it as boys. The centerpiece of this game was a pitcher locked in fierce combat with a batter, throwing a rocklike sphere at a man with a club in his hand. This primeval match-up provided the classic man-to-man face off, all staged before the backdrop of the standard double-arc defense, three outfielders spread across a vast expanse of turf while four infielders ranged across the scrubby grass and bare dirt of the infield. Professional baseball now connected many men to the baseball of their youth.

"I used to play the hot corner," a white-haired fan stated, memories of hard smashes to his left and right flooding his mind.

"I was a pitcher," said a bald gentleman standing next to the former third baseman. "Had a decent fastball that bought me two seasons with a semipro team in Baltimore some thirty years ago. The Lords, they was called. Then I threw out my shoulder and it ended before I turned twenty-one."

Big league baseball crowds included all ethnic, racial, and class lines. Any person could marvel at a great curveball and a deftly-turned double play. The World's Championship Series, a match-up between the upstart American League and the "Senior Circuit" National League, debuted in 1903 and further spurred the popularity of the game. For the first half of the twentieth century, baseball, in the words of Bill Veeck, "was the only game in town."

The World Series of 1906 matched Chicago's two baseball clubs, the only time this has ever occurred. The Cubs 1906 regular season winning percentage of .763 (116-36) is the best of all time. They built an ex-

July 9, 1883 Brooklyn, New York

A heavy wave of warm air settled over the Brooklyn neighborhood, bringing the residents out of their dwellings to the stoops, steps, and porches. A dark-haired boy stumbled out onto Coffey Street in front of the row house in which he lived, his vision still blurred from a blow to his head, and blood streaming from a cut below his eye. Breathing heavily, tears ran down both cheeks as he headed across Ferris toward the shore of New York Harbor. Past the alternating rows of cucumbers and tomatoes in Mr. Gordon's vegetable stand, past the smelly fish store and the hundred dead fish-eyes that followed him, the boy's gait steadied and the blood stopped flowing. He leaped over a splotch of vomit on the pavement and nimbly navigated between numerous small heaps of horse manure and a clogged sewer. An ice wagon with ironclad wheels clattered by the boy as he followed the cobblestone street down to the beach. The sun momentarily dazed the child, while the waves lapped gently on the dappled brown sand and shreds of newspaper tumbled in the wind. Eight years old, he sat down on the beach, burying both hands in the warm sand, his eyes exploring the horizon. Out to his left he saw the giant lady, the statue called Liberty. Dead ahead lay what he knew as Gubners Island. He knew the giant lady stood for freedom while Gubners Island, a short distance across the Buttermilk Channel, held a military prison known as Castle Williams. His thoughts returned to his father, who had just beaten his mother and him in a drunken rage. The tears ran harder now.

Three older girls jumped rope in the sand forty feet north of the boy. They sang in rhythm with the cadence of the rope and the sounds washed over the waif.

> *From the Army*
> *Run away!*
> *Castle Williams*
> *There you'll stay.*
> *Forever, forever,*
> *Forever and a day.*

On the beach not far from the boy lay a rotting, dead fish. He took a closer look and saw hundreds of small, white, wormlike creatures twisting as they consumed its flesh. A chill ran up the boy's spine, and he averted his gaze. Gathering his courage, the boy returned to his home. He walked slowly, head down. Unexpectedly, an old man in a rumpled gabardine suit, the family doctor, greeted him at the door.

"It's your mum, Percival. She fell and hit her head against the chimney stones. I am sorry to tell you she just passed. She's with the Lord now, boy."

He heard the wailing and moaning of his father inside but he could not bear to see that man again. He turned and ran, mechanically, without stopping or thinking for thirty minutes, until the warm flow of urine down his legs brought him back to this earth.

From the Journal of Kid Durbin

I decided to stay in Chicago until spring. My father and a few of my brothers still live in Lamar but it is time for me to make my way in the world. My mother, Clarra Sinclair Durbin, died about five years ago of consumption—the saddest day of my life. She was a genteel woman. She worried that baseball would lead me to excessive drink and the chewing of tobacco. She told me how the other farmer wives made fun of her unwillingness to butcher the hogs or a steer. Mom would hire the traveling tooth-puller/butcher/silhouette artist on butcher day every November—four bits for every hog, and a dollar a steer. Once one of these traveling tradesmen used a revolver to kill a 200-pound pig but the bullet passed through the animal's head and struck the man in his foot. Ma applied a tourniquet and saved his life so he butchered for free the next three years. He failed to return the fourth year. Mother thought he might have shot himself again.

An educated woman, my mother taught some school and got me interested in reading early. When I turned nine she gave me a copy of Tip Top Weekly, a dime novel that featured Frank Merriwell. I loved it and read it every week for years. Frank Merriwell, the hero and Yale college man, possessed great athletic abilities and superior intelligence. The perfect model for a small boy. While I am no college boy, thanks to my mother's encouragement I have progressed beyond the weeklies to read my share of the classics and good literature. And I am a professional athlete. I get paid to play! I'd like to think that some of Frank Merriwell rubbed off on me.

It is time for me to get used to the big city because there is a good chance I will be living here from now on. I just rented a furnished apartment on the West Side for $5.50 a week. The landlady is nice but a little nosy. Yesterday I found her sniffing around my flat when I returned. She acted like it was no big deal, saying, "I'm just checking for vermin."

My wardrobe, although sufficient for Lamar, now needed some help. I figured I could use another suit. So, heeding the circular given to me by a ten-year old newsagent on Madison Street, I wended my way to "Strauss Brothers—Master Tailors of Chicago" on Monroe Street, just west of Dearborn. As I walked in, a customer, an older fellow in a checked suit, said to the salesman, "I'll be back," and left. The salesman, who turned out to be one of the Strauss brothers, said to me, in a mock-confidential tone, "If I had a greenback for every 'be-back' I'd be a wealthy man." He then cheerfully steered me around his "clothing emporium," sensing that I was a bona fide buyer. I had a choice of black, brown, gray, or green, all with waistcoats, with three prices, sixteen, eighteen, and twenty-five dollars, depending on the quality of the "finest imported British fabrics." While the twenty-five-dollar fabric felt smooth and silky, the eighteen-dollar material, a wool worsted, also appealed to me. I figured I could use the extra seven dollars to buy a shirt and pair of shoes, so I chose a blue suit in the middle range. Mr. Strauss measured me up and down and wrote all the measurements down in a book with a brocade cover. I did select a pair of leather shoes and a white shirt so my total bill came to $25.75. I took the shoes and shirt with me. They said I could pick up "the garment" after one o'clock the next day. First time I ever bought a "garment."

My next stop was "John Campbell Anderson's Tonsorial Studio," on Adams Street near State. Three large leather barber chairs and the sweet smell of cigar fumes greeted me. Mr. Anderson seated me immediately underneath a colorful metal sign that read, "We Use Antiseptilene. It Kills All Germs." Mr. Anderson seemed impressed when I told him I would be pitching for the Cubs.

"I am a great admirer of the Cubs," he stated. "Especially Frank Chance and Johnny Evers. I have had the honor to provide a great range of tonsorial services to them on several occasions. Look here." He removed a shaving mug, one of hundreds, from a shelved cabinet along the wall. It bore the name Frank Chance. Mr. Anderson cut my hair (fifteen cents), gave me a shave (ten cents), and seemed appreciative of my nickel tip. "You now have another rooter when you pitch against the Giants," he told me.

The city offered many attractions, and as I walked east down

Monroe Street after getting my hair cut, the colorful show bills outside the Majestic Theater, advertising the awesome feats and abilities of a magician, caught my eye. Evidently "The Great Thurston" had only recently returned from a "triumphal tour of the Continent." I didn't know which continent the sign meant. One poster described Thurston as the "King of Entertainers and Entertainer of Kings," while another showed a beautiful white-gowned lady floating in air over a gasping audience. In the poster, little angel cherubs like the ones that I had seen in pictures of the baby Jesus supported the floating woman—all at the command of Thurston. I had never before attended a demonstration by a professional magician. But I had read the newspaper reports just a month ago about a fellow named Houdini who, while handcuffed, jumped off a bridge in Detroit into a hole in an ice-covered river—and came out of that hole fifteen minutes later! My mind was open regarding the spirit world and conjurers. The lady in the poster struck me as particularly attractive too, so I figured my education would benefit from being exposed to, as the show bill put it, "the Secrets of the Cosmos." The matinee began in only forty minutes.

One thing in the back of my mind made me hesitate about buying the ticket. Two days before, on my way to the Cubs office, I walked right past the massive columns of the Colonial Theater on Randolph Street. This theater had burned only three years ago, when it was known as the Iroquois Theater. More than six hundred people, mostly women and children attending a matinee, died there. That fire was big news in Lamar. The Lamar Democrat ran articles for two weeks detailing the horror of the fire and carried an illustration of a pile of burnt bodies. The Iroquois Theater, brand new when it burned, had advertised itself as fireproof. Six hundred people were incinerated in their seats or trampled to death trying to escape. The Majestic is brand new too, only one year old, with a placard boasting "Latest safety features; quarterly inspected by the Chicago Fire Department." My inner voice convinced me that the city authorities must have learned some lessons from the Iroquois, and that lightning wouldn't strike twice. Nevertheless, I decided to buy an aisle seat near an exit door, just in case I had to leave quickly. The ticket cost me one dollar, twice what it costs to see the Cubs!

I sure got my money's worth from that matinee. A fancy the-

ater, it had blue velvet seats, decorated walls and ceilings, and expensive box seats for the rich people. But when the lights dimmed the show truly transported me to other places. The Great Thurston appeared in a spotlight, center stage, dressed just like in the posters, a black evening suit, white gloves, and a sparkling top hat. He seemed like a distinguished, educated gentleman, speaking in a deep, clear voice that carried throughout the theater. I couldn't believe some of the things he did. For example, he had a pitcher that could hold maybe a gallon of milk, but he must have poured twenty gallons out of it! And he brought a man out of the audience and pulled a dozen baseballs out of one of his pockets.

Early in the show a beautiful lady named Princess Falow joined Thurston on the stage. She lay under a lace sheet and he pointed his wand at her and said, "Rise, Fernanda, I command you to rise! Rise as you rose in the Temple of Krishna more than one thousand years ago!" At that precise moment the princess floated gently upward, above Thurston's head, where she seemed to hover like a hummingbird over a flower.

Thurston then said, and I am not sure I can remember this part exactly, "There she sleeps, alone in space, suspended by nothing but the power of thought. There she can remain in peace for two hours, two weeks, or two years. But the slightest sound, even a whisper, can disturb her sleep." The theater went quiet as a night on the plains. And while I could observe no cherubs or devilish imps holding her up like in the posters outside, there weren't any wires either, because Thurston had her pass through a solid steel hoop. So I figured that maybe the cherubs—or whatever types of spirits cooperated in this enterprise—were rendered invisible at this performance. Which made me wonder whether I should have waited for the evening show. Maybe if you paid the $1.50 in the evening you got to see those spirits. Thurston levitated this Princess high over the audience and then said, in a ringing, solemn tone, "I will now show you something which you will remember your whole life!" At that instant the princess went "poof" and she disappeared, vanishing into the ether! Thurston never did bring her back, which made me wonder whether he had to get a new princess for every show or whether he could coax her back from the cosmos somehow. And like the man said, I truly believe I will remember that moment for the rest of my life.

But the most exciting thing happened right after the intermission. Thurston requested volunteers from the audience to go up on the stage to participate in an "exhibition of the power of the mind." Maybe fifteen young men offered to participate. I got carried away when a fellow near me raised his hand to volunteer—in the excitement of the moment I, too, raised my hand. Thurston selected me and six other young men. We all sat in a line of chairs across the front of the stage, facing the audience. With all the stage lights shining, I couldn't see the faces of the audience members. Then Thurston told a story about a Frenchman named Mesmer, who had developed the science of mesmerism, or hypnotism. Thurston said that hypnotism could "transform" human beings. I had no great desire to be transformed. I felt pretty satisfied with the way my career had progressed. But I thought it would be great fun to float across that stage like Princess Falow or vanish into thin air. When Mr. Thurston told the audience that people under hypnotic influence would not commit any act that they would not ordinarily do, I decided it would be harmless fun to participate in his demonstration.

I found myself second in the line of volunteers up on the stage. A little nervous at first, but then I realized I had pitched before bigger crowds in the Western League. Thurston quieted the audience and began to ask us questions about ourselves, our names, our occupations, whether we were married. The gentleman on my right, a tall man of thirty or so with thick black hair slicked down behind his ears with a considerable amount of pomade, told the audience his name, Percy McGill, and said he earned his living as a traveling salesman for a firm named Midwestern Manufacturing. Thurston asked him another three or four questions and then turned to me. I gave my name and noted, proudly, that I had just been signed to pitch for the Chicago Cubs. The audience applauded, but one blonde kid in the front row booed. "Evidently we have a White Sox fan in the audience," boomed Thurston, and the audience laughed. Thurston asked me if I had met "the Great Frank Chance" yet, and applause greeted the mere mention of that name. I answered honestly, admitting that I had yet to meet any of my new teammates.

After introducing the other volunteers, Thurston started with McGill. He held up a small crystal, just inches from the fellow's eyes, *and told him to peer deep into it. "Find the inner light," he commanded. Thurston continued to whisper to the man for another minute until the fellow slumped back a bit, his eyes closed, and he seemed to lapse into some kind of trance. Thurston came over to me, dangling the crystal above my nose. I felt a little nervous but the calmness and certainty in Thurston's tone allowed me to concentrate. He said some of the same things to me that he told the other guy and I started getting sleepy, even though I'd slept a good nine hours the night before. The crystal light and the soothing voice of the magician took me where he wanted me to go. When he told me that my eyelids felt heavy, they did! Next thing I know I am in what I can only describe as a waking sleep. I knew my whereabouts but everything seemed a little fuzzy and I couldn't open my eyes until Thurston told me I could. Then things got very hazy and confusing.*

When I awoke, I felt pretty good, but I had no memory of anything after Mr. Thurston put me asleep. When I returned to my seat the twelve-year-old boy sitting next to me filled me in. He told me that just as promised by the magician, I had been transformed.

"Transformed into what?" I quickly asked.

"Why, a rooster!" the boy informed me, with obvious glee. "Don'tcha remember?"

"Not at all," I answered.

The boy told me that every time Thurston had pointed out the sun rising I had yelled out a hearty "cockle doodle doo." The other gentlemen on stage had assumed the identities of a cow, a horse, a pig, a dog, and a donkey.

The boy said to me, "You made a great rooster—but I liked the pig the best."

The Game   Father, Son, and Holy Baseball

It occurs so often that it has become a part of the fabric of our national life, an idiom of Americana. The first preliminary to the game of baseball: father and son playing catch. It begins with a gentle arc and words of encouragement. A parent, a child, two gloves, and a red-stitched ball. It is a ritual, part of growing up, memorialized in American culture.

Playing catch with his son is an act of love by a father. For the boy it is an opportunity to relate to his father and to demonstrate his developing skills. The simple back and forth of the throw and catch gathers a rhythm, a cadence of movement and sound. The baseball, like quicksilver in a mercury switch, connects the two contacts and the current flows between them. Love and affection carried like electricity on a sacred cowhide baseball, from father to son and back again, over and over again. A holy trinity.

To father, son, and holy baseball,
The Game that we adore,
Be everlasting honor paid
Now on and evermore.

At St. Procopius, in Toledo, Ohio, a priest raises his hand in the familiar gesture of blessing, extending the index and middle fingers and the thumb, and curling the other two fingers down. The three extended digits represent the Holy Trinity. And the position of the hand, in the act of the blessing, is the same as used to grasp and throw a baseball. As the priest gives the blessing, a father in Sacramento, California, says to his boy, as his father once said to him, "Let's play catch." And the ritual continues like a scene in a stage play, performed with little variation, day after day. The child extends his glove over his head and the ball drops into the webbing. "Good catch!" the father exclaims.

January 13, 1907 Chicago, Illinois

The fog of last night's drinking lifted, and Mike Fitzgerald found himself walking slowly down Clark Street, his fingers and toes stinging from the cold. Gray and brown buildings towered over him on both sides of the street, confining his movements and his spirits as well. Slowly spiraling down to a wretched death, a victim of alcohol and himself, the scruffy man shuffled down the cobblestones with no destination in mind. Lingering memories of his childhood and better days drifted through his addled skull. Once he was a hard worker, starting his life of toil at seven years of age in the Armour slaughterhouse as a broom-boy, standing ankle-deep in animal blood twelve hours a day, pushing the blood down metal vents to collection vats below. *In the summer we worked from dawn to dark*, he remembered, *and in the winter, we worked from dark to dark.* The packinghouse owners did not heat the premises, so on cold winter days the blood would freeze to his boots and trousers. On the way home his pants froze stiff, making walking difficult. There were other jobs, and later a wife and a child.

He met Theresa on a Sunday morning at St. Joseph's Church. *Where was St. Joseph's?* he now asked himself. *Was it 38th Street?* He could not remember. They wed at that church six months later, on a cold, crisp, April afternoon, and the girl was born ten months after that. A new life, for whom he was responsible. He worked to support his family at a series of menial jobs. He carried bricks at construction sites, dug muddy ditches for the city, and unloaded barges. All the jobs ended as the result of his drinking. There had been an apartment too, on the South Side, filled with furniture and food. Friends visited him there, the baby cooing in the bedroom while his wife brewed coffee and drapes flapped in a gentle spring wind. Sometimes Fitzgerald felt haunted by the memories of the past. Other times he considered these same memories a blessing.

My daughter must be about fifteen now, he thought, sipping on a Schlitz beer in a Levee watering hole. He remembered her as an infant, and the sadness of losing her overcame him again, but only briefly. The alcohol soon erased the discomfort.

Beer, wine, whiskey, and "medicines" with 30 percent alcohol ate away at Mike's ability to work or care about anything except the next drink. He worked unskilled labor jobs, like digging foundations at construction sites, or carrying crates in factories, earning twelve to fourteen dollars a week. The ten-hour workdays ended the same way, with Mike on a barstool in a gloomy smoke-filled tavern, drinking until the bartender pushed him out on the street. His wife screamed at him when he came home filthy drunk. She was justified, but he could not see this through the alcoholic haze. Sometimes he worked himself into a rage and beat her, or tried to, but mainly he fell asleep on the kitchen floor until she woke him at six and the cycle started again. She threatened to leave him, to move back home. One day, a long time ago, after losing another job for a reason he no longer remembered, he drank all night and just didn't go home. He never went back, rationalizing that she and the girl would do better without him. He never wrote, and he never saw or heard of them again.

Fitzgerald thought about them almost every day, before he drank. "The other life," he called it. He lamented that he would not recognize his own child if he ran across her. Lacking a photograph of his wife Theresa, he realized that he could no longer create a mental picture of her. He remembered her blond hair, warm hazel eyes set close together, and a wide smile, but he had lost the ability to piece the features together. The memory of Theresa's soft arms and delicate fingers was strong. He remembered the urgency of their lovemaking early in their marriage. And the joy the child brought them. But the image of Theresa was muddled in a fog of whiskey and the haze of time. It did not matter—he was married to the bottle now, and faithful to his new spouse.

Mike was a tall man, with hefty arms and a slight stoop. Gray eyes peered out from teary lids. The hair was gone from the crown of his head, and dark patches of brown hair circled his ears. A scruffy beard stretched from ear to ear. Shuffling from place to place, dressed in rumpled, unkempt working clothes, he looked much older than his forty years. But he remained a strong man, able to defend himself when necessary. Working men in Chicago who could not use their fists or a knife in a tight spot often ended up in the morgue.

Days were spent on the streets, begging or working small jobs. Mike wielded a pick axe doing county construction and foundation excavation projects. One day's work usually earned him fourteen bits ($1.75), enough to buy him sufficient drink and a caged bed in a flophouse for two days. But some days he could not hook a job.

Nights, at least from October through April, were the worst. He had seen the stiff pale corpses of his fellows, fallen prey of the bitter cold, carried off in wagons in the same way they removed horses that died on the streets. He remembered the wide-open, unseeing eyes of his good friend, Harry Chaney, lying on his back and staring into the indifferent gray sky on a frigid December morning a year back. Mike had shared a bottle with Harry just five hours earlier. *I woke up. He didn't.*

Thousands of homeless men trudged the city streets looking for food and warmth. The *Chicago Courier* prescribed a remedy for its readers: "When a tramp begs you for bread, put some strychnine or arsenic on it and you will find that he will trouble you no more." Some commercial establishments let men like Mike spend the night, such as Hinky Dink's Workingman's Exchange saloon on South Clark Street. The Harrison Street Police Station also allowed hundreds of men to sleep nightly in the halls of the jail wards. Tramps sprawled across the damp, crowded floors and a thick, foul air hung over the place, but a coal-fired furnace provided enough heat to sustain life. Sleeping on the mucky concrete floor meant you woke up groggy, with aches in every nook and cranny, but you were alive for another day.

Five cents bought Fitzgerald a narrow spot on a wooden floor splotched with tobacco spit in a lodging house on Madison Street. He remembered to lay newspaper on the floor, but he hadn't arrived early enough to find a place near the stove, so he slept in his coat and shoes. The fire burned out at four in the morning, but the whiskey kept Fitzgerald asleep until dawn.

In the morning he walked aimlessly in a haze for hours. At noon, he found himself at Michigan Avenue and Jackson Street, with forty cents in his pocket and a deep thirst for a beer. *I need a corpse-reviver bad,* he thought. He had to decide whether to spend an hour begging on State Street, or to immediately wend his way to the Exchange for a beer or two. The beer won out—an easy decision.

The Era   The Yards

By the turn of the century the confluence of geography, technology, and the entrepreneurial spirit made the Union Stockyards the largest livestock market and meat processing center in the world. The "Great Bovine City of the World" consisted of a network of railroad tracks, fenced corrals, and grimy slaughterhouses, all designed to feed a nation hungry for meat. As a result of a massive national advertising campaign, the American consumer now willingly purchased meat shipped a thousand miles in refrigerated rail cars. The Yards provided fifty thousand mostly immigrant workers with their first job in the New World. A few enterprising businessmen like the Swifts, Wilsons, and Armours grew rich turning Chicago into the nation's slaughterhouse, while the armies of Pole, Czech, and Lithuanian workers got by, barely, until they or their children moved up a notch in the workplace.

The rail lines transported the animals to the South Side. Each day more than twelve thousand head of cattle, five thousand swine, and hoards of sheep, goats, and other animals were prodded from their pens into the mechanized mazes designed to kill and process swiftly, avoiding decay and waste. The slaughterhouses were organized into "disassembly lines." Workers herded cattle into ever-narrowing corridors and chutes, sometimes following a Judas steer who escaped in a last-minute exit while the followers headed to their death. A brawny blood-spattered man, the "headman," slammed each animal in the head with an iron sledge hammer, usually killing them, sometimes just knocking them unconscious and bleeding onto the bloody floor. A chain slid around the cow's right hind leg, and a steam hoist yanked it up, to hang inverted, from an ever-moving chain that conveyed the steer about the slaughterhouse. Then came the man called the sticker, who slit the throat of each animal, more than eighty an hour at peak. The arterial blood spurted an average fifteen seconds, some of it spraying the sticker and the rest trickling into channels where child workers pushed it along with brooms to vents that sent it down to collection tubs. Nothing of the animal went to waste save the urine, which flowed out of the slaughterhouses in lengthy tin gutters. "Every bone's a penny," the foreman would bark. They collected the bones for the cutlery factories for use as handles on knives. Stacks of animal hides sat outside the packinghouses, awaiting shipment to the tanneries. Workers swept up the hair of the animals, removed extracts from certain glands, and ground up bull testicles and goat horns for shipment to Asia. Hills of manure, thirty feet high, surrounded the slaughterhouses, destined for Midwest farm fields. Collected intestines ultimately served as casings for sausages while the fat went into oleomargarine. The men bragged, "We use all of the hog except the squeal." After the sticker did his job, others gutted the animal and halved it into two sides of beef. Dressing of the meat came last, and then men loaded it onto refrigerator cars for shipment.

The pens full of skittish animals never emptied. As workers herded each group of doomed hogs or lambs into the killing areas, other animals, just off the stockcars, replaced them. The animals could sense their approaching fate—they could smell it in the air from the blood of the fresh kills. The cattle would moan and fidget, on edge and alert, and moo in a rapid, frantic manner. Some men could not stomach the butchery and stench in the Yards, while others did whatever they had to do to keep their jobs. Every day the elevated trains brought thousands of visitors, fine-dressed Chicagoans or tourists, for organized tours of the slaughterhouses, where they could see every step of the kill and disassembly of the animals. During the Columbian Exposition of 1893, more than ten thousand came each day at the invitation of the meat-packers. The packers concealed nothing from the crowds, from the headman and the sticker to the final product, fresh-cut carcasses hanging in lines, swinging gently from great steel hooks in the railway refrigerator cars.

The smell of the stockyards could not be forgotten. An amalgam of shit, sweat, blood, decaying hides, steam rising off freshly cut flesh, and the reek of brains and splayed organs. One strong whiff could knock an unprepared man to his knees. The white-collar men in the Yards would wink when someone mentioned the odor, saying, "That smell means employment." The smell lifted above the Yards, the winds carrying it afar, a part of the time and place, a Chicago landmark no less than the Loop skyscrapers and the Chicago River.

January 13, 1907 **Majestic Theater, Chicago, Illinois**

Howard Thurston earned a reputation as the greatest magician touring the United States. Stage magic reached its zenith with the Great Thurston. Seven years of touring abroad, from the Orient to Europe, earned Thurston large sums of money, much of which he poured back into elaborate apparatus for his theatrical productions. He traveled with a crew of twenty, needing six or seven railway baggage cars for the equipment and scenery he used on the best stages in urban America. Thurston maintained a full-time workshop the size of a small factory on Long Island, along with several warehouses filled with contraptions devised under his direction. He mastered every phase of the business, from card tricks and stage hypnotism to his popular large-scale illusions. Thurston injected humor and beautiful "assistants" into a vocation that had previously consisted of semiformal, didactic presentations. But he soared to stardom on his ability to gain the confidence and affection of the audience and his meticulously-crafted showmanship.

"The key to my success on any night," he told his friends, "is whether I can radiate good will to the audience. There is only one way to do it and that is to feel it. You can fool the eyes and minds of the audience but you cannot fool their hearts."

Howard Thurston peered through the red stage curtain to gauge the audience, a sizeable matinee crowd. He would tailor the show to fit the audience. This day he viewed a large number of women and children, a well-dressed audience, filling half the theater. One little urchin scampered out of his seat and advanced toward the stage before his mother chased him down. Thurston conferred with George White, a young black man who served as the backstage assistant, and Pete Cannard, the production manager, to finalize the program, and then retreated to his dressing room to prepare for the show. He anticipated no problems this afternoon.

But something did go wrong in the hypnotism segment of the show. Thurston always knew that certain subjects under hypnosis might act in unpredictable ways. If the subject possessed a low moral character, a substantial risk existed that he could misbehave on stage. Uneducated subjects could misinterpret the commands of the hypnotist. Thurston prided himself on his selection of "volunteers" for the hypnotism segments, excluding shady-looking men, the ignorant, and those under the influence of liquor. The seven volunteers on stage today included Thurston's two regular shills, Roger and Timothy, boys of seventeen and eighteen who traveled with the show on salary at fourteen dollars weekly. Thurston easily placed both in a hypnotic state. But the gentleman who sat in the first chair at stage left, Mr. Percy McGill, gave Thurston pause right from the start. While he said he worked as a salesman for some manufacturing concern, Thurston, a fine reader of human responses, knew him to be lying. And while men frequently misrepresented their lines of work, the cold demeanor and peculiar mannerisms of this fellow worried Thurston.

Next to McGill stood a professional baseball player, a likeable, small man, with a mane of fine, crisp red hair, named Blaine Durbin. He had high, prominent cheekbones, a serious glint in his intelligent eyes, and a strong chin. Dressed in a cheap, light-gray suit and vest, Durbin told the audience that all his friends called him Kid. Thurston asked Kid Durbin about the Cubs, his baseball team, and Frank Chance, the manager, but the young pitcher had not yet played for the team.

"I haven't met nobody on the team just yet except the owner," he admitted.

"And how did you get along with the owner?" asked the magician.

"Just swell… he signed me up!"

Thurston then interviewed Roger and, as he always did, informed the audience that he employed Roger as part of the Thurston team. But Thurston did not mention that Timothy too served as part of the team. Disclosure was fine, to a certain degree. This McGill fellow and the other volunteers went under well, with no particular problems. Typically, Thurston found that he could hypnotize three or four out of the five non-shill volunteers. One or two would not go under, and Thurston could always recognize this, but the volunteers would usually play along. That is why they raised their hands—they were extroverts, happy to be on stage, performing for an audience. Both the hypnotized and the play-alongs could be commanded to eat imaginary pies and they would do so. But when it came time to stick a five-inch needle through a forearm, Thurston chose the hypnotized subject, who truly felt no pain, rather than the play-along who would probably bolt off the stage at the approach of the needle.

The program began well. After the volunteers sunk into a somnolent lethargy, Thurston addressed them. "Gentleman, please stand up." The seven men stood next to their chairs. "Now you can hear only me, only my words. You are now at Hawthorne Race Track. You are jockeys standing next to your horses. Please mount your steeds."

At this point the men straddled their chairs. Thurston, stage left facing the "jockeys," announced: "On the count of three the race will begin. Your horse will not move but it will seem like you are racing around the track at a tremendous speed. You can win this race if you ride well. One. Two. Three!"

The men started hopping about the stage, whipping their "steeds." Each man believed he rode a horse around a track. Durbin jumped up and down and hung on to his chair like it was running away from under him. Roger clung to the back of the chair for dear life, his knees on the seat of the chair and the legs extended in back, kicking furiously. When Thurston instructed them that they would approach the finish line in five seconds, the men pushed their mounts to the limit. In a mock-serious tone, Thurston informed the seven that they had finished in a dead heat. Each of the men smiled, satisfied with the victory, wiping at their brows. The audience applauded loudly, and exhibited an equal response to the next exercise, where Thurston had the subjects nurse "babies" made out of rolls of newspaper. Durbin and the others gently cradled their newspaper babies in their arms, exhibiting sincere paternal devotion to their little bundle. The problem arose in the final scene, which Thurston introduced as the Bucolic Farmyard Episode. As he always did, Thurston caused each volunteer to assume the identity of a different farm animal. Today, McGill transformed instantly into a pig, Durbin became a rooster, Timothy a sheep, Roger a cow, and the others a horse, a donkey, and a dog. Thurston commanded the "animals" to go about their business in the farmyard, at which point the rooster began to crow, the donkey to bray, Roger mooed strongly, etc. McGill, as a neophyte pig, did a fairly good oink and rooted about the farmyard. The other animals also acted in appropriate barnyard form. But then something occurred that Thurston did not anticipate. Without warning, the pig leaped onto Timothy the sheep's back, and began to mimic, all too realistically, the act of copulation, there in the middle of the Great Thurston's stage, during a matinee filled with women and children. The pig's haunches heaved up and down repeatedly on the sheep's rear end, while Timothy was too startled to even utter one baaaaa. Some mothers covered the eyes of their children until Thurston quickly intervened, scolding the pig.

"Mr. Pig, you cannot ride a sheep like men ride horses. Pigs do not ride sheep. You are very hungry. Go eat your corn—it is right over there."

The pig came down off of Timothy and started to nibble eagerly on the nonexistent shredded corn. Thurston wrapped up the hypnotism segment early, sending the volunteers back to the audience to scattered applause and a strange undercurrent. Thurston took one last look at McGill, marking him in his memory. Oblivious to what he had just done, Percy McGill took his seat again in the audience. A matron of fifty, seated next to him, muttered under her breath, "The pig!" and left the theater in a huff.

February 10, 1907 **Chicago, Illinois**

He woke up on the stone corridor floor of the Harrison Street police station, muddled, a ringing headache plaguing his every move, his clothing damp with urine. Digging the sleepsand out of the corners of his eyes and rubbing his fingers through his thinning hair, he thought, "That bastard next to me must have pissed in his sleep." He pulled his leg back to kick the still sleeping man before he realized, from the location of the wetness, that he had wet himself. It was not the first time. Others roused themselves from the night's sleep, street bums like Fitzgerald, homeless children as young as six, and the insane, babbling and shouting at their demons. The cops began to shoo them out of the station.

Mike Fitzgerald faced another cold Chicago day with thirty cents in his pocket and no plans other than to get drunk as soon as possible. He could not remember much about how he had come to spend the night on the floor outside the jail cages in the basement of the police station. The cops began to poke and push the men out and the noise woke the caged prisoners, who begged the departing men for money or assistance. *This scene repeats itself every day*, Mike thought. Many times he witnessed this same scene from the other side of those metal fences. Mike shuffled out the front door of the police station.

The first order of business for Fitzgerald—he needed to find warmth. He prayed that the sun shone, as that would do the trick. Out on the corner of Harrison and Pacific Street he smiled, as the warm sunshine played off his brow and his eyes adjusted to the sharp light. In no time at all he shook off the cold. For a short time he hung about the iron fence that surrounded the brick building, pondering his next move. But a fat police officer, nibbling on a pickle, noticed Fitzgerald enjoying the sun, smelled him, and growled, "Get the fuck outta here, you stinking bum, or we'll take a walk right back into the station!" The cop delivered his command in a strident, high-pitched tone, designed to persuade. The officer's right hand nervously fingered the nightstick on his belt. Fitzgerald took the hint and immediately headed away from the cop, east on Harrison. Knowing that the tiniest delay would buy him a severe kick in the ass or worse, he smiled as the blue-coated lawman ambled off in the opposite direction. Mike then headed to State Street, the best place to cadge nickels.

February 10, 1907 **Wilton, Iowa**

Constance Dandridge, twenty years old and terrified of life passing her by, purchased a one-way ticket to Chicago for $2.73, deposited the twenty-seven cents change in her purse next to a white envelope containing her life savings of $176, and sat down on a varnished oak bench in the station to wait for the train. Connie did not view her departure from Wilton as running away, but rather as a passage out of life as it had always been to a new life. Connie's mother died soon after Connie turned eight. Her mother's sister raised Connie after that, but she had recently passed on. Connie's mother told her that her father died of consumption when she was an infant.

All my relatives gone, she thought, clutching her handbag to her chest. A sigh escaped from Connie's unpainted lips. She mused on her existence to that point, a life of hard work, simple joys, and unmet expectations. Nothing happened in Wilton, Iowa. Literally nothing! Life ticking by, one tedious day after another. The biggest event in the last three years was the hullabaloo at Mr. Crittendon's poultry farm. John Crittendon lost hundreds of layers and pullets to some sort of fowl epidemic. He buried all these poor creatures in a shallow trench. The gases built up and exploded. Feathers and chicken parts rained down as far away as a mile.

Remaining in Wilton meant marrying Theodore Helton or, God forbid, William Cordell, neither a happy prospect for Connie. Connie read books suggesting that life could be a dazzling series of adventures, and Chicago seemed to offer such limitless possibilities. Fine department stores hired girls like Connie to work in a city filled with broad streets, theaters, mansions, and finely-dressed women. After her aunt's death she had agonized for a month about leaving. In the end the decision came easily. She made her plans, informed a few friends, and left.

Miss Dandridge stood 5'3". A pretty girl but not a beauty, her brown eyes gleamed a sad note beneath curly auburn hair carefully arranged to frame her face. On this day she wore a look of steely determination along with a deep blue narrow-brimmed hat, a long, gray dress that covered her ankles, and a black wool coat that draped below her knees.

In the midst of her revery, a tall man in a black suit, green cravat, and bowler hat sat down opposite Constance. With a graceful charm he removed his hat, revealing thick black hair pulled back on each side. Constance averted her eyes from him, but when he asked her if she was traveling to Chicago she looked at him and answered, "Yes." A conversation followed. The man soon learned of Connie's plans.

Constance observed that he had an agreeable countenance, large blue eyes, a decent set of clothes, and a kindly, educated manner of speech. Helping her with her valise as they boarded the train, she did not decline his invitation to sit across from him on the coach. After a bit he brought her a drink from the water bottle on the far end of the railcar, in the tin cup that served as the communal drinking vessel for the occupants of the coach. As he handed her the water, she noticed a gleaming gold ring on his hand. He introduced himself as Percival McGill and told her that he sold machine parts for Midwestern Manufacturing.

McGill lied. He did not work as a salesman. Instead, he owned a house of prostitution in Chicago's Levee District. Percy McGill excelled at drawing into his business a supply of ever-needed new flesh. The customers demanded new girls and he had lost a whore one week earlier. He made the Iowa run monthly.

February 10, 1907 **Kansas City, Missouri**

In 1899, when he pitched for and managed the semipro Kansas City Schmeltzers, Johnny Kling traded two uniforms and a bat to acquire a young infielder named Joe Tinker. They fast became friends. As the Cubs starting catcher since 1902, Kling did not attempt to hide his Jewish heritage and never resented that Tinker, Evers, and a number of other Cubs called him "the Jew." The nickname was used affectionately and his teammates meant him no disrespect. Kling had a second nickname, "Noisy John," because he chattered behind the plate, encouraging his teammates and distracting opposing batters with insults and insightful observations. The best receiver of his time, Kling provided a hard-hitting offense combined with a great defensive effort, including perhaps the best catcher's throwing arm in the majors. And Kling possessed remarkable skills in calling pitches and dealing with pitchers. Only 5'9" and 160 pounds, the dark-complexioned Kling had a dimple set in his chin, sad brown eyes, and thick eyebrows. A student of the game, Noisy John befriended black ballplayer Bruce "Buddy" Petway, a catcher barred from the majors as the result of his skin color. Petway taught Johnny how to throw to second base from the crouch, what Buddy called his "flat-footed snap throw."

"You catch that sucker, throw your shoulder forward, and snap it to second," Buddy taught him. "You don't stand up before you throw," Buddy added, "it ain't necessary or smart."

Kling caught on to the snap throw from the crouch quickly. The flat-footed throw enabled Kling to throw out many base stealers at second and third, and to occasionally pick off a dozing runner at first base. One of his victims called it instant death. Most catchers in 1907 still squatted three steps behind the plate, as a safety measure, until after the second strike, when they inched up in order to ensure catching the tipped balls for third strikes before they bounced. But not Kling. He positioned himself—at all times—directly behind the plate as do modern receivers.

Kling puttered around his Kansas City billiard parlor this day in a sour mood. Two weeks earlier Kling sent his 1907 contract back to the Cubs unsigned. He sent a one-sentence letter with it: "This is entirely inadequate." Kling never drank or used profanity. But he enjoyed betting on horses with Frank Chance and other forms of gambling.

His chest heaved with agitation. "The cheapskate sends me a contract and has the nerve to say he is offering me 'a princely sum.' A princely sum is it? I will not play for $3,500," he told his wife. "Just who do they think they are dealing with, Lillian? I am underpaid at $4,000 and I deserve a three-year deal." Lillian agreed.

Kling did have one viable alternative to playing for the Cubs. He figured he could make a decent wage developing his new billiard establishment and playing professional billiards. Maybe he could earn enough to enable him to take a year off from professional baseball. Maybe then Chubby would break down and pay up. Johnny did not think highly of Pat Moran, the backup catcher. *Moran's over the hill,* he thought. *They can't win without me behind the plate.*

Kling did not know that the Cubs had invited minor leaguer Warren Seabaugh, a rookie catcher, to the spring camp, as well as Mike Kahoe, a veteran backstop and former Cub.

February 10, 1907   On a train to Chicago, Illinois

The trip to Chicago afforded Percy sufficient time to impress the young woman with his animated conversation, fine manners, and charm. He gave her his business card and she listened to his stories of life in Chicago, its politics and personalities, asking many questions, mainly about the fine department stores and theaters. When he could not answer her question, he made up a response quite nimbly. Percy never allowed an inconvenient fact to interfere with business goals.

As the train approached Chicago, McGill nonchalantly offered Connie a ride to her hotel. "My driver and car are meeting me at the train. It would not inconvenience me in the slightest," he stated, his voice dripping sincerity, peering directly into her eyes.

Connie considered the offer, but declined.

He persisted. "Please, Miss Dandridge. I do not wish to see you in the clutches of these dreadful hacks. They are notoriously rude and will no doubt charge you more than a lawful rate. Some are nothing more than rascals, or worse, common criminals. Perhaps you are unaware of a tragic incident but three weeks ago. An Italian hack—a swarthy, reprehensible creature—took advantage of a young woman in his vehicle. The newspapers spread word of this attack, further humiliating the victim. It would be improper of me, indeed ungentlemanly, if I did not offer you the safety and convenience of my automobile. My driver will drop you wherever you choose."

Connie relented. Percy conveyed the bearing and appearance of an honest and decent man. She viewed him to be a proper young man, generous and kindly.

After the train came to a rest in the station, McGill assisted with her luggage and she accompanied him to a cobbled street on the west side of the depot, where a shiny black vehicle waited. The driver, a small man dressed in a rumpled suit of clothes, packed the bags in the trunk of the vehicle and Connie and Percy climbed into the rear seat. The engine puttered noisily, then lurched forward when the driver engaged the gears. As she peered out the rear window, Connie smelled an unfamiliar vapor. *Not gasoline*, she thought. Turning to ask McGill if he smelled the odor, she instinctively recoiled as he leaped toward her, stuffing a heavy cloth in her face, the material reeking with the same pungent smell. Connie struggled and gasped to breathe but the vapor dragged her down. Losing consciousness her head slumped sharply against the side window, a small smear of blood bubbling on the glass as the automobile sped south on Dearborn Street.

Connie awoke slowly, confused and dizzy. She found herself alone on a damp bed in a dark room. As she stirred she grew nauseous. Rolling over, she vomited quickly and softly on the floor by the side of the bed. That done, she lay back and rested. She thought back on McGill and the assault. The fear heightened as her senses sharpened. Drugged and abducted! A chill ran down her spine as she considered her situation. For the first time in her short existence, Connie felt her life to be in jeopardy. She looked for her purse and her belongings but they were not in the room. She tugged at the handle of the only door in the room but it held fast, locked from the outside. Tears welled in her eyes but she gathered her courage, vowing to survive. *I will not let my life end before it has even begun*, she thought.

A short time later she heard a key twisting and the turn of the doorknob. Light from the hallway outside flooded in on her, obscured for a second by a dark shape that entered the room and slammed shut the door. It was McGill. He approached the bed, removing his waistcoat as he advanced, tossing it on the floor.

Connie sprung to her feet, shouting, "Stop this instant," but he did not.

The expression on Percy's face, or lack of it, caused a cold fear to spread over Connie. The look of a crazed person, calm and steely but strange. The eyes, in particular, seemed to shimmer with cruelty.

"Take off your clothes," he commanded. He spit out this instruction in a cold monotone. "Now!" he shouted.

Although the terror leaped into her throat, Connie responded firmly, "I will do no such thing. I gave you no reason to treat me in this manner. Please, sir, in the name of God, do not do anything that you will later regret or for which you will have to answer to the police."

McGill smiled ever so slightly. "Honey," he drawled, "what I am about to do to you I have done many times before, and I have never once regretted it. Quite the contrary. I enjoy my work. As for the coppers and the shit-heads they call judges, well, I pay them more than the fuckers deserve. It is a business expense that I must bear. Now," he purred, the smile growing broader, "where were we?"

She shrunk back, terrified, overcome with the horror of the moment, but McGill reached quickly toward her, grabbed the collar of her blouse, and ripped downward, shredding the garment and exposing her corset. Connie shrieked, but the scream cut short as McGill's fist struck her left cheek. She reeled back onto the bed, stunned and hurting. She heard him ripping at her dress and pulling away her undergarments, touching her breasts and then fingering between her legs, mumbling or humming as he did so. A few seconds passed as he kicked off his shoes and then his pants. Trying to rise off the bed, Connie felt the full force of McGill's bare foot smashing onto her chest, stomping her back down, and she lost her breath. Then he dropped down on her, exploring first with his hands and then thrusting hard in and out, panting a liquored breath into her face. Her tears and crying did not stop the rape. He finished in a moment, but that moment stretched endlessly for Connie.

February 11, 1907 Chicago, Illinois

Connie was imprisoned in a panel house at 1233 South State Street. Known as *Lila's*, the three-dollar bordello (three dollars for one-half hour) housed seven prostitutes, a madam named Mrs. Kelly, and the owners, Percy McGill and his confederate, Little Johnny Laughlin. A panel house was simply a whorehouse with a number of bedrooms that had sliding wooden panels. At *Lila's*, certain customers—not all—ended up in the panel rooms. The prostitute made sure the trick placed his clothing on the chair by the wall, the only piece of furniture in the room. As the prostitute entertained the customer, a hidden panel slid open and arms popped out to grab every bill in the gentleman's wallet. Most of the time the men never noticed the theft until they ordered a beer at the saloon across the street. Panel houses did not do great return business, but they reaped large profits from the initial visits. Plus *Lila's* had a stable of regular customers, mostly locals, who were spared the robbery. The police demanded higher bribes due to the nature of the establishment, but all in all, the seventy-five-dollar monthly honorarium to Officer Jensen and similar payments to the aldermen allowed McGill to make a handsome living, even counting the freebies that Jensen had been demanding and receiving lately.

Locked in the dark bedroom with just two wooden chairs, a commode, some towels, and a bowl of water, the time passed slowly for Connie. The only window had thin metal bars on it, offering no means of escape. Twice daily a woman entered the room with food and carried away the contents of the commode. The woman, maybe fifty years old, said only her name—Mrs. Kelly—and warned, "Do not ask me to help you. It will be easier if you simply abide his wishes."

Connie pleaded with Mrs. Kelly. "Are you a Christian lady? In the name of all that is right, Mrs. Kelly, do not let this continue. He has attacked me. Please contact the police or get me out of here. Please!"

Connie looked in Mrs. Kelly's eyes as she pleaded but they remained dull and lifeless. The woman acted as if she could not hear a word and left the room, locking the door from the outside as she had done many times in the past with many different girls. The door closed with a soft thud that echoed off the hardwood floors.

February 13, 1907 Chicago, Illinois

McGill raped Connie twice in the next two days, each time beating her bloody to obtain compliance. She resisted every step of the way. The last time he brought his partner in with him, to leer and laugh at her humiliation.

"This is my associate, Little Johnny. A funny man, Mr. Laughlin is. He prefers to watch this sort of thing," said Percy. "Isn't that so, Johnny Boy?"

"True as rot," answered the greasy little figure, his right hand exploring a large pocket in a gray cardigan sweater that draped over his slouching shoulders. He wore a large smirk on his face and Connie soon recognized him as the same individual who had driven the car from the railroad station. She now observed that he had a scar on his left cheek and red pimples on his chin. Little Johnny sat himself down on a chair by the bed and took a paper bag out of his pocket, the crinkling clatter of the bag distracting Percy. Little Johnny removed a ham sandwich from the bag and began to eat.

"Enjoying yourself?" Percy inquired of Johnny.

"Oh yeah," he answered. "You wanna bite?" Johnny raised the sandwich to affirm the genuineness of the offer.

"No thanks. You wanna bite of this?"

Johnny gurgled a laugh, a heavy phlegm bubbling in his throat and nasal passages. He spat onto the floor.

McGill again leaped onto Connie.

McGill's attempt to "break" Connie—to beat and degrade her such that she felt she had no alternative but to work as a whore at *Lila's*—had succeeded with others many times before. Battered, ravished women, in the grip of fear or drugged beyond rationality, acceded to prostitution. McGill and his cohorts employed drugs when rape and force did not gain their ends. McGill used opiate injections, laughing when the needles broke in the arms of the struggling woman. Three of the seven prostitutes at *Lila's* had been forced into whoring by McGill. Two others he had acquired in trades with bordello owners in Milwaukee. Only twice in five years had McGill's efforts failed to force his victim into prostitution. In both of these instances Percy had given the women an ultimatum: work as a prostitute or die. Slaughterhouse workers found the two women floating in the Chicago River near the Yards, nude, their throats slit. Police never identified the bodies or took any action to investigate the crimes.

Percy slipped into the room while Connie lay asleep. He sat gently on the bed, listening to her breathe, the slow in and out rhythm of a sleeper. He caressed her ankle, causing her to wake and withdraw, without a word or sound, from his touch.

"You have a decision to make, Carmen," he began.

"My name is Constance," she interrupted.

"You are mistaken. Your name, from this moment on, is Carmen. You will be employed by me, in this establishment, for significantly more money than you would make at the Boston Store. You will have no tedious chores other than the company of men, some of whom you will find quite charming. And some of whom will be stinking sots. Think of this as an educational institute, if you will. After a five-year curriculum you will be free to leave, and if you save your money, you will have many opportunities. Life will not be as you planned it, but it will be gay and remunerative. And you will not have to work as most women do. You will not be on your knees scrubbing floors. You will spend time on your knees, of course, but, as I said, not scrubbing floors. Oh yes, there is one more thing. You *will* start turning tricks for me tomorrow. If not, then Little Johnny will slit your throat. Ear to precious ear, darling. I've seen his handiwork. The man is a wizard with a razor."

Connie examined Percy's face as the hate grew inside her. Percy stared back at her, cold and blank, oblivious to her pain and terror. The face of a madman. A terrifying image of the leering Little Johnny, knife in hand, entered her mind. In a quivering but emphatic voice, she stated, "No. The answer is no. Forever no."

February 14, 1907 Bubbly Creek

Two boys, both eleven, stood playing catch just over the dirt embankment that led down to Bubbly Creek. They wore tattered clothes and their shoes had holes, but they were enjoying themselves. The boys tossed a homemade baseball back and forth, but an errant throw sent it slipping down to the creek where it rolled onto the crud that layered the surface. They paused at the crest of the embankment, looking down at their ball and their predicament.

Bubbly Creek stretched out before them, not a creek at all, but a small tributary of the Chicago River, the dead end South Fork of the South Branch of the river. A hundred fifty feet across, it served as an open sewer, the main drainage receptacle for the wastes and runoff of the Union Stockyards. Numerous gutters and pipes, blocks long, carried the frothy yellow animal urine to the creek. Worse, every day the stockyard workers tossed in spoiled and diseased animal torsos, along with toxic chemicals and grease. The carcasses mixed with the other substances and caked three feet thick on the benthic bed of the primordial pool. As the animal remains decomposed, they oozed huge bubbles of foul-smelling gases which burst at the surface, giving the creek its name. The grease eventually congealed, creating a scummy surface that cats and vermin could run across. It caught fire on more than one occasion, requiring the fire department to extinguish the sooty flames.

The boys had reservations about approaching the creek to retrieve their baseball. Their mothers, on numerous occasions, had warned them of the perils of the creek.

"Let's get a long stick to fish it out." They guided the ball toward the rock-strewn edge. But as they approached the ball, another secret of black Bubbly Creek was revealed. Not six feet from the shore, a woman's mottled arm extended from below, a bloody palm skyward, as if beckoning the boys to a dance at the bottom of this watery hell.

February 16, 1907 Chicago, Illinois

Fitzgerald worked State Street that morning, collecting twenty-four cents for his efforts. His technique did not vary. A defeated look on his face, a tin cup, and two pennies. He slipped all newly won coins into his pocket. The two clinking pennies produced a pathetic, spare sound. Not like the vibrato of a cup filled with change. The lonely coins cried out an invitation for good citizens to deposit more.

By the size of the crowds and the many families present, he figured it must be Saturday. That meant that he could head over to Clark Street, near Van Buren, to the Workingman's Exchange, the saloon of Alderman Hinky Dink Kenna. A poor man could pay a nickel there and get what Hinky Dink called "the largest and coolest schooner of beer in Chicago." With the beer came a sandwich, but on Saturdays the bartender laid out trays of food. Getting there early meant getting a seat at the bar, so, after only two hours working the crowds, Fitzgerald wandered down Van Buren Street under the elevated train tracks toward Clark. An el train rumbled thirty-five feet above him, shaking loose clumps of snow that rained down softly onto the cobbled street. Three stray dogs chased across Van Buren, their tongues hanging out and their exhaled breath turning to steam in the cold air. When he spied the dogs Mike clutched for his pocketknife, but the animals did not turn.

Eight-inch letters on the window spelled out "M. Kenna's Workingman Exchange" and, next to it, "Manhattan Beer." Empty thirty-one-gallon beer barrels lined the sidewalk in front of the building, stacked two high. A bartender with red and white suspenders, a busted bottom lip, and a greasy white shirt turned over a tin sign on the door, from "Closed" to "Open," as Mike slipped through the front entrance. Hinky Dink had yet to convert the place to electricity, so a series of dim gas lamps still provided the lighting. Mike would get his stool at the bar and a good position for the food trays that afternoon. Mike knew these wooden floors well. He had slept on these same creaky planks on many cold nights over the last few years. A little girl, who had entered the saloon right behind Fitzgerald, tugged on his pant leg, plaintively asking for a penny. Mike shook his head and quietly, almost kindly, said, "You ought not beg the beggarman, darling."

The bar stretched sixty feet from the front of the establishment to the rear. Mike knew exactly where to sit to assure the best access to the assortment of breads, meats, and pickles. As other tramps filed in and took the seats next to him, Mike placed a nickel on the bar. The bartender scooped it up and soon a large schooner of Manhattan beer sat before him. The strong scent of the alcohol welcomed Fitzgerald like an old friend.

Fitzgerald respected Alderman Kenna. Two years earlier he had come here to speak with him. After only ten minutes an employee led Fitzgerald back to Hinky Dink's crammed office, filled with cigar smoke, spittoons, whiskey bottles, and political cronies.

The alderman looked up from a mountain of papers and extended his small hand. "How may I help you, sir?"

"I could use a job. I'm not afraid of hard work."

Without hesitation Kenna went into action. "Very well. I want you to talk to Bobby Fenton over there, the fat man with the big Havana cigar. He will sign you up for the City Water Department. It's hard work, like you say, but you look like you're up to it."

"Thank you. God bless you, sir."

Getting a job was that easy in Chicago. Speak to the man with clout, and many things could be arranged. Fitzgerald laid water pipes on the West Side for three weeks until a jailing for public drunkenness caused him to lose the job. He didn't even go back after his release from jail. The urgent need to get drunk again grabbed first priority.

Fitzgerald knew that Alderman Kenna could no longer help, but he remained loyal. "This town is the better for Hinky Dink," he told his drinking associates. "He speaks for us, the working stiffs and the down-trodden."

Fitzgerald settled in for a long session. After four beers a gentle numbness overtook him, and his despair and misery faded into the smoky darkness of the saloon. Fitzgerald didn't even look up when a noisy scuffle broke out, with two smelly drunks screaming and trying to bite off each other's ears and noses. His gaze remained frozen on the world that danced and beckoned within the mug he cradled on the bar, where a multitude of bubbles shot to the surface and burst in tiny explosions, sending little sparkles of light careening through the glass.

Connie Dandridge awoke on the sixth day of her nightmare. A dull pain rang in her ears and dried blood crusted an eyebrow and her upper lip. Before falling asleep she had weighed the idea of taking her own life. She could tear the bed sheet into strips and hang herself from the steel window grill, but her desperate desire for a measure of revenge halted all thoughts of suicide. *Percy had to be punished.* Tears again flowed from her eyes, the salty rivulets stinging her bruised cheeks.

Curled up on the bed, Connie heard a scraping noise and startled at the sight of a wooden panel of the wall sliding open. Lit by a candle flickering in the dark, the face of a woman appeared, whispering "Come!" As Connie cautiously approached, she made out the form of a woman with pearl earrings and heavily rouged cheeks. At the woman's beckoning, Connie climbed through the opening into a passageway behind the wall where a narrow corridor led off into the darkness. The woman carefully replaced the panel, quietly secured a locking wedge, and signaled Connie to follow. Connie did so without hesitation while praying to the Virgin Mary, "Please, let this be my salvation!"

The passageway led to a clammy, narrow flight of stairs. Connie followed the woman and the flickering light of the candle down several flights to a damp, cold, and cluttered cellar where water dripped down the unfinished brick walls and collected in small pools. For a moment Connie hesitated, fearful that she may have leaped from the frying pan into the fire. But the woman's expression exhibited concern for Connie. Her liberator turned and closely examined Connie's face and neck, then pulled out Connie's arms to inspect them. Besides the blood crusted on her cheek, Connie had bruises on her face, arms, and hands. Her feet were dirty and bare and she wore only filthy, tattered scraps of clothing.

"Did he stick you with the needle?" she asked, looking at Connie's arms.

Connie shook her head "no."

"You are a frightful mess," the lady observed. "Are you still hurting?"

Connie, too edgy to reply, instead asked, "Can you get me out of this place?"

"Yes, dear, that is my plan. I need to first clean you up a bit and have you put these clothes on." She pointed to a chair with some shoes, undergarments, a dress, and a coat on it. The woman identified herself as Jennie and said that she worked at *Lila's*. Jennie, a brunette, wore a navy blue housecoat with bright red slippers. She told Connie they must be quick and quiet. As Jennie helped clean Connie with a series of wet towels, Connie asked her why she had risked her life to help her.

"I heard you crying all yesterday and today. My room is directly above yours. It tore me up and reminded me of how I came to this place, over a year ago. I had to do something."

After Connie dressed she asked Jennie how she could get out of the building to the street. Jennie pointed to a rickety wooden ladder leading to a storm window. The window had been opened.

"Can you climb that ladder?" Jennie asked.

"Yes. Aren't you coming with?"

Jennie shook her head. Her eyes glazed over, and tears welled. "I am lost. There's no turning back for me now. You still have a chance."

Connie embraced Jennie heartily and urged her to accompany her. "It will be easier," she said, "if we are together." But Jennie would not change her mind. Jennie put two crisp one-dollar bills into Connie's hand as tears flowed from both women's eyes. Climbing the ladder with great determination, Connie pushed aside the window and stepped out into a cold Chicago drizzle.

Jennie's last words to Connie: "Walk north on State Street, toward the Loop. Stay away from a fat cop named Jensen. He is in Percy's pocket and will take you right back to this hellhole."

The Game Catching the Fly Ball

The first time it is impossible. The ball leaps off the bat and climbs skyward. You are ten years old, standing uncomfortably alone in right field or some far stretch of grass. Your eyes and brain have never before teamed up to attempt this task. You see the small speck of white streaking across the blue. The ball arcs upward in a trajectory shaped like a wave. You stagger in three steps until you realize, too late, that the white sphere will sail over your head. At the instant of this realization both legs wobble and there is a stutter-step, an external sign of the rampant confusion in the nervous system.

To catch the fly ball you need to consider the angle of the ball off the bat, its force, spin, velocity, and the effect of the wind. The mind and eyes must weigh these factors in a split second and direct the feet to run to the precise spot on the field where that five-ounce, hide-covered ball of yarn is destined to land. A typical fly ball comes off the bat at a thirty-five degree angle, moving seventy miles per hour, achieving an apex at sixty feet, and traveling two hundred fifty feet. The whole process takes about 3.6 seconds. You cannot catch it the first time. The second attempt you come closer. Each ascending fly ball weaves a new thread of experience that entwines with all past attempts, until the skill is there, built up like a quilt stitched together from each prior effort. Ultimately, the crack of the bat and the flash of the sphere draw you effortlessly to the exact location where you know, without thinking, the ball will descend into your grasp.

February 16, 1907 Chicago, Illinois

Fear grew inside Connie. She navigated a path around the three-story wooden building to get to the street in front, where she had no difficulty discerning north as the tall buildings in the Loop popped out over the horizon. A few people, mainly men in dark overcoats, walked up and down the street, a broad avenue lined with saloons, diners, gambling houses, and a variety of other establishments. Nervously, Connie headed north, looking behind her every few steps. She regarded each step away from that place a small victory.

And then she shuddered, seeing him only twenty yards ahead. Worse, he saw her. Percy McGill doubted his eyes at first. This had never happened before.

How in the hell did she get out? he wondered, and then, *Someone will pay for this!*

He saw Connie's eyes grow large with fear. She stopped dead in her tracks and swiveled about.

McGill increased his pace and Connie figured she had no more than ten seconds to do something. A young man exited a saloon to her left, pausing to place his derby hat on a mass of red hair. She did what she had to, approaching the stranger with palms up, pleading.

"Sir, I am terribly sorry to intrude, but this is truly a life and death matter. A man abducted me a few days ago, he has assaulted me, I escaped, and…"

The red-haired man cut her off, politely but firmly. "I am afraid I do not have any money for you, Miss. Just spent the last of it." As the young man prepared to walk away, Percy hurriedly arrived on the scene, placing his right hand firmly on Connie's arm.

"We really should be going now, dear," he said. "Come, Connie, we need to go to your doctor."

Connie cringed at the touch of Percy and vigorously pulled away from him. She turned to the young man and cried out in a chilling manner, "Please! You must help me, sir! This is the man that has taken advantage of me and I fear he will kill me. I do not exaggerate! I implore you, sir!" Connie pointed to the left side of her face and said, "Look what he has done to me!" As she spoke Percy again gripped her arm and began to tug her away from the other man.

"Hold on there, Mister," the young man said. He looked at the pair, the way the man pulled at the woman, and the abject fear she exhibited. She began to cry and he observed a bruise on her face, where she pointed. As the young man peered into Percy's cold blue eyes, something about him seemed familiar.

Percy spoke again, explaining that the lady, his wife of two years, suffered from a "serious ailment" and that no man should interfere in the "vicissitudes of marital relations."

Connie, crying now, denied every statement of Percy, labeling them lies.

"You see," she said, pointing to her hand, "there is no wedding ring."

At that instant the young man, Kid Durbin, remembered where he had seen this man before, but a few days ago. "I know you, sir. Your name is Percy something, correct?"

"Yes, but…"

"We shared the stage at the Majestic Theater several days ago. The Great Thurston. Do you remember?"

For the first time, Percy scrutinized the man and remembered. "Oh yeah, you were right next to me, the ballplayer, the kid on the Cubs, right?" While Durbin nodded, Percy kept on. "Well that's fine, but this is still my wife and you are trampling on my rights as her husband. We bid you good day."

Kid put his hand on the shoulder of the taller man and said, in the most forceful voice he could muster, "Hold on, sir. There's a bit of a problem here. When you were on that stage with me you told the Great Thurston and the audience that you were not married. Now you say different. We had better find a police officer to sort this matter out."

McGill released his hold on Connie and stepped toward Kid, his face taking on a pained expression. He articulated his words in a measured, menacing tone. "Listen, little man," he said, "you don't know what you are getting involved in. This is not your concern. You could get hurt, maybe a broken arm, perhaps never play ball again. Lose your ability to make a living all over a two-bit whore."

This clinched it for Durbin. *The woman is telling the truth*, he thought, *this man is a criminal*. Kid put his hand on Connie's arm and said, "Let's go." They walked briskly toward the Loop.

Percy spat on the sidewalk as Kid and Connie departed.

He shouted after them, "You just made the biggest mistake of your life, sonny boy. I know where to find you. Think about that. And you, Miss Bitch, don't even think of taking this any further. Women like you get fished out of the river every day."

As they fled, Connie turned once to look back. Percy smirked and threw her a kiss. Connie stumbled as the fluids in her stomach shot up into her throat.

February 18, 1907 **Chicago, Illinois**

Mike Fitzgerald was mildly drunk, still enjoying the bounteous culinary delights at the Exchange. He chewed on his third beef and cheese sandwich, wiping it down with cold beer every so often. For Fitzgerald, it couldn't get any better. He could eat as much as he wanted. Hinky Dink, the alderman/owner of the Exchange, once fired a bartender who told a customer he had taken too much food. "After all," Kenna scolded the barkeep, "*this is a voter.*"

A small man, a stranger, sat on his right, equally engrossed in the business at hand. The saloon buzzed that afternoon, as rows of hungry men jostled for position behind the men on stools at the bar. One of these men, a youth of twenty, with curly blond hair, blue eyes and a decent, unblemished overcoat, tapped Fitzgerald on his right shoulder to announce a proposition.

"Hey old-timer," the young man began, "what say you let me have your seat in exchange for this here five-cent piece?" The boy stood tall, maybe six feet, and he waved the nickel back and forth in front of Fitzgerald like it was a silver dollar.

Mike half-turned on the stool, looked the boy up and down, and simply said, "No thanks, sonny."

Undeterred, the boy tried again. "Excuse me, but I didn't make myself clear. I want your chair. I will give you five cents for it."

"I heard you the first time. The answer is still no." Mike spoke with little emphasis, still peering straight ahead at the bottles and mirror against the wall.

The blond-haired boy placed his hand upon Fitzgerald's right shoulder and tugged at him.

This time Fitzgerald swiveled fully around, tugging free of the boy's hold. "If you touch me one more time, I will put your right eye out."

The youth stared into Fitzgerald's face and started to laugh, saying, "Put my eye out will you? Maybe a long time ago, pops." He again placed his hand on Fitzgerald's shoulder, this time forcefully gripping his coat, and pulling him forward off the stool.

Fitzgerald moved quickly, simultaneously kneeing the young fellow in the groin and grabbing the flaxen hair by the roots with his right hand. The four fingers of Fitzgerald's left hand grabbed the boy's right ear and the thumb slipped over the eye, and, without hesitation, burrowed into the glassy orbit, bursting the vitreous body. The eye fluid and remnants spilled out over the thumb, running down the cheeks of the howling youth. Fitzgerald casually wiped his thumb on his coat, perched again on the stool, and reached over to his stein to gulp a quantity of beer. The boy lay on the floor and lapsed into unconsciousness. A dirty one-legged man pretended to attend to the boy but, instead, rifled through the lad's pockets and stole his wallet.

The small man sitting next to Fitzgerald took careful note of the great physical skill wielded by Fitzgerald and chuckled with a phlegm-like sound. He turned a pockmarked face toward Fitzgerald and commented, "Very impressive display, sir." The man rocked back and forward on the bar stool. "Can I buy you a drink?" he asked, his small eyes shifting slowly from side to side.

"I never turn down the offer of a free drink. Are you an Irishman?"

"That I am, although 'tis a burden to admit that in certain quarters of this city. The name is Johnny Laughlin. People call me Little Johnny."

From the Journal of Kid Durbin

February 19, 1907

The woman is named Connie Dandridge. She has only been in Chicago a short, terrible time. It appears that I helped her escape the clutches of a dreadful rogue, Percy McGill, one of the men on stage with me at the Majestic Theater. I didn't remember his surname when I saw him with her on the street, but I had written it here, in my journal. Connie says he assaulted her, kept her locked up for four days, and stole all her money. She hinted that McGill committed more evil acts but she didn't elaborate.

Since she needed help, I called the one person I knew in Chicago, Mr. Murphy of the Cubs. I asked for his guidance and he went to bat for the young woman. He and his wife, Marie Louise, had no hesitation in agreeing to put Connie up and help her get back on her feet. So she is living up north now, with them, on Lincoln Avenue. Mr. Murphy even had his doctor come and take a look at Connie the day I took her there. The doctor said she was bruised up pretty bad but she will be fine.

Mr. Murphy is not sure if Connie should report McGill to the police. He feels there could be what he referred to as "detrimental repercussions." Maybe she should put this matter behind her, he wonders. But she seems determined to do something, whatever the consequences might be. Connie agreed to give it a few days' thought, as Murphy suggested, but she is stirred up something awful about all of this, and I cannot say as I blame her. Murphy did say that he knows an honest man in the Cook County State's Attorney Office, a prosecutor named William Wilen. I promised Connie I would accompany her if she chooses to pursue this matter. I feel terribly sorry for her. Mrs. Murphy is looking after her and helping Connie the best she can. The day after I brought Connie to their home Mr. Murphy confided to me that Connie brought back to the Murphys "the golden memories of their own daughter," who had died of consumption three years earlier.

When I think back on my confrontation with McGill I wonder if I should have popped him one. I admit that I felt a little streaked when he advanced on me and the young woman. But my father told me that fear is a healthy thing, a signal from the angels to tread carefully. If I had let Percy beat me—he is no sickly child—he might have been able to keep ahold of Connie. My actions allowed me to remove her from danger.

I used to have quite a temper. That's how I got my nickname, Kid. Ornery men in Lamar got that nickname. A few years back I just might have lost my composure. People change. Getting Connie away from that hooligan proved the best course of action. I didn't need to prove anything with Percy. There are better ways to deal with this guy.

Connie grew stronger and more resolute to press on against McGill. Murphy arranged for her to meet with the prosecutor one afternoon and Kid Durbin agreed to accompany her. He took the streetcar north and walked one block to the Murphy residence. The cold winds still howled down the broad avenues, and Kid shivered as he approached the house, a large, Tudor-style brick building. Entering the building, Durbin found Connie ready to go. She welcomed Kid with a handshake.

"I very much appreciate you taking the time to do this," she said.

"It's no problem, Connie. How are you doing?" he asked. His green eyes looked down into hers.

"Just fine, Blaine. A lot better than when we met." She pulled on a toque, a small hat garnished with black ribbons and white lace. She asked about the weather and they left the house.

Kid looked at Connie differently now. He thought her very pretty, but he also observed a great sadness. *This poor woman has endured a great deal*, he thought. He wanted to help her move on with her life. He was glad that fate had tossed Connie into his life.

Through the assistance of Mr. Murphy, Connie had obtained employment in the Masonic Temple Building at a flower shop on the atrium floor. Kid asked her about her work and Connie glowed.

"I enjoy it. I cut and arrange flowers. Wonderful colors, great fragrances. I work with another girl who is very nice. We can talk while we work. It's a good job. I get Sundays and Wednesdays off! I was lucky—at least in this respect."

They climbed on the streetcar heading south to the Loop. A sign above them stated "SPITTING PROHIBITED." While they talked the city sped past them in a blur, and sunshine flashed in and out of the car sporadically. The streetcar rolled smoothly down the center of Clark Street, its great iron wheels clacking a muffled beat every three seconds.

"How long before you join the team?" she asked him.

"We leave for training in Indiana on March 2."

"And when do you return to Chicago?"

"About a month. We'll spend a week in southern Indiana and three weeks in New Orleans and a number of other southern cities. I'm looking forward to it."

"I am sure you will be a great success," Connie stated. "You seem very determined to realize your goals."

Kid thanked Connie for her kind words. They hopped off the streetcar one-half block from City Hall and the county offices, which occupied a large columned building on LaSalle and Washington. Up a flight of ten stairs that led within, they found a dimly lit and cluttered structure. A sign informed them that the State's Attorney Office occupied the third floor, and an elevator took them up.

Beyond a double-door entrance, dozens of desks, cabinets, and clerks crowded the dark premises. A receptionist directed them to Mr. Wilen, who occupied a spacious office overlooking Dearborn Street. Many boxes cluttered the space, each a file marked with names like "Schaap, Giles," and "Robertson, Kenneth." A carved ivory sign on the man's desk said "William Wilen." Fifty years old, two inches short of six feet, he owned a full head of white hair combed neatly across his head. A white mustache extended across his upper lip, gold-rimmed spectacles sat on the bridge of his nose, and his eyes truly twinkled in sincerity. He spoke in a firm, measured voice, but when he became excited, his head bobbed and the voice cracked a little. He had a warm smile and began with small talk about the miserable weather and how he hated February.

"The winters are too long! February is always so tedious. Of course I am a veteran of Chicago winters and worse, having grown up in Dakota. All's I can say is I ache for spring."

Then he got serious. "Mr. Murphy informed me of the nature of your problem. These are grave allegations. I will have to speak to you alone, Miss Dandridge, in order to preserve the confidentiality of our discussion."

Kid excused himself and headed for the waiting room.

Wilen began in earnest. "I need you to tell me everything that happened, leaving out no facts, even those you feel are peripheral. I must know every detail if I am to take action against the person who violated you. If you remember the exact times events took place I want to know these. I will want you to describe every person you mention, their height, weight, and appearance, and the exact words they used. A shorthand secretary will transcribe every word you say and I will ask for more information than you will be able to provide so please forgive me in advance. I do this so that we—the State of Illinois and the County of Cook—will be armed with enough facts to overcome any and all defenses."

The secretary, a young woman of nineteen, came in and they began, Connie nervous at first, but composed until it became necessary to describe the details of the rapes. She wept at having to relive the horror of what had been done to her, but Wilen showed a sensitivity to her needs and gingerly elicited what he needed to know. Toward the end, after an hour and thirty minutes, Connie made one final point.

"You must be delicate in the matter of the woman who rescued me, the woman named Jennie. If her role in my escape is revealed, her life will be in jeopardy. Can you promise me that you will act accordingly?"

Wilen agreed. And then he concluded, warning Connie of the difficult road that lay ahead.

"Miss Dandridge, our case rides or falls on your testimony, unless we are able to convince an employee of *Lila's* to testify against their employer. That is an unlikely prospect. This man McGill has no scruples. He no doubt has money, and as he already told you, he will try to use that money to interfere in the normal workings of our judicial system. We do have seven excellent judges who would afford us a fair and proper trial. Unfortunately, there are twelve other judges."

Connie understood.

The Game   Frank Chance, the "Peerless Leader"

Frank "Husk" Chance grew up in a prosperous Fresno, California, family, his father a businessman and banker. As Frank gained a place of stature in the game a story developed that he had attended college and dental school out west, but he had not. He did not even graduate from Fresno High School, despite an undeniable intelligence. Chance had other priorities. Early on Frank Chance shone as a baseball player, his pure talent marked by deceptive speed, intelligence, and a gritty determination. He played catcher for a number of California semi-professional baseball teams and broke into the majors with the Cubs at that position in 1898. A good defensive backstop, foul tips broke the fingers on both of his hands numerous times, maiming his hands. But the man played like it meant more to him than anything else. It did. Baseball was his mission.

Snarling at the pitcher, he always hugged the plate, inviting the brush-back pitch. But one thing set Chance apart from every other hitter, then and now: he never backed off from an inside pitch, never even evaded the fastball targeting his body. He did not even duck away from pitches aimed at his head. A strategy of sorts, the pitchers came to know that you could not brush this man back, that if you threw one close in you were likely to hit the bastard. The downside was painfully obvious. At a time when batting helmets had yet to be invented, pitches struck Frank Chance in the head, and elsewhere, more than any player of his time. In one doubleheader in 1904 he took five hits to the body, including one to his head. In about 4,300 major league at-bats in a career stretching between 1898 and 1914, 137 pitches plunked the Cubs manager. In contrast, Cubs shortstop Joe Tinker got nailed only ten times in more than 6,400 big league batting appearances.

When bloodied by a ball, Chance spat tobacco juice and saliva into his hand, rubbed it on the wound, and played on. When he did not arise immediately after being struck by a beanball, his players carried him to the Cook County Hospital across Polk Street from the West Side Grounds. The repeated beanings took their toll. By 1907 Frank could not hear well out of his left ear and suffered severe recurring headaches.

In the history of the game, not many individuals have successfully managed a team and played at the same time. Frank Chance, perhaps the finest playing manager of all time, produced as a player and managed the Cubs better than anyone since. A natural leader, his teammates elected him team captain under the prior Cubs manager, Frank Selee, and he stepped into the role of manager when Selee's health forced an early retirement. Chance studied the game and retained the "smart" ballplayers like Johnny Evers, Joe Tinker, and Johnny Kling. A good judge of pitchers, he acquired Jack Pfiester and Orval "Jeff" Overall, two strong young arms for the Cubs, in 1906. Every aspect of the game came under Chance's scrutiny. His Cubs employed bunts, hit and run plays, stolen bases, and stealing opponents' signs to eke runs out of every scoring opportunity. Chance and Evers made meticulous observations of National League players, carefully cataloging the pick-off motions of pitchers, the quality of catchers' and outfielders' throwing arms, how quickly the outfielders could field a ball, and the circumstances when opposing teams used a pitchout or a hit and run. Chance and Evers took careful pains in positioning their defense, and may have been the first ballclub to use the shortstop to cover second base when a lefty batted with a runner at first. By 1906 the Cubs were seldom surprised by an opposing team's field maneuvers. Nor did Chance hesitate to use a measure of intimidation on the opposition and umpires, as well as an occasional resort to "dirty baseball." His view: "If they do it, we're gonna do it."

Chance had some failings as a field manager. For example, he did not believe that the batting order made much of a difference. He often simply sent the three outfielders up first, the infielders in the next four slots, followed by the catcher and pitcher. The center fielder often led off, the first baseman generally batted cleanup, and the third baseman was mostly fifth. Utility man Solly Hofman, who was born to bat second, would find himself leading off when he played center, batting cleanup when he subbed for Chance at first, and batting sixth when covering shortstop duties for Tinker. Another quirky policy of the Peerless Leader was his order to not shake hands with opposing players while in uniform. "You are a ballplayer and not a society dancer at a pink tea," he screamed one day. "I want to see some fight in you and not this social crap." Violation of this rule brought a ten-dollar fine, a stiff penalty for that time. Chance, always the strict disciplinarian, often reminded his players of his managerial motto: "We do it my way or we meet after the game and let our fists decide who is right." On many occasions he unleashed his furious fists on his own or opposing players, always bloodying the opponent. "Gentleman" Jim Corbett, former heavyweight boxing champion and Frank's drinking buddy, called Chance "the greatest amateur fighter in the world." He liked to drink but he did not overdo it. Chance encouraged his players to loosen up and drink a few beers following a ballgame. Constantly urging the Crab, Johnny Evers, to have a few drinks with him, he succeeded only once or twice. With but a few exceptions, the players loved him, looked up to their "Peerless Leader," and tried their best to earn his respect.

On the field Chance displayed excellent skills. A fine defensive first baseman, he gradually developed into an accomplished hitter. From 1902 through 1906, Chance never hit under .310. He spent countless hours studying the mannerisms and deliveries of opposing pitchers. It paid off. For a big man, he stole an amazing number of bases. In fact, he led the league in swiped bases in 1903 and 1906, and the sixty-seven bases he stole in 1903 remains a season record for a first baseman, as does his career total of 401 stolen bases. In April 1906, Chance set the tone for that year when, with two out in the ninth, he stole home against the Reds to give the Cubs a 1-0 victory. On a number of occasions, after being hit in the leg by a pitched ball, he would feign a limp as he took first base. Then, as the pitcher wound up to toss the first delivery to the next batter, Husk would scamper down to second base, slide in successfully, stand, and curse out the pitcher.

"Hit me again, asshole. See what it gets you!"

February 24, 1907 **Chicago, Illinois**

Mike Fitzgerald walked slowly toward *Lila's* on South State Street as the result of Little Johnny's promise of employment, work that paid significantly more than Mike usually received. Mike understood that Little Johnny's "job" probably involved criminal activity, with the risk of prison if things went bad, but that possibility did not trouble him. A big payday far outweighed his concern of getting caught. The wind blew strong across State Street from the east, whipping little whirlwinds of dust and paper scraps. Men and women scuttled down the street, holding their hats. As Fitzgerald arrived at the whorehouse, a bell somewhere rang nine times. He was right on time.

An older woman, dressed drably in a gray frock, answered the door and led Mike to Little Johnny who welcomed him into a parlor off the entrance room.

"You ain't been drinkin' today, have ya?" said Johnny, more of an observation than a question.

"No. Figured I oughtn't," replied Fitzgerald, half-truthfully. He had limited himself to three beers in the last twelve hours.

"Good," Little Johnny remarked, "I like that. You come ready to work. No shenanigans. So let me explain what the deal is. You ever take someone out?"

"If you mean kill someone, no…" said Mike.

"Yeah, that's what I mean. I gotta take someone out tonight, and I need a new backup man. That would be you. This one will be a cakewalk. You don't have to do nothin' 'cept if sumpin goes bad. I'll give you a gun, a pistol. You ever fire one?"

"Sure," Fitzgerald lied. "Used to own one."

"All right then. You just need to use it in a emergency… and you gotta help me afta… with the body. My old helper got religion and is now runnin' with some preacher guy. Can you 'magine that!"

"I seen it before. Uh, what does this job pay, Johnny?"

"I was gettin' to that. This first time out is fifty dollars. It's a easy piece of work—probably don't need a second man but it's always good to have a man behind ya. Next time, if ya work out good on this one, it's one hundred dollars. If ya can't stomach this job now's when ya gotta tell me. Not later. You in?"

Fitzgerald nodded yes. Fifty dollars could buy a lot of drink.

Little Johnny handed Fitzgerald a revolver, pointed out the safety, and stuffed the six chambers with bullets. Fitzgerald examined the pistol carefully, the cold chunk of steel resting comfortably in Mike's large, weathered hands. He kept the safety on and stuffed the weapon under his belt, pointing it away from his crotch. Little Johnny told him the job would go down right there at *Lila's*, and had Fitzgerald follow him up two dark flights of stairs. With each step Fitzgerald grew more apprehensive, but he steeled himself for the task. Johnny found a particular room with an open door, and signaled Mike to enter with him. Inside the sparsely furnished room a young woman leaned forward on a chair before a cracked mirror, applying rouge to her cheeks. They entered and Johnny closed the door behind them.

"Jennie," Laughlin said, "I want you to meet my friend Mike."

Jennie turned and said, "Hello." She gave a puzzled look to Little Johnny. "You know I'm not on til later."

"'Fraid I have some bad news for you, girl," Johnny said, his eyes cutting into hers, "a message for you from Percy right here in my pocket."

Jennie became alarmed. "What kind of bad news?"

"The worst kind, Jennie," he explained, pulling a long steel razor out.

Johnny jumped at the girl like a demon and slashed the razor deep, across her throat. She screamed, more in horror than in pain, but in less than five seconds it ended in a low gurgle, as the blood spewed from the severed artery, spattering the wall as she fell, and puddling under her on the rough-hewn wood floor. She died at their feet. Mike's heart pounded at the ghastly scene he had just witnessed and he did not move, even when the body lay still. A cold shudder ran through him as Little Johnny bent over the victim, examining his work.

Johnny spoke calmly, not a trace of emotion evident. "Ya need to get me the sheet and blanket there, Mike. We gotta wrap her up and get her outta here."

Mike hesitated for an instant and then went to work. *That girl was gonna die whether I helped or not*, he told himself, at the same time knowing he had simply rationalized a senseless murder. A moment later, as they rolled the corpse into the sheet, Fitzgerald looked right into the lifeless eyes of the dead girl. *This was wrong, all wrong*, he thought, *I helped Little Johnny kill a young woman*. The realization that he had committed a murder sank into him like a knife into his heart. He never believed he would sink this low. *Is this how murderers are made?*

Little Johnny locked the door to the room and the two men spent almost five hours drinking beer across the street. They didn't talk about the murder. Around 2:00 a.m. they returned to *Lila's* and carried the body to an automobile. Laughlin drove west on 22nd Street until they hit the river, where they dropped their package into the languid dark waters. The body, rocking gently in the water, slowly floated south as Laughlin and Fitzgerald made their way back to the auto under a three-quarters moon. When they reached the vehicle Johnny spun around and dug into his pocket, the same trouser pocket from which he had earlier withdrawn his razor. For an instant Mike worried that blade might soon sink into his flesh, but Johnny instead pulled out some gold pieces, handing Fitzgerald two double eagles and an eagle.

He grasped the coins, thinking now it did not seem like that much money.

February 28, 1907 **Chicago, Illinois**

It took prosecutor Wilen but four days to obtain an indictment for the attack on Connie from the standing grand jury. Two Cook County sheriffs arrested McGill, barging into his bedroom at *Lila's* at ten in the morning, rousing the dazed man from his bed, and dragging him downtown to the Harrison Street Police Station. In 1895 Chicago had adopted the Bertillon Method of prisoner identification, an anthropometric system that used separate measurements of the prisoner's bony body parts to classify persons for later identification. As a consequence, a handcuffed McGill endured the careful measurement of the circumference of his head, his outstretched arm, and, among other things, his middle and little fingers.

"You gonna measure my dick?" he wisecracked.

An officer cuffed McGill on his head. "Shut your filthy mouth."

Percy turned back to the technician who began to measure his knee.

"What happens if I get fat? Ain't it gonna make these measurements wrong?"

The technician, a young man with a bushy black mustache, shook his head.

"Your knee won't gain fat. These fingers aren't going to get longer or shorter. Some parts of the body don't change."

Not long after, McGill found himself peering up at Judge Wilfred Martin for a bail hearing. Martin, a respected judge, lived by the motto that "no decision is final until it is decided right." Wilen argued that bail should be denied because McGill posed a risk of fleeing the jurisdiction. Judge Martin agreed, declaring the charges "significant, warranting detention until adjudicated at trial." Wilen had won the first skirmish.

A horse-drawn patrol wagon transported McGill to the Bridewell Prison, on West 26th Street and California Avenue. A stone structure, the building housed about six hundred inmates and three times as many rats. McGill quickly acclimated to the smell of urine and the constant sobbing of two mentally unbalanced inmates on his wing.

Percy shared a ten-foot by ten-foot cell with a young Italian fellow, Pasquale Aiuppa. A small man with a scar on his neck, Aiuppa spoke very little English. Right from the start McGill determined that Aiuppa belonged to the Black Hand, the not-so-secret criminal society of southern Italians. He had been charged with the murder of another Italian, a grocery store owner who refused to pay monthly tribute to the Black Hand. Ordinarily McGill would have nothing to do with Italians, whom he usually referred to as "dagoes" and regarded as an inferior race. In fact, as a sixteen-year-old, Percy ran with a street gang that regularly targeted the Italians moving into his neighborhood for beatings and worse. That is where Percy first learned of and came to admire the Black Hand.

Circumstances dictated that Percy approach his cellmate differently. He took no action to upset Aiuppa. Instead, McGill went out of his way to treat this particular Italian with respect. It didn't make sense to alienate someone who could slit your throat while you slept. The prison guards forced Aiuppa to join the work gangs in the limestone quarries behind the prison each day, even though prisoners awaiting trial—as opposed to convicts—ordinarily did not have to labor in the quarries.

McGill put his cellmate in touch with the alderman who "handled" the problems of Italians, Johnny Powers of the West Side's Nineteenth Ward, and soon Aiuppa's duties on the work gang ceased. Powers, known as the "Prince of the Boodlers," had pulled a few strings. McGill also "lent" Aiuppa two hundred dollars to expedite his situation. With the help of the alderman and the money, Aiuppa easily obtained a new hearing on bail. A reduction in bail, to fifty dollars, allowed Aiuppa to walk. He thanked Percy profusely for his help.

"I maybe give you the help in tomorrow days," he told Percy as he gathered his belongings from the cell.

Aiuppa's murder trial never took place. Things could be done in Chicago.

Percy mapped his own course of action. His anger steadily grew each day he spent in the stinking Bridewell cell. He first needed to overcome the criminal charges, so he reached out and retained Benjamin Franklin Cole to represent him. McGill had availed himself of Cole's services on one prior occasion and Cole had performed admirably. A young man of thirty-two, he had excellent connections to Alderman Kenna and other city council boodlers. An ingratiating manner, a Harvard law degree, and a willingness to do what is necessary brought Cole quick wealth and powerful friends. Earlier in his career Cole acted as a bagman, delivering brown envelopes stuffed with money to aldermen or those they designated to receive it. Now he handled more complex matters.

In the afternoon Cole visited McGill in the Bridewell Prison. They met in a dingy room with only a table, one chair, and scattered mounds of rat turds. McGill took the chair. Cole wore a derby hat, a black single-breasted, wool-tweed overcoat, which he removed and laid carefully on the table, and a gray wool three-piece suit, his "jail suit" as he styled it. He had dark hair, a mustache, and a pale complexion, with acne scars pocking his cheeks. He did not remove the black gloves he wore.

"So what approach do you wish to take to these charges?" Cole began. "Shall it be a vigorous litigation or some other device?"

"Some other would seem to be the safest approach, would it not?"

"Yes, that is true," Cole answered, dryly and honestly. "Yesterday the Chief Judge assigned your case to the Honorable Winston McCall. As fate would have it, I am dining with Winnie next Wednesday evening. Shall I put in a good word for you on that occasion? Or perhaps I could put in something more substantial than mere words?"

"How substantial are we talking?"

"I believe five hundred dollars would accomplish our goals. My fee is an additional five hundred dollars, and there will be costs of approximately fifty dollars." A greasy smoothness marked Cole's manner, particularly when it came to the subject of his fees.

"Can we round that off at nine hundred dollars?" Percy asked. "Dinner won't cost you fifty dollars."

Cole looked at him cooly and said, "We can round it off to $1,050."

Percy attempted no further negotiation. "My man will bring round the money to your office tomorrow."

Cole left as quickly as he could. *No need to hang about in a dungeon longer than is absolutely necessary*, he thought. He despised the filth and dampness of the jails. He despised the clients too, such as McGill, uneducated, base men who used violence in their business like Cole used money in his. But these vile criminals made up the lifeblood of his law practice. These sullen clients paid top dollar for Cole's services. And they paid in cash. Attorney Cole enjoyed an adept ability to resolve their problems, achieving their goals, one way or the other. "Complex, difficult situations," he told his paying clients, "often have simple solutions."

Stepping out of the prison gates Cole looked west, observing a bright and cloud-free sky. *Great things await me*, he thought. *Perhaps a life in politics. Who knows?* He could not imagine that three years into the future, one of these vile, uneducated clients, souring on his lawyer's demands for more money, would deposit two lead bullets into the back of his pomaded head.

March 1, 1907 Chicago, Illinois

The seasoned prosecutor knew the case would be difficult. His investigator had checked out *Lila's*, the whorehouse on South State Street run by Percy McGill. The madame who ran the place, a Mrs. Kelly, proved as hard as nails. She might have been McGill's mother but that could not be established yet. A secondary operator, a slimy, lowlife character named John Laughlin, owned a record of burglaries and misdemeanor assault convictions, mainly against female victims. *A real tough guy*, thought Wilen. The six prostitutes who worked *Lila's* refused to give up anything. Didn't see anything or hear anything out of the ordinary. *What in the hell is ordinary in a brothel?* Wilen wondered. Connie had mentioned getting help from a prostitute named Jennie, but the investigator could not locate the woman. Mrs. Kelly said she returned home to Boston and identified her as Jennie Smith. Wilen had his investigators interview the johns who frequented *Lila's*, while doubting any useful information could be gained from this source. That left just the victim and Blaine Durbin as witnesses for the prosecution, not as much as Wilen would have liked. To make matters worse, Wilen learned of the case's assignment to Judge McCall, not one of Wilen's favorite jurists, and not on Wilen's unwritten list of clean judges.

Wilen received a motion earlier in the day. McGill had retained Ben Cole as counsel. *Another bad sign*, thought Wilen.

"The man reeks of impropriety," he told his young law clerk.

Entitled "Motion to Quash the Indictment," the ribboned document occupied fourteen typewritten pages, with three accompanying blue-backed affidavits. The motion argued that insufficient evidence existed to sustain any criminal charges against the defendant. The last affidavit took Wilen by surprise: a sworn statement from a Chicago police officer named Charles Jensen. Jensen's allegations, ludicrous but damaging, read as follows:

I, Officer Charles P. Jensen, being first duly sworn, state under oath as follows:

1.   The affiant is a respected and decorated member of the Chicago Police force, having entered into such service on March 23, 1904.

2.   Prior to March 23, 1904 the affiant was a member of the United States Army, serving as an infantryman and member of the military police for two years and three months.

3.   On or about May 6, 1904, the affiant first came to know the defendant, Percy McGill, having met this man during religious services at Holy Name Cathedral, 735 N. State Street, in the City of Chicago, Illinois.

4.   The affiant is now assigned to a beat which includes the area in which the defendant operates a tavern known as *Lila's*, at 1555 South State Street, in Chicago, Illinois.

5.   In the years that affiant has known the defendant as a result of his employment in the area of the defendant's business, the defendant has conducted himself and his business in a lawful and Christian manner, observing to the letter all state and municipal statutes and ordinances.

6.   The affiant has, on numerous occasions, observed the defendant providing alms to the poor, food to worthy Negroes, and shelter to Christian souls who lacked same.

7.   On or about February 21, 1907, the affiant observed a young woman named Connie Dandridge milling about in front of *Lila's*. This woman appeared to be under the severe influence of alcohol and would only leave the vicinity of *Lila's* under threat of incarceration.

AFFIANT FURTHER SAYETH NAUGHT.

Signed, this 28th day of February, 1907.
Charles P. Jensen

Wilen threw down the affidavit on his law clerk's desk and shouted, "Observe, young man, the power of the almighty dollar."

The Game   Fear of Getting Hit

A great part of the art of good hitting is the ability to step into the batter's box, sidle up to the plate, and swing clean and true at an object like a rock which is hurtling at you between eighty and one hundred miles per hour. The batter has precious little time to decide whether to stride into the ball and swing or hang back, waiting for the next pitch. Maybe half a second on the average to make the decision, or .41 seconds on a one hundred miles per hour fastball. At some point in his life the batter has been struck by the pitched baseball. And struck again. The pain of these incidents leaves an indelible mark in the psyche of the hitter. A palpable fear lingers with some would-be sluggers, interfering with their ability to hit the ball. They may pull off the pitch ever so slightly as it whizzes inside. Or fail to sufficiently stride into the pitched ball to hit it with authority. Some can overcome this fear while others cannot.

The pitcher uses this fear like it is an extra pitch. The fastball, the curveball, and the inside pitch. The inside pitch is designed to intimidate, to stake a claim to the inner third of the plate, and to upset the rhythm in the next few swings of the batter. Frank Chance once managed a rawboned rookie Cubs pitcher too timid to throw inside at batters who crowded the plate. Chance required the young hurler to deliberately hit a batter in the first inning of each game. Any batter. The rookie did this and it worked, pushing the opposing batters off the plate, so the kid could gain some strikes on the outside corner of the plate.

This is how it works: The batter digs in at the plate, literally, kicking depressions in the soft earth of the batter's box to create toeholds for his steel-cleated shoes. His batting stance encroaches on the plate. His head may actually hang over the dish, like a leaf off a twig. The pitcher peers in to the plate, in a disapproving scowl: *This batter is invading my space.* The next pitch is launched more like a spear at an invading warrior than a baseball in an afternoon game. The pitch is a weapon in the ancient battle between pitcher and batsman. The pitch hurtles toward the head of the batter, who twists and drops to his knees to avoid the darting missile. The baseball may graze the batter or strike him flush, bruising the tissue or breaking a bone. Most of the time the batter dodges the bullet and, seconds later, the contest begins again. The batter rises from the dirt, brushes the dust off his uniform, and swings the bat briskly over the plate, inviting the next pitch. Come what may, the batter must exhibit no fear, or the battle will be lost. The pitcher gets his sign, sets, and throws, the ball once again speeding toward home.

March 1, 1907 Chicago, Illinois

McGill's defense counsel scheduled the motion for two o'clock on another chilly, gray Chicago day. Wilen had prepared diligently for the event, including beefing up the record with copious counter-affidavits from Miss Dandridge and Mr. Durbin. His investigator could not unearth any police officer willing to chip away at the reputation of Officer Jensen. Other officers showed little respect for Jensen but he wore their colors. The investigator did learn that Jensen had been reprimanded twice for "conduct unbecoming a police officer," departmental code for taking bribes. Wilen also filed a certified copy of these two reprimands with the court.

The entire cast of characters sat waiting in Judge McCall's courtroom. Ben Cole leaned over the defendant's table, dressed in an expensive, finely tailored black suit, a silver watch-chain hanging from his waistcoat. Next to him McGill slumped to the side of his chair without affect until he eyed Connie, and smiled in her direction. Cole, observing his client do this, placed his hand on McGill's shoulder and warned him against making any further attempts to communicate in any manner with the young woman.

"There will be a proper time for that," he advised McGill. "I want you to fade into the background just now." Before fading into the background Percy sauntered a few steps toward a brass spittoon that sat in the middle of the courtroom and launched a stream of amber-colored spit into it.

Connie sat next to Kid Durbin in the first row of chairs. Wilen assembled his documents in piles on the state's table and then stepped over to greet Connie and Durbin, wearing a smile that lifted the left corner of his mouth. A moment later Judge McCall took the bench and the bailiff called the room to order.

"Oyez, oyez," shouted the bailiff. "All those with business before this tribunal, please draw near. The Superior Court of Cook County is in session. God save this Honorable Court."

Sixty-five years old with scruffs of white hair amidst pink bald spots, Judge McCall had a ruddy red face with a prominent nose, thick reading glasses, and a black judicial robe that rode up high on his neck. Arranging a stack of papers on his high bench, he told the clerk to call the first case.

The clerk belted out, "People of the State of Illinois versus Percy McGill."

Cole and Wilen approached the Judge who signaled Cole to proceed. Cole argued for a half hour, belaboring each fact in the six affidavits, focusing on the sworn statement of Officer Jensen. He referred to Jensen's statement five times until Judge McCall finally urged him to move on.

"You are repeating yourself, counsel."

Cole concluded with an impassioned argument. "It is unmistakable, Your Honor, that the State cannot meet its burden in this matter. Every allegation of the indictment is uncorroborated and implausible balderdash. The state's case is entirely based on one questionable source, a woman of dubious character, who admits she boldly accompanied a man in his automobile, a man she had only just met. A respected officer of the law observed this same woman, in an inebriated state, in front of defendant's tavern on the very day she claims to have been imprisoned. Yet Officer Jensen observed her on the street in a demonstrable state of intoxication. There simply is insufficient evidence to permit this matter to go to trial. To subject the defendant to the jeopardy and expense of a trial would violate his rights and simply delay the day of judgment, for no judge or jury can possibly convict this man on the allegations of this lady, Officer Jensen's 'Lady of the Street.'"

The jibe crushed Connie, and she leaned against Durbin for support. Durbin noticed little beads of perspiration forming on her forehead. The court invited the state's attorney to proceed.

Wilen began in a calm and reasoned manner, marshalling the facts and building in intensity. He addressed the court for forty minutes, carefully detailing all the evidence in his plea that the case be submitted for trial.

"We cannot know what the truth is in this matter, your honor, until the witnesses have their say and are subject to cross-examination and the impartial scrutiny of the trier of fact," Wilen thundered. "There is a victim here today who has suffered at the hands of the defendant.

She represents every decent woman in Chicago. She has been grievously assaulted and, despite the mischaracterizations of opposing counsel, she has acted at all times with propriety and decency. Constance Dandridge is pure of heart and innocent in all respects. She deserves her day in court. We owe her that. She must be allowed to mount the witness stand and set out the cruel circumstances that befell her but weeks ago in this jurisdiction. She pleads for a trial. A civilized Chicago requires a trial. Majestic justice demands a trial. What happened here can happen again. What happened here must be tested by the crucible of a trial. Only then will the truth emerge, like the sun from behind a cloud. The state respectfully prays that this court deny the defendant's motion and set this cause down for trial."

Wilen took his seat and the judge rocked back in his chair, while shuffling several documents. After a pregnant twenty seconds he looked up and surveyed the courtroom.

"My course is clear," he began. "I have carefully examined the motion, its supporting documents and the counter-affidavits introduced into the record by able counsel for the state. I have also considered the oral arguments of the learned counsel, both of whom have given compelling presentations. I must conclude that the state has not met its burden of establishing a *prima facie* case. The indictment is quashed and the defendant shall be released forthwith."

It hit Connie like another fist to her face. She exploded in tears. Durbin, shocked by the judge's decision, cradled Connie to keep her upright in the chair. Percy approached the weeping figure.

"I told you not to bother, Carmen," Percy spat. "All you've accomplished is to stoke the anger in the horrid beast. Not smart at all. Who knows what happens now?"

A searing hurt knifed through Connie. She could not utter a word and her breathing became labored. The courtroom spun around her. She saw McGill approach and speak but could not hear a word he uttered. Durbin heard the not-so-veiled threat, longed to jump up and throttle McGill, but had to attend to Connie. Wilen went to get her a glass of water but for three minutes she could not drink it. Finally Kid helped her to her feet and they began the return trip to the Murphy residence. She continued to cry, quietly. After a short period she asked Durbin what McGill had said.

"I will tell you later," he said.

She shrieked, "Now. Tell me this moment!"

"He said something like, 'You stirred up the beast and who

knows what could happen.' But you must not fear this man, Connie. I heard Mr. Wilen talking to McGill's lawyer. He told him that if anything happened to you that Wilen would devote the rest of his life to seeing Percy hang. McGill just wanted to inflict more pain, Connie. Don't let him get to you."

They made it back to the house and Mrs. Murphy helped Connie up to her room where she dropped off to sleep.

Over the next few days Connie grew more and more despondent. She could not work or eat much. For many days Connie uttered no words and refused to leave her room. The Murphys summoned the doctor again, and he prescribed "Paine's Celery Compound," a worthless concoction, 20 percent alcohol, advertised to rectify "thin, pale cheeks." It did not help.

Durbin visited the Murphy home the night before the Cubs departed for Indiana, but Connie's health did not allow her to see him. He left a note that said, "Please rest and let the Lord speed your recovery. Do not dwell on the past but look to the future. I will see you in one month. Blaine"

March 1, 1907 Chicago, Illinois

The March morning dawned on the type of day for which Midwesterners yearn, the first glint of spring, the sun melting through the haze of winter with unlimited promise. The thin ice coatings on every blade of grass dissolve, the cold liquid dripping into the earth. It is a moment in time like the instant in a baseball game—the players call it the "break"—when an errant peg or a double down the line rips the fabric of the afternoon and All Is Changed.

Joe Tinker, the Cubs shortstop, had briskly walked his West Side neighborhood that morning, observing the promise of spring. He had napped in the cool afternoon before catching a taxi with his wife to lunch downtown at Henrici's.

A curl of brown hair spilled down over Tinker's broad forehead. A handsome man of average stature, Tinker had bright eyes and sensuous lips. The hint of a dimple marked the base of his chin. Ruby noticed he had only picked at his meal, and she saw the shudder as he eased up from the table. "Are you all right?" she asked, scrutinizing her husband's face.

"No, I am not feeling well," he replied slowly. Placing his hand on his right side he explained, "I have a pain right here."

Tinker began to speak again but the words gurgled in his throat and, for him, The World Turned White. He awoke one hour later in St. Anthony de Padua Hospital. Ruby stood at his side and a number of white-clothed persons milled about. He smelled antiseptic fumes, alcohol, and his wife's perfume.

"Dr. Donlon says it's appendicitis, Joe. They want to remove your appendix. It should be routine." He noticed the lines at the corner of Ruby's eyes as she said this, and a tear glistened from the left eye.

"Sure," he answered, "so long as I am ready for Opening Day."

As the ether trickled down a tube in the apparatus, Tinker choked briefly and then slipped into a pleasant dream. A sunbathed ballfield, Tinker lolled at shortstop on a smooth, chocolate brown dirt surface, back near the outfield turf. The emerald green grass surrounded Joe like a wooden harp framed its strings. A sharp, bounding ball squirted his way. He lunged to his left to spear it in his glove, and smoothly flipped it over to Johnny Evers at second for the force play. Three outs.

From the Journal of Kid Durbin

March 2, 1907

President Murphy instructed me to be at the Dearborn Street Station today in time for the 10:30 a.m. train, to meet up with Manager Frank Chance and a number of other players. We would board the Monon Railroad train to French Lick, Indiana, a journey of seven hours. While I felt some jitters about meeting Mr. Chance and the other Cubs, I figured the Cubs plucked me out of the Western League because I had something to offer. I firmly resolved to justify their faith in me.

Hundreds of milling people filled the station. Thirty minutes early, I looked about for Frank Chance and the Cubs without any luck. I did notice a number of attractive women but they did not seem to pay me any heed. I purchased a hard-boiled egg in the lunchroom and then found a copy of today's Chicago Courier at the newsstand. I munched on that egg while reading the paper for a good ten minutes. The Courier had a story about Frank Chance arriving in Chicago and conferring with Pres. Murphy. I am reading this article and what do you know! My name was in it! In the same sentence with Johnny Evers! It said: "It is expected that Johnny Evers, Carl Lundgren, Orvie Overall, Catcher Seabaugh, and Pitcher Durbin will report today or tomorrow for the start." I nearly spit out that egg as I read it!

A few minutes later I wandered over to where a tall chain link fence marked the entrance to the passenger boarding area. I knew Frank Chance the minute I saw him. He towered over me at six feet, bull-necked and strong, like a boxer, and he had this firm jaw and clear gray eyes that looked right through me like sunshine through a clean pane of glass. But his mouth curled up in a genuine smile as he extended five thick, gnarled fingers and said, "I'm guessing you would be Kid Durbin, right?"

"You guessed right, Mr. Chance."

"Kid, you need not call me 'Mister.' 'Husk' or 'Cap'n' will do just fine. You are a Chicago National now."

Owing to a faulty air brake, the train left Chicago five minutes late. Those five minutes enabled the Cubs trainer, Jack McCormick, to make the train. He huffed on at 10:34 a.m., cussing up a storm about the "goddam elevated railroads in Chicago." Seems he had been stuck for an hour in an el train on the Union Loop. The bushy-browed, ruddy-faced man tossed his medicine valise and a case of witch hazel onto an empty seat and composed himself.

John F. McCormick started as "rubber" for the Cleveland Spiders in 1881, becoming very adept at using liniment to rub the aches and pains out of Spider muscles and joints. Now fifty-five, the amiable man carried a flask and a few too many pounds around with him. Born in Scotland and a baseball lifer, he knew which ointments and dope would take care of the variety of maladies that pestered ballplayers.

Jack had other useful talents. Besides being an expert rubber, Trainer Jack knew how to treat a wet infield with sawdust to get it back into playable shape. He had worked for Cap Anson on two championship Cubs teams in 1885 and 1886, and Cap recommended him to Frank Chance.

The train lurched as it started out of the station, the squeak and rattle of the undercarriage cutting through the coaches until the normal clatter of the iron wheels on the rails took over. Trainer Jack withdrew a leather-covered porcelain flask from a vest pocket and sucked down a small amount of whiskey, remarking, to no one in particular, "That shoor hits the spot!" Catching the eye of center fielder Jimmy Slagle, he added, with a wink, "Preparation, my boy, 'tis the key to success!"

Jack grabbed three Cubs rookies, Billy Sweeney, Newt Randall, and Warren Seabaugh, and gathered them around him.

"Boys, as the official trainer of the Chicago Nationals, I am duty-bound to advise you regarding the rules of our Peerless Leader and my own rules on dietary matters. In fact, it is required in my contract. So listen up."

"There ain't too many rules you need to know. Rule number one: When the season starts you gotta be in your hotel room by midnight and they is no exceptions to this. We will check up on you most nights too, so forget about pullin' any shenanigans after twelve. We will then telephone your room at eight o'clock in the morning to get you up if you ain't already up, and if you are not down for breakfast by nine o'clock—well, then you don't get no breakfast. Now some advice about your diets."

Randall interrupted. "Any dietary problem in sharing a sip of that flask with me, Jack?"

"Oh no sir, not at all," said Jack as he passed around the whiskey.

"Fermented barley is a staple for all athletes. But you fellows need to also remember to eat vegetables and fruits to stimulate the juices of your digestive tracts. Spinach, cauliflower, corn, and chickpeas is your best vegetables and apples, pears, and melons will do fine for your fruit. And don't go near the strawberries as they have their seeds in the skin on the outside and these will absolutely debilitate your intestinal walls!"

"So long as I can eat a juicy steak most nights, I can take the vegetables," said Seabaugh.

Jack continued. "If youse gotta a pain in the stomach region, let me know and I'll fix you up a dose of treacle. A secret recipe of mine that will do the trick. And if your nose is runnin' something awful and you think you got the catarrh, whatever you do stay away from the catarrh powders available from your local apothecary. These will no doubt contain cocaine and you will soon find yourself a slave to a cocaine habit and unable to pitch or bring a baseball. I seen it happen!"

"To who?" asked Randall.

"To none of your business, that's who. Now I hafta tell you also that the prime cuts of beef will provide you the protein your muscles need to grow and strengthen. But you should also partake of fried pork and fried chicken on a regular basis, gents. The lard in which these fried foods is cooked is an oil derived from hog fat. This oil will lubricate your joints and ward off the rheumatism. You might instruct your cook to fry your biscuits in lard—it's very important for all athletes. In fact, a medical doctor has proved that a diet with too little animal oil will result in your testicles shriveling up into tiny critters no bigger than a pea."

Sweeney went weak in the knees at this revelation. During the next seven days these three Cubs rookies ate fried chicken at least once a day, Newt Randall boasting that he had persuaded the hotel cook to serve him cold fried chicken for breakfast.

Chance and Charles Dryden, a *Tribune* sportswriter, sat alone together in the smoking car. The two men respected each other and worked well together. Each year, at the start of the Practice Season, they sat down to catalog the current Cubs, position by position. Dryden had a small mouth, a broad forehead, and warm, expressive eyes. The two men nursed schooners of beer and Chance smoked a pipe. Though late in the day, Chance still wore a neatly pressed suit and tie.

"We're strong at first base," Chance began. "Big fellow there hit .319 for us last year and scored over a hundred runs. Managed to steal fifty-seven bases too. He's gotta slick glove and he brings some other good qualities to the team."

Dryden smiled at Husk's description of himself. He admired the Cubs skipper, even coining Chance's nickname, the Peerless Leader. Playing along, he said, "Yeah, but he has a nasty temper and has not endeared himself to the umps."

"True, but he put the bacon on the table last year. Anyways, let's waste no more time on first base. The guy on second, Mr. Evers, he's probably the most valuable asset to this team. Winning clubs need a 'glue-man'—somebody who glues together everyone else on the field. Johnny's our glue-man. The glove is matchless and the bat comes through when you need it. A fearless base runner. He's got more sand than any ballplayer I've ever seen. I'm not so sure folks appreciate his contributions as much as they should, him being a little guy and a difficult character and all."

"Difficult? That's putting it mildly, isn't it? That man with a permanent smirk on his face is a quarrelsome fellow, almost bitter, don't you think?"

"No, not really. Look, you gave him the nickname Crab and it stuck for a good reason. He's an edgy guy, an ornery, high-strung fellow. He's gotta sharp tongue and he's a loner. Not many of the guys pal around with him much off-field. But they trust him on the diamond, knowing he can do so many things to allow us to win. Johnny has the best baseball brain in the game. He knows everything worth knowing about baseball. He knows the goddam official rules backwards and forwards—I think he sleeps with that book. Woulda' made a fine lawyer. The man likes to delve into the details of every goddam thing. He is always scheming up a new play, a new defense, or a different way to approach a situation on the field. He's the sparkplug to our nine. He didn't hit that much for us last year but with his glove and his mind at work we did swell at second. I wouldn't want anyone else there but the Crab. My only problem with Johnny is his constant yapping on the field. It drives me crazy. You know I can't hear much outta my left ear. Well it's a goddam shame it ain't my right ear that's near deaf! Then I wouldn't have to listen to all that crap."

"But it also drives your opponents batty."

"Yeah, I've seen it work. He made McGraw crawl under the bench one time last year. Tell you something else. My guess is that if Johnny let off a little steam every once in a while his disposition might improve a notch or two. He keeps it all bottled up inside him. Maybe if he got himself laid every once in a while…"

"Well, that isn't a difficult proposition in New Orleans."

"Yeah, well, Johnny's not one to get laid the easy way. Lord knows I have suggested that to him. Would loosen him up like the other boys. It's no secret Johnny needs a wife. Life without love stinks."

"Yeah, well, life without baseball also stinks. What about short? With Mr. Tinker out of commission you have a bit of a problem there for a while now?"

"No, I heard that guys can make it back from this kind of operation fairly soon. And in the meantime we have the best replacement man in baseball, Solly Hofman. He can play almost every position. His best defensive work is in the outfield but he's gotta solid glove—they don't call him Circus Solly for nothin'. And he wields a decent bat. Artie would be a starter on any other team. We'll do fine at short."

"And what do you think of Mr. Steinfeldt at third? He's as dumb as Evers is bright, no?"

"Yeah, well, it don't always take a lot of brains to play this game. You know that. A good glove and a level swing can get you pretty far. Like a lot of Krauts, Steiny loves his brews. But he hasn't let the suds interfere with his job. Harry got something like 175 hits for us last year! Hit about 327 percent and his defense is as good as it gets. Notice he gets rid of the ball faster than any infielder I've ever seen and his arm is as strong as a pitcher's. We got us a good one at third base."

"And your backstop?"

"I don't want to talk about the Jew right now. Kling's hat size has got so big it can't get any bigger. He seems to think he's worth more money than anyone else on the team. Until he can come down to earth Pat Moran will be catching for the Cubs."

"Your outfield—no changes there?"

"I don't think so. Last year Sheckard comes over to our club from Brooklyn and he did swell—just what we hoped for. Picked up over 140 hits, ran the bases well, and he's another good glove man. We gotta chalk up his failure to hit in the Championship Series as a bad case of nerves. He'll be fine this time around. Jimmy Slagle didn't hit that much for us but he made up for it in center—the name Rabbit fits him well. He outraced a whole lot of fly balls last year. And in right you got a guy who may be the best in the business. Frank Schulte is a slugger. He hit 281 percent, drove home a ton of runs, and swatted something like seven home runs for us. He hits 'em deep and runs like the wind. And he produced runs in the Championship Series too. A real gem."

"So let's talk about your slabmen. I hear you got a yannigan who can throw the ball through a brick wall."

"You mean Kid Durbin. I haven't got to see him throw yet. But folks who have say his stuff is big league quality. Fact that he's a southpaw don't hurt neither. So we think we improved the club with that acquisition."

"He's the little redhead, right?"

"Yeah, that's him. He doesn't knock you flat when you see him but the arm is strong. Pitched in the Western League."

"He doesn't figure to get many innings, does he?"

"Maybe not, but you never know. Our staff of twirlers figures to be very strong.

I got five guys I can count on. Miner Brown pitched better than anyone in the National League last season. No question there, and no reason the same shouldn't be true this time around. He won twenty-six and only lost a handful. He could be the best fielding pitcher in the history of this game. I mean that. Another thing about Miner—he can come into the fag end of the game to put out a fire when my starter craps out. And two days later he's pitching nine. He's a soldier! Your buddy Cy Sanborn calls him the Royal Rescuer!"

"He's got one flaw, Husk. Your opponents have no problem running on him."

Chance paused and gulped his drink. "Yeah. We don't want to mess with his delivery to address that. But not many guys make it to first with Miner to begin with!

Reulbach's better at holding 'em close at first and he is now a reliable twirler. Real good curveball but it's his fastball that can be so goddam overpowering. Went nineteen and four and he tosses a one-hitter against the Sox in the Championship Series. Sky's the limit for Big Ed. And Jack Pfiester came out of nowhere—a twenty-eight-year-old rookie winning twenty for us! He gave us a whole lot of innings and you guys are calling him Jack the Giant Killer because he can handle the fucking McGraw crew. Carl Lundgren's no slouch either—he won eighteen games for us—"

"Seventeen."

"Okay, seventeen. I think he's just coming into his own now."

"Why didn't you use him against the Sox?"

"As good as he is, I wanted to go with my top three in the Series—Brownie, Big Ed, and Pfiester. Simple as that. I got another guy who can pitch as good as these others—Jeff Overall. He comes over from the Reds last year and really shows us a thing or two. The boy has a great drop ball. The trick with him is not to overuse him—I played against him in California. I know that he will do his best if he gets plenty of rest between starts. We expect good things from him. He's coming into his own."

"Jeff's another college boy. You seem to favor college boys for starting pitchers, Husk. You've got Overall, Lundgren, and Reulbach from the campus quadrangles."

"Well, it's worked for us so far." Chance eased back in his chair.

"Jack Taylor's no college product, although you could say he's old school. You picked him up from the Cardinals and he contributed twelve victories."

"Right. Taylor can still throw. He is a control pitcher, able to hit the corners of the zone. But he's pitched a lot of innings in his career and, as you surely know, he's a pain in the ass. We picked up Chick Fraser from the Reds this winter just in case Taylor shows signs of goin' back."

"You and Fraser have some history, don't you?"

"You done your homework. Yeah, my first game in the big leagues, nine years ago, Chick was on the hill for Louisville. And they had Wagner at first too. Chick got hit hard but he made an impression. He'll give us a capable extra arm."

"Any other rookie besides Durbin I should keep my eyes on?"

"Check out the outfielder Randall. Newt Randall. He seems ready. Fast as hell, too! I don't think Sweeney or Perdue are gonna cut it. By the way, what's this crap with your paper calling us the Spuds lately?"

"Well, it's a tribute to Chubby Murphy's ancestry. I've never liked the name Cubs. Sounds too cuddly for me. You don't really care a corn-husk, do you?"

Chance said he preferred the Chicago "Nationals." Dryden asked his last question. "So, when you put all these guys on the field to play— how good are they?"

Chance replied without hesitation. "Charlie, this team don't have no weak links. My job is to get them to see with their own eyes just how good they are. If I succeed in that, it's gonna be as good as it gets."

The Game   Deadball Baseball

Deadball baseball brought an era of clever nicknames, collared, heavy wool flannel uniforms, and low-scoring games. The term "deadball" originated because the ball did not spring off the bat like it does now. Baseball manufacturers deliberately produced a ball designed not to soar. For example, one advertisement of a baseball manufacturer in 1871 promised baseballs the "deadest of all." A spherical lump of Para rubber, imported from the Amazon jungles, formed the center of the ball. Alternating layers of woolen yarn were wound around that core, the ball being dipped in rubber cement at two separate stages of the production process. Two pieces of horsehide, adorned with the name A.G. Spalding and Brothers, were sewn together with 108 red and black stitches to create the National League ball. Balls did not begin to leap off the baseball bat until manufacturers introduced the more resilient cork center in 1911. An even livelier ball came about before the 1921 season, when new yarn-winding machines wrapped the yarn tighter, giving the balls more bounce.

Because the team owners paid fifteen dollars per dozen for baseballs, umpires did not routinely replace scuffed and damaged balls during the game. In fact, prior to 1900 one ball might last an entire game. By 1907 it was not uncommon to introduce several new balls into play during the game, but umpires remained stingy in this regard. Small boys scampered after foul balls, getting a free ticket to another game as a reward for retrieving them.

The spitball, introduced in 1903, took its toll on the ball and those trying to hit it. The legal doctoring of the balls by pitchers transformed the baseball during the course of the game. A ball that started out white and firm ended up soft, lopsided and almost black from the dirt, tobacco juice, slippery elm, licorice, and saliva. Until 1908 the rules permitted the pitcher to grind a new ball into the soil to "improve" the feel of it. Balls darkened by dirt and other substances proved harder to see and thus harder to hit, especially at twilight. Occasionally, during the game, the stitches would unravel, and the horsehide covering would flap about. After being whacked about for a number of innings, and literally spat upon, a soggy, misshapen deadball did not exactly leap off the bat. Honus Wagner described it "like hitting a chunk of mud." The baseball in this state could hardly be induced to travel more than two hundred feet. So outfielders played shallow, two hundred feet from home plate. American League center fielder Tris Speaker, for example, played so close to the infield that he frequently participated in rundowns. Speaker even recorded two unassisted double plays in 1918. Since outfielders corralled most fly balls, pitchers of the deadball era tended to pitch up high rather than low. The low pitches could be lined between the infielders or chopped over their heads. Pitches at the level of the armpits ended up as fly balls that could be chased down. Infielders could not get to or cleanly grab as many ground balls as now due to the small, inferior gloves. The gloves, often half the size of current models, lacked webbing, padding, and pockets. Catchers in particular suffered from the lack of padding, sometimes inserting a half-inch cut of meat in the catcher's mitt before the game. A fifteen cent piece of flank steak worked fine.

Given the sluggish nature of the deadball and the fact that most fly balls could be caught by the outfielders, it did not pay for batters to swing from the heels and attempt to drive the ball over the outfielder's head. It seldom could be done. Batters had an incentive, instead, to shorten the arc of their swing, meet the ball with the bat, and hit it on the ground. Most batters choked up on the bat for better bat control and some, like Ty Cobb and occasionally Honus Wagner, used a split-hand or gapped handgrip, the hands spread apart on the lumber. Bats were heavy, up to forty-eight ounces or more, with thick, ungainly handles, not the thin molded handles of today. Deadballers sometimes referred to bats as "wagon tongues" and in fact some bat manufacturers actually scrounged the country to purchase old wagon tongues for their sturdy, cured wood. One result of the portly bats and the more controlled swings: many fewer strikeouts than now.

Deadball baseball made every run critical and low-scoring pitchers' duels the norm. Managers angled for one run rather than the big inning. Pitching dominated the game and the fifteen-inch mound (it has been ten inches since 1969) aided pitchers in their endless battle against hitters. Because runs were a scarce commodity, each base advanced meant a great deal. The team that pushed across three or four runs usually won the ballgame. Runners attempted more steals and seized an extra base every time the opportunity came. Batters bunted and sacrificed more frequently, even the star hitters. Fielders jealously guarded the base paths, placing themselves in front of second base, third, and home plate. The runners retaliated with slides designed to knock down the men on defense or to spike them to soften them up for the next time. And the critical value of the catcher reached its zenith. A receiver capable of nailing base runners with larceny on their minds could literally make the difference between victory and defeat. Managers and many players spent a great deal of time strategizing ways to advance runners one base or to prevent that from happening. As Johnny Evers put it in 1925: "[I]t was as much a battle of wits as a trial of strength and speed. Everything was trying to outguess the other fellow and we used to spend hours doping out plays…"

Stadiums were shabby affairs, mainly rickety wooden structures not meant to last more than twenty years. These ballparks were built reflecting the shape of the city block that they occupied, sometimes resulting in shallow left or right field bleachers and monstrously deep center fields. Baseball fields lacked the well-manicured, garden-like lawns and grounds that later graced the major leagues. The outfield grass was often uncut, rutted, weedy, and pitted with broken bottles and other debris. Ty Cobb, in his autobiography, recounted how a Baltimore Orioles outfielder, chasing a fly ball, vanished, falling into a sewer hole covered, ineffectively, with boards and turf. Batted balls hitting unkempt infields strewn with pebbles swerved and bounced crazily. Field conditions and primitive fielding gloves meant many more errors than in current times. Lumpy, ripped, and unevenly filled bases often marked first, second, and third. Dugouts rarely rested below field level—the wooden team bench, with a ceiling of corrugated metal to seal it off from the fans, sat on the same level as the field.

Umpires did not have small whisk brooms to clean home plate prior to 1910. Instead, a full broom lay on the field, just ten to fifteen feet from home plate. The ump used the broom to clean the plate and then tossed it back where, once or twice each year, a catcher pursuing a foul pop-up would stumble over it.

Many cities still enforced blue laws prohibiting Sunday games. Chicago allowed baseball games on Sundays after 1896, when a jury acquitted Chicago Nationals outfielder Walter Wilmot of violating the Sunday blue laws. In the National League in 1907 only the three "western" cities, Chicago, St. Louis, and Cincinnati, permitted Sunday baseball. To generate extra money for the players and the clubs, many big league teams played exhibition games—in towns that lacked blue laws—on their Sunday off-days, although a number of players refused to play ball on the Sabbath. Weekday games, except for doubleheaders, began around three o'clock and lasted no more than an hour and a half. Men could attend the game and easily make it home before the six o'clock meal.

The deadball made home runs rare, as did the huge dimensions of the ballparks and the fact that almost every batter choked up on the bat and punched at the ball. Almost all home runs were the "hit it past the outfielder and run like hell" variety. With the outfielders playing shallow, and with outfield walls so distant, hard hit line drives in the gaps between the outfielders could translate into triples or home runs. The deep outfield fences allowed team owners—when needed—to rope off large areas in front of the outfield walls and charge patrons twenty-five cents each to stand there or sit on folding chairs. Police and vendors often wandered on the field during games along these ropes. Very few home runs soared into the stands. Frank "Home Run" Baker led the American League in home runs three years straight, yet never hit more than twelve. Dave Brain led the National League in homers in 1907 with ten.

Until Babe Ruth changed everything, pitching provided the focus of the game. Young fans worshipped pitchers as the heroes of the diamond. Because batters put the ball in play and struck out less, the typical game might require a pitcher to throw no more than eighty pitches, considerably less than now. Aside from allowing pitchers to throw more frequently, this also meant that complete games were the rule rather than the exception. Relief pitchers—hurlers whose only job was to enter the game when the starter ran into trouble—did not exist, though some starting pitchers also came in to put out fires. A good "swing man" could start a game on Monday, pitch three or four innings to lend a hand on Wednesday, and start again on Thursday or Friday. The Cubs' Three Finger Brown performed admirably in this capacity. But for the most part, the starters went all the way.

A typical deadball game in 1907: a 4-2 final score with both pitchers turning in a complete game.

From the Journal of Kid Durbin

March 2, 1907

As fate would have it, I found Warren Seabaugh sitting next to me on my first train trip as a Cub. Warren played against me in the Western Association. He caught for the Springfield, Missouri, club when I toiled for Joplin. So we were both headed for our first major league training camp, a little edgy and excited as we watched the flat Illinois and Indiana landscape slide by.

After one hour, we found ourselves in the midst of a sea of barren cornfields. A ten-year-old butcher boy came through our car selling apples, beef jerky, and Hershey bars from a big wicker basket. I paid two cents for a large apple. After the boy left us Warren got this serious look on his face and says to me, "Kid, you 'member that day in Joplin when you was facing me with two out in the ninth? We was down a run..."

"Course I do, Warren," I replied. "I threw the first pitch for a strike, low and away. Then I whizzed one high and tight, nearly nipped you, I recall."

"Nearly nipped me? Hell, my recollection is that pitch more than any other I seen came the closest to getting me right between the eyes!"

I believe in speaking the truth, so I leveled with Seabaugh. "Warren," I said, "I didn't intend to hit you. As a catcher you know that I have to pitch like I own that plate. I needed to stake out my territory—you know what I mean. Besides, if I had wanted to nail you, I would have plunked you in your more than ample behind."

Seabaugh accepted my unapologetic apology with a slight grin. We did not speak of what happened after the inside pitch, but I rolled it over in my mind later. I came back with two outside pitches, two good ones on the outer quarter of the dish, and he missed both to end the game. Pitchers remember these things.

When the sun slipped away I met three veteran Cubs I knew from the sports pages, Jimmy Slagle, Jack Taylor, and Mike Kahoe. Maybe the beer made them want to talk, or maybe it was just part of being a team on a train headed off to the start of a new campaign. But these vets shared some time with me.

"Rabbit" Slagle, our center fielder, had the look of a cherub, a small and wizened man, already wrinkled and old at thirty-three. He had a large nose coming down from a creased forehead and a receding hairline. A big smile exposed some crooked teeth. But Trainer Jack told me this old man could still run well and had a great glove. Some of the players called Jimmy "Shorty" or "Midget," but he much preferred "Rabbit." Along with Frank Schulte and Jimmy Sheckard, Slagle belonged to an all-"S" and all-German Cubs outfield. Sometimes these three called for fly balls in German.

Rabbit smoked a cigar and coughed like a barking dog. I tried not to get too close to him, what with his cough and the strong tobacco breath. "It's the croup," he explained, but he went out of his way to introduce himself to me. He and his wife lived in farm country, as I had, so we had that in common. He harkened from Worthville, Pennsylvania, which he described as "no bigger than Schulte's rear end." He also mentioned that, like me, he came out of the Western League, where he played outfield for Kansas City. Speaking proudly of his business in Worthville, a flour, feed, and grist mill, he claimed that, "It jus' set a record-- forty barrels o' wheat and ten o' buckwheat flour in a day!"

"There's gonna be so many buckwheat cakes in Worthville this spring there may be an ep-ee-demic of pimples. It's a good thing my milk wagon got me out o' that valley! I think I'm comin' down with the croup. Hope like hell it ain't the grippe!"

Jimmy took a package from his pocket and rubbed Magic Croup Salve across the top of his upper lip. He inhaled it and shook his head back and forth murmuring, "Thass damn good!" We talked a bit about my background before Rabbit started grousing about what he called "the unfairness of it all." In the middle of a decent season in 1906, in which he contributed to the Cubs' great year, an injury kept him out of the World's Championship Series.

"What can you say?" he asked. "Sometimes the good Lord just has a different plan for us than we figure. I growed up with that belief. But it's damned inconvenient, ain't it?"

Jack "Brakeman" Taylor was no spring chicken either. A pitcher in his mid-thirties, he parted his blondish hair down the middle. I noticed a number of small wrinkles on the skin beneath and alongside his eyes. Not a big man but he tried to act like a heavyweight. He told me to call him Brakeman because he used to work the off-seasons as a brakeman for the Union Pacific Railroad. When I told him my father still worked the railroads he warmed up to me. He talked like a railroad man, with some of the same language my father used. On the other hand he also referred to the porter as a "nigger," which did not sit right with me. My folks taught me not to use that word or other terms of disrespect.

Jack, an Ohioan, also came out of the Western League, playing for Connie Mack's Brewers in Milwaukee around 1897. He had been pitching nine years in the National League, coming from the Cardinals in 1906 for his second go-round with the Cubs. Jack owned a very good major league record, which he did not endeavor to conceal from anyone. But he had a dark look about him, like he was trying to hide something. On the other hand, he talked to me as a teammate, at least it started as such. After a while I realized that Jack was talking to himself, not really to me. Killing time, not really conversing. After boasting of winning 20 games the year before, he grumbled something about "not being appreciated by the so-called Peerless Leader." Then he got around to complaining that his pickle crop had failed.

"Yes," he said with a sigh, "the cucumbers only grew four feet long this year, instead of six feet as in former years. I tell you," he said earnestly, "there ain't no way to account for this 'lessen the Ohio soil is losing its grip."

I smiled back at the Brakeman when he related this story, considering whether I should relate the story of my Uncle Jed's mammoth watermelon, the one that took a team of four horses to move it to market. But I didn't think it prudent to try and one-up his story. Not my place, *a yannigan fresh out of the Western League, to do that. So I sat quiet, listening intently. Jack Taylor could talk the hind legs off a donkey. When he shuffled off to get another beer, I slipped away.*

Another Ohioan introduced himself to me when I escaped the Brakeman, Mike Kahoe, a thirty-three-year-old journeyman catcher, trying to hook on with the Cubs after not playing major league ball in 1906. Mike looked forty, losing his hair and wrinkles popping up all over his face. He had that weathered look I've seen before on older ballplayers—too much time in the sun. Like Taylor, Mike wanted to talk, and I offered a willing audience. He had a full bottle of beer in his thick, scarred catcher's hands, and he waved the bottle with his right hand when he made a point.

Mainly Mike wanted to talk about the old days. He told me about his early years with the Cincinnati ballclub.

"I messed up two or three shots with them," Mike confessed, as he wrestled with the bottle of beer. "The first time I was just about your age. Couldn't hit the goddam curveball. Now that I think about it, I couldn't hit the goddam fastball either. In 1900 I hit only .189! Fucking 189 percent! The Reds cut me loose the next year and the Cubs grabbed me—only they called themselves the Orphans then. This was three or four years after Anson. My average was only two-twenty-something that season so the Orphans cut me loose and I caught on with the St. Louie Browns. We played in the brand new ballfield. Strange thing is—it seems like so long ago but my first year in St. Louie wasn't more than five years ago."

"You must have had some great times along the way, Mike."

"Sure. There were women, lots of booze, and always my teammates. The women and booze made my teammates bearable."

I smiled and Mike smiled back.

Mike had a load of advice. "Kid, it goes real quick in this business. One day you're a rookie trying to catch on, like you. Next thing you know you're over the hill, trying to eke out just one more year. Time don't mean nothing to a hog, but for a ballplayer it's every-damn-thing. First base now seems a mile away to me when I stand in the batter's box. My legs are gone and they're takin' the rest of me with 'em. So enjoy every moment of it. Everyone says—and it's true—that numbers matter a lot in this game, like your average and the amount of runs you score or don't let score in your case. But there's another number that's more important, that two-digit number that grows every year, your age. When you hit thirty in this man's game you don't got much longer to go."

Kahoe sucked down some beer with a gulp and dried his mouth on the sleeve of his shirt. He continued with his fatherly advice: "A great man once said, 'Always do what you are afraid to do.' That's a useful notion, son. It will get you more snatch and take you more places than otherwise. I'll shut my trap in a minute, 'cause I got just a couple more things for you. Number one, you gotta play all twenty-seven outs. Full out. Right to the last fuckin' groundball. You keep going till the bastard in blue tells you you're done. And number two, when you get knocked down you gotta get right back up. Don't give 'em the satisfaction. You get to your feet quick when they knock you down. Simple as that, Kid."

Due to what the porters called "mechanical problems," we arrived late, at nine o'clock or so. A voice rang out, "All out for French Lick and West Baden Springs!" The arched, house-sized station hummed with activity. Many colored boys, resplendent in the hotel colors, awaited us, throwing our luggage onto the hotel stage, drawn by a splendid team of bays. The cool air refreshed us after the stale, dusty stench of the railroad cars. We climbed down the stairs of the passenger car, carefully using the step stools put there by the porters, onto a white gravel that crunched beneath our shoes. A number of horse-drawn carriages waited for us. I climbed into the carryall with some teammates and the stage lurched forward under the crack of a whip. We traveled down a gravel avenue lined with spreading locust trees. Jimmy Slagle told us the hotel was swell, described some of its amenities, and warned us about the spring water.

"What's wrong with the water?" I asked.

"Jes' wait an' see," is all he would say.

The West Baden Springs Resort Hotel lived up to Slagle's description. Built as a resort hotel five years ago, the brochures at the railroad station described it as "the Eighth Wonder of the Modern World." As we approached through the surrounding trees and a lingering night mist, a huge dome, the largest in the world and bigger, we were told, than the dome in St. Peter's basilica, loomed out of the dark, covered in strings of light. *Four large structures with huge turrets surrounded the dome. I couldn't help but wonder how this amazing structure had come to be placed here, in forgotten Indiana, and more to the point, how I had ended up here.*

Cap'n Chance caught up to us in the lobby. He told Seabaugh and me that we were rooming together. He gave us a set of room keys and told us to meet in the lobby at 8:00 a.m. Trainer Jack then invited us to have a beer with him and Harry Steinfeldt at a tavern he knew in French Lick, a ten-minute walk. Seems the hotel did not allow alcoholic beverages on its premises. But the beers I drank on the train already had taken their toll. I was licked so I begged off, as did my roommate. Warren and I made it to the sixth floor and room 622. Darned if we didn't have our own bathroom, including a cast-iron bathtub with claw feet! We quickly threw on our nightshirts and collapsed into a large bed that comfortably fit the two of us. A welcome sleep came swiftly.

March 3, 1907   West Baden Springs Resort Hotel,
West Baden Springs, Indiana

West Baden Springs, a small, sleepy town buried in Southern Indiana's Valley of Lost Rivers, hosted this world-class resort hotel. Rich folks came here from all over the country to "take the waters." Three dollars a night for the room, meals, and amenities—more than the Waldorf-Astoria charged! The hotel possessed many charms beyond the vast dome over its lobby and dining area. Each of its five hundred rooms had hot and cold water, steam heat, and a telephone. The hotel grounds boasted sunken gardens, an opera house, a tenpin house, billiards, a large indoor swimming pool, and a series of sulphuric mineral springs, including the world-renowned Spring No. 7. And a one-third-mile long, double-decked bicycle and pony track. The track encircled an uncovered ballfield where the Cubs, Pittsburgh Pirates and Boston Pilgrims opened their Practice Season. But the crowds—and the ballclubs—came for the natural springs and bottled spring water. The general wisdom held that the ballplayers, fat and out of shape after a winter of drinking and sloth, would benefit by taking the waters and cleansing their systems. Trainer Jack McCormick called it "the water cure."

The Cubs, as instructed, met in the lobby at 8:00 a.m., garbed in the hotel-issued dark-flannel robe over their bathing gear. Trainer McCormick waited impatiently for the stragglers, Solly Hofman, Mordecai Brown, and Jimmy Slagle. When all the Cubs assembled, he looked them over carefully, tilting his mustachioed head to the left and squinting some. He addressed the group.

"You boys is a sorry fucking lot," he began. Pointing to Harry Steinfeldt he said, "Look at you, Steiny! You musta put away a thousand beers over the winter. Your belly is pushin' out like you was with child."

A few of the players laughed. Miner Brown maneuvered the chaw of tobacco in his mouth and spat a good amount of tobacco juice and saliva toward Trainer Jack.

"That stuff ain't gonna help you none, Brownie. And you, Solly, you're as flabby as a razor strop. You're likely to spring a hock. You coulda done something other than eat and sleep the last five months. Look, I just want to make sure you don't fuck up this Practice Season. Stick with the plan, gents. Drink the water like we tell you and don't overindulge the female pulchritude."

Billy Sweeney turned to Warren Seabaugh and asked him, "What the hell is he talking about?"

"I think he means tits."

Trainer Jack directed the group to "go down to number 7 and lap up a gallon." Brakeman Taylor, in the jaws of a vicious hangover, wore his usual scowl. He told Trainer Jim to "eat dung" but Jim took no offense. He led the ballplayers outside, into the damp, cold morning. Gray mist still clung to the ground in places. The grip of winter was ebbing but the players grumbled about the chill. They walked a hundred steps or so to a small white structure with a sign that denoted Spring No. 7.

Enclosed by a white, wooden structure with numerous windows, Spring No. 7 flowed into a concrete basin, as the warm sun penetrated from many angles. Inside the little building, several other guests of the hotel clustered around a counter where a white-shirted hotel employee dispensed the fresh spring waters—the Number 7 variety—in crystal glasses. Pipes pumped the spring water up from below the earth, into boiling tubs from which hotel employees served it, hot and steaming. Hotel staff warned the boys to drink it hot, because the lukewarm spring water tended to cause nausea. Another hotel employee, a white man aged thirty, called it Sprudel Water. He explained it to the Cubs in a patter that suggested he had told this story many times before.

"A long time ago, maybe five thousand years past, all of Indiana was covered by an ancient sea filled with millions of sea creatures. When those fish and mollusks died, their shells and skeletons settled to the bottom of the ocean, and over time this material formed layers of limestone. You dig down twenty or fifty feet anywhere around here and you will find the limestone bedrock that extends a couple hunerd feet down. The water you will be enjoying comes from way down below, from the bowels of Mother Earth. Down there it starts to perc-u-late through 284 layers of the earth, by my cal-ki-lations, through all the min-ral beds and the porous limestone bedrock. These min-rals, and a number of gases, is dissolved into the water by what the professors call cosmosis. The earth swirls the waters about like it's gargling and then pushes it up through tiny holes in the limestone that act as filters. When the water reaches the surface it is pure and medicinal. Even the Indians hereabouts called it 'the healing water.' So drink up, gentlemen. Drink and then move about. A brisk walk will aid the action of the water."

It could be drunk straight or with a dash of salt, but for most people both ways proved unsavory. It smelled like bad eggs and tasted worse. The *Tribune* reporter, Charlie Dryden, who had a way with the English language, said it tasted like a "cheese cocktail." Down a flight of seven stairs the sulphurous spring waters bubbled away at fifty-three degrees

Fahrenheit, too cold in which to bathe. But Trainer Jack led the young men on a short walk to the bathhouse where, for the bargain price of fifty cents each, they could bathe in heated tubs of the venerated sulphur water and imbibe additional quantities of the spring water, all under the direction of trained attendants. The hotel also offered Turkish, Russian, and mud baths.

As the Cubs pondered their next move, Cap'n Chance burst into the bathhouse, a whirlwind of energy and advice.

"Boys," he said, in a carefully cultivated, soft, earnest tone, "listen carefully. We are here in this forgotten place for a reason. You veterans know why. This water is magic. This water is a gift from God. It will clean your gullets, and it will remove from your alimentary canals the impurities you have ingested and digested in the last four months. This water will rejuvenate you, boys. It will seep into your muscles, cleansing and fortifying every fiber. We will ask you to drink prodigious amounts of this sparkling liquid. We will also direct you to immerse yourself in it thrice daily. And you will benefit greatly from this—it is my steadfast promise, boys, my guarantee. I have seen it work wonders, and felt its salubrious qualities. Give yourselves up to the Sprudel Water, boys. You will not regret it."

He raised his glass over his head and then downed the twelve ounces in two seconds. After quickly imbibing a second glass, Chance removed his robe, exposing a strong, scarred barrel-chest, took five long strides and immersed himself up to his neck in a sulphur spring-water bath tub. He gave a quick shout of "hurrah" and the rest of the team soon climbed into other tubs.

The Cubs faced a rigorous morning schedule. After leaving the bathhouse, the trainer led the group to the track, a two-tiered, canopied, elliptical wooden edifice. The bicycle and running track occupied the second floor while the ground floor, a dirt course, was reserved for ponies. One-third of a mile long, the track circled the outdoor grounds where the Cubs would practice. Jack had the players run sprints for a half-hour and then led the boys down to Spring No. 1, where they had to drink more Sprudel Water. Then back to the track and on to the bathhouse. By noon the players were exhausted and the mineral water made them desperate to relieve their bowels.

The Era   Chicago, Illinois; Aldermania

Michael "Hinky Dink" Kenna, one of two aldermen from the First Ward, owned two saloons on South Clark Street. Hinky Dink, an intelligent man who never showed his emotion, used some of the great sums of money he stole in office to care for the poor and homeless in his ward. Charity made good politics.

One of the alderman's bars, the Workingman Exchange, took care of the tramps, the homeless and the down and out. Kenna allowed over a hundred street dwellers to sleep in the bar every night. The other establishment earned Hinky Dink a great deal of money because he did not have to pay for the alcohol he sold. The distributor, the O'Dell brothers, provided it without fee, in return for a lifetime of "favors." When, for example, a nephew of the O'Dell brothers—Tommy Clausen—faced a murder charge after beating Billy Campbell to death in an alley in the Levee, the police officer who heard Clausen's drunken, on-site confession ("I'll kill the fucker again if he gets up") and found him covered in the victim's blood, suddenly did not remember the incident. Given the missing testimony, the court dismissed the case, demanding only a small bribe. Alderman Kenna subsequently "sponsored" the officer's promotion to sergeant. The system worked for everybody except the dead guy. Policemen obtained their jobs through the politicians and quickly realized they were joined at the hip with the local ward organization. If the ward boss had a good year, so did the copper.

Hinky Dink had a partner in every crime, the other First Ward Alderman, Bathhouse John Coughlin, and these two truly became the "Lords of the Levee." While Hinky Dink was short, thin, and smart, Bathhouse John was tall, portly, and dumb. Coughlin was dumb enough to steal Princess Alice, an elephant, from Chicago's Lincoln Park Zoo, for his Colorado Springs getaway home. And dumb enough to give Princess Alice great quantities of whiskey to cure her colds. "That's how I cure my ailments," he explained. The elephant became an alcoholic, begging whiskey from the flasks of visitors, spending all her days and nights soused, hung over, or passed out.

Coughlin, fond of outrageous colors in his wardrobe, frequently garbed himself in lime green waistcoats and red stockings. He also claimed to be a poet and songwriter, producing such profound works as "She Sleeps By the Drainage Canal" and "They're Tearing Up Clark

Street Again." But what Bathhouse John lacked in the way of intelligence he made up for with street-sense, a practical conviviality, and his strategic alliance with the clever Hinky Dink. Still, John Coughlin struck an unusual pose, even for the times. The mayor of Chicago once asked Hinky Dink if Bathhouse John was crazy or addicted to drugs. Kenna said no to both, telling the mayor, "To tell you the God's truth, Ma-aar, they ain't found a name for it yet."

Money being the lifeblood of politics, the First Ward duo "earned" huge sums from three sources. Protection money, between twenty-five and one hundred dollars weekly from each Levee house of prostitution, produced a steady flow of cash. In return for this tribute, the whorehouses could operate without police interference. Boodle provided another source of funds. Most Chicago aldermen sold their votes or their influence on a wide variety of municipal ordinances, zoning laws, tax proposals, and permits. While a vote for minor legislation often did not cost more than twenty-five dollars per alderman, special legislation on major projects sometimes garnered Kenna and Coughlin up to twenty-five thousand dollars each. A "fix," such as halting an indictment for pandering, started at one thousand dollars, depending on how messy the situation. Finally, the two aldermen garnered a big chunk of money, ultimately about fifty thousand dollars, from each year's annual First Ward Ball. The December affair, a lascivious, drunken revelry, attracted thousands of Chicagoans, a bizarre mixture of two-thirds pimps, prostitutes, and thieves, and one-third leading lights of society. The Ball soon evolved into an annual ritual, presided over by the Lords of the Levee, a winter night's homage to influence, corruption, and sexual excess.

The two men reduced elections to a science. The legions of poor workingmen, rail hands, thieves, and the jobless received fifty cents to a dollar for their votes. These voters were rounded up by First Ward party workers who held city jobs and transported to a polling place. Although these men were loyal to the Lords of the Levee, before they entered the polling place the aldermens' workers provided them with ballots that had already been filled out—the aldermen took no chances. The voters then took the ballots they obtained at the polling place out with them, to give to the workers so the whole process could be repeated. Coughlin also devised a system to move a group of tramps from polling place to polling place on election day to vote numerous times, calling it "hobo floto voto."

Kenna and Coughlin forged a smooth working relationship and never lost an election. The lowest point in their partnership occurred in

1906 when Bathhouse John learned that Hinky Dink had given a freebie to a local businessman who needed a zoning variation, something that ordinarily cost a bribe of twenty-five dollars. Coughlin was flabbergasted.

"Dink, ya can't give nobody nuthin' fer nuthin'! It's yer reputation at stake."

March 4, 1907 Chicago, Illinois

Release from prison, while not unexpected, gave Percy an excuse to drink and whore around for three days. Percy specialized in these two tasks, and adopted a routine that did not vary. A hearty lunch, usually sausage, spinach, and boiled potatoes, washed down with three or four beers, followed by a two-hour nap. Then a session drinking hard liquor at the Vendor's Saloon, across the street from his establishment, until 2:00 a.m. Once or twice a day, when the spirit moved him, he utilized the services of a woman at *Lila's* and then returned to the glittering bottles. When he paused to think during this period, not a frequent occurrence, he assured himself that in due time he would craft a careful plan to deal with Connie and maybe the meddling ballplayer.

That bitch cost me over a thousand dollars and got me thrown into the county jail. I'll spend whatever it takes to get her.

Sitting at the saloon bar as the night winds howled down State Street, Percy downed a shot of cheap rye and wiped his wet lips with his sleeve. He chomped on peanuts and pickles while smoking a fat cigar. Smoke from fifty cigars and cigarettes hung in a cloud over the place while sawdust covered the floor. A drunken man, with a leather cap pulled down over his head, hunched over the bar to the left of McGill, cradling a stein of beer. The man suddenly jerked to his right and vomited, dribbling a few drops on the cuff of Percy's pants. Percy flashed an angry sneer at the drunk, who made the mistake of smiling back at him, while emitting a smelly current of bile-breath. McGill edged off the three-legged bar stool, picked it up over his head, and brought it crashing down on the man with the leather cap, who cried out in pain and landed on his back on the floor. Blood began to flow from the man's head as Percy laid a dollar on the bar and calmly walked to the exit.

Doctor Kent had a dual diagnosis for Connie Dandridge: hysteria and neurasthenia. He explained his view to the Murphys.

"She has suffered severe swings of mood and temperament, and now we observe a clear excess of emotion. The attack on her physical person and subsequent events have resulted in a form of grief and a depth of emotion which has simply overwhelmed this child. Her reactions comport with the terrible experiences she has undergone. But hysteria has magnified her problems. She exhibits signs of *globus hystericus*, a blockage of the throat, and a closing of the breathing passage, a symptom we often see in conjunction with spasms of the esophagus. There are gastric problems as well, and it is not unusual for these symptoms to continue for months. But the chief symptom of the hysteria is her inability to emotionally cope with what has befallen her. In denying there is a problem she delays addressing the problem. As for the neurasthenia—it is not often associated with the female patient, but the fatigue, irritability, and extreme despondency of this young woman compel this diagnosis."

"What must we do to help this child?" asked Mrs. Murphy.

"Just what you have been doing. She needs the shelter of this home, rest, and a caring hand. If we have to, we can consider other treatments later. Perhaps an opiate derivative like laudanum or paregoric if she does not shake the disequilibrium in the next thirty days."

March 4, 1907 West Baden Springs

They stood in the cold, on the practice field, within the ellipse formed by the double-tiered track. The Cubs, at least those who had made it there in a timely fashion, crowded around the Peerless Leader, who leaned on a bat and exuded a strength and dignity that could not be missed. Close by, the tall, dark complexioned and skinny Solly Hofman crouched above the still-wet grass, an easy smile on his face, as he joked with Trainer Jack. Every few seconds Hofman puffed on a cigar.

The turf seemed spongy, giving a bit with each step, while a few puddles still marred the field. Almost all the Cubs dressed in their high-collared, flannel-pullover jerseys, with knickers. These pants had a buckle under the knee to keep the stockings in place. The stockings were made out of a heavy wool designed to protect the wearer during slides. Some sported the new team sweaters, thick gray woolen garments with a black, rolled collar, while a few others, like Durbin, wore navy blue, hip length, belted Cubs team jackets. They wore rounded, close-fitting caps with small bills.

Jack Taylor paced at the side of the group, gripping a dirty baseball. No jacket for Taylor. He denounced those wearing sweaters and jackets as "sissy-boys." Jimmy Slagle, still sniffling, sat calmly in the forefront, along with Durbin, Steinfeldt, Chick Fraser, Seabaugh, Miner Brown, Hub Perdue, Newt Randall, and Kahoe. Frank Schulte, an eccentric man, stood in back of the group, humming and whistling as he always did in such meetings, to the consternation of the Peerless Leader. Tinker failed to show due to a recent attack of appendicitis. Johnny Kling, "the Jew," did not put in an appearance either, having yet to resolve his salary dispute with management. Nor had Evers yet made his appearance as he still tended to his shoe store in Troy, New York. Orvie Overall would meet the team later, in New Orleans, and catcher Pat Moran remained in Chicago seeking surgery on his nose. Just before Chance began to speak, Jack Pfiester, ace lefty pitcher just in from Cincinnati, jogged onto the field, as did team secretary Charlie Williams, dressed in a black suit and not wearing an overcoat. On the edge of the field, six uninvited, derby-hatted locals observed. They didn't say a word, for fear of being required to leave.

Chance, clean-shaven and robust, had plenty to say. He peered out over the heads of his charges, speaking to the horizon, but as he warmed to the topic his gaze pierced into the players. "Boys," he began, "welcome to the commencement of our grand campaign." He paused for effect, clenching the bat he held before him, and his face darkened. "We was beat by those White Stockings last year, but there is one thing that I will never believe and that is that those cock-suckers are better than us. But maybe now you sons of bitches have learned a lesson as to what happens when you underrate the other sons of bitches." Chance truly hated the cross-town rivals. He scorned their fans too, calling them pig-stickers due to the proximity of South Side Park to the stockyards.

He paused and relaxed. "This is the last you will hear me speak of the events of aught six. We will not look back. Our focus is now on winning the World's Championship Series this year. We have all the strength of last season and new men enough to plug any weak spots that injuries may produce. I simply cannot see where or how any other team can take us. We will work as a unit; we will compete as a team. We will play to the limit of our abilities; we will fight hard and devise strategies to cover all contingencies. The result of all of this careful planning and hard work is inevitable. I promise you we will win."

The players shouted a chorus of cheers but in the back row the Brakeman, Jack Taylor, shook his head and told Newt Randall, standing next to him, "That fucker never gave me the ball against the Sox."

At two o'clock the players assembled in the second story of the covered bicycle track, the field outside being too wet to be used. Several Cubs leaned against the white wooden walls while one veteran, Miner Brown, lay on the wooden floor, stretching his limbs and exercising vigorously in a regimen he had carefully developed in past years. As the Cubs pitcher performed his thirtieth leg lift, Jimmy Slagle poked fun at him, telling him, "You gonna stretch your muscles too far Brownie, and then where will ya be, by gum? Don't come cussin' round me when ya pull yer killie's tendon!" The general consensus of professional ballplayers of the time held that exercise did not benefit baseball players and could, in fact, impair performance.

Chance directed Kid Durbin to warm up with Seabaugh taking the tosses. The Cubs manager suggested they start out only fifty feet apart. The second pitch that Durbin cut loose bounced hard and crazily off the planked floor of the track, clipping Seabaugh in the cheek, splitting it pretty bad below the ear. A crimson trickle seeped from the cut.

Brakeman, passing by, yelled out, "Great way to start the season, Kid!"

Kahoe took over for Seabaugh while the trainer applied some cayenne pepper and plaster to the rookie catcher's wound. After ten minutes Kahoe and Durbin moved to sixty feet six inches and the young pitcher let it out, throwing with all he had as Chance looked on. One pitch dropped as it ripped across the plate and made a popping sound on impact with Kahoe's glove.

"Don't you go and strip your gears!" yelled Chance. "You don't want to throw away your arm just yet."

Ballclubs in this era did not have pitching coaches—or any coaches for that matter—but the veterans made sure the youngsters obtained some instruction. In this vein, Jimmy Slagle asked Miner Brown to show Durbin how to throw the change-up. Miner expressed a willingness to oblige, and Kid tried hard not to stare at the mangled right hand that gripped the baseball in front of him.

"You hold the ball like you hold it when you're flinging a fastball," Miner began. "But you don't grip it tight. No, for a good slowball you hold it kind of loose, in the fingers, which, by the way, you will find easier to do than me since you got more fingers." Durbin smiled at the joke and Brown continued.

"You throw the pitch overhand, as hard as you can with the loose grip, and you want your delivery to be exactly like your fastball motion. The ball comes out of your hand pretty fast but it quickly loses speed on the way to the batter. Should fuck up his timing if you do it right."

Slagle carefully observed Durbin's first seven attempts to throw the change of pace pitch, as Brown encouraged and assisted him. The ball flew off the young hurler's fingertips and then died halfway to the plate.

"Seems like we got ourselves another pitcher," said Slagle, to no one in particular.

Kahoe groused that his trunk still hadn't made it to the hotel while Durbin couldn't quit thinking about the bloody mess he made of Seabaugh's face. After Durbin had his turn, Hub Purdue threw for thirty minutes to Kahoe, experimenting with a sidearm and overhand spitball. Perdue bit down on a chaw of tobacco, spit into his right palm, and rubbed the saliva and tobacco juice into the white horsehide. Then he whipped the ball toward the catcher. Kahoe hated catching a spitball artist.

"It's a goddam mess," he said.

The Game   Jack "Brakeman" Taylor

Brakeman Taylor is forgotten now, but the sidearmer set a record that will never be broken. From 1901 through 1906, Taylor started 187 games—and finished them all! One hundred eighty-seven complete games in a row. This stretch included a nineteen-inning complete game and an eighteen-inning effort as well as one day when he started and finished both ends of a doubleheader. No one ever accused Taylor of failing to finish what he started. Brakeman Jack earned a second nickname during these years, Old Iron Arm. By late 1906 Old Iron Arm did not know how many complete games he had pitched in a row, but he couldn't remember the last time he had been removed from a game.

Taylor discouraged his catchers from conferences on the mound, brushing them off with harsh words and walking away from them. He would shout at them as they approached, "Lord knows you ain't pitching today. Get your fat catcher's ass back behind the plate!" Though not a big man, Taylor came across as a rough character, willing to use his fists to make a point. "Beware the man who enters the pitching box to remove Jack Taylor from the game," he had bellowed on more than one occasion. Then, in August 1906, the day arrived. In the midst of a poor performance, a manager yanked Taylor from a game. Who had the guts to pull Taylor out of a game to break the streak? Frank Chance.

Not a strikeout pitcher, Taylor threw a lot of junk—slow pitches, which he judiciously mixed with a good fastball, and much of what he threw cut the corners of the plate. "Corner working is his forte," one sportswriter noted. He may have been the best pitcher in baseball in 1902, when he went 23-11 for Frank Selee's Chicago Nationals, with a stunning 1.33 ERA. In June of that year Taylor pitched and won a 3-2, nineteen-inning effort against the Pirates. The Pirate legend Honus Wagner went 0-8 against Taylor in that contest. Taylor mastered the change-up, called a slow ball by the deadballers, and befuddled Wagner by mixing it in amongst his heat. Toward the end of his magnificent career Wagner, perhaps remembering that afternoon, expressed the view that the toughest hurler he ever faced was not Christy Mathewson or Mordecai Brown, but Jack Taylor. Wagner, who loved to tell stories, also told the story of a June 1903 afternoon when Taylor handcuffed him terribly his first three times at bat. So on his fourth stroll to the plate Honus batted lefty, the only time he ever did that in his career. And, as Wagner told it, "Damned if I didn't hit the ball squarely down the right field foul line for a double!"

Brakeman's blond hair darkened by 1907, and his high cheekbones pushed up against the orbits of his eyes, narrowing them to slits. He gained a reputation as a mean son of a bitch, a drinker, and a gambler. Worse, several accusations of bribe-taking marred his career. In 1903 the Cubs and White Sox began an annual matchup, after the regular season, called the City Championship Series. If nothing else, much local pride rode on the outcome of these exhibition games. The first City Series proved the longest. Lasting fourteen games, the White Sox, who had finished a lowly seventh place that year, surprised the baseball community by winning seven. Shortly before the series Taylor asked then-team president James Hart for additional compensation to pitch these games. Hart refused. While Taylor dominated the Pale Hose in the opening game, tossing a shutout, in his next three starts he pitched poorly. Hart suspected Brakeman of tanking these contests, but lacked evidence to take action. Instead, the Cubs traded Taylor to St. Louis that winter for an unproven young pitcher with a mangled right hand, Mordecai Peter Brown.

When he returned to Chicago's West Side Grounds with the Cardinals, for a regular season game in early 1904, Cubs rooters still smarted from the City Series. They jeered at Taylor for his poor performance in the October matchup and openly accused him of taking money to lose. Taylor, no shrinking violet, yelled back at the crowd, "Why should I have won? I got one hundred dollars from Hart for winning and five hundred dollars for losing."

Cubs owner Hart, getting reports of this statement, publicly accused Taylor of accepting a bribe but National League officials did not pursue the matter.

Taylor proceeded to secure twenty victories for the Cards in 1904, but in July of that year he again faced accusations of taking money to throw a game, this time against the Pirates. Taylor denied the charges, the league allowing him to continue pitching until a formal investigation took place in February 1905. At that time Taylor testified that he pitched badly in the Pirates game because he spent the night before and the morning drinking and gambling with his teammate Jake Beckley and Pittsburgh gambler Slim Deneen. Taylor put it this way:

Slim... was introduced to me that night and went downtown with us. We had a couple of hours sleep and foolishly renewed drinking when we woke up. We stopped in a saloon on the way to the hotel and Slim said, 'Taylor, I'll bet $10 if you pitch today.' I told him I was not in shape to pitch for any man's money and hoped [Cardinal's manager] Nichols would not work me... They made seven hits off me but I was wild, giving five bases on balls and hitting a couple of basemen.

I am not a saint. I have generally kept myself in shape during the playing season, but at times have dissipated. I have shot craps, and have played poker. But that doesn't show that I am a baseball crook and I challenge anyone to prove that I ever made a dishonest dollar on the diamond.

The Board of Directors of the National League acquitted Taylor of throwing the game. But the board found sufficient evidence to find Taylor guilty of "bad conduct" and to fine him three hundred dollars. He refused to pay and the league never pressed for the money.

One month later, due to continued pressuring from Cubs President

James Hart, Taylor found himself again having to defend against the charges arising out of the 1903 Cubs-Sox City Series. This time the National Commission, a three-person body that ruled the American and National Leagues, conducted the inquiry. At the hearing Hart tendered three affidavits from fans who heard Taylor make the crack about the five hundred dollars. The commission found the evidence "insufficient." Taylor's hearing reflected the approach big league officials then took toward possible scandal: Don't rock the boat unless there is no other choice.

Taylor did not change his ways. In fact, history repeated itself in 1905 when the two St. Louis baseball teams, the American League Browns and the National League Cardinals, had their own autumn City Series. Once again Jack Taylor found himself accused of accepting money to throw several of these games. The statistics do not seem to justify the charges. Taylor won his first two appearances, lost his third appearance 2-1, and lost the final game of the seven game series due to two Cardinal errors. But Cardinal management had tired of the Brakeman at this point. In the summer of 1906 the Cards traded Jack, strangely enough, back to the Cubs, who had new ownership, where he performed admirably, going 12-3 to help the Cubs make it to the 1906 World Series against the White Sox. But Frank Chance did not let Brakeman throw a single pitch in that Series, partly because he did not trust him. Taylor never forgave Chance for this.

From the Journal of Kid Durbin

I found out what per diem means a few days ago. Charlie Williams, the team secretary and treasurer, gave me three crisp green dollars, saying "that's your per diem." Ten minutes later Warren Seabaugh told me it was meal money. I reckoned I could easily save a dollar a day.

I woke early this morning and took a walk down toward the baseball field they have here. It was cold and damp but pretty, the trees just budding and a wispy morning mist still hanging in the branches. The quiet of the morning was disturbed only by an occasional call of a wood thrush and the soft drone of bugs. As I grew closer to the ballfield I heard a familiar sound: a pitcher throwing to his catcher, the ball smacking into the leather with a "thwack" every fifteen seconds or so. Through the mist I finally made out two guys. Before I got up close on them I figured it must be two Pirates, but it certainly wasn't. It was two colored guys dressed in overalls.

I watched from the pony track as the black moundsman threw some dangerous lightning. A lefty like me, the guy's shoots came in quick and then exploded at the last minute, twisting off to the left or right. Then he started with the curveballs. They flew out of his hand high and outside and just came arcing into the glove like the catcher had a giant ball-magnet hidden there. Great stuff!

I introduced myself and told them I pitched for the Cubs. The pitcher, a six-footer with a big smile on his face, was Pat Dougherty. I have forgotten the name of the catcher, a smaller man, but I think he said "Strothers" or something like that. When I said I played with the Cubs they told me they played for the West Baden Sprudels. The Sprudels, it turns out, is a team made up of colored waiters from the hotel. Dougherty told me the Cubs used to spar with the Sprudels in "exhibit games" but that Frank Chance had put an end to it. The catcher told me that their manager was trying to line up a game with the Boston club that would be coming into the hotel a few days after we departed. The catcher offered to take some tosses of mine but I told him that Chance wouldn't want me warming up without him around. Shaking their hands, I wished them luck and set off back to the hotel.

At three o'clock I relaxed in the lobby of the hotel, drinking the Sprudel Water with Doc Gessler, a twenty-six-year-old veteran out-fielder. He arrived today and we struck up a quick friendship. Doc joined the Cubs mid-season last year after playing a number of years with Brooklyn. Doc is a genuine medical doctor who prefers playing baseball to practicing medicine. A Pennsylvanian like Rabbit Slagle, Doc completed medical school and then started playing ball professionally for an independent club in Punxsutawney. He worked his way to the Brooklyn Nationals before being traded to the Cubs. But not seeing much action in the last campaign, Doc, like me, hoped to make a good impression this Practice Season. I liked Doc right off. He didn't put on any airs about the sheepskins he had earned.

We watched Lefty Leifield and a few other Pirates horsing around with a medicine ball. They were getting a pretty good work out from it. Lefty asked us if we wanted to join in but, knowing Chance's views on fraternizing with the enemy, we begged off. I did ask Lefty if Mr. Wagner had arrived. He burst out a quick "Ha!" and said, "Ol' Hans always finds an excuse to miss most of the Practice Season and this year is no different."

Seeing the Pirates prance about the immense hotel lobby got me thinking, which, as my father says, can be dangerous. There is a cold rain outside so we cannot take the diamond for practice. While this massive atrium and its huge dome are almost big enough to allow a game inside, we would smash too many windows and probably break a bone or two on the mosaic-tiled floors. But observing this large enclosed space makes me believe that baseball can be played indoors. I know that there are indoor baseball games in Chicago during the winter but those fellas aren't playing real baseball—they use some sort of mushball and play in small gymnasiums. I'm thinking of something grander, a ballyard built just for baseball indoors.

If baseball is played indoors fifty years from now, there would be no reason why it couldn't be played in the summer or the winter, in the day or in the night. Bugs could go to a game in January, after work, and electricity would fill the ballpark with plenty of light and heat. The season could stretch all year! Baseball players will probably travel directly to the giant ballfields in dirigible balloons, maybe landing on the roofs. Probably sixty passengers will travel over eighty miles per hour on these crafts! We could have Sunday doubleheaders with the first game in Cincinnati and the second game in Chicago! Indoor games will mean more ladies attending, since they won't have to worry about the wind or a sun shower disturbing their hair and there can be fancy tables and chairs for the ladies, like in the atrium here.

Maybe the rules of the game will change too, like six years ago when the National League started to count the first two foul balls as strikes. That really helped us pitchers! Fifty years from now the batter might be allowed four strikes or possibly a walk would take only three balls. Or maybe instead of nine three-out innings we can go to seven four-out innings per game. It would be swell too if in 1957 the players owned the teams and voted on important decisions like firing the manager or increasing the ticket prices. I can see ticket prices going as high as two bucks and a beer costing as much as thirty cents. More people will be reading about baseball on a daily basis in 1957 because most newspapers will probably have photographs in them like some gazettes now and even towns like Joplin will grow big enough to support their own major league team. There will probably be six major leagues by then, and sixty teams fighting it out every year to make it to the World's Championship Series. We might even have teams from Tennessee and Georgia.

The average ballplayer will probably be making more money in the future, maybe as much as ten thousand dollars a year! And if the players have that much money coming in, we might move up the social ladder, too. Right now we don't get a whole lot of respect from the white-collar crowd. Those guys will go to a game and root for their hometown favorites and hoist a few beers with the players after a great victory or a hard defeat. But if a ballplayer wants to court their daughter, they start calling us "rowdies." That should change once ballplayers are flying around the country, making good money, and getting their photograph in the local papers.

In 1957, if I live that long, I will be an old man. What now lies ahead of me, my career as a pitcher on the Chicago Cubs, will then be a faded memory. I suppose this journal is partly that old man in me telling me to write things down so I don't forget them. So I will do just that. Funny—while I can come up with all sorts of ideas about the future of baseball, I have no ideas at all about how I will change over the course of the next fifty years. I only pray that I will still possess two things I learned from my parents: to always strive to do better and the belief that great hope mixed with a little bit of courage can accomplish anything.

March 6, 1907 Chicago, Illinois

On the fifth day of his drunk, Percy turned philosophical. Observing the sunset from the third floor of *Lila's*, Percy relished a line of purple clouds into which the sun had dipped and threatened to disappear. Naked, he turned to his employee, a young prostitute named Jill.

"Come here, Missy. You have got to see this." He called all his whores Missy.

Jill, reclining on the bed, in a similar state of undress, glanced at Percy and responded, "I see that sort of thing six or seven times daily."

Percy laughed. "No, Missy. I am not referring to the angle of my dick. I am suggesting you get your pretty ass out of that bed and view a truly majestic sunset. You do not see this six or seven times a day."

Jill came to the window and peered out at the horizon, just in time to see the final piece of the sun sink slowly into the now violet-orange cloud bank. For a few seconds the clouds which hid the sun seemed to bubble, and then they were still, as the bright globe dissolved under the line of the horizon.

"Very nice," she commented.

Percy sidled up behind the woman and smoothly slid his penis into her.

"So the sunset was just a ruse, was it?" she inquired, as Percy pumped in and out.

"Perhaps." He lifted her off the ground and began again. As Percy turned to carry Jill back to the bed, the door flung open and two men barged into the room.

Percy dropped Jill near the bed. He swiveled to scream at whoever had the temerity to intrude on him, especially in the middle of his staff "evaluation." But one look at the interlopers stopped Percy dead in his tracks.

The two men held pistols and wore khaki military uniforms. The United States Army. They took one look at McGill and knew they had their man. Jill strolled slowly to the bed, unfazed by the *coitus interruptus* and the two interlopers.

One of the men spoke to the cornered Percy. "Mr. Percival McGill! We are happy to make your acquaintance. We bring you greetings from the United States Army, Office of the Adjutant General. You, sir, are charged with being a deserter from the army, an offense punishable by a sentence of up to seven years hard labor." At this point the soldier looked down at Percy's flaccid manhood. "I said *hard* labor, Mr. McGill."

"This is a great mistake," said Percy.

"Good," said the other soldier. "Then your attorney shall have no difficulty winning your court martial proceeding. Now shut your fucking mouth, prisoner. You have two minutes to clothe yourself for a long journey. To Gotham. New York City. We leave in two minutes whether you are dressed or not."

March 6, 1907 West Baden Springs

The practices took their toll on the players, sore arms and legs abounding. But Trainer Jack rubbed the players down with liniment and arnica, allowing them to plod on. After the morning immersions, the Cubs found themselves tossing the ball and playing pepper on a wet field. The drizzle ceased but the temperature dipped uncomfortably cold. The sandy dirt did not provide good footing, so the players moved about slowly, inhibited also by the chill in the air. The vets wore coarse, gray cardigan Cubs sweaters, while most of the rookies sported coats. To complicate matters, seven Pittsburgh Pirates, including pitchers Lefty Leifield and Vic Willis, shared the diamond. Lefty brought a soccer ball to the field, and all the players, Cubs and Pirates, enjoyed kicking the leather ball around, until Husk appeared on the field and flatly told the Pirate players to get the hell out. Husk would not tolerate fraternization with players from other teams even during the Practice Season. No Pirate said anything to Chance. They knew that Frank would just as soon smash them as spit.

Trainer Jack worked hard at getting the sandy dirt infield dry enough to allow the boys to field grounders off it, spreading and mixing several hundred pounds of sawdust into the dirt. Six players formed a large circle and warmed up with the season's first game of high-low. They tossed the ball quickly to each other, purposely throwing too high or too low, or to the right or left of their target, forcing each other to stretch. Steinfeldt grabbed the ball off his shoe-top, pretended to throw to Durbin, but sailed it over to Randall to his left. The rookie wasn't paying attention and the ball squirted by him. Shrugging off a few good-natured catcalls, Randall retrieved the ball and the game resumed. After five minutes they were all sweating profusely.

Then Chance signaled the players to take the field. Husk took his familiar place at first, Hofman, a versatile utility player, covered second, rookie Bill Sweeney played short, and Steiny grabbed his normal third base spot. In the outfield an ever-shifting group shagged fly balls. Kahoe and Durbin took turns hitting grounders and fly balls to the fielders. Durbin took the mound for ten minutes but when he broke off a nasty curve to Steinfeldt the Cubs third-sacker walked away from the box, grumbling, "It's too early to face that kind of stuff."

After two hours the Cubs retreated to the hotel, allowing the Pirates to take the grounds. Pirate manager Clarke, a toothpick dangling from his lips, led his team out to the practice field. Clarke, as usual, wore a serious look on his face. As they passed, Chance asked Clarke if Wagner had shown up yet and Clarke responded, "Ain't his nature."

Husk directed Trainer Jack to look at Sweeney's ankles—both of them—after the practice. Sweeney limped slowly to a bench, his ankles swelling up and turning red. Jack appeared stumped by the problem until he questioned the young shortstop awhile. Sweeney reported that he skated literally every day in the winter, in Newport, Kentucky. That information gave Jack enough to diagnose the problem.

"I seen this before. You got strapitis," Jack declared. "Those ice skate bindings you was using is as tight as Chubby Murphy is with a dollar. They cut off the circulation good in your little feet. Now here you go running and jumping on those dogs without the binding and the blood is rushing down there mighty fast, filling those feet with more blood than they need. This rapid circulation is toughest on those veins. And that can cause a whole lot of pain." The trainer gave a simple prescription for treatment: "Don't worry about it, Billy boy. This ain't gonna hurt too long. Give it a few days and it will pass."

After the day's activities the Cubs relaxed in the hotel, trading stories and drinking beer. Durbin did not drink beer that night as he had developed a strong affection for Spring No. 7's Sprudel Water. He took a lot of kidding from his teammates for that.

Looking at Kid guzzle the smelly mineral water, Brakeman winced, and observed, "He must be a masachoid!"

Husk corrected Taylor. "You mean a masochist, Jack."

Jack shot a nasty glance at Husk. "I said what I meant."

Husk let it drop. Addressing the whole group he said, "You know who's a big rooter for the Sprudel Water? Wagner. Says it puts pepper into your blood."

The *Tribune* reporter, Dryden, convinced Newt Randall, a twenty-seven-year-old rookie from Canada, to allow him to publish a letter that a female admirer had sent him. Dryden termed the letter "the first mash note of the season." It read as follows:

I found your name on the sporting page, Newton Randall. The name has a singular quality to it. The article said you are a minor league player with great promise of joining the ranks of the major leagues this year. Do you know what that means, Newton Randall? You may soon be a shining light in baseball. I am hoping that you can become my shining light. What I have been seeking for a long time. Please send me some postals and a photo and I will do the same. I have one of me in low neck attire; I shall send you that one. If you can send me a diamond comb set or some jewelry that would be swell. Wishing you the greatest success, I beg to be yours only,

Miss Dorice Lind
Schofield, Wisconsin

Randall penned a short response, which Dryden printed in the paper the next day:

Thank you for your kind note. I hope you can come down from the land of milk and cheese to see me performing for the Cubs. Owing to the uncertain state of my future, I cannot ship you jewelry just now. And diamonds are too tall for me just yet. However, by this mail I send you a comb with fine teeth that you will see are set close together. Trusting that we may grow as close as the teeth of this comb, I remain your faithful admirer.

Newton Randall

March 8–10, 1907 New York City, New York

At the Grand Passenger Station on Canal Street in Chicago, the two military police checked the cuffs on McGill and tightened them. They also placed heavy leg irons around his ankles and dumped him into a steel wire cage, five feet square, in an unheated baggage car. Leaving him, one of the soldiers said, "Parting is such sweet shit." Percy did not reply.

Six feet away, in a similar cage, a large German shepherd dog named Prince Leopold, who did not suffer the indignity of handcuffs or leg irons, nervously pawed the metal wiring in a corner of his enclosure. The dog, moreover, had a soft straw bed at the base of his cage, while Percy lay upon a steel bed for the journey. Twice the soldiers undid the handcuffs, allowed Percy the use of a toilet, and fed him a hunk of bread and an apple. Other than those two interruptions, Percy made the trip alone, save for the dog, in the long cold night and the stuffy, warm afternoon. Once, when Percy awoke in the middle of the night, he could hear the dog whimpering, perhaps afraid that no human being would ever again stroke his back.

"Take it easy, fella," Percy called out. "Like you, I don't care beans for this railroad and these accommodations. But there must be a reason for all of this. The morning will be better."

By the time the train pulled into Grand Central Depot on Park Avenue, Percy's body screamed out in a parade of cramps, aches, and pains. He had a difficult time crawling out of the cage when ordered to do so—the military men dragged him out and rudely yanked him up off the floor. Each hobbled step he took sent seething pains down his legs from the lower back to his toes. But if he hesitated the soldiers rapped him on the side of the head with their brass knuckles. He did not complain, not wanting to set off his guards. Percy devised a saying for the occasion, a lesson he could tell his son, if he ever got around to having one: "Son," he would instruct, "when you are hogtied and the bad men are hovering over you with a mean spirit in their hearts and weapons in their hands, comply with their wishes and do nothing to provoke them. In return for this, the Lord may grant you another hour of life."

Percy then found himself in a taxicab, traveling thirty miles per hour down a broad avenue in Manhattan, where a few farms still dotted the area. As a fresh wind filled his lungs, Percy thought back on the events that brought him to this predicament. When he turned twenty-two years old, in 1898, he had enlisted in the United States Army to fight in the Spanish-American War. It did not take him long to figure out that he had made a grievous mistake, perhaps the dumbest decision of his life. He had never resolved whether to blame strong whiskey or his stronger hatred of the Spaniards for enlisting, but two months and three days into a six-year enlistment Percy left the army base in Georgia, never to return. Percy, who grew up in Brooklyn, living with his aunt after his mother's death, knew he could never return to his home there. He fled to the Midwest, to Cleveland and ultimately to Chicago, a town tailored to his needs. The army listed Percy McGill as a deserter, but he eluded their notice for nine years. *Why now?* Percy asked himself.

Percy did not become discouraged. Life, from his perspective, consisted of a series of skirmishes. A vigorous fight in each separate battle generally allowed one to advance to the next. You know you're going to lose the last battle, but the fight you are in now need not be the last.

The taxicab pulled up to Pier No. 7 on the southern tip of Manhattan, and the three men exited. On this breezy, bright Sunday afternoon a number of people milled about, including some finely dressed tourists. Gulls flew in close to the tourists while the harbor water lapped against the wooden pier with lilting, smacking sounds. The soldiers looked for a particular ship, a forty-eight-foot vessel named the *Barcelona*, which they found moored toward the end of the pier. Dragging Percy between them, the soldiers approached the *Barcelona* and hailed the captain. After a moment a crusty sailor stuck his bald head out of the pilothouse and asked the men their business.

"We need to transport this piece of shit over to the Castle," shouted the soldier.

"And I 'spose you boys is wantin' to do that now?" asked the captain.

"That would be our desire," the man said.

"Well sirs, get your jo-fired army asses on board and as soon as I find my trousers we'll shove to."

During this interchange, Percy peered south, to a spot of land out on the harbor. He remembered the place from his boyhood, although he had never viewed it from this direction. He knew it as Governors Island, sitting a half mile off the southern tip of Manhattan and the same distance from the Brooklyn waterfront. Castle Williams, an old fortress used as a federal military prison, perched on the northwest corner of the island, close to the water's edge. The jump-rope rhyme of the girls in the Red Hook neighborhood came back to haunt him now:

> *From the Army*
> *Run away!*
> *Castle Williams*
> *There you'll stay.*
> *Forever, forever,*
> *Forever and a day.*

He remembered something else about "Gubners Island" and Castle Williams. A fact he had stored away in his childhood. *Could be just a legend*, he mused, *or maybe it was true. A tunnel!* Long ago he had heard that army engineers dug a tunnel under the waters of New York Bay, under the Buttermilk Channel to Brooklyn, connecting the fortress Castle Williams to a now crumbled waterfront fort in Red Hook. The older boys told Percy of the tunnel, boasting how two of them "crawled out to Gubner's back in '81." Percy remembered the exact words of one of the boys, Chester Landingham, who said, "We was wet but we was alive."

March 8, 1907 West Baden, Indiana

Johnny Evers sauntered into the hotel around noon, just four hours before the team's scheduled departure for New Orleans.

"How you boneheads doing?" he greeted them.

Only twenty-five but looking a good deal older, Evers stood 5'9" and weighed in at 138 pounds in his polished black leather shoes. A big head perched on a small body, Evers had squinty, hooded eyes above a strong, square jaw that framed a permanent smirk. He had protruding ears, crowned by a shock of chestnut brown hair, a lock of which he occasionally brushed back from his forehead. The face of a genial Irishman. But Evers could not be described as genial. A moody, sad man, so prickly and testy that even his friends called him "The Crab." This marked his sixth year with the Cubs. Even after all this time he could not forget the indignities of his first week with the Chicago Nationals. The Cubs could not find a uniform small enough for his tiny frame, so he played his first five games in knickers that scraped the dirt. A few players threatened not to take the field with the then 110-pound infielder, afraid they might injure him.

On Evers' first day as a Cub in 1902 Jack Taylor took a look at the diminutive Irishman and said, "Not bein' much bigger than a rabbit is gonna hurt. You ain't gonna make it, boy. You'll be going home in a box, a little box."

Evers responded with, "Why don't we work this out with our fists, asshole?"

But Taylor would not oblige Evers, and over the years the two came to a grudging truce. Taylor and the others who prematurely judged this ballplayer based on his small stature soon admitted their error. Evers worked hard to become a valuable asset to the Cubs, a great defensive second baseman who hit well in the clutch. But more than his skills with the bat and the glove, Evers earned a reputation as an aggressive and smart player, a pepperpot who used the gray matter to figure out new plays and new ways to win ballgames.

The vets mobbed the Crab, genuinely happy to see their teammate. Slagle and Hofman insisted he drink a schooner of Sprudel Water and when Husk joined in the request Evers acceded. The look on his face as he drank the magic water drew a host of laughter from the group.

"Good God, that is awful!" Evers remarked. "It ain't got any better since last year, gents."

"Trainer Jack forces that crap down our throats every three hours," Slagle told Evers. "And we gotta bathe in that stink twiced a day."

His friends asked Evers about the state of affairs in Troy, New York, his hometown, where he owned a shoe store.

"Still a little cold up there," Evers related, "but business has been strong."

"Ain't exactly been the tropics here, Johnny," said Solly Hofman. "Between the rain and the cold we haven't been able to cut loose once."

"Wait till tomorrow," Johnny offered, "gonna be hot in N'awlens."

"Nights might be really hot, Crab," Brakeman said.

"I wouldn't know about that, Jack," Evers replied. While Brakeman Taylor had a reputation as a drinking man and a carouser, Evers was the opposite. On a typical night Evers would curl up in his hotel room with a Hershey's chocolate bar and the baseball rules book.

After the pleasantries Husk introduced Evers to Durbin, Randall, and the other rookies. Evers broke the ice with each in a comfortable, gracious manner. When informed that Billy Sweeney played shortstop, he said, "Good, we could use a new shortfielder."

A nervous laughter rippled from the vets at that remark, but the rookies did not understand the joke. Evers meant what he said. He and Joe Tinker had played next to each other in the middle of the infield since Evers broke in. While Evers and Tinker clicked as a double play combination on the field, the two could not stomach each other outside the lines. By 1905 they spoke not at all, except when absolutely necessary while playing. Tinker blamed it on an incident where Evers grabbed a taxicab without waiting for him. Evers blamed it on a ball Tinker heaved at him from ten feet away, breaking his finger. Whatever precipitated their split, the pair refused to acknowledge each other's existence off the diamond. At times Evers wanted to beat the crap out of Tinker, but held back, having witnessed Joe's handiness with his fists. Evers knew of Tinker's surgery—it had been all over the newspapers—and looked forward to playing alongside Sweeney or Artie "Solly" Hofman for the first part of the season.

The introductions over, Evers sat alone with Chance who nursed a beer while the scrappy second baseman drank coffee. Chance enjoyed talking baseball with Evers, once described by legendary sportswriter Hugh Fullerton as "a bundle of nerves with the best brain in baseball."

"You say that little lefty pitcher Durbin is out of Missouri?" Evers asked.

Chance nodded. "Yeah… pretty good fastball. Question is if he has any control."

"That's always the question with a young twirler. You remember the youngster from Missouri when I first joined this team, Jimmy St. Vrain?"

"Five years ago. How could I forget him? I even remember he was out of Montana, not Missouri."

"Montana, Missouri, what the hell!" Evers sipped at the coffee.

"I know what you were thinking about, Crab. St. Vrain's the guy who tried to bat lefty 'cause he couldn't touch the ball righty. First time he did that we was up against the Pirates. He swings from the left side—'an experiment' he calls it—and hits a ground ball to Hans Wagner. The kid puts his head down and starts running full chisel, only he's running to third base instead of first!"

"Right! What I remember most is the look on the Dutchman's face when he saw the Saint going straight to third! Why, his eyes nearly bugged out of their sockets. He seemed more stunned than anyone. He must of hesitated a full five seconds before he threw over to first. I thought he was gonna try and gun Jimmy down at third."

"Yeah. That kid acted like a bone-bean. In over his head. Durbin has more going for him, at least in terms of his bean."

"Good. That's half the battle."

Chance smiled. "What you said about the look on the Dutchman's face made me think about that stunt Germany Schaefer pulled last year."

"What stunt?"

"You remember Schaefer. He played with us your first year here."

"Course I do. A real cut-up! Good fella."

"Exactly. Well, Schaefer's playing for Detroit and the Tigers was up against the Cleveland Naps in Cleveland, at League Park. Germany was on first base with Davey Jones on second. The Tigers then pull a double steal, Schaefer ending up on second and Jones over at third. Germany then yells over to Jones at third, 'Let's do it again.' On the next pitch Schaefer tears off the base—not toward third but back toward first base!"

"Honest to God?"

"So help me! He hoped to get the catcher, a fellow named Harry Bemis, to throw over to first, but Bemis just stood there with his jaw dropped down to his kneecaps, stunned like everyone in the ballpark, so Jones had to stay put at third base. Hell, Jones got so flabbergasted by what he'd just witnessed that he couldn't move anyways. The Cleveland manager protested to the umpire, I think it was Billy Evans, but Evans told him there weren't no rule against running back to first. So the play stood. And on the very next pitch Germany tries to steal second base for the second time in the same inning! Bemis whips the ball to second but Germany beats the throw and, imagine this, Jones takes that opportunity to thieve home plate and makes it safely."

"Did not hear about that. Great story. My recollection is that Germany wasn't the strongest hitter."

"Yeah. His game is mostly his glove. A real nut though. He pinch hit a few years ago at South Side Park and hit one into the bleachers. So he doffs his cap and proceeds to slide into first base, then second, third, and home. The Sox bugs did not appreciate it."

"Back to Durbin for a moment. Does he have enough stuff on his ball to make the grade?"

"Yes. The ball moves. But he'll need some luck as well."

Chance didn't say it but he knew Durbin faced tough odds. The team had plenty of good arms in 1906, remarkable pitching in fact, and the acquisition of the veteran Chick Fraser from the Reds wouldn't leave much room for an inexperienced pitcher to get a shot. Still, he thought, Durbin's got a strong arm and other guys have overcome similar obstacles to make it in the big leagues. He'd seen it happen many times.

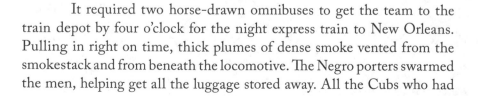

It required two horse-drawn omnibuses to get the team to the train depot by four o'clock for the night express train to New Orleans. Pulling in right on time, thick plumes of dense smoke vented from the smokestack and from beneath the locomotive. The Negro porters swarmed the men, helping get all the luggage stored away. All the Cubs who had been on the team in '06 sported impressive, forty-dollar alligator hide suitcases, souvenirs of the World Series. Secretary Williams assigned the rookies to Pullman sleeping berths directly above the wheels while the vets got the better berths, lower berths away from the clatter. As always, the superstitious Frank Chance took upper berth 13, the smoothest ride on the train.

The Cubs spread out over the train, many heading for the club car for liquid refreshment. When a black waiter clad in white announced, "Dinner is served in the dining car up front," almost all the players dashed past him for a steak dinner. Newt Randall, ailing with a stomach problem, retired to his berth and wasn't seen till the next morning. Evers and Chance talked baseball for a few hours in the Pullman car filled with the smoke of cigars and cigarettes before Evers begged off. In his berth Evers munched on a chocolate bar and read the *Sporting News* before going to sleep at 8:15 p.m. By that time a poker game raged, with Slagle, Chance, Steinfeldt, Kahoe, and Chick Fraser sitting round the narrow table, pushing quarters, dollars, and an occasional quarter eagle ($2.50) into the pot. Playing five-card draw, Mike Kahoe cried out "For the love of God!" when his flush ended up second best to Harry Steinfeldt's full house, jacks over threes. Harry, dead drunk, exclaimed, "God ain't got nothin' to do with it, Kahoe!"

The train rocked and swayed through the darkness. Durbin slumped in a window seat, reading *Sapho,* a novel by a Frenchman named Daudet that had become popular once a number of reviewers deemed it "an unwholesome French novel with a morbid focus on sex." Sapho, a beautiful woman, seduces a number of men in the course of the novel, but ends up paying the price for her misdeeds. Sweeney and Seabaugh smoked cigars and downed beers at the bar in the club car. A sportily dressed thirty-year-old man joined them and bought a round of drinks but they asked him to leave when he kept pumping them for information. "Must be a sharper," said Seabaugh.

When the train paused in Memphis, Cubs pitcher Carl Lundgren and his wife boarded. The twenty-seven-year-old Lundgren was a handsome Swede, with piercing eyes and dark hair parted down the middle. His teammates welcomed the seventeen-game winner with handshakes and he introduced his wife to them. A conductor, breathing heavily from some exertion, informed the passengers that there would be a delay in leaving Memphis "owing to a staffing situation," by which he meant that the engineer scheduled to take the train south was on a drunk and they were out scrambling for a replacement. The train chugged out of Memphis two hours late. Most of the Cubs ended up in their berths around midnight, as the train streaked through the northern Mississippi flat land in the cold clear light of a luminescent moon. Brakeman and Steinfeldt, ensconced in two stuffed armchairs in the parlor car, sipped bourbon and discussed baseball and women. Steinfeldt told a sheep joke and then suggested that the rookie Randall "had a mean pair of dogs," by which he meant the kid had some speed. Brakeman disagreed. "Hell, I could outrun that youngster home to first three times out of four." Around 3:30 a.m. Steiny retired, sleepy from the alcohol and no longer able to stand the bitterness that spewed like vomit from the old sidearmer.

From the Journal of Kid Durbin

Last night we arrived in the Crescent City. The train station is still under construction and isn't much more than a giant shed, with some kind of wrinkled tin roof and no walls. In the station, which is right off of Basin Street, a little guy no more than ten years old stuck a small pamphlet called the Lid in my hands. The Lid consisted of a dozen advertisements for saloons and more than one hundred women's names and telephone numbers. Figuring that the Brakeman could put me wise to this, I asked him about it. He looked over my shoulder and said those names are the local church choir members, but from the snickers of the other guys I knew he lied. Jimmy Slagle, always the decent fellow, jumped in and told me, "Them's the local whores." So that's how I found out about Storyville. By the way, some of the women's names had a "J" written after them. Jimmy explained that it stood for "Jewish." Jewish whores! Seems like they got 'most everything in this place.

The dampness in the air hits you right in your face and takes a whole lot of getting used to. It's like breathing soup. There seems to be more colored people here than St. Louis and Chicago combined, but they seem pretty damned skittish of white folks. When I say hello to a colored man here he seems to find it necessary to remove his hat and gaze to the ground in making his response, "How do, sir," to me. I suppose that is how they train the colored folk to act down here. While we didn't have any coloreds in Lamar, I can't imagine we would have forced them to act like that.

A huge carryall pulled by six horses took the team from the station to the St. Charles Hotel in the business district, a block or two from the French Quarter. The hotel is a solid, red brick building, about seven stories tall. Seabaugh and I are on the fourth floor, room 422. It's a good thing Warren is not a restless sleeper because we are again sharing a bed that is fairly small. Even though we are right by the Quarter I haven't yet had a chance to explore much. But six of us did go to a fine new restaurant called Galatoire's on Bourbon Street for dinner last night and the trout there is a huckleberry above any other restaurant's persimmon. We came straight back to the hotel after eating, resisting the numerous temptations of this place. By the way, I brought with me from West Baden two cases of Sprudel Water, not mentioning this to any teammate. In fact, I am drinking some now.

It is five o'clock and the reason I am writing this is because today was the first game of our Practice Season. The Cubs played the New Orleans Pelicans, a Southern Association team managed by Charlie Frank. We dressed into our uniforms at the hotel because there's no visitors' dressing room at Athletic Park, the Pelicans' ballpark. Then we had a carriage parade to the ballgrounds. My first carriage parade. The way it works is like this—all the Cubs in their uniforms crowd onto two large carriages, what Slagle calls "tally hoes." Trainer Jack threw colored blankets over the horses with large letters saying "CHICAGO NATIONALS." It's not much of a parade but some bugs do follow us all the way to the game and pay their way in, which I suppose is the reason we do it. The Cubs have these parades all the time, except in New York, where the bugs started to throw bricks at the players. It seems Mr. Murphy is a big believer in carriage parades, but Jack Taylor takes the opposing view.

"The coon teams do this," Jack offered, "because it's the sort of thing a coon does. White men shouldn't hafta do this. Next thing ya know they'll have us bunkin' in a nigger hotel."

Athletic Park is a rickety wooden ballpark on its last legs. To say this place is falling apart is being kind, because it couldn't never have been much to brag about even when it was new. Now it reeks of beer and urine and hasn't been painted in a decade.

The first thing I noticed when we entered the park was Henry the Ape. You cannot help but see and smell Henry. Turns out he is the mascot of the Pelicans, a huge orange monkey, an orang-outang from the wilds of North Borneo. Henry, who stands about four feet tall with long, muscular limbs and stringy orange hair hanging off him, is kept tethered to an iron stake in the grandstand area directly behind home plate. We strolled in an hour before they let the bugs in, and Henry took a close look at us, got very agitated, and let out a strange, high-pitched holler. Either Henry was a devoted Pelican bug or he didn't take kindly to the smell of us Cubs. He got used to us after a bit, but I began to feel sorry for him. Later, some nasty kids came up behind Henry and threw stones at him. I thought about chasing those ruffians away but Henry handled the situation nicely. He picked up some of his own shit and flung it at them and they quickly scattered. Still, Henry would have been better off if the Pelican ballclub had left him swinging on the trees in Africa (if that's where Borneo is). Anyhow, I never played ball in front of an ape before.

I ran across Jack Taylor sitting in the outfield grass, with a large glass jar. His cap lay next to him and he seemed hung over and grumpy but I had to ask him what he was doing with that big jar. He showed me these little lizards infesting the field. "Chameleons," he called them. They were everywhere. These lime green creatures averaged three inches, and their color changed when you put them against different colored backgrounds. When he held one against his gray uniform, the chameleon turned gray! I asked Jack why he collected this menagerie.

He said, "Wouldn't it be splendid if the Crab slept with some of these fellows tonight?"

I did not comment. I could smell the alcohol on Jack's breath. If he still wanted to play a prank on Evers when he sobered up that was his business. After he placed about forty or fifty of these little critters in the jar Jack screwed the metal cover on. I told him they'd die without air and he bellowed, "You think I'm a fuckin' dummy? Get out of here." I kept my distance, but about five minutes later I saw him punching numerous air holes in the jar's cover with a screwdriver and hammer.

One hour before the game Husk comes to me and says he wants to see the new guys perform so I am the starting pitcher! I took a deep breath while the Cap'n gave me one bit of advice. "Don't overdo it and blow out your arm." I think he waited till then to inform me so I wouldn't have a whole lot of a chance to worry about it. Anyhow, just as he is telling me this, while most of our guys sprawled about stretching their limbs, the skies darkened over Athletic Park. The temperature must have dropped twenty degrees in two minutes and then a cold rain starts to pelt us. This brought out a great many moans and groans from my teammates since we *had been rained on just about every day up in Indiana.*

Jimmy Sheckard, a dark-haired, good-looking guy about my height but heavier, complained the loudest. "We was watered to death in West Baden. Drinkin' that goddam Sprudel Water six times a day, sittin' in the stinkin' water for hours, and the good Lord bringin' the rains down on us every day. And now the skies is openin' up on us again. Maybe we should start building an ark."

It's fitting that Sheckard moaned about the rain because this is one guy who actually hated water. Old fashioned in this regard, he never bathed but once or twice a year when his roommate couldn't stand the stink anymore. Jimmy truly believed that water made you sick, that germs and contagion streamed through most non-alcoholic fluids. He said, "Only the alcoholic drinks is free from those critters and safe for a body."

Trainer Jack had to threaten Jimmy with a ten-dollar fine to get him into the West Baden waters. I will never sit next to him on the train.

While we waited for the storm to pass, Husk passed the word that he would pay two bits for every base hit by a pitcher during the Practice Season. I told Seabaugh, "I'm gonna be a rich man." The storm died away after an hour, the sun came out nice and bright, and the groundsmen fixed up the field proper for baseball. I warmed up with Warren, happy to see my curveball working. The fastball did not have much zip on it but at least it tailed off to the left at the last moment. Any movement on a fastball is a good thing. When my hummer is not moving it usually spells trouble, especially because I don't yet have a third pitch. I threw for twenty minutes and then took a seat on the bench.

The game started out with our guys ripping apart the Pelican slabman in the first. We scored five runs on four hard hits and two walks. So after the third out, there I stood, in the pitcher's box, twirling for the National League champion Chicago Cubs in the first game of 1907. I felt a little jittery but once I started throwing to the Pelicans I didn't have time to think much.

Kahoe was the receiver and the old vet signaled one finger for a fastball to begin the game. That's what I gave him and the umpire called it a strike. That felt good. But the second pitch sailed off from the plate, as did the next two. I tried to get too cute with the 3-1 pitch and walked the leadoff man, never a good move. Walking the leadoff guy in an inning is an invitation for trouble. I got the number two batsman on a decent curve—he popped it up to Cap'n Chance at first. But then things turned ugly. I walked another Pelican and the next guy bounded a ball to Sweeney at short. Billy scooted in to get it but on the muddy field it slid under his glove, and the base runner never stopped running, scoring from second. I did retire the next two guys so the first inning was no major disaster. I breezed through the second inning but then I'd have to say I lost my composure in the third frame, walking two batters after an error and then giving a pass to the next batter, allowing a run to trot home for free. Giving up so many bases on balls like that in one inning embarrassed me.

Husk trotted over to me from first and said, "Kid, don't you go getting lazy in your noodle when you're throwing for this club. I don't want you thinking about the last pitch. Focus on your next pitch. You're trying too hard to strike out everyone. Ease up and enjoy yourself."

Those words calmed me down some and helped me get the next guy out. I think my confidence grew toward the fourth and fifth innings, my last frames. My totals: five innings, three runs, and four hits. The worst part is that I walked six, unusual for me. Maybe it had something to do with the ball being fairly wet. We won the game 11-8 and I got credit for the victory. Husk came up to me afterwards and told me that all the runs I gave up scored as the result of errors and that I had done fine in my debut. So as I write this, just a few hours after our victory, I am feeling tired but satisfied. I will sleep just fine tonight. Oh—I almost forgot—in the first inning when everyone smacked out hits, I got one too! So Husk flipped me a quarter for this when we got back to the hotel.

Couple more things. When I was a boy and a St. Louis rooter, the Cards had a player by the name of Charley Frank. So once the game ended I asked the Pelicans manager if he played for the Cardinals a while back. Mr. Frank said "yup," but he didn't seem to want to talk much about it, saying only that he played for the Cards two years and really never got much of a chance. He seemed sort of bitter about this.

And then Brakeman and I jogged to the outfield fence to get the jar of chameleons, to take them back to the hotel with us. But the heavy rain had poured in through all those air holes, filling the jar to the top with rainwater and drowning every trapped chameleon. Brakeman shook his head.

"They's all dead as a can of corned beef. Kid, you were the smart guy that told me to punch those air holes into the jar top. That's what killed 'em."

Although I wanted to tell Brakeman straight out that he's what killed 'em, I held my tongue. But Jack must have seen some kind of disapproving look on my face because he looked at me, his lips drawn and tight, and said, "You best be on your way, rookie."

THE BEST TEAM EVER

March 11, 1907 New Orleans

Husk did not schedule a game for this day. Just a workout session at the Pelican's ballpark and a swim at the local YMCA afterwards. "One practice each day is enough for me," Chance told two reporters, "and what's good for me is good for the other fellows. Too much exercise is weakening in a climate like this."

The infielders took ground balls on the no longer muddy diamond, Billy Sweeney trying to show that his two errors the day before were a fluke. Trainer Jack knocked some fly balls to outfielders Slagle, Schulte, and Hofman. Carl Lundgren, the college boy pitcher from Illinois, displayed the form that resulted in a 17-6 record in 1906. Miner Brown, a frumpy, impassive man, showed his stuff to the reporters and a few bugs who snuck in, while Jack Taylor spent a half hour commiserating with Henry the Ape.

The Cubs finished their practice at three o'clock and were set free until the next day. Husk took a group of Cubs to the racetrack, claiming that he had some inside information on two races. The information may have been "inside" but nobody shared that dope with the horses. Meanwhile, Brakeman Taylor cajoled two Krauts, Harry Steinfeldt and Frank Schulte, into accompanying him in a foray to Storyville. Brakeman had been tipped off about a joint on Basin Street that sold something besides liquor and women.

Steinfeldt wasn't looking for anything other than a few beers. It hadn't been hard for Brakeman to convince Harry to accompany him. Harry, a garrulous descendant of hard-drinking Germans, played a great third base and drank more than his share. The walk from the hotel to 210 Basin Street took only ten minutes, but the afternoon heat, rising off the sidewalks in visible waves, took its toll on the three men. Water that trickled on the pavement from the carts of street vendors gave off tiny curls of steam. The narrow avenues were almost deserted, not many people braving the midday heat. On the way over Schulte engaged in his usual superstition of searching for hairpins in the streets and on the walkways. He truly believed that each hairpin he found represented a hit he would get in his next game. And the bigger the hairpin, the bigger the hit. He even believed that hairpins bent to the left meant a base hit to left, and vice versa. He called it his "hairpin hunt." By the time the three sweating men reached their destination, Schulte was swearing about failing to find a hairpin and Steiny's need for a cold beer had greatly intensified.

The strong smell of alcohol greeted the three men as they entered the *New Monte Carlo Saloon.* A chipped and patched mahogany bar stretched along one wall, while two dozen round tables, most of them empty, filled the place. It wasn't as hot inside the place as outside, but it wasn't cool either. The trio grabbed two stools at the long bar, Steiny ordering them three drafts. The beer could have been colder but it served its purpose. Taylor asked the long-sleeved bartender where he might find Professor Sam and an extended arm directed him to an old, white-haired black man, sitting on a stubby stool before a piano.

The old man sat alone, staring at the piano keys in a reverie, nursing a whiskey, stirring it with an ancient finger. He wore an aged suit, once blue, now of uncertain hue. Brakeman introduced himself and said, "I wanted to talk to you about some of your magic powder."

Professor Sam swiveled around and asked, with a deep, throaty delivery, "Ya jes wanna talk about dis or is ya fixin' to buy de zaggeratin powduh?"

Jack reassured the old man, telling him, "I am a buyer, but I wanna know the properties of this powder. What it's all about."

Smiling to reveal a fine set of teeth minus one, the professor said, "I be happy to 'splain all ya needs to know suh. All de 'propa-tees' as ya puts it. I been makin dis powduh long 'bout thirty yeas now. De zaggeratin powduh—it be a gif of Mudder Natcha, and it be mo' powaful dan de juju grass. De powduh is made from de mushrooms dat grow outta de cow-shit. Where day is cows day is cow-shit. And where day is cow-shit, day is de mushrooms. Ya needs not worry suh. We does not use any of de shit for de powduh, no suh, we clean de shit offa de mushroom. Den we lays dem mushrooms in de sun for two days until all de moisturity is 'vaporated outta dem. We is able den to ground it up into a fine black powduh, which we call de zaggeratin powduh. De powduh gots to be eatin' wid sompin' cause if ya eats it all by itself ya gonna be sick. So ya takes dis powduh and ya mix it up wid yo red beans and rice and den ya eats it. Maybe one hour afta eatin' it ya sees why day calls it zaggeratin."

"And why is it called that?" Jack queried.

"Because it zaggerates mos' everything and all dat happen to ya. Fo instance. If ya's havin de bad day, de type o'day where ya wish ya nevah be bone, ya does not wanna eat dat zaggeratin powduh dat day. No suh, not dat day because den yo day be two times bad. But if ya be happy and wid a woman-friend maybe, de powduh make it two times bedder. Dat woman-friend she be evah so mo' bootiful afta ya's eatin de powduh. De food taste bedda den evah. An' de music is zaggerated too, it goes deep into ya head like it nevah sound so good befo'. Dat powduh make you undastand de music is how I 'splain it."

"Does it do anything else?"

Professor Sam leaned back and then eased forward, toward Jack. "Yessuh, dis powduh been known to stir up de 'magination sumpin' fierce. Folks say day see tings dat ain't dare, like rainbows and colors where dare ain't no rainbows. But maybe dose rainbows *is* dare, only ya needs da powduh to sees dem."

Jack asked Professor Sam if anybody ever got hurt from the powder.

"No suh," answered Sam, "ceptin maybe dat gentaman Sad Henry bout two yeas back, a color'd man like me. Eighty years ol' he was and he eat de powduh and den goes to Sister Sally's to party wid de ladies. Passed onto de next world wid a zaggerated smile on dat face, he did. But I do not blame de passin' of Sad Henry on de powduh. Jes a Quincy-dance! Y' ain't eighty, is ya? I cain't tell wid de wide folks."

Jack laughed and shook his head. "How much does this powder cost?"

Professor Sam, all business now, stated, "Yessuh, my partnuh over dere can let ya have two bags fo de regla price of three dollars. Fo' bags fo' a fin."

Jack paid the professor's partner, tucked away the powder, and rejoined Steiny and Schulte, who entertained four patrons with tales of the National League, some of the stories featuring each other.

Steinfeldt told one of his sheep jokes.

"There was this guy, a small-town boy, and he was complaining to his friends. He says to his buddies, 'Why does everybody in this town call me "sheepfucker?" Explain that to me, will you. I dig ditches the last ten years and they don't call me "ditchdigger." I play baseball three times a week for twenty years and they don't call me "ballplayer." I been a Lutheran all my life and nobody calls me "Lutheran." But I fuck one sheep and...'"

The drinking men laughed and in a few moments Jack, Schulte, and Steiny walked back to the hotel, the sun less intense as it sank low in the sky.

"What was that all about, you and the old nigger?" asked Steinfeldt.

"Magic, Harry. Magic in a brown paper bag."

New Orleans had its own Levee, a legalized prostitution district called Storyville. Twenty square blocks, three thousand whores and one hundred saloons. Legislated into existence in 1898, Storyville sat close to the French Quarter, bounded by Basin Street, Canal Street, Claiborne Avenue, and St. Louis Street. Any sexual act could be purchased in Storyville. Independent prostitutes called "crib girls" worked out of ramshackle "cribs," rows of dilapidated shacks consisting of nothing more than an exterior door leading into a room just big enough to hold a bed and a chair. Crib girls charged fifty cents to a dollar for various sexual services, but competition frequently cut prices to twenty-five cents during weekday afternoons. On the other extreme, Lulu White ran a well-appointed brothel where the "menu" included mother and daughter combos and the prices ran from five to fifty dollars. Men from the upper echelons of New Orleans society frequented *Lulu's*, winking gingerly at each other the next day at tamer social events. The Crescent City boasted white whorehouses and colored houses. And all the larger houses had a dance area on the first floor, where the customers met the girls, and black bartenders sold low liquor at high prices while a "Professor" played music on a piano. The music came to be known as jazz.

The sportswriters did not report everything that happened in the Practice Season. They saw themselves as guardians of the game's reputation, especially since the teams paid their travel and hotel expenses. Certain subjects were deemed unworthy of reportage, such as the drinking and the whoring of the players. Of course the reporters drank as much as the players, perhaps more. Dryden and the other newsmen would have utilized the services of the Storyville women just as much as the Cubs had they been paid as handsomely as the ballplayers. Sitting around a saloon table, Warren Seabaugh, Doc Gessler, Billy Sweeney, and several other Cubs planned a visit to Storyville. Gessler, with black hair deeply parted down the middle, deep-set brown eyes, and a broad forehead, took charge. He briefed Warren on what to expect once the young Cub confessed that he had never "engaged" a prostitute before.

"First thing buddy," said Doc, "you don't *engage* a whore. You fuck her."

Warren blushed but said nothing, while the others chuckled.

"Second, I am no red-light district man but I was here last year with the Superbas. We have to choose our spot carefully," Doc continued. "I suggest a place I know where we can get a few drinks and lie with a woman and not spend more than five or six dollars, assuming you do not overdo the drinking part. And they'll treat us white. We won't get rolled."

Warren, who did not mention that he was a virgin, assented. He looked forward to this evening, and its uncharted territory, with excitement and some anxiety.

Doc continued, this time assuming the air of a medical man.

"Now when you go upstairs with the young lady, she will quickly remove her garments. Very quickly. Probably only be wearing a chippie to begin with. She will be naked in less than thirty seconds. You see, their profit margin demands volume, so things will not take all that long. You will then remove your clothes and the first thing she will do is to grab your prick and give it a good yank."

"That's a gob of spit, right?" asked Warren.

"No. On the square, buddy. The lady *will* grab your dick first thing. She's not doing this for your excitement and certainly not for hers. They do it to see if a puss leaks out, indicating you are diseased." Doc delivered his explanation in a clinical tone.

"They do it for their own protection. So just be ready for it. The rest is as you would expect."

Warren did not know what to expect although he had a fairly decent idea of the mechanics involved.

Warren did have another question. "Doc, what if *she* is diseased? I've heard some scary tales of something called 'the gleet.'"

"Yeah, that's what the locals call gonorrhea. Look, there is risk involved when you visit a sporting club. But if you choose a young woman who is relatively new to the job, you cut down your risk significantly. By the way, Warren, you know that sexual congress and the game of baseball have very much in common."

Warren had a puzzled look on his face. "Truly?"

"Yeah. You've heard of getting to first base with a woman? Well second base and third base—they're just two more steps on the way to home. Your doubles and triples are foreplay, in a manner of speaking. The goal is to come home. Remember—home plate is the very place you started from. Another way of looking at it is that all men enter this world from a woman's quim, and we all are trying to come back to that place— home base if you will—as darn near often as we can."

"I never thought about it like that," Warren said, a pensive look on his face.

"No doubt. But one more piece of medical advice for you, buddy. The reason men go to whores is because it's a sure thing—in baseball terms you're gonna bat 1000 with a whore. So when you come around third base tonight and you're headed for home plate, it's okay to slide into home, Warren, but for God's sake don't slide feet-first!"

The boys, including Warren, laughed heartily at this. They ate their dinner at a seafood place two doors south of the St. Charles and then sauntered off in the direction of Storyville, several of them lighting up fat cigars. By eight o'clock a cooling breeze blew off Lake Pontchartrain. As they walked down Canal Street, a ballyhoo truck pulled slowly along, and three different bands of black musicians played on the flatbed, each band trying to outdo the other. A banner from the side of the truck proclaimed "The Devil's Dance," an affair scheduled for the upcoming Saturday night. A few minutes later the sounds of the ballyhoo truck gradually evaporated into the cool night air. Doc and Warren ended up outside a joint that Doc had visited before, a place called *The Studio*, on Basin Street next to the firehouse.

The boys entered in a good mood, and left their hats with a small boy. The madame of the house, Emma Johnson, greeted them warmly. A Negro, she looked fifty or so, and wore a formal, peach chiffon velvet dress that showed more of her than the two men cared to see.

Warren whispered to Doc, "Is this a colored place?" and Doc shook his head no.

Emma overheard the exchange and winked at Warren. "Don't ya worry none, honey. My girls is whiter than you is. But some day you boys ought to expand your horizons, maybe wet your end in a mulatto girl. You gets the best of both worlds. Just let me know."

She led them to a large room off to the right, where other customers drank and mingled with the prostitutes. A young colored man in a fine gray suit played a ragtime piece on the upright piano, while several couples danced to the syncopated tunes. Dressed in a manner to stir, a pretty young girl approached Warren. Her black silk dress came down only to mid-thigh, where the horizontally striped silk stockings took over. The low-cut decolletage displayed a great portion of her bosom, immediately grabbing Warren's attention. The girl then grabbed Warren's crotch, briefly, but long enough to make her point. She introduced herself as Edna, and before he could look back at Doc, she led him off to the bar. He purchased two whiskeys, noticing that hers contained little, if any, whiskey. The barkeep stood in back of a brass-plated, electric National cash register. Warren paid him one dollar plus a quarter tip. The whiskey relaxed Warren, and the second drink, five minutes later, removed any lingering doubts. Edna had dark hair, creamy, smooth skin, and brightly painted red lips. Warren guessed she was eighteen.

"Shall we go on up?" Edna smiled as she asked. "It's a different world upstairs."

Warren didn't take any convincing. He followed Edna up the wooden stairs. Trailing behind her he smelled her flower-like perfume but his eyes stayed glued to her long legs as they ascended the stairs. The temptation to reach out and caress her bottom overwhelmed Warren but he successfully resisted. All things in due time, he thought.

The bedroom stood right at the top of the stairs, and Edna closed the door behind them in a practiced motion. She asked Warren for four dollars. He paid and she tucked the money away in a dresser drawer. Before he realized it she sat nude, on the edge of the bed, her dress laid across the chair. Warren eyed her body with amazement, beautiful breasts that jiggled as she moved and a dark triangle of downy hair between her legs. Just as predicted by Doc, she grabbed his cock and twisted it just so, inspecting the tip to see if anything emerged. That done, she lay back, pulling Warren down on top of her, and inserting him inside.

"Do it to me darling," she urged, and Warren obliged. He looked into her eyes, but they were closed. She moved in a steady circular grind beneath him, allowing his penis to dig deeper. He bore into her and each thrust demanded another. It did not take long. After forty seconds Warren ejaculated inside her, and then rolled off, onto his back next to her. A great relief overcame the young catcher. Now that he had spilled his seed in a woman, he had crossed some strange threshold as a member of a great secret society. *Maybe this was what the Masons was all about*, he thought.

Twenty-five minutes after entering *The Studio*, Doc and Warren stood on the street holding their hats, stretching their backs and their stories. "I fucked her twice," Warren lied. The boys headed toward the St. Charles in the heat of the darkness. After walking two blocks they came to a wooden building with a sign proclaiming it the *Tuxedo Dance Hall*. A strange, beautiful music streamed out the front door, literally stopping the two men in their tracks.

"What do you think?" asked Gessler.

"Let's give it a try."

They paid their quarter admission charge and struggled back through the dancing couples, some in close embraces while others flung their limbs in wild abandon. Smoke from cigarettes, cigars, and what the locals called ju-ju weed filled the place, and Gessler and Seabaugh finally made it to the back wall to observe the six Negro musicians on the bandstand. The two Cubs stood twenty feet from the band admiring a sound which they had never heard before. A cornet, trombone, clarinet, guitar, drums, and bass fiddle. The sound leaped from the instruments in a series of cold, clear currents and open tones that wrapped around each other, creating the new music called jazz. The Buddy Bolden Band made this music and Buddy Bolden blew a powerful cornet. Like no one else then or since.

Seabaugh and Gessler found a small square table, drank several lagers, and listened attentively to a sound unfamiliar to their ears. Politely rejecting solicitations from two Creole prostitutes, the two men slid back in their chairs and let the music take hold of them. The band played a version of "Bucket's Got A Hole In It" that lasted twenty minutes and included several improvised solos. Around midnight, when the musicians took a break, the two Cubs left and made for the *Cafe Du Monde*, as Jack Taylor had recommended, each trying their first beignet and washing it down with chicory coffee.

"Damn tasty critters, don't you think?" Gessler asked.

"Brakeman steered us right."

Seabaugh displayed his serious side. While savoring the pastry, he asked Gessler, whom he rightly regarded as an educated man, if Doc ever thought about "the Great Beyond."

"You know, matters we humans cannot figure out, no matter how hard we try. The spiritual and mystical aspects of life."

Doc's eyebrows raised up on his forehead. "The Great Beyond? Shit, right now I'm looking at a young woman strolling over there and I'm thinking more about the Great Behind!"

Warren's preoccupation with the spiritual evaporated into the New Orleans night air. "Any chance you want to head back to the Studio for a second round?"

"My thought exactly. Must be these beignets!"

* * *

Frank Chance knew a lot of people in New Orleans. The town offered Chance all that he desired away from home—good company, sporting women, and splendid drinking spots. His favorite watering hole in all the world, Tom Anderson's *Annex Saloon,* stood on the corner of Basin Street and Iberville, right across from the train station. It opened in 1901 with 102 electric bulbs, the first saloon in the nation to be illuminated solely by electricity. Anderson, a stout, blue-eyed Irishman with a bushy handlebar mustache, earned the nickname "Mayor of Storyville." He fought his way to become the political boss of the Fourth Ward and then got himself elected as a state legislator despite the public's knowledge that he ran numerous houses of prostitution in Storyville and carried on liaisons with some of his employees. The gregarious Anderson, who traded free passes to his bordellos for political favors, maintained many contacts. He could get things done.

He knew that business and politics went hand-in-hand. Anderson also realized that celebrities frequenting his places of business increased the grosses, so he cultivated friendships with the famous, especially sports and entertainment figures. He included among his many friends Frank Chance and Frank's old friend, Jim Corbett.

Chance arranged to meet Corbett at the *Annex* for a few drinks. By now Corbett was forty years old, still fit at 185 pounds, and earning a living by doing three-round exhibitions and some vaudeville appearances. Local hero "Gentleman Jim" Corbett never had to spend a dime for drinks in New Orleans. Here, in 1892, he defeated John L. Sullivan for the heavyweight championship of the world.

Chance and Corbett first met each other in September 1900, in Corbett's *Broadway Cafe*. It could not be described as friendship at first sight. Chance took the opportunity, in his initial meeting with the boxer, to accuse the father of modern boxing of fixing a fight with Charles "Kid" McCoy one month earlier. In that bout, Corbett knocked out McCoy in the fifth round, but evidence surfaced shortly after the fight that McCoy made a bundle of money on bets to lose the contest. Chance expressed his views on the matter to Corbett and it quickly degenerated to a fistfight. Others joined in and the brawl spilled out onto the street. Chance remained proud of the fact that he had started the brawl and that others had to pull him off of Gentleman Jim. Corbett and Chance patched matters up the second time they met, in England one winter, Corbett remembering and complimenting Chance on his right hook. They had much in common, both being native Californians, professional athletes, and sharing an appreciation for fine wines and not-so-fine beer. Chance also played against Jim Corbett's younger brother, Joe, who pitched for the Cardinals in 1904.

Meeting at the bar in Anderson's, the two men embraced in a bear hug.

"How the hell are ya?" asked Corbett.

"Couldn't be sweller," said Chance.

"How long do you figure to be in town?"

"The team's here about a week and then we start our trek back north."

"Let me buy you a drink, Mr. Baseball Man," Corbett said. "Tom has introduced me to a number of beautiful ladies in the last few days. I've a notion that you may desire to make the acquaintance of one or two of these young women, Husk."

"Sounds good, Jimmy. It's been a long spring already."

March 13, 1907 Castle Williams, Governors Island

Dark clouds rained down on New York Harbor while small waterspouts swirled off the southern tip of Manhattan. Percy McGill found himself one of 235 inmates on Governors Island, in the federal military prison called Castle Williams, a fortress completed in 1811 to protect New York City from the British. Rusting cannon and pyramids of crumbling cannonballs still decorated the old structure. The army had used Castle Williams as a prison for Confederate enlisted men during the Civil War and now used it to house those charged with or convicted of criminal acts while they served their country, from deserters like McGill to murderers like several of Percy's eleven cell-mates.

In the few days he spent in the prison Percy carefully noted the dimensions and physical characteristics of Castle Williams. Viewed from the top, the fortress took the shape of a horseshoe or a giant "C," with the walled portions facing out toward the bay. Percy estimated the diameter of the premises to be about two hundred feet, and the height of the three-tiered building to be about forty-five feet. The imposing walls had been constructed out of a solid red sandstone, seven or eight feet thick. Percy could gauge the thickness of the walls from the portals built into them, window-like openings on each tier that allowed the cannons to fire out onto attacking ships. The central portion of the giant "C" opened to the sky, like an atrium, and here the prison boasted a broad lawn and garden. The three floors of the prison all overlooked this green space. A spiral stair-case inside a tower connected the floors. Both the front and rear entrances to Castle Williams always had a contingent of four guards and a double-door system. It took two different sets of keys to gain entrance or exit.

The prison sergeant, Sgt. Lorenzo Bell, maintained his quarters and his offices on the first floor of the castle. The dining rooms, bake shop, carpentry shop, laundry, and kitchen also occupied the first floor of the prison. The prisoners occupied the second floor. Twenty cells housed eleven to twelve inmates in each. Some boasted iron-barred portals over-looking the bay and others had barred doors leading to the garden area. Percy hadn't learned much about the third floor yet except that it contained the solitary rooms the prisoners called the dungeons. Prisoners who broke the rules spent time in the dungeon, usually three- to ten-day stints. Percy estimated a distance of fifty feet from the outer castle walls to the ten-foot stonewall, which the bay waters constantly battered. Finally, Percy confirmed his childhood memory: the island seemed equidistant from the shore of Manhattan (to the north) and Brooklyn (to the east), about a half mile from each. A difficult swim, with strong currents. He had never swum that far in his life.

Sgt. Lorenzo Bell commanded the prison, its staff of sixty-eight soldiers, and the numerous civilian employees that commuted to the island. Honest but pragmatic, the thirty-eight-year-old soldier appeared trim and neatly uniformed. In his first meeting with McGill, Sgt. Bell addressed McGill with a stiff formality that McGill had not seen since his brief military tenure. Two brawny privates flanked McGill for security purposes.

"Private McGill, your court martial is being arranged. Should you desire to obtain counsel for those proceedings that will be facilitated. In the interim we must assign you a job. You will work at that job until your court martial is conducted. Should you be convicted in the court martial proceedings, this job assignment will likely continue during your period of confinement here. Please tell me what form of work you have been doing since your separation from the army and I can make an informed work assignment for you."

Percy looked directly into the dark eyes of the sergeant. "I have two requests, Sergeant."

"Requests? Such as?"

"First, you need not address me as 'Private McGill.' 'Mister' would be more appropriate, as I have never been a member of the United States Army. I am afraid the army has made a grave error. My name is Percival McGill, but I am not the fellow with that name who served and deserted. I am afraid you have dragooned the wrong Percy McGill."

"Yes, well that is why we have proper evidentiary hearings to resolve these thorny issues. What else, Private?"

"My second request is for your ears alone. Any chance these two gentlemen could wait outside? In the interest of privacy?"

"No chance whatsoever. Did you wish to say anything else?"

"Well, sir. It's this ring." Percy pointed to the gold ring that circled a finger on his right hand. "It's a valuable item as it is gold and studded with diamonds that form an 'M.' 'M' for 'me.' Might be worth as much as seven hundred or eight hundred dollars."

"And?" Bell grew impatient.

"And I thought that you should have it—just for safekeeping of course."

"Just for safekeeping, Private?"

"Yes sir. And maybe I could be relieved of any work requirement in the meantime, if you could do that for me sir?"

Bell expressed his indignation. "Private McGill, you have just attempted to bribe me. For that you will spend the next twenty-four hours in solitary confinement. Do you understand that?"

"I do, sir."

"Fine. Now, if you will please tell me what occupation or skill you possessed in the world outside, Private? You will need to work, just like every other prisoner, once you are released from solitary."

"I see. Well, as for my occupation, Sergeant, for a number of years now I have been self-employed. Yes sir. A self-employed procurer. I am a pimp, a purveyor of human flesh. Of women, to be precise. I shall be quite happy to continue those endeavors here at Castle Williams although I shall certainly need your assistance to import a number of the fairer sex to this hellhole. For how useless is a pimp without his whores? I think we should start with a dozen, don't you?"

※   ※   ※

As Percy relaxed on a cot in a dark solitary confinement cell, he congratulated himself on what he considered a most successful interview with Sgt. Bell. When the Barcelona carried him over to Governors Island, Percy had promised himself that he would be off the island by autumn, one way or another. He dedicated everything he did from that moment on, beginning with his careful observations of Castle Williams and its surroundings from the deck of the Barcelona, to the goal of escape. As the result of his conference with Sgt. Bell, Percy had accomplished three goals at one sitting. He needed to see the third floor, the location of the "dungeon," and now he sat there, albeit in solitary confinement. He also wanted to draw the most menial work assignment, the rock crew. Prisoners consigned to the rock crew maintained the shoreline rocks of the island, to stave off the constant erosion of the island's soil. The channels cutting across the harbor on either side of Governor's Island had literally whittled the island in half by the end of the nineteenth century. But in 1900 the sensible decision to take the landfill from the building of the Lexington subway line and to cart it across the channel had restored the lost acreage of Governors Island. The rock crew work was tough and dirty, moving huge boulders into place to create seawalls around the island, to prevent further erosion. But this work would allow Percy to learn every inch of the island's shoreline, important information for any escape plan. Telling Sgt. Bell that he worked as a pimp proved a sure ticket to the rock crew. And the final item, the gold ring, caused Percy to chuckle to himself. He stored that memory away, just as, no doubt, the Sergeant did. No way in the world would the Sergeant forget that ring.

March 13, 1907 New Orleans, Louisiana

An exhibition game against the Pelicans started at one o'clock while a fierce sun still ruled the day. The Cubs slotted three veteran pitchers to throw three innings apiece, Miner Brown, Jack Pfiester, and Chick Fraser. Eight hundred bugs paid to be admitted, most of them in the six-bit, covered seats, shaded from the direct rays of the sun and the ninety-three degree heat. But dozens of white-sleeved black men sat in the open-planked bleachers, the twenty-five-cent venue. Although the game itself was not memorable, two events transpired that marked this day for all the Cubs.

The trouble began during batting practice. Women's screams and shrieks pierced the air. Everyone behind home plate fled the area. Frank Chance looked into the stands and saw men stumbling and pushing to get out. The source of the problem then leaped up onto the Cubs' dugout. The goddam monkey! Somehow Henry the Ape had escaped from his stake behind home plate. The orangutan grabbed a metal trash can and flung it at an old man, knocking him down. Henry advanced toward a cowering child and then leaped over the boy to attack a young woman whose eyeglasses reflected in the ape's eyes. The woman shrieked as Henry pummeled her, and two brave men tried to grab the ape's arms from behind, only to find themselves clubbed and bleeding as the orangutan boxed and scratched them. At one point Henry straddled one of the gentlemen, kicking him gently to see if he still lived, and losing interest when the man feigned death. It took a half hour for the Pelican stadium hands to subdue the ape with a net pulled down from the third base area.

The groundsmen returned Henry to his proper place none the worse for wear, although the ape carried one souvenir, a young bug's straw hat that he happily consumed. The workers who inspected the ape's tether labelled the caper an "outside job." Meaning someone cut the rope tying him to the stake. But the culprit who freed the ape could not be discovered.

Henry's adventure provided more excitement than the game as the Pelicans did not put up much of a fight on this day. But another scary moment came in the bottom of the third inning, as Frank Schulte meandered to his spot in the tall left field grass. When he turned to face the infield, he began to scream and hop. His teammates rushed out to him. A snake had wrapped itself around his left ankle, and coiled like a grapevine around his stout leg. After shouting for assistance, Frank ripped the serpent from his leg, grabbed a piece of a plank that leaned against the outfield fence, and killed the greenish-brown creature with several blows. Jack Taylor, a self-proclaimed herpetologist, took one look at the creature and declared it a water moccasin, fresh from the canal that crossed right outside Athletic Field.

"It couldn't have hurt me, could it?" asked Frank. "Is it poisonous?"

Brakeman laughed. "Shit, Frank. That's a cottonmouth." He opened the jaws of the dead snake and exhibited its white palate. "These critters can sink these here fangs deep into fat Krauts like you, deeper than ticks on a hound. They can shoot so much venom into your body that you'd be lucky to last an hour. Yeah, they can do some damage." Taylor hung the corpse of the snake on the scoreboard and the game resumed.

Schulte got two hits after the incident and the Cubs won easily, 6-0. Chance spoke with pride of Mordecai Brown's performance.

"Did you see what Brownie did with his curveball today?"

But the yellow ape and twisting reptile are what the players remembered of this day. From then on the Cubs referred to that game against the Pelicans as "the day at the zoo."

March 15, 1907 **Governors Island**

Percy McGill was allowed to send a telegram to lawyer Ben Cole, requesting the name of a New York City attorney that could help him in his current predicament. Cole located for him a man who, Cole said, "knew how, when, and where the army brass wiped their asses." The attorney, James K. Kenton, visited Percy on a pleasant spring-like day.

Kenton, a forty-year-old blue blood, wore spectacles and a red bow tie, and never cracked a smile. The two men sat at a table in the prison dining room, three guards just out of earshot. The first order of business, he informed McGill, concerned his fee.

"You don't want to hear about the case first?" Percy inquired.

"No. Cole filled me in on the basic facts. You either deserted or you didn't. Either way my fee is the same. One thousand five-hundred dollars."

"That's stiff. I need to find out a few things first. Let's say, just for the sake of discussion, I am guilty as charged. That I left the army prematurely. If we play by the rules and have a court martial, is there any chance I can beat this with your help?"

"Yes. Given the length of time since the alleged desertion, the army may have trouble locating and presenting witnesses who can establish your identity. Some of the soldiers who served with Private McGill, whoever he is, did not survive. Some have moved West and will never be found. Then too, should we lose the trial, should you be convicted, my assistance could reduce your sentence."

"From eight years to five?"

"Perhaps."

"That ain't worth one thousand five-hundred dollars to me," McGill spit out. "Another thing... is there a different way for me to play my cards? Can the judge be persuaded outside the court room?"

"No." Kenton moved closer to the table. "It's not one judge. You will be tried by a panel of five judges, all army officers. We need two of these gentlemen for an acquittal. You would need to 'persuade,' as you say, two ranking military officers. This tactic is not possible. Not a realistic option."

"And the prosecutor?"

"You mean the Judge Advocate. Straight as an arrow. No chance for mischief there either."

"I see. So we roll the dice and see who the army can dredge up to identify me. I take my chances for one thousand five-hundred dollars."

"That is the sum of it." An unintended pun.

Percy rolled back in his chair, his decision made. "Fine. I'm a gambling man. Let's take a shot at justice. You will get your money soon. But I need one more thing from you. I need to know how the army learned about my whereabouts now, nine years after the fact."

"I may be able to answer that for you right now based on what I've seen in other cases. Tell me, have you recently been charged with a felony?"

"Yes. But I beat it."

"No matter. That is how it happened. The army pays the clerks of criminal courts in major cities to send it a list of felony defendants every month. Those lists get cross-checked with the army's list of wanted soldiers. It happens to be a very efficient way for the military to locate men who choose not to make their whereabouts known. The only good thing about this process is that some of these men then become my clients."

Percy's thoughts again turned to Connie.

March 15, 1907   New Orleans; Inexplicable Perversions of Judgment, or, the Work of a Bullet

After a debilitating practice in stifling heat, the Cubs showered in the shabby visiting team locker room at Athletic Field and then dragged themselves onto two buses to return to the hotel. As one of the buses neared the hotel, Brakeman Taylor approached Durbin with an invitation.

"Kid, how'd you like to go fishing now with me and my cousin Daniel? He's a local guy. He has a boat and he knows what he's doing. Your buddy Warren informs me you been fishing since you were three."

"I've fished some," Kid answered, a look of casual interest spreading across his face. "What kind of fish are we talking about?"

"Not sure. Of the saltwater variety." Brakemen could tell by the look on Kid's face that he had hooked him. "I think he said redfish and flounder. We'll be going out on Pontchartrain on Daniel's boat. Probably eat dinner before or on our way out. Should be great fun. We'll make it back by nine. You can do this, Kid. You're free, white, and twenty-one, ain't you?"

"Free, white, and twenty. But old enough to go fishing with a teammate, I suppose." Kid said yes. A little surprised that Brakeman chose him, he correctly guessed that a whole lot of the other guys must have turned him down first. That didn't matter. Kid wanted to go fishing, even if it meant sharing a boat with the Brakeman. He grew up fishing Stockton Lake in Missouri with his father, pulling in white bass and catfish. Fond memories for Durbin.

Daniel met them outside the hotel at 4:30 p.m., driving a beat-up Buick automobile with a thick layer of Louisiana mud plastered over the fenders and the running boards. Daniel Robinson, thirty-one years old and almost entirely bald, stood six feet tall and weighed no more than 140 pounds. Dressed in blue overalls and a sweaty, oil-spattered undershirt, Daniel spoke little at first. He had a habit of rubbing his forehead with his knuckles. Since the knuckles invariably were covered with oil, smudges streaked Daniel's brow. Jack introduced Durbin and they jumped into the idling vehicle, Jack in the front passenger seat and Kid in the comfortable and ample rear seat. Kid learned that Daniel had lived in New Orleans for a decade, moving here from Pennsylvania.

"What brought you to the South?" asked Kid.

"An iron horse and my pappy," said Daniel.

"You like it here?"

"Suits me just fine," Daniel said, while honking at a horse and buggy that occupied the center of the road.

Brakeman here interjected. "Daniel is a fine mechanic. He can fix just about any automobile. Has a way with engines and such. You were an apprentice for some guy for four or five years, weren't you Daniel?"

"Yup. This here is his gas-buggy. Been tuning it up and adjusting the crankshaft for him."

"Where we headed?" Jack asked.

"I'm fixing to head east and north on Highway 11, toward Slidell. I know a place we can eat near where I keep the skiff. We can fish right up to sunset."

They drove twenty-three miles down a road that went from macadam to gravel to dirt with many potholes. Most of the time Lake Pontchartrain formed a vast expanse to their left, with the sun at their backs. It took forty-five minutes before they pulled up at a roadside diner named Wilbur's. A second sign, reading "Restaurant and Bait," did not encourage Durbin. Not much more than a shack surrounded by some stately old willow trees, Wilbur's boasted four tables and two magazine photographs of Jesus and Robert E. Lee, pasted unevenly on the rough-hewn walls. Daniel spoke to Ida Mae, the fifty-five- year-old wife of Wilbur, as the three sat down around a circular table. Ida Mae wore a blue dress with white buttons, her hair pinned back in a bun.

"This here is my cousin, Ida, and his friend. They's both profes-sional baseball players from up North."

"I won't hold that against y'all," she said, in a serious tone.

Jack asked "What—being baseball players or being from the North?"

"Why both," she answered, matter-of-factly. "We all gotta make a livin'. And you boys was born Yankees. Didn't have a choice in it, did ya? Say, they ain't no niggers on your team now, is there?"

"Naw, the coons got their own teams," Brakeman responded.

"You can cook us up some Creole fixins'?"

"Yessir," said Ida, "you'll like it. We make everything with Southern hospitality."

"Just make mine with Tabasco sauce!" retorted Brakeman.

She took their orders and scuttled back to the kitchen, humming under her breath. The three men talked about fishing before Ida returned and placed steaming plates of shrimp, crawfish, beans and rice before them, commenting, "There ya goes, gents."

Without giving it a whole lot of thought, Brakeman removed a small bag from his pocket and sprinkled a black powder onto his beans and rice, prompting Durbin to ask him about the substance.

"Just some cayenne pepper, Kid. Got it in the Quarter."

Brakeman figured now was as good as time as any to try out the zaggeratin powder. He mixed it in good with the rice and beans and washed it down with a cold Dixie beer. He finished the meal and two bottles of beer in ten minutes but didn't feel anything unusual except that he perspired more on the way out of the place than on the way in. He blamed that on the Tabasco sauce. The bill for all three totaled eighty-five cents. Taylor threw down a dollar with a flourish and the boys headed out on the bumpy road again.

Fifteen minutes later the three fishermen skimmed across Lake Pontchartrain. The craft rode low in the stern, the hull slapping the placid surface and the reflection of the sun dappling the rippled waters. The skiff was powered by what Daniel called a "rowboat motor," a tiny, gasoline motor that emitted a stream of black smoke. Brakeman watched the smoke ooze out of the motor, get sucked down into the choppy turbulence of the propeller, and then emerge from the wake where it lingered for a moment and dissolved. The patterns of the smoke fascinated Jack. Black and gray vapors twisted and collapsed, with small purplish explosions marking the line between the air and the water. Daniel took the small craft out a little more than half a mile, puttered east another quarter mile, and then cut the engine.

Only the water sloshing in the bottom of the skiff and the gentle waves lapping at its wooden sides broke the silence. Daniel handed out the gear and gave Jack and Kid each a worm to thread onto their hooks. Kid readied to drop his line while Jack still pondered the worm, the creature coiling and uncoiling in his palm.

"Ya got a problem with that there worm, Jack?" Daniel asked, a note of irritation present in the delivery. "I got a whole lot more if that one don't suit ya."

"You think the hook kills the worm, Daniel?"

"Hell no," Daniel said, "It's the water that does that. Drowns 'em. But the fish don't give a shit. A drown worm's as good as one still squirmin' to them."

"I don't wanna drown this particular worm, Daniel." Brakeman held the worm an inch from his face, carefully examining the twisting creature. "He has a certain personality, a real nice disposition. So many segments! He's had a tough day already. He seems a little chilled…"

Daniel erupted, "What the fuck you talkin' about, cuz? You corned on two Dixies?"

"No suh! Da debol made me do dat!" Jack looked up with mock fear on his face.

Daniel quickly tired of the Brakeman's actions. He grabbed the worm from Jack's fingers and flung it into the lake.

"Ya needn't be concerned no more Jack."

Without a second's hesitation Jack rolled over the side of the skiff into the water, shouting, "We can't let him drown!" Durbin and Daniel, stunned by this turn of events, had to steady the boat before they could take action. Jack floundered about, flailing his arms and legs, and finally disappeared under the surface for fifteen seconds.

"I better go git the fucking lunatic," Daniel said, standing up and taking off his pants.

Before Daniel could dive in, Jack surfaced, poking his head up a yard from the side of the boat.

"I got the little guy," Jack shouted.

"You crazy bastard!" Daniel exclaimed, as Jack latched one arm onto the skiff. "Don't you try to climb in the boat right there 'fore you turn us over. Let us get in the stern here and then you climb in the bow. Hold up for a minute, will ya?"

Jack followed Daniel's directions and struggled to pull himself into the bow, managing it on his second attempt. A frightful mess, he babbled something the boys could not decipher. He had the worm in his left hand but in the struggle to get into the boat he crushed it. He started to cry.

"Jack, take it easy buddy," Kid offered. "It's okay."

Jack's words became understandable. "I killed a hundred chameleons yesterday. Today I killed this here innocent worm. I must be stopped, Kid. You gotta stop me. I mighta killed Henry too the way that got outta hand. You can't let me keep this up… promise me Kid, will you?"

"Sure Jack. Just calm down a bit and you'll see everything is fine." Kid turned to Daniel and suggested they head back in.

Daniel drew his knuckles across his brow. "Suppose you're right. No tellin' what this darnfoolski might do if we stay out here. Damnedest thing I ever did see."

On the trip back to shore, Kid asked Jack if he had cut loose Henry the Ape the day before. Jack readily admitted the deed.

"Whenever something happens that shouldn't and people suspect someone of doing something... I'm that guy, the guy they suspect," Jack said, shaking his head as he spoke. "Of course, it's usually me that done wrong." He paused. "You know how there's always one player on a team that just doesn't fit in? That's me. I'm always that guy."

A couple of tears rolled down Jack's cheeks and Durbin pretended he didn't see it. Then Jack picked up the bailing bowl and started to bail water from the boat into the lake, feeling a great sense of accomplishment. He filled the bowl with water once again and stopped, peering into the vessel with a great curiosity. The sun seemed to light the water into a luminescent mass that glimmered just above the bowl. Jack was enchanted. He did not budge for five minutes, until a shadow destroyed the glowing magic in his hands.

Disgusted with his cousin, Daniel said little as he moored the boat and tied her in. Durbin assisted Jack off the boat and took a look at his teammate. *What a strange drunk*, Kid thought. *Jumped into the lake to save a worm and then cried when he couldn't. All as the result of two beers.* Kid helped Jack find his way to the automobile. He seemed lost and dazed and murmured nonsense words.

But when they made it to the automobile, Jack refused to get in.

"Hell no, I will not do it. The road's too bumpy for me just yet."

Kid and Daniel both took turns trying to convince Jack to hop in the auto, to no avail. He folded his arms and sat on the auto's running board, his back resting against the door. In the midst of this, a Louisiana State Police motor vehicle pulled up, and two state troopers emerged.

Daniel knew one of them, Earl Pickens III.

He greeted the officer. "Hey Earl, how ya doin?"

"Jes fine, Daniel. Whadda we got here anyhow?"

"These is just my cousin and his buddy. We was fishin' and now we be headed back to town."

"Don't see no fish, Daniel. And it don't rightly look as if you actually is headin' back now, do it?"

As he said this, Brakeman pushed Daniel away from him and blurted out, "Much obliged, sir. I am not headed back to town, as you just observed. We gotta stick right here for the burial."

Kid and Daniel both groaned, and the right hand of each officer slowly moved to the handle of their guns, as they studied Brakeman more carefully.

"Whose burial would y'all be referrin' to sir?" Earl asked.

"Why my friend the worm. A little guy about two inches tall, same color as a nigger, almost drowned and then I crushed him though a grievous error."

Earl turned to Daniel. "What the fuck is goin' down here Daniel? Give it to me straight."

"He's just a little tipsy from some beer, Earl. A strange drunk is all I can figure. He's harmless."

"Why's he all wet?" the cop asked.

"Just a little accident in the lake, Earl."

At this juncture Brakeman stood up and threw his arm around Durbin, drawing the diminutive redhead toward him. "We're team mates," he beamed. Durbin tried, without success, to squirm out of Jack's hold.

The cops shook their heads. The second cop, a small, nervous man named Cotton Randolph, looked at the little red-haired fellow being squeezed by the wet, larger man and said, "Looks to me like we got two Nancy-boys here, Earl. These here might be gen-u-ine cocksuckers—the real McCoy."

Daniel shook his head and protested. "No sir. They ain't no such thing! They are ballplayers. In Chicago."

Earl sneered. "And 'zactly whose balls they been playin' with Daniel? Yours maybe?" Both troopers bent forward laughing. They finally eased off when Earl discovered that Brakeman was the same Jack Taylor who had pitched for Earl's beloved St. Louis Cardinals as recently as a year ago.

"You are Old Iron Arm of the Saint Looie Cardinals?" Earl asked.

"One and the same!" answered Taylor.

Earl apologized to Taylor and Durbin and, taking pity on the predicament of the Brakeman, asked Daniel to wait an hour or so before returning "to give the Brakeman a chance to catch his breath." That being agreed, the cops took off after their next adventure.

Brakeman did not sober up in the next hour, which he mainly spent remarking about the clouds.

"Chrissakes, look at that one," he yelled, pointing to the sky, "it's like a horse head with three baseballs in its ear!" A minute later he whistled and said, "That one is the spitting image of Teddy Roosevelt! Can you believe it?"

Eventually Durbin conned Jack into the back seat of the car by suggesting there might be another worm back there. So, as darkness fell over the trio, they prepared to return to the hotel. But Daniel could not get the vehicle's headlamps to work. He fumbled under the steering wheel to inspect the black fuse box attached to the steering column, opened it up and removed the top fuse, a burned, metallic object half the size of a thimble.

"Damn it," he lamented. "A blown fuse and I don't have a spare. Maybe I can find something that will do the job instead of a fuse," he mused.

"Just don't use a worm or any other of God's creatures, all right?" Jack begged.

Daniel ignored the remark. He took a penny out of his pocket and tried to insert it into the fuse box but it did not fit. Then Daniel hit upon an idea. He had a .22 caliber pistol in the tool compartment of the auto, wrapped in a heavy canvas cloth under some wrenches. He retrieved the gun and examined it. Jack looked over at Daniel fingering the gun and asked, "You fixin' to kill us all now?"

"Jes keep your trap shut. I'm busy."

Daniel removed one of the bullets from the chambers of the gun. Palming the bullet, he inserted it into the fuse receptacle and pulled the lever for the headlamps.

"It's workin' like a charm," he said, delighted with his clever electric ploy.

They finally began the trip back. Daniel cranked the vehicle and it started with a "bam, bam" and a spurt of smoke. The headlamps of the old Buick lit the way on the dark and deserted highway. Daniel pushed the gas buggy for all it was worth and the wind whizzed through the hair of the three men. They passed Wilbur's at the dizzying speed of twenty-seven miles per hour. A dim light seeped out of the restaurant as they sped by.

Daniel turned to Brakeman and shouted, "Goddam good headlights, don'tcha think?"

Brakeman turned to Durbin in the back and said, "Daniel's just told me he's got head lice." Neither Durbin nor Daniel heard what Taylor said.

Half a mile past Wilbur's, it happened. An explosion ripped the fuse box apart as the overheated bullet discharged and ripped into Daniel just as he slowed the vehicle at an intersection. He cried out in pain and the auto veered off the road, stopping with a lurch in a shallow drainage ditch. Daniel fell back against the door and moaned, then lapsed into unconsciousness. Durbin, scared silly by the "blam" of the bullet and the jolting end to their ride, bruised his right elbow against the side of the vehicle but not seriously. Jack Taylor showed no effect from the crash. He took the accident in stride, remaining calm, and climbed into the front seat to examine the mess below his cousin's waist, pulling the tattered pants away to assess the damage.

"It seems that Daniel has blown off his balls," he proclaimed, in a quiet, matter-of-fact tone.

The Game   March 16, 1907; Augusta, Georgia; A Man Possessed

The Detroit Tigers finished way out of the running in 1906. Tiger management pegged their hopes for a run at the pennant in the '07 American League campaign on their talented but raw center fielder, Tyrus Raymond Cobb. Cobb played in his first major league game in 1905, at age eighteen. Now just twenty, Cobb's frenetic style of baseball thrilled the Tiger fans and promised to translate into many Tiger victories. He played a rough and tumble game, running the bases with wild abandon, bunting for hits, slashing the baseball to all corners of the field, and often stretching singles into doubles and doubles into triples. Shocking opponents and teammates alike, he would dash home from second base on infield grounders and routine fly-outs.

Cobb, a fierce competitor with an antagonistic, combative attitude, spent every moment of his waking life trying to find an edge. Sometimes, in a game already lost or won, Cobb attempted to take an extra base on a single where he knew he had no chance, or to advance from first to home on a routine single, simply to set the stage for the future, to plant, as he put it, "the threat." He knew the opposing team's outfielder would remember this recklessness, and might later tense up and fumble the ball. And if he spiked the shortstop or the second baseman in the tag-out at second, or the catcher in a play at the plate, he knew that man might not block the base as aggressively the next time around. Sometimes it backfired, the fielder remembering the incident and trying to slash Cobb with an errant spike on their next confrontation on the diamond. The lean six-footer used his fists on those occasions. In Cobb's view, the game of baseball was "as gentlemanly as a kick in the crotch."

But for all his ability on the field, Ty Cobb was a man possessed, a victim of his own demons. Ernest Hemingway, who observed Cobb close up on a hunting trip, said he had a "screw loose." Today Cobb might be classified as a violent psychotic. Cobb's twisted behavior started even before his mother killed Ty's father with a shotgun one night in 1905. She gained an acquittal on a charge of murder, the court believing her claim that she thought she shot a prowler. But this shattering event took a big toll on Cobb, who had idolized his father. Nor did being one of the relatively few Southern boys playing baseball in the North aid Ty's mental balance. He complained bitterly about the persistent, mean-spirited hazing of his Detroit teammates, such as when Tiger pitcher Eddie Siever told Cobb, "You're still a Dixie prick whose folks live off nigger slaves." As a bitter old man Cobb still blamed his teammates: "These old-timers turned me into a snarling wildcat."

Cobb, a loner, exhibited an outrageous temper and an overriding, untempered racism and hostility toward Catholics and Jews. Cobb used violence and the threat of bodily harm, on and off the field, to get what he wanted when he wanted it. Selfish, surly, self-absorbed, vindictive, given to fits and rages, Cobb's teammates and opposing players hated him. A 1907 story in the *Detroit Times* stated that Cobb had not a single friend on the Tigers because his "temper" had estranged his teammates. Early on in his career the Georgian carried a gun, a Belgian-made revolver, for the express purpose of staving off attacks from his own teammates. He had dozens of fistfights with his fellow Detroit Tigers, umpires, fans, and anyone—man, woman, or child—who Cobb perceived to have slighted him.

Cobb suffered a mental breakdown in the summer of 1906. The Tiger owners arranged for his placement in a sanitarium near Detroit, informing the local newspapers that Ty had "stomach problems." He spent forty-four days in the rest home before returning to the Tigers in September.

For the 1907 Practice Season, the Tigers trained in the red clay country of Augusta, Georgia. Cobb, a Georgia boy, broke into organized baseball with the Augusta Tourists minor league team, so he considered this small, sunbaked Southern town's Warren Park home turf. But as the Tigers dressed for an exhibition game, Cobb still rankled over the fact that someone had scissored off several fingers of his favorite glove two days ago. On the day he discovered the vandalism, Cobb deduced a likely suspect, Bungy Davis, a black groundskeeper he had known since 1905. Cobb confronted the groundsman.

"Nigger man, tell me why you destroyed my tip."

Bungy, a small man who cowered before the lean, muscular Cobb, denied doing it.

"No suh. Don't know nuthin' 'bout dat."

Cobb gripped Davis by his collar. "Just lemme know who did it!"

"I dunno suh."

Cobb cursed under his breath and sulked away.

Bungy made the mistake of thinking that Cobb had forgotten the matter. Two days later, prior to a ten o'clock practice session, Bungy approached Cobb, patted him on the shoulder, and said "Hello, you Georgia Peach!" Cobb flew into a rage, pounded Davis to the ground with three blows, and then kicked the black man in the head. Bleeding from the nose, Bungy managed to get to his feet and run to a small shack alongside the clubhouse, underneath the third base bleachers. But Cobb, not satisfied, ran after him, screaming obscenities and racial epithets. Bungy hid in the shack but his wife, a large woman who served as the clubhouse cleaning lady, saw Cobb chase after her husband and intervened.

"Go away, white man. Leave Bungy alone!" she shrieked. "If you hurt my man I'll have the law on you."

Cobb yelled, "Get out of my fucking way!" When she did not, he pushed Mrs. Davis to her knees in front of him and began to violently choke her. Tiger catcher Charlie Schmidt, a big, husky man with some boxing experience, rescued the stunned woman. Schmidt, a Southern boy who impressed his teammates by pounding nails into a hunk of wood with his fist, hated Cobb and jumped at the opportunity to demonstrate his feelings for this odd teammate.

"You lousy, rotten skunk," shouted Schmidt. He slammed home a punch on the side of Cobb's head that instantly ended Cobb's attack on Mrs. Davis. Cobb rolled to the ground, dizzy for three seconds, then sprung to his feet, fists poised against Schmidt.

Schmidt yelled at Cobb, "Whoever does a thing like that is a coward!"

"I don't see as it interests you," Cobb replied, slowly and deliberately. He edged toward Schmidt again but by now the Tiger manager, Hughie Jennings, and five other players formed a ring around Cobb, restraining him as he struggled to get at Schmidt.

Five minutes later Cobb justified his action to Jennings by claiming that Davis had been drinking and had been too familiar with him, "Especially for a darky in the South."

"Why in God's name did you put your hands on Mrs. Davis?" Jennings queried.

Cobb stated he did not remember doing so.

The newspapers picked up this story. In the North the headlines proclaimed "Baseball Player Attacks Groundsman," while the Augusta, Georgia, *Herald* had a different slant: "Georgia Peach Defends the Honor of the Southland." The Tigers spent the next week trying to unload Cobb. But no other team would have him.

From the Journal of Kid Durbin

Yesterday's events still trouble me some, what with Jack acting like a loon and Daniel losing part of his manhood. I told Jack this morning that I felt bad that Daniel wouldn't be able to have any more kids. Jack said that since Daniel already had seven children it was actually a blessing, and that when Daniel's wife found out about the accident, her first words were, "Did he catch any redfish?"

"I take that to mean she ain't heartbroken over Daniel losin' his balls," Jack explained.

Jack half apologized for his conduct, describing it as "a momentary lapse of reason." I told Jack the lapse lasted four hours. Anyhow, the truth of the matter is that Jack, when he had a brick in his hat yesterday, was a kinder, more likeable fellow than he normally is. While I didn't tell him that, I told him he had nothing to apologize for from my angle.

Today I took another turn in the pitcher's box against the Pelicans. With the sun burning down on our backs something fearful, we swept out of the dugout like regular hellions, all chesty, taking that field like we owned it. This Saturday game attracted more bugs than the last few games. Mike Kahoe handled the catching chores while Doc Gessler played first base for Husk, who injured a ligament under his shoulder blade the other day. And Solly Hofman patrolled the shortfield position. By the time I tossed my first pitch we led 1-0. My half of the first inning did not go exactly like I wanted. Their second-sacker leadoff man nicked me for a Texas Leaguer and then, would you believe it, the normally reliable Solly Hofman muffed a ground ball for an error. To make it even worse, their next hitter, a Creole guy named Nadeau, bunted the horsehide past me down toward first base and I could not make the play. Bases loaded and no outs! For a man on the mound there can be no worse predicament! This guy on first, Nadeau—I never did get his first name—starts bellowing at me, "Hey Doo-bin! You stay out of my restaurant. Don't you go back to Galatoire's! They say you eat with your tiny prick!" I guess that kind of bullyragging works on some but it didn't get under my skin. I took a few deep breaths, bore down, and got the next three batters with no one scoring. That felt sugar sweet.

The second inning went three up, three down. My fastball seemed to zip across the plate—I had speed to give away! And my inshoots and outshoots moved nicely. I gave up a run on two hits in my final inning, the third, but, all things considered, it was a good outing. Orvie Overall and Carl Lundgren pitched the rest of the game without giving up any runs, so we killed them 14-1.

I sent a number of letters to Connie Dandridge but so far she has not responded. I am going to write the Murphys now to learn how she is doing.

I agonized over whether I should write this next section. It may not reflect right on me. But this journal is meant for me, so it shouldn't matter how it "reflects." It should be what happened and I'm going to set it out straight, best I can.

As I mentioned above, in the train depot here in New Orleans a boy handed me a pamphlet that contained the names and phone numbers of quite a few local prostitutes. I know that many of my teammates are frequenting these whorehouses in Storyville. It wasn't a secret and nobody but Carl Lundgren and Chick Fraser spoke against it, and they maybe felt compelled to do so given their wives are traveling with us. I know that even the Peerless Leader, who is a married man, spends a whole lot of time at Anderson's Saloon in Storyville. Anyhow, after to-day's ballgame I started thinking about that pamphlet and the girls listed in it. You might say that my curiosity got the best of me. You could also say my prick got the best of me, but whatever it was, I could not resist this temptation. Sure, I had a regular Catholic upbringing so I knew that it was a sin, but my Aunt Delia told me playing baseball for a living was a sin and I didn't let that stop me.

The pamphlet, called the "Lid," had an introduction that said:

The names in this booklet are the 'class women' as de-
fined in the famous Blue Book. So no matter which one
you choose to ring up by telephone you can rest assured
that you will be well answered.

*I puzzled over that information a while and then decided to go
ahead. The urge had to be satisfied. So I found a telephone in the hotel lobby
and asked this nice young hotel employee how to work it. After figuring
that out, I randomly selected a woman that listed an address of 1550 Conti
Street. Her name was Maud Livingstone and the telephone number said
"1406." I called the operator and asked to be connected to 1406.*

*Five seconds later a woman answers, a sweet voice that says,
"Hello, this is Maud speaking." I told her that I had picked her name out
of the Lid. She asked me if I was a local or a visitor to New Orleans, and
I explained that I pitched for the Cubs, a baseball team from Chicago. I
got the impression that Maud didn't know a whole lot about baseball.
Maud asked when I wanted to get together.*

I said, "Are you free now?"

*She replied, "Darling, I am not free, but I do have one slot I could
fit you in."*

*I laughed and said I could be there real soon. She asked for my
name and I told her "Blaine." I took a motorized hack over there to avoid
getting all sweaty beforehand. A machine sat next to the driver, making noise, and I asked what it was. He called it a "taximeter." It figured
out my fare. But I felt uneasy as the amount kept going higher. When
we arrived, the taximeter registered forty cents and I gave the driver a
nickel tip. The address, 1550 Conti Street, turned out to be a big wooden
"sporting house" named Trilby's. Nervous as hell, I managed to pull myself together and enter the place, where a Negro all dressed up in a blue
suit asked me whether I had an appointment. He then seated me on a big
gold brocade davenport in the parlor while I waited for Maud. The place
was fixed up swell for a whorehouse, what with expensive furniture,
drapery, and oil paintings of the sea and English landscapes.*

Maud did not keep me waiting long. She swept into the room in a red satin dress that clung to her every curve. I guessed she was twenty-five. She had light brown, almost golden hair, that came down long on the sides of her face, with rouged cheeks and lips painted a glowing pink. Lips that invited a kiss. I stood up, removed my hat, and before I could say anything she kissed me full on my lips.

"Let's have a drink and discuss business," she said.

The Negro brought two colorless mixed drinks and Maud suggested I pay him two dollars plus a dollar tip. I complied. The man took the three dollars without any expression on his face.

"You seem a like regular gentleman," she began. "Shall we discuss your options?"

"Yes. Sure," I replied, the anxiety growing.

"Seven dollars will get you what you want but no extras. Seven minutes of heaven. You will be happy but the time goes by very quickly. An eagle buys you a half hour with many delights, including French mysteries. Fifteen dollars provides an hour of pleasure, everything I have to offer with nothing out of bounds—carte blanche."

The bone truth is I had no idea that sexual relations was as complicated as all this. All these options and decisions I never realized I'd need to worry about. I had been with a woman but twice in my life, both times with the same girl back in Lamar, and all the time we were going at it (in her barn in the winter) we were looking over our shoulders to make sure her daddy didn't barge in. I did not know what "French mysteries" or "carte blanche" meant but I wanted to find out.

One thing troubled me so I raised it with Maud. I told her about Connie, who had been beaten and almost forced to become a prostitute. I asked Maud if she was being forced to do this work. She answered "no," that she considered herself an independent agent and that she wanted someday to open her own place of business. But Maud said that she thought it "gallant" of me to ask. So I told her, "Let's do it up right, Maud, one hour's worth." She grabbed my hand and we went upstairs. Nervous all the way, I calmed myself by the time we reached the top of the flight of stairs, figuring that for that kind of money I should relax and enjoy each moment of the evening.

We entered a big room with a huge canopied bed, one wall of

flower-framed mirrors and pictures and another wall of shelves filled with hundreds of books. A window on the other wall looked out over Conti Street. Lots of little throw rugs littered the floor. After I paid her the fifteen dollars, Maud excused herself and went to the bathroom. I wondered whether that time would count against the hour I had booked when she came out, the silk dress gone, wearing only a bodice, tight underpants, and black silk stockings held up by garters. I became very excited, and more so when she tiptoed over to me and unbuttoned my pants, letting them drop to the ground. She pulled down my underwear and took a firm hold of my manhood, twisting it back and forth. Before I knew what was happening she taught me my first French mystery, pulling my prick into her mouth and sucking it in and out in a manner much like the act of copulation itself. I didn't want to shoot my seed just yet, so I removed it from her grasp and shook off all my clothes.

A stepladder stood in front of the wall of books, mounted on tracks in the floor and ceiling. I asked Maud if she would please climb the ladder four steps. She was only too happy to oblige. Up on this stepladder, she bent over and stuck her ass right at the level of my face. I slowly eased down her undergarment and spread her apart. Her glorious quim was moist and ready for the fingers that I then inserted. Maud moaned lowly as I caressed the wet places inside her. In another moment I learned another French mystery, what Maud described to me as the ancient Roman practice called cunnilingus. At first I did it to oblige Maud, but I soon realized I enjoyed it plenty. I then undid her bodice and we lay naked, wrapped in each other's arms on the bed. I spent my seed twice in that amazing sixty minutes, once within her and once across her breasts.

Ten minutes before our hour ended Maud turned to me as we lay in that great bed.

"Do you know what lagniappe is, Blaine?"

"No," I replied. "Is it something along the lines of what we was just up to?"

"No. It's a New Orleans custom. To give something extra. Like a baker might throw a cookie into your bag when you buy a cake. Or a grocer giving an extra apple to a customer. I have one for you."

"A cookie?" I asked, realizing too late that wasn't what she had in mind.

Maud gave me a lagniappe that I will never forget! But since I will always remember it, and owing to the curious nature of the matter, I will not set it down here. I did ask Doc Gessler about the word "lagniappe" in order to be able to spell it right. Doc said it's a French word—there's a whole lot of French words used around this city—so you don't pronounce the "g." Comes out in English like "lan-yap."

As I sit here now writing this I must confess I am still shaking as I remember the delights of the hour I spent with Maud. But the Catholic boy in me is praying that my acts have not sentenced me to a life of sin and degradation and an eternity in hell.

Oh yes, one more thing. I eased my way out of Trilby's, but just as I exited the place, in walked Newt Randall, Fred Osborn, and Billy Sweeney.

Sweeney took one look at me and started to laugh. "From the smile on your face, buddy boy, it looks like this is gonna be a fun place."

I don't remember what I said in response. At that moment I was still in a state of rapture.

March 17, 1907 New Orleans to Mobile, Alabama

The Cubs broke camp to head for the next stop of the practice season, Mobile, Alabama. Only 130 miles east of New Orleans, it should have been a four-hour jaunt on the Louisville & Nashville Railroad, but a series of problems delayed the trip. Charlie Williams chartered a day coach for the trip. But the rail yard men decided to strike two days earlier, and the fill-in switchmen could not figure out how to couple the Cubs' day coach to the train. Then a rail worker with two weeks experience on the job stumbled beneath the wheels of the rolling coach car and both his legs were severed beneath the knees. The seven o'clock departure time passed as the team waited in the New Orleans depot.

After an hour and a half the Cubs walked out to board the train. Air and smoke hissed from the undercarriage as they climbed the stairs. The locomotive pulled slowly out of the Crescent City and switched onto tracks headed east. Disappointed to learn the train had no lounge or dining cars, the Cubs scurried to make themselves comfortable. Brakeman got creative, piling the alligator suitcases that had been stored on one end of the car into a flat platform upon which he now lay. In ten minutes his snoring increased enough to force several Cubs to move away from him. Trainer Jack McCormick slept in his chair as in a coma, his mouth agape. Chick Fraser stuck a cigar in the trainer's mouth and it hung there, drawing no reaction from old Jack. Solly Hofman pretzeled his body across two seats and lapsed in and out of consciousness. Durbin curled against a window reading a Dickens novel.

The two ladies on the journey, the wives of Carl Lundgren and Chick Fraser, sat together in the middle of the car.

Mrs. Fraser worried about her niece. "Her mother caught her holding hands with with a boy. She is only eighteen and so headstrong."

"Goodness!"

"The girl—Georgina is her name—could not grasp the gravity of her error. She does not seem to realize what passions might be stimulated in the young man, what desires could be unleashed."

"Or that her own strength could be undermined," added Mrs. Lundgren.

"Indeed. Her mother has taken appropriate steps and Georgina and my sister will be going abroad soon. Oh! I must tell you two additional sad commentaries on my niece. The last time I saw her she was standing on the lawn of her next door neighbor, chatting, without a hat!"

"Outdoors without a hat? My, my!"

"Yes, and Georgina recently purchased and wore a vulgar garment called the 'peekaboo shirtwaist.' Have you heard about these?"

"Worse. I saw a young woman in a shop here yesterday wearing one. It had dozens of eyelets on the forearm of the blouse that exposed the girl's bare arm to the public, and, believe me, men ogled her to no end! It was a disgusting display of imprudence. This garment encourages the mashers."

"The young are reckless. They need a strong, guiding hand."

"And less holding hands."

Five seats away Chance and Evers talked until midnight, when the train paused at Ocean Springs, Mississippi, to pick up a load of oysters. Evers always sat to the right of Husk, Husk having lost much of his hearing in his left ear as the consequence of a beaning a few years back.

Chance read a March 11 copy of the *Chicago Record-Herald*.

"Says here, right on page one, 'Existence of the Soul Proved Beyond Doubt.' Would you like me to read this to you, Johnny? Could be big."

"Yeah. Let me hear it." Evers bit into a Hershey's chocolate bar.

"It says: 'Five Massachusetts physicians claim to have demonstrated beyond doubt the existence of the human soul through experiments conducted in Haverhil over the last six months. In remarkable tests, these doctors carefully weighed live human bodies shortly before death and then again immediately after death. Dr. Duncan MacDougal reports that the bodies seem to lose between one ounce and one-half ounce at the instant of death. MacDougal states that there can be no other explanation for this loss of weight other than it represents the human soul departing the body.'" Chance looked up at Evers with a smile curling around his lips. "What do you think of that, Crab?"

"I think those doctors are full of shit. What is wrong with them? You needn't try to prove the existence of the infinite by weighing the dead and the dying. Those idiots! The proof is all around us—a leaf on a tree, a snowflake, the goodness of..."

"...the whores in Storyville?" Chance interrupted.

"No, not the ladies of Storyville," Evers continued, "the goodness of ordinary people, people willing to help their friends and neighbors. That's proof of the human soul."

"You know, Crab," Chance added, "I'm betting that your soul weighs much more than an ounce. You gotta have a two-ounce soul!"

"Thanks, Husk. I believe you are complimenting me."

"I am, indeed. Why don't you broaden your horizons with me and a few of the boys tomorrow night? Just a few drinks among teammates."

"No thank you, sir. I will be asleep at nine, as is my custom."

At 2:00 a.m. the train eased into Mobile, and the roused athletes staggered down the steps as Secretary-Treasurer Williams figured how to get them to the Bienville Hotel. Chance patted Evers on the back and said, "If we had walked from New Orleans we might of got here faster."

March 18, 1907 **Governors Island**

McGill bided his time in Castle Williams, studying the daily rhythms and tedious routines of prison life. Who did what and when they did it. As always, a bugle called out reveille at 6:00 a.m. The prisoners roused themselves from their cots, grumbling and stretching, and assembled for breakfast, the first shift at 6:30 a.m. and the second at 7:00 a.m. since the mess hall could not contain all the prisoners in one sitting. The menu this morning was not untypical: fried bacon, fried potatoes, bread, and coffee. After breakfast Percy assembled on the lawn with all the others to be counted for the morning tally. After the completion of the tally, the prisoners headed for their work details. For McGill, this meant meeting Corp. Hanson, his crew chief, and the six other members of the rock crew out by the rear door of the castle, a huge iron gate some thirty feet tall. Getting out took two different keys, for an inner door and the iron gate, the two keys never in the hands of the same guard. On a typical morning Privates Jahn and Relkerd owned the keys, and fiddled with them for thirty seconds in order to undo the two separate locks in the giant door.

The rock crew left the prison walls but did not have to walk far today. They headed for Fort Jay, the other military installation on Governors Island. Now mainly a barracks for six hundred soldiers, the old fort stood only one thousand feet east of the prison. Many soldiers went about their business on the roads and lawns between the prison and the fort. It took just five minutes for the crew to make it to Fort Jay, where they found the two large wheelbarrows and boulders they needed. Percy took this opportunity to mentally chart the fort, observing it to have low, outer stone walls, no more than three feet high, in an odd shape. He later learned that the fort took the shape of a five-pointed star. Gently sloping manicured lawns surrounded Fort Jay. Four barracks formed a square in the center of the fort.

The prisoners started to load the boulders into the wheelbarrows, sometimes needing two men to lift the bigger rocks. McGill did what he was told, not wanting to upset any applecarts just yet. He chose to work with a bigger man than he, rightly figuring it would make the job a little easier. That man turned out to be Private James Lincoln, nicknamed President. Lincoln was serving his first year of a four-year sentence for murder. They talked as they worked.

"How come they only gave you four years for killing a man?" asked Percy.

"Cause I didn't kill a man," Lincoln explained. "I killed a Chinaman."

"Shit," Percy responded. "They used to give soldiers medals for that. How the hell did you run into this Chinaman?"

"I got drunk in New York one night and ended up in a den. So I paid this old Pigtails a dollar and he set me up on a platform with a pipe. I was smoking for a few minutes when I noticed a white woman— alone—on a platform just across from me. She was dreaming the dreams of the poppy smoke when a goddam filthy Chinaman came up on her and slipped his dirty Chink hand under her dress and right up between her legs. I could not let this yellow dog assault the white race in that manner so I warned him to leave the lady alone. He didn't pay no heed so I slit the fucker's throat. A couple of other pigtailed Johnnies told the judge that *it was my hand* between the lady's legs and that the yellow fellow was defending her honor. I sure as hell don't remember it like that. Anyways, there was this dead Chinaman and someone had to pay. I got stuck with it. My lawyer says I'm lucky."

"How's that?"

"Lawyer says you could get ten years for killing a Chinaman in the civilian courts. In a court martial you get three or four. So it turns out I'm a lucky bastard to be here cracking my back on these rocks for the next forty-three months."

The men carted the boulders to the shore, about 250 feet north. The waters of the bay cut hard into the island, eroding the soil and gravel and dragging it under the waves. The prisoners rolled the boulders into the waters to slow nature's clawing action. Without any machinery to assist them the job required backbreaking exertions of effort. They inserted logs under the larger rocks to move them to the water. By noon the men headed back to Castle Williams for a dinner of roast pork, mashed potatoes, and rice pudding. But by 1:30 the members of the rock crew again found themselves on the shore, heaving the smaller boulders into the muddy edges of the island. The corporal gave them five minutes rest each hour, and if a prisoner showed signs of slacking, the corporal threatened three days in the dungeon.

McGill noted the jagged rocks surrounding the island. It would be extremely difficult for a boat to approach the island other than at the dock used by the Barcelona. But he learned that a detachment of soldiers manned the dock day and night.

By six o'clock the prisoners found themselves locked within the walls for the night, the evening tally completed, and supper served at seven o'clock. McGill lay on his cot, waiting for the second call to mess, listening to the banter of his cellmates. Two inmates near the back of the cell shoved each other and one furiously struck the other, dazing him, ending the conflict for the moment. Next to McGill, a twenty-year-old hothead, Robert Deanne, lay on a cot complaining about a soldier who had clubbed him. Sentenced to three years for rape, Deanne worked in the prison boiler room since his conviction six months earlier. McGill got Deanne to talk about something other than his run-in with the guard.

"What do you have to do in the boiler room?" asked McGill.

"Mainly shovel coal into the furnace. Pile after pile. It never ends. I shovel so you guys get your steam heat and the warm water for your weekly bath." The prison had been updated in recent years. Electric lights and steam heat made life in Castle Williams a tad more bearable.

"You get much rest time there?"

"It ain't bad."

"Does somebody have to work all night there?"

"Only in winter."

"What's the size of the working crew?"

"Jest me and Sandy. You know Sandy?"

"No, not yet. Only one door in and out of the boiler room?"

"Yeah, it's the one next to the bake shop."

McGill pressed a little more. "Any other doors of any sort in that boiler room?"

Deanne answered, "Well, now that you mention it, there is one more, a locked door on the east wall. Never seen it used. Why? You lookin' for a shortcut outta here?"

"Naw," Percy responded. "I'm gonna be on a detail next week painting all the doors in this joint. Just trying to figure out how many doors we'll need to work on."

March 19, 1907 **Mobile, Alabama**

The Cubs had no problem defeating the Mobile Oysterman

this day. The only regulars in the Cubs lineup were Evers at second and Schulte in left. Husk, suffering from a cold that he picked up on the ride over from New Orleans, put outfielder Doc Gessler at first, aware that Doc played over a hundred games at first for Brooklyn two years earlier. He slated Artie Hofman at short, Billy Sweeney to cover third, Seabaugh behind the plate, and Fred "Ossie" Osborn and Randall to fill out the outfield. Miner Brown took the mound and pitched like a god for five innings. In fact he pitched the same way he did in 1906, when he produced a phenomenal 1.04 ERA to go with his 26-6 record. Six batters went down on strikes, most baffled by the curveball that snapped down tightly over the plate after tracing a wide arc. In the second inning Brown hit the Oysterman shortstop Ross in the head, the ball bouncing off the crown of the young man's cranium into the stands. Ross hesitated and trotted down to first. Before the next pitch he stumbled off the bag and collapsed in a heap. Doc Gessler tagged the heap but umpire Jim Ellery said, "No, sir. I will not declare a dead man out!"

Kneeling next to Ross, Gessler protested, "He ain't dead! There's signs of respiration."

"What medical school did you attend, smart guy?"

As he searched for a pulse Doc answered truthfully, "Johns Hopkins."

The ump was not impressed. "Don't sass me asshole. I don't need no answer."

March 20, 1907 Mobile, Alabama

The Cubs assembled at the Mobile Depot at 7:15 p.m., only to learn that the Louisville & Nashville to Birmingham, their next destination, would not leave until ten o'clock. Blue-eyed Orvie Overall came up with a solution.

"I know a bar, a swell place on the waterfront, within walking distance."

Six Cubs, Overall, Chance, Fraser, Gessler, Sweeney, and Hofman, took a hike to the aptly named Chicago Buffet. Orval led the Cubs into the tavern, a sailor's dive, with faded, torn wallpaper, wooden floors, and wainscoting stained with two decades worth of errant spits of tobacco juice. Six brawny sailors in white uniforms milled about a pool table and the bar. One former sailor, an older man lacking both legs, swept the floor with a broom that towered above him. He lurched about the room on a small triangle of wood with little wheels under it. The pool table also missed a leg, but a beer keg pinch-hit nicely. Two signs graced the walls, one asking patrons to refrain from spitting on the tables and the other reading, "Donation to buy Jack White a pair of crutches." Chick Fraser dropped a dime into the donation box and then stepped up to the bar and ordered six beers.

Sweeney saw Fraser slip a dime into the box and asked, "Wouldn't it be cheaper to just saw off the top of the broom rather than buy some crutches?"

"You are heartless, sir. You need a beer. A cold one may warm your disposition." Fraser gave him a sweating bottle that dripped beer as he handed it over.

One of the sailors, a boy of nineteen with close-cropped blond hair, approached Overall, asking if the group of six were locals.

"No. We play for the Chicago Nationals professional baseball team—the Cubs—and we are headed to Birmingham later this night."

"Chicago Nationals? Never heard of 'em," said the sailor, with a country twang.

Orvie chuckled. "You will, sailor. You will!"

March 21, 1907 Birmingham, Alabama

Dubbed the Pittsburgh of the South, Birmingham was one of the few places in the world where coal, iron ore, and limestone, the three minerals used to make steel, were found in close proximity. The foundries in this steel town gave off a great deal of smoke and a haze frequently muted the sun. The Birmingham Coal Barons, the next sparring partner for the Cubs, won the Southern Association championship in 1906. The name of their ballpark, Slag Pile Field, reflected the fact that a huge iron slag heap, dubbed Mt. Slag by some, lay just beyond the right field wall.

As the Cubs changed into their uniforms in a small and dirty visiting team locker room, "Big Ed" Reulbach, one of their best starting pitchers, walked in and the handshakes and hugs began again. Dark-complexioned, Ed stood 6'1" with brown eyes flashing from deep dark sockets under bushy eyebrows. A spark of compassion lurked in the shadow of his eyes. A dimple marked his cleft chin, and a small mole graced his left cheek, an inch from his nose. Coming off a 19-4 record in 1906, he had pitched and won a one-hitter against the White Sox in the Series.

Big Ed did not drink or chase women; his hobbies were reading and chemistry. He believed that abstinence from alcohol should be a required clause in every player's contract. Two weeks earlier in March, Reulbach had asked the Cubs to trade him or pay him more. President Murphy flat out rejected these demands, telling Reulbach he must honor his contract. Reulbach stewed for ten days and then caved.

Chance introduced Big Ed to the rookies and then everyone went back to preparing for the game. Chubby Murphy came in from Chicago to join the team and conferred with Frank Chance right before game-time. Item one in their discussion: Mr. Johnny Kling.

Manager Chance and Johnny Evers held a small training session before the game, instructing rookies Sweeney, Perdue, Randall, and Osborn in the art of the force bunt.

"You don't drop the ball dead at the plate 'cause the catcher nine times out of ten will gun you down," Evers drawled. "Before you come to bat you watch the slab artist at the end of his delivery. If he's ending up on the first base side of the mound you're gonna push the ball to the third base side. And vice versa. You hafta push it with enough juice to scoot it by the pitcher." With Durbin on the mound, Chance demonstrated, pushing the ball down past Durbin, out toward the second baseman. Each of the rookies took a turn at bat and laid down three force bunts. Randall's bunts all slipped by Durbin.

"Keep it up, Newt," Chance shouted, "very nice!"

Chance then took Durbin aside, his arm slung over the young man's shoulders.

"One piece of advice for you, Durbin. When you know in your gut that a batter is gonna try to lay one down on you, put all the jump you got on your pitch, every bit of lightning you still got. S'more likely you'll get him to pop up that way." Durbin nodded and returned to the mound.

For the slated contest the Cubs sent regulars Slagle and Sheckard to the outfield and Evers to second base. Rookies or newcomers covered every other position except that dependable Artie Hofman manned the shortstop duty in the absence of Joe Tinker. Gessler took over at first, old Mike Kahoe played behind the plate, Newt Randall trotted out to right field, and Billy Sweeney, who no longer complained about his strapitis, dug in at third base. On the mound Jack Taylor fidgeted with the rubber and made ready for his first Practice Season outing. In the top of the first Brakeman retired the side 1-2-3, but in the second inning he allowed three hits and two walks, permitting three Barons to cross the plate. Jack grew irritable on the bench. He and Kahoe pulled off a strikeout with a "quick pitch" on an unsuspecting green kid, tossing it by the minor leaguer before he set up in the box. But Taylor gave up another two runs in the fifth inning and muttered a number of curses at the umpire as he left the mound.

Husk had Kid Durbin warm up to finish the last three frames. When Durbin entered the game in the seventh, the Cubs had already posted seven runs to lead 7-5. Kid never pitched better. The fastball broke down and away from the righties and the curve broke in on them. The red-haired rookie even experimented with two changeups as instructed by Miner Brown. One found the plate for a strike and the other got nailed as a hit. He struck out five Barons and allowed no runs.

Durbin's only mistake came in the eighth, when he plunked the Baron right fielder, Smith, in the shoulder. Kid took some ribbing for this because Smith stood only five feet three inches and could not have weighed more than 130 pounds. Jimmy Slagle remarked, "My goodness! He ain't much of a target. The guy's so skinny it's a mystery how you was able to nail him!"

Final score: Cubs 11, Barons 5. Husk shook Durbin's hand on the final out and whispered, "You keep that up and we'll be seeing more of you on the mound." In the dressing room after the contest Jack Taylor sat quietly as he pulled off his uniform, shaking his head over his performance.

Chick Fraser noticed Durbin guzzling a bottle of Sprudel Water. His bushy eyebrows raised up high on his forehead and he yelled out, "Holy shit! This is how the Kid does it! Sprudel Water is his secret!"

Husk took Charlie Dryden, the *Tribune* reporter, aside to talk to him about Johnny Kling.

"Print this, Charlie," Husk started. "If I do not hear from him within a week, he will be traded. I have deals pending for two young backstops, either one of whom will develop into a star in fast company. The way Kling has behaved disgusts me. He is a grand catcher but he isn't too good to be traded."

"Do you mean it, Frank?" Dryden asked.

"Sure as shit, Charlie. This is the last chance for Noisy John."

March 23-24, 1907 Memphis, Tennessee

The journey from Birmingham up to Memphis went smoothly. Thirty-one-year-old reserve catcher Pat Moran joined the club in

Birmingham for the trip north, still bearing a bandage on his nose, broken while he played indoor baseball—a professional softball league—in Chicago. The Cubs obtained comfortable accommodations in Memphis's Cordova Hotel, and the weather cooperated, ratcheting down on the heat they had experienced farther south. About twelve Cubs took in the new Memphis Zoo at Overton Park before the first game, enjoying greatly the antics of several baboons and two copulating antelopes.

After the visit to the zoological gardens the Cubs did well in Red Elm Park. They knocked off the Memphis Turtles (known until recently as the Egyptians) twice in two days, the second time marked by a complete game effort by Big Ed Reulbach. Ed told Husk he wanted to go the full nine and that's exactly what he did.

Reulbach, the Cubs' number two starter behind Mordecai Brown, burst into the majors with the Cubs in 1905 with eighteen wins, quickly winning Chance's confidence. A graduate of Notre Dame, the six-footer then won nineteen games in 1906 while losing only four, and threw a one-hitter in the second game of the World Series to bring the Series even. Off the diamond Big Ed often wore eyeglasses, but never on the field. While he said, "My eyes get better on the mound," Chance ordered Kling to paint his glove white when catching Reulbach. A brainy player, the twenty-four-year-old often outguessed the hitter, throwing a magnificent curve when the batter expected something else. A no-nonsense guy and a loner, the married Reulbach got along fine with his roommate, Carl Lundgren, another college boy.

After Big Ed's nine-inning victory the Cubs lounged in the hotel. Jack Taylor got in a squabble with Chance and Pat Moran and walked out of the hotel bar in a huff. But around four o'clock a fire in a home across the alley from the Cordova drew many of the Cubs out of the saloon's lair. Firemen rushed into the smoke and flames. Frank Chance, Hub Purdue, Newt Randall, Fred Osborn and Doc Gessler followed them in, looking for the residents. Finding none, the players helped carry out some furniture and other items into the alley. Frank Chance wrapped his head in a wet towel and dragged out a mattress. Firemen doused the small fire quickly, and the home owner politely asked the players to bring the furniture back into the residence.

"Last time I'm ever gonna play fireman," commented Chance to the newsmen who reported the fire but did not enter the burning dwelling. The next day the *Courier* reported the Cubs' involvement with the fire under the headline "Amazing Rescue of Furniture."

After supper a number of Cubs sat in the lobby of the Cordova, telling stories and ogling some of the women. Most of them held a stein of beer and some smoked. They were joined by a number of bugs and sporting men, the generous term for gamblers and sharpers. A few of these same sporting men had accepted bets from some Cubs and other players in the past. Harry Steinfeldt noticed one pretty girl of twenty or so, a brunette carrying a box of chocolates.

"Darling, are those chocolates for me?" he asked.

"I surely don't know. Are you a professional baseball player?"

"Honey, you are looking at one of the finest professional ball-players in the world. Harry Steinfeldt is the name. I play third base on the Chicago Cubs, the current champions of the National League. You are…?"

"Winifred Colson, a native of Memphis."

"It is a great pleasure to meet you. I have a soft spot in my heart for natives. Please do me the honor of sitting down for a moment."

In the ensuing two and three-quarters hours Steinfeldt shared two chocolates with Winifred, bought her three bourbons in the hotel bar, walked her to his room, kissed her for a full minute, removed her clothes, nibbled gingerly on her engorged nipples, inserted his penis into her vagina, and, after considerable friction within that region, withdrew and ejaculated an ounce of sperm and seminal fluid onto her stomach, some of it settling in her navel.

By 10:30 p.m. Winfred departed and Steiny sat again in the hotel bar nursing a beer in the company of Jack Taylor and Chick Fraser.

"We saw you glom onto that Baseball Sadie," said Taylor. "She was a looker! Did you hammer that nail of yours?"

Steinfeldt grinned. "Well, let's just say that I did my part in up-holding the reputation of our National Game."

From the Journal of Kid Durbin

I find myself getting a little nervous about whether I am ever going to get much chance to pitch on this team given the pitching staff in place. Two days ago Big Ed took the mound for the first time this spring and reeled off nine innings like it was nothing. Yesterday Jack Taylor, who isn't even slated to be a starter, pitched a complete game, mowing down the Egyptians like they didn't exist, giving up only one run. Taylor throws his fastball with a long, fluid motion, so that when the ball leaves his hand it seems to come up on the batter quick as a lick. He had the nerve to ask Cap'n Chance if he could pitch again today! Typical Brakeman! The guy always wants more. Chance declined the offer, saying he wanted to give Carl Lundgren a chance to show his stuff. Carl did just that, blanking Nashville for six innings and then allowing three runs late in the game when it didn't matter a whole lot. Husk did have me warming up in the seventh inning when Carl began to lag, but I never got the call. By the way, the Nashville ballpark—Sulphur Dell—has a screwy right field. It is steeply sloped so that the right fielder has to run uphill backwards to catch a deep fly ball. Poor Newt Randall had to dash back—and up—on seven flies during the contest and he managed to corral five of them. Doc Gessler assumed duties at first base today because Husk still has shoulder problems. Gessler used this opportunity to impress the Cap'n, banging a double and triple to spark two rallies. It dawned on me after the game—we haven't lost yet this spring. This seems like a good omen for the regular season. Husk seemed satisfied at the results today but on the way back to the hotel he scolded several guys for not taking enough pitches, especially early in the game.

"The best hitters in this game are good waiters. Your first time up I don't want you to even think about swinging until that third pitch. You need to get a good idea of the speed and the movement before you can hit the bastard. So take a close look at a couple of pitches first and then take

the bat off your shoulder. Ain't never gonna be no first-ball hitters on this man's team."

When we reached the hotel Jack Taylor received a letter from his wife that shocked him. It seems that Nelsonville, Ohio, has flooded, and his wife is living on the second floor of their home because the first floor is under water. Jack expressed great concern for his business establishment, a pool hall. Husk allowed Jack to break camp, so he took a train north and will hook up with us again next week in Cincinnati or Columbus. Some of the guys commented that we will have a pleasant week with Brakeman busy elsewhere.

March 27, 1907 Nashville, Tennessee

Before the game the Cubs sold Hub Perdue to the Nashville Egyptians for five hundred dollars. Under the terms of the agreement the Cubs could reclaim Perdue after the 1907 campaign for one thousand dollars. Chance told the young spitballer the club would do so if he had a good year, although the Cubs skipper was not fond of spitballers. Hub acted delighted by the deal because he and his wife grew up and still live in Bethpage, Tennessee, a small town just 26 miles from Nashville. He told the reporters "I knew I couldn't stay with a good club like Chicago. I haven't shaken all the hayseed out of my hair yet. But I have pegged three holes on one deal from Class D to a Class A league. I'll make good here and will see Michigan Avenue before 1908 blows over."

Nashville took possession of Perdue and pitched him against the Cubs two hours later. The youngster pitched credibly, holding his former teammates to two runs in four innings. But veteran Cubs twirler Chick Fraser pitched ten innings and the Cubs put across what proved to be the winning run in the top of the tenth on a double by Newt Randall. Husk approached Randall soon after the game ended.

"Good going, but you can't overstride like that. Your front foot shouldn't stride out more than six to eight inches. A smaller stride will keep you more balanced."

Randall thanked Husk and the two walked to the dressing room.

At the hotel after the game Hub Perdue had to pack up his stuff.

"This is a good thing for me," he told roommate Randall. "I'm not sure I'm ready for the fast company of the big leagues just yet. I can get in a whole lot of innings in with these guys."

"Yeah… but you gotta pitch in an oven here in July and August."

Hub laughed. "You know I grew up here. I'm used to the heat. You Canadians just can't adapt to a little sunshine."

The two had a final beer together along with Durbin and Gessler and then Perdue walked over to the Fairmont Hotel to start his new life as an Egyptian. He never did make it back to the Cubs, but after toiling four more years in the minors he earned a berth on the Boston Nationals in 1911 and pitched in the National League for five years. "Those years pitching the horsehide were the best damn years of my life," he told his grandson shortly before his death in 1968.

When Randall took off to make a telephone call, Durbin cornered Gessler outside the hotel.

"Doc, would you mind if I asked you a medical question that's bugged me a whole long time?"

"Go right ahead," Doc offered, "but be advised that the four beers I just consumed may affect my answer in an otherwise unpredictable manner."

"It's about self-abuse, Doc. I have this worry that sexual self-gratification could unbalance a person, maybe drive someone insane. I was taught this in high school back in Lamar. Mr. Schlessinger, my mathematics instructor, warned the young men of this danger in our hygiene curriculum."

"You're asking me if masturbation can lead to insanity?"

"I guess so."

"Well, in my first year in medical school I too had a professor who claimed that masturbation—he called it self-pollution—could lead to insanity. He conducted a study in an asylum. He said that almost all the male inmates were observed masturbating and concluded that this is what drove them insane. Dr. Clannon was just one of many doctors who credited masturbation with causing imbecility, blindness, tumors, epilepsy, impotence, and a dozen other maladies. Hell, Clannon probably thought it was masturbation that caused Teddy Roosevelt to get elected. Dr. Clannon had a cure for masturbation. He performed infibulations, inserting silver wires through the foreskin of the poor patient's penis to prevent any further 'improper' stimulation of the organ."

"Ouch! Doesn't sound pleasant. So you don't believe the insanity stuff?"

"From what I've seen, most males inside or outside asylums masturbate and don't end up in straight-jackets. There's plenty of other things that drive people crazy, like syphilis, opium and alcohol. Clannon and those of his ilk are idiots. I don't give a dead rat if *most* physicians believe that masturbation harms you--it just isn't so. You know, if the majority are insane, it's the sane who hafta go to the hospital. There's another lesson here, Kid. Beware of men calling themselves 'doctor.' If some sawbones tells you he wants to operate on your prick, you run the other way."

March 28, 1907 West Baden, Indiana

After the Cubs and Pirates left West Baden Spring the Boston Pilgrims moved in. The Boston club had named outfielder Charles "Chick" Stahl their player-manager over the winter. But the moody Stahl did not undertake the new responsibilities with relish. The stress of his private life—he had married in the off-season—and running the team took their toll on Stahl. A week into the Practice Season he resigned as manager. But jettisoning the managing responsibilities did not lift his spirits as he had hoped. He still carried the look of a lost man.

While the sun poked through the trees and foliage of the grounds at eight in the morning, Stahl walked about the perimeter of the West Baden Springs Hotel, carefully inspecting the ballfield. Before nine he met with the owner of the hotel to obtain bathhouse tickets for the Pilgrims. He then took the tickets up to his room. His roommate and old friend, Jimmy Collins, had just finished dressing for the morning practice when Stahl entered the room.

"Hey Jimmy, you 'bout ready?"

"Yessir, Chick. Looks like we got us a sunny day for a change."

Chick grabbed his woolen uniform and walked into the bathroom. He used his new Gillette razor, which he had recently raved about to Collins, to carefully shave yesterday's stubble. He then stepped into his Boston pants and wrestled on an undershirt, and, that done, calmly drank the contents of a glass bottle that he had earlier placed on the shelf in the corner. The effect was immediate. Stahl staggered out of the bathroom, eyes flashing pain, and fell face down on his bed, convulsions wracking his body. Collins rushed to his teammate's side, rolled him over, and gulped when he saw a white froth emerge from Chick's mouth and the eyes roll back in the man's head.

"What the hell's going on here, Chick? Talk to me!"

But Chick never talked again. He died fifteen agony-filled minutes later. In the black-and-white-tiled bathroom they found an empty four-ounce bottle of carbolic acid and a note penned on an envelope, which simply said, "Boys, I couldn't help it. It drove me to it." Cy Young, the legendary Boston pitcher then one day shy of his fortieth birthday, collected the stunned team about him. "It is mighty tough, boys," Young told them. "I never dreamed of such a thing. In fact, none of us could imagine Stahl doing away with himself. Players may come and go, but there are few Chick Stahls."

The "it" mentioned in Stahl's last note has never been definitively identified. It could have been Stahl's long-standing battle with depression, drugs, women problems, or something else. Chick may have indulged in opium or laudanum, drugs freely available in those times. Then there was Lulu Ortman, an Indiana resident who had previously punctuated a long tempestuous affair with Stahl with two attempts to shoot him. Lulu may have attempted to visit Chick in West Baden. To complicate matters, there were rumors of an unnamed twenty-year-old girl who visited Stahl the night before he took his life; she is alleged to have informed Chick that he had impregnated her. And recent bride Julia may have learned of this liason. The something else theory has Chick torn between his devout Catholic views and a homosexual relationship with David Murphy, a Fort Wayne engineer. Murphy, a friend of Stahl's, took his life a day after Chick did, in the same manner as Stahl, by ingesting carbolic acid. Murphy left a note reading "Bury me next to Chick."

Thirty-four years of age at the time of his suicide, Stahl, in ten years of major league service, knocked 1,500 hits and ended with a .305 batting average. Not the first Boston American to kill himself, a former teammate, catcher Martin Bergin, took his life seven years earlier after murdering his wife and two children. The Boston newspapers played up the Bergin-Stahl connection on the day of Stahl's funeral. Because Stahl took his own life, he was denied a Catholic burial. Stahl's wife Julia was dead from drugs and alcohol one year later.

March 28, 1907 Louisville, Kentucky

The Cubs departed Nashville at seven o'clock the night before for a scheduled six-hour trip to Louisville. Only it took over thirteen hours. The train seemed to meander about Tennessee and Kentucky aimlessly, pausing in every rural hamlet for a ten-minute sojourn. Pulling in to get water in one tank town, the engineer learned that the storage tank had sprung a leak, leaving no water for the locomotive. Rail workers located a tank of water and made do.

A weary team arrived in Louisville's 7th Street depot at 8:30 in the morning. Compounding the Cubs' problems, an Elks convention had taken up most of the rooms at the Piney Woods Hotel, so three and four Cubs crammed into each room, with only four baths for the whole team and two toilets on the floor. The rooms had chamber pots—which Shorty Slagle liked to call "slop jars"—for use when the toilets were occupied.

Slagle complained. "A few days ago we was taking baths every time you turned around. Now's we gotta wait two hours to take a bath. What gives?"

Chance set a two-hour workout for noon, telling the players to eat beforehand. The schedule called for a game with the Louisville Colonels at three o'clock. Chick Fraser led a contingent of Cubs around the

Louisville business district before lunch. Chick knew the territory well, having spent his first three major league years pitching for the Colonels when they were one of the original National League clubs. "We should eat at the Galt House," he suggested, "they serve a great meat loaf."

Although cool and pleasant conditions prevailed, only four hundred fans showed up for the contest at League Park, by far the smallest crowd of the spring. The first inning proved decisive as the Cubs pushed five runs across the plate on a pair of walks and hits by Slagle, Sheckard, Randall, and Chance. Randall took Frank Schulte's place in right field because Schulte nursed a sore wrist, while Billy Sweeney covered third base since Harry Steinfeldt had traveled to his home in Cincinnati to be treated for a charley horse. Johnny Evers nailed three hits in the game even though he boasted a swollen right hand as the result of being spiked at second base the day before. Jack Pfiester pitched all nine. The lefty's sidearm delivery took a number of the Colonel batters by surprise, as the ball seemed to come at them from the right side of the infield. But some Colonels saw the ball fine and he gave up four runs, three of them late in the game as he tired. Still, the Cubs won 8-4, maintaining their perfect Practice Season. It also marked the fourth game in a row that a Cubs pitcher twirled a complete game.

Back at the hotel after the game Evers joked with Slagle that no one had heard from Jack Taylor yet.

"Brakeman might've been swept away and drowned by that flood, Rabbit."

"Nah. Odds is against it. Durbin tells me Jack's a fine swimmer."

Frank Chance received a phone call from Jimmy Collins of the Boston Pilgrims (one year later dubbed the Red Sox) fifty-six miles away in West Baden Springs, informing him of Chick Stahl's suicide. Husk shook his head and informed a number of the players who knew Stahl. The Peerless Leader sat down with Johnny Evers to talk about Stahl's death.

"I knew that Chick used dope, Johnny. But I never said nothin' to him about it. Figured he must have it under control."

"Yeah, well, you can't blame yourself. If you'd a said something he would have just barked at you. Those things Chick had to deal with himself. Has to come from inside."

"It's strange. Just days before he drinks the acid we're holed up in the same hotel guzzling that Sprudel Water. Chick and us, we're all swinging at baseballs and hopping on trains and eating steak dinners. But we drank the mineral waters and he drank the fucking acid. We're choosing life and he's choosing death."

"It's an old story, Husk. Happens every day. Probably always will."

"A bad death, Crab. Not the way to go."

"Ain't no such thing as a good death, Frank."

"Yeah, well quick is better than slow."

"Could be *too* quick, Husk. You die in your sleep and you might not know you died. I wanna know when it's my time. I wanna be able to look back and look ahead, even if it's only for a few seconds."

"Nah. None of your looking this way and that. Give me a shot in the back of the head while I'm walking down a street on a full stomach. The work of a bullet."

Shortly after this conversation, Chance received another call notifying him that his old Cubs teammate and current Boston Nationals outfielder, Harry "Cozy" Dolan, lay hospitalized in Louisville with malarial fever. Chance planned a visit to Cozy the next day.

March 29, 1907 Louisville, Kentucky

More bad news hit the Cubs this day. Still reeling from the suicide of Chick Stahl, Frank Chance learned in the morning that Cozy Dolan had died the night before in the Northern Infirmary, a hospital not more than three miles from the Cubs' hotel. The story of Dolan's death disturbed the Cubs pilot. The thirty-four-year-old ballplayer fell sick two weeks earlier in West Baden Springs as the Boston Nationals, who had just changed their name from Beaneaters to Doves, enjoyed the waters there. The doctors diagnosed his illness as malarial fever but expressed optimism, suggesting that bed rest alone would cure him. Being too weak to accompany his club on the trek south to Georgia, the Doves transported Cozy south across the Ohio River to a hospital in Louisville. His wife arrived from Boston and immediately became alarmed. She summoned Cozy's sister, a nurse, and the sister called in a second physician, a man of considerable reputation, who soon determined that Cozy did not suffer from malaria. The new diagnosis: pneumonia and typhoid fever. Six hours after getting the new diagnosis Dolan succumbed.

President Murphy joined the Cubs a few days later, taking charge of the Dolan situation on behalf of the National League. He and Mrs. Murphy consoled Mrs. Dolan and Cozy's sister, both of whom complained to the news reporters of the "neglect" of the doctors who misdiagnosed Dolan's malady. The Cubs Secretary Charlie Williams made the transportation arrangements for the two women to accompany the body back to Boston, Murphy paying for everything. The grieving widow and sister departed on the two o'clock train. Down in Thomasville, Georgia, the Boston Doves canceled the remainder of their Practice Season and headed back to Boston for the funeral.

Although their heart wasn't in it, the Cubs players dressed for an afternoon game against the Colonels. They were relieved when a persistent, cold drizzle forced the cancellation of the game. The damp, gray weather perfectly reflected the low spirits of the team. Slagle told a group of Cubs what he had heard of Dolan's last hours.

"The wife and sister swear Cozy kept calling out Chick Stahl's name. They couldn't figure all of what he was sayin' cause he was fucked up. But they's positive he was talkin' to Chick. Say he used Chick's name many times last night 'fore he passed. And the wife and sister had no idea that Chick was already on the Other Side. And a course Cozy couldn'ta known Chick was a dead man either. They said they didn't know till *after* Chick passed. But now it's tolerable clear. Chick was helpin' Cozy in his last hours, while's he's on his deathbed."

"I've heard stories like that before," Jimmy Sheckard offered. "Spirits, especially the new spirits like Chick, they are still interested in engaging the living. Chick was just trying to ease the passage of someone like Cozy, who was leaving this world and headed for the next."

"Yeah," said Frank Schulte, "a person who dies can get caught between two worlds, so to speak. Maybe they're not sure which way to go at first. They linger."

Durbin contributed a different view. "I'm not so sure. Seems to me like the folks on the Other Side might have more important matters to deal with than messing around with the living or the dying. They got to sort out what they did and didn't do while they walked the earth, don't they? Spirits might be too busy with celestial doings to have any time to concern themselves with us."

Slagle remained unconvinced. "Sonny boy, Chick and Cozy was good buddies. Cozy had this restaurant in Cambridge. A swell place. Chick used to take his lady friends there and Cozy never charged Chick nuthin'. So I'm thinkin' that once Chick went on over he couldn't help but notice an old pal nigh to leavin' this side. No doubt in my mind that Chick eased the way for Cozy, tit for tat, no doubt about it."

The conversation turned to West Baden Springs.

"That is the last nail in the coffin for West Baden. No fuckin' way am I ever gonna take the waters there again." Slagle kept going. "Can you figure how Chick can go and drink acid and dissolve away his innards? Ain't no explanation other than the fuckin' Sprudel water, drinkin' it and swimmin' around in it everday's 'nuf to drive some people over the edge. And Cozy took sick there too! First they said 'twas malaria. Then they calls it the typhus and pneumonia. Where do ya think he got it? The goddam water in West Baden."

Sheckard agreed. "Yessir. I been telling you boys about the dangers of that stuff for some time now. I can't see any team heading back to that place anytime soon. You can call it fear or you might just call it common sense. Two men died this time around. I sure as hell won't go back there."

Durbin, who earlier in the day had consumed twelve ounces of Sprudel Water, fell silent here. He knew it wasn't the water that caused these deaths. But as a new man he could not inject reason into this discussion.

The team's departure was delayed until nine o'clock. A full moon hung in the sky, a mere quarter-million miles away, winking wildly and bathing the players in a sickly pale orange light as they boarded a train for Columbus. After the long day, the players slept soundly in their berths. Not even the piercing whistle of the locomotive disturbed their slumber.

The Era Typhoid Fever, Hygiene, and Houseflies

Typhoid fever posed a terrible threat to Americans at the turn of the century. It killed more men in the Spanish-American War of 1898 than did hostile action. While medical authorities of these times understood the causes, they lacked the antibiotics that now easily cure the affliction. The source of the disease, a unique strain of salmonella known as *salmonella typhi*, is found in another human being, or more specifically, the feces or urine of another human being. The germs are spread when one individual ingests food or water contaminated by waste products of an infected person.

How, then, did this disease get transmitted in an America that boasted flush toilets and knowledge of sanitation needs? In some places the problem arose when infected feces and urine contaminated bodies of water used for drinking purposes. This is precisely why the Chicago health authorities reversed the direction of the Chicago River in 1900. Prior to that great engineering feat, waste products deposited into Lake Michigan, where Chicago also drew its supply of drinking water, infected residents of the city with typhoid fever. The death rate from typhoid fever in Chicago in 1891 ran 174 per 100,000. But this form of contamination did not often occur in urban areas by 1907, where public health departments monitored the quality of the drinking water and treated the sewage. The most common manner in which typhoid spread resulted from poor hygienic habits. A food preparer who carried the disease, like the infamous Typhoid Mary in New York City, would fail to properly wash his or her hands after urinating or defecating. The germs leaped from stool to food, as the hands of the infected person touched food such as fruits and vegetables that would not be cooked. Lettuce could kill.

The ever-present two-winged pest, the common housefly, *Musca domestica*, also assisted the spread of typhoid germs from stool to food. Sadly, houseflies do not eat in the same manner as do most human beings. They cannot ingest solids and yet solid food is their preference. So evolutionary forces have provided the housefly with a process that enables them to gorge on nonliquid foods. They alight on a morsel of food, a piece of cake for example, and regurgitate onto the cake a fine mixture of their digestive juices, saliva, and enzymes, a blend, incidentally, which carries bits and pieces of their last meal. The fly's vomit-like substance readily dissolves the particles of cake, liquifying the tasty mass. *Musca domestica* comes equipped with a funnel-like tongue, its proboscis, which is then utilized to suck up the "pudding" it has created, or at least most of it. And there lies the rub, for the housefly is not a tidy creature, and it always leaves behind some remnant of its vomit and pieces of its prior meal, either from its spongy mouthparts or hairy, sticky legs. Flies have this nasty habit of wiping their feet on our food. If the fly last dined on human waste products infected with typhoid germs, those germs may be transferred to the cake on which the fly has set down for his next repast. Little wonder then that in past days when typhoid fever stalked this nation like a specter, houseflies earned the labels "Typhoid Flies" and "messengers of death."

Flies have prodigious abilities to reproduce. A fly egg takes twelve days to become a maggot. Female flies lay about 150 eggs. Under optimum conditions, one pair of flies could multiply to eight million in one season! There are fewer flies in twenty-first century America than a hundred years ago, primarily because we have moved from horses to automobiles. A favorite spot for the female fly to deposit her eggs is a warm, dead carcass. But lacking that, a soft, moist pile of horse manure offers an equally promising venue on which the eggs can transform into maggots who are delighted to ingest the horse dung. Chicago's horses produced enough manure in 1900 to breed more than seventy-five billion flies. Twenty-five pounds of horse manure per horse each day adds up. Fewer horses, fewer flies, and better hygiene have reduced typhoid fever to nuisance levels in modern America, with most cases now hitting travelers returning from undeveloped areas of the world.

March 29, 1907 Governors Island

The rock crew, eight inmates today, trudged slowly down Carder Road past Fort Jay, along the north side of the island, and then around to the south, along the island's east coast. The morning sun ascended to their left out of the haze of Brooklyn as they passed the old Governor's House, the Dutch House, and the Admiral's House. Percy gazed out across the Buttermilk Channel at Brooklyn and the memories of his despised father chilled him like a winter's draft. Ten yards away, choppy waves pounded the large rocks on the island's edge, spraying a salty mist over the prisoners. They walked another two hundred yards south toward a small mound of boulders that a barge had deposited three weeks earlier. The crew chief today, Corporal Andrew Tollington, ordered the men to disperse the boulders up and down the eastern shore of the island. James Lincoln and Percy lifted a two-hundred pound rock, carried it ten yards south, and heaved it into the ocean in a bare, muddy spot, the stone making a loud "thwop" as it landed. They then rolled another, heavier rock to the same spot and shoved it over a ledge. In the midst of his work Percy looked out over the harbor waters. He observed a red and white buoy some fifty yards off the point where he stood. As he turned around to note his exact location, Corp. Tollington called out to Percy to "get your ass back to work."

The men labored for an hour. A new man had joined the detail this day, a strong, lean fellow named Harold Conners. Percy scrutinized the man. Conners seemed about thirty, a little taller than Percy with short, dark hair. He had thick lips and a small nose, a baby face fixed in a scowl. Conners had just drawn the rock crew assignment after attacking a guard and serving one week in a third-floor solitary cell. Around ten o'clock, with little warning, Conners became agitated at his partner, Joe Lavertine, and grabbed a pick axe to attack him. Conners swung the axe back, over his head, ready to bludgeon Lavertine, but James Lincoln ripped the axe out of his hands and stepped in front of him.

Conners immediately desisted.

"No more of this crap." Lincoln spat out the words. "You gotta come after me before you go for him."

Percy waited an hour and then asked Lincoln why he had intervened.

"Is that Lavertine guy a friend of yours?"

"No," Lincoln replied, as he picked up a hundred-pound rock. "I just don't like Conners."

"You know him before today?"

"Yeah. We was in the same unit. We never did get along much. Then one day we came to an understanding."

"What kind of understanding?"

"We got in a scrap and I busted his jaw. Doc had to wire it shut and he couldn't eat real grub for a long time. Had to drink his meals. We didn't have any problems after that."

March 30, 1907 Columbus, Ohio

The Cubs' train jerked to a halt in Cincinnati and the conductor announced, "You got fifteen minutes!" The team took a quick breakfast on stools at a grill inside the station and wolfed down hamburgers and grilled frankfurters. Harry Steinfeldt had promised to rejoin the team in Cincy, where doctors treated his charley horse, but he failed to show at the station. Chance didn't even have time to telephone Steiny before the train resumed its journey. They pulled into Columbus around 11:00 a.m. and made tracks for the hotel. Cold winds greeted the players.

Jack Taylor met the boys in the lobby. He had a fine story to tell as his teammates pulled up armchairs around him.

"I couldn't believe it myself, boys. The floodwaters nearly wiped my town off the map. On the train coming into Nelsonville we seen driftwood and cornstalks hanging from the telegraph poles and wires above us. I can't even guess how high the waters rose in town, but I made out fine 'cause of my friends. They piled everything in my pool hall on the shelves and on top of the tables. Water stopped right below where it could have really damaged the pool tables. Six inches more and I'm cooked! Didn't even lose a box of cigars or a stick of chalk. The grocer man in the store next to me wasn't as lucky. He too had all his stuff piled up high, but at the worst moment of the flood a cow swam into his place and tipped everything over. He lost most of his inventory."

Newt Randall spoke up. "What about your wife? She okay?"

"Oh, she got a little shaken up. The rats is mostly what scared the bejesus out of her. But she's good to go now. I got her stashed upstairs. You guys will meet her later."

"What rats?" asked Durbin.

"Rats are good swimmers but they'd just as soon get into a nice dry house rather than get bounced about in the floodwaters. They got a little testy once they left the water, too. Maybe they didn't appreciate all the cyanide we left for them. After the water went down, we shoveled more than a hundred dead rats out of my place alone."

Durbin, aware of Jack's propensity to exaggerate, calculated there must have been about six rats.

Jack Taylor convinced the youngster Fred Osborn to join him for lunch after six veterans begged off. Finding a diner one block down the road from the Cubs' hotel, Osborn ordered the lamb stew while Brakeman chose a large steak even though the game loomed only a few hours later. The two dug into their meals.

"How's the lamb stew?" Jack asked.

"Much ado about mutton," responded Fred.

Osborn's wit was lost on the Brakeman. Instead, he began to tell Osborn his life story and all the terrible things that had come his way. The stories of his job as a brakeman never failed to impress the ballplayers, at least the first telling.

"Railroad is the most dangerous job there is," Taylor started. "The brakeman puts his life and limb on the line day after day. It's only a matter of time till the brakeman is crippled or dead. The easy part of being a brakeman is finding the hobos and running them off, maybe knocking their heads with a lantern. But other parts of the job can be hard. Nearly lost my left arm once at a water stop in Virginia. My coat got stuck on a nail and the pumping hose almost ripped the arm out of the socket. But the nail tore loose before my arm did. And that was my salary wing too! 'Nother time a train rolled a whole lot closer to my foot than I thought it could. Looked down and my boot was gone—pulled right off my foot—but damned if my foot wasn't still there!"

"You ever see anyone get hurt?"

"Sure. The worst was this boomer who was working with me and a hogger—that's the engineer—to string together eleven cars in the Youngstown Yard. The boomer rode on the front of the lead car while I was back with the hogger in the kettle—the locomotive. Must have been a little wet and slippery that night because the boomer slipped off his perch. Train went right over him. He was all torn up and dead when we found him."

A moment later Taylor started on another subject that he enjoyed talking about—his disdain for Frank Chance. "Peerless Leader my ass! He's a vindictive son of a bitch."

"I ain't seen nothing like that yet."

"You will. Last year I seen it right up close. There was this pitcher, on the Reds, name of Jack Harper. You can ask Chick Fraser about him 'cause Chick was his roommate for a while a year back. Chance had some history with Harper. In a doubleheader back three years or so, Harper nails Chance two or three times. Then early last year the Cubs come into Cincy and Harper's toiling and Chance is scowling at him like he used to do when I pitched against him. Harper throws one high and tight to Chance and, like usual, he doesn't move—he lets the fucking fastball hit him in the head. He goes down and he ain't moving for ten seconds. Frank gets up off his ass a minute later and yells at Harper, 'I won't forget that!'"

The boys ordered dessert.

Taylor began again. "So a month later Chance convinces President Asshole Murphy to purchase Harper from the Reds. Lies to him about how we really need him. Hell, we needed another arm like we each need another dick. When Harper arrives, first thing Chance does is to force a three-thousand-dollar pay cut down his throat. Harper accepts it—he has no choice. Then the fucker tells Harper he ain't gonna be seeing much action. He pitches him one lousy inning and that's it. Harper asks for more work and Chance tells him it ain't gonna happen. Harper appeals to the National Commission and loses so he quits. You notice he ain't pitching this year. He was only twenty-eight and won more than twenty games a couple of times and yet Chance drove him out of the game to make a point. That's our Peerless Leader."

A moment later Taylor expounded on his political views.

"See here, Ossie. America is certain to lead the world from now on. We have the responsibility to guide the colored nations and the declining countries like our enemy Spain and even England with all those Irishmen. It's as if God gave us this duty. Teddy Roosevelt is just the man to teach all those foreigners a thing or two. And baseball is a prime example of all this. We lead the world in baseball and no foreigners will ever be able to play baseball at the level we do."

"Hold on, Brakeman. You know the Japs sent a team to California to play our boys just about two years ago. The Japs licked the U.S. team fair and square in a series of games."

Brakeman shook his head. "I don't believe it for a moment. You're sayin' those little brown fellers with oily black hair beat a white American team?"

"I read it in the papers, Jack."

"Well, I could only accept that if I seen it. Maybe those boys laid down there."

The waiter brought dessert—two huge slices of pecan pie and vanilla ice cream—while Jack boasted about his "long and illustrious baseball career."

"You know a sporting writer in St. Louis once called me the George Washington of National League pitchers. Probably because..." While Taylor spoke, Osborn's eyes rolled back in his head, his head tilted to the ceiling and he started shaking violently. He fell out of the chair, convulsing, squirming, and murmuring on the restaurant floor for thirty seconds before he quieted down. Taylor did not rise from his chair. He continued to eat as if nothing happened. A waiter came to the aid of Osborn, helped him up and got him back into his chair. The restaurant had gone silent as Osborn yelped on the floor but now the customers resumed their normal conversations.

"You done with that crap?" asked Taylor, not looking up from his plate.

Osborn first cleared his throat. "Yeah. Sorry. I gotta medical problem."

"What is it for God's sake, the eepiloxy?"

"No. It's the strangest thing. Two different doctors tell me I got Catuchmen's Syndrome. Bet you never heard of it."

"Damned right. What the hell is it, kid?"

"It's what the docs call a psychic imbalance. For reasons no one can figure out I react when I hear those two dreaded words, the name of the first president. Those two words make me collapse."

"You mean the words George Wa..."

Osborn raised his arms. "Don't do it, Brakeman. I beg you,

please! I can't take it again, so soon."

"Ossie, just kiddin' you. I wouldn't do that to a teammate. Don'tcha worry none. It sounds more like there's a hoodoo on you than some Hootchman's Disease. By the way, can you pick up this check? I'll get the next one."

The team prepared for a game against the minor league Columbus Senators, winners of the pennant in the American Association in 1906. Columbus boasted two significant assets beyond its talented players: a magnificent playing field and good management. The Columbus club built Neil Park, the first concrete and steel stadium in America, in 1905. The beautiful, double-decked structure seated ten thousand and predated the first major league concrete and steel stadium, Shibe Park in Philadelphia, by four years. The manager of the Senators, thirty-three-year-old Bill "Derby Day" Clymer, owned a reputation as a smart baseball man. The nickname came from his chant at the start of each game, "It's Derby Day today!" Robert Quinn owned the team and provided a solid, intelligent approach to minor league ball. Columbus supported the team, as it led the American Association in attendance in 1906. But today a sparse crowd of only 1,500 fans braved the cool weather for the game.

Husk gave Ohioan Fred Osborn a chance to start in right field today, and the kid made the most of it. No worse the wear from the lunch episode, Ossie drove in the Cubs' initial tally with a screaming double down the line in the first inning. Second time up he drew a base on balls and scored a moment later. Chance pulled Osborn aside when he returned to the bench.

"When you are turning second base, heading for third, and the center fielder is fielding the ball, you can help yourself. Just come into third base from the same angle you think the ball will be coming in from. To do this you just gotta run an extra step out toward the outfield when you cross second. Damn hard for the outfielder to throw you out at third when you are between him and the base."

Osborn soaked it up like a sponge in dishwater. His third at-bat produced an out, a ringing shot directly at the right fielder. In his final appearance Osborn drove in two runs with a hard single. When Osborn returned to the bench, Jack Taylor winked at him and said, "You oughtta ka-tooch yourself more often." Jeff Overall, Ed Reulbach, and Miner

Brown each pitched a decent three innings and the Cubs grabbed another victory by a score of 7-2.

Kid Durbin congratulated Osborn after the game.

"One heck of a performance, Ossie! A few more like that and you could be a starter."

"Hell. I'd settle for just making the team. Them three S's ain't going anywhere."

The three S's constituted the Cubs starting outfield: Slagle, Sheckard, and Schulte. Osborn knew he couldn't crack the starting lineup as an outfielder, so he pegged his hopes on gaining a berth as a reserve.

From the Journal of Kid Durbin

On the night train to Columbus Charlie Williams assigned Billy Sweeney and me to lower berth 22 on the Pullman car. Around eleven o'clock we turned in and I took the inner side of the berth while Billy slept on the aisle side. Maybe a half-hour later, before I fell asleep, someone opened our curtains a foot or so, and an arm came in, poking about. I shoved Billy and whispered to him about the arm and he told me it was only the porter grabbing our shoes "for to shine 'em." At one in the morning, while in a deep sleep, some racket awakened me and I learned Rookie Rule No. 1: Never sleep in the aisle berth. The curtains to our berth flew open and two pairs of hands grabbed Sweeney and he was gone. Sweeney got dumped on the floor of the car and someone poured molasses all over him. What a mess! It sounded like Steiny and Artie Hofman but neither of us is sure who did this. The porter and the brakeman assisted Billy but he couldn't get all cleaned up until we made it to the hotel. Newt Randall didn't get much sleep last night either. At eleven o'clock Chick Fraser corralled him, handed him a lantern, and told him about some emergency. Newt had to stand on the platform of the last car of the train, waving the lantern to prevent another train from overtaking us. Chick said Randall had the "11:00 to 2:00 duty." Newt didn't know any better—I might of done the same in his situation—and he stood out there in the cold waving the lantern for almost two hours before a porter wised him up.

They call Columbus the "Buggy Capital of the World" because of all the buggy factories here. I may forget that but I shall long remember today's game against the Columbus Senators. We had Jack Taylor on the mound and he had real good stuff. But some fireworks started early, in the bottom of the third. With one out and a man on first a quick grounder scooted out to Evers midway between first and second. Johnny fielded the ball smoothly, tagged the base runner gliding by him, and made a hurried toss over to Chance at first base. The ball sailed wide, eluding

Husk. White-haired "Porky" Sullivan, the sole umpire, called both base runners safe, ruling that Evers missed the tag. The ump then turned his back on the fielders, not noticing that the batter had taken off for second base after the bad throw. So Sullivan didn't see Husk send a bullet to shortfielder Artie Hofman who tagged the runner out by a country mile at second. Sullivan clean missed it and never called the runner out. A number of the boys started toward Porky at home plate to explain what had just happened. Sullivan seemed threatened even though the boys just wanted to talk. He started to wave his arms and beckoned the coppers down onto the field. Four bluecoats came running out to home plate and Sullivan ordered them to remove Chance from the field. Frank got all worked up and started cussing. He took a seat on our bench, spat a torrent of tobacco juice in Porky's general direction, and refused to leave the premises. Sullivan threatened a forfeit so Frank exited, telling Sullivan to "Go fuck yourself."

Sullivan must have been feeling his oats because at this point he turns to our pitcher, the Brakeman, and tells him his day is over too. Jack, who had not said a word, started to steam but pulled himself together and kept his head, not wanting to embarrass his wife who sat just above us in the stands. Evers then runs off to locate Husk to see who the Peerless Leader wants to pitch in place of Taylor. Believe it or not, when Johnny came back on the field Sullivan ordered him too out of the game, for no reason at all. Johnny had some choice observations at this point, my favorite being, "You're dumber than a codfish and don't smell as good!" Rather than reply to this comment, Sullivan called the police back onto the diamond to escort Evers out of there. Johnny took the hint and skedaddled.

Sullivan then must have forgotten that he threw Taylor out of the game because he pointed to Brakeman, who still sat on the bench spitting tobacco juice and snarling, and told him to resume pitching. Only he put it this way: "Get your sorry ass back out here, Taylor." And so Jack took the mound again like he hadn't been tossed. That delighted about twenty folks who had come from Nelsonville, sixty miles up the road, to see their buddy pitch. Doc Gessler took over at first base for Husk and Frank Schulte, always an outfielder, tried patroling second. Frank did not look too confident at second. He booted one of two chances.

The game stood at 2-2 when the Senators brought in a spitball pitcher, a right-hander by the name of Rube Geyer. He struck out Jimmy Slagle on three wet ones but the catcher couldn't hang onto the third strike and Jimmy made it to first. He then stole second base and came around to score what proved to be the winning run on a single to center by Jimmy Sheckard. Taylor wore a smile after the game because he put on a good show for all his hunting buddies. This team plays to win! By my reckoning we still have yet to lose a game in 1907.

One more thing. Miner Brown, who is a friendly guy, spent some time the other day in the hotel lobby telling me and Chick Fraser the way he approaches pitching. He says the trick is to work against the hitter's batting stance. The main goal, according to Miner, is to "take the power away from the hitter, and you do that by keeping him from putting much wood against the ball." The way to do this, Brown says, depends on how the batter is standing in the batter's box. If the batter is set up away from the plate, Miner says pitch him away, feed him outside pitches. If the guy crowds the plate, you have to pitch him in tight. And if the batter is crouching, Brown advises pitching him a little high, so he cannot get around on the ball. "You want a ground ball, maybe a double play?" he says. "Then pitch low and outside, not inside." I listened carefully to Miner's advice because he has gone far in this game.

April 1-2, 1907   Columbus, Ohio

Cold mists wafted off the Scioto River in downtown Columbus. The game should have been called on account of the frigid thirty-eight degree temperature but the Senators wanted to play. The grounds were dry and the sun shined bright, but the cold cut through the air like a coyote's howl on a clear winter night. The two teams took the field in a deserted Neil Park, only two hundred fans brave or foolhardy enough to attend. Umpire Sullivan, a little skittish over the previous day's events, ran his fingers through his white mane and joked nervously with two cops he'd arranged to stand behind home plate.

Right before the game Evers and Chance informed Jimmy Sheckard that they had been suspended by National League President Pulliam for three days as a result of their run-ins with Porky Sullivan. Sheckard started to groan. "I oughtta punch that fat sonofabitch in the jaw. He rightly deserves it!" But when the game started Evers and Chance suited up and Sheckard soon figured out he was the butt of an April Fool's Day joke.

"Nice goin' guys," he said to them in the dugout as the game begun. "What if I hadda socked that bastard on account of what you said?"

"That would have suited us just fine," said Evers, his thin lips sporting a wide grin. "He had it coming."

The chilly weather forced the Cubs to wear coats over their uniforms for the entire game. It wasn't pretty and it made fielding ground balls an unwieldy chore, but it kept them warm. The Cubs hurler, Carl Lundgren, owned the nickname "the Human Icicle" before this game, due to a history of effectiveness in wintery outings. Today's performance cemented that sobriquet. Lundgren could not be touched, the cold and his overpowering fastball conspiring to result in a two-hitter. The Senators' five errors, three by their frozen-fingered shortstop, helped the Cubs plate ten runs on only five safeties, and the Cubs won the game 10-1. The players call games like this, where one team is never in jeopardy of losing, "laughers." But no one laughed during this ninety-minute ordeal. Too damned cold for that.

President Murphy departed Columbus after the game to return to Chicago, intent on preparing for the start of the Championship season. He made a point of telling the reporters that he had telegraphed Johnny Kling, inviting him to a "conference" in Chicago.

"I will discuss terms with Kling when he meets me," Murphy said, "and if we find it impossible to agree on terms perhaps something in the way of a trade can be arranged."

Frank Chance spoke bluntly with the news boys. "That fucking Jew is trying to extort this club. We'll just see how far that gets the prick. Hell, he already makes more than any other player on the team." The writer for the *Courier* modified Chance's statement for the newspaper audience: "Mr. Kling is asking for a great deal of money. His demand may be unrealistic."

Before the game the next day Husk called a meeting in the hotel parlor. He did not speak long but he spoke with force and conviction. While Frank Schulte hovered on the fringe of the group, nervously humming, Chance told the players that they must "hit up their speed" now to prepare for the start of the new championship season.

"We hung bells on those bastards yesterday, boys. That's what I want each and every day. I want a good start. Every game must be hard fought. Go as fast as you can. Think what must be done next. Each move you make on the field should be clean and smart. Start today!"

The Cubs complied. They played hard and smart. The temperature shot up to forty-two degrees and the Cubs wore the team sweaters during the game, another laugher. Slagle and Sheckard each knocked out three hits while Chick Fraser threw nine innings of five-hit, two-run ball. The West Side crew unleashed a fusillade of base hits that ripped apart two Senator twirlers for sixteen runs. Next stop on the road back to Chicago: forty-five miles due west to Springfield, Ohio.

April 3, 1907 **Governors Island, New York**

The Army set the court martial for April 9, a Tuesday. In the meantime, Percy continued to assemble information about Castle Williams and its surroundings. A cellmate named Thomas Conant offered a tantalizing morsel.

"The way off this island is not over the waters of the bay," Conant claimed, "it's *under* the waters."

"You got a submarine ship, Tommy?" asked Pete Gomina, a short-termer convicted of insubordination.

"No. That's not what I mean. The thing is, there may be a tunnel, connecting this island to Brooklyn. A tunnel east under the bay.

Supposedly dug to allow the bigwigs in the Governor's house here to get to Brooklyn if the British stormed this rock."

Percy interrupted. "Where did you get this from, Tommy?"

"I heard two guards talking about it yesterday. The story is that the tunnel building equipment is rusting away over on the east side of the island, by the South Battery. It's all smashed up now but supposedly still there. But the guards weren't sure of it. They said it might be only a rumor. They ain't never seen no tunnel and they can't be positive what the bastards used the old equipment for."

"Did they talk about where on this island the tunnel begins?"

"Nah. They don't got that kinda information. They just suspect there's a tunnel."

Percy said nothing. Telling these men that he had heard of such a tunnel as a child in Red Hook would not help Percy in any way. But if the tunnel really existed, he wanted to be the one to learn its secrets.

From the Journal of Kid Durbin

We finally took one on the chin yesterday, after nineteen straight Practice Season victories, losing to the lowly Central League team here in Springfield, Ohio. If we wanted to blame it on something other than ourselves we can say it's because the train arrived at two o'clock and the game started at three o'clock. Had to scramble just to suit up in time. But, truth be told, we simply did not play a good game. Our boys committed six errors and only managed three base hits even though nobody compared the hurler to Mathewson. Brownie and Pfiester pitched their tails off but the offense never materialized. Another way to look at things is that nineteen out of twenty is more than respectable. But Chance did not hide his disappointment. He told us we needed to think about what we did wrong and work to avoid those missteps from now on.

Today's game got scrubbed on account of rain. The only bad thing about that is the fact that we wanted to gain a measure of revenge today for what those sandlotters did to us yesterday. Harry Steinfeldt came in from Cincy last night. He saw me drinking Sprudel Water in the hotel lobby—I was gabbing with Johnny Evers and Chick Fraser—and he says to me, "You know that spud water's gonna kill you, right?" He and Jack Taylor lit out from the hotel around four o'clock and we saw them later, drunker than bums on the street. Hell, you couldn't tell they weren't drunken bums. They invited me and some of the boys to join them in a gambling establishment but we declined. It's a good thing Husk didn't see them that way.

The plans for the next few days are in flux, but it looks like we are going to split the team into two squads, the A team and the Zeepho team. I am assigned to the Zeepho squad and Husk asked me to play outfield for that bunch since that is what we will need. I agreed. The Zeephos will boast an outfield of Randall, Osborn, and me. The infield will feature Gessler at first, Lundgren (yes, the Human Icicle!) at second, Sweeney at

THE BEST TEAM EVER

short, and Jack Taylor at third base. I don't know that Taylor has ever played third base but he begged Husk to do so. We will have Seabaugh as our backstop and Fraser and Reulbach to throw. The way I understand it, we all go to Indianapolis for a game tomorrow. But after that contest, the A squad heads to Springfield, Illinois, for Saturday and Sunday games while the Zeephos stay in Indianapolis for a Saturday game and then move to Dayton for a Sunday game. And then we all get back together on Monday in Champaign, Illinois. As confusing as all this sounds, at least I will be on the field for a change, even if it's only in the outfield.

April 5-6, 1907 **Indianapolis, Indiana**

The weather again turned icy cold, featuring a deadly, knifing wind, but the game with the Indians, the doormat of the American Association, did not get scratched. "Jeff" Overall took command for the Cubs, allowing the minor-leaguers only four hits and one run, while striking out eight batters. The six-footer displayed masterful control, the ball cutting the perimeter of the plate time after time. He did not walk anyone and only went to three balls on one Indian. He threw no curves. One pitch sailed over an Indian batter's head, getting recorded as a wild pitch, but both teams recognized it as a purpose pitch. In the bottom of the ninth the Indians leadoff hitter stroked a triple over Jimmy Slagle's head in center. Big Jeff bore down magnificently, getting the next batter on a pop fly and whiffing the last two hitters.

"I determined to go only with the fast stuff and an occasional slow ball," Overall said afterwards. "I worried that if I tried to bend anything my arm might break off like an icicle."

As they had in most of the Practice Season games, the Cubs dressed for the game at their hotel and took three fine—and warm—carriages to the ballpark. Somehow, however, Chance exited the hotel late, and the boys did not have one of the carriages wait for him, each group thinking another would remain. That forced Husk to take an open streetcar. Freezing on the journey over, Husk plotted his revenge. After the game he slipped out quickly and told the carriage drivers to return to the city. When the Cubs emerged from the park to find the carriages gone, they faced a long, cold walk back as most had not brought any carfare. The boys scrounged around and discovered that Trainer McCormick had a dollar on him, enough to get the whole squad back on a streetcar. From that point on, the carriages always waited for the Peerless Leader.

The owner of the Indianapolis club made a big stink about the regular Cubs not taking the field, and, with a series of telephone conversations, persuaded Chubby Murphy to keep the main squad in Indianapolis for the second game of the visit. So the Cubs sent the Zeephos over to Springfield. Before they left, "Manager" Jack Taylor and "Surgeon General" Gessler of the Zeephos issued a challenge for an inter-squad game next Wednesday in Chicago. "It will be a death struggle," Taylor deadpanned, "for the heart and soul of this team." Frank Chance accepted on condition that the weather was favorable.

The Zeephos had no luck against the Springfield nine. With pitchers Chick Fraser, Kid Durbin, and Jack Taylor handling duties at second base, right field, and third base, the unit may have been doomed from the start.

But Durbin and Taylor didn't get any fielding opportunities, and Fraser performed flawlessly with the three grounders squibbed in his direction. Big Ed Reulbach had an off day, walking six Springfield batters and giving up eight hits. One moment of levity came in the eighth, when Brakeman slashed a bounding drive to right field and loped toward first base. The Springfield right fielder, trying to be cute, threw the ball to the first baseman but Taylor beat the throw by a step. Lone umpire Setley, however, who did not get a good look at the play, ruled Taylor out. When the Zeepho Cubs mounted a vigorous protest the man in blue gave the next batter, poor Mike Kahoe, two strikes before he even stepped into the batter's box.

"Why punish me?" asked Mike. "I kept my mouth shut about you blowing that call!"

"You want I should call you out right here and now?" the ump asked.

Kahoe said nothing more. Swinging and missing the next pitch, the umpire called him out on strikes. The final score: Springfield 5, Zeepho Cubs 2.

Back in Indianapolis, cold weather and dark clouds still gripped the town so manager Chance called on the Human Icicle to address the Indianapolis bats in game two. Lundgren responded professionally, spinning a one-hit shutout. The regular Cubs squad found the Indian's southpaw pitcher difficult but managed to push two runs across to win 2-0. Evers impressed the crowd with fourteen flawless chances. He hurt his foot sliding back to second base to escape a tag at one point, but Trainer Jack pronounced him fit and he continued on.

Frank Chance talked with the *Tribune* reporter over a beer after the game, expressing optimism for the upcoming campaign. "We ought to win again for I can't see where any other club in the league has anything on us."

Mordecai Brown, Harry Steinfeldt, and Jimmy Slagle took dinner at a cheap steakhouse. Steiny asked Brown how he became a pitcher.

"Pure accident, back in Indiana, when I played with the best amateur team ever put together, Coxville. We were all coal miners on our team. They spent most of their days chipping away at the black diamond. I was lucky—my job kept me up top. But on Saturdays we played ball. You guys might know some of my Coxville teammates, like Tub Noonan and Bob Berryhill and a pitcher name of Clayton, what a great curve he could conjure. All these guys went to fast company later."

"You mean Billy Clayton?" asked Slagle. "Tall, lean fellow?"

"He was tall all right, but I can't remember his given name.

Anyways, one Saturday we had a game against a salaried team out of Brazil, Indiana. All our buddies in Coxville bet every cent they had on us. A lot riding on that game. But on the day of the game Clayton shows up drunker than a miner on a Saturday night after payday. Pickled to the gills. He can't walk, let alone pitch, and he was our only twirler. I played third and never pitched an inning in my life. So John Buckley, our manager, comes to me and says, 'Brownie, you have to pitch 'cause we are up against it.' I told him I couldn't do it but he said mine was the best arm. Well, I walked out to the pitching box and damned if I didn't go seven innings and no one reached first base. We beat that salary team 9-3. Right there I began to be a pitcher in my own mind. The Brazil guys must've liked what they seen in me because the next spring they signed me up and started payin' me ten dollars a game—enough for me to leave the mine. Great old days, those. The big leagues ain't the only place you can have fun."

Steinfeldt, who had managed to consume three beers while the others stuck to one, asked Brown when he hit his stride as a pitcher.

"That's easy. Just three years ago, the first time I pitched with Johnny Kling behind the plate. I'm not ashamed to admit that I was just a so-so pitcher before I teamed up with Kling. He's made all the difference. He knows what pitches when and he can keep the goddamned base runners nailed to the spot. And the Jew can remember every swing and every hit of the other guys! He knows which guys will fish for the low ones and which guys will turn their noses up at those. If Fred Clarke hits one of my pitches for a double, Kling ain't never gonna let me throw that pitch to Freddy again."

Brown and the rest of the regular squad players hopped a midnite train to Springfield, Illinois, absent Frank Schulte who had left for Chicago to get more medical attention for his charley horse.

April 8, 1907 **Kansas City, Missouri**

Four reporters visited Johnny Kling as he left his brother's billiard parlor around five o'clock. They knew Kling had signed a contract yesterday to catch for the Chicago Cubs.

"How did you get together?"

"I can't tell you anything about the agreement except to say it is acceptable to me."

When asked if he received more than his salary for 1906, Johnny replied, "They are paying me a satisfactory sum. I will be ready for the first game." He said nothing more.

The *Tribune* reported that Kling wanted a three-year contract at $4,800 per year, but had settled for two years at $4,700. The papers inflated the real figures. Kling actually signed for the Cubs original two year offer of $3,500 a year.

In a taxicab with his business partner a minute later, Johnny fumed.

"Murphy is a cheapskate! And a blustery, arrogant man. Always threatening to do this and that. Saying he's gonna deal me over to the Pirates. I told him, 'Go ahead, Chubby. Barney Dreyfuss is an honorable fellow. He will pay me what I'm worth.' You know what Murphy said? He said, 'You mean he's Jewish, right?' Murphy couldn't part with a miserable extra one hundred dollars, and he refused to go the third year. Mark my words buddy, Chubby Murphy will live to regret this. Under no circumstances will I play for the Cubs in 1909. They had their chance. For Chrissakes, I batted 312 percent last year. Only Husk and Steiny beat that!"

"You shouldn't get yourself all discombobulated about this shit, John. It'll strain you bad."

"I suppose. But I have to live with this for the next two years. You know, we had great pitching and defense last year. Well, I am the guy who called every pitch in over a hundred games. A lot of the credit for our great pitching goes to me. And I'm the guy who signaled Steiny at third to edge in when a bunt was about to be laid down. I'm also the one who kept the fellers on the other side from stealing second and third when they did get on base. My right arm is why they didn't run! That ingrate! A hundred bucks!"

"Take it easy, John. You said it yourself. The fat man is gonna live to regret the way he treated you."

April 9, 1907 Governors Island

"A great day for a court martial!" So said Percy's lawyer, Jim Kenton.

"How so?" asked a handcuffed Percy McGill.

"We have two witnesses on the issue of your identity, you and Mr. Laughlin. They have only one identity witness. And an expert graphologist has graciously agreed to testify in your behalf. Ergo, we have a chance to prevail."

"A possibility for justice!"

"Who said anything about justice? I said we could win. And I have to hedge this because one of our witnesses is feebleminded."

"You referring to me or Johnny Laughlin?"

"The latter. This fellow is actually your business partner?"

"For five years. He has his strengths."

"I don't want to know what those may be. But the English language is certainly not one of them. I am not sure the panel will find him credible. His criminal record is no asset either."

"Will that come out in the trial?"

"Yes. Very likely to."

The court martial convened in a two-story colonial style office building just south of Castle Williams. The courtroom, a large rectangular room with dark paneled walls and a creamy white ceiling, had four windows on one side to let in plenty of air and sunshine. The floor consisted of large squares of wooden tiles, while two short tables abutted one very long table where the panel of army officers sat. Percy sat slumped at the table, handcuffed and dressed in a blue wool suit. Five army officers constituted the court: Lieutenant Colonel Robert Waltz, who chaired the panel, two majors, and two lieutenants. The Judge Advocate, Lieutenant Gerald Brickell, acted as prosecutor. Kenton made no objection to the panel as constituted, and both sides waived opening statements. A clerk swore in the first witness for the army.

"State your name and home address for the record." Brickell asked the first question loudly, in a gravelly voice. He wore a khaki dress uniform, as did all the officers that composed the panel.

"John F. Baker, 112 Clinton, Akron, Ohio." Baker, a small, dark-complexioned man, wore spectacles, a gray suit, and a green tie. He spoke softly, but articulately.

"Mr. Baker, you served as a soldier in the United States Army at one time?"

"Yes sir."

"When did your tour of duty begin sir?"

"I served from February 1897 to February 1903."

"Where were you based in March 1898?"

"Fort McPherson, Atlanta, Georgia."

"And while stationed at Fort McPherson did you happen to meet a person named Percival or Percy McGill?"

"Yes, I did." As he answered the question Baker's gaze turned to McGill.

"Do you see Mr. McGill today?"

"I sure do. He is that gentleman, there." Percy looked back at Baker without any emotion, as if he had never seen the man before in his life. Kenton had suggested that he do that.

"Let the record reflect that Mr. Baker has pointed to the defendant."

"How did you meet Mr. McGill, sir?"

"He was a private in our unit. Part of the Fifth Infantry Division. We worked together doing kitchen duty for at least one month."

"Describe your relationship with Pvt. McGill."

"We were friends. At least I thought we were."

"Please tell the panel the date you last saw this man."

"Around the middle of June 1898. He deserted."

Kenton rose and objected to the characterization. The chair sustained the objection.

The prosecutor asked again. "What did you observe in mid-June 1898?"

"One day he was there and the next he was gone. He took off. Never saw him again until today."

"Anything further you remember about this man?"

"Yes. The last night I saw him he asked me to lend him fifty dollars. Every cent I had. I lent him the money."

"No further questions."

The chair of the panel, Lt. Col. Waltz, turned to Kenton. "Cross-examination?"

"Why yes, thank you, sir. Mr. Baker. Has 'Baker' always been your family name?"

The Judge Advocate stood up. "Objection. Immaterial." The chair overruled the objection.

"The name was changed. My father changed it when he arrived in this country. In Europe the family name was 'Bakovich.'"

Kenton walked a few steps closer to Baker, smiled, and asked, "Is Bakovich a Hebrew name?"

"Objection!" Brickell jumped up. "This line of questioning has no relevance whatsoever. There is no excuse for this."

"On the contrary, your honor. I will soon show this tribunal the relevance."

"I'm going to let him proceed," answered the chair.

"It is a Hebrew name, isn't it, sir?"

"Yes."

"Mr. Baker, a few moments ago you were sworn in, sworn to tell the truth, correct?"

"Yes."

"You placed your right hand on a bible, on the King James version of the bible, correct?"

"Yes sir."

"But you do not accept Jesus Christ as the Son of God, correct?"

"That is correct. But…"

Kenton interrupted. "But nothing, sir. Your sworn statements are based on your oath, and your oath was grounded on a bible which means nothing to you."

"Objection! Counsel is not asking a question." Col. Waltz sustained the objection.

"Sir. The cunning Jew plays with the truth and uses lies and deception as a matter of course does he not?"

Brickell, outraged, leaped out of his chair. "Objection! This question is irrelevant and outrageous. Mr. Kenton has exceeded all bounds of decency."

The chair nodded. "Objection sustained. Go on to something else, sir."

"How many men were in your division, sir? Several thousand?"

"Yes."

"Please name for us the fellow who slept in the bunk next to you in June of 1898."

Baker looked about, stammered, and stated, "I do not recall."

"Nine years is a long time, is it not? Please name for us the fellow who slept across from you in the bunkhouse."

"I cannot. I don't remember."

"Nine years is a long time, is it not? This Mr. McGill wears a mustache. Did your Private McGill have a mustache?"

"No he did not."

"You did not bear arms or fight in Cuba or anywhere else for this nation, did you?"

"No, I never left Georgia."

"One more thing. Your Private McGill stole your last fifty dollars from you, did he not?"

"He did."

"You have never forgotten that deed, have you?"

"No, I guess not."

"You have had a long time to think about that theft of your few pieces of silver?"

"Objection to the characterization."

The objection was sustained.

"I will rephrase. You have had a long time to think about that theft of your money, correct?"

"Yes."

"You wanted justice all these years, didn't you?"

"Yes."

"And today you feel you have secured a measure of justice?"

"I suppose."

"And Mr. Bakovich, oh, excuse me, Mr. Baker, as long as you feel you received a bit of justice it doesn't matter who gets sent away for desertion, does it?"

"No, that is not true. That is Percy McGill."

"Correct. Any Percy McGill will do for you, right? Nothing further, your honor." Kenton returned to his chair next to McGill.

Brickell asked but one question on his redirect examination of Baker.

"Mr. Baker. Did Percy McGill, this man here, did he know you were a member of the Jewish religion?"

"Yes. I didn't hide it. I told him this early on, when we first met."

At this point the chair excused Baker. He shuffled from the courtroom, expressionless, averting his eyes from McGill. The army then called a young staff sergeant to introduce documentary evidence showing McGill's enlistment materials, including a signature from "Percival McGill" in 1898. Kenton waived cross-examination of the witness. The final witness for the army, a Castle Williams clerk, introduced into evidence a document signed by Percy at the time of his admission into the island prison. The two signatures were similar. Kenton asked but one question to this witness on cross-examination: "You do not claim to be an expert in the science of handwriting comparison, do you?" Shortly after this the army rested its case.

Kenton called Percy as his first witness, and the prisoner slouched on the stand in a most un-military way, in a manner suggested by his counsel. Percy denied ever entering the army or deserting. "You can't desert if you never joined up," he concluded. Percy claimed he started working in Chicago with Johnny Laughlin in 1897. He denied ever meeting

John Baker, saying, "Today is the first time in my life I ever laid eyes on the man." Brickell's cross-examination did not damage the thrust of Percy's testimony. Kenton then called Johnny Laughlin to testify, and the forty-year-old Irishman strolled into the room and up to the stand. He wore a green suit that had seen better days. Pomade plastered down his hair and the scar on his left cheek stood out in the courtroom light.

Laughlin raised his right hand as the court clerk administered the oath.

"Do you solemnly swear to tell the truth, the whole truth, and nothing but the truth, so help you god?"

Laughlin hesitated a moment and then said, "I do." He appeared nervous and fiddled with the buttons of his suit coat as he spoke.

Kenton began. "Please state your name and address for the record, sir."

"John J. Laughlin, 2233 South Dearborn, Chicago, Illinois."

"And how long have you resided in the city of Chicago, Illinois, sir?"

"All's my life. A few times I been to Cleveland."

"Tell the court when you first met Percy McGill, the defendant in this matter."

Laughlin got the story out, sometimes with a bit of prompting. Kenton had prepped him well. His testimony, which did not change on cross-examination, had him meeting Percy in 1897 in Chicago and going into business shortly thereafter, establishing the "saloon" known as *Lila's* in early 1898. He stated that Percy had never left Chicago for more than two days in 1897 to '98. The cross-examination revealed that Johnny had been convicted of a number of misdemeanors like assault and public nuisance, but Johnny did not retreat from any of his statements regarding Percy. The chair excused the witness but he paused before leaving the witness stand.

Turning toward the clerk Laughlin asked, "Can you unswear me now?"

Lt. Col. Waltz intervened. "Address me, sir. What is it you are asking?"

"He swore me in before. Now I would respectably like to be unsworn, so that when I leave here I don't have to tell the truth no more."

Several panel members laughed, and seeing this Johnny grew a broad grin. But Lt. Col. Waltz was not amused, dismissing Johnny with, "Please stand down now, sir," and Laughlin exited, looking back at Percy with a crooked smile. Kenton whispered to Percy, "I told you that little man was an imbecile!"

With the end of Johnny Laughlin's testimony the court recessed for the noon dinner. The officers of the panel ate a sumptuous meal of glazed pork and red potatoes while Kenton and the still handcuffed Percy made do with a loaf of rye bread and cold cuts of ham and bologna. When they resumed the court martial, at two o'clock, Kenton called a surprise witness, one Dr. Donald Kepplinger, a sixty-year-old, white haired, stout man who carried a bunch of papers with him to the witness stand. After being sworn in, Kepplinger described himself as an "examiner of questioned writings and graphologist," an expert in handwriting analysis. The chair allowed Dr. Kepplinger to testify as an expert witness for the defendant over the Judge Advocate's vigorous objection. Dr. Kepplinger's testimony presented no surprises. Kenton paid Kepplinger one hundred dollars to testify that the signature on the Castle Williams admission record was from a different hand than the army enlistment signature of Percival McGill from 1898.

Kepplinger pulled out two nine-inch square photographs of the two signatures, in which he had enlarged the handwriting samples dramatically. He used a foot-long wooden pointer to focus on specific areas of the photographs.

"As is obvious to even the untrained eye, the 'P' in 'Percy' is looped in a different manner, angle, and intensity in these two signatures. The 1898 signature is firm, untroubled, and unbroken while the 1907 signature has a break and an unsteady waver, right here at the base of the vertical shaft of the 'P.' All of this constitutes a variant form level." Kepplinger pointed out nine other discrepancies or variations in the signatures that his trained eyes had located.

Kenton inquired, "Given these marked differences between the two signatures, have you formed an opinion based on your years of training in forensic science?"

"I have indeed. The same person did not sign these two documents."

Brickell mounted a largely ineffectual cross-examination of Kepplinger, save for the witness's grudging admission that the defense paid him one hundred dollars and expenses for his testimony. This ended the testimonial portion of the trial, leaving only the closing arguments of counsel.

After a recess of twenty minutes, closing arguments commenced. Lt. Brickell began by stressing the "unimpeached" testimony of John Baker. Brickell argued that Baker had no ulterior motives and no reason to finger the wrong man.

"Eyewitnesses like John Baker, who worked with the defendant day after day for weeks on end, do not make mistakes."

The Lieutenant looked into the eyes of the panel members and told them that the attacks on Mr. Baker's religion were entirely unwarranted and repugnant to any court of justice. He urged the panel to closely examine the two signatures themselves and to ignore the "paid testimony of the charlatan doctor." Brickell characterized Laughlin's testimony as "lies of a loyal friend, a friend with a troubling criminal history." As for Percy, Brickell referred to him as "the worst form of human detritus, a man with no conscience, a man who deserted his comrades in arms and let others fight in his place at a point in time when our nation needed to rally all its resources and citizens." Brickell concluded by exclaiming that "Percy McGill is a coward and a liar. This panel must cut through the lies and deceit and find him to be what he is: a deserter plain and simple. And worse, a deserter in time of war!"

After an appropriate pause, Jim Kenton stood behind the lectern to address the panel. He spoke in a firm, confident voice as he delivered his closing remarks, threading together nicely what he labelled "the uncontradicted statements" of Mr. Laughlin, his expert witness, and the defendant. Kenton painted McGill as a victim in a case of mistaken identity. Kenton raised his voice only once during his closing, when he discussed the testimony of John Baker.

Inflecting his voice to a higher pitch, Kenton faced the panel.

"Gentlemen of the court martial, we spotted this man to be what he is the first moment we laid eyes on him. The International Jew is not subject to the bounds of truth and decency as are Christian men and women. John Bakovich will change his name and his story at the drop of a hat, for reasons you and I and decent Christian gentlemen will never be able to fathom. The Jew is not to be trusted in a matter as important as this, when a good man's life and future is on the line. In the first place, how can a Jew positively identify a Christian man? Just as most Christians cannot tell one Jew face from another, Jewry cannot readily distinguish the facial characteristics of one Christian from another. Confusion is to be expected when racial identification is the issue. And secondly, you cannot award any credibility whatsoever to the testimony of a man whose oath of truthfulness is suspect and compromised at best." Kenton urged the panel to reject the testimony of the "swarthy son of peasants" and accept the evidence of science and common sense. "You must accept the judgment of science, as clearly and positively laid out by Dr. Kepplinger. The scientific evidence has not been rebutted. The signature of this Percy McGill is not the signature of the McGill who left the army."

In rebuttal, a calm Lt. Brickell labelled Kenton's arguments "reprehensible and inflammatory," and urged the panel not to be swayed by factors not germane to the issues raised in the proceedings. Nor should they be swayed by the pseudo-science of a witness paid to testify. "Kepplinger is a fraud, gentlemen. His testimony constitutes a fraud on this court." But as he sat down he feared that the Jew-baiting might buy the defendant votes on the panel. The proceeding concluded and the panel adjourned to deliberate on their verdict.

In the lock-up area Percy thanked his lawyer.

"You did a fine job. The handwriting expert was clever, and that 'kike' stuff was damned effective."

"Yes, Percy. I knew you would appreciate that segment."

"You needn't patronize me, counsel. After all, that 'International Jew' crap was your idea, not mine."

"True indeed. Guilty as charged."

"So what's my chance here?"

"Cannot say. I never attempt to predict the unpredictable. We will know soon enough."

The panel took two hours to deliberate. They smoked cigars and drank small quantities of claret as they performed their duty. The room sported comfortable chairs and a fine spring breeze. Lt. Col. Waltz organized the deliberations to allow each officer to speak freely. One officer expressed grave reservations about the testimony of "the Hebrew witness." Another officer mentioned that the prison sergeant, Lorenzo Bell, had learned that the defendant worked as a pimp in Chicago. Yet another panel member looked at the two signatures and remarked that they looked "suspiciously alike." One lieutenant commented that Johnny Laughlin seemed quite nervous while he testified. "Maybe he was lying." Another suggested that "Mr. Baker's testimony seemed *too believable* to be true." After a spirited discussion the panel voted, achieving a 4-1 verdict.

All the parties reassembled in the courtroom to hear Lt. Col. Waltz announce the court's decision. He waited until the courtroom quieted down and then read the verdict.

"On the sole charge against the defendant, desertion from the United States Army during time of war, we find the defendant guilty. Our verdict is 4-1. He is sentenced to six years confinement at hard labor." Percy gritted his teeth and looked down at the grainy table. A minute later two burly military guards led him away.

April 10, 1907 Governors Island

The day after the verdict Little Johnny Laughlin returned to the prison, as instructed. He met with Percy in a small, grimy room, after the second work detail and before the evening meal. Johnny had purchased a new suit in Brooklyn, and it hung loosely on him, but he still had the look of a lower form of being. Sweat seemed to congeal in clumps in his hair and dripped down the sides of his head.

He greeted Percy with a limp handshake. "It's a terrible thing, boss. Ya can't get justice 'less you pay for it."

"'Tis true, Johnny. I had a certain amount of hope that the military tribunal would recognize the grave error done to me and rectify the situation. I shall now have to take things into my own hands."

"What can I do, boss?"

"I do not need your assistance here. The Italian gentlemen that Aiuppa put me in touch with are quite capable. But I want you to attend to one important matter back in Chicago."

"Anything at all."

"It is the matter of the young woman. Connie Dandridge. It does not sit well with me that while I am shackled and humiliated behind these walls the bitch flits about freely. I am caged while the cause of this circumstance is enjoying life. This is not justice."

"I know just the thing to put this right. Where do ya think I can find her, boss?"

"You ever watch the Cubs play baseball, Johnny?"

"The Krauts at West Side Park? No. I like the Irishmen on the South Side."

"Of course. But the bitch probably still cavorts with a pitcher for the Cubs, an Irishman, name of Kid Durbin. So you will be able to find her through the Cubs or, if that fails, you can get her address from the State's Attorney office, the assholes that prosecuted me. One more thing, Johnny. Not from behind. Don't do her from behind. I want her to see it coming. I want her to have to think about it for a moment and suffer, knowing it is coming. Understand?"

"It's all taken care of boss. You just take care of things here."

April 11, 1907 Chicago, Illinois

Connie continued to deteriorate, her mind unraveling in tiny bits and pieces each day. She could not concentrate and frequently became agitated, screaming and crying. An hour later she would apologize and then, without warning, it would happen again. Opiate injections did not help much, so Dr. Kent switched to a relatively new treatment for anxiety, barbital, a derivative of barbituric acid. He prescribed one five-grain capsule daily for Connie. She used it each night but it did little for her save allow her to sleep.

She did not cooperate with the doctor. When confronted about her angry outbursts, lack of communication, and failure to eat she became irritated, denied any problem, and rationalized her actions. Each day she became more testy and moody. She lost weight, her complexion sallowed, and dark rings formed under her eyes. Some days she never left her bed. The Murphys cajoled her into taking a walk one day in Lincoln Park. The sun shined brightly and a warm spring breeze blew off the lake. But after ten minutes, Connie appeared fatigued and they had to return home.

Dr. Kent expressed his concern.

"We need to try something else. The medicines I have prescribed are clearly not assisting Miss Dandridge. She needs something more than I can give her. The time has arrived where we need to take drastic action to avoid the most serious of consequences."

Murphy asked if Dr. Kent had any ideas on an "innovative remedy."

"Yes," he replied, "there is the field of hypnosis. Very controversial. Physicians here and on the Continent are split on the effectiveness of this method. Many alienists have used these techniques. For a long time I myself believed hypnosis a false treatment, and worse, until I observed a skilled mesmerist in England two years ago, in a prolonged public demonstration of the remedial powers of hypnosis. This remarkable fellow worked with patients with maladies similar to Connie, young women suffering from hysteria—in some cases more severe than her condition. I followed the treatment over an eight-week period. I personally witnessed the absolute cure of four of five patients the man treated with nothing more than hypnotic suggestions. No opiates, no medicines of any sort."

"Was this man you speak of a licensed physician or an alienist?" Murphy asked.

"Actually, no," Kent replied, "he was neither. The power of hypnotism rests in the skills of the hypnotist. Whether it is a medical man or not is of no matter. The skill is what is critical. Why do you ask?"

"Because I recently met, quite coincidentally, an extremely gifted hypnotist. He is not a physician. Maybe this could be the man we approach. I speak of an entertainer, a man named Howard Thurston," Murphy noted, in a calm tone.

"Why, sir," Kent answered, "the coincidence is compounded. For Thurston is also the man of whom I speak!"

April 11, 1907 West Side Grounds

An ugly structure from day one, by 1907 it had earned the label "shabby." The Cubs erected West Side Grounds, Chicago's first double-decked baseball stadium, in 1893, on the city block bordered by Polk, Wood, South Lincoln, and Taylor Street. In actuality the park took up only 80 percent of the square block, leaving room for apartment buildings, stores, and a Hebrew School along the south side of Taylor Street. Not unlike other ballfields of the time, the sole aim of its designer was to cram as many people as possible into one city block. A wooden stadium, it almost burned down in 1895. Home plate sat in the northwest corner, so as the sun set in the late afternoon, it shone directly in the eyes of Jimmy Sheckard in left field. A large grandstand stretched in an arc from first base to third. It had a tiny upper deck, limited to eight rows of seats, supported by an extensive system of beams. Those beams, almost ninety in number, obstructed the view of a third of the twelve thousand seats in the park. Later, when the Cubs' success dictated expansion, the team extended the upper deck down the lines, increasing the capacity to sixteen thousand, with new beams obstructing the view of a great many more. A series of bleachers surrounded the rest of the field, with nooks and crannies everywhere, and a wooden scoreboard sprouting twenty feet off the ground in left-center. The dimensions of this field were cavernous, 340 feet down the left field line, 431 feet to left-center, and a gargantuan 560 feet to center field! No one ever drove the ball into the center field bleachers, but balls hit past the center fielder could roll a long time. Pitchers from both teams used the outer reaches of the outfield to warm up. Spacious foul areas allowed fielders to catch up with many a foul ball. Both foul lines were marked in the outfield with a flattened hose painted white. On occasion a fielder would trip over the foul line hose. The Cubs built a brick, colonial-style clubhouse in straightaway center field in 1905. The *Chicago Tribune* erected a huge sign above the wooden bleachers, stretching from center field all the way to near the right field line. Ten-foot high white letters screamed, "THE TRIBUNE ALWAYS MAKES A HIT WITH ITS SPORTING NEWS."

The West Side Grounds rested in a residential area. Crowds of spectators lined the roofs and specially built rooftop bleachers on apartment buildings overlooking right field and across from the park, on South Wood, to watch the games for free. Chubby Murphy threatened to take action against the building owners for "infringing on the Cubs' rights" but never got around to it. Billboards outside the stadium advertised "Owl Cigars now 5 cents." Inside the West Side Grounds a sign proclaimed, "No True Lover of Baseball Will Risk Any Injury to the Players or Interfere With the Game By Throwing Bottles On the Field." Running up and down the foul lines, the field announcer used a yard-long megaphone to make pertinent announcements. "Attention, attention, please! Have your score card and pencil ready and I will give you today's starting nine for the Chicago Nationals…"

The field itself had a large expanse of infield, the skin extending well past the bags at first, second, and third. An immense foul territory sat along the foul lines. On warm days, the fans sitting in the first row draped their suit coats over the short wooden fence. When large crowds necessitated it, the Cubs seated overflow fans on planks laid down behind home plate and along the foul lines from home plate to just past the edge of the outfield turf. Fans also stood behind a rope in center field when the park sold out its regular seats. The team benches sat at field level exposed to the dangers of the game. Wicked foul balls took their toll on inattentive players.

Inside the main entrance scorecards cost a nickel while seat cushions could be purchased for a quarter. Vendors in white coats and white hats, carrying willow wash-baskets filled with peanuts, popcorn, bottles of beer, and cigars, walked the aisles of the park. Whiskey and pigs' knuckles rounded out the menu. A bag of popcorn cost five cents. No hot dogs; for that you had to go to the home of the New York Giants, the Polo Grounds. One vendor sold nickel bottles of Coca-Cola, hawking it as "the temperance drink."

While signs proclaimed "No Wagering Permitted On These Premises," men with little stacks of paper receipts prowled the stadium, loudly announcing the shifting odds and taking bets on numerous aspects of the game. The great number of wagering fans often put a negative edge on the tone of the crowd. A man who is about to lose money on a ballgame casts about for scapegoats and villains. With few exceptions, men wore black bowler hats on cold days and straw boaters on warmer occasions. But a rule prohibited the fans seated on the ground behind the plate and down the foul lines from wearing hats, as that would interfere with the view of those behind. As a result, on sunny days these fans wrapped ample white handkerchiefs about their heads for protection from the sun. The effect was like a sea of turbaned Arabs.

Across the street from the park, Cook County Hospital stretched over a city block. Teammates frequently carted injured players there for treatment rather than wait for the horse-drawn ambulance. Batboy Howie Huhn had a friend in the hospital kitchen who provided free scraps of meat on those days when the players brought their dogs to the park.

"Kid" Durbin, Opening Day

PHOTOS ON PAGES 209-217 FROM THE CHICAGO HISTORY MUSEUM.

LEFT: Cubs President Charles Murphy

BOTTOM: Cubs player/manager Frank Chance, the "Peerless Leader" (c. 1905)

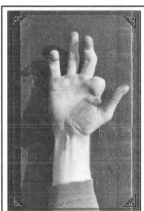
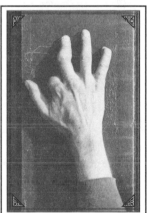

TOP: Mordecai Peter Centennial Brown

BOTTOM: The Hand of "Three Finger" Brown

The Best Team Ever

Left Page: TOP: The Browns and Chances; MIDDLE: Seabaugh, Durbin and Randall bundled up for Practice; BOTTOM LEFT: The Overalls; BOTTOM RIGHT: "Kid" Durbin swings at West Baden Springs.

Right Page: TOP: Downtown Chicago Crowds; MIDDLE LEFT: Billy Sunday; MIDDLE RIGHT: Hinky Dink Kenna; BOTTOM RIGHT: Stockyards.

214   The Best Team Ever

Left Page: TOP LEFT: Johnny Evers leaping; TOP RIGHT: Joe Tinker at bat; MIDDLE RIGHT: "Brakeman" Taylor; BOTTOM: Horse and Frank "Wildfire" Schulte.

Right Page: TOP: Jack Pfiester, sidewinder; MIDDLE LEFT: Harry "Doc" Gessler with bat; MIDDLE RIGHT: Dog and Mike Kahoe at WSG; BOTTOM LEFT: "Kid" Durbin in traveling uniform.

The Best Team Ever

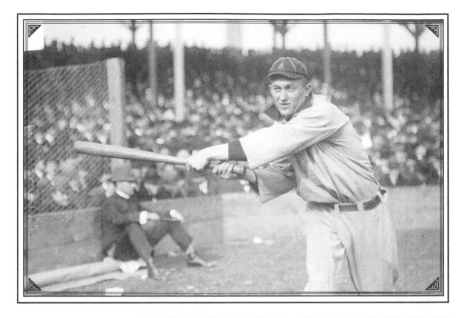

Left Page: TOP; Johnny Kling (at bat); MIDDLE LEFT: Ty Cobb, Detroit Tigers, and Jack Fournier, Chicago White Sox; MIDDLE RIGHT: Christy Mathewson, NY Giants; BOTTOM: John McGraw NY Giants.

Right Page: TOP: Ty Cobb at the 1907 World's Championship Series; MIDDLE LEFT: Andrew "Rube" Foster, Leland Giants pitcher MIDDLE RIGHT: Pete Booker, Leland Giants catcher; BOTTOM: Honus Wagner, Pittsburgh Pirates.

ABOVE: The Great Thurston

From the Journal of Kid Durbin

It is Opening Day. We are back in the Windy City and today we met the Cardinals in the West Side Grounds to start the year's official campaign. Before the game Trainer Jack gave us each two new uniforms, a gray one for the road and a white one for home games. We also received new stockings and two new caps. The home uniform has a "C" over the heart while the road jersey has "Chicago" spelled out across the chest. My name is stitched into the front tail of the jersey and the pants in little one-inch black thread—first time a ballclub ever did that for me. The road cap features a blue bill, with the main part of the cap in gray with blue pinstripes and a large blue "C." Jack told me each outfit cost Mr. Murphy $23.50, making it the most expensive set of clothes I have ever worn. I like to fasten the top button on the jersey and wear the collar up high, even though it sometimes itches my neck. Hell, the whole uniform itches because of the coarse wool fabric, but that's just the way of it.

The big league teams really make a to-do of opening day. Charlie Kuhn, the groundskeeper, has been working on the field for two months. Mr. Murphy had a bunch of boys slap some fresh paint and whitewash all about the park and two carpenters worked for a month replacing rotten wooden planks. Flags and bunting hung from the grandstands and dozens of floral arrangements lined the foul areas. When we finished our pre-game practice a band took the field and gave a concert. I was too nervous to enjoy the music, even knowing I had no real chance to see any action today. A singer with a deep voice and a large megaphone sang a number of songs. Over nine thousand bugs showed up for the affair, even though the sun never came out and the temperature hovered around forty degrees. Cap Anson, a legendary Cub, lent his presence to the opening-day festivities. A tall, fit man with gray eyes, he came bundled up in an overcoat and chewed on a toothpick while the cameramen clicked away at him. Then he visited our bench and personally gave each of us a silk umbrella in a pasteboard box marked "National League Champions," courtesy of the Board of Trade. I took the opportunity to introduce myself to this great player, now a politician running to be re-elected City Clerk. He had a firm handshake and offered to buy me lunch sometime. Old Cap tossed the first new ball of the season onto the field and the Cubs starting nine raced out to their positions with the band playing "My Country 'Tis of Thee, Sweet Land of Liberty..."

Later today I heard that Cap played twenty-two years with this club, and that at age fifty-four he still plays ball with a local semipro team he owns, Anson's Colts. Shorty Slagle told me that Anson might be the best batsman ever. Slagle said, "Old Cap could hit a baseball as easy as you and I can spit." Brakeman, hearing this, spat out some tobacco juice and said, "Shee-it, the pitching way back then wasn't nowhere near as good as it is today." Slagle reminded Jack that Anson played up until 1897, and that Taylor started his career with the Cubs in 1898. Taylor said, "There you go. The caliber of pitching increased considerably once I entered the league—my point exactly."

When Taylor took his leave Slagle looks at me and says, "That guy's got a bad case of a swelled head."

Husk penciled himself in at first and started the three S's in the outfield. Evers covered second, and Steiny took his regular spot at third base. Joe Tinker, still recovering from his surgery, was sitting in a box seat observing the affair. Artie Hofman played short, while Pat Moran caught. Our regular catcher, Johnny Kling, finally showed up yesterday. I met him and he seems like a right fine fellow. He's still in Husk's doghouse so he may not get to catch for a bit. The guys around here say no big league player has ever held out like Kling, refusing to sign his contract until after the Practice Season. Mr. Murphy and Chance are still fuming about the situation. Brakeman had his own opinion on the matter, telling a group of us that "the Jew wanted more money and what's so unusual about that?"

I also met our mascot, a kid named Howie Huhn. He's a good-natured boy, maybe twelve or so. He helps out Trainer Jack on game days, keeping the bats sorted out and separated, cleaning up the spit box, and stuff like that. When we need cigars, chaw, or lunch, Howie can scoot across the street to get these for us. The little guy seems to be a hard worker and while he doesn't have a lucky hump on his back or frizzy hair like some of the mascots, he's a friendly little fellow. Slagle has the kid spit on the bat before he hands it to him to get rid of any jinx, but I asked him not to spit on mine. Jack's got Howie fixed up in a little uniform, a miniature version of ours, but his spikes seem about three sizes too big. Brakeman asked me if Howie was wearing my duds and I said my stuff was too small for him. I am beginning to push back when pushed.

Cardinal rooters could be heard in the bleachers early in the game, but they soon quieted down. Jeff Overall took the mound and whipped his weight in wild cats! The Cardinals could manage no more than four hits and only Solly Hofman's miscue in the ninth prevented a shutout. But Solly had a fine game at the plate, smacking a triple and scoring four of our six runs. The most excitement in the game came in our half of the second frame. Evers, a left-handed hitter, choked up on the bat as he always did. He beat out a bunt hit, but Umpire Carpenter called him out. I thought Johnny would rip his head off but instead he just scowled for ten seconds. A long ten seconds, with no words exchanged. Evers gained a little revenge his next time at bat. When Carpenter called the first pitch to Evers a strike, Johnny, with a great sweep of his little left arm, took off his cap and wiped the plate with it, as if to say, "Ump, you need some help." Carpenter did not appreciate the gesture but the Cubs fans loved it.

Trainer Jack collected our uniforms after the game. He folded them and threw them in a big wooden slatted box, ready to hand out to us again the next day. He noticed me looking at him and said, "I hafta launder these every night."

"We only got them cleaned once a month in the Western Association," I told him.

"Well, the big leagues is different," he said, but I saw some of the boys smiling and realized Jack was just funning me. Turns out Jack gets our stuff washed about once a week, after they start reeking pretty bad. Washed, not dry-cleaned like the way the Boston Doves did it.

Chance spoke to the news fellows after the game, saying, "The team looked better than I even hoped it would. The boys were on their toes and hit well for the condition of the grounds." Then he asked, "How did New York come out?"

Chance invited the boys from the newspapers to join him and a bunch of the Cubs, me included, for a beer at Biggio Brothers, a convenient watering hole across the street from the ballpark, on the corner of Polk and Lincoln. The place was loaded with bugs and they paid for our drinks. Everyone had a fine time.

This great day ended on a musical note. Half the team headed to the Whitney Opera House as guests of the house. My first opera and I am glad I didn't have to pay for my ticket because the whole thing was in Italian! Another problem was the story—none of the characters are likeable except maybe the girl, but even she kept singing at the top of her lungs while she did some stupid things that proved her downfall. The main character in the opera is a hunchback named Rigoletto. I met a hunchback once, a mascot on a team we played in the Western League. The players thought that if they rubbed his hump it would bring good luck. In the opera Rigoletto is a mascot after a fashion. He's a fat guy with a three-pointed hat that has bells on it, working as a jester for a duke. He has a beautiful daughter named Gilda. I wondered how in tarnation this fat hunchback happened to have such a gorgeous child. But that part never got explained.

Rigoletto's boss, the Duke, is a very nasty fellow. The Duke spends all of his time seducing women, including Gilda, but Rigoletto doesn't find out about Gilda and the Duke right off. Rigoletto is not the nicest guy either, and when he insults the father of one of the Duke's victims, that guy puts a hoodoo on Rigoletto. I have never seen a hoodoo succeed in my experience, but they always work in books and plays. When Rigoletto learns about the Duke and his daughter Gilda, he hires an assassin with a long Italian name to kill the Duke. The hired killer is supposed to murder the Duke, stick his body in a big burlap bag, and deliver it to Rigoletto. But things get fouled up and the assassin, instead of killing the Duke, stabs the first man who walks into his inn. It turns out the victim is Gilda, dressed up like a man. Poor Gilda actually sacrificed herself for the rotten Duke. Love, apparently, makes people do dumb things. The killer sticks Gilda in the burlap bag that he gives to Rigoletto. Of course Rigoletto is thinking it's the Duke in the bag. Then Rigoletto sings a song about how happy he is that the dead Duke is in his bag. Unfortunately,

Rigoletto soon finds out who's really in the sack. Gilda still has enough life left in her to belt out one or two last songs with her father before she dies. As we filed out of the auditorium I must have been shaking my head because Lundgren, a college graduate, felt obliged to tell me that opera is "an acquired taste." I took this to mean that if I attend more opera productions I might begin to like them. I didn't particularly like beer when I first tasted it either, so maybe there is something to what Carl says. On the other hand, I have never acquired a taste for the cauliflower, so who knows?

Near the end of the opera, while I watched poor Gilda being betrayed by the Duke, my thoughts turned to Connie. She too fell under the influence of an evil man. It strikes me that this is a common theme both in literature and in life in general. Whether it's Italy two hundred years ago or Chicago today, men frequently take unfair advantage of women. At least Connie didn't have to deal with an Italian assassin.

One sad note to report. Yesterday we released Doc Gessler to the Columbus Senators of the American Association, one of our opponents about two weeks ago. Doc covered first base when we played the Senators so they must have liked what they saw of him. He took the news like a professional and told us he had been assured his salary will not be cut by the Columbus team. I learned that Doc hit .290 for the Brooklyn Nationals in both 1904 and 1905 so I am betting he will make it back to the major leagues soon. A swell guy, we will miss him. He never treated me like a yannigan even though I am one. Baseball has this reputation we are trying to live down—that of a game played by rowdies and rapscallions interested chiefly in fast women and hard liquor. While he certainly admires the ladies, Doc Gessler is a first-rate fellow, a learned man who does not put on airs. We could use more like him in this sport. Last thing he said to me: "Remember this, Kid. There is always a scientific explanation for everything, except for half the time."

April 12, 1907 Chicago, Illinois

Frank Chance knew of Howard Thurston's engagement at the Majestic so he telephoned the theater and contacted him. Thurston welcomed hearing from Chance, a man whom he genuinely liked and respected. The magician offered Chance tickets for the eight o'clock show and suggested dinner afterwards. Frank took him up on both proposals.

Frank had attended Thurston's show once in Paris, but it now included many new illusions and improvements in other acts. Such changes drew his audiences back again and again. Tonight's show featured the girl within a box spectacle. As the audience filtered in they observed a small wooden chest, hoisted by ropes, near the theater's ceiling, fully eighty feet in the air. Many ticket-holders pointed to the box and drew it to the attention of their companions. That box remained hanging over the audience's heads through the entire show—its unveiling held until the last act that night.

Chance sat third row, center, alone, as his wife Edythe tended their ailing nephew on the North Side. He enjoyed Thurston's presentations, only a few of which he had witnessed before. Thurston opened the show by pouring a hundred gallons of milk out of one coconut. After a series of card tricks Thurston raised a black stallion thirty feet above the stage, on a broad wooden platform, and made it vanish. The audience literally gasped at the sight. The hypnotism segment intrigued Chance. He observed carefully as Thurston, in Frank's honor, had seven hypnotized subjects engage in a delightfully comedic baseball game, with imaginary bats and balls. Thurston's "Day at the Ballpark" act included a volunteer from the audience slamming a home run over the head of the center fielder and running gingerly about the bases.

For the final act, the magician borrowed a crimson scarf from a lady in the front row, wrapped it around the neck of a pretty female assistant, placed her in a large steel cannon pointed directly at the box on the ceiling, and fired the cannon. The "boom" of that cannon resounded through the cavernous theater, with white smoke billowing out of the mouth of the giant weapon.

Thurston then commanded his assistants: "Lower the chest."

Stagehands carefully lowered the box from its perch near the ceiling to the stage and Thurston quickly opened it. His two male assistants lifted a second box from inside the outer one, placing it next to the bigger box. As the assistants removed a third box, it opened, and out of it jumped the same woman who had just been fired out of the cannon! She removed the crimson scarf from her neck, returned it to the lady in the front row who verified its authenticity, and then bowed deeply as the audience applauded. Thurston bid them "Adieu" and the curtains closed for the evening.

In the third row a young man of thirty turned to his wife and suggested Thurston used twins for the final act. One twin spent the whole show in the box and the other pretended to be shot out of the cannon. His wife protested, "But the scarf around her neck…"

The man said, "Maybe the lady with the scarf was in on it?"

Another man, hearing this remark, pitched in. "No she weren't! That was my Aunt Mildred."

Chance and Thurston dined at the Palmer House Hotel restaurant after the show. They both spoke fondly of Paris—Chance spent three weeks there while Thurston performed for six months in that venue. Their wives had spent a good deal of time exploring Paris and its environs. They talked about a magnificent Parisian day the four of them had spent together, capped with a nighttime visit to the top of the Eiffel Tower. Thurston brought up the World Series but soon sensed that Chance preferred a different subject.

"Our club was the better team, Howard. We won 116 games in the regular season. Only lost thirty-six. That's the best record yet! We fully expected to win the Series. I knew my toughest job was gonna be to convince the boys it wouldn't be a walkover. We all lost a helluva lot of money that we bet on ourselves. So I guess it was my boys' own heads that did them in when it came to the Championship Series. Call it overconfidence, or taking too many things for granted, or whatever, we just could not perform in the Series like we did the whole season. We were running the bases with weights chained to our feet."

"The mind can help or hinder athletic performance. I suspect that an athlete who is performing at his peak is able to focus his psychic energy to propel him forward. Conversely, if the mind is not in harness with the body there is a chance that performance will suffer."

Chance nodded, and Thurston resumed.

"Frank, the game of baseball is a strange and unique enterprise. It is a team sport, correct?"

"Absolutely."

"Yet when the team assumes the defense, each member of the

team stands alone on the field. Alone in a discrete bounded area, relatively distant from his teammates. And on offense, one solitary member of the team faces off against all the defense. It's like a mixture of a team sport and an individual sport."

"Yeah, but every member of the team is connected, Howard. They're all connected by the ball. Trace the path of the ball through the game and you have the links between every player."

Moments later Chance startled Thurston.

"Howard, I want pennant *and* World Championship this year. I think you could help. What would you think about coming to work for us?"

April 14, 1907 Governors Island, New York

An Italian man with a small retinue came to visit Percy. He brought with him a beefy bodyguard named Vito. He gave the prison authorities the name of Martin DeVitalli. A member of New York's Black Hand, his friends and associates called him Caesar. The son of Neapolitans, DeVitalli arrived in America in 1878, a seven-year-old waif with a nose that never stopped running. His father, a cobbler, died of tuberculosis one year later, leaving the boy's mother to earn a meager living by washing clothes for her neighbors. Martin lived in a malodorous tenement with windows looking into a narrow air shaft that was slowly filling with garbage.

The child learned of life and gained his education on the streets of New York's lower East Side. In the beginning he stole to eat. Apples and vegetables to supplement the pasta his mother provided. Later he joined a gang called Vesuvio. These teenaged gangsters beat up other pimply young men and boys, helping themselves to their wallets and whatever else they carried. On occasion an attack of this sort yielded several dollars and a bag of new clothes but sometimes considerably less, such as the time when the gang bludgeoned the Negro Sammy Chase for a dime. But the risk was low because these incidents did not get reported to the police. And the boys truly enjoyed their work. Coming back after a hard night's work with bloodied knuckles was a badge of honor. Martin DeVitalli exhibited natural leadership qualities. By the time he turned twenty-two he ran Vesuvio. Around 1897 he realized that businessmen and others would pay money to Vesuvio to avoid beatings and attacks. "Protection money" soon provided a comfortable income for DeVitalli and his top lieutenants. His mother no longer needed to scrub sheets and linens.

Percy began. "I am deeply grateful that you have come to visit me here, Mr. DiVitalli."

DiVitalli smiled. The thirty-six-year-old man owned a full head of jet-black hair with gray just beginning to appear at the temples and on the edges of a small, well-trimmed mustache. His nose was large but not big enough to detract. He wore spectacles and a finely tailored green suit. "Please call me Caesar. I will call you Percy.'"

"Good. As is evident, Caesar, I am in need of your assistance. The army has made a terrible mistake and I am stuck here as a result."

"My nephew, Pasquale Aiuppa, also needed help. Your aid to Pasquale has earned you our gratitude. How can we assist you?"

"Do you have the acquaintance of any architects?"

April 14, 1907 Chicago, Illinois

As the players dressed for the game Husk and President Murphy escorted Howard Thurston into the clubhouse. He wore an expensive suit, carried a black cane, and had a sophisticated bearing about him. Thurston had not been in an athletic locker room since he was a child, and he was struck by the smell, a pungent amalgam of sweat, liniment, cigar smoke, and shoe polish. But before Husk could introduce him to the assembled Cubs, Kid Durbin burst out, "It's the Great Thurston!" Husk looked over to the Kid and said, "You got that right, Durbin." Turning to the group he stated, "I would like you gentlemen to meet a genius, a man of science, and a good friend. He is a master magician. In fact, those in the know would say he is the world's leading stage magician. Boys, meet the Great Thurston!"

Husk introduced Thurston to the entire crew. Then, in a serious tone, he stated: "Gentlemen, I think I have impressed on you how important it is for us to take advantage of every angle we can if it gets us even one step closer to our goal of World Championship. Well, the Great Thurston here offers us an avenue that can help us accomplish our goals."

At this point Jimmy Slagle asked, "What's he fixin' to do, Husk? Put a fog over the Giants' batsmen when Miner pitches?" A few guffaws greeted the remark.

Here Thurston interjected. "No, boys. Would that I had such

powers. But Frank has asked me for my assistance and I have devised a program that, as far as I know, has never been attempted in connection with any professional sport. I have given this considerable thought. I am talking about using the power of suggestion, the power of the mind, the power of thought. Think of hypnosis as a different form of sleep. In ordinary sleep, the mind is unleashed, free to wander as it pleases. You may have pleasant dreams or nightmares. Hypnotic sleep is different. The mind is leashed, focused by the operator, through the simple medium of suggestion. I am talking about harnessing the power of your minds to enhance your physical performance on the field. Our objective will be for each one of you to maximize your God-given talents, to be able to draw on 100 percent of your abilities at any given time. We will work on your minds like Trainer McCormick works on your muscles. It will be on a strictly volunteer basis, and your Peerless Leader has enthusiastically agreed to be the first volunteer."

One man rose to question the plan. Jack Taylor.

"And what if we think that hypno-pocus is a pile of crap, like some pygmy hoodoo?"

"Then you do not participate," replied Thurston. "But let me tell you something I usually mention when hypnosis is challenged as fakery. And that is animal hypnosis. Animals do not fake their responses to hypnosis. They are not capable of pretending to be hypnotized. They either are or they are not. And I am telling you that animals have been hypnotized on hundreds of occasions. One gentleman I had the privilege of meeting, a Hungarian named Volgyesi, hypnotized almost every animal in the Budapest Zoo. From a canary to a lion. A Frenchman hypnotized a flock of turkeys, turning them into rigid statues, forty of them, still and quiet until he undid his work. A living organism, whether it is a turkey or a pitcher, is subject to the same biological laws of nature. Hypnosis is real. I know that to be a fact. It can be used to help someone help themselves, to utilize every ounce of their talent."

April 14, 1907 Chicago, Illinois

Cold air, rain, and snow made it impossible to play the Cards on Friday and Saturday, forcing the scrapping of these games. But Sunday brought some sunshine even though the temperature clung to the low thirties. While the field remained damp and clumpy, Chance decided to play the game and pitch the Human Icicle, Lundgren. Chance penciled himself in at first despite suffering from a terrible cold. Pat Moran got the catching assignment as Husk still nursed some anger regarding Kling's holdout.

The Cardinals dressed at their hotel and took carriages to the game, complaining loudly to the press of the conditions in the visitors' clubhouse. Jake Beckley, thirty-nine-year-old veteran first baseman of the Cards and former drinking buddy of Jack Taylor, took one of the reporters aside. Jake, once a handsome man, now sported a mouth full of gold teeth, one crossed eye, and one of only three mustaches in the major leagues.

"You got one little room, one shower spigot, one small wash basin, and those lockers are vets of the War Between the States. And the place ain't even heated right. The cold damn near chilled us to death on Opening Day. It's a disgrace for a moneymaking championship club to provide these quarters."

Over ten thousand fans attended and the Icicle did not disappoint. He tossed a four-hit shutout, striking out eight batters and going the distance. Former Cub Fred Beebe, the Cardinals pitcher, did not do badly himself. But he gave up two runs, one more than the Cubs needed. Frank Chance scored the first run in the second inning, walking, advancing to second on a slow grounder, and then coming around on a sharp single by Solly Hofman. When he took his seat on the bench Chance realized he could not continue in the game—his sneezing and coughing kept growing in intensity. So he put Johnny Kling out at first base and tried to keep warm at one end of the bench, but his misery grew as the day wore on.

After the game the Cubs clubhouse had a visit from a very familiar face, Joe Tinker, on his feet again. He threw his arms around Chance and proclaimed his readiness to return. The team mobbed the shortstop and asked to see the scar from his operation. Joe obliged. Tinker met the new boys, Durbin, Osborn, Seabaugh, Sweeney, and Randall. Learning that Sweeney played short, Tinker quipped, "For your sake, I hope you can play some other positions as well."

A small crowd gathered around Tinker but Johnny Evers stayed across the room, carefully tying his necktie and adjusting his vest. A vague tune came whistling out of Evers's mouth, but he did not say a word to Tinker. Never even looked in his direction.

President Murphy asked to be present at the first session, when Thurston hypnotized Frank Chance. Neither Chance nor Thurston objected, so Chubby Murphy and Chance traveled together to the Palmer House Hotel, where Thurston resided on his lengthy Chicago sojourn. Thurston had a double suite on the fifth floor, and had prepared the premises comfortably for his stay. Pictures of Thurston and his wife sat on the tables.

All three gentlemen wore suits and ties, and Chance greeted Thurston warmly in the anteroom. Chance introduced Murphy to Thurston and the three reclined in sumptuous armchairs.

"I can offer you a glass of water, Frank. I do not want you to drink alcohol just now."

Husk took him up on the water.

"Let's talk about what I plan to do, both with you and your players. First, you should know that I have used hypnosis in my act and in other endeavors for about fifteen years now. None of my subjects, to my knowledge, has ever been injured or suffered detrimental consequences from my induction of hypnosis. To the contrary, most of my subjects feel pleasantly refreshed and invigorated after a session. Second, the key to hypnotizing a person is their cooperation. If you or a certain pitcher does not want to be hypnotized and refuse to cooperate, I cannot assert my skills against that will. Third, I cannot make your players into something they are not. Consider the man who runs to first base on ten occasions— and the times range from 4.3 seconds to 5 seconds. I cannot make that man run to first base in four seconds. What I can do is to get that man to run to first base in 4.3 seconds more often than he would have without my intervention. The goal is to get your players to play at their peak."

"So you won't be able to increase the speed on Miner's fastball?" Chance jested.

"No," answered Thurston. "No such luck. But we should be able to keep him pitching crisp fastballs longer into the game, and perhaps we can assist his control, reducing the number of bases on balls a tad."

"Yeah, you should also work on the wildness aspect with Durbin," Chance mentioned.

"Very well. Shall we begin?"

From the Journal of Kid Durbin

I am writing this late at night, in my apartment in Chicago. This is another day that I never want to forget. Husk finally allowed the Zeephos—that's me and the other subs and yannigans—to play the regulars in a real game. We Zeephos took the field at 2:30 this afternoon, although we needed a few vets to fill out our squad. Our skipper for this affair, Jack Taylor, put Lundgren out in right field, Kling at first, and Chick Fraser at second base. Chick volunteered for second because he said he'd fooled around at second on a semipro team before he started pitching. On the mound for the Zeephos was a dashing young lefty from Lamar, Missouri, a redheaded kid with a wicked curve. Me.

Even though the winds blew frosty cold, about four thousand bugs attended—maybe because the admission price was only two bits. Jimmy "Pony" Ryan, an outfielder for Cap Anson's championship teams, served as umpire and did a bang-up job of it. I decided to go flat out so Husk could see what I had. It's too bad that he still had his cold and didn't take the field 'cause I sure would have enjoyed pitching to him. But I did get to face Evers, the three S's, Moran, Steiny, and Circus Solly. And I did my job, besting Big Ed who threw for the regular squad. I pitched five innings and gave up no runs. They only made two hits off of me! I knew I would be okay after my first couple of warmup pitches. The fastball had some pop on it and the curveball curved sweetly. I heard Jimmy Ryan talking to the sports writers after the game, which we won 5-2, and he said, "Young Durbin pitched great ball. And the way his shoots and benders took effect was wonderful." I copied these words down exact so I would have them forever. I am going to write my father and Connie now and share all of this with them. I probably will leave out the part about the two guys I hit with pitches—Shorty Slagle and Frank Schulte.

Two more things: The rule is that the players get to split all exhibition game gate receipts 50-50 with the club. The players' share of the gate today amounted to five hundred dollars or so and as a result I am getting an extra twenty dollars. This is money I truly earned.

After the game Chance informed me that I would not make the trip to Pittsburgh with the Cubs since I had pitched today and wouldn't be available to pitch against the Pirates. He told Big Ed the same thing so I didn't feel bad, but three other guys who aren't traveling east, Kahoe, Sweeney, and Osborn, took this as a bad sign, like writing on the wall. Sweeney said to me, "Does make a guy wonder if he's gonna be with the club a whole lot longer."

April 17, 1907 Pittsburgh, Pennsylvania

A month earlier a terrible flood inundated Pittsburgh. The water rose more than ten feet in parts of the city and covered the diamond at Exposition Park, the left field wall of which sat only a hundred yards from the north shore of the Allegheny River. Pittsburgh still stunk from the muck, mold, and mildew. But industrial Pittsburgh always smelled from the steel mills. The never-ending smoke and grimy soot, which often masked the sun at midday, earned it the label Smoky City. Cold weather still plagued the Cubs, threatening the Wednesday game. A light snow even dropped on the area in the morning but the groundsmen cleared the field by game time, when the temperature peaked at thirty-five degrees.

Chance selected Jack Taylor to face off against the Pirates and their great star, Honus Wagner. Always seeking an edge, Chance knew that Taylor could usually handle Wagner.

During pre-game practice, the Cubs, particularly the yannigans, paid close attention to the Flying Dutchman, already a legend and anointed "the best shortstop that ever played the game." But, truth be told, Wagner did not look like a ballplayer. Ace sportswriter Fred Lieb described him as "a bulging, squat giant." A massive chest, two trunk-like legs bowed out like he was straddling a barrel, long arms with huge hands, he looked like a hairless ape. A plain face with a square jaw, he had a large nose set off by hooded eyes and thin lips. Wagner gave off the image of a good-natured salesman uncle. Frequently munching on a chaw of tobacco, with scrap (loose tobacco) bulging one pocket of his pants, he was neither graceful on the field nor a sight that appealed to the women in the stands.

But he covered the shortstop position with lightning quick moves and a facile efficiency, scooping up ground balls along with chunks of infield dirt and gravel with large, long-fingered hands, and flinging the ball and the debris together to first base. The former Pirates first-sacker, Kitty Bransfield, said, "I just tried to catch the largest object headed my way!" Wagner's mitt-like hands served him well. On post-season barnstorming tours, Honus sometimes delighted the crowds by removing his glove and fielding his position with bare hands.

Wagner owned an extraordinarily powerful arm. Once, slipping on the perennially muddy infield at the Pirates' ballpark while cornering a groundball at deep short, he fell onto his ass, embedded in four inches of mud. From that position he launched a bullet to first to nip the runner.

Wagner quickly earned a reputation as the finest fielding shortstop to play the game. Yet Wagner's hitting skills exceeded his defensive abilities. Using one of the heaviest thick-handled bats made, he hit .381 as a rookie and ultimately won eight batting championships. Baseballs shot off the muscular German's bat like rockets. The strange-looking Pirate came alive on the base paths, leading the circuit in stolen bases in 1901, 1902, and 1904. He possessed decent speed, running low and close to the ground, but the stolen bases came more from his adept ability to read the pitcher's moves and his mastery of the art of the hook slide. Not a wild, mean-spirited baserunner like Ty Cobb, but coldly efficient, Wagner maintained that he could always find a "tell" in the pitcher's windup that would give away whether the moundsman intended to throw to first or the plate. The Dutchman stole more than seven hundred bases in his career. He possessed a keen sense of the game. John McGraw said he had "the quickest baseball brain I have ever observed."

Frank Chance suggested a game plan to the Brakeman to deal with Wagner. "Use the cold to your advantage, Jack. Come in on the Dutchman. Inside, on the hands. Show him the outside pitch, but make it way off the plate so he won't be tempted. Then come back in on him. Jam the fucker."

Over the left field wall barges cruised lazily down the Allegheny River, while across the river in downtown Pittsburgh smokestacks poured dense black smoke into the air. The winds blew stiffly as a small crowd shivered in the stands, waiting impatiently for the start of the contest. The first two Cubs batsmen grounded out to begin the game. Vic Willis, a tall veteran righty with expressive eyes and a long, straight nose, threw for the Buccaneers.

Frank Schulte sauntered to the batter's box as the third hitter. The Cubs outfielder adopted an unusual batting approach for the deadball era. One of the first free-swingers, he used a forty-ounce, thin-handled bat and gripped it at the base rather than choking up on it. To the consternation of the cost-conscious Cubs, Frank broke fifty bats a year, but he would not shift to the thick-handled lumber all his teammates used. Schulte usually waited until the last possible instant before snapping his bat through the zone. Johnny Evers said Frank possessed a "lightning cut."

Willis possessed a first-rate curveball and just a decent fastball. He wasted two curves, although one cut the corner for a strike. But then the Buc pitcher grooved a fastball that Frank got around on, blasting it over the head of left fielder/manager Fred Clarke. Schulte really poked this one because Clarke always positioned himself deep in left—he had trouble going back on fly balls and preferred to run in on balls hit his way. The ball rolled all the way to the outfield fence, some four hundred feet from the plate, and Schulte easily beat the relay throw for a home run. One player on the Cubs bench did not cheer as outfielder Clarke chased after the ball. Chick Fraser sat quiet, since Clarke was his brother-in-law!

The first time Wagner came to bat the Brakeman dug in on the mound, determined to get the best of the Pirate star. As always, the right-handed hitting Dutchman positioned himself all the way back in the outside corner of the batter's box, as far from the plate as possible. This gave him the room, he told his teammates, to stride into the ball while fully extending his arms. His legs were spread wide apart, maybe five feet. The burly Pirate began to wave the bat toward the pitcher in small circles, until Taylor began his delivery. The first pitch came way in on him and he took it for a ball. The next pitch also flew inside, but Wagner, with the weight on his back foot, strode into the ball with his left leg, swinging at the same time, and fouling it back of the plate. He didn't miss it by much. Taylor wasted the next delivery, a curve that sailed outside for ball two. The fourth offering, designed to come in on the Dutchman's fists, missed the mark—he swung and hit it solid but the ball darted right at Steinfeldt at third who caught the line drive before it hit the dirt. Taylor realized that only Lady Luck and Steiny's quick reflexes prevented the ball from ending up in left field. After tipping his cap to his third baseman, Taylor reminded himself to bring it in closer to Wagner next time, even if he ended up nailing him.

Taylor pitched fine and scrambled out of the few jams that arose. Wagner did little that day against the Brakeman, who pitched a complete game and held the Pirates to two runs while the Cubs managed to push six tallies across the plate.

"I still got it in me," Taylor told the reporters after the contest.

"And on you," retorted one of the boys, referring to a few extra pounds Brakeman had picked up along the way.

"Well, ask the Dutchman about my stuff. See what he says."

Three Chicago reporters did talk to Wagner, who conceded that Taylor got the best of the Pirates that day. "But there's another hundred and fifty games to play," Wagner commented, "we're just startin' here." The Dutchman then invited the newsmen to accompany him to a local saloon. "It's on me," he told them.

April 18, 1907 **Pittsburgh, Pennsylvania**

Two huge four-sided Queen Anne Towers jutted up into the sky at the entrance to Exposition Park. The name "Pittsburg" was spelled out across the bleachers, "Pittsburg" without the "h" at the end because in 1890 the United States government ordered all cities with names ending in "burgh" to drop the "h." A young hurler on the rise, Albert "Lefty" Leifield, stalked nervously about the mound, wearing a white home uniform with a red "P" on the jersey pocket, and long, blue stockings with a horizontal red stripe in the middle. The 6'1" Leifield produced his first solid season in 1906, going 18-13 with a 1.87 ERA. But his opponent for the day's contest, Miner Brown, pitched the Cubs to a World Series in '06, going 26-6 and leading the league with a 1.04 ERA.

Umpire Hank O'Day stood behind the plate, the sole referee that day. A dour Irishman and former National League pitcher, O'Day earned a reputation as a courageous arbiter, never favoring a boisterous home crowd as weaker men did. The game started out like neither team would be able to score but in the bottom of the third the Pirates got lucky. Their first batter, catcher Ed "Yaller" Phelps, lobbed an easy fly ball out to Rabbit Slagle. Jimmy waited for the ball, corralled it in his glove, and tried to make a quick throw all at the same time. The ball slipped out of his fingers and umpire O'Day said he didn't have possession long enough to constitute an out. Chance steamed and jawed but O'Day would not budge. Chance almost got himself ejected at this point, calling umpire O'Day a "fuckin' stupe." But O'Day did not react. As a result of this call, Phelps ended up on second base, advanced to third on a sacrifice, and trotted home when Goat Anderson pushed a gentle bunt past Brownie, out to Husk by first base. That one run is all it took as Leifield responded masterfully any time the Cubs landed a base runner. Miner Brown gave up only two hits but Slagle's miscue resulted in the 1-0 defeat.

President Murphy met with the news reporters an hour after the final out, but did not want to talk about the game. Instead he chose to respond to the press reports of the Cardinals' complaints regarding the visitors' dressing room at the West Side Grounds.

"I spent over six hundred dollars fitting up quarters for visiting teams on the West Side," Murphy stated, "so the Cardinal crabs will find them better than visiting teams' quarters in other cities. St. Louis has provided no quarters whatever for visitors at its grounds."

Frank Chance echoed this sentiment. "The Cardinals were sore over not getting a game out of us, and had to kick on something."

Jack Taylor, who had pitched for the Cardinals the year before,

Jack Taylor, who had pitched for the Cardinals the year before, offered his views on the controversy. "Those fuckers ought to keep their mouths shut and play ball or they might just end up with less teeth than they got now."

Chubby Murphy also responded to press inquiries regarding possible trades. He revealed that the Cubs had an offer from the Boston Doves to purchase Fred Osborn and that Pirate owner Barney Dreyfuss had expressed interest in Warren Seabaugh. But Murphy suggested that nothing had progressed very far on these fronts as yet. One of the reporters asked if Kid Durbin might be dealt away. Murphy stated, "All offers for Durbin will be refused."

From the Journal of Kid Durbin

April 20, 1907

It is more difficult than I thought to stay here in Chicago while the team is out east. Each day I read the Tribune and the Courier to keep up but it doesn't give me too much to go on. Yesterday's paper, on the other hand, might have given me too much—it really packed a punch. The paper reported a tough loss as a result of Shorty Slagle dropping one. But the Tribune also quoted President Murphy talking about trading or selling Fred Osborn and Warren Seabaugh. I got this lump in my throat when I read that. And I am sure that Warren and Fred must have felt like they got kicked in the behind when they heard about it. But in the same story Mr. Murphy said he would refuse all offers on me. That sure did allow me to sleep better last night.

I telephoned Mrs. Murphy today about Connie and she said that nothing in her condition had changed. She said that the doctor hoped some new medicines might do the trick. I am very worried about Connie but Mrs. Murphy doesn't think it would be helpful for me to visit her now so I have to bide my time. I continue to think that Connie is a strong girl who can fight this problem and beat it.

Mr. Thurston has given me two "treatments" in the last couple of days, along with Lundgren, Sweeney, and Osborn. Mike Kahoe is here in Chicago too but he has declined the sessions, saying "old dogs get dizzy from new tricks." The four of us go to the Palmer House for our sessions and we have lunch together after. Sometimes we all go to the Palmer House barbershop for a trim, a delightful place to get your hair cut because the floor is tiled with silver dollars. As for the sessions with Mr. Thurston, like when I transformed into a rooster on stage at the Majestic, I do not recall much of what takes place. Mr. Thurston says I am a good subject. Meaning he can hypnotize me in a snap and do all the suggestion stuff without a whole lot of preliminaries. I still have confidence that he can help me improve my game.

It's strange. Even though I received a good deal of coaching from my manager in the Western League, the guy who taught me more about pitching than anyone else was my buddy Bucky Gunderson back in Lamar. Probably 'cause I had a whole lot more to learn in those days. Bucky taught me the elementary stuff, how to hold the ball and how to use the seams, when we were fourteen. He showed me how to snap off a curve with the twist of my wrist. His advice hit right on the mark. Said he learned it from a blacksmith who played semipro ball for his hometown in West Virginia. On a great many summer days we played catch for hours, taking turns as pitcher and catcher. Since we both wanted to pitch first, I would spit on a flat stone and toss it up in the air. Bucky would call it "wet" or "dry" and that would determine who went first. We'd play until the sweat poured out of us in torrents and then we'd race down to Maddy Kelvin's swimming hole. I'll never forget those days.

Bucky and I both pitched for the Lamar Grange Association. Saturday mornings would find eighteen young men spread out on a green grass field under that blue Missouri sky. All wrapped up in a game so that nothing else mattered 'cept the game itself and whether that dark cloud might drop some rain on us. Those games took us away from the problems of our ordinary lives, like whether I should send Sears Roebuck and Company that $8.92 for a new wooden icebox. Bucky, being smaller than me, couldn't get the speed on the ball like I could so he got nicked for a lot of hits when he threw something besides his curve. Time passed and Bucky got sucked into his family's undertaking business while I went off to pitch professionally. I should write Bucky but it don't hold with me to sound like I'm showing off. I think I will just thank him for teaching me how to pitch and for being a good friend and all.

"Ossie" (Fred Osborn), Billy Sweeney, and I met in the Loop yesterday for an adventure. We had two goals: link up with a friend of Billy's who lived a mile south and visit the Levee District, a natural destination for fellows our age and inclination. But rather than hop on a train we walked, and, for the hell of it, we chose not to stick to the main streets. We got more than just a glimpse of the real Chicago. These back streets themselves shocked us, strewn as they were with debris, manure, and garbage. Sometimes we could see patches of the rutted and rotting wooden

pavement (Billy Sweeney said these were cedar blocks) beneath the clutter but many of the streets lacked pavement. Shabby gray tenement build-ings, three and four stories high, lined the streets on both sides, with car-tons of garbage and overflowing trash cans sitting on the curbs. Wooden sidewalks fronted the buildings but often these walkways were ripped up or dangerously splintered. Raggedy men with pushcarts methodically searched through the mounds of garbage and the cans as if they held bur-ied treasure. Street urchins—little kids in tattered clothes—popped out of basements and discarded cartons to beg us for money. Sometimes we gave them some pennies and a few times they thanked us.

Shortly before we reached our first destination we saw two kids, maybe thirteen years old or so, jump another boy in a blue jacket across the street from us. They began to pummel their prey. We started to cross over to help the boy but he didn't need our assistance. A tough little bastard, he managed to keep knocking the other boys down. An ice wagon, drawn by an old horse with blinders, clattered up to the fight and the driver began to applaud and scream encouragement to the kid in blue. After another moment the instigators ran off and the boy, not much the worse for the wear, climbed up on the ice wagon to sit next to the driver. Billy asked the ice wagon driver what was going on.

"Dose Polacks leaved their neighborhood to come after my boy, Albert," said the driver. "Next time dey will need to bring more Polacks, no?"

We found the tenement where Billy's friend from Kentucky lived and sure enough, the postal box inside listed James Fox as residing on the fourth floor. Up we went, a dark, narrow staircase, which sported rotting celery and a pool of urine on the third floor landing. The stench hung in the air and almost knocked us down. The top floor had no light whatsoever. One of the apartments had its door open so we knocked and entered. The place, one room and a small kitchen, seemed empty, but we heard a noise in the corner. I figured it might be a rat but we found a baby, maybe two or four months old, wrapped in rags and sleeping in a pile of linens and newspapers. We knocked on the door of the next flat and asked if they knew about the baby all alone next door. An old man with white hair said, "Sure, that'd be Maggy's little-un." He said the

240

mother "mopped floors downtown, in the employ of the sobbering State of Illinois." Evidently he looked in on the child every once in a while. He also told us that Jimmy Fox had taken off for Wisconsin on business so we never did make that connection.

On the way to the Levee the three of us talked about life in those tenements.

I said, "Folks in those tenements are as poor as Job's turkey."

"It's worse," Billy stated. "Those buildings are death traps. Dirty and smelly. One man or woman gets consumption and it spreads through the whole place. Heard a fellow once call one of those places a 'lung building' after the tuberculosis killed seventeen people there. They got no toilets, no baths. The tenants throw their shit into the air shafts. And if you wanna bathe you have to go stand in a line for the city bath over on Jefferson and Canal. It's a goddam shame."

Nights can get very lonely here. Beer helps lighten up things a little. There is a saloon by the name of "Teddy's" right on the block where I live. It has what I call the "saloon stink," the product of ten thousand cigars, one hundred thousand streams of tobacco juice spittle, and sawdust, all blended together with alcohol. So it may smell but it's got a friendly air about it and the bartender/owner, whose name is George and not Teddy, is a strong rooter of the Cubs. Which means I usually get at least one free round a visit. The only beer they sell there is Peerless because George has a contract with the Peerless Brewing Company and they don't allow him to sell any other brand. Peerless isn't my favorite, but I may eventually acquire a taste for it.

Yesterday I visited a nickelodeon to kill an hour or so. The moving pictures usually do not appeal to me a whole lot more than the opera. At least the title cards are in English. But one of the films did knock me over, a long one—maybe nine or ten minutes—entitled "The Modern Pirates." It wasn't about the Pittsburgh team. Instead, some nasty criminals manufactured an armored motor vehicle that allowed them to rob and steal with impunity. They pulled into one town and swept up all *the town chickens in a collector at the front end of the vehicle. The police bullets just bounced off this fearsome motor car and the rotten men inside it shot and killed half the townsfolk from within. When this armored vehicle sunk in a river and all its occupants drowned, half the people in the theater, including me, got up on their feet and applauded. But I felt bad for the chickens.*

Last night, while walking home from "Teddy's," I slipped back into thinking about Maud Livingston from New Orleans. I really thought I smelled her perfume. Just thinking about her made me want to lay again with a prostitute (and do some other stuff too!) but I obtained release the other way—a lot cheaper and far less complicated.

One more thing. I continue to drink the Sprudel Water religiously, at least three one-quart bottles daily. I ordered a load of the stuff because it settles my system and keeps me strong. I learned that Spring No. 7, the source of the Sprudel Water, only dated back to 1892 when geologists first uncovered it. The West Baden Springs Company ships me the twenty-four quart cases for $2.50 per case plus seventy-five cents a case shipping fee, and I get a fifty-cent rebate when I ship the empty case of bottles back to Indiana or their Chicago office. I have twenty cases in my apartment and I intend to acquire, when I can afford it, a whole lot more. I may store the water in Lamar. By my calculations I am paying about thirty-five cents daily for the Sprudel Water, a tall price, but my health is worth it.

The Pirates called off yesterday's game due to "inclement weather." Snow showers and freezing rain made it impossible to play a game in which hands, fingers, and toes play important roles. Falling snow mixed with the soot spewed out by the steel mill chimneys and came down gray and speckled. The players had suited up to perform but learned of the rainout at two o'clock. Frank Chance commanded the whole team to change into their street clothes and then accompany him to a saloon he knew one block from the park.

"I'm buying," he announced.

The rookies learned that Chance frequently did this sort of thing on rainy afternoons. All the players took advantage of the Peerless Leader's generosity, although Evers, Kling, and Reulbach stuck to Coca-Cola.

Cold air still blanketed Pittsburgh twenty-four hours later, but the snow stopped falling and the ground, while slippery in the outfield, offered enough traction to get the game in. Frank Chance again called on Carl Lundgren, the Human Icicle, to work his frosty magic. Johnny Kling got his first start of the year at catcher while Artie Hofman manned shortstop for Tinker, who had remained in Chicago. The three S's patrolled the outfield, the fourth S (Steinfeldt) hunkered down at third base, and Husk and the Crab took their normal positions.

The box score reveals how the Cubs grabbed an easy victory, plating five runs on six Pirate errors, nine hits, and three walks. Meanwhile, Lundgren held the opposition to five hits and one run.

One play in the top of the sixth raised the ire of Husk and Steinfeldt. Steiny opened the inning with a line drive down the left field line. He scampered round the bases, ending up on third base. Circus Solly Hofman, the next batter, hit a wicked liner between short and third. Wagner leaped to grab it, batted it down, but Solly beat the toss to first and Steiny wisely held at third. Evers then fouled out on a tough inside pitch that he didn't mean to swing at. Chance signaled Kling to lay down a squeeze bunt and Steiny prepared to scoot home on the play. As soon as Kling deftly pushed it down the right side, Steiny took off for home plate. At least he tried to. But Tommy Leach, the Pirate third baseman, grabbed hold of Steinfeldt's belt from behind, and the only umpire officiating the game, Hank O'Day, didn't catch it as he trained his eyes on the ball over at first base. Steiny finally broke loose and sped toward home but the throw from the first baseman beat him. Steinfeldt and Husk protested to O'Day to no avail. Back in the dugout Husk looked at Steinfeldt and shook his head.

"Harry, you've done the same thing to base runners many times, right?"

"Yes. Anytime I think I can get away with it."

"So then you oughta anticipate that the other guy is gonna do it to you. And make sure it don't happen to you. Make sense?"

"Yes, Cap'n. Won't happen again."

The eighth inning began with Steinfeldt cracking a triple in the gap between left and center. Artie Hofman came to bat determined to plate Steiny. Artie's normally large brown eyes grew larger as the first pitch sailed right down the middle. He swung evenly but did not hit it square—a fly ball shot up in the air to center, deep enough to give Steiny a fair chance to score. When the ball dropped into the outfielder's glove, Steinfeldt started for home plate, just then feeling third baseman Leach's grubby hand loop into his belt from behind. But Steinfeldt had unhitched his belt buckle a few seconds earlier, so Leach ended up standing at the bag with Steinfeldt's belt in hand while Harry made it home to score. Players on both benches laughed at the sight of little Tommy Leach stuck holding Harry's blue belt. Leach tossed the belt to Chance in the coacher's box while umpire O'Day shook his head disapprovingly.

The Cubs caught a nine o'clock sleeper for Cincinnati. At the station President Murphy told the press that the deals to sell Osborn and Seabaugh collapsed and Husk joked that "it's still possible for us to win 153."

The Era   Baseball and Show Business

Nobody ever described Harry Steinfeldt as a bright man. A fine hitter and a great defensive third baseman, he had an incredibly strong throwing arm. But while Harry excelled on the field he lacked common sense and good judgment. As Evers put it, "Harry ain't always home, upstairs." Nor did Steinfeldt have the benefit of much formal education. He was born in 1877, in St. Louis, Missouri, his father a German immigrant. His family relocated to Fort Worth, Texas, around 1882, and Harry ran away from home to join a minstrel show when still a teenager.

Outside of alcohol and prostitution, the minstrel show became the most popular male entertainment of the nineteenth century. White men, and on a few occasions, black men, painted their faces black with greasepaint or burnt cork and took to the stage to mock black culture, lampoon African-Americans, and make racist jokes, all to the beat of song and dance and to the delight of the white audiences. Under the cover of black face-paint, white men engaged in otherwise forbidden acts. Three recurring characters appeared in the traveling minstrel shows: "Mr. Tambo," an exuberant musician, twirling his tambourine and fiddling a fiddle; "Jim Crow," an athletic, carefree slave; and "Zip Coon," a free Negro, who put on airs, lacked self-control, and always failed in his attempts to rise above his station in life. Mark Twain spoke highly of the "old time nigger show," and included minstrels in *Tom Sawyer*.

In the mid-1890s Steinfeldt toured with Al Field's minstrel show for several years, donning the black face and singing the songs of his troupe. While playing Jim Crow in Texas and singing *Dixie* three times a day, Harry tried out for a local ballclub and discovered he had a talent for baseball that could earn him a living without having to paint his face. In 1895 he jumped to the Fort Worth team in the Texas League, debuted as a major leaguer with the Reds in 1898, and never looked back. But Steiny never forgot the old routines. With four or five beers fueling him, Harry could be convinced to perform Jim Crow's most famous soliloquy:

> *First on de heel tap,*
> *Den on de toe.*
> *Eb'ry time I wheel about*
> *I jump Jim Crow.*
> *Wheel about and turn about*
> *An do jes so,*
> *An eb'ry time I wheel about*
> *I jump Jim Crow.*

When drunk, Harry performed the Jim Crow dance that he'd done in the minstrel show across the Midwest and the South. Inflating his lungs, Harry belted out the old songs over and over until he passed out or found himself alone. One night he told the story of his last days as a minstrel to Frank Chance.

"Maybe it was '95 or thereabouts. I had a powerful hankering to do somethin' else. My boss, Mr. Fields, introduced us to a new member of the troupe, a guy I'd never heard of but I should of. Name was Daniel

Emmett, a real old coot. I mean old like in the Bible, Mefoolsalot old. Eighty years old he was! The best minstrel performer I ever seen. Al told me he was maybe the first minstrel ever! Turns out he wrote *Dixie* and *Turkey in the Straw*. You know those songs—everybody does. Sure, I felt honored meetin' Mr. Emmett. But I didn't want to end up like him, you know, touring them one-horse Texas towns like Toadsuck and Bucksnort for thirty dollars a week and train fare. Then the chance came to play ball for a living. I grabbed hold. Never even told Mr. Fields I was quitting."

Many major leaguers, like Harry, performed on the stage as well as on the diamond. Dozens of professional ballplayers supplemented their baseball incomes with vaudeville appearances, perhaps starting with former Chicago White Stockings great Michael "King" Kelly reciting "Casey at the Bat" on the stage of the Palace Theater. Other ballplayers, including Joe Tinker, Ty Cobb, and Christy Mathewson, followed in his steps. Eastern promoters paid John McGraw three thousand dollars a week for fifteen weeks to mount the stage and recite anecdotes. While some elements of society looked upon both ballplayers and show people with a jaundiced eye, the vaudeville audiences demanded to see their athlete heroes up close and were more than willing to pay for that privilege.

New York Giants' "Turkey" Mike Donlin presented a curious example of the ballplayer/stage performer. Donlin, a handsome, talented, and troubled outfielder, could hit but he could also drink. Enjoying showgirls and alcohol more than baseball, he missed most of the 1902 baseball season serving a six-month jail sentence for assaulting two chorus girls and urinating in public. He was thrown in jail in 1906 for attacking a conductor and waving a pistol in the face of a waiter on a train while in a drunken rage. "Mr. Gun talks loud," he proclaimed. Donlin played only twelve years in the majors but his career batting average of .333 ranks him in the top twenty-five of all time. But vaudeville—not alcohol—cut short this great hitter's career. Donlin missed the entire 1907 campaign, abandoning McGraw's New York Giants, to team up with his wife, songstress and comedienne Mabel Hite, in an extremely successful road show. Missing that season did not impair Turkey Mike's batting eye, as he hit .334 when he returned to the Giants in 1908. The lure of the greasepaint again took Mike away from the game for the 1909 and 1910 seasons. Donlin again came back to baseball in 1911 and again surpassed the .300 mark. Vaudeville proved more financially rewarding to Turkey Mike than baseball. Donlin's wife Mabel died of cancer at age twenty-seven, in 1912. After her untimely death, Donlin's close friend John Barrymore helped Mike begin a silent film career, which ultimately led to appearances in more than forty films, including baseball reels like *Slide, Kelly, Slide.* An early teammate of Donlin's, Ossee "Schreck" Schreckengost, once told Turkey Mike that he had "a million dollar arm and a ten-cent head." Donlin, sober enough to realize the remark had hit the nail on the head, took offense and beat Schreck senseless.

April 21, 1907   Cincinnati, Ohio

The schedule must have been drawn up by a drunk. It called for the Cubs to travel from the Smoky City to Cincinnati for a one-game "series" with the Reds, and then for the Reds, the Cubs, and umpires Carpenter and Johnstone to hop on the same train and journey to Chicago for three games in the West Side Grounds. The teams caught a break, weather-wise, in Cincinnati. The temperature zoomed and so did the attendance, some eighteen thousand Ohioans making their way into the Palace of the Fans, a concrete and wooden stadium designed to resemble a Greek temple, with white Corinthian-style columns supporting the grandstands. Though only five years old, Cincinnati building inspectors complained of its decayed supporting structures, cracked girders, and dangerous flooring. The stadium, built in an industrial area adjacent to the Crystal Oil Company, featured concrete opera boxes called "Fashion Boxes" that overhang the field and sold for a significant premium.

The crowd overflowed the stadium this day, occupying much of foul territory down both the lines. Encroaching on the field, the unruly fans delayed the start of the game twenty minutes, until the police managed to push them back. On the Reds' bench sat their mascot, a ten-year-old black boy named Ralph, garbed in a loud pink outfit and a red cap. Before each Reds batter headed to the plate he would vigorously rub Ralph's head of hair for luck. If a Reds ballplayer got a double he might give Ralph a nickel after the game. Charlie Dryden, the sportswriter, brought a huge smile to the face of Harry Steinfeldt by telling him, "That coon looks like a strawberry sundae topped with a prune."

A legend managed the Reds. Forty-nine-year-old "Foxy Ned" Hanlon gained fame and fortune managing the rough and tumble Baltimore Orioles to three National League championships in the 1890s, with players like John McGraw, Wee Willie Keeler, and Hughie Jennings. The Orioles under Ned Hanlon, harkening back to Charles Comiskey's St. Louis Browns of the early 1880s, played "Inside Baseball," moving runners around the bases in carefully crafted moves—sacrifice bunts, squeeze plays, and double steals—capitalizing on game situations. Hanlon's Orioles may have invented the hit-and-run play and some less than ethical moves, such as having the base runner go from first to third directly, straight across the infield, when the umpire was distracted. The Orioles also, on occasion, concealed spare baseballs in the tall outfield grass and shined mirrors into the eyes of opposing batters. Hanlon, and McGraw after him, also espoused what they called "disorganizing baseball," a rough and rowdy game with spikings and umpire-baiting, all calculated to upset the opposing team's game plan. In addition to his legendary success with the Orioles, the savvy Hanlon won two championships with the Brooklyn team in 1899 and 1900. But now Hanlon piloted the hapless Reds, off to a 3-3 start and not figured to contend. In fact, quipsters said that Cincinnati was famous for having the first professional baseball team back in 1869 but the city hadn't had one since.

Manager Hanlon experimented with his pitching staff, selecting rookie Cotton Minahan to make his major league debut against the National League Champion Chicago Cubs. The kid had never pitched in front of more than five hundred fans in his life, and today thousands of vocal rooters leered at the boy and closed in on him from all sides. At least that's how he perceived it. Worse, several Cubs sized up the situation correctly, and bullyragged the yannigan.

"Did you bring your suitcase with ya, rube? The one you'll need to take you home to mama after the game?"

Evers, in his high-pitched screech designed to drive men mad, let him have it right before his first pitch. "You ain't gonna throw strikes today kid! You're a busher!" The abuse continued throughout the game.

Unnerved by the situation, Minahan pitched a wild and wobbly five innings, giving up six walks and three runs.

Orvie Overall threw well for the Cubs. He had pitched for the Reds the year before and he wanted to show his old teammates—particularly his buddy Hans Lobert—how much he had progressed. His performance was marred by three unearned runs resulting from a sixth inning error by Hofman at short.

In the seventh, Overall faced a tough left-handed batter while the locals grew uneasy. Behind the plate Kling placed his index finger straight down and then moved it to a horizontal position above the catcher's glove. Out near second base Evers, learning that a high, outside fastball was coming, dipped his hands into the infield dirt, signaling Hofman of the pitch, who tapped his right hand on his mitt, indicating he understood. Evers next put his ungloved hand on his right hip, to signal left fielder Sheckard of the impending outside fastball. Informed, Sheckard moved closer to the left field line. As Overall wound up, Evers yelled over to Chance and Hofman alerted Steinfeldt so that as the ball came out of the pitcher's hands, the infield edged left, into the expected trajectory of the ball. The ball met the bat and sailed out to Sheckard, two steps from where he stood.

Twice in the game Frank Chance barely avoided serious injury. In the fourth he and Kling collided going after a foul ball, and Frank had the wind knocked out of him. He bent over, gasped for breath, but hung onto the ball. Later, in the sixth, Hans Lobert, the Reds' blue-eyed thirdsacker, bunted his pal Overall's first pitch and barrelled into the Cubs manager at first base after a high throw. Lobert did not intentionally stride into Chance—the two drank together in the past, as Husk had managed Lobert briefly in '05. Lobert still respected him. Hans asked Husk if he had been hurt after the incident. He said, "I'm good." But back on the bench, Evers observed a large bruise on Chance's left arm. In the end, the Cubs earned another victory.

No one noticed an event at the top of the eighth inning, as the Cubs prepared to come to bat. Frank Chance stood calmly in front of the Cubs bench, slowly surveying the Palace of the Fans and the two contesting teams under the arc of a blue and white-clouded sky. The trace of a warm smile crossed the Peerless Leader's face. Maybe it was the fluid way Johnny Evers scooted over to second, pivoted, and threw to first base. Or it might have been the way the ball leaped off of Schulte's bat all day or the manner in which Overall's curveball dipped at the last second. He couldn't put a finger on it, but he recognized perfection on the baseball diamond when he saw it. This team had something. Something more than last year. Something that made him happy to be standing on that field, at that instant of time. *One of them.*

The Game The Bizarre Early Days of Team Mascots; Making Men Into Pets

While large costumed chickens and parrots now parade about major league stadiums as official team mascots, in the early twentieth century teams adopted or jettisoned a mascot without much thought, on the spur of the moment, usually based on the belief that certain persons could bring luck to a team. Or to bring bad luck to the opponent, in the capacity of what the players called a "jinx dispenser." The white men playing ball in the major leagues did not normally associate with blacks, mentally disabled persons, or the physically deformed. As a result, the "novelty" of an African-American, a hunchback, or a retarded individual rendered that person suitable to serve as a team mascot. A ritual then took place, as the players would rub the hump of a hunchback or the frizzy hair of a black child before every at-bat. Or shake the tiny hand of a midget—for luck.

In 1888 to 1889 the Chicago White Stockings, as the Cubs were then known, circled the world playing a team of National League All-Stars in fifty exhibition games in San Francisco, Honolulu, Australia, Egypt, Rome, Paris, and London. The White Stockings, piloted by Cap Anson, brought with them a team mascot, a young black man named Clarence Duval. Duval's duties included entertaining the players and hauling the bat-sacks about. After the tour Anson critiqued Duval's performance: "Outside of his dancing and his power of mimicry he was, however, a no account nigger, and more than once did I wish that he had been left behind."

In 1901, a homeless black man by the name of "Lucky" Williams walked the streets of Chicago until chance linked him up with several drunken Philadelphia Phillies ballplayers who, after a few more drinks, concluded that "Lucky" was indeed lucky. They induced Mr. Williams to accompany them to the ballpark the next day and to allow them to rub his "large African head" before each batting appearance. Williams' head and his engaging personality contributed to a Phillies winning streak, so they persuaded Williams to accompany them on the road. But the Phillies organization did not allow this black mascot to ride the train with them. Instead, he traveled with the sandwich meat and cold cuts, tethered to the roof of the railroad car, getting so covered with locomotive soot that the Phillies had to scrub him clean at stops. When Williams turned to alcohol the Phillies unceremoniously deserted the weeping man in a New York train station.

Many teams used apes or other animals as mascots while others used young boys, black and white, to do menial chores and serve as good luck charms. Some big league outfits enlisted dwarfs or hunchbacks to grace their benches. Louis Van Zelst, both a hunchback and a dwarf, went to work for Connie Mack's Philadelphia A's in 1910. With Van Zelst as the mascot over the next five years, the Mackmen won four pennants and three World Series. But in 1915 the small man died. The A's proceeded to finish dead last in the American League for the seven seasons following Van Zelst's death.

The most celebrated hunchback mascot, Eddie Bennet, began his mascot career at age fourteen, when White Sox outfielder Happy Felsch rubbed his hump before a Sox victory over the Yankees at the Polo Grounds. After the game Felsch invited Bennet into the Sox dugout and, two victories later, convinced the teenager to travel with the team as their mascot and bat boy. He accepted, and the White Sox won the 1917 World Series with the help of Eddie Bennet. Bennet's "luck" ultimately led other clubs to seek his services and he grew up—to 4' 8"—on the road. The Dodgers grabbed him in 1920 and won the pennant. The Yankees offered Bennet more money and obtained his services for 1921-1928, winning six pennants in that eight-year span. Rumor had it that Bennet made more money than some players. Babe Ruth, who had his own mascot (a child named Little Ray Kelly), grew very fond of Bennet. One of Bennet's regular chores consisted of bringing bicarbonate of soda cocktails to the Babe after Ruth consumed too many hot dogs. Many years later, billionaire Warren Buffett cited Eddie Bennet as a managerial model. "It's simple," Buffett said, "to be a winner—work with winners." But in 1933, when Bennet died, alone and penniless, the winners did not remember Eddie. Not a single Yankee attended his funeral.

Ty Cobb discovered a small, affable black man by the name of Ulysses Harrison outside the Tigers' ballpark in July 1908. He christened him "Li'l Rastus" and enrolled him as team mascot, arranging for Harrison to sleep beneath his bed on the road. The Tigers availed themselves of Li'l Rastus' services for three months but, despite their successes, terminated his services in September. Frank Chance, ever the master psychological strategist, tracked Li'l Rastus down and engaged him to work for the Cubs in the 1908 Cubs-Tigers World Series. Cobb fumed at the presence of Li'l Rastus on the Chicago bench while the

Cubs, with the assistance of the black mascot, defeated the Tigers, four out of five. The Tiger Hall-of-Famer, evidently persuaded anew that Li'l Rastus could help, rehired him to be the Tiger mascot for the entire 1909 campaign. The Tigers won the pennant but Li'l Rastus could not gain them the World Championship. Li'l Rastus never mascoted again. Cobb collected enough money from his teammates to send Harrison down to Augusta, Georgia, where he employed the diminutive man in a number of different menial jobs.

One of the strangest mascots ever was a man named Charles Victor Faust. Described by some as a lunatic, a madman, or the village idiot of Marion, Kansas, Faust suffered from hebephrenia, a form of schizophrenia characterized by childish mannerisms, delusions, and hallucinations. A tall, thin man with a peculiar look to him, Faust lived with his parents on a farm. In 1911 he traveled to Wichita, Kansas, to consult a fortune-teller who predicted that Faust would join the New York Giants and pitch them to a pennant. A few months later the thirty-year-old Kansan journeyed to St. Louis and talked his way into John McGraw's hotel room. McGraw, as a lark, agreed to let Faust try out for the team before that afternoon's game. At Robison Park, still garbed in a suit and derby hat, Faust threw to McGraw himself. Whether McGraw called for a fastball or a curve, the lanky Kansan would lean back like a windblown tree, twirl his arm three times, and unleash a ball with nothing on it. After a few pitches McGraw dispensed with the catcher's glove and caught him bare-handed. Yet when the "tryout" ended, McGraw gave the genial Faust a uniform and told him to suit up and join the Giants on the bench.

The Giants, who had been stuck in third place, began to win, and the superstitious ballplayers gave Faust the credit. McGraw asked Faust to travel with the Giants as their mascot. He entertained players and fans alike with an enthusiastic display of pitching, defense, and base running during batting practice before each game. And if the day's events included a marching band, "Victory" Faust, as the Giants now called him, took his place in front of the band, a bat in hand, skinny arms pumping every which way out of the Giants uniform. Occasionally, when the Giants needed a rally, McGraw allowed Faust to warm up in the Giants bullpen, his exaggerated windmill wind-ups amusing the Giants and the crowds. In a number of instances this spectacle sparked a rally for the club.

Just after the Giants clinched the pennant in October, McGraw acceded to Faust's constant quest to take the mound for the Giants in an official game. He let Faust pitch in two major league games. Faust's statistics are respectable: two innings, two hits, one earned run, a 4.50 earned run average. As the only mascot in the history of the game to actually play in a game, he acquitted himself quite well, although it is not clear how hard opposing players tried to hit the odd Giants hurler. Charlie also batted in one contest, on the last day of the season. The opposing pitcher, quite accidentally, hit Faust, who proudly took his base. Faust then stole second and third bases, with a herky-jerky lope, to the great amusement of a sparse crowd. Scoring on a grounder, Charlie greeted his teammates with, "Who's loony now?" The "delusional" diagnosis evaporated. *Faust was a New York Giant.* The prediction of the fortune-teller had come true. The Giants went 37-2 when Faust was with the team, causing manager McGraw to state, with tongue only 90 percent in cheek, "I give Charlie Faust full credit for winning the pennant for me." Less than four years later, in 1915, Victory Faust died of tuberculosis in an insane asylum in the State of Washington.

Flash forward almost ninety years to September 28, 2004, as the Boston Red Sox fought to gain their first world championship since 1918. Pedro Martinez, the team's star Dominican pitcher, surprises his teammates by bringing thirty-six-year-old countryman Nelson De la Rosa to the Sox clubhouse for a visit. De la Rosa, an actor who appeared with Marlon Brando in the movie *The Island of Doctor Moreau,* is a midget, barely twenty-nine inches tall. Martinez introduced his diminutive sidekick enthusiastically.

"My friend is Nelson. He's... a very funny character and very animated. Everybody is happy with him. He is our lucky charm now."

Many of the Boston players treated the little man like a toy, placing him on their laps for photos. Derek Lowe asked, "Can I buy one of those?" Lowe later confessed, "It gave me the heebie-jeebies," and Kevin Millar agreed: "It scared the shit out of us." Manny Ramirez was less philosophical. "His dick is bigger than Millar's."

Two weeks later the Red Sox overcame the Curse of the Bambino to win their first World Series in eighty-six years.

April 21, 1907 Chicago, Illinois

She sat on the edge of her bed, feet flat on the small circle of carpet, eyes down, staring at a pair of red slippers about one foot from the base of the bed. "Red slippers," she mused, "like Jennie's red shoes in the house of horrors. Or should I say house of whores?" The red hue of the slippers reminded her of the blood on her hands, and the blood between her legs after Percy raped her. She did not want to revisit those four days again, for it brought agonizing memories and physical pain in her stomach and loins. She turned her gaze to the floor where the circle of carpet gave way to polished wood. The wood-grain patterns pleased her, parallel waves of dark and light fibers, like desert landscapes. She saw herself at the top of a sand dune, skipping merrily, and then tumbling down its angled side, the granules of sand tickling her arms and legs, her head toppling over heels. Falling. Falling down into an endless chasm. Her hands came up to cover her eyes as she no longer wished to see. She dropped back onto the bed and felt a cold draft blow over her, chilling her quickly. Climbing under the sheets, she settled there to fight the coldness. But under the linen sheets, in the darkness, a voice from nowhere, a deep insisting voice, proclaimed, "Satan calls for you!" And then again, "Satan calls for you!" She pulled the sheets down from over her head and the room gleamed cold and empty. But the red slippers winked and laughed at her from their perch on a small sand dune in the desert that had been her floor.

She thought, *Why would Satan want me?* And then she knew the answer. She had sinned. She had lingered with a strange man on a train, bringing all this down on herself. She asked herself, *Is he a man or something else?* She had never seen a human being act as this one had. Until that day she did not know such things could happen in civilized places. She spoke aloud: "I must pay the price." The red slippers gleamed redder and the voice became louder and more insistent.

"Now! Satan demands you now!" She did not think to resist. There was nothing to fight. Connie rose from the bed and walked to the chifferobe, opening the top drawer and withdrawing the bottle of barbital capsules. She shook a handful of capsules out into her right hand and swallowed them with some water, thinking, *Satan must be served.*

Marie Murphy padded down the hallway at ten o'clock to check on Connie. Light from within Connie's room spilled out from underneath the closed door. She knocked softly but heard no response. Quietly opening the door, she gasped at what she saw. Connie lay naked, face down on the wooden floor, her arms splayed out in hard angles. The bottle of barbital lay broken on the floor, capsules spilled around the glass shards. Mrs. Murphy ran to the girl and turned her over.

"Connie, Connie, how could you? Please darling, talk to me."

Connie did not respond. Not a word, not a sound. Chubby Murphy came to the doorway and looked in, terrified.

"Call a doctor quickly, Charles. I am not sure she is still with us." Murphy ran downstairs to the telephone and called Dr. Kent's home. The doctor had taken another house call, so his wife gave Murphy the number of an associate. He then telephoned the associate, Dr. Timothy Kelmon, and convinced him to come immediately.

Connie did not respond and did not appear to be breathing. Mrs. Murphy and a servant moved her to the bed and dressed the girl in a nightgown but when she pressed her ear to Connie's chest she could not hear a heartbeat. Mrs. Murphy's own daughter had died in this bed. Trembling, she recognized the face of death and cried, as much for her daughter as for Connie.

Dr. Kelmon arrived at the door of the Murphy's home fifteen minutes later. A stocky old man with thick bushy eyebrows and a head of white hair, he carried a battered black bag full of medical instruments. Mr. Murphy quickly led the doctor upstairs to Connie's bedroom. Entering the room, still huffing and puffing from the stairs, they observed the pale, still girl, reclining on the bed, with no signs of breathing. He pressed a stethoscope to her breast to listen for a heartbeat, but found none. Placing his hand on the girl's forehead he felt it to be cold to his touch. Dr. Kelmon inspected Connie's eyes, but they did not dilate when he shined a light into them. He turned to the Murphys, who stood at the end of the bed.

"She can feel pain no more. She is dead."

Mrs. Murphy wept. Dr. Kelmon pulled Mr. Murphy aside and asked to see the pill bottle. He learned that Connie must have taken twenty tablets. He knew little about barbital, a relatively recent medication.

"I will issue the death certificate tomorrow morning, when I return to my office. I am afraid I must report this as a suicide."

"I understand," said Murphy.

"Shall I send for the coroner's wagon or will you be making arrangements for the interment?"

"We will put her to rest."

April 22, 1907 Chicago Illinois

The body of Connie Dandridge was transported to the Tanner Funeral Home & Garden on Halsted Street. Two attendants from the home, dressed in dark green uniforms with red trim, arrived at the Murphy residence at eight o'clock. They wrapped the corpse in a series of sheets, carried it down the stairs on a stretcher, and swung it into a horse-drawn wagon parked on Lincoln Avenue. Murphy made all the arrangements for the funeral, scheduling it for 9:30 a.m. the next day.

Charles Murphy grieved over Connie's death. He blamed himself for not thinking the girl capable of such an extreme act. If only he had realized this he could have taken precautions. She should never have been left alone. He should have had the house girl with her at all times. If only. He thought back to his own daughter, and the pain of her last days. He'd gone over these same thoughts a hundred times before.

Murphy took a cab to the West Side Grounds to inform Kid Durbin of Connie's death. Tiny Hellanson, a janitor, let Murphy into the locked stadium, along with Jimmy Slagle, who had just arrived. Murphy found Durbin in the Cubs locker room, climbing into his uniform. The young man paused to tinker with his glove, which had a small rip in it. Murphy sat down in front of Durbin and asked him to sit down. Durbin, puzzled at the request, took a seat. Murphy, his eyes on the floor, then broke the news of Connie's death. Kid took it hard. The color drained from his face as he stood up, and a woozy feeling overcame him. His knees buckled and he would have fallen had Murphy not grabbed him under the armpits.

"This can't be true!" Durbin cried. A strained quiet settled over the locker room.

"I am afraid it is, Blaine. She took her own life last night. Some pills. I don't think she knew what she was doing. It was quick and she did not suffer."

The tears welled up in Durbin's eyes but he did not let them flow. He listened as Murphy tried to console him, but a numbness overtook him, making him feel like a drowning man separated from the living world by a thick layer of water. His thoughts turned to the last time he saw Connie, shuddering in the courtroom, devastated after the dismissal of charges against McGill. He blamed McGill for Connie's death.

Murphy told Durbin about the funeral and gave him directions to the home.

"Is it all right if some of the boys come?"

"Of course. I will talk to your teammates." Murphy directed Durbin to go home. The young man slowly removed his uniform, donned his street clothes and shuffled out of the ballpark, his eyes clouded like a gray Chicago winter day.

Hanlon and his Reds did not seem intimidated by the growling, sneering throngs of Cubs fans at the West Side Grounds.

"Hey little man with the big ears! You bums ain't gotta shot today!" screamed a fan in the first row at the scrappy little Reds second baseman. Miller Huggins glared at the fan and launched a hefty stream of tobacco juice in the bug's direction. Frank Chance selected Big Ed to start for the Cubs, figuring the tall righty to be well-rested from a week off. To throw for the Reds, Hanlon picked lanky right-hander Charley Hall, a second-year fast-baller out of the West Coast. Chance could not play due to lingering effects of the two collisions the day before in Cincy. He told Evers "the bones and muscles are aching every which way." So Johnny Kling trotted out to first base and veteran Pat Moran covered home plate for the West Siders. Moran earned his reserve catcher spot on the roster by being a smart, solid receiver, but he couldn't hit.

The game began at the routine three o'clock weekday starting time. The first inning almost doomed the Cubs as Reulbach could not find the plate. He walked the first three batters before getting the fourth hitter to ground out, a run scoring on the putout. An error on catcher Moran allowed a second run for the Reds before Big Ed tamed the next two hitters. But when he walked the second and third batters in the top of the second inning, Chance declared Reulbach's day to be over, replacing him with Jack Pfiester. On the bench Chance shook his head, troubled that Reulbach's control had deserted him.

Charley Hall ripped Pfiester's second pitch for a tough line drive to Schulte in right field. Schulte raced in, grabbed the sinking liner at his knees, and casually tossed to Evers at second base for the third out. The runner, standing befuddled at third, never thought Schulte would make the catch. That proved to be the last Reds threat, as Jack Pfiester gave up only two more hits the rest of the day. The Cubs tied it up in the bottom of the third. It looked like the game would go to extra innings, as it remained tied in the bottom of the ninth, with two outs and nobody on. But the baseball gods dictated no extra frames. Rabbit Slagle whacked a fastball for a base hit to left-center, and promptly stole second. Jimmy Sheckard then laced one off the pitcher's shin, the ball thudding down between his feet. Hall swiveled around wildly looking for it, but before he located the object of his desire, Sheckard stood on first and Slagle perched at third. Schulte advanced to the plate and fouled off two pitches before hammering a low liner safely to center, bringing Slagle around to end the game 3-2. Behind home plate three thousand men stood to applaud, their derby hats forming an undulating black wave as the Cubs jogged joyfully to the clubhouse in center field.

※　　　　　　　　※　　　　　　　　※

Steinfeldt, Schulte, and Sheckard dressed hurriedly and grabbed a cab to the Levee after the game, destined for a saloon favored by Steinfeldt, The *Lucky Lady*, on Dearborn near 22nd Street. A typical Levee establishment, The *Lucky Lady* offered a choice of beers and other alcoholic concoctions, free sandwiches, loose women, and games of chance in a rear room. The stale smoke of cigarettes and cigars hung thick in the air. Six brass spittoons sat on the wooden floor. The *Lucky Lady* employed numerous persons, but only two blacks. One of them, James Dennings, a twenty-two-year-old piano man, sang suggestive ragtime songs for ten dollars a week plus tips. His employers referred to his position as the "coon shouter." The other black employee of the saloon, "Coon Charlie," donned his gloves every six hours, emptied each spittoon in the alley, and washed the vessels in a big wooden tub. Frequently he found coins in the muck he dumped out of these cuspidors. Earning but ten cents an hour, Charlie did not hesitate to pluck this treasure from the mire.

The three Cubs displayed a beer-drinking mood this night, although Steinfeldt drank two for every one that Sheckard and Schulte polished off. Gradually Harry's face and the whites of his eyes grew red.

"Give us a sheep joke, Steiny," said Sheckard, as he the three men relaxed at a quiet table in a dark corner of the saloon.

"Why sure," responded Steinfeldt, reclining in his chair. "A man walks into his house carrying a sheep under his arm. He goes to the bedroom where his wife is lying in bed, wide awake. He says, 'I want you to see the pig that I've been sleeping with.' His wife looks at him and yells, 'You stupid idiot, that's no pig. It's a sheep!' He says, 'I wasn't talking to you.'"

Sheckard and Schulte cracked up.

"That's a good one, Steiny!" said Schulte. "Where'd you hear it?"

"My dentist," Steinfeldt replied, pointing into his open mouth. "While he was pullin' this one!"

By eight o'clock, having downed a dozen beers and enormous portions of cow tongue and salami sandwiches, Steiny had settled down into a convivial stupor. After spitting out the punch line of the sheep joke to a table of strangers, Harry leaned back to admire the surroundings. And that is when a plumbing supply drummer named Joseph Colbert attempted to engage Steinfeldt in a learned conversation.

Colbert inquired of Steinfeldt, "You know where I can get some good pussy tonight, buddy?"

Steinfeldt paused to collect himself and then turned to his left to address Colbert. "What do I look like, a pimp?"

Colbert retorted in an ill-advised manner. "Now that you have made that observation, good sir, I would have to answer, as a matter of fact, you do. Veritably so."

Steinfeldt's jaw tightened, and his face scrunched up into a severe scowl. Jimmy Sheckard, four steps away and aware of the storm stirring in his teammate, attempted to get close enough to Steinfeldt to restrain him but couldn't do so in time. Harry lashed out at the stranger, his meaty fist casting a glancing blow to Colbert's chin as the man dodged disaster at the last instant. But Harry wanted more. He lunged onto the man, driving him to the floor, slugged him once in the face, and dumped the contents of a nearby spittoon over the moaning man's head. Owing to Coon Charlie's diligence, there wasn't much fluid in the spittoon.

Sheckard pulled Harry off of the salesman. The two tracked down Schulte and left the *Lucky Lady* without delay. They spilled into the cold night air of Dearborn Street, gaslit and alive with newspaper boys, drunks, working women, and horny men.

April 23, 1907 Chicago, Illinois

Durbin, Chance, Slagle, Seabaugh, Sweeney, and Evers joined the Murphys at the funeral home, as did Prosecutor Wilen and several employees of the flower shop where Connie had worked. Durbin and the Cubs met outside the funeral parlor and walked in, where the Murphys greeted them. Inside, organ music came from the main room. Durbin braced as he neared the entrance. A polished wooden coffin rested on a platform at the front of the room, white flowers surrounding it on three sides. Connie rested inside an open casket. Durbin immediately walked to the coffin and laid his hands on it as he peered inside. Connie lay there, dressed in a white crinoline gown, dimpled with black lace and ribbons. Her head rested on a black satin pillow, her arms folded together at her waist, a bouquet of white roses on top of her gloved hands. The face, rouged and powdered, seemed tranquil. Without thinking, Durbin bent over her and kissed her lightly on her lips, whispering "Goodbye." This time Durbin couldn't stop the tears.

Durbin looked at Connie and cried for what might have been. The loss cut through him. He thought of the brute that did this, again blaming himself for not stopping that monster when he had the chance. He realized for the first time how much he cared for Connie. He loved her. Deeply. But she would never know. *What might have been*, he thought. Over and over it played in his head. *What might have been!*

As Durbin looked at Connie's powdered cheeks, tears began to run down his face again. No one else was near so he did not try to staunch the flow. He bent over again and kissed her lightly on her fragrant hair. Feeling weak, he gripped the wall of the open coffin, struggling to suppress the sounds gurgling within him. Just then the flowers fell from the clasped hands of the body, startling him. As he moved the flowers back into place Connie's right hand seemed to tremble. At first he doubted his own eyes. But then he saw her fingers move again. Now he knew for certain. He placed his hand on her forehead, expecting to feel a cold, lifeless flesh. It was not cold. His left hand resting on Connie's forehead, an icy chill arced up Durbin's spine as Connie's lips moved.

Durbin shouted. "She's moving! She's not dead!"

Talbot Tanner, the owner of the funeral home, rushed to Durbin's side.

"Please sir, I assure you the young woman is…" As he spoke the body stirred, and heaved a breath. Tanner turned paler than Connie and changed his tone.

"Good God!" he cried out. "I'll get a doctor."

Connie Dandridge emerged from her deathlike coma gradually. The first day she lay still, her legs and arms twitching periodically, and her lips trying to part. The second day her eyes opened and she could follow movements. In the course of the next few days she regained all of her faculties. Dr. Kelmon, who had pronounced her dead and signed the death certificate, retired four days later. Connie's "re-vivification" forced the old doctor to realize that he had diminishing observation skills. He had never seen a patient who had overdosed on barbital, which had only been available for three years. Nor did Dr. Kelmon even know that barbital, a central nervous system depressant, can make it exceedingly difficult to detect a pulse or to observe spontaneous respiration.

Back at the Tanner Funeral Home & Garden, Mr. Tanner fired the two young employees who were paid to embalm Connie but did not do so. Although their dereliction saved her life, they had not done their job.

"Those bastards even had the nerve to charge me a dollar for the arsenic embalming fluid," Tanner complained.

From the Journal of Kid Durbin

  God must have heard me crying because Connie is alive. When Mr. Murphy told me she had passed on I truly felt my world crumble, like everything ripped asunder. I nearly fell over in a panic. She is more important to me than anything. I attended her funeral with a number of the Cubs. As I stood over her coffin and looked down at that sad pale face, I saw her move. The spark of life! God brought her back to me and I will forever be grateful. The heavy sorrow is gone and I am truly reborn. The emotions I experienced are equal to what I felt when my mother died. Now that Connie is back with us, I can tell her about my feelings toward her. Maybe she will feel the same about me.

  Johnny Evers witnessed Connie's return from the dead. An hour later, while a doctor tended to Connie, he said to me, "Kid, I don't consider myself an overly religious man. But this day has got to make you stop and think that someone or something is out there, helping or guiding us. And giving you a second chance. So make the most of it."

April 23, 1907 **Chicago, Illinois**

After a hypnosis session, Chance and Thurston retired to the Berghoff Restaurant for dinner, and Chubby Murphy tagged along. Murphy related the events regarding Miss Dandridge, her "death" and resurrection. He made arrangements for Thurston to visit Connie.

Thurston spoke. "The story of Miss Dandridge reminds me of a mentalist, Mr. Washington Irving Bishop. At age twenty, not yet having made my mark in this business, Bishop befriended me and guided me to follow my strengths, to pursue my ideals. His advice helped me enormously." Thurston paused to take a drink.

"Bishop, as I said, worked as a mentalist. He had an impressive ability to discern information by 'reading' the faces and slightest movements of others. For him the smallest tremor of a muscle revealed a wealth of information."

"Sounds like he would have been a good poker player," said Chance.

"He was. No one played poker with Bishop a second time. His show featured one act in which an audience member unknown to Bishop concealed an object, such as a pocket-watch, in the pocket or purse of another member of the audience. While the audience knew what the object was and where it was concealed, Bishop did not. At least at first. Blindfolded, Bishop would find that hidden object solely by touching the hand of a randomly selected person from the audience who knew the location of the hidden object. Bishop did not use shills or other chicanery. He could discern things simply by holding the hand of a man or woman and sensing their pulse and their breathing. On one occasion, reported widely in the press, he was double-blindfolded and hooded. His wrists were linked to the wrists of three strangers with copper wire. The strangers knew where a small pin was hidden one mile away. Bishop led these gentlemen to a horse-drawn carriage, grabbed the reins, and drove blindly through the streets of New York. Several times he nearly struck a pedestrian. He pulled up to the Gramercy Park Hotel, leaped from the carriage, and rushed into the lobby of the hotel, dragging his companions with him. Heading straight to a bust, he picked it up, and located the hidden pin beneath it."

"Impressive," stated Murphy.

Thurston drank from the stein and leaned on the table. "Yes. He was gifted. One night Bishop was performing at the Lambs Club in New York, a private club for entertainers and their friends. In fact, I believe I once met your Mr. John McGraw there."

Chance snorted. "He ain't *my* John McGraw."

"Bishop's act dazzled his fellow performers. But in the middle of the performance, the heat and the blindfold took its toll on Bishop. He collapsed in a lifeless heap in the midst of his peers. Two members of the audience, prominent New York physicians, men of high station and excellent reputation, meticulously examined him as he lay there. No pulse, no sign of breathing. Both doctors pronounced him dead. But here, gentleman, is where this story becomes strange.

"The two physicians had been quite astounded by Bishop's show. They conferred and decided to examine Bishop's brain before it cooled, so they could ascertain whether it contained any unusual vascular structure that would explain the magician's phenomenal abilities. The doctors rushed the body to St. Vincent's Hospital, neatly sawed the top of the head off, and removed the still warm brain."

"I would wager they discovered no anomalies," said Chance.

"You are correct, sir. They determined the brain to be quite normal and healthy, and other than the fact that it weighed 15 percent above average, the autopsy uncovered no peculiarities in the organ. But shortly after the autopsy, a note was found in the trousers of the dead man. It read:

> *To any person who may find me in a lifeless state: Please be on notice that I, Washington Irving Bishop, suffer from a rare form of catalepsy that can place me in a coma-like condition for several days at a time. During this attack I will appear to be without life, unbreathing and still. But I am alive and I will, God pray, return to normal if left undisturbed. My temperature will not fall dramatically and thus will prove that I remain alive. Please refrain from any premature autopsy or treatment by ice or electricity while I am in this trance state.*

> *Signed,*
> *Washington Irving Bishop*

"So the doctors killed him?" Murphy asked.

"Yes. They tried to cover up their pernicious interest in Bishop's brain. These physicians probably killed a number of their patients while picking the pockets of New York's elite. You see, I am no great believer in these so-called men of science, who carry morphine and worthless nostrums in their black valises. But this particular death generated headlines, and the victim's mother sought justice for the wrongful murder of her son. New York prosecutors indicted the doctors for murder."

Chance asked the outcome.

"The judge dismissed the case before trial. The prosecutor did not contest, knowing that the defendants would testify, with no witness to contradict them, that Bishop died before they cleaved open his head. The fact that the defendants were wealthy figures in the City's society circles played no small role in the state allowing the matter to fade away."

"Justice was not served," Husk concluded.

"No," Thurston agreed. "However, as Longfellow observed, 'Man is unjust but God is just; and finally justice triumphs.' So let us drink to ultimate justice."

The men hoisted their mugs, clinked them together, and drank.

The Era   Bishop's Brain, Diagnosis of Death, and Premature Burial

Thurston's version of Washington Irving Bishop's death missed the mark, partly due to Thurston's friendship with the mentalist and partly because much of what he knew about Bishop's demise came from flawed press reports. Bishop did spend his last night on earth performing for a group of friends, entertainers, and wealthy New Yorkers at the Lambs Club. In the excitement of a mind-reading demonstration, he collapsed and lost consciousness. But an old friend of Bishop's, Dr. John Irwin, informed the crowd that Bishop was a cataleptic, and that he had recovered from similar attacks in the past. When Bishop came out of the trance they carried him upstairs to a bedroom. At this point he insisted on finishing the demonstration, which had been interrupted by his attack. He begged Dr. Irwin to observe the finale. Unfortunately, the strain once more overpowered the young magician and he fell into an unconscious state again.

Dr. Irvin summoned one Dr. Charles C. Lee but the two physicians could not revive Bishop and Lee left at 4:00 a.m. Several hours later Dr. Irwin and yet another physician performed a series of tests and declared Washington Irving Bishop dead. They took the body to a funeral home where Bishop's wife came to view it in a glass-topped coffin. She asked the owner of the funeral parlor to comb the corpse's hair, but when an employee dragged the comb through the hair, the top of Bishop's head came with it, revealing an empty cranium. Bishop's brain was gone!

Bishop's wife swooned, realizing that the brain had been removed as the result of an autopsy—an autopsy that she had not authorized. She screamed, "They have killed my husband! He was murdered by these doctors… to get his brain."

She may have been right, but the truth will never be known. The doctors admitted doing an unauthorized autopsy and removing the brain for examination. They later testified that they performed the autopsy because they had been impressed by Bishop's "powers" and had heard Bishop boast on several occasions that his brain must contain unique features. So they removed the brain for examination but found no anomalies. Following the autopsy the doctors placed the brain in the chest cavity, where funeral home employees found it after Mrs. Bishop demanded an investigation. As for the note warning against an autopsy, which Bishop called his "life guard" and always carried, the doctors denied ever seeing it and it never surfaced. The most likely scenario—the doctors discovered the note after the autopsy and destroyed it.

Authorities arrested four doctors, including Irwin and Lee, in connection with the coroner's inquest into Bishop's death. The inquest produced fascinating testimony that Bishop had been declared dead years earlier by two physicians, who observed no respiration, no pulse, and "no indication of life…" The young magician awoke twelve hours later. The testimony of friends and other physicians established a number of such incidents. But the jury, mainly "dry goods men and jewelers," handed down a verdict of not guilty for all the defendants. After all, no one could definitively establish that Bishop's heart still beat at the moment the doctors sawed into his skull. Dr. Irwin received a minor censure for his hasty, unauthorized autopsy on his friend. Bishop was buried and forgotten.

The death of Washington Irving Bishop exemplified a serious problem of the times—medical practitioners often erred in the diagnosis of death. Doctors had not determined definitive signs of death and, as a result, unconscious and comatose patients were sometimes mistakenly pronounced dead. Dramatic consequences often followed. Bishop is one example, but the more frequent scenarios involved the victim being buried alive or narrowly escaping that fate. How often this happened is uncertain, but enough to create a widespread fear in Europe and America of what Edgar Allen Poe called "premature burial." Terrifying tales of people buried alive circulated from the Middle Ages to the twentieth century. *Burial Reformer,* the magazine of the Society for the Prevention of Premature Burial, began publication in 1905, collecting macabre stories from around the world. One variety described lucky escapes from premature burial under clever headlines such as "A Dead Man Jumps Out of His Coffin" and "A Corpse Asks For Beer." In its first issue, the magazine recounted a story from the *Manchester Guardian* about Mrs. Elizabeth Holden, a resident of Accrington, England. Declared dead and laid out on a table in a mortuary, the undertaker observed a twitching of her eyelid. Soon she could talk again, grateful that she had not awakened in her casket, underground. The magazine also printed a great number of reports describing the opening of crypts or the digging up of coffins and gruesome descriptions of the findings: coffins with scratched markings inside from the clawing of fingernails, corpses that freed themselves from their shrouds and bodies with chewed fingers—consumed by the dying to stay alive (or more likely nibbled by vermin).

The Germans did not take their fear of premature burial lying down. They did something about it. A brick and mortar approach. Starting in 1792 and continuing through the nineteenth century, city governments constructed dozens of "waiting mortuaries" across Germany. Morticians transported the dead to the local "Leichenhaus" where they were placed on "beds" for days until evidence of putrefaction—the only sure sign of death—could be observed. On-site staff at each Leichenhaus guaranteed the presence of someone in case one of the "inmates" suddenly revived. Not a job for the squeamish because the bodies gave off a horrible stench and occasionally jerked about due to normal physiological phenomena. In some of these "houses of the dead" strings or ropes connected the wrists or the toes of the corpses to bells, so that a man or woman waking from apparent death could quickly summon assistance.

Entrepreneurs devised technological approaches to address the fear of premature burial. Early on, relatives interred shovels and crowbars with the dead so that they might dig their way out should they revive. Many ideas for "security coffins" were patented after 1850. Most involved coffins equipped with air tubes and ropes connected to bells above ground. Those awakening in a casket beneath ground had air to breathe and a means of alerting the world above of their plight. Other more elaborate designs included air filters, air pumps, lamps to light the coffin, and food and drink to lessen the horror of the predicament. One design replaced the bell with a rocket.

A Russian nobleman, Count Michel De Karnice-Karnicki, designed a security coffin that gained rave reviews at the Sorbonne in 1897. The coffin had numerous advanced features, including a mechanism that triggered a flag to automatically deploy when the body inside stirred. The Count designed the apparatus after witnessing the burial of a Belgian child. The girl awoke from her "death" while cemetery workers shoveled dirt onto her casket. The screams of this child deeply affected Karnice-Karnicki.

Some physicians took another approach to prevent unwarranted burials. They developed "tests" for those pronounced dead, procedures designed to awaken those still alive by triggering the vital spark of life. One such test actually did revive an Italian man, Luigi Vittori, who had "died" of an asthma attack. A physician inserted a burning candle up Vittori's nostril. It worked, causing Vittori to leap up from the platform on which he had been laid. Thereafter he proudly explained the history of his scarred nose. Other doctors used extreme and outlandish methods in attempts to revive the fresh dead. Hot iron pokers were inserted in the anus of the dead. Physicians used bellows to force foul-smelling substances into the mouths and noses of corpses and administered enemas of tobacco smoke. There are also more than a few recorded incidents of cadavers awakening as medical students poked and probed inside.

American doctors also struggled with the questions of life and death. Sometimes laypersons made the call when doctors were unavailable. Mistakes occurred, and patients still clinging to life were buried alive. The last words of George Washington reflected his fear of premature burial:

> I am just going. Have me decently buried, and do not let my body be put into the vault in less than two days after I am dead.

Doctors still make errors in declaring death. Found stiff and motionless on her living-room floor, the Albany, New York, coroner pronounced eighty-six-year-old Mildred C. Clarke dead in 1994. She endured ninety minutes in a body bag in the city morgue before an employee noticed movement in the bag. Ms. Clarke lived another week. But widespread worry of the possibility of being buried alive no longer exists. Embalming the dead or cremation has ended the threat of premature burial.

Contrary to common belief, the term "fan" did not derive from the word "fanatic," but rather from the term "fancier," as in a "fancier of baseball." But in 1907 "fans" were more commonly called "bugs," or sometimes rooters, boosters, "cranks," and (the females) "cranklins." Rooters might come to the ballparks in groups, outfitted in unusual hats and marching to the beat of a bass drum, klaxons, or cowbells. But most bugs came to the ballpark dressed as they did on their jobs, with suits, ties, starched collars, and bowler or straw hats. The crowd was overwhelmingly male. The few women in attendance wore long dresses that covered their ankles and colorful, obligatory hats of all forms. The men gambled on the game and guzzled beer. The era featured animated crowds. "Cranks," as the name implied, could get nasty. If the umpire made a bad call a fan might throw an empty bottle in his direction. If the umpire blew a call that cost the home team the game, a drunken fan might run out and throw a punch at the man in blue. A thrown pop bottle knocked Umpire Billy Evans unconscious and almost killed him in 1907. A sign in a Kansas City ballpark, circa 1886, read: "Please do not shoot the umpire; he's doing the best he can."

Too often the players gave the umpires more than just a hard time. Players frequently physically attacked the umpires in the course of a game or as post-game entertainment. In Indiana in1899 and in Alabama in 1901, bat-wielding ballplayers actually killed two minor league umpires during ballgames. National League umps had it worse than their American League counterparts because the league leadership rarely cracked down on errant players. Almost a hundred years later, Umpire John Rice described the brutalization of umpires in these terms:

> I've been mobbed, cussed, booed, kicked in the ass, punched in the face, hit with mud balls and whiskey bottles; and had everything from shoes to fruit thrown at me... [A]n umpire should hate humanity.

In the early years of the twentieth century each league employed only six umpires, guaranteeing the staffing of most games with a single umpire. Not until 1911 did the two-man umpiring crew become standard. A lone umpire often could not see the mischief and outright cheating that occurred behind his back, the "bumping" of base runners rounding third base, runners saving five steps by turning toward home plate without bothering to tag the bag at third, and a dozen other common schemes. Worse than this, given the large size of the playing field, umpires arbitrating a game on their own frequently were forced to make calls on plays they had not seen. When they botched the call under these circumstances it drove players and fans crazy. An unwritten rule of thumb existed for umpires in such situations: "If you didn't see the play but you gotta call it, give it to the home team. Less chance of problems that way."

Steadfast courage became a critical requirement for the job of umpiring due to threats and physical attacks from fans and players. The first umpire to make a name for himself, Bob "Death to Flying Things" Ferguson, acquired the great nickname from his ability, in his playing days, to "kill" fly balls by catching them. Ferguson, reputed to be baseball's first switch-hitter, played infield for Anson's Chicago Nationals in 1878, dabbled in umpiring while still a player, and became a full-time umpire when he retired in 1884. Ferguson's umpiring philosophy is recorded:

> *Never change a decision, never stop to talk to a player—make 'em play ball and keep their mouths shut and never fear but the people will be on your side and you'll be King of the Umpires.*

Players of the time considered "Old Fergy" smart, impartial, decisive, and fearless. He worked games without a protective face mask, which raises questions regarding his sanity. On a sunny afternoon in 1873, Ferguson, still an active player, volunteered to umpire a game between Hartford and the New York Mutuals. Nat Hicks, the catcher for the Mutuals, said something to Ferguson that caused Old Fergy's blood to boil. Hicks's exact statement has dissolved in the fog of history but it proved sufficient to push Ferguson to pick up a bat and crack Hicks with it, breaking the catcher's arm in two places and instantly ending the squabble. No other player challenged the umpire that day. When a constable advanced to arrest Ferguson after the game, the injured catcher, still present on the bench, declined to press charges. Years later, when an enraged mob of fans encircled Ferguson on a baseball diamond, threatening to kill him, Fearless Fergy again picked up a bat, vigorously swung it about him a number of times, and yelled, "I don't know what drove you men into the arms of anarchy but you will surely come to regret it. I'm only one man to your thousand, but if you don't think I can protect myself just pitch in and give it a trial." The mob crumbled.

Bill Klem, perhaps the greatest umpire of the modern era, umpired in the National League for thirty-seven years, from 1905 through 1941. An innovative ump, he regularly worked the slot, the space between the catcher and the batter, lining up his eyes on the inside corner of home plate, his chin right at the top of the catcher's cap, much like modern umpires do. Klem didn't invent the signaling of balls and strikes—that probably happened ten to fifteen years earlier, when a deaf outfielder, Dummy Hoy, convinced a number of umpires to gesture "strike" or "ball" so he would know the count from his perch in the field. But Klem always employed signals for balls and strikes, and probably invented the hand signals to denote "out" and whether a ball landed "fair" or "foul." He is also the first umpire to position his rear end away from the crowds at home plate when using the whisk broom to clean home plate.

Klem, a small man with slick, black hair that lay flat on his head and parted down the middle, had ears that stuck far out from his head. He called balls and strikes in an exuberant, demonstrative style. Piscine lips earned him the nickname Catfish, but players soon discovered that uttering that term within earshot of Klem guaranteed an ejection from the game. When surly managers or ballplayers approached the 5'7" Klem, he sometimes scraped a line in the dirt, crossed his arms, and shouted, "Don't cross the Rio Grande or I'll put you off the field." Those that stepped over the line earned instant ejections from the game. In a legendary incident, Klem delayed signaling a call at third base, and when a player asked, "Well, what is it, safe or out?" Klem barked, "It ain't *nothin'* till I call it." Klem umpired with a dignity and integrity that earned him great respect and, ultimately, election to the Hall of Fame. The Giants honored Klem in a ceremony before a game at the Polo Grounds in 1949. Klem told the crowd: "Baseball is more than a game. It is a religion to me."

Umpires get little recognition or respect from ballplayers and even less from the fans. Spat upon and attacked, until recently they've been terribly underpaid. In spite of these enormous drawbacks, history has recorded no instance of any minor league or major league umpire accepting a bribe to influence a game. Not a single incident of corruption! In a hundred years that has seen a vice president, a dozen Chicago judges, numerous baseball players, and innumerable politicians guilty of bribery, not one single umpire has crossed that line. All of us could learn a lesson from these faithful servants of the game of baseball.

From the Journal of Kid Durbin

April 24, 1907

Big Ed, who couldn't throw strikes two days ago, pitched to the batting practice for both teams today. Chance wanted him to get the extra work and the Reds manager allowed it. Ed liked the idea, wanting to work on his curveball some.

We beat the Reds for the third straight time yesterday, so today they came gunning for us like they had something to prove. They proved it too. Things went to smack right from the start. To begin with, Husk hates the umpire, Jim Johnstone, on account of Johnstone serving as the National League umpire in the Sox–Cubs World's Championship Series. "Never gave us a break!" Husk said.

Brakeman, who got the start, mouthed off before the game, telling us it was gonna be four in a row because his old iron arm felt strong. Evers told some of us, outside earshot of the Brakeman, that Jack drank so much the night before that he couldn't beat a drum today. When Taylor warmed up, he shot some nasty glances at Reds second-sacker Huggins, so naturally when Huggins led off the game he nailed the second pitch into center for a solid hit. Taylor scowled at Huggins at first but Huggins paid no attention. He raced over to third when the second batter, another little guy named John Kane, sliced a single to left. Then it got uglier, and by the end of the first inning we fell behind 4-0.

Ballplayers are a superstitious bunch. I don't put much belief in superstition except for the powers of mascots, which I know about from experience. A good mascot is worth his weight in gold. But your average ballplayer thinks there are all sorts of supernatural forces behind everything that happens on the diamond. That kind of thinking affects some games. Like the big mistake our mascot Howie made right before today's first pitch from the Reds twirler in the bottom of the first. Howie's main job during the game is to keep the bats lined up on the turf in proper order, with Husk's bats first. Under no circumstances must the bats ever get crossed, with one bat lying across another, since most players think that's a bad sign—a signal of bad luck on its way. Somehow Howie didn't pay attention. Maybe it was the ruckus Jack Taylor made kicking up a storm of dirt and trouble as he returned to the bench after his bad inning. At least three bats were crossed in front of the bench and Jimmy Slagle cussed and wailed, "Jesus Christ! The sticks is crossed! Uncross 'em for god sakes!" He continued to rip Howie for messing up. The kid started crying and ran back to the clubhouse. Trainer Jack had to run over and straighten out the bats and then go tend to Howie.

Slagle spoke for most of the boys when he said, "This game's nigh gone. It's one thing to battle against the Reds when they got a four run lead. But to hafta battle against a curse at the same time. Cain't be done."

Husk had me warming up to go in during the first, and then again in the sixth when Taylor gave up five more runs on a slew of base hits. Husk finally pulled the Brakeman, and as Taylor left the mound he walked past Jim Johnstone, the umpire, and said, "You fucked me good to-day, Jimbo!" Johnstone glared at Brakeman but let it go, figuring he was headed to the clubhouse anyways. At that Husk sent me out to pitch—my first time on the mound in the majors. And as I'm making my way to the pitcher's box Umpire Johnstone looks at me and says, "Not a goddam word out of you, redhead!"

The jitters grabbed me. We were getting our asses kicked, half the boys saw the game as hexed, and the ump spat and cussed in a foul and nasty state. Shaking a little, I took the mound with a powerful aim to do well.

Husk says to me, "Give it all you got."

I said, "Yessir, Cap'n. That's what I'm fixing to do."

We had two outs when I entered with Kane hugging first base. The first guy for me to face in the big leagues, Lefty Davis, an ugly, hairy fellow, snarled at me and waved the bat over the plate in a menacing sort of way. "Come on you busher!" he yelled. "Give me a pitch I can hit. Or can you even throw it this far?"

Mike Kahoe came in to catch me—his first appearance of the year also. He squatted behind the plate, signaled for the fastball, and I threw one too good for Lefty to resist. He stung it right past my left ear into center, so the Reds now had two men on base and the number four hitter, hard-hitting Hans Lobert, coming up to bat. I took a few seconds to get my bearings, figuring I'd throw the ball to third if it came back to me. Kahoe gives me the sign for a curveball and I got strike one called as the ball nicked the outside corner. Then I threw a blistering fastball wide to make it a 1-1 count. The third pitch, another fastball, killed me. Lobert didn't get around on it but he swatted it out to right field and a run scored. Two batters, two hits. Not the way I pictured my first big league outing.

Husk danced over to me from first and suggested I should relax and let it fly given the 10-2 score. While Frank returned to the bag, I remembered Trainer Jack's comment from the day before. He told me that the next Reds hitter, John Ganzel, their tall first baseman, had a tough time hitting low stuff. So that's where I threw him. He missed one shoot, and on the next hit a weak pop fly to Husk at first to end the misery of the inning. As I walked to the bench, Chance came over to me and said, "The way you pitched to Ganzel—that was first rate. That was major league, Kid." Those few words really buoyed me up.

I came to bat in the next inning. Husk directed me to bluff a bunt twice. Only Chance always called it a "put" rather than a "bunt." He said, "Make like you're gonna put—two times—then slam it down their throats." I'd seen Jimmy Sheckard, a fine bunter, do this a number of times so I had the general idea of it. On the first pitch I squared away as if to bunt and then pulled the bat back. The ump called it a ball. With the second pitch I again faked the bunt, this one called a strike. So on the third pitch both the first baseman and the third-sacker are coming in to field what they are sure is gonna be a bunt. I laid the bat out over the plate for the third time but at the last second I pull it back and slap the ball past the ear of the first baseman who's only twenty feet in front of me. It worked like a charm so I got credit for a base hit my first time at bat in the big leagues.

I threw a scoreless seventh and eighth innings, following Chance's command to "move those fuckers off the plate." But I ran into trouble in the ninth, when two singles, a walk, and an error by Evers cost us two

THE BEST TEAM EVER

runs. The boys all said I did fine but I knew I could have done better. Jack Taylor sulked. He sat in the clubhouse with an awful frown on his mug, a look that said, "If you come anywhere near me or talk to me I'll knock you down." No one went near him.

Husk looked equally sour and finally exploded. "You're a fine lot of bastards, you are! You ought to be ashamed. We didn't give it everything we shoulda." Most of the Cubs hung their heads low. No one looked at Chance when he spoke these words.

Shortly after his outburst Chance informed Sweeney, Kahoe, and Seabaugh that the Cubs were shipping them to Columbus. The look on Billy's face! I thought he might start crying but he held it in. Chance said they'd worked out an arrangement with the Columbus club so the Cubs could get all three back in a pinch. Warren Seabaugh, my roommate, also took it bad, and nothing I said made much of a difference. Kahoe knew the decision was in the works so he didn't react much. Two hours later they were gone.

I bought the evening papers to send the stories of my first game home to my father. He will be pleased to read about me, I think. The papers show the Cubs in first place, our 7–2 record slightly better than the Phillies at 6–2 and the Giants at 7–3.

April 24, 1907 Chicago, Illinois

Connie began to speak two days after her funeral. Single words for a day or two and then sentences. Thankfully, she had no recollection of the events that had befallen her, neither the suicide attempt nor the strange occurrences thereafter. The Murphys hired two nurses, each on a twelve-hour shift, to provide full-time care for the girl, never leaving her alone. Chubby Murphy viewed Connie's return from the dead as a gift from God.

Kid Durbin visited Connie in the afternoon. Sunshine dappled the bed where he found her sitting up, reading a newspaper. The nurse hovered alongside her with a tinkling cup of steaming tea while Emma, the cleaning girl, tidied up the room.

"How are you, Connie?" he asked.

"I will be fine, Blaine." She did not speak of the past.

Durbin could not figure how this woman could have tried to take her life. She seemed so cheerful and vibrant. He decided to match her tone, and lightly queried, "Anything new and interesting in the paper?"

"There is a story about the Cubs. Mr. Murphy is in it but they don't mention you."

"That's all right. I'm still getting my bearings."

"Your time will come." Connie looked into Durbin's eyes and smiled.

"I want you to do whatever it takes to get better. Did Mr. Murphy tell you about Howard Thurston?"

"He did. Sounds a little strange to me. Maybe not proper. After all, he is not a physician. What do you think?"

"I have confidence in this man, Connie. He is capable of much good. Please give him a chance to help you. Will you?"

"Since you trust him, I will do it. Bring on your magic man."

April 25-28, 1907 St. Louis, Missouri

Kid Durbin felt happy to be back in Missouri. His father, a short man with sandy brown hair, brought Kid's eleven-year-old brother Howard down to St. Louis to see his big brother in a Cubs uniform. Kid had exacted their promise to root for the Cubs rather than the Cardinals. Howard and the senior Mr. Durbin visited Kid in his room at the Southern Hotel, where he impressed them by calling room service for soda pop. The chief desk clerk, Jack Ryan, a genial thirty-five-year-old who always catered to the ballplayers' needs, quickly sent the drinks plus complimentary cookies.

Durbin's kin didn't see any baseball on April 25. The skies opened up and pelting rains spilled over Robison Field, washing away the game. With no game to report, the newspapermen accosted the Cardinals and tried to stir up a story, harking back to the criticism the Cards had leveled about the visiting team's dressing room at West Side Grounds. But Jake Beckley and Manager McCloskey denied the whole story, and it fell flat.

On Friday, Chance handed the ball to Orval Overall and the lumbering Californian responded with a gritty complete game performance, holding the Cards to seven hits and three runs. The Cubs, behind Shorty Slagle's three hits and Kling's first two hits of the season, pushed five in to win. The next time up after gaining his first hit, the superstitious Kling meticulously repeated every move he had made the previous at bat, including stepping to the plate in his earlier footprints. *It worked the first time,* he thought. Kling also discovered his inflated, rubber chest protector had a small leak in it, so he had to keep blowing it up, but an inner voice persuaded him that he could only inflate the device in the odd innings.

A lone umpire, Hank O'Day, monitored the event, and both teams tried to cut some corners on the field when O'Day looked elsewhere. But he kept spinning around and catching the boys at their mischief. In the bottom of the eighth inning the Cards' leadoff man, outfielder Al Burch, lined a gapper to right-center field. As Burch charged out of the batter's box, Johnny Kling purposely flipped his catcher's mask between the runner's feet. The single ump didn't see it, but Burch didn't stumble, making it all the way to third.

Back on the bench, Chance sidled up to Kling. "That was a good idea, Jew. But the next time you toss your birdcage under somebody's feet, make sure the cocksucker goes down."

The Redbirds put up a tough fight on Saturday, dragging the contest into twelve innings before the Cubs pulled out a 4-3 win. Fidgety Jack Pfiester pitched all the way, the crafty southpaw slipping out of jams as easy as his nightshirt. His curve proved impossible for left-handed hitters like Beckley and O'Hara, who went one for eleven between them. For Beckley, it signalled the approaching end of his two-decade big-league career, as the Cards released him a few weeks later. Newt Randall played left for the Cubs in place of Schulte, who nursed the same charley horse that plagued him in the Practice Season. Starting to warm up to the major leagues, Newt knocked two key hits, one of them a double. The Cubs scored the go-ahead run in the twelfth when Artie Hoffman, who earlier committed two errors at short, led off with a double. A big smile on his face afterwards, Artie said, "I had to make amends."

"Amen to that," Evers quipped.

Sunday afternoon brought a doubleheader as the two teams made up the rainout from earlier in the week. With more than twelve thousand in the stands and the field warmed by a gentle April sun, Jack Taylor started the opener. Brakeman, edgier than usual, paced on the mound as the game began. The umpire tossed him a new ball to begin the contest. Jack bent to his knees to rub it up in the grass, as many hurlers did with new baseballs. Brakeman threw scoreless ball until the fifth, when Doc Marshall, the Cardinal backstop, tagged a ball over Sheckard's head in left field. As the ball rolled all the way to the entrance gate, Taylor loudly cursed Sheckard for playing too shallow. The unhappy pitcher stomped around the mound, disgusted that Doc Marshall, a slow runner, could circle the bases. But the bags were empty before Marshall homered, so the Cubs maintained a 2-1 lead. Jack cooled down and did not let things get away from him, pitching inside, then away, not serving up anything fat.

The game went into extra innings tied 2-2. A Frank Chance dribbler down the first base line scored the go-ahead tally in the tenth. The ball would have likely spilled into foul territory if Jake Beckley hadn't grabbed it, and then compounded his miscue by missing the tag on the lumbering Cubs player-manager. Taylor smelled victory as he took the mound in the tenth and mowed the hapless Cardinals down with ritual fervor.

Taylor's comments to the three sportswriters that approached him centered on Sheckard letting Marshall's hit go over his head: "If Jimmy hadn't of fucked up we wouldda won this a lot earlier. But I showed those bastards today."

Game two featured a brilliant performance by the Cubs number seven starter, Chick Fraser. Fraser disposed of the first eighteen batters in a row in an effortless blaze.

On the bench in the top of the seventh Evers commented to Chance, "Only two or three pitchers ever pitched a no-man-reach-first game. Maybe we're watching another one?"

"Takes nine more outs, Crab…" Husk mumbled.

Chance thanked his lucky stars that the Cubs picked up Chick Fraser in the off-season because the veteran righty still had plenty in the tank. A natural starter, he could also relieve when someone ran out of gas. With Brown, Overall, Reulbach, Pfiester, Lundgren, and Taylor, the Cubs now possessed seven solid starters. Durbin was hungry, and still might pan out. No matter how you looked at it, the pitching marked an improvement over the 1906 staff, which produced 116 victories.

Fraser lost the perfect game by walking the leadoff man in the seventh. In the eighth, he lost the no-hitter when thirty-nine-year-old Jake Beckley, after greeting Fraser with his characteristic one-armed twirl of the bat, laced hit number 2,918 of his career, a clean double in the left-center gap between Sheckard and Slagle. The Cards could do no more, so Fraser's one-hitter gave the Cubs a 1-0 victory. At day's end the Cubs, 11-2, sat atop the National League. The unhappy St. Looie crowd filed out of Robison Field onto North Vandeventer, shaking their heads at the twin loss.

April 16-30, 1907 **Chicago, Illinois**

Thurston, with plenty of time on his hands between performances, hypnotized thirteen Cubs after Frank Chance. Each of them received two sessions, the first to test the limits of their receptivity and lay a groundwork, the second to hammer home the message. The top five starting pitchers, Brown, Lundgren, Pfiester, Reulbach, and Overall participated. Slagle, Taylor, Fraser, and Kling refused. Thurston conducted the sessions in his suite at the Palmer House Hotel. Durbin convinced many of his teammates to try the treatment, although he never revealed the rooster incident to them.

During the same period Thurston treated Connie Dandridge on three occasions, each instance at the Murphys' home. Initially nervous, she developed into a compliant subject, easily put under while Mrs. Murphy looked on.

Thurston took a number of approaches, frequently urging her to recognize and examine her inner strength and to directly confront any problem.

"You are a strong woman," he told her in a calm, assured tone, "quite capable of dealing with any problem that befalls you. You are a fighter. You never give up. The world might present problems but you have always overcome any difficulties. No obstacle can stop you! God has a purpose for you. You will be a wife and a mother. There will be a loving husband and a number of precious, tender children. Life has a great deal to offer you. Your future is wondrous and filled with love and happiness."

He had her raise her right arm, told her that she had the strength of three men, and that no one could force her to move that arm. He asked

Jean Murphy to attempt to move Connie's arm but she could not.

"The physical strength you possess is matched by your strength of will. You will survive simply because you want to, and because you desire to achieve the bounties of your future. Say these words after me: I will endure. I will overcome. I will achieve!"

Her eyes closed and her mind locked in an intense focus, Connie dutifully repeated the phrases. More than that, these words were converted into electro-neuronic impulses and carried in neurofibrils to a place deep inside her mind where they were processed, engaged, and absorbed.

Thurston finished on a high note. "Tell me the instant in your life when you experienced electric joy, the greatest happiness you can recall."

Connie slipped into a slight dream and responded, "I was twelve or so. I had a boyfriend for six months. His name was Danny and I fell head over heels for him. We had a moment I will always remember. My first kiss."

"Good, Miss Dandridge. The joy of that moment. The supreme happiness of it. Think on it now. Remember the exquisite beauty of that moment. Experience that same feeling now."

April 26, 1907 Chicago, Illinois

Mike Fitzgerald agreed to meet Johnny Laughlin this night "for a hundred-dollar job." Although he had told himself after the first job that he could never do it again, Fitzgerald could not resist the powerful lure of one hundred dollars, enough money to buy him two months of clean beds and ample liquid refreshment. Even if it meant, as he assumed it did, another gruesome murder. Fitzgerald no longer wrestled with his conscience. He had done it once, he could do it again. It was easier to just not think about it. To blot out any nagging thoughts. There would be time to think afterwards, when the whiskey would wash away all doubts and regrets.

They met at *Lila's*, sharing a beer in a corner of the parlor. Johnny laid out a sketchy plan as the two men sat at a small table covered with an elaborate lace doily.

"Bossman says we gotta take out another whore. All you need to know is that this bitch done wrong. Big time wrong. She thinks she's too good for this place. She is living with some bigwig baseball team owner, fella that runs the Cubs. In his big house on the North Side. Been watching the place for a week now. Got it all figured out. I pretty much know who's gonna be home and who's not. We take the train to get there, I do her, and we get out. We don't hafta clean up the place or nuttin' like that. We do the job and then get the hell out. You carry the gun in case somebody makes trouble."

"How do we get in?"

"Easy. Jus' like I done once before on another job. We carry these small toolboxes and I got us badges sayin' we're from Commonwelt' Edison—the electric company. And we wear these caps pulled down low on the noggin. Pretty nice, huh?"

The two hopped on a red electric streetcar headed north on State Street. After getting off in the Loop they walked a block to catch another streetcar north and twenty minutes later found themselves on Lincoln Avenue on a cool, brisk day in mid-afternoon, facing the Murphy residence. As Laughlin knocked on the front door, Fitzgerald slipped his hand into his pocket and flipped the safety on the pistol. Emma, the seventeen-year-old servant girl, answered the door, wearing a white apron over a black dress.

"Yes?" she asked, looking at the two strange men. A sweaty sheen covered Fitzgerald's forehead and upper lip.

"We're from Commonwealt' Edison. We hafta check your wires. We think ya got a problem here." Johnny started in.

"Please wait here while I get the missus."

A minute later Mrs. Murphy greeted the two men.

"What is it, gentlemen?"

"We have to check all the wiring, ma'am. We know there's a circuit problem somewhere. Gotta find out where. Could be serious if we don't find it."

"You are from Edison?"

"Yes'm. This here's my badge."

"Well, alright. Maybe you could start down here and not bother the young lady upstairs?"

"Uh, no, sorry, ma'am. We're supposed to begin with the wiring upstairs. Won't take long."

"Oh well." She sent them upstairs with Emma.

As they trudged up the stairs Johnny said, "Maybe we should start with the young lady's room and get it over with."

Emma took them to Connie's room and knocked.

Connie sat at her desk writing as the three walked in. Johnny pulled his hat down over his head and hung behind his partner.

"Miss Dandridge, these two gentlemen need to look at the electric wires in here."

Connie began to speak when Little Johnny grabbed Emma from behind. He squelched her cries by stuffing a rolled-up cloth in her mouth and quickly tied her hands in back of her. He then locked her in the closet. All the while Fitzgerald pointed the gun at Connie, but when he heard Emma address her as "Miss Dandridge," a cool shiver fell over him.

"What is this all about?" Connie demanded, a slow terror overcoming her as she observed the man with the gun.

Now Johnny sprung forward, removing his hat, his yellowed teeth bared by a wide smile. Connie took one look at him and remembered the face. The same hideous grin he wore eating that sandwich while the madman ravaged her. She screamed.

Johnny took out a large knife, his greasy fingers set off in stark contrast against the flash of the silver blade. Fitzgerald edged up behind him and looked carefully at Connie's auburn hair and brown eyes.

He turned to Johnny and asked, "What's her Christian name, Johnny?"

"Her name is Connie Dandridge. She ratted out McGill. No one does that and lives."

Fitzgerald turned pale, a riveting pain shooting up from deep in his gut. "Let me ask her one question, Johnny. Just one question."

"I don't have time for games here! One question."

"Your mother, what was her Christian name?"

Connie trembled. "Why, for God's sake?"

"Please! Her name?" Fitzgerald was begging.

"Theresa."

Fitzgerald stiffened and peered into the large eyes of the girl he now knew to be his daughter. In those eyes he saw his wife and himself, a perfect blend. Connie, his daughter, alive! At least for the moment, as he remembered that he was here to kill her.

Johnny took a step toward Connie but Fitzgerald suddenly placed the gun at the left side of Laughlin's head and pulled the trigger. Nothing happened. A sickly silence fell over the room. Connie swooned.

"What the fuck!" shouted Johnny, his scarred face contorted with fear. He then suddenly smiled.

He spoke without raising his voice, but the words came from deep within his throat, edgy and pointed. "You must be outta bullets, big boy.

A real shame. You picked a fuckin' bad time to go nuts on me." Raising the blade in Mike's direction, he then looked away, as if something else caught his eye. But it was a deception. Laughlin pivoted and slashed the knife at Fitzgerald, who jumped back at the last instant. The blade still caught his left arm just below the elbow. It sliced into Fitzgerald's flesh.

Mike remained calm. He pushed the safety catch with his thumb, and stabbed the gun into Laughlin's gut. This time the pistol fired and Laughlin jerked back, dead before he hit the floor. The leering grin remained stamped on the dead man's face.

Fitzgerald turned toward Connie, who shrank from him, afraid that she was next.

"My name is Michael Fitzgerald. I am—I think—your father."

"What? No... it cannot be!" Connie grew dizzy.

"I am so sorry. I married Theresa Dandridge. We had a baby girl, Constance. Your hair color. Your eyes. Theresa's mother was from Cleveland. A sister in Iowa."

"Yes! But—you came here to kill me?"

"I didn't know. I didn't realize. There is no way to explain— nothing to say except that I am sorry. You have another chance. Forgive me, girl. I truly loved your mother. I loved you, but long ago I was lost." He turned to leave and then looked back. "Is she still alive?"

He knew the answer from Connie's face. Another stab of pain in his chest buckled his knees. Fitzgerald looked down and saw the gun in his right hand. He put it in his pocket, gently touched the hand of his daughter, turned and reeled toward the door. Waves of emotion swept over Fitzgerald like cold winds barrelling across the Illinois prairie. He did not look back.

Fitzgerald stumbled out of the Murphy residence in a daze, trying to choke back the stinging tears. Head down, he walked without a destination, his legs grinding out a steady trudge, as if they possessed their own purpose or goal. The gun weighed heavily in his pocket, and the smell of burnt gunpowder still lingered in his nostrils. He put his right hand to his nose and the unpleasant sulphurous odor overwhelmed him. I could use this gun one more time, he thought. A bullet in my brain. No more of this madness. One simple pull of the trigger. He tramped on, not looking up, afraid to peer into the eyes of another human being. For the first time he felt the sting of the knife wound below his left elbow. Stopping to examine it, he ripped a piece of his undershirt to tie around the arm and staunch the bleeding. He looked up once as a young couple approached him, averting their eyes from the bloody man in tattered clothes. The woman's face was Connie's, until it slowly changed into the face of a passing stranger.

Fitzgerald looked down at his blood-caked hands. He sensed the stink of the murder seeping into his palms. His finger pulled the trigger that killed a man. A loathsome and mean man, but still a man. *I snuffed out that life*, Mike thought, while realizing that the deed saved the life of his daughter. His legs kept pumping out their steps, taking him south toward the Loop. The wind kicked up a swirl of dust and litter, propelling a small piece of cardboard against Fitzgerald's leg. Its bright yellow hue penetrated the haze that enveloped Fitzgerald. He stooped and grabbed it with the same hand that had killed a human being twenty minutes earlier. *Perhaps the hand is guilty and not the man?* He looked at the small piece of cardboard, discerning it to be a ticket. A ticket to a stage play in the Loop, at the Temple Theater. A play entitled *The Wizard of Oz*. Fitzgerald had never heard of this play. The ticket was for tonight's performance, two hours later.

Mike treated the appearance of the ticket as a message from on high. He must see the play. "I got a free pass for tonight's performance," he thought. "A reason exists for this good fortune. There will be time to blow my brains out later."

April 26, 1907 Chicago, Illinois

Introduced in Chicago in 1902, the play known as *The Wizard of Oz* swept the nation off its feet. Successful from coast to coast, it broke box office records in every venue. Installed at the Temple Theater, in the Masonic Temple Building, the return engagement sported a lesser cast than the original Chicago production. Fitzgerald made it there as the doors opened for a meager Thursday night crowd. He laid the ticket, emblazoned "Fred J. Hamlin's Musical Extravaganza," into the readied palm of a bald ticket-taker who wore a green jacket embroidered with golden crests and epaulets. The ticket-taker did not look up at the unkempt, bloodied, and reeking man who presented the ticket. A young usher showed Fitzgerald, who did not check his coat, to his seat, twentieth row on the right side, and handed him a one-page stage bill. Fitzgerald had trouble reading the handout and finally gave up, leaning back in the well-padded chair and dozing for ten minutes.

The stirrings of the orchestra awakened him. The opening scene of the play did not grab Fitzgerald, as young Dorothy Gale, her cow Imogene, and some other characters gamboled about Kansas. But then came the cyclone. The whirling storm tore up Kansas and yanked Dorothy, Imogene the cow, waitress Tryxie Tryfle from Topeka, and Tryxie's boyfriend Pastoria, skyward and deposited them in the land of Oz. The depiction of the cyclone enthralled Fitzgerald. Dizzying magic lantern images of Dorothy, her house, Imogene, and the others swirled about on a giant gauze screen, terrifying a third of the audience and delighting the rest.

The play progressed with numerous show songs that had nothing to do with the plot. The story was carried by vaudevillian repartee, puns, and topical humor, and dozens of beautiful girls in skimpy costumes, all legs and clavicles. Fitzgerald never did understand that the character Pastoria was in fact the former King of Oz, who had been tricked out of his kingdom by the man from earth who assumed the position of Wizard in the Emerald City. Pastoria reminded Fitzgerald of men like Hinky Dink Kenna, fast-talking politicians who bought him drinks and secured him jobs in exchange for his vote. These men stole and cheated but provided help and sustenance for those in need.

Fitzgerald found himself pulled into the tale by the comic interplay between the Scarecrow and the Tin Woodman. When the field of poppies enveloped Dorothy, Pastoria, Tryxie, Imogene, and the Lion in a deep, dangerous sleep, Fitzgerald cheered as the snowflakes fluttered down from the heavens, killing the poppies, and reviving the travelers, ending Act I to the thunderous applause of the audience. He found himself concerned, actually caring that Dorothy and the others might persuade the Wizard in the Emerald City to assist them in their plight.

The Scarecrow and his wobbly walk amused Fitzgerald greatly—he walked in this manner when the whiskey filled his gut. The Scarecrow's motives were pure and simple—he sought the brain his maker had not provided. His song delighted the audience:

> *When brains are lacking in a head,*
> *It's usually the rule,*
> *That wisdom from the man has fled,*
> *And he remains a fool.*
> *So tho' my charms are very great,*
> *As I am well assured,*
> *I'll never reach my full estate,*
> *Till brains I have secured.*

Fitzgerald marveled at the scene in which the Scarecrow was cut up and reassembled, although it brought back troubling memories of the pigs and cattle in the slaughterhouses he had worked. Later, when Imogene the cow nibbled on pieces she had plucked out of the Straw Man, Fitzgerald convulsed with laughter, rolling back and forward in his seat. *This Scarecrow cannot feel the pain of the flesh*, thought Fitzgerald. *In that respect he has an advantage over mortal men like me.*

The Tin Woodman also intrigued Fitzgerald, whose wildest dreams had never included a man made of metal, let alone an iron man seeking a lost heart. This poor creature, once a normal being named Niccolo Chopper, loved the beautiful Cynthia, a Munchkin girl. But the Wicked Witch disapproved. She charmed Chopper's own axe to cut off his arms, legs, and body, leaving only his head. A kindly tinsmith replaced Nick's limbs and body with tin versions but could not restore the heart he had lost to Cynthia. Then came Dorothy to the rescue! The Tin Man accepted Dorothy's invitation to seek a heart from the great Wizard of Oz.

And while the cowardly lion scurried about on all fours with a giant head and uttered not a single line during the play, he too drew the sympathy of Fitzgerald and the audience. For what is a lion who lacks courage if not a sad and useless creature? This groveling beast could also be cured by the great wizard.

The play included three romantic threads: Dorothy and the poet Dashemoff, Pastoria and Tryxie, and the Tin Woodman and Cynthia. But these relationships held no particular interest for Fitzgerald. He longed for resolution. Emotion overcame him as the Scarecrow found his brain, the Tin Woodman his heart, the Lion his courage, and Dorothy her home in Kansas.

I am like them, he thought. *I have lost my heart, my reason, and my will. And like Dorothy I have lost my way.*

He walked out of the play emptied, a man in desperate search of his soul.

April 27, 1907 Governors Island; New York

The meeting with the Italian gentlemen proved fruitful. One week later Percy obtained the information he needed, architectural drawings of the prison and other parts of the island. A lawyer with muddy trouser cuffs, allowed to provide Percy legal documents, smuggled the drawings into the prison for a small fee. The documents, forty years old, did not provide everything that Percy needed to know, as the prison had been modified in recent decades. But these dusty papers gave Percy valuable information. To Percy's dismay the plans revealed that no tunnel connected the island to Manhattan or Brooklyn. The boys of Sandy Hook had lied. Two different drawings, however, confirmed something else about Castle Williams that could be very helpful to Percy, if he could just locate one particular door.

After his work detail, a one-sentence telegram arrived for Percy. The prison authorities opened it, recorded its contents, and gave it to him after supper. The guard who handed it to Percy read it first. The yellow-brown message read:

Regret to inform you of sudden death of John R. Laughlin.

Mrs. Wm. Kelly

For Chrisakes! Percy thought. *What on earth is happening? From bad to worse!* The very next thought that popped into his head: *If you want something done right, you got to do it yourself.*

April 28, 1907 Chicago, Illinois

William Wilen learned of the attempt on Connie's life from Charles Murphy. The news made his blood boil. Anger and frustration fueled his every step. He had warned McGill to leave the girl alone, and yet McGill reached out from his prison cell to kill her. This man would not listen to reason and acted without regard to Wilen's warnings. The silver-haired prosecutor must take forceful steps to protect Miss Dandridge.

He dropped everything else to investigate the matter. Wilen knew that the dead man, John Laughlin, worked for Percy McGill. As yet he did not know the identity of the other man who had killed Laughlin and fled. Wilen ordered everyone at *Lila's* whorehouse interrogated but nothing productive surfaced. He had two investigators do a quick ask-around in *Lila's* neighborhood to come up with the name of another male employee of the business. They drew a blank. Mrs. Kelly refused to talk, so he had her confined in the County Jail on charges of running a house of prostitution. Wilen then took steps to close *Lila's* down. When the Chief of Police finally agreed, Wilen arranged to board it up.

Wilen personally purchased a ticket on the Twentieth Century Limited, a first-class, express train that could get him to New York City in fourteen hours. He boarded at the LaSalle Street Station, striding across the New York Central Railroad's bright red carpets, just as they advertised. Wilen's goal: to confront the scoundrel McGill. Wilen quickly consumed a small dinner in the dining car, sharing the table with a recently married young couple, returned to his own sleeping compartment, and dozed off by 9:30 p.m. A troubled sleep did not refresh the Chicago prosecutor. A disturbing dream plagued him that night, a vision of a huge hulking wolverine, hungry and dangerous, a black-maned beast in the Canadian forest. The creature, frothy juices dripping from its jaws, stalked a herd of sheep on the forest edge. It bolted toward the herd and leaped upon a ewe, its jagged teeth eviscerating the helpless animal with one mighty bite and a tug of its head. When he awoke to the Pullman porters' shouts of "New York City," Wilen recalled the dream, and knew without a doubt that he would be visiting that wolverine in a few hours.

Wilen had visited New York City only once before, with his wife, to attend a session of the American Bar Association. They had stayed at the Waldorf, wandered the lively streets of Manhattan, marveling at the bridges and the Statue of Liberty. But now Gotham seemed different, less welcoming. Smoke hung low over Manhattan, like a filthy shroud over the city. Hack-drivers seemed surly and dour, and the streets seemed filled with the hungry and homeless. Wilen, too, grew sullen and morose, questioning his approach to the problem at hand. He had always worked within the law to gain justice and serve the public good, but in this instance his lifelong respect for the rule of law did not work to protect the young woman. He wondered if he should consider a less principled strategy.

The short boat trip to Governors Island gave the prosecutor some pleasure, as the clouds dissolved and a warm sun enveloped him. A calm harbor made the jaunt easy, but the tension within Wilen gradually rose as his thoughts returned to the reason for his journey. Six young working-class women and several children shared the ferry. They told stories of their lives waiting for prison sentences to run their course. When the ship moored on the island, Wilen let the young women and the kids disembark first, and then bolted up the causeway toward the entrance to Castle Williams. *I could,* he pondered, *arrange an accidental death for Percy McGill. These things happen in prison.* His pace slowed. *Maybe I am the wolverine in the dream?*

Fifteen minutes later, the warden of the prison, Sergeant Bell, greeted Wilen and whisked him out of the small, stuffy visitors' waiting room.

"You wanted to interrogate McGill?"

"Yes, Sergeant. It is important."

"Very well. Can you tell me anything about the purpose of your visit, counselor?"

"Yes. We believe prisoner Percy McGill conspired with a Chicago fellow named John Laughlin to kill a young woman. I am guessing that your visitor records will show Laughlin met with McGill shortly before Laughlin and another man attempted to murder the girl."

"You are guessing right, Mr. Wilen. John Laughlin came here as a witness in McGill's court martial. Met with Percy McGill both before and after the trial."

"I see. I will need a record of those dates before I leave. I will also need copies of any letters or other communications to Mr. McGill and copies of his responses."

"Of course. You wish to meet with McGill now?"

"Yes."

"And would you like me to be present or would you prefer to meet him alone?"

"Alone would be best, sir," Wilen responded, getting up out of his chair as he answered.

Sgt. Bell led Wilen across a courtyard to a pleasant room that turned out to be Bell's office. He seated Wilen behind an ornate cherry-wood desk and provided him paper and a Conklin fountain pen. Soon a uniformed guard led the shackled McGill into the room, leg-irons causing the prisoner to shuffle to his seat. The guard prodded McGill to the other side of the desk from Wilen and then left.

In a gray, striped prison uniform, McGill looked unchanged to Wilen. The same cold eyes and impertinent countenance. Percy slid back in the chair, as if to luxuriate in the moment.

"What brings you to this god-forsaken place, Willy?" asked the prisoner, allowing a small grin to form at the corners of his mouth.

"You surely know the reason."

"No sir. I am at a loss. Please enlighten me."

"The subject that brings me here is the same woman whom you viciously assaulted in Chicago not so long ago. Constance Dandridge."

"Judge said I didn't do it. She's just a two-bit whore. She give you a free fuck, did she? Wild and wet was she, Willy, like a bucking bronco?"

Wilen expected as much from McGill, and had steeled himself for this manner of provocation. He had heard such things many times before and didn't bite at the bait.

"I will not trade insults with you, McGill. It would accomplish nothing. I am here simply to tell you that you have miscalculated. We have taken certain actions in Chicago."

McGill said nothing but he leaned back, waiting for Wilen to explain.

"Your colleagues' attempted murder of Constance Dandridge—"

McGill exploded with a laugh. "Absolute rot. I had nothin' to do with any of that!"

"Shut up, McGill, or I will walk out of here and you'll have to wait a week to learn what we have done. Your foolhardy actions have already cost you dearly. The house of prostitution—*Lila's*—which has financed your criminal activities, has been shuttered and no matter what you do or try to do, it will never re-open. I have seen to that. No amount of boodle will alter that fact. *Lila's*, by the way, is about to be condemned. It will be auctioned in the summer and the proceeds will go to pay the considerable fines attached to the property. Your friend, Officer Jensen, now walks a beat on the West Side, far away from *Lila's*. The woman who calls herself Mrs. Kelly now resides in the Cook County jail. We are holding her on a number of charges, including conspiracy to attempt murder. You may contact her in care of my office. I am sorry to say she does not seem to be doing so well. Head colds, melancholia, and the like. Prison can be difficult for the gentle sex. Finally, as you are well aware, your associate John Laughlin and another man attempted to kill Miss Dandridge. Unsuccessful as you well know, although one good thing came of it, a silver lining so to speak. Your confederate, the late Little Johnny Laughlin, ended up with a bullet in his cold heart."

McGill spoke softly and without emotion. "You had no right meddling in my business. I had nothin' to do with any of that attempted murder crap. I have my own problems right here."

"Let me finish. The investigation of the attempt on Connie Dandridge's life is continuing as we speak. You may soon find yourself back in Chicago, facing a hangman's noose for all of this. If we locate the man who killed your friend Johnny, we may be able to tie you into this. Or maybe Mrs. Kelly will shed some light on this affair. She seems out of sorts in her current surroundings. Desperation sometimes lubricates the memory and loosens the tongue."

"You ought not treat an old woman like that."

"When it comes to the treatment of women, sir, I will take no counsel from the likes of you."

"You call her 'Miss Connie Dandridge.' Well, I call her 'Carmen' or 'Missy' or whatever the hell I want to call her. You think of her as a human being. I don't. She's a stinking piece of shit. Nothing more. You've had your fun with me, Willy, shutting down my business and all. That's okay, because I've had my fun with her. A bobcat, Willy, a true bobcat. And who knows what will happen when I get outta this place."

A dull pain rolled around in Wilen's gut. McGill's steel blue eyes flashed cold and unblinking, piercing and hateful. Wilen looked away, fearful that he would lose his composure and physically attack the prisoner. Maybe drive the fountain pen through McGill's heart or into an eye. Disgusted and disappointed, he called for the guard to remove the man.

April 29, 1907 **Cincinnati, Ohio**

Sleeping all night in their Pullman berths as their train rumbled across Illinois, Indiana, and Ohio, the Cubs arrived in Cincinnati at 8:30 a.m. The boys left two black porters smiling with generous tips, although Jack Taylor did not contribute, commenting that "those bedbugs did not apply a proper shine to my shoes last night."

The players boarded the Black Line trolley to the Sinton Hotel, and by nine o'clock Secretary Williams stood in the lobby, checking them in. The hotel clerk, towering over a small marble-topped registration desk, knew many of the Cubs from prior visits and winked at Johnny Evers as the diminutive athlete grabbed a piece of hard candy from a bowl on the counter. Most of the Cubs took their rooms and relaxed for two hours, but a few, like Taylor and Steinfeldt, explored the streets of downtown Cincy looking for adventure, finally settling for a game of billiards and a few beers at Schubert's. After lunch the team changed into their uniforms at the hotel and endured a carriage-parade to the Palace of the Fans. One curb-stander spotted Frank Chance as the procession passed and bellowed, "Chance, Muggsy McGraw's gonna beat your ass this year!" Husk sneered and swiveled around to locate the source of the insult, but the man slunk back into the anonymous crowd.

Under clear skies and a gentle breeze, a few thousand fans watched the Reds take the field. While the Cincinnati record stood at only 4-8, the beginning of a game in a young season offered boundless possibilities. Every Red and most of their fans held out hope that this team would compete.

In the opening frame, with a runner on first, Jimmy Sheckard bunted to advance him. The Reds pitcher didn't grab the ball cleanly and pegged high to first. Sheckard figured he beat the throw but umpire O'Day called him out. The Cubs outfielder approached him for an exchange of views, but O'Day didn't want to chat. Jimmy kept beefing. The fans yelled loudly, urging O'Day to "put him out!" O'Day, in a low tone, told the Cubs outfielder to "quit jawing like a chatterbird." Sheckard let loose a string of insults, finally calling the man in blue an "old Gazeka." It is not clear whether O'Day, or Sheckard, or any of the assembled multitudes for that matter, had any idea what the term "Gazeka" meant, and learned discussion afterwards could not determine its meaning. The mystery left O'Day little room.

"Get the fuck outta he-ah," shouted the umpire, with his finger pointing to the horizon.

Frank Chance, observing the dispute from the bench, became very agitated, muttering between huge spits of tobacco juice.

"I should kick that umpire's ass," Frank vented.

Instead, he leapt onto the field and kicked the hell out of the leather ballbag that lay next to the Cubs bench, sending eleven stitched spheres in different directions. Chance commanded Durbin to collect the balls and return them to the bag, where they remained until the fifth inning when the Cubs pilot again assaulted the sack. Schulte and his charley horse replaced Sheckard in left.

Miner Brown hadn't thrown for ten days, since Shorty Slagle dropped the fly ball against the Pirates, so the stolid hurler advanced to the mound feeling strong and confident. Brownie cut down the first twelve batters like weeds under the blade of a scythe. The dipping curveball, time after time, resulted in infield grounders and easy pop-ups. But the Reds twirler, six-footer Bob Ewing, matched Brown's performance pitch for pitch through eight innings. Ewing had learned how to throw the spitball three years earlier, and it transformed his career. He used it ruthlessly against the Cubs this day. The two teams headed into the last frame locked in a scoreless tie. Slagle, Brown's roommate, took matters into his own hands in the ninth, powering a fastball over the head of the Reds center fielder. The smash had triple written all over it but a relay got away, allowing Jimmy to circle the bases and score. That made it 1-0 Cubs. Miner congratulated Slagle when he returned to the bench, huffing and puffing.

"You sure put a mule-kick into that one, Rabbit."

Chance also congratulated Slagle.

"You put that fuckin' spitballer outta business, Jimmy!"

Slagle lit a Sweet Caporal cigarette, inhaled deeply, and smiled, a happy man. Only a few men, like Husk and Slagle, risked being viewed as effeminate by smoking cigarettes rather than cigars.

A monarch butterfly flitted about near the Cubs bench. Spying the insect, Slagle let out a hoot. "We gonna win this one. Got the red butterfly for luck!"

Durbin asked teammate Sheckard to explain Slagle's comment.

"It's as simple as pie. Red butterflies mean you win. White butterflies mean you're about to get your ass kicked to Kahokia. Don'tcha know that?"

The Reds gave the Cubs a scare in the bottom of the ninth. With runners on second and third, Brownie pulled out all the stops and, with the help of the red butterfly, the Cubs pocketed their fifth victory in a row. The former coal miner walked slowly off the field, concealing his exuberance. He shook hands with his teammates and promised himself a great big Delmonico steak for supper.

May 2, 1907 Cincinnati, Ohio

Husk slated Jack Pfiester to pitch. Almost six feet tall, Pfiester, not a handsome man, lacked a real chin and his narrow eyes squinted from the shadow of their brows. Worse yet, protruding ears could not balance a large nose and black hair, which hung down over his forehead in strings. But Jack's teammates liked the diffident southpaw, and he had a wide circle of friends, some of whom honored the native Ohioan prior to the game. A girl of seven presented Pfiester with a bouquet of flowers and a kiss. But once Jack toed the rubber and gave up a few runs, Jimmy Slagle began to blame the flowers for the weak performance.

"Ya just cain't accept nuthin' from the other guys and expect to beat 'em," Jimmy opined on the bench. "There's a sayin'… 'Beware of Greeks with boring gifts.' Maybe they snuck some kinda powder onto those roses."

The flowers affected more than Pfiester, as the Cubs made four errors, including two by Hofman. They managed only six singles and one run off the tall young Reds hurler, Del Mason, while his teammates bunched eight hits to score three tallies. Rookie Randall came to the plate and swung wildly at the first two pitches he saw, going into the hole 0-2. He held off from swinging at the third pitch, which broke outside the strike zone by a foot, but Hank O'Day called him out. Surprised, Randall looked umpire O'Day in the eyes and whined, "You missed that one, Ump!"

"Well, you missed the first two," O'Day replied, "so I'm one up on you."

As this exchange occurred, Johnny Evers and Chance screamed obscenities at the man in blue from the bench, but he pretended not to hear. Randall sulked toward the bench, having a genuinely bad day. Besides the strikeout, the rookie dropped an easy fly ball and got nailed trying to steal second. When the last Cub grounded out to end the game, the Cubs learned that the New York Giants had won, tying them with the Chicagoans for the National League lead.

Slagle knew why the Cubs lost. "We hit a hoodoo. No doubts about it."

The sportswriters found out after the game that President Murphy spoke with Reds owner Gary Herrmann about selling Fred Osborn to him, but Herrmann did not bite. Cincinnati also announced that pitcher Cotton Minahan, the rookie who had imploded against the Cubs in their earlier confrontation, had come down with a malarial infection. In truth, the young man had syphilis, but in this era both the ballclubs and the press used "malaria" as a code word for a variety of sexually transmitted diseases. Minahan never again pitched in the big leagues.

From the Journal of Kid Durbin

May 3, 1907

I did not learn until two days ago of the monstrous attempt on Connie's life. It sickens me that this poor woman should have to experience something of this nature on top of everything else that she's gone through. There's no doubt in my mind as to who is responsible for this unspeakable act. That wretched excuse for a human being, Percy McGill. Mr. Murphy told me that Mr. Wilen has taken steps to deal with this and is now in New York to sort things out. I have prayed for Connie's well-being. It is difficult for me to put my feelings about this down on paper.

 The rains cost us another game today. Frank Chance called me into President Murphy's office after the game got cancelled and I thought maybe he had sold me to the bushes. But it wasn't that at all. Seems my father sent Husk a letter. Here's what he said:

Dear Mr. Chance:

My name is James F. Durbin and I am Blaine Durbin's father. I believe you and his teammates call him "Kid" and most everyone hereabouts does likewise except for me. For me he will always be "Blaine."

As you can well imagine I am very pleased that the Cubs extended a generous offer of employment to Blaine. Half the town is excited that a native son of Lamar is now wearing a uniform for the Chicago Nationals. The other half are Cardinal fans.

I hope you will give my son a few opportunities to show you what he can do. You will see that he has great talent and a fierce, competitive spirit. I have seen that since he was a small boy.

Sincerely,
James F. Durbin

I apologized to Husk when he showed me the letter, but he told me it wasn't necessary. Instead, he apologized to me! The man has a heart of gold. He told me my day would come and that we all have to pay our dues sometimes before we get a break. I told him I'd be ready when he needed me.

I took an early supper alone, at a steak place in the Loop. While expensive (it cost $1.05), they gave me a huge cut of juicy red beef. The waiter, a not-too-friendly fellow named Grover, had a big wart on his neck, with many hairs sprouting from it. While Grover had brown hair, the hair on the wart was white. I had seen the same sort of thing on a sow back in Lamar. I resolved to concentrate on the steak rather than the wart so as to enjoy my meal. Dousing the meat with Worcestershire sauce, I must have eaten a full pound. I paid the bill, threw down a tip of fifteen cents, and strolled out of the restaurant, a full stomach and three beers under my belt.

During my supper, I kept rolling that discussion with Husk over and over in my mind. He did not promise me any opportunities to pitch and I can't say I blame him given how well our slabmen are doing. I will just have to be content pitching to the batting practice for the time being.

After supper I wandered south on State Street to take in a dime museum I'd seen there. The broad street teemed with beggars, tourists, and prostitutes. A man in a clown suit carried an advertising sign that said "Clothing Sale at the Boston Store," only he carried the sign upside down, making it tough to read. Six or seven bicycle riders shot by me going north at a great speed while a little boy offered to sell me a pair of shoestrings for a nickel.

I stopped below a huge, colorful banner that hung outside the dime museum, "Ricardo's House of Wonders." The banner stretched from the third floor to the ground, with large illustrations of men with two heads, a half-man, half-fish creature, tiny people, and the Circassian Princess, a beautiful woman wearing a delightfully skimpy outfit. Near the door a shiny metal sign proclaimed: "See the fish that learned to read!" It cost a quarter to enter. I asked the old man who took the admission fees why a dime museum cost a quarter. He said, and from his tone I figured he must have said this a thousand times over the years, "Dime

museum is the name of the institution, sir, not the price of admission."
I entered.

What a strange place this was! Right in the main hall, under three large chandeliers, the Fish Man swam in a huge metal and glass tank of water. He seemed like an ordinary fellow. I didn't see any gills or scales. He wore a green leather tunic around his legs to give him the look of a mermaid, or merman, and surfaced every minute and a half to gulp some air. Children who put their faces right up to the tank delighted in the funny faces the Fish Man made at them. In another corner of the main hall I found a shrunken head, a fetus with three arms, and a skull with a unicorn-like horn coming out of the forehead. The next room had an exhibit called "Honest Abe's Last Defecation." A pile of shit, now hardened and shrunken, which the sign said came from President Lincoln's deathbed. I took one look and turned away in disgust.

In the next room I saw a large exhibit entitled "Direct From Coney Island—Dr. Couney's Miniature People." It cost another ten cents to get in, but lots of folks paid it. Eight large glass boxes lined the walls of this room, each with two little babies asleep inside. And when I say little I mean little. One look told me these were not ordinary babies. Each baby was only seven or eight inches long and the sign listed their names and weights. They weighed between one pound, eleven ounces and three pounds. It seems these babies got themselves in a heap of trouble by being born too soon. I learned that the boxes housing the infants were called electric incubators, and that by keeping the babies very warm and filtering the air they breathed these tiny kids stood a chance to live. Dr. Couney's daughter, a nurse, explained that hundreds of babies like these gained the chance for a normal life at her father's Coney Island facility. She said most hospitals, both in New York and Chicago, had yet to invest in incubators, and that those that did reserved them for "their wealthy, paying clients." I asked her how hospitals without incubators treated these "too soon" babies and she said they let them die. One lady next to me said she had been coming every day for the past week to observe one of the infants on display, "Baby Julie." The woman seemed pleased because Baby Julie had gained another two ounces since her last visit and looked rather pink.

The "Zulu Warrior" in another room also interested me. A tall, very dark Negro, he wore a grass skirt and lots of feathers. Another man beat a drum and the Zulu fellow danced about wildly, getting all sweaty and losing a feather or two in the process. But after his exertions I heard him ask the drummer for a glass of water. He spoke English with a Southern twang so I doubt he came direct from Zululand like the sign proclaimed.

The Circassian Princess made up for the Zulu and Lincoln "exhibits." A gorgeous woman in a skirt that reached just to her knees, she sang and danced for five minutes on a small stage in a room packed with men of all ages. Blond and petite, she had a warm smile and a winning personality. And magnificent legs. At the end of her show, following a sustained and heartfelt applause, she announced that a special one-man show would begin in fifteen minutes, starring Mr. David Bates, "the famous bigamist." The topic of Bates' address would be "How to Win a Woman."

Bates had been convicted ten years earlier in Chicago of marrying six different women. He would have breakfast with one wife, lunch with another, and so on. Following a brief prison stint, Bates now earned a living lecturing on his favorite subject—women and how to woo them. As I figured I could use some advice in this regard, I paid the extra dime to hear from an expert.

Bates was not a handsome man. About forty-five, somewhat stout, with thinning hair, a mustache, and spectacles, his voice boomed out to the crowd of a hundred men. I'll do my best to put down what he said:

> A man has to plan his conquest of a woman like he plans any great enterprise. Two overriding principles must govern your campaign: observation and sympathy. First, careful observation is critical. You must observe the woman closely, studying her needs, her likes, and dislikes. Do not let her know that you are scrutinizing her, but do so regularly and thoroughly. If you note that she has a preference for lilies rather than roses, mark that preference down in your mind for future use. Sympathy is the other key. As a species, women are extremely susceptible to sympathy. She will have troubles and if you

are there at her side, providing comfort and a calm hand, you will be rewarded. The close attentions of a manly presence will be appreciated and reciprocated.

Blonds, when angered, will attack you like a crazed tigress. But their temper is short-lived compared to dark-haired girls. Brunettes, with their deep, quiet nature, let their passions simmer and stew, extending any tempest.

All women admire mustaches. Wear one and keep it neat. Much depends, too, upon your feet. If possible, wear patent leather shoes. Do not wear a pink tie or red shirt. Women do not want their men dressed in the colors reserved for their gender. For brunettes, you should wear dark and quiet clothes. Loud clothing annoys the dark-haired woman. Blonds are more tolerant. You can wear large checks for a blonde if you like. Blonds seem fond of blue and white neckties.

The time will come for a kiss. Do not grab your girl like a cake off a hot griddle. Proceed slowly. Place one hand on the side of her head, perhaps in the region of her neck, but, by all means, do not dishevel her hair or her collar. The kiss is a critical step on the road toward winning her heart. If you do not study the principles of kissing you will find it difficult to achieve your goals.

Never should there be a hint of liquor on your breath. Nor should you indulge in sassafras, cloves, or cardamon seed, all of which girls view as a subterfuge.

Should the time come (or times in the case of Bates the Bigamist) when you must ask her the momentous question, you should be dressed in your best frock coat. Wait for the precise right moment, when she is possessed of a receptive humor. And you do not need to kneel—it will make you appear unmanly.

The crowd applauded Mr. Bates at the end of his speech. The fact that this ordinary-looking fellow had snagged such a great number of women certainly helped him sell tickets. Lacking experience in matters of the heart, I'm not sure what to make of much of what he said. But it cannot hurt for me to study these suggestions of Bates the Bigamist. By the way, I never did get to see the fish that learned to read.

May 3, 1907 Chicago, Illinois

Excluded from organized baseball, black men formed their own teams in Chicago, Philadelphia, New York, Kansas City, and other large cities. No black leagues existed, but sometimes the black teams traveled from city to city to face black competitors and an occasional white team. Prior to the 1906 World Series the owner of the black Philadelphia Giants, who had gone 108-31 that year, extended a challenge, addressed to the winner of the Cubs-Sox World Series. Play his team, he suggested, "and thus decide who can play baseball the best, the white or the black American." After winning the Series, the White Sox declined the invitation.

Chicago's premier African-American baseball club used the name Leland Giants, and Johnny Kling watched them play on more than one occasion. A Friday off-day provided Kling a perfect opportunity to visit an old friend, a man he hadn't seen in a year. He grabbed Durbin and Big Ed Reulbach and the three of them rode a cab south. The Leland Giants had a late afternoon game slated with the Philadelphia Giants. Kling wanted to see Buddy Petway, the skilled twenty-three-year-old catcher of the Philadelphia Giants. Frank Leland owned the local Giants, having assembled a legendary crew that mercilessly beat up on other black ballclubs. In fact, Leland raided the Philadelphia Giants for a number of players after the 1906 campaign.

The Leland Giants played in Auburn Ball Field, a small park at 79th Street and Wentworth. Kling paid seventy-five cents for admission for the three white men, and they found their way down to the field where the Philadelphia Giants took batting practice. Kling and the two others huddled out of the way, by the third base coach's box, as the batters sprayed line drives about the field. The rich, unmistakable sound of bat on ball drifted over the field and into the stands. Kling asked a small boy who lounged behind third base where he might find Bruce Petway.

"You might find Buddy in the toilet," the child answered.

The kid ran away, and a moment later a young black ballplayer approached, not tall but strongly built, about 5'7" and 175 pounds. He wore the uniform of the Philadelphia team and, recognizing Kling, opened his arms to welcome and embrace the Cubs catcher.

"Why Mr. Johnny Kling," Petway exclaimed, "I do declare you are a sight for sore eyes. What brings you here?"

"A day off and a desire to see some good baseball."

"You're in the right place for that."

"Lemme introduce you to my teammates, Buddy. This here is Big

Ed Reulbach, a pitcher who throws hard and in. Won nineteen games and lost only four last year."

Reulbach, surprised that Johnny knew his record, and slightly uncomfortable in these surroundings, spoke loudly as he extended his hand to the Philadelphia catcher. "Very glad to meet you, Buddy. Johnny has told me many good things about you."

"And this youngster," Kling interrupted, "is the newest addition to the Cubs pitching staff, Kid Durbin. He's a lefty, Buddy."

"I do like the southpaws. Glad to meet you, Kid."

After a few more minutes of conversation, the black catcher took his leave to prepare for the game and the three Cubs took seats that Buddy had arranged for them in the first row.

Another black man in uniform approached the trio, this fellow wearing the uniform of the Leland Giants.

"You're the guy I met in West Baden Springs," the tall man said as he advanced toward Durbin. "I remember the red hair."

"That's right, I'm Kid Durbin. And you're the guy with a smoking fastball, Mr. Dougherty, I believe."

"Just call me Pat. My fastball ain't been smokin' so much lately. What brings you gentlemen here?"

Durbin introduced Dougherty to Kling and Reulbach and they chatted for a few minutes before Dougherty needed to return to his pregame responsibilities.

"How did you meet Mr. Petway?" Durbin asked Kling, curious about how Johnny came to know this black man.

"Came out here for a look last year. Buddy was playing with a fine ballclub, called themselves the Cuban X-Giants. I told one of the guys I was a catcher and he asked me if I was lookin' for a job. It was Buddy, and when we got to talking it didn't take me long to figure out he knew the game backwards and forwards. He showed me the snap throw from the crouch and a few other things. I helped him with a few ideas on some signs, like where I pick up some dirt and toss it to the right it's a signal to Evers I'm going to try to pick off the guy at second on the next pitch. That kind of stuff."

Durbin asked Kling what kind of money the black players made.

"Not like we do," Kling replied. "These fellows, most of them, are lucky to make sixty bucks a month. They play because they love baseball, pure and simple. And Buddy gave up medical school for the game too!"

"Honest to God?"

"Yes. A school for colored doctors in Tennessee."

By the time the game started 1,400 fans filled the ballyard's rickety bleachers. Every one of them black except for twenty or thirty whites sprinkled about the place plus the white umpire. The black teams frequently used white umps because they figured the white ones wouldn't care who won.

Durbin looked around and said, "I ain't never seen so many coloreds in one place."

Kling laughed. "You feeling uncomfortable?"

"A little…"

"Well, now you know how a black man feels at the West Side Grounds, or most anyplace in Chicago."

A large, fat man took the mound for the Leland Giants. Standing six feet tall and weighing a menacing 240, Rube Foster warmed up quickly, sweat beading on his forehead and dripping from the tip of his nose. The portly right-hander didn't have the look of a ballplayer, but he threw the ball hard and it moved as it crossed the plate, sometimes dropping and sometimes breaking away from the batter. Kling and Reulbach tried to gauge the man's stuff. The owner of the team, Frank Leland, brought Foster to the Giants only weeks ago to pitch and to manage the team. Foster took the nickname "Rube" a few years back after besting the famous white pitcher, Rube Waddell, in an exhibition game. Kling judged the fastball as good or better than any Cub's, including Miner and the big man sitting next to him. Reulbach agreed.

"That man throws bullets," said Big Ed.

"Yeah," Kling responded. "He went 51-4 for the Cuban X-Giants four years back. And there's a rumor that McGraw hired Foster in the spring of '03 to teach Mathewson the fadeaway. Matty won thirteen or fourteen games in '02 and then he up and wins more than thirty after Rube's schooling."

Foster struck out the side in the top of the first. Foster's version of the fadeaway also impressed the Cubs trio.

"Did you see that one break?" Durbin exclaimed.

"Surely!" replied Reulbach. "That guy can pitch."

In the bottom of the first the third batter beat out an infield dribbler down the third base line. Two pitches later the base runner broke for second and Petway, from his knees, snapped the ball effortlessly to second. The ball whizzed out to second like an arrow, right on top of the base, an easy putout for the shortstop.

Kling turned to Reulbach and said, "Now, that was sweet!"

The game was hard fought, with Rube Foster only allowing five hits. Meanwhile, the Lelands' catcher, Pete Booker, a square-jawed, husky man, put on a display of his formidable skills. He laced three line drives for hits, two to center and one, a long ball, to right. The Leland Giants beat the Philadelphia team 4-1. In the ninth inning Durbin asked a question he had never asked before.

"These guys are good. As good as us. Foster could be pitching for the Cubs if he weren't colored. How come they aren't playing in the majors?"

"You should ask your friend Cap Anson about that," Kling responded.

"What do you mean?"

"Some folks will tell you it was Cap who drew the color line. Only it wasn't just Cap. Twenty years ago Cap's team, the White Stockings, had an exhibition game scheduled with the Newark team out of the International League. Cap learned that Newark planned to pitch a black man that day, a Canadian named Stovey. I don't remember the kid's full name. Anyways, Anson threatened to pull his team from the game if Stovey played. Said something like 'baseball could not survive the mixture of the races.' The Newark team agreed to pull the kid. That same night the International League bigwigs announced that no colored guys would get contracts after that season. It's been that way since. The coloreds can't play in the white leagues so they have their own independent teams. Thing is, Cap couldn't have done this all alone. He had lots of help."

"What happened to Stovey?"

"All I know is he won more than thirty games that year for Newark, but because of the new rule they couldn't re-sign him."

Shortly after the final out Pat Dougherty popped out of the dugout and brought Foster over to the three white ballplayers.

After introductions Foster spoke. "I asked Pat to introduce me to you guys. For two reasons. I seen you two fellows play last year in Philly. You whumped the Phillies good. So it's a damn pleasure to shake your hands. And second, I am most determined to see if we can set up a game between the Leland Giants and the Cubs."

May 4, 1907 Chicago, Illinois

The gentle cool air reminded Fitzgerald that spring would make life easier, since he could sleep outdoors and survive. He heard the lilt of music as he approached the corner of Dearborn and Monroe and soon gazed on eight young women and four men of varying ages, all singing hymns. A big sign in back of them proclaimed "The City of Zion Welcomes You." He stood at the edge of a small crowd and listened, and before too long a gentleman stood on a sturdy wooden soapbox and started to lecture. Fitzgerald guessed the speaker to be about forty, a blond man with eyeglasses and the hint of an Eastern accent. First he delivered a stern warning to the crowd that had formed, scolding them, saying, "Many of you worship mammon and Bacchus. They are your lords and kings. Unless you submit to the word of God, you will be dragged into the depths of hell. No matter what, no matter how you resist. Only the word of the Lord can save you." After warning the listeners of the dire consequences of not "setting things right with Jesus," the speaker told the audience of a wondrous city on the lake, some forty miles north of Chicago, the City of Zion. This, he said, was a City of God, a city where "the light of the Lord shone the way and where all was peace, tranquility, and godliness." He stated that thousands of Christians had committed their lives to this endeavor and lived there now, building a church community that grew each day. That city, he informed the crowd, welcomed all those who desired to live God-fearing lives under the guidance and tutelage of General Overseer Voliva.

Fitzgerald stood entranced, ripe for the picking. Two tears formed in the corners of his eyes.

One of the young ladies approached him, a short, dark-haired girl about twenty. She greeted him with "Peace to thee," to which he did not respond. The words then began to flow from her mouth, promising Fitzgerald a new life in a new place, a City of God open to all of god's children.

"You must see the City of Zion with your own eyes, brother," she pleaded. "My simple words cannot do it the justice it merits. It is truly heaven on earth. My name is Julia Bessant, and my family has lived in the City of Zion for three years. Three years which have drawn me into the warm embrace of the living god."

Mike Fitzgerald had no doubt of the sincerity of this child, and her name, "Julia," struck a chord. His mother's name. He remembered now a piece of an old poem she recited to him so often that it lingered in the back of his mind. A poem by a man named Herrick:

Whenas in silks my Julia goes,
Then, then, methinks,
how sweetly flows,
That liquefaction of her clothes.

He wondered if this was another sign. In a trembling voice he asked her, "How do I get to Zion?"

"We will take you there brother, on the railroad to heaven. We will leave in an hour and we will arrive there one hour later. There will be no expense for you to incur. Please sit here, and my brothers will register you."

Fitzgerald grabbed hold of a wooden folding chair and eased into it, convinced that a divine hand pointed the way for him. His body ached and heaved, deprived of alcohol for a day. But the promise of God's help overwhelmed him.

Just at that moment a man in a dapper new suit, enjoying a cigar, walked by.

The girl Julia, who had spoken to Fitzgerald in a calm and soothing tone, now became a banshee, screaming at the passerby, like he was the devil himself!

"Stinkpot!" she shrieked, "you abysmal, horrid stinkpot! The tobacco you burn does the work of Satan." Surprised but unfazed, the man inhaled on his cigar and walked on.

Precisely sixty-five minutes later, Fitzgerald, two other recruits, and the group from the City of Zion boarded a northbound train at the Grand Passenger Station just west of the Loop. The church people used the travel time for "productive godly purposes," meaning efforts to convert the recruited. Julia told Fitzgerald that everyone needs spiritual healing and that they would deal with that in Zion. But she also inquired if he needed any physical healing. The Church of Zion believed in the physical healing power of faith. Their General Overseer had cured many afflicted people. Fitzgerald had been taught by his Sunday School teacher that sickness and injury were a sign of god's love. But Julia's church taught the opposite, that sickness and deformity are "gifts" of Satan.

"No," she said, "the Lord is not the source of maladies. It is the devil that shrivels limbs and palsies hands. The devil's work, I am sure, can be undone. The Lord's curative strengths can be brought to bear, funneled or targeted to heal, by instruments of the higher power."

So when Fitzgerald revealed the cut on his arm, Julia and her fellows, particularly a gaunt boy named Wendell, started wailing, tears pouring out of their eyes, lamenting to the Lord as if the end of the world approached! Examining the wound, Wendell cried out, "Your arm is infected with the devil's venom. If we don't attack the problem it could spread to the rest of your body."

Fitzgerald almost snorted. "This ain't the pox. Ain't nothin' but a

The Best Team Ever

scratch, boy. A touch of witch hazel will contain the damage. You gotta doctor in Zion?"

Fitzgerald discovered that he had made two doctrinal errors.

Julia explained. "Do not place your trust in the mortal hands of doctors, sir. Physicians are instruments of the devil. They attempt to usurp the healing powers of the Lord. No, the Lord himself shall heal, not the slimy, dollar-grabbing heathens with their black bags and quack remedies. Moreover, alcohol in any form is evil. Christian men and women do not imbibe the devil's brew. Nor do they apply witch hazel or liniment to the flesh. Why do you think they call it *witch* hazel? General Overseer Voliva will heal your body. Prayer and General Overseer Voliva will cure the devil's work to your arm."

Fitzgerald did not question their assertions. *After all*, he thought, *the wound to his arm actually was the work of a devil. A dead demon, but a demon to be sure.*

He turned to Julia and said, as earnestly as he could, "Please Miss Julia. Show me the way to God!"

Smiling radiantly, Julia told him, "We're on the way, Michael."

From the Journal of Kid Durbin

I visited Connie tonight. Mr. Murphy invited me to share their dinner table and I accepted before he finished asking. Connie wore a white dress and blushed when I said she looked like a beautiful bride. After dinner we took a stroll around the neighborhood. The sun still hung in the sky and the first fragrance of spring caught us by surprise. I smelled her perfume and held her hand. There came this one moment—an instant when she bent her head toward me and her hair brushed across my face and lips. A heavenly experience!

We talked at great length of her travails and her recuperation. Connie told me about the two men who tried to kill her but I got the feeling there was more to the story, like she wasn't sharing everything. I can't put my finger on it but something just seems odd about the whole horrible episode. We also talked of my struggle to establish myself in the big leagues. She had the most generous observations about Mr. Thurston, whom she now regarded as her friend and healer. She thanked me for this, Mr. Murphy having told her that I had a hand in bringing Howard Thurston into the Cubs family. We shared many thoughts. I even disclosed to her the story of my transformation into a rooster on the stage of the Majestic Theater, something I had not told anyone else. Mr. Thurston must be a discreet man, for he had not mentioned this to Connie.

I wanted to say more to her but it did not happen. Still, I am heartened by her healthy cheer and the warmth she showed me. I left the Murphy home with a definite spring in my step.

The locomotive, emblazoned with large white letters proclaiming "The Chicago and Northwestern Railway," pulled into Zion at 5:38 p.m., a new station with a giant white cross sitting to the west of the tracks. Here, halfway between Milwaukee and Chicago, a new city, the City of God, six years old, grew out of the prairie. Mike Fitzgerald gazed out of the windows, feeling the same excitement he experienced during the cyclone scene in *Oz*. He hurt all over from not drinking for more than twenty-four hours, but he truly believed he had come to the land of Oz. Julia and Wendell were Munchkins leading him to the Wizard. As they disembarked the train, an older man addressed Julia.

"Peace to thee, Miss Bessant."

"Peace to thee be multiplied, Mr. Conklin," she replied. A standard, almost ritualistic, greeting and response.

The man asked Julia, "How many visitors today to the Christian Catholic Church?"

"Three, sir."

"Fine. They shall be our guests for supper in the Meeting Hall." Conklin turned to Fitzgerald and the two other visitors, a rumpled bookkeeper and a weeping woman of thirty.

"Good people, I am Elder Conklin and this is the City of God. Welcome. I pray God shall provide you an ample appetite and efficacious digestion."

They walked through the station and emerged on the other side, where numerous horse drawn drays awaited them. Out to the west, twenty buildings could be seen, all painted white and surrounded by newly planted trees and shrubs.

Fitzgerald and the others hopped into the carts and were carried six blocks to a large clapboard structure that bore the sign "Meeting House." Walking up a wood-planked path to an open doorway, they entered. Elder Conklin took the men to a large lavatory where they cleansed themselves. Fifty steps from the lavatory the men came into a large room with forty-two silent, well-dressed men and women seated at seven tables, hands clasped in prayer. Elder Conklin directed the seating of the new recruits, sprinkling them at three different tables. He then advanced to a podium at the side of the hall and everyone in the room bent their head for a prayer.

"Brothers, sisters, and visitors. We pray that God in his wisdom shall make this day meaningful, shall give us the strength to endure when others flag, and shall infuse us with the knowledge of his intent for us, that we shall rise to his challenges. Amen! May we now share victuals to fuel our mortal vessels."

Six young women carrying trays of food and drinks emerged from two doors. Fitzgerald looked down in front of him to see a plate of beef stew, boiled potatoes, and a glass of milk. He could not remember the last time he had tasted milk, and the plain glass it occupied reminded him of a beer glass used at Maynard's Saloon. Rather than thinking about the beer and whiskey that his gut craved, Fitzgerald grabbed a hunk of bread from a bowl to his left, dug it into the stew on his plate, and chomped happily on the first food he'd had in a day. He did not drink the milk. A woman to the left of Fitzgerald, Sister Nellie Singleton, asked him to tell the group at the table something about himself.

"Ain't much to tell," he responded between bites. "I'm a drunk and a criminal."

No one at the table reacted to the statement.

"We have heard worse. You are a sinner in need and you have come to the Lord's house for aid. You shall find it here in Zion."

"I hope so, ma'am."

When supper finished, the men showed Fitzgerald his new quarters, a small room that he would share with a college student named William. Two beds, a table, and two chairs. Fitzgerald looked forward to a fine sleep. He had not slept on a mattress for a long time.

Meeting time started at seven o'clock. The Meeting Hall, a large wooden building that could hold six hundred souls, was packed this night. Mike Fitzgerald sat in the first row, Julia to his side. The night's agenda, according to Julia, would be an opening prayer by Elder Conklin followed by an address by General Overseer Voliva. He started to doze as he waited for the meeting to begin, but Julia gently nudged him.

Elder Conklin walked to the podium, a four-foot high maplewood box sitting on a platform three feet off the ground.

"Peace be to this house!" he began.

The assembled group responded enthusiastically, in unison, "Peace to thee."

"Heavenly Father," he began, "we thank you tonight for allowing us to build your kingdom here on the Illinois plains. We are now endeavoring, at your prompting, to bring heaven to this earth. We are working with every ounce of our mortal strength to achieve your perfection in the here and now, as you have commanded.

"We are all humble sinners, Lord. We have all engaged in unclean practices. We beseech you to cleanse us, keep us strong, and free of sin. We have with us tonight, by your grace, Lord, several visitors who seek a glimpse of your perfection. Show them, Lord, what we in Zion have accomplished in your name. Let them see what fine possibilities exist, that they may join us in our quest.

"Now I am honored to introduce our rock and our spiritual link to the Almighty. I speak of our beloved General Overseer Voliva."

Fitzgerald could sense the change in the mood of the group as Voliva approached the podium. Those sitting around Fitzgerald stiffened in their seats, an air of anxious expectancy filling the hall. Voliva, a short man dressed in black with a silvery-blue necktie, bounced jauntily to the task.

"Members of the flock, visitors, friends, and worshippers, I bring you the word of the Lord. And tonight the Lord tells us in Zion City to fight against the tide of modernism. That which is new is not necessarily right. Those who call themselves scientists are not always what they claim to be. Those who proclaim themselves doctors—we know—can heal neither the body nor the spirit. They are butchers and nothing more. All of you have seen real healing here in Zion. The blind now see. The crippled now walk. The tumors disappear. How does it happen? Not with opiates, not with the scalpel, and not with worthless nostrums. Not from the hands of surgical butchers. But solely from the hands of God.

"There are those so-called men of science who peer into the night firmament, trying to snatch a glimpse of the heaven that we can see, feel, and indeed experience every day in Zion City. They build telescopes to aid their feeble attempts. A decade ago some university men constructed the largest telescope in the world, just fifty miles from here, in Williams Bay, Wisconsin. They squint into this tin tube hour after hour. They profess an ability to see spheroid worlds and they claim that the earth too is shaped like a ball and moves through the cosmos. I say hooey! What has come of these men spending their nights in their observatory? Nothing! The bible gives us our astronomy. Our earth is a stationary plane, resting on water. Stationary in the heavens—we do not move. There is no such thing as the earth's axis or the earth's orbit. This is silly rot, born in the egotistical minds of infidels. Neither is there any such thing as the law of gravitation. The bible says nothing about orbits or an axis or gravitation. These silly notions derive not from the Lord but from the deranged minds of heathens."

It interested Fitzgerald that Voliva preached about a flat earth. An earth that hung in one place in the sky. He had never given the idea much thought. But cosmology is not what drew him to Zion City. The possibility of redemption brought him to the doorstep of Zion. And so Fitzgerald paid close attention as Voliva concluded his remarks with that subject.

"We built a city with no saloons or breweries. A city with no gambling hells, no houses of ill repute, no drug or tobacco shops! No hog raisers, no hospitals or doctors' offices, no dance halls or theaters. No secret lodges or apostate churches! We have cleared an expanse on this earth where all is possible. We are all here to get right with Jesus. We are all here to have our sins washed away, to be cleansed in the blood of the lamb. Zion City is a sacred place that symbolizes God's victory over Satan. It is a place that gives its residents an opportunity to find the salvation and purity that will smooth our path to heaven. All who join this endeavor and commit their lives to it will find the true path."

Voliva looked straight into the eyes of Fitzgerald and concluded, "All—without exception."

May 5, 1907 Governors Island; New York

Instead of eating lunch, Percy McGill made his way to the boiler room, looking for the locked door that Robert Deanne had mentioned. It wasn't hard to find. Positioned in a dusty corner, the ancient oak door was painted a dull green and secured solely by an iron padlock that hooked through eyelets in two steel anchors, one in the door and one in the oak doorjamb. McGill examined the padlock carefully. It had a brass dust cover that slid across the keyhole. On the reverse side he found the name "Russel Erwin Manufacturing Company." McGill now needed to find someone who could pick the lock. *I'm in the right place for that*, he mused.

McGill asked around. "Who's the best lock-picker in the house?" The answer was always the same. "Your man is Jimmy 'The Pick' Costello. He's serving a ten-year sentence for burglary," Pinky Williams told McGill. "He can pick any lock, break any safe."

Percy tracked down the Pick at supper. Costello looked older than his thirty years, a short, balding man with huge shoulders but tiny legs. Small, dark eyes peered out from above puffy cheeks. Not an impressive specimen of manhood. Military officials did not allow facial hair in Castle Williams but Costello's dark, heavy stubble was tolerated. He sat alone, pondering a muffin.

"I'm told you can pick locks."

"Who told ya?" The Pick looked up indifferently at McGill and took a big bite out of the muffin.

"About five different soldiers. You got a good reputation when it comes to locks."

After chewing for a bit, Costello spoke, a slight Italian accent to his voice.

"Yeah, well, what's it matter if I can pick a lock? My pickin' ain't gonna get us outta here. I can't get us past the gates."

"Can you pick an Erwin padlock? It looks pretty old. Had a dust cover made out of brass."

"Sure. I done many of those."

"What about the locks on our cells? Can you get outta your cell and come get me outta my cell?"

"Yeah, I could do that. But even so I can't get us out the double-doors, front or back."

"I know. Can you swim?"

"Not to Brooklyn I can't."

"That wasn't my question. Do you know how to swim?"

"Yeah. I can swim some. Whaddaya got cookin?"

McGill explained his plan, at least part of it, to the Pick. The Pick's face lit up like a bright light. He wanted in.

"Here's the deal, Pick. I need you and you need me. We keep all of this discussion just between the two of us and maybe one more guy I have in mind. That's all there's room for. We don't tell nobody nothing about this. That's very important. If I find out that you even hinted about this to somebody you are out and I sneak up on you some day when you're eating a muffin and I cut your throat. Capiche?"

A bead of sweat started to roll down the Pick's forehead, pausing briefly and then diving into a bushy eyebrow. "Yeah, sure. I get it. When do we go?"

McGill smiled. "You'll be the first to know."

May 4-5, 1907 Chicago, Illinois

Unseasonably cold winds and low, scudding clouds blew across the West Side Grounds on Saturday and Sunday, keeping the crowds down to five thousand or so. The Pirates managed but one run in the two contests, Cubs pitchers Lundgren and Overall using the cold to their advantage and stifling all offensive threats. Honus Wagner went 0 for the weekend. On Saturday, a nervous Frank Chance kept sending bat boy Kuhn up to the press box to get the Giants' score from the Western Union wire. Finally the telegraph man told the kid the Giants beat the Superbas, keeping the Cubs a half game behind. But the Cubs took both games from the Bucs and with the Giants not playing on Sunday, the Cubs found themselves in first place, their record going to 15-3.

On Saturday night Frank Chance invited four teammates to his North Side home for a game of poker. Chance was alone in the house save for a servant, his wife having traveled to California to visit a relative. Jimmy Slagle, Frank Schulte, Harry Steinfeldt, and Chick Fraser all took cabs to the two-story brick home. Chance provided plenty of Pabst beer and pretzels, and the men played five-card draw into the night. As always, Husk kept the beer flowing. The stakes were not low. Charlie Dryden wrote more than one story in the *Tribune* about how Chance limited the bets to a quarter, but Dryden knew full well, having played in many of the games, that the stakes were higher. High enough to take a big bite out of a player's wallet. On this night the largest pot of the evening, maybe twenty-five dollars, went to Fraser as his spade flush beat Steinfeldt's straight. When the two men showed their hands Steinfeldt reached for the pot, having forgotten that a flush beats a straight. Withdrawing his pipe from his mouth and exhaling a stream of smoke, Husk gently reminded Harry of the relationship between straights and flushes. The third baseman apologized.

"Oh sure… I'm sorry. Don't know what I was thinking."

"You wasn't thinking," said Slagle.

The men enthusiastically downed a number of beers before Steinfeldt got around to recounting his famous yarn about a collision at second base with a yannigan when playing for the Fort Worth team in the Texas League. All the men except Fraser had heard this story at least twice, but they encouraged Steinfeldt to relate it again.

"I thought I had a good jump on the pitcher but the Dallas catcher gets off this fine throw to second, like an arrow coming off a bow. I seen it's gonna beat me there. So I barrelled into the little nubbin who's grabbing the ball right over second base. He couldn't have been much more than five feet high if you count the hair that shot straight up on his head as I came at him. Sure, I wanted to bust that ball loose from his tip, but I wasn't fixin' to hurt the little pecker."

"What, did you catch him with your spikes?" asked Fraser.

"No. Like I says, I didn't want to bloody the tiny fellow. Hell, the cleats mighta cut clean through him. He was all skin and bones and not much bones. So I just sort of landed on his legs. He fell backwards and started moaning. Over and over he was yellin', 'Jesus wept!' Umpire calls me out. The feisty little bastard held onto that ball. I get up to leave but I stick around for a few seconds to see if this guy's ever gonna get up. Whiles he's still sitting on the ground in back of the base, he unlaces and removes his left shoe. I seen him shaking that shoe back and forth, and he gets this strange, puzzled look on his face. Finally he turns that shoe upside down and dumps out, right onto the bag, three of his toes!"

All the men laughed.

"Didn't you say two toes the last time I heard this story, Steiny?" Chance asked.

"No Cap'n!" replied Steinfeldt. "Three toes it was."

Husk insisted the game close down at eleven o'clock so the men could be in bed by twelve. Five minutes after they left, Husk walked out the door and hopped into a taxicab.

"The Everleigh Club," he told the driver.

From the Journal of Kid Durbin

We've been stuck in Brooklyn for three days, but the weather has only permitted us to get in one game. Pittsburgh four days ago and Chicago just before that. Off the diamond, baseball in the big leagues is a set routine—from the train to the hotel to the ballpark to the hotel to the train. Nights spent lollygagging in the hotel lobby or a saloon. The train rides seem to bring the members of the team together some, if only in poker games, drinking bouts, and eating. Oh yes, in singing too! Lots of these fellows spend good amounts of time belting out some fine tunes. Baritone Jimmy Sheckard and Artie Hofman, for example, are a good duet. I do not join in as I have no talent in this regard. The only song I have, on occasion, given voice to is the old English tune, "Greensleeves," a melody that has haunted me since I first heard it as a small boy.

We had a dismal trip from Chicago to Pittsburgh and then got rained upon there so we never got a game in. This marked my first time in the Steel City and the only good thing was that I could sleep and read a good deal when they postponed the game. On the journey over here from Pittsburgh I finally got to talk with Joe Tinker a bit, as he has now joined up with us. Joe is a new father—his son is about a year old—and like many new dads he will talk your ears off about his child. He mostly pals around with Johnny Kling, who he first met when they both played on the Kansas City Schmeltzers in 1899. The two hit Pittsburgh's hot spots last night and they saw a great actor—David Warfield—in his most famous role, in the play "The Music Master." Tinker told me that during the famous attic scene—where Warfield's character shares some tears with his daughter—he looked over at Kling and saw "the greatest catcher in the world bawling like a baby girl! Huge tears rolling down red cheeks," is the way Joe described it. Tinker said that when he observed the Jew crying like that he couldn't help but let out a roaring howl of a laugh, to the consternation of those seated in close proximity to the pair.

"*The Jew was stunned to see me laughing,*" *Tinker related. "He looked at me and said that any man with a heart would be weeping just then. Hell, Warfield was good but not good enough to get my eyes wet and misty.*"

When Johnny Kling heard about Tinker's version of their visit to the theater, he flatly denied the whole story, claiming he didn't shed a single tear. Wasn't the first time I heard a teammate deny weeping or try to cover it up when it happened. Men don't want to appear unmanly or come across like a sissy. There's a whole lot of unwritten rules in this regard. A man can cry only in a few situations, like if his mother or wife is dying. But not when David Warfield is emoting in a stage drama.

Joe Tinker did not say a word about Evers but it's clear that he has nothing good to say about the man. I also get the idea that Joe and Harry Steinfeldt aren't exactly the best of friends. It's funny that Joe plays between two guys he hates. But he's still happy about returning to the shortstop position as soon as possible. Joe said one other thing to me that I probably need not write down here because I won't forget it. He said, "If you don't honestly and ferociously hate the Giants, you will never be a real Cub." I took that to heart.

We played a sloppy game against the Superbas two days ago, but our boys pounded out sixteen base hits and twelve runs so we never had to fret. Even Miner Brown picked up two hits along the way. There couldn't have been more than three thousand bugs in the place today. Half of them left midway through the fracas when we made it 6-0. The other half were too drunk to get up out of their seats so they stuck around for the fag end of the game. I shouldn't be too nasty about those cranks, though, because they are the ones paying the freight.

The afternoon papers put us in second place, as the Giants have won one more game than we have. The Superbas, by the way, now have a record of 1-16! Guess what place they're in!

I'm saving the most troubling thing for the last here. A few days ago Husk approached me and told me that management—meaning him and Mr. Murphy—wanted to farm me out to a minor league team for the rest of this season. Chance put it this way: "You'll get an opportunity to shine like a nigger's heel—a whole lot more of an opportunity than you will have with this squad."

I took it fairly hard. Chance could see my great disappointment.

He said, "If this happens you can come back with us next year and your salary will not be cut."

I went to bed that night thinking my days as a Cub were coming to an end.

But curious forces have conspired to keep me here, at least for now. Turns out the only way I can be sent to the minors is if every other National League team signs a waiver on me. But when the Cubs sought these waivers, Mr. Barney Dreyfuss, the owner of the Pirates, refused to sign, blocking my reassignment. Dreyfuss wanted to buy my contract and Mr. Murphy wouldn't sell me, so it appears that I am staying put for the time being. The fact that these two owners hate each other—I heard Mr. Murphy refer to Mr. Dreyfuss as "that Jew bastard"—might explain what happened. Life is sure packed with surprises and strange twists.

May 10, 1907 Governors Island; New York

Ten men composed the work detail, with Corporal Tollington supervising the activity. Inmate Harold Conners approached Percy as they tramped past the Dutch House. Sunshine peeked in from thick, fluffy clouds that swept by. Sidling up to McGill, Conners introduced himself. His next words took Percy by surprise.

"I wanna go with you when you jump off this fucking rock."

McGill paused, looked disdainfully into the eyes of Conners, and then spit, narrowly missing him.

"What makes you think I'm jumping off?"

"Pick told me so. Says you need him to crack some padlock."

"Well, Pick is a fucking liar. I don't know what the hell he's talking about."

Conners chuckled under his breath. "Look, McGill," he said, "let's not play games with this. I'm not a patient person. You got three days to think about this. You tell me I can go within three days or the sergeant hears about your plans. Capiche?"

Percy didn't answer. He moved away from Conners toward the sparkling blue-green harbor.

Percy sought out Pick at the first opportunity, the last mess call that night. He sat alone, disheveled and absorbed in his meal. Pick tore into a piece of beef with his hands and teeth, oblivious to anything else.

"Didn't I fucking tell you that I would slit your throat if you told anybody about our plans? Didn't you believe me?" The look on Percy's face matched his cold and threatening tone.

Pick did not seem worried. "Yeah. You told me. So I ain't told nobody."

"Not even an asshole named Conners?"

Pick shrugged, guiltily, and snatched a glance at Percy before answering. "Oh yeah. Conners. I told him. I guess I fucked up, right?"

McGill scowled. He began to realize that Jimmy "The Pick" Costello wasn't playing with a full deck.

"Jimmy, how did you get into this place? What did you do?"

Pick's flabby face expanded in a great, genuine smile as he happily explained the sequence of events leading to his imprisonment. A year earlier he lived above a pawn shop in Harlem. One night he dug a hole through his floor to the pawnshop below, but his drill cut into a gas line, igniting the gas. In the consequent explosion he fell through the pawn shop ceiling, landing on a glass display case filled with musical instruments. Pick told McGill, "The doctors removed a hundred shards of glass and a brass harmonica from my ass!"

"Christ Almighty!" said McGill. "That true?"

"All of it except the harmonica part," winked Pick. "I always add that part for some sympathy."

Percy grew impatient. "Jimmy… one more time. Are you sure you can open up an old Erwin padlock like we talked about before?"

"Yeah. Sure I can. Like I says, I done it lots of times before."

"Listen to me, Jimmy. When I told you not to tell anyone else about this plan, I said that because there's only room for three guys in this escape. So we can't tell anyone else. Can you understand that now? No one else can hear about this or they'll rat us out and we won't be able to go. You'll be stuck here another ten years. Get it?"

"Yeah. I'm sorry. Look, Percy, I let you down with Conners. I won't fuck up no more. I really need to get away from this place. I'll keep my mouth shut from now on." Jimmy got up with his meal tray and waddled away, leaving Percy to wonder whether Jimmy, a dimwit at best, would further endanger the plan.

May 12, 1907 **Paterson, New Jersey**

Fueled by their desire to earn a few extra dollars on a Sunday off-day, the Cubs detoured from their normal paths, ending up twenty miles north of New York City in "The Silk City," Paterson, New Jersey. The schedule called for a match-up against the Paterson Intruders, champions of the Hudson River League. For the locals this game marked the high point of the season. The rickety stands of Olympic Park trembled with an overflow crowd as Mayor John Johnson shook 264 hands in the course of the afternoon. A marching band performed and both teams paraded around the ballpark in an electric streetcar as part of the pre-game festivities. The ballpark stood in the cold shadow of Garret Mountain, its lush greenery a stark contrast to the many unpainted industrial buildings of the small town. "Ain't much of a mountain," opined Jimmy Slagle between spits.

"Ten years back Honus Wagner played for these galoots," offered Jimmy Sheckard. "He might have looked out yonder and said the same thing."

Chance selected Big Ed as the point man in the skirmish, and Joe Tinker made his first appearance of the year, although Husk slated him at second rather than shortstop to ease him back. Frank Schulte observed the proceedings from the bench, still sore from having his tonsils removed several days earlier, while Newt Randall stood in Schulte's place in right field. Husk took the day off, placing Moran at first base and Kling behind the plate. While fielding a fly ball in the outfield during batting practice Jimmy Sheckard cried out, "Dammit to hell!"

Rabbit Slagle, thirty feet away, asked, "Whatsamatter?"

"I just stepped in some dogshit!"

Coming closer to inspect the damage, Slagle said, "That ain't dogshit. It's goatshit."

"How in the hell can you tell that?"

"Cain't ya see the green cast to it and the big turds? Sure as hell not dogshit. Why, it's as plain as the nose on your face, Jimmy."

"Those turds are as big as the nose on your face, Rabbit!"

Sheckard warned the Cubs about the hazards in the outfield, and soon the exhibition game commenced. Big Ed had better outings. He could not find the plate, walking nine Paterson batters and plunking one with a wicked fastball that got away. That and the six hits he surrendered allowed five tallies by the minor league squad. But former minstrel Harry Steinfeldt once again put on a show, cracking three hits, including two deep doubles. One of Steiny's hard hit foul balls ripped through the crown of a spectator's three-dollar derby, to the delight of those close enough to observe the carnage. Joe Tinker celebrated his return by adding two safeties, knocking in the winning run in the seventh inning.

By the third inning the Cubs had solved most of the signals employed by the Intruders that day. Like many minor league squads of their time, they used oral signs. For example, if the manager called out a player's last name, it meant nothing. But if he yelled at the player using his first name, such as "Come on Jocy," that signified the hit-and-run play or, if directed toward the base runner, a steal. Evers figured out a curve was on its way whenever the manager called out, "Cut one loose!" Using this information, Chance called for two pitch-outs and Kling cut down both base runners. After the second pitch-out, the Intruders switched their signs. It took Evers only one more inning to figure out the new ones.

Besides tossing out two would-be base-stealers, Kling followed his usual practice of establishing a good working rapport with the umpire, a tack that frequently benefited the Cubs. He sometimes alerted the ump—out of earshot of the batter—to be on guard because the next pitch would be a curveball. "If they know a curve is coming," Johnny explained, "they can do their job better and we're more likely to get the call." Kling worked the umpires carefully, knowing which ones could be softened up a little bit. He complimented them when they got the call right and never openly criticized a plate umpire. The closest he came to criticism was to whisper, "Looked to me like it might have nipped the corner, Hank." But he was merciless with opposing batters, particularly the youngsters. Noisy John's steady stream of chatter and derisive comments often distracted unfocused hitters.

As the eighth inning opened, Harry Steinfeldt grabbed the chewing gum out of his mouth, stuck it to the button on the top of his cap, and stepped into the batter's box. Many of the gum-chewers did that to aid their concentration at the bat, popping the gum back into their mouth after leaving the batter's box. When the pitcher wound up to launch the first pitch, Steinfeldt peeked back at the catcher to see where he had positioned himself. Noting that the catcher crouched on the outside corner of the plate, Steinfeldt moved a step closer to home, but did not swing at an outside offering. The catcher did not appreciate Harry's peek—an unwritten rule prohibited batters from doing this. As payback, the young backstop, whose left cheek bulged from a chaw of tobacco, spat half the contents of his mouth onto Steinfeldt's left shoe. The Cubs third-bagger reacted immediately, kicking the catcher in his groin and jumping on him. The two players rolled about in the dirt for thirty seconds, cursing angrily. When the umpire yelled, "Stop it, you dumb fuckers," the two finally quit and the game resumed. Steiny's chewing gum suffered the worst from the scuffle, becoming covered with enough dirt to prevent even the adventurous Steinfeldt from chewing it again.

About three thousand attended the exhibition game, delighted to see the likes of Joe Tinker, Harry Steinfeldt, and Johnny Kling. The Cubs' share of the gate receipts amounted to about $1,800, with $900 going to management, and each player's share at $45. Secretary Williams passed out the cash on the train from Paterson to Philadelphia, fueling three separate poker games.

Fred Clarke, player-manager of the Pirates, telegrammed a protest to the National League offices, complaining that New York Giants catcher Roger Bresnahan should not be allowed to wear the shin guards (actually white cricket leg guards) he had introduced to the game on opening day. Clarke argued that the shin protection gear violated league rules and interfered with base runners coming to the plate, particularly in squeeze plays. Off the record Clarke questioned Bresnahan's "manliness" and threatened to equip Pirate infielders with shin guards if the league did not take action. Johnny Kling, who had experimented with shin protection, supported Bresnahan's actions. "Let Fred Clarke squat behind the plate and take a few foul balls in the knees. Then we'll see what he says." New York newspapermen labelled Clarke a "spiker." The Pirates dogged Bresnahan with chants of "sissy" at every opportunity. But Bresnaham never again caught a game without the apparatus. The utility of the protective equipment soon overwhelmed all opposition.

May 13, 1907 Governors Island; New York

A cold wind blew off the harbor as the prisoners on the morning work call filed past the South Battery, toward Craig Road South. The trees moved in tune with the wind while choppy white waves pounded the shore. Each inmate carried a heavy sledgehammer to crush rocks, a brutal task that took a heavy toll on hot summer days. But today the men had things going their way, as the cool breeze offered relief. Percy breathed in the sea air, simply happy to be alive. He thought, for the briefest of moments, of Little Johnny. A crude and stupid confederate, but Laughlin had shown him true loyalty to the end, testifying for him and linking him up with the Italians. A shame that he died trying to carry out business. It would be difficult to find a man to replace Johnny. Difficult but not impossible. Many men are hungry for the sporting life, and willing to do anything necessary to achieve their goals.

In the midst of these ruminations Harold Conners ambled up to Percy.

"We gotta deal, McGill?" he asked, his eyes shrinking into narrow slits.

"You got nigger lips, Conners. Your mama a nigger?"

Conners was amused rather than angered. "I ain't a hothead, McGill. You can't get me thrown into the dungeon so easy, so that I come outta there and find you and Pick is gone. I'm smarter than that. Let me ask you one more time, McGill. Do we gotta deal or what?"

McGill offered a look of resignation to Conners. "Yeah, I suppose so."

Conners flashed a smile. "Good. There's more you oughtta know. I'm now in Pick's cell. I'm bunking right next to him. He goes nowhere without me. If he gets up in the middle of the night to piss I'm right there with him. You won't be able to pull this off if you forget me."

"Yeah, okay. You and Pick are real close. Anything else?"

"My mother. She's whiter than you Percy. It's my father who's a nigger."

Percy snickered. "Get away! You don't mean that."

Conners stared blankly, saying nothing for a second or two, but he held the sledgehammer on his shoulder, at an angle that would have allowed him to smash McGill's skull.

Then he spoke. "You don't have anything against folks of African descent, do ya?"

McGill cracked a small grin. "Why, no. It don't mean nothin' to me one way or the other."

✳   ✳   ✳

The noon meal completed, Percy asked for leave to see the prison doctor, Dr. Conrad Malhern, a fifty-year-old alcoholic, regarding a sore arm. Percy did not have a sore arm, but men on the rock crew often developed problems in their limbs, so an officer approved Percy's request to visit the prison physician. Boxes, medical journals, vials of medicine, and chemicals cluttered the doctor's office. A large scale, dusted with a yellow powder and clumps of a white substance, shared the desk with stacks of papers. The doctor sat at his desk reading a newspaper and devouring an apple. Percy, yellow prison pass in hand, smelled the presence of alcohol on Malhern's breath when he slouched into the chair across from the doctor. Dr. Malhern, disheveled and absorbed in a newspaper, rubbed his left hand against his beard and spoke.

"What is it sir?" asked Malhern, not looking up from the *Times*.

"Nothing too serious, I think," responded McGill. "I just want you to bury my body here, on this island."

Malhern looked up from his paper.

May 13, 1907 **Chicago, Illinois**

Talk about bad omens. In Chicago, banners festooned the South

Side Park at 39th Street and Princeton. The first place White Sox prepared for ceremonies as they faced off against the Philadelphia Athletics. The A's threw their best pitcher, a strange character named Rube Waddell. In a pre-game ceremony the Sox raised the pennant to celebrate their 1906 World Championship. As the groundsmen raised the pennant, the flagpole snapped, dropping the victory flag into a muddy puddle. Sox owner Charles Comiskey cursed the groundsmen and stalked off the field. The South Siders also had bad luck with Waddell, unable to handle his stuff. The A's batters pounded Roy Patterson, the Sox hurler. Final score: A's over the Sox 9-1.

May 14, 1907 Philadelphia, Pennsylvania

Two umpires officiated this game, with Bill Klem behind the plate calling the balls and strikes. About 5,600 fans spread out in National League Park, which could hold eighteen thousand. An odd little ballpark in a bleak industrial district, three huge faux-castle structures supported the double-decked grandstands. Center field and right field sloped up in what the locals called "the Hump," the result of a railroad tunnel beneath the park. The unusual shape of the park resulted in a short right field wall, only 280 feet from home, but a forty-foot fence made it tough to hit one out.

Joe Tinker played his first official game of the 1907 season, looking and feeling right at home at the shortstop position. Only three balls came his way in the field and he dispatched them flawlessly. At the plate he managed a base hit and a walk in five tries. In another laugher, the Cubs assaulted the Phillies with fifteen hits and nine runs. Artie Hofman, the Cubs super-sub, covered left field for Jimmy Sheckard and smashed four hits, and Steinfeldt stroked three more. On the mound, Cubs starter Jeff Overall overpowered the Phillies, holding them to three hits and no runs. He gave up only one walk, that to center fielder Roy Thomas, whose ability to foul off good pitches led him to lead the league in walks almost every year. The Cubs' season record went to 19-4 but they found themselves in second place behind their arch-enemies, John McGraw's New York Giants.

As the Cubs sauntered to the visitors' dressing room following the final out, manager Chance congratulated Tinker on a successful return.

"I hope I can help out some," said the Cubs shortstop.

Harry Steinfeldt could not resist a verbal jab. "We was doing just fine without you."

Tinker did not let it pass, turning slightly to address Steinfeldt over his left shoulder, and said, "Harry, there's good and bad about coming back to this team. You're in the 'bad' category."

Steinfeldt jumped Tinker from behind, pulling him down on the turf, and whacked him on the neck and face. Harry pushed Tinker's face into the moist ground. Tinker staggered under the repeated blows, but managed to slide the bigger man off his back. One quick blow from Tinker caught Steiny's ruddy red nose and the blood erupted. By now several teammates pulled the two men apart, with Steinfeldt yelling, "Let me at the asshole," and Tinker responding with, "The man's an idiot. Let me go!"

Husk had the final word: "Fuck off, the both of you. You ought to be thinking about smashing the goddam Giants next week."

Durbin turned to Jack Taylor, who walked alongside him. "Joe really handed Steiny a wollop! Never seen two teammates go at it that hard."

"Shit," said Taylor, "stick around a bit, Kid. This was round three for these two. And I saw Joe punch the shit out of Evers last year too. Still, it's a friendly team compared to some."

May 18, 1907 Boston, Massachusetts

The Boston Beaneaters finished in eighth place in 1906—dead last—so in 1907 the new owners, the Dovey Brothers, changed the team nickname. Being creative fellows, they chose to call the club the Boston Doves. The new ownership did little else to improve the plight of the team, which still lacked fans, talent, good management, and a decent ballpark. The Doves played at the South End Grounds, a tiny piece of property jammed between the New York, New Haven & Hartford rail yard and Columbus Avenue in south Boston, just across the tracks from the Boston Pilgrims' home field, Huntington Avenue Grounds.

Seven thousand fans crammed into South End Grounds to see the Doves' pitcher Big Jeff Pfeffer, who was coming off a season in which he lost twenty-two games. Out of the University of Illinois, the Cubs knew him because he broke into the major leagues with them two years earlier. Carl Lundgren, another U of I alumnus, took the mound for the Cubs. The first four innings saw both pitchers in control. But with two down in the fifth, Joe Tinker got the second of his three singles for the day and, two pitches later, stole second base. Jimmy Sheckard then stroked a chopper to the Doves shortstop, which bounded over his head, allowing Tinker to scamper home for the first run of the game.

The bottom of the sixth would stick in the memories of the bugs on hand. It began with ancient Boston first baseman Fred Tenney drawing a base on balls and stealing second. The next Doves hitter struck out. Beetle-browed left fielder Del Howard then dropped a perfect bunt down the third-base line, so perfect that Kling had to eat the ball. At this point outfielder Johnny Bates sent a grounder to third baseman Steinfeldt who let it get by for an error. The tying run scored on the miscue.

Then came a string of events that decided the game and displayed all too graphically the forlorn futility of the second division ballclub. On the second pitch to the next batter, Ritchey, Bates broke for second base and slid in, only to find stunned teammate Del Howard still hugging the other side of that now too-small canvass bag. Clutching the baseball tightly in his right hand, Cubs catcher Johnny Kling shed his mask and made out for second. As Kling approached second, Bates spun around and retraced his steps back to first. But Kling caught up with Bates from behind, tagging him squarely on the back for the second out. Hearing a chorus of shouts from his teammates, Kling wheeled around to see Howard sprinting for third. Kling gave chase but, realizing he could not catch Howard, whipped the ball over to Steiny at the bag. Howard then reversed his course and headed back to second. Steiny chased him down and tagged him for a freak double play.

This errant baserunning took the wind out of the Doves' sails and they could not score again. Steinfeldt made amends for his error by pushing across the winning run in the eighth. Lundgren gave up only three hits on the day, and his teammates patted him on the back as they jogged off the field. But when the Cubs read the Beantown newspapers the next day, they found that the New York Giants won their seventeenth game in a row and still possessed first place in the National League. The Cubs looked forward to their first contest with the Giants on Tuesday.

May 19, 1907 Zion, Illinois

Mike Fitzgerald found a warm welcome in Zion. The residents of this theocratic community recognized a lost soul, for they had seen men and women of his ilk many times before. The followers had faith that God could help men like this. Their souls would be saved.

For three days Fitzgerald had no responsibilities other than to observe the rhythm of life about him and to listen to the encouraging comments of four elders who tended to his spiritual needs. On the fourth day they placed Fitzgerald as a laborer in the local lace factory. Fitzgerald carried forty-pound boxes of doilies from conveyor belts in the packing room to wagons outside the loading shed. *A piece of cake,* thought Fitzgerald. *I could do this all day.* He did do it all day. For nine hours a day, six days a week, Fitzgerald received $13.50. Although not required, Fitzgerald voluntarily donated 10 percent of his paycheck to the church. Mike developed a good working relationship with his boss, an Englishman named William Millingham, who spoke with a thick cockney accent. Church officials, who ran the facility, imported Millingham and other English laceworkers to assure the success of the business.

The daily life of Zion gave Fitzgerald the order and regularity he needed as his battered psyche struggled to stabilize. Twenty years of alcohol pickled every organ in his body, including his brain. But the horror of his recent criminal acts provided an incentive. He could not allow himself to return to that life. As the alcoholic fog slowly lifted, the clarity of his participation in two murders sharpened in his mind. Guilt germinated in this new believer. In the past, Fitzgerald always pushed aside remorse of this sort—especially in relation to the abandonment of his family. He now wept frequently, with church members encouraging him to "let the tears stream forth." His desire for renewal spurred him to persevere, to ignore the pangs for drink and the call he sometimes felt for the "freedom" of the street. Fitzgerald quickly grasped that his life was on the line. If he missed this chance there would probably not be another. For the first time since he could remember, Mike cared whether he lived or died.

May 21, 1907   New York City, New York; The Most Remarkable Man in America

John McGraw stood no more than 5'6" and sported a small paunch at his mid-section. His size and his genius on the baseball battleground earned him the nickname "the Little Napoleon." Formerly a rowdy infielder and now a bullying, no-nonsense field pilot, his ballplayers worshipped and feared him. A number of attributes made him one of the winningest managers in baseball history. He infused his players with the desire to win and extracted the best from every one, even those of limited talent. A ferocious competitor on the field, off the diamond he had a soft spot that down-on-their-luck former players exploited for "loans" and other assistance. McGraw controlled every decision on the field of play, calling every pitch and every play. He told his charges: "Do what I tell you. I'll take the blame if it goes wrong." Even his best pitcher and close friend Christy Mathewson thought McGraw's managerial style reduced his players to "puppets on a string." But it worked, ultimately garnering his Giants ten pennants and eleven second- place finishes. While his veterans could call him Mac, those new to the team addressed him as Mr. McGraw. Behind his back some called him Muggsy, a name he detested, while English dramatist George Bernard Shaw labeled McGraw "The Most Remarkable Man in America."

While the Polo Grounds' fans adored McGraw, crowds in opposing camps detested the swaggering, belligerent Irishman. He purposely baited them, swearing and gesticulating emphatically so that the whole ballpark got his point. Mathewson said, "I have seen McGraw go onto ballfields where he is as welcome as a man with the black smallpox… He doesn't know what fear is."

There was no love lost between John McGraw and Frank Chance, Christy Mathewson and Mordecai Brown, or for that matter, the Giants and the Cubs. Competition often breeds contempt, but contempt is not a strong enough word to describe what had developed between these two original National League teams. McGraw piloted the Giants to National League pennants in 1904 and 1905. But the Cubs' dominance in 1906, finishing twenty games ahead of second-place New York, cut into McGraw like a knife. He promised it would not happen again. Frank Chance disliked McGraw intensely, and never passed up an opportunity to let him know it. When the Little Napoleon argued with an umpire, Chance would yell, "Get your ass off the field."

The year before, on a wickedly hot August day, McGraw had battled ferociously with umpire James Johnstone in a game with the Cubs at the Polo Grounds. Johnstone had ejected McGraw for calling him, among other things, a "damn dirty cock-eating bastard." At least that is what witness Harry Steinfeldt later testified in a formal statement requested by National League President Harry Pulliam. Muggsy took his revenge against Johnstone the next day, locking him out of the Polo Grounds. McGraw required the gatekeeper to exclude Johnstone on the trumped-up grounds that the police could not guarantee his safety. The Giants skipper asked Frank Chance to allow Giants reserve (and former Cub) Sammy Stang to act as a substitute umpire, but Chance flat-out refused. As the Polo Grounds crowd repeatedly screamed, "Play ball," umpires Emslie and Johnstone declared the game forfeited to the Cubs.

Now, a little less than one year later, a splendid spring Tuesday afternoon matched the first-place New York Giants and Christy Mathewson against the second-place Chicago Cubs and Three Finger Brown. Christy, also known as Big Six or The Christian Gentleman, was tall, blonde, blue-eyed, broad-shouldered, and the first modern athlete/ superstar. Like none that came before him, Matty was no coarse country boy. Revered on the field and off, the charismatic college-educated Mathewson provided a superb role model for American boys. While he could be rowdy with umpires and fans at times, he came to be known as a true and honest sportsman. Big Six's arch-rival, on the other hand, Mordecai Brown, gained notoriety mainly for his maimed pitching hand and the ever-present chaw of tobacco bulging in his left cheek. Cubs rooters crowed that Brown's efforts in 1906, 26-6 with an ERA of 1.04, dwarfed Mathewson's performance of 22-12 with an ERA of 2.97. But Giants fans grumbled that Big Six had suffered a bout of diphtheria in 1906, which cost him some starts and weakened him well into the season. "Besides," the Mathewson supporters pointed out, "look at 1903-1905! Christy won more than thirty games three years in a row!"

The horseshoe-shaped Polo Grounds stood facing the Harlem River in Upper Manhattan, between 157th and 159th streets. The double-decked ballpark could seat about sixteen thousand, with its wooden grandstands stretching from first base around to third and bleachers extending out to left and right field. More than twenty thousand rabid fans filled the Polo Grounds for this eagerly anticipated encounter. The wooden bleachers in center field, named Burkeville in honor of the Irish immigrants who spread out there, overflowed, fans spilling out behind ropes in center field and down the foul lines. The cheapest seats of all, up on Coogan's Bluff, which rose 115 feet behind the grandstands, provided an elevated perch for those without the price of admission. Droves of fans also occupied the elevated train structures and every electric light pole with a view. Right before the first pitch a tipsy fan on the elevated railroad tracks slipped and fell to his death. Another equally drunk young man filled the dead man's space twenty seconds later.

Unlike many ballparks, the Polo Grounds had a visitors' dressing room. Chance addressed his teammates in his usual calm and firm manner. "Set your minds and spirits to the goal of winning and accept nothing less. We are the better team. There is no question about it. So play your hearts out and think before every pitch. And I want each of you now to pick one of those Giants assholes—Trainer Jack will make sure we cover every starter—and you work on that bastard the whole game. Never let up. Call 'em everything in the book. Let me take care of Muggsy."

Mathewson made his appearance in his trademarked manner, waiting until ten minutes before game time, then slowly crossing the outfield from the center field clubhouse, wearing a linen duster like auto drivers wore that came down to his high-top spiked shoes. A ten-year-old boy in a Giants cap followed four steps behind Mathewson, as if to provide a retinue. At each determined step of the Christian Gentleman the applause of the partisan crowd roared louder. A horde of photographers captured every stride.

He took the mound promptly at 3:50 p.m., the large letters "N" and "Y" gracing the collarless, pullover jersey of the New Yorkers. Mathewson immediately took control of the game, displaying all the tricks of his trade, blurry fastballs that broke down or away, curves of several varieties, and the famous "fadeaway" that was later called the screwball, a slow pitch which broke in on right-handed batters. The Cubs could not touch him in the first three innings, each pitch a small work of art. But the masterpiece began to crumble in the fourth. Rabbit Slagle led off and worked Big Six for a base on balls. Tinker came up next, carrying the longer bat he had used the last few years against Mathewson. Joe's early lack of success against the big Giants right-hander transformed when Tinker began to use the extended lumber. It worked again this at-bat, as he gave the leather a ride to right field for a double, with Slagle gliding into third.

Jimmy Sheckard strolled to the plate. Bresnahan, the brown-haired, blue-eyed, muscle-bound Irish catcher, did not squat behind the plate. He stood, with a slight crouch, even after he got the signal from McGraw on the Giants bench. Muggsy wanted a curve. Sheckard took a hard swing and grounded in the direction of Giants second baseman Corcoran, who flung the ball home trying to nail the Rabbit. Roger Bresnahan stood like a rock at home plate, his controversial white shin guards gleaming in the sun. Slagle slammed into the Giants backstop at the same moment the ball arrived, and when the two untangled umpire Hank O'Day called the runner safe, the ball having trickled out of the catcher's glove for an error. Before the dust settled, McGraw leaped off the Giants bench to protest, arms flailing and profanity flowing until he spied the ball on the ground behind his catcher and walked back to his seat, kicking the dirt and muttering. Standing on deck, Frank Chance's face darkened as he called to McGraw.

"Stick it up your ass, Muggsy!"

"You fuckin' cementhead!" McGraw countered, his eyes crinkling up into two little hateful triangles.

Play resumed with Frank Chance hitting Mathewson's second pitch to Corcoran, and again the second-sacker threw home, with Bresnahan easily putting the tag on Joe Tinker. Chance stood on first while Sheckard now occupied second. One pitch later, with Steinfeldt at bat, Chance danced around first base enough to draw a throw from the pitcher, and Sheckard used that throw as an excuse to successfully steal third. Six photographers camped near third base to catch the action. Steinfeldt swung mightily at the next Mathewson curveball, but merely topped it three feet in front of the plate. Bresnahan pounced on it like a tiger siezing its prey, and whipped it to first for the second out, with Sheckard racing home on the throw. Frank Chance exulted under his breath, "Two runs off Matty!"

Chance intently watched the Giants whip the ball around the infield prior to the bottom of the fifth. They fired it at great speed at the insistence of McGraw. "It's a symbol we mean business," McGraw told people, "even in the little things." Chance thought it idiotic and dangerous. "Someone's gonna break a hand some day." He peered out toward center field as Cy Seymour waved to the Giants pitcher that he was ready. The outfield in the Polo Grounds sloped slightly down from the infield, so sitting on the bench, Chance could only see Seymour and the other outfielders from the waist up, tiny figures dwarfed by huge signs proclaiming "Irish Whiskey" and "Ideal Milk Chocolate." "I hate this fucking place," Chance told Evers.

Three Finger Brown pitched a steady game. Midway through the contest, with a Giants runner at first, a New Yorker pounded at the ball but managed only a chopping grounder to short. Joe Tinker bounded in to snatch the ball, picked it out of his glove, and shoveled it to second without even looking. Evers, in one fluid motion, speared the toss from Tinker while dragging his foot across the sack, and launched a rocket to first for the double play.

Tinker to Evers to Chance.

As the teams headed into the bottom of the ninth the Cubs led 3-2. Bresnahan came to bat first, choking up on the bat almost one-third to the top. He pried a walk out of Brown. Switch-hitting first baseman Dan McGann, his cap pulled down low on his head, stepped into the batter's box. Back from a broken wrist in the Practice Season, he took a few pitches and then slashed a tricky groundball to Evers. Evers

THE BEST TEAM EVER

snagged the ball out of the dirt, side-stepped twice to his left attempting to tag Bresnahan, and threw out McGann. But Bresnahan had altered his course to avoid the lunging Evers and ended up on second, untouched.

Extending his arms out to their limits, Evers yelled over to Umpire "Wig" Emslie, "He was way outta the base path!"

Wig waited two long seconds and then called Bresnahan out, with a wide sweep of his arm, to the delight of Evers and the Cubs. The Giants bench erupted, and Bresnahan leaped at Emslie, screaming at the umpire, "I never left the base path, Wig!" McGraw stormed the field, thrusting out his chest and gesticulating to the fans, egging them on. He charged up to Emslie and spit his quid of tobacco at the feet of the umpire.

"What the fuck did my guy do wrong?" he began.

With a stern countenance, Wig looked into McGraw's eyes and said, "You know what he did. He took three steps out of the path to avoid the tag. Now get back to the bench so we can finish the goddam game."

McGraw was commenting on Emslie's hairpiece when the hot-tempered Bresnahan lunged toward the umpire. The crowd exploded but McGraw grabbed the Giants catcher by the arm and yanked him away. Two pop bottles came hurtling out of the swirling grandstands toward Emslie but they did not have the range. One smashed on impact and scattered shards of glass about the infield. McGraw and Bresnahan retreated to the bench, spitting and cussing all the way. A moment later the final Giants hitter flied out and the Chicagoans claimed victory on enemy turf.

But the final out precipitated a wave of rowdy acts among some drunken fans. Every crowd is a mob in the making. The warm afternoon of beer and dashed hopes had taken their toll on the multitudes. Dozens, then hundreds of young men jumped out of the bleachers and grandstands and raced helter-skelter toward the two umpires. Both men, along with the players, clawed their way toward the dressing rooms. Taunts became threats and someone tossed a large apple that bounced off O'Day's back. A runt of a boy heaved a bottle at the umps but it fell short, striking a fan in the ear. Seat cushions rained down on the umpires but did no harm. Five Pinkerton security guards rushed to the aid of the men in blue, but could not stop a young man who emerged from the swarm and smashed the bristle end of a broom on Emslie's head. The umpire staggered but did not fall. He began to fear for his life and searched wildly for an escape route. Now the throng transformed into a deadly mob, and the lives of these two umps hung in the balance. Several Giants and

Cubs, including Steinfeldt, Reulbach, and Durbin, ran over and placed themselves in front of the umpires, but the crowd pressed on. Two New York City policemen appeared, screaming at the fulminating mass. The cops drew their pistols, fired skyward, then pointed the guns at the nearest miscreant. Like all mobs, this one lacked backbone, and the sound of the shots drove them back, enabling the Pinkerton men, ballplayers, and cops to spirit the umpires out of the ballpark. They raced up a ramp to the elevated train station, and barricaded themselves in a small room there for a full hour. By then passions had ebbed, and the two umpires made a safe escape.

The next day, the *Chicago Tribune* box score read: "Two base hits—Mathewson, Tinker, Strang. Three base hit—Shannon. Riot—1."

From the Journal of Kid Durbin

May 22, 1907

I saw Matty yesterday, the great Christy Mathewson. A regular Frank Merriwell, he is. Tall and good-looking, the man can throw the baseball like no other pitcher I've ever seen. The New York cranks have made him a God. So sore about losing were they that they tried to kill the umpires after the game. Don't get me wrong—I'm no friend of the umpires. But I don't believe an umpire deserves to die when he messes up a call. That's not part of our Jew-Deo-Christian upbringing. At least not mine.

The Giants came straight at us today, bats blazing and spikes flashing. We never had a chance. Every seat in the Polo Grounds was occupied. Speculators had the only tickets available for the game, some going for as much as ten dollars. When I first set foot on the field, I spied the scheduled Giants pitcher, Joe "Iron Man" McGinnity, with a dead rat in his palm, tossing the long-tailed carcass up and down like a baseball. I didn't say nothing to the man but he saw me staring and he says, "What's with you? You never seen a pitcher get ready to pitch?" He had a strange look in his eyes so I didn't respond.

A Chicago bug, sitting maybe five rows back, one of only a few Cubs rooters in the ballpark, called out a word of encouragement to the Peerless Leader. Hearing this, Mr. Bresnahan, the Giants catcher, gave the Cubs bug the evil eye and yelled up at him, "Close that trap, you stew, or I'll come up there and get you!" The chattering crowd laughed and the man held his tongue after that.

Husk put Jeff Overall in the pitcher's box, and Jeff muddled along until the fifth when all hell broke loose and the New Yorkers scored five times. But a play in the third inning still sticks in my craw. Joe Tinker had the ball in his glove, ready to tag Giants outfielder Cy Seymour, who rumbled toward second base. The bastard Seymour springs up as high as he can and spikes Tinker in the wrist, arm, and face. Tinker is bleeding in all three places and there is a gash right below his right eye. Nothing justified this malicious act. Husk had to come over and restrain Joe once he picked himself up out of the dirt. I asked Joe later what Husk told him. Husk said, "We're gonna skull that yellow drunk."

Later in the game Husk huddled with our new pitcher, Big Ed Reulbach, and everyone in the park knew what was coming next. Seymour entered the batter's box a little wary, rightly figuring that the incident at second base had not been forgotten. The Giant outfielder possessed an odd batting stance, his weight shifted forward while the bat projected over his shoulder, parallel to the ground. The first pitch, a fastball, sped right at his ear, and only a gymnastic leap saved the outfielder from a knock on his coconut. Seymour ducked away from the second pitch, aimed at his ribs, and the ball hit the bat and trickled foul. Reulbach tried three more times to hit him but the Giants slugger nimbly dodged each attempt and trotted to first on a pass. So it looks like we will have to take care of Cy Seymour some other time. Charlie Dryden's comment to Big Ed summed it up nicely: "You pitched well except for your failure to kill Seymour."

Three errors by Evers did not help our cause. But the main problem was McGinnity, who certainly put on a show. He'd be throwing with an overhand delivery and then, without warning, he'd come in with a sidearm pitch. But that's not all! He had another pitch called "Old Sal," a curveball that he threw underhand. And with that same underhand delivery he also had a rising fastball. Our guys said McGinnity's submarine pitches seemed to spin right up off the ground at them. And he's always coming in right at you—throwing inside—and has a reputation for hitting a lot of batsmen.

All of his stuff worked today so we just couldn't knock many safeties off that rat-man. He got us coming and going. Plus McGinnity is what we call a "quick-return artist." A batter has to be ready the minute you step into the batter's box with the Iron Man, because he will pitch without waiting for a sign. Today he caught a few of our guys napping even though Evers warned every man about this before the game. So we got clobbered 7-1. Husk told us after the game there would always be days like this when the bad guys did bad things and still won. He reminded *us that McGinnity had won twenty-seven games last year so we ought not feel like we did not measure up. In the end, he said, we would prevail because we had "more sense, more talent, and more internal fortitude."*

From the rear of the room I heard someone mutter "internal fucktitude." I knew without looking it was Jack Taylor.

May 23, 1907 New York City, New York

The final game of the three-game set pitted Carl Lundgren against left-handed side-armer Hooks Wiltse. Wiltse, a gaunt, dark-eyed, skinny six-footer with a mouth full of chewing tobacco, got the nickname Hooks as a result of a large, aquiline nose. Hooks was coming off a decent 16-11 season with the Giants. At twenty-six, his best seasons lay ahead of him, but there wouldn't be many. Evers had a history with Hooks. Both natives of the state of New York, they played together on a team in Evers' hometown, Troy, New York, when Evers broke into the professional ranks in 1902. Wiltse often told the story of just how small Evers seemed in those days. The punchline: "He coulda used one of his big black cee-gars as a bat!"

The Cubs jumped all over Wiltse in the first inning, plating two runs, while Lundgren held McGraw's men scoreless for the first five frames. Although the opportunity arose several times, McGraw, as usual, would not employ the sacrifice play to advance a runner. Except occasionally with a pitcher, he could not bring himself to intentionally give up an out, even as a tool to advance a runner. Every other National League manager regularly employed the sacrifice, but not Muggsy. Normally an edgy man, McGraw seemed even more irritable today. When the Giants batted he stood in the coacher's box, hunched over, spitting out comments like, "What the fuck did you think you were doing, you big stiff?" and "Run, you fuckin' ice wagon!"

McGraw, an early proponent of summoning help from the bullpen, kept his reserve pitchers working this day. The "warmup pen" in the Polo Grounds sat deep in right-center field, between the bare benches in the bleachers and the fans occupying the roped-off outfield standing area. When he judged that Wiltse did not have his good stuff, McGraw brought in another slabman to corral the Cubs. The first reliever proved unable to tame the West Siders, so McGraw got cute and starting using a new pitcher every ten minutes. Ultimately he employed six pitchers in the game, about as many as the Cubs used in the previous six contests.

The top half of the fifth decided the game. The score stood at 2-0 Chicago and Muggsy brought in his Golden Boy, Mathewson, for a return engagement. Mathewson had volunteered to McGraw that he "wouldn't mind taking the mound in a pinch." Lundgren opened the inning against Matty with an easy fly to the outfield, but Jimmy Slagle then stung a liner to center for a base hit. Tinker, the little nemesis of Mathewson, poked another groundball through the infield, resulting in two Cubs on with one out. Mathewson kicked at the rubber and focused on the job at hand, trying to get the next batter to ground into a double play. He resolved to keep the ball in the lower part of the strike zone. Jimmy Sheckard resolved to smash the first pitch that appealed to him. He took a couple of low pitches and then golfed a fly ball deep to right-center, far over the fielder's head. As the outfielder gave chase, all three Cubs circled the bases, Sheckard grinning all the way.

Back on the bench Slagle congratulated his teammate. "You gave it the business, Jimmy! What'd you hit, a fadeaway?"

"Shit, I dunno what the hell it was," responded Sheckard. "All's I know is that I could see the ball real good. Like I was able to see the stitches on the damn thing. It come in big and I seen it get scrunched on my bat and fly off of it like a Chinee' rocket. Sure felt good."

Sheckard's home run altered the landscape of the game. It was the break in this one. McGraw somberly removed Mathewson and brought in Dummy Taylor, whose deafness prevented him from appreciating the utter silence that had fallen over the Polo Grounds like a fog. Because of Dummy almost all the Giants had learned sign language for the deaf, and McGraw frequently used it to signal for steals, the bunt, and the hit-and-run. But McGraw no longer used hand signals when the Cubs were the opponent, knowing that Johnny Evers had gone out of his way to learn the language of the deaf so he could steal the Giants' signs. Dummy, with his unusual corkscrew delivery, mopped up in an admirable manner, but the Cubs now led 5-0 and the Giants could not come back. The defeat shook a great many Giants fans and reminded their players of last year's frustrating campaign.

As the Cubs walked off the field, McGraw shot a dirty look at Evers. Johnny turned and took the time to signal "Fuck you" in perfect sign language to the Giants manager. McGraw turned away before it all got spelled out.

In the Giants clubhouse McGraw railed at the umpires and "those assholes Chance and Evers." He kicked over a trash can, spilling garbage under a table near the showers. Most of the Giants showered and dressed in a hurry to escape the wrath and ravings of Little Napoleon.

May 30, 1907 Pittsburgh, Pennsylvania

After taking two of three from the Giants, the first place Cubs landed in Cincinnati for four games with the lackluster Reds. But the Reds reared up, splitting the four games and sending the Cubs back east for a three-game series with Wagner and the Pirates, starting with a Thursday double-header. The Cubs made camp in Pittsburgh at the Monongahela House on

Smithfield Street, a fine hotel where Abe Lincoln once slept, and which now sported a huge sign on its roof advertising "ROOMS $1.00 AND UP." The Pirates ballpark was a short walk away, across the Sixth Street Bridge, on the other side of the Allegheny River, in what was then called Allegheny City. Gamblers congregated in the lobby of the Monongahela House, taking bets on both the local horse races and the ballgames. Frequently, Cubs players bet on their own games, almost always to win, although the unfavorable odds this year diminished their profits. The players knew that league rules prohibited betting on baseball, but no one—the Cubs or the League—enforced the rule. The gamblers often bought the players drinks and attempted to befriend them, if only to learn some scuttlebutt that would give them an edge. "So Big Ed's arm is still hurting him?"

The twin bill started at ten in the morning. When game one ended, workers emptied the stadium for a half-hour, after which ticket takers admitted the crowd for the one o'clock game. A gentle sun poured down on Pittsburgh, perfect baseball weather were it not for the ever-present smell and smoke of the foundries. Two blocks north, picnickers on Monument Hill looked down on the ballpark for free, but the grandstand roof blocked their view of the batter's box and most of the infield.

The picnickers could not see Jack Taylor as he took the mound for Chicago. In a foul mood, Brakeman stormed about the rubber and challenged numerous calls of Umpire Rigler. When he retired Wagner in the first inning, Taylor grinned, raised a fist, and yelled at the Dutchman, "Go on back to your hole, you cur." Wagner just shook his head. Taylor stopped grinning in the bottom of the third, when Wagner and the Pirates plated four runs. After the fourth run, the Pirates shook their fists at Taylor and raised a ruckus. One leather-lunged youngster yelled out to Taylor, "It's time you go home to your rocking chair." Taylor ignored the taunts.

Returning to the bench, the Brakeman slammed his glove down on the wooden plank floor.

"Those bastards got lucky. Or maybe they slipped Rigler a quarter-eagle. Goddamnit!"

Evers could not restrain himself. "They hit you hard, Brakeman. Why don'tcha just shut the fuck up and pitch?"

Taylor let it pass, not even looking up. He knew that if he slugged the little second baseman, Chance might pull him from the game. He calmed down and didn't give up another run the rest of the contest. The Cubs put together a couple of rallies, erupting for four runs in the sixth and seventh, two scoring on a double by Steinfeldt. Taylor walked off the field with a victory in his pocket and a big smirk on his face.

Chick Fraser faced off against Pirates hurler Vic Willis in the afternoon game. Although Fraser's brother-in-law, manager-outfielder Fred Clarke, nicked Fraser for two singles, Fraser easily outdueled Willis, allowing but one run while the Cubs pushed across seven. Steinfeldt again nailed the key hit, another double in the seventh.

In the sixth inning of the second game, a shot rang out outside the park, and a fan in the bleachers caught a bullet in his face. The ballgame continued without interruption while fans dragged the unconscious man to the Pirates dressing room where two doctors probed unsuccessfully for the bullet. The unlucky man died four hours later, his fourteen-year-old son by his side. The Pirates' Secretary convinced the local press that the story was not newsworthy, so it did not appear in the Pittsburgh papers.

After the game, President Murphy announced that Cubs rookie Fred Osborn had been claimed on waivers by the Phillies. Secretary Williams purchased a $2.95 rail ticket to Philadelphia for Osborn. The young outfielder bid his teammates farewell and caught a cab to Union Depot. Ossie was upbeat. He had a better shot to play with the Phillies than with the talent-rich Cubs.

June 2, 1907 Chicago, Illinois

Back home, the Cubs prepared to meet the Pirates for a three o'clock Sunday afternoon matchup at the West Side Grounds. At noon, Howie the boy mascot arrived at the clubhouse where a few Cubs already gathered. Harry Steinfeldt, nursing a mild hangover, gave Howie a quarter to pick up some chewing tobacco and sodium bicarbonate. The kid returned with the two items and fifteen cents change. Harry gave him a nickel tip, which Howie pocketed with a smile. He then loaded the seventy Cubs baseball bats, packed in six canvas bags, onto a battered hand cart, which he pushed across the field to a spot directly in front of the Cubs dugout. He set the bats carefully on the ground in a long, neat row, starting with Chance and Evers' clubs. Mainly spruce, ash, and willow, each bat cost the club seventy-two cents, and Chubby Murphy winced every time a player discarded a broken stick. Howie then trudged back to the clubhouse with the cart to fetch the catchers' gear, a box of water bottles, some towels, and a stack of pails.

The Swede, Carl Lundgren, took the slab for the Cubs today, facing Sam "Schoolmaster" Leever, a bald, thirty-five-year-old Pirates moundsman with a career on the downslope. A large crowd, twelve thousand or so, welcomed home the first-place Cubs.

With the Bucs batting in their half of the third, Lundgren launched a high hard one at Pirates catcher Harry Smith. Smith froze, and the ball cracked loudly off his left temple. The dazed batter fell backwards in a slow arc, his rigid body thudding the ground, where he lay silent and unmoving. As a hush fell over the ballpark, Umpire Klem called for water and ice chips. Fearing the worst, Lundgren rushed to the plate, his pallor white as a new baseball, while the Pirates trainer sprinkled cold water on Smith's face. The liquid did not revive the fallen batsman, so six players, including Wagner and Newt Randall, clumsily picked up the unconscious player and carried him to a covered area down the foul line where they deposited him on a cot. A physician attending the game volunteered to examine him, and after ten long minutes he finally stirred. Forty minutes later Smith dragged himself off the cot and pronounced himself "a little dizzy but fine." The doctor, relieved by his patient's recovery, suggested a visit to the hospital but Smith declined.

The beanball upset Lundgren's concentration, and he quickly ran into trouble in each of the next two innings. By the end of the fifth the Pirates led 3-1.

As the game played out its normal rhythms, the quiet buzz of the dugout was interrupted by Artie Hofman. The lean utility man called out, with two outs and Joe Tinker advancing to the plate, "Who's up after Tinker?"

Jack Taylor loudly responded, "The Pirates!"

In the top of the seventh, Bucs' first baseman Jim Nealon smashed a line drive that caught Lundgren on his shinbone, knocking him out of the game. He limped off the field with the help of Harry Steinfeldt. Chance brought in Mordecai Brown to finish up and he proved flawless. Leever was not sharp. The Cubs pushed three runs across in the seventh, two knocked home by Kling, and the last by none other than their three-fingered pitcher. The Cubs had eked out another victory.

Chance congratulated Brown. "You did it all today, Brownie. You hit as good as you pitched. I can always count on you when we're down."

The first place Chicago White Sox also played in Chicago this day, losing 4-3 to the Tigers at South Side Park. An omen of things to come. In the ninth inning an intoxicated bleacher fan tossed a pop bottle at outfielder Ty Cobb, narrowly missing him. Cobb spun around and searched the crowd for the jerk who threw the bottle, without success. He shouted, "You fucking coward," and then turned his attention to the game.

From the Journal of Kid Durbin

June 3, 1907

Connie Dandridge is making wonderful progress in regaining her health. She still sees Howard Thurston once a week, and Dr. Kent says these sessions have been the key. In fact, I visited her yesterday at the Murphy residence and sat down with Thurston right after he met with Connie. I hadn't seen him in a while, but he expressed delight to run across me again. He is so genial a man he must have many friends around the world. He asked me if my pitching had shown any signs of improvement and I leveled with him.

"Not really," I said. "But mainly because I haven't been pitching. I've been warming a bench since Opening Day."

Just like Frank Chance, Mr. Thurston told me my opportunity would come, that I had youth on my side. I then changed the subject, asking him if he thought Connie might be receptive to me in "more than a friendship way." He said "absolutely," and encouraged me to take "all appropriate steps." When I asked how a young man would know if he was in love, I stumped the Great Thurston. "I can't put it in words for you, son," he said, "but I am quite certain you will recognize it when it happens."

I then made my way toward Connie, after an extended (or so it seemed to me) conversation with Mrs. Murphy and her friend Mrs. Wilson. We discussed the Cubs and beefsteak.

A maidservant finally led me to Connie, who reclined on the back porch, still "recovering" from the session with Thurston. Wearing a tan dress with buttons down the back, she seemed relaxed and in fine spirits. After our initial greetings I steeled my nerves and asked her if she had any supper plans, suggesting the possibility that we could dine out. She accepted my invitation immediately, but then said she must seek the approval of Mrs. Murphy. Excusing herself to find Mrs. Murphy, she walked past me and my knees started to wobble at the sight of her and the smell of her perfume. Something else happened too. I got a hard-on right then and there! Right when and where I didn't want to. This wasn't what Thurston would call an "appropriate step." The guilt that immediately overcame me soon withered my dick so that when Connie returned I could stand and greet her normally, but I'm not sure my face wasn't still a little red.

We had a delightful supper together—just us two—at a small restaurant near the Murphy residence. The waiter, bald and thin, wore a white shirt and apron, and scurried about the place like a lizard runnin' from a hound dog. We ordered a bottle of red wine, and I chose a sirloin steak. Connie selected chicken. We talked for an hour about the Cubs, Chicago, Teddy Roosevelt, and Howard Thurston. After all this time Connie still hasn't seen Thurston's show, so I promised to take her. The dinner bill came to $2.45. Trying to impress Connie, I left two quarters as a tip. We walked back to the Murphy's home, holding hands. At her door I looked into her eyes and wanted to kiss her, but hesitated. Then the moment was gone, my only regret of the night.

I returned to my flat in a very good mood. I got out of my clothes, into my nightshirt, and sat on my bed reading the Courier. Three articles interested me greatly. The first told the story of a Chicago millionaire, one Raymond Trustlow, smitten by the aptly named Miss Marie Love, a native of Atlanta, Georgia. Trustlow had pursued Miss Love, without success, for three months. Last night, Mr. Trustlow, or his agent, forced his way into Miss Love's bedroom and attempted to chloroform her. Miss Love's screams deterred her attacker. He dropped the bottle of chloroform and escaped, leaving this note:

I am taking Marie for my wife whether by fair or foul. It is futile to oppose me. She will be my happy bride by June 16.

Raymond Trustlow

I thought about this story while sipping Sprudel Water. By the way, I am no longer concealing the Sprudel Water from my teammates. They taunted me about this water for a while but now that has passed. As for Mr. Raymond Trustlow, what in tarnation is wrong with this guy? Can't he accept no for an answer? He must be a very addled rich man.

The second article recounted the recent death of Dr. Marvin Chapin. Chapin died of old age, having made it through eighty-six summers on this earth. His daughter, Mrs. Edward Browne, informed the Courier that forty years ago, in 1867, her father had been diagnosed with a terminal case of tuberculosis. Physicians had given him but a few hours to live. But Marvin Chapin absolutely refused to accept their diagnosis. He leaped out of his deathbed, telling his wife that he'd "just as soon die standing up," and that he "might as well die in Ohio." He grabbed a train heading in that direction. On the journey there he learned that job opportunities existed in the Ohio oil fields and he soon found himself employed on an oil rig. "He cured himself," Mrs. Browne added, "by ingesting crude oil."

"Ingesting crude oil?" I made a mental note of this story. If I ever come down with tuberculosis I may have to try that. The thought does not appeal to me.

The next story about Bishop Samuel Fallows of St. Paul's Reformed Episcopal Church really set my mind to work. The subject of Bishop Fallows' regular sermon: "Is Chicago Hell?"

I paused to consider the question unaided by Bishop Fallows' views. I have observed but one devil in Chicago, the monster known as Percy McGill. Maybe there are more, especially in the Levee District and other sinful places. But not all who spend time in the District are sinners. Heck, I myself have passed some time there. Besides, many good people, like Connie, Mr. and Mrs. Murphy, and Frank Chance, reside in Chicago. And some evil people ultimately are saved, transformed. I decided Chicago is not hell. But New Orleans, on the other hand...

Bishop Fallows, according to the article, also arrived at the conclusion that Chicago is not hell. Hell, Fallows declared, is located within the hearts of individual sinners, within the doers of evil deeds. It satisfied me that I came to the same conclusion as the bishop. But I have to say that Bishop Fallows' next comment stunned me. He said that missionary work would someday be required to heal those in need on other planets. In the words of the bishop:

The Earth is but a tiny speck in the great universe of God. This Earth has been the setting of God's richest revelation. But the fruit of this knowledge must be spread. There are countless other worlds and countless other souls inhabiting these worlds who need redemption from sin to the same extent as those dwelling in this small sphere called Earth.

I chewed on this thought. Souls on other worlds? Like Mars? I imagined being a missionary on the Red Planet, bringing Christ to the people of Mars. The thought turned over and over in my imagination, and began to blur with the other stories in the paper. I pictured Miss Love and Dr. Chapin, sharing a warm cup of Ohio crude on a windswept Martian plain, while reformed millionaire Raymond Trustlow and the Bishop Fallows climbed a spiral Martian staircase to ring the doorbell of a Martian sinner.

"Good evening, Mr. Jxztrse," Dr. Fallows would begin. "We are from Earth and we are here to bring you good tidings!"

June 4, 1907 **Governors Island; New York**

McGill stood by the barred window in his cell, watching the sun decline slowly over Lady Liberty and drop into the urban horizon to the west. For a few moments the sunlight danced white and gold off the harbor waters. This was it, the night he had selected for the escape. A sliver of a moon would provide sufficient light for his needs, and not enough to make their presence obvious. His instructions to Pick had been simple enough for the man to understand—at least he could hope as much. "At midnight, get outta your cell and come get me outta my cell. If Harold Conners wants to come with you, let him." McGill asked Pick whether he had a watch.

"Yeah I gotta watch. Why? What's it to you?"

Disgusted, McGill said, "I just want to make sure you're gonna know when it's midnight. You'll need a timepiece to do that."

Pick knew that if he went to sleep that night he would miss his midnight appointment. Sleep right through it. So he lay in his bed determined not to succumb to the drowsiness that soon pulled at him. He began to worry that he would doze off, so he looked over at Conners, four feet from him.

"You still up, Conners?" he whispered.

"Yeah. Why?"

"This is the night. We go at midnight. Can you wake me if I fall asleep before then?"

"Why didn't you tell me yesterday?" Conners asked.

"I didn't know yesterday."

"Well why didn't you tell me an hour ago?"

"I dunno. I forgot to."

Connors scowled. "Do you have a timepiece?"

"Uh, huh. Why?"

"So I'll know when it's time, asshole!"

Pick gave Conners his watch and quickly fell asleep. In what seemed to Pick like just ten minutes, Conners nudged him on his shoulder to awaken him. The minute Pick opened his eyes he said, "Gimme my watch back." Conners gave it to him and the two men quietly made their way to the cell door. Jimmy Vanders, a prisoner who slept nearest the door, awoke and saw the two men standing there. Conners saw Vanders stir and told him, quietly but sternly, "Go back to sleep, Vanders." Vanders pretended to do so.

Pick had a rusty eight-inch nail in his hand. He inserted this tool in the cell-door lock, probed for five-seconds, then twisted it up and around. The lock sprung open, impressing Conners and Vanders, who had peeked out to observe Pick in action. The two men emerged from the cell, looked up and down the gangway, and then set off for McGill's cell, some forty feet away. As soon as they reached the steel-barred door to Percy's cell, Percy jumped up from his bed and woke cellmate Jimmy Lincoln. Pick again attacked the lock, this time taking only five or six seconds to spring it.

Percy praised him. "Good work, Pick." Percy leading the way, the four men now headed for the staircase, the Pick straggling behind slightly. Nothing now stood between them and the oak door in the prison boiler room. Percy knew these two hallways were not guarded with sentries. The men walked quietly down the spiral staircase to the first floor, their steps echoing softly off the stone walls. Percy peeked out of the archway from the staircase. He saw nobody. They scurried to the boiler room door, which had no lock. Percy opened the door, lit a candle, and the four men entered the room. Percy shot over to the green oak door, and the men followed.

"Pick, this is the padlock, just like I explained."

Pick's jaw dropped as he placed his pudgy left hand about the old brass lock. Three beads of sweat grew on the Pick's forehead. He lightly inserted the rusty nail in the keyhole but immediately withdrew it.

"What's the matter?" Percy asked, a clear tone of concern in the question.

"Uh. Could be we gotta problem." Pick took the candle and placed it next to the lock, sighed and then tried to stick the nail in the keyhole more forcefully than his initial attempt, but it only went in a short way.

"What's the problem?"

"Ten years of crud and corrosion. This child's been here a long time. The salt air from the sea has turned the insides of this lock into mush. Ain't nobody can open this lock, even with a key. We need to saw through the fucker."

"Jesus, Pick, there ain't no fuckin' saws. If I'd a had a saw I wouldn't need you."

James Lincoln approached the door and slowly palmed the padlock in his meaty right hand, inserting two fingers inside the shackle and closing his fist around the lock. Hesitating for one second, he then yanked violently. In one clean, uninterrupted yank, punctuated by splinters of wood flying in all directions, Lincoln pulled the padlock and one of the steel spikes right off the door.

"Do you want to take this with?" he asked, dangling the lock from two fingers.

"No, James. We can leave it here."

Percy pulled at the door, and after a small struggle, it gave way. A dank, sickening sweet smell wafted out of the doorway. Placing the candle in front of him, Percy looked in.

A dark tunnel stretched out in front of the men, its packed, earthen floor girded with wooden support beams along the walls and wooden arches overhead.

"Don't tell me this fucker will take us to Brooklyn?" Conners asked.

"No such luck," responded McGill. "This tunnel takes us out of Castle Williams."

"To where?"

"To Fort Jay."

"Fucking Fort Jay? With five hundred soldiers? Outta the frying pan into the fire, don'tcha think?"

"No. They ain't exactly expecting us."

The men started into the tunnel.

The endless darkness scared Pick.

"How do you know where this tunnel goes?" he asked.

"I know," replied McGill. "It won't take us long to get there. Five or ten minutes at most."

Soon the men waded in water eight inches deep. Pick whined until Percy growled, "Shut your yap." Pick lapsed into silence as the cold water sent an icy chill up his legs into his crotch. In another moment the angle of the tunnel tilted upwards and they reached dry floor. They were approaching Fort Jay.

Percy saw the staircase first, a set of six or seven thick stairs, covered with a layer of mud and grime, leading up to another oak door. He pulled the men around him to discuss their plan.

"Number 1—we gotta be quiet. We're going to open this door, one way or the other. Lincoln will rip the damn thing off its hinges if we have to. If we run across a soldier we need to somehow take him out without waking up half the barracks."

McGill grasped the brass handle of the doorknob and turned it to the right. Unlocked, it opened with a slight hitch, and a dim light filtered in through the crack of the door. Percy stuck his head out into a Fort Jay storage room, lit by one electric bulb. The men tiptoed into the room while Percy extinguished the candle and put it in his pocket. Percy told the men to look for weapons, rope, or clothing.

"What do we need rope for?" asked Pick.

"To hang your carcass if you don't shut up," Percy quickly responded. Percy took Pick's rusty nail and began to pry open some wooden crates strewn about the room.

They did not find any rope or weapons, but Percy opened a box of blue army caps and each man donned one. A moment later Conners discovered a box of blue army shirts. The men discarded their striped jail shirts and replaced them with the army issues. Pick swam in his while Lincoln could not latch all the buttons.

Percy spoke to the men. "I'll search for a way out while you three stay here. We can't have the four of us skulking around this place."

Conners objected. "We can't be sure you'll come back for us. I go with."

Percy held in his anger. "All right, asshole, let's go. You two keep quiet and we'll be back real soon."

McGill and Conners returned after an absence of only ten minutes, but for Lincoln and Pick it seemed like an hour. Still breathing heavily, Percy informed Lincoln and Pick that they had located a safe exit from the Fort. The group stealthily slipped out of the storage room and retraced the path McGill had found. In five minutes they walked out an unguarded kitchen door to a vegetable garden on the south side of Fort Jay. Percy and Conners observed two sentries that walked along that side of the Fort, so the convicts timed their hike across the lawn to avoid the soldiers. In another minute they jogged southeast to the shore of the island.

Stopping in an area protected by trees, Percy asked Pick the time. It was 1:10.

"Here's the plan, boys. A couple hundred yards south of here is a muddy place where we can enter the water. About 250 feet off shore there's a buoy. It has a bell on it and we should be able to hear it. We swim to that buoy at two o'clock because a boat will pick us up there at 2:15. Take off your shoes and outer clothes when you swim. They will have some shoes and coats for us on the boat. I made sure of that."

"Why doesn't the boat come in and pick us up along the rocks?" asked Pick.

"Too dangerous. We stay here for now. They won't see us under these trees. In forty minutes we slip down to the water."

A tiny filament of silvery moon lit the clear night, and the rhythmic smash of waves against the rocks kept the men awake and aware. As they waited, each man pondered his plans. Percy would exact revenge for the detour his life had taken. James "President" Lincoln dreamed of opium in the dens of New York City. Conners pictured a black prostitute named Candace. Pick had no dreams. He would not be leaving the island.

At 1:50 all four men headed to the shore, alert for the sentries. From his understanding of the night patrols, Percy did not believe there would be any soldiers in this area, and he guessed right. At the shore, the men began to peel off their clothes. Except for Pick. Percy came up to the little man.

"You can't swim, can you?" Percy asked, matter-of-factly.

"No. Never could."

"So why in hell did you tell me you could swim?"

"I wanted in on the action, no matter what."

"What now?"

"I wish you well and I go back."

Percy's eyes examined the little man's face. He knew he had nothing to fear from Pick.

"Okay. Once we jump in, go back to those trees and go to sleep. At dawn you walk back to the Castle. We'll be long gone when you turn up. Get it?"

"Yeah."

"One more thing. Tell them we forced you to come along to pick the locks. They may believe you because you can't swim, and only an idiot would come along on this escape if he didn't know how to swim."

"Good. That's what I'll say. You made me do it. Thanks."

Percy considered killing the pudgy lock-picker—bashing his skull with a rock—but figured that even if Pick squealed it would make no difference. He informed Harold and Lincoln that Pick wasn't going, and the three men entered the water in a muddy spot near some large boulders. At first, the swim was not difficult, but the cold currents took their toll. The buoy, equipped with a bell and a light and bobbing four feet out of the frigid waters, beckoned them. The shivering men made it at 2:10, each grabbing hold of the floating marker, wrapping their arms in and around its beams and resting. Percy searched the horizon for any sign of the boat, but saw nothing.

Lincoln said, "I couldn't have made it much farther."

Conners said, "I dunno. Brooklyn looks close from here."

"Looks can be deceiving, Conners," Percy offered. "Like me, for example. You think I rolled over for you as you forced your way in on this."

"Oh fuck you, McGill. In an hour you'll never see me again."

"You're wrong, Conners. Your timing is off by an hour." While looking calmly into the eyes of Conners, his words still flowing without the slightest rise in intonation, Percy plunged Pick's rusty nail into the base of Conners' skull. Percy jerked the imbedded steel barb back and forth, as a gush of warm blood spilled over his fingers. Conners' left arm flailed in a spastic motion, and his eyes fluttered wildly for a few seconds until he went limp. The buoy bell ringing loudly in their ears, Percy and Lincoln unwrapped Conners' right arm from the buoy. Percy then slipped off his own ring and worked it onto the dead man's finger while Lincoln clasped Conners by the hair.

"It fits just fine," Percy whispered. The two let Conners sink into the harbor, small bubbles marking his departure.

"Think about it, Lincoln," Percy said, "I just gave a diamond ring to a dead nigger!"

The sound of a motorboat grabbed their attention. Two Italian gentlemen steered toward them.

The afternoon newspapers of June 6 contained the sanitized story of the escape—three men, under cover of darkness, escaped the military prison with the aid of saws, outside confederates, and a boat.

Military authorities did file escape charges against Pick, but a court martial acquitted him. After all, why would a prisoner who could not swim agree to participate in an escape that required a 250-yard swim in New York Harbor?

June 5, 1907 Zion, Illinois

Fitzgerald put together three straight weeks of sobriety and gainful employment, his longest efforts at both in twenty years. And then he slipped. Finishing up work at the laceworks in Zion, he walked briskly over to the railroad station, like a man on a mission. He purchased a ticket, briefly fidgeted for twelve minutes, and hopped the next train to Waukegan, seven miles south. At first, he told himself he needed a steak dinner, something unobtainable in Zion. But on the way to Waukegan, all he could think about was whiskey. After fifteen minutes he stepped off the train, walked north on Lewis Avenue past the A & P and Edna's Bird & Animal Store and halted in front of Harry's Tavern. A jolt of electricity jumped through Fitzgerald when he smelled the vapors waft out of the saloon's open door. Sweat poured out of him and his mouth grew dry. Every fiber in his body told him to buy a bottle and drink it as quickly as he could.

He stood frozen on the wooden planks outside the tavern's entrance. As he hesitated a man slowly emerged from the door. Shabbily dressed, stumbling over his own feet, and mumbling incoherently, the red-faced drunk stank of vomit and alcohol. Another sign from God, thought Mike. A picture of what I was. And could be again. Mike took a step back, both literally and figuratively, a step back from the precipice. He walked north, humming to himself, "What a friend we have in Jesus..." Looking for a steak place.

June 5, 1907 **Chicago, Illinois**

The second-place Giants invaded the West Side Grounds for the first time in the '07 campaign. Their ace, Christy Mathewson, took the hill with five days rest under his belt. At the last moment, Frank Chance decided he wanted Mordecai Brown to hurl for the Cubs, even though he had thrown in relief three days ago. Chance asked Brown, "Are you ready for the slab today?" Brown answered, "I'm like a smoked ham, Husk, always ready."

For many Chicagoans, this was a must-see game. The Grounds could hold eighteen thousand, but over twenty-one thousand fans paid to see this match-up. Cubs management evicted both teams from their benches to allow paid attendees to sit there, forcing the players to occupy wooden planks laid out for them near the baselines, with fans to their sides and in back of them. When the Giants took the field for batting practice, a good number of raucous Cubs rooters, still upset over Cy Seymour's vicious spiking of Joe Tinker in New York, tossed dozens of lemons at the New Yorkers to let them know how they felt. Extra police, who staffed the park in anticipation of trouble, rushed in to stop the ruckus.

As in New York, Mathewson's early performance shined. The Cubs eked out a run against Matty in the first, but the score stood 2-1 Giants after four. In the bottom of the fifth, Kling, Brown, and Tinker all singled to load the bases. Sheckard sacrificed deep to right to tie it up. The big break for the Cubs came in their half of the sixth. Johnny Evers bounded the ball ball high over Mathewson's head. As the Giants legend broke back off the mound, he twisted his right ankle. Mattie tested the leg gingerly, putting weight on it, then easing off. Rather than give in to the injury, he pushed on, but did not pitch like Christy Mathewson the rest of the game.

The seventh inning proved critical. With one out, Tinker stroked a base hit. Chance had Jimmy Sheckard bunting, knowing that Mathewson still nursed his ankle. Sheckard beat out a nifty roller, Mathewson no longer agile from his position. Chance then lined a double to right, Tinker coming around to score. Steinfeldt hollered greetings to Joe, entered the box, and swatted a base hit between short and third, driving in both Sheckard and Chance. While the Cubs manager and Sheckard walked away from home plate, a rhubarb developed in back of the planks holding the Giants. A couple of drunken Cubs fans had jumped two Giants reserves. Several cops rushed to their aid, with Chance and Sheckard running over to lend a hand and calm the crowd. The altercation quelled, the game resumed with Artie Hofman bouncing one deep to short, and Steinfeldt beating the throw to second. Evers made an out but Johnny Kling's double down the line brought in Steinfeldt. The inning ended with the Cubs in front 6-2. By the top of the ninth the Cubs led 8-2, and Howie the mascot, figuring that there would be no bottom of the ninth, started to collect the bats. Steinfeldt and Fraser put a quick stop to this, fearing it would jinx the pending Cubs victory. But Howie's faux pas did not alter the course of the game, as Brown neatly handled the Giants in the ninth.

A satisfied Frank Chance savored the victory. Mathewson suffered only his second loss of the season, both coming at the hands of Mordecai Brown. Pulverizing the Giants ace like this, getting fifteen hits off the legend, could set the table for the remaining two games with the New Yorkers. Husk sat in the clubhouse wondering why the hell John McGraw let Matty stick around once he hurt his ankle. Husk would have immediately pulled the pitcher to guard against further injury. But that wasn't McGraw's style. Chance figured that McGraw was gambling for all the marbles in this contest, and was sticking with his ace no matter what. That pretty well summed up McGraw's general philosophy: all or nothing. In this case it was nothing. The Cubs now had won four more games on the season than McGraw's boys.

A few feet away from Chance, Three-Finger Brown also wore a satisfied smile. He had now beaten Matty in their last five confrontations.

June 5, 1907 **Chicago, Illinois**

At 3:30 p.m., prosecutor William Wilen received a telegram from Sgt. Lorenzo Bell in New York City informing him that Percy McGill escaped from Castle Williams the night before. Wilen, standing while he read the telegram, sat down behind his desk, removed his polished spectacles, and read the document again. Cursing under his breath, he yelled out to his secretary and asked him to telephone Sgt. Bell on the long distance wire. Ten minutes later he spoke with Bell, anxious first to learn the exact number of hours that had passed since McGill's escape and the names of the other escapees. Bell estimated fourteen hours at the outside, but more likely in the neighborhood of twelve hours. And Bell told Wilen that Harold Conners and James Lincoln made it out with McGill.

Sgt. Bell promised to send him photographs of the men. Wilen scribbled down the name and telephone number of a district attorney in Manhattan who could help the investigation. He then called him, and asked if the New York police could monitor Grand Central Depot for the escapees. The D.A. told Wilen they had already done so, as soon as the military alerted them.

"Did any trains depart before you were informed of the escape?"

"No, sir. We received notification of the escape at 7:30 a.m. and the first train did not leave until an hour later. My detail did not observe any of your three escapees board that train or any subsequent train."

Wilen then personally called Mrs. Murphy. He knew the Cubs owner would be in his box at the ballpark, rooting for his club. Mrs. Murphy informed him that her husband would be home at six o'clock.

"It's urgent that I meet with him then, Mrs. Murphy. Do you think that is possible?"

"Why, of course," she responded. "I will tell him. You will come here?"

"Yes. Thank you."

Wilen then called his liaison at the Chicago Police Department and secured two police officers to guard the Murphy residence full-time for the foreseeable future. They would begin duty at eight. While Percy could not make it back to Chicago that quickly, there was no need to take a chance.

June 5-8, 1907 **Chicago, Illinois**

Dispirited by Mathewson's loss to Brown on Wednesday, McGraw tried to rally the Giants on Thursday. He stomped around the visitors' dressing room exhorting his players.

"Give it everything you got today. These guys got nothin' on us,"

McGraw growled. "They got a washed-up piece of shit on the slab today."

But Jack Taylor showed no signs of being over the hill this afternoon. The Brakeman had good velocity and movement on his fastball, keeping the Giants at bay most of the game. The Cubs won 3-2, and McGraw sulked, refusing to talk to anyone, including the press.

A rainstorm washed out Friday's game. When the umpire made the call, players on both teams hurried to leave the park, some taking advantage of the rainout to start their carousing early. A group of five New York Giants, including Cy Seymour, headed to the Levee District to drink, gamble, and whore. At midnight, heading back to their hotel, they passed three Cubs on Dearborn Street. The two groups did not greet each other. The Cubs still seethed at Seymour's slashing of Joe Tinker. Trouble would have erupted if Tinker had been there.

On Saturday, Frank Chance did something he knew would enrage McGraw. Chance named Mordecai Brown to come back on two days rest for the final game of the series. When McGraw learned that Brown had been slated, he exploded in a fit of anger.

"That sonofabitch has seven starters and he's throwing that three-fingered fucker at us again!" Chance had succeeded in getting the Little Napoleon's goat.

Brown pitched his heart out. Starting out like a demon, he struck out the first three batters. Giants hurler Red Ames also had good stuff going, and he checked the Cubs' bats. Ames, a thick-lipped right-hander sporting a day's growth of beard, tired late in the game, walking two Cubs in the eighth and two more in the ninth. With the game tied 3-3 in the bottom of the ninth, one out and the bases loaded with Cubs, McGraw stewed on the bench.

Mumbling to the reserves on the bench, he said, "If Red thinks I'm gonna send somebody in to rescue his ass he's nuts. It's his game to win or lose."

Two pitches later Shorty Slagle connected for a clean single into center and Evers pranced across the plate with the winning run.

The huge crowd exploded with joy and covered the field like a swarm of locusts. The players fought their way off the field with the help of seventy-five Chicago police officers. McGraw randomly selected one small middle-aged man and knocked him down with a blow to the side of his head. The Giants manager disappeared under the stands before the crowd could retaliate.

The Cubs now held first place by five and a half games. In the Cubs clubhouse, Frank Chance sat in his red flannel underwear on a bench in front of his locker, still sweating heavily and trying to fight off a terrible headache.

"We can whip these guys' asses on any given day," he snorted to Tinker. Husk then withdrew into himself, waiting for the aching and ringing in his head to subside.

June 9, 1907 Chicago, Illinois

The Phillies marched into the West Side Grounds in third place, seven and a half games off the pace set by the Cubs. Husk's buddy, Gentleman Jim Corbett, sat behind the Cubs bench, attracting dozens of visitors, many of the soft gender. Although the pitchers of the day sported cold nicknames, a bright sun warmed the air. Carl Lundgren, the "Human Icicle," took the mound for the West Siders, facing off against "Frosty Bill" Duggleby. At thirty-three, right-hander Duggleby was on his last legs as a major league pitcher, having suffered nineteen defeats in '06, and not showing much in the start of this campaign. The Brakeman's analysis of Duggleby: "His heat ain't so hot no more."

The Cubs jumped on Frosty Bill for two runs in their half of the first, Evers cracking the first of his three hits in the game. While Duggleby readied to pitch to the next batter, Evers went into his regular routine at first. Up on his toes, he grabbed a long lead and did a little dance in the dust six feet off first. The pitcher ignored him and retired the side.

Later in the contest, Carl Lundgren felt the fire of the sun on his neck and the sweat dripping down his back. He did not have his best stuff, walking seven opposing batters, but managed to slip out of the jams. In the top of the ninth, with the Cubs ahead 4-1, who should appear as a pinch hitter for the Phillies but erstwhile Cub Fred Osborn. Wanting more than anything to show the Cubs their error in dumping him, Osborn sent a single into center field and proudly assumed his place at first base.

Two pitches later Osborn took off for second base and slid in under Kling's throw.

Following an easy out, another Phillie sliced a hit to the outfield, and Osborn took off from second, intent on scoring. Jack Taylor could wait no more. As Osborn came chugging around third, Jack jumped up from the Cubs bench and shouted, "George Washington!" Nothing happened. He tried a second time, again shouting "George Washington!" at Osborn. But Ossie kept coming and scored without incident.

"What was that all about?" asked Chance.

"The kid's got the Hootchman's disease, or something like that. I thought I could slow him down by yelling that out."

"Yeah, well, maybe you just oughtta sit down now." Husk shook his head.

Right after the Cubs secured the 4-2 victory, Osborn loped over to the Cubs bench to confront Taylor.

"I thought you promised you'd never use that trick on me, Brakeman."

"No sir. I told you I'd never say that to a 'teammate.' Way I see it, you ain't no teammate of mine no more. All's fair in love and baseball, right? Say, anyways, you got the cure?"

"Yeah," replied Osborn, "I got the cure." Osborn had the cure in his left pocket. Two wax plugs he'd just removed from his ears.

June 11, 1907 **New York City, New York**

Percy advised James Lincoln against returning to any of his old haunts or relatives. Those would be the first places the military authorities would stake out in their search for him. He gave the man fifty dollars of the five hundred provided by the Italians and the two split, unlikely ever to cross paths again. Percy believed that no matter what advice he provided, Lincoln would return to the opium dens and probably end up dead or back on the island in Castle Williams. Percy carefully prepared Lincoln on what to say if captured.

At Percy's request the Italians rented a small flat for him in a lower-middle-class Bronx neighborhood. He needed to wait for a better time to leave the city on a train. The Italians were thoughtful, filling the ice box in his apartment with beer, pickles, and half a ham. McGill's first beer in months electrified him.

Every morning, a delivery boy dropped the *New York Journal* outside Percy's door, and he meticulously read through the entire newspaper, searching for the story that would help determine his next step. On June 11 he found it:

> *June 10. A body that washed ashore yesterday in Brooklyn was positively identified as Percy McGill, an escaped prisoner from the Castle Williams United States Army Military Prison on Governors Island in New York Harbor. Dr. Conrad*

Malhern, an Army physician, determined that the body was that of McGill, one of three prisoners who, with outside assistance, escaped on June 5. Dr. Malhern listed the cause of death as drowning. McGill had been serving an eight year sentence for desertion.

It had gone precisely as Percy hoped. He now had three days to deliver three hundred dollars to Dr. Malhern's mother in the Bronx. If he failed to do this, the doctor suggested he would "correct" the identification of the body. The sacrifice of the gold ring probably helped, assuming the fingers remained on the body when they fished Conners out of the harbor. He would stick around New York another week or so and then head back west to Chicago to attend to business.

Sgt. Bell telephoned William Wilen in Chicago with the good news.

"I wanted to tell you myself. They found Percy McGill's body yesterday. Dr. Malhern here has positively identified it."

"What was the condition of the body?"

"From what I heard, it was extremely bloated and the fish had nibbled away much of the soft pieces of the face, the lips, ears, and eyes. But Malhern states there is no doubt that it is McGill. And the body had a gold ring—McGill's ring—on it. It's his ring all right. He once tried to bribe me with it."

"And the cause of death?"

"Drowning."

This puzzled Wilen. "I thought they used a boat to escape."

"Yes, they did," Bell explained. "But we know the boat picked them up off the island. They swam out to meet it at a buoy. McGill drowned swimming out to the rendezvous."

"You seem certain."

"We have corroborated all that I have told you because we picked up one of the other escapees, James Lincoln. He confirmed that McGill went under while they swam to a buoy."

Wilen was satisfied. "Thank you, Sgt. Bell. A number of people here will be very relieved to hear this news."

June 11, 1907 West Side Grounds

Cottonwood trees dotted the Chicago creeks and riverbanks. Each tree produced thousands of seed capsules, which hung like miniature grapes off vines. The capsules contained seeds and a white fiber resembling cotton. In June, these cotton masses burst open, and the white fibers extended to catch the breeze, carrying some seeds for miles. Today they filled the air, floating down on the West Side Grounds. A large web of tendriled fibers accumulated in one corner of the Cubs dugout like a mass of unginned cotton, a nuisance to be avoided or scooped up and stuffed into a teammate's glove. Jack Taylor had another idea. He lit a match and tossed it into the clump, which burst into flames with a loud "whumph." But the fireball leaped into the spitting box, a sawdust-filled wooden crate in front of the bench. Taylor worked quickly to beat out the flames with a wet towel to prevent a disaster. Thick smoke poured from the dugout.

The Crab, looking on with disdain, shouted, "Nice going, Brakeman. You wanna burn down the fucking place, maybe?"

The Brakeman glared from the dugout, heaved out his chest, and shot back to Evers. "Fuck off, Crab. I was just foolin' a bit. No harm done."

Evers scowled and muttered as he walked over to take batting practice.

Husk gathered the starting nine around him before game's start.

"The Phillies are throwing Fiddler Corridon. He pitched for us three years back, so some of us know his stuff. Look for him to stick mainly with his lightning, and he'll come inside on you plenty. You won't see the curveball too often, but he's got a decent slow ball and every once in a while he'll toss a spitter. Just go out there and whack it if it's over the plate."

Chick Fraser started for the Cubs, but he walked the first batter and things quickly got out of hand. Two runs came across for Philadelphia in the first, and when two more scored in the third, Chance summoned Pfiester to the mound. The lefty responded well, checking the Phillies effectively.

Newt Randall left his glove out in right field after every inning. Many outfielders did the same, simply dropping the glove on the turf as they trotted in to the bench. But when Randall retrieved his mitt in the top of the seventh it was covered with tobacco juice.

"The fucker juiced my glove!" Randall muttered.

Swearing, he rubbed the gooey substance off on the grass and cursed the name of Phillie right fielder, Silent John Titus. At the recording of the third out, Randall went down to his knees to tie his shoelaces. Titus jogged out to right field, a toothpick hanging out of the left side of his mouth underneath a bushy mustache. Randall headed toward the Cubs bench, head down, passing near the Phillie outfielder. At the last possible moment, Randall abruptly grabbed Titus by the arm, twisted him down to the ground, and spit a wad of tobacco in his face. The surprised Titus, normally a mild-mannered fellow, responded with a half-hearted swing at Randall's chin, which the Cubs outfielder deftly avoided. Randall then sat on Titus's chest and reached back to slug him. But he thought better of it. He sprung up and walked back to the bench.

The umpire, Hank O'Day, who had raced out to the brawl, turned around and headed back to home plate.

"Ain't you gonna toss the fucker?" asked the Phillies manager.

"No. It's a spittin' match. No one threw a punch. Play ball!"

The Cubs went into the bottom of the ninth down 5-3. Artie Hofman got things started with a base hit, but a slow grounder by Evers forced him at second. Evers then stole second and held there while Kling flied out. Tinker, pinch hitting for Pfiester, coaxed a base on balls. When Slagle knocked another hit, Evers, looking very pleased, scuttled in for the fourth Cubs run. Randall, fresh from his assault on Titus, stood in next. He drove the ball over the second baseman's head to tie the game. But the hits stopped, and the game went to extra innings.

The tenth inning resolved the contest. While Pfiester gave up only one run in his six innings, Kling told Husk that the Cubs pitcher had lost a little on his fastball, so Chance called on Orvie "Jeff" Overall to take the mound. Jeff, now twenty-six, stood well over six feet tall and owned more than 210 pounds. He came over from the Reds in '06 for Cubs hurler Bob Wicker and two thousand dollars. Overall went 12-3 for the Cubs while Wicker earned only six victories for the Reds and retired. Evers called the trade "the joke of the season." Husk now looked on Overall as his number two man behind Brown. Orvie's out pitch was a "drop ball," which fell off the table. He perfected the pitch while throwing for Tacoma in the Pacific Coast League. Jeff walked briskly to the mound, determined to hold the Phillies.

But it was not to be. Overall missed with a curve and three drop balls to the leadoff man, Phillies second baseman Otto Knabe, walking him on five pitches. The heavy humidity grabbed the ball, causing it to drop precipitously. John Titus grounded one to Steinfeldt who cleanly snared it and threw to second. But both Evers and shortstop Hofman had run over to cover the base. Hofman reached for it at the last moment, but dropped the ball, leaving the Phils with two men on and no outs. Outfielder Sherry Magee, the Phils' best hitter, came next. Overall, stung by the error, threw too hard to Magee, walking him to load the bases. The Cubs moundsman bore down on the next batter, Kitty Bransfield, but still could not tame his drop ball. He walked Bransfield, forcing in the go-ahead run. Overall then managed to shut down the Phillies, but the Cubs went 1-2-3 in the bottom half of the tenth, giving the Phils a 6-5 victory.

A dejected Chance did not say anything in the clubhouse. He had seen the bottom drop out before. *You can't win 154*, he thought. *But ya gotta try.*

June 13, 1907 **New York City, New York**

As agreed, Percy put three hundred dollars in a sealed envelope, addressed it to Dr. Conrad Malhern, and delivered it personally to Malhern's mother in the Bronx. The gray-haired old woman answered the door herself, telling Percy she had expected the delivery.

"You must be Mr. Johnson, right?"

"Yes ma'am. I am Johnson." He pulled the envelope out of his vest pocket. "You'll make sure your son receives this?" Percy asked.

"Don't you worry none. I'll give this to him tomorrow," she said. "He comes for supper every Friday night. A good son."

Percy doubted that Malhern had informed his mother of their deal, but he figured that the old lady would transmit the envelope to her son. He turned around and headed to a smoky saloon where female companionship could be purchased.

Around three o'clock in the morning, McGill headed toward his Bronx walk-up, stumbling every so often, his first drunk in months. But not soused enough to stop him from reassessing his plans. He realized it would be safer for him to delay his departure from New York for an extra week or two. The local coppers would still be looking for Conners at the train stations, and they had probably been given photographs of both of them after the escape. He knew they wouldn't be looking for him, but they had seen his photo recently. Better to wait while memories dimmed. He would buy groceries in the morning and let time pass at the apartment.

One block from his flat Percy heard the sound of footsteps behind him. Two men came up on him quickly, running while he could not.

Before he could muster a turn he felt their hands grab his shoulders and twist him around.

"What do you want?" Percy shouted.

The men, bearded bums in tattered coats stinking of body odor and urine, did not respond. They punched McGill in his stomach and when he fell to the ground they kicked him senseless. He sunk into the blackness while the men rifled through his pockets for his wallet and money. But Percy had nothing more than a few coins left. Incensed, the men kicked again.

Three hours later Percy awoke, the pain flooding his senses. He could not walk. A policeman, beginning his daily beat at dawn, found Percy moaning in the gutter and used a signal box to call an ambulance.

They took Percy to the Lebanon Hospital. At noon Percy learned that he had a broken nose, two broken ribs, and a broken left leg. Doctors set the leg and applied a plaster of paris cast to it. Percy asked how long he would be laid up. "Two to three months," said the doctor.

"Doc, can you do something about the pain?"

The doctor prescribed laudanum.

June 15, 1907 Chicago, Illinois

Brooklyn limped into the West Side Grounds with a 15-32 record and lost two more to the Cubs. The new Superbas road uniforms, which featured a small blue and gray check pattern, amused some of the Cubs.

"Those new duds might explain why you guys ain't winnin'," Jimmy Sheckard told his old teammate Heinie Batch. Jimmy broke in with the Superbas and spent nine years with them—his best seasons—before being traded to the Cubs in time for the 1906 season.

The third game of the set found Elmer Stricklett, a little man who made Evers look like a giant, occupying the mound for the Superbas. Five years earlier, Stricklett, pitching for Sacramento in the Pacific Coast League, developed a sore arm and contemplated retirement. An outfielder on the team, George Hildebrand, demonstrated to Stricklett the effect of a gob of spit on a pitched ball. His teammates gave Elmer the nickname Spitball, and he now threw little else. Jeff Overall warmed up for the Cubs.

The Cubs lineup had some changes. Billy Sweeney, back from his stint in the minors, patrolled shortstop because Joe Tinker still suffered from his undiagnosed ailment. Artie Hofman manned first, Chance choosing to rest a bad back while the Cubs faced a weak adversary. And Randall occupied right field as Schulte could not shake what the newspapers called a charley horse. Trainer Jack scoffed when he read about Schulte's injury.

"Charley horse my ass," Jack spat. "Papers 'fraid to print he's got a pulled muscle in his crotch. 'Groin's' too crude for their namby-pamby readers!"

The Cubs nicked Spitball Stricklett for single runs in the fourth, fifth, and seventh while Overall shut out the Superbas through eight. But the promise of an easy victory dissolved in the top of the ninth inning on a barrage of Brooklyn hits and two errors, including Billy Sweeney's fourth error of the game at short. Three runs crossed the plate, and the Cubs could not score in their half of the ninth so they went to extra innings. At the start of the tenth, Chance told Sweeney he was playing too deep, moving the young infielder in four steps on the dirt. Sweeney appreciated the advice but wondered why Chance waited until the tenth to move him.

With one out in the bottom of the eleventh, Johnny Evers cracked his fourth hit of the game, a single to center. Kling came up next, and Chance signaled for the hit and run. The Cubs catcher responded by walloping the ball over the right fielder's head. Evers scampered around the bags to score the winning run. He lingered at home plate as Kling jogged in.

Evers patted Kling's back and said, "Nice hit, Jew."

Kling winked his appreciation. Umpire James Johnstone, still hovering around home plate, asked Kling if he was Jewish.

"Would it help me or hurt me gettin' a call from you, Jimmy?"

"Don't half matter," replied the man in blue.

"Then I'm half Jewish."

From the Journal of Kid Durbin

June 16, 1907

We took the first three in a row from the Superbas and had high hopes of sweeping the series with a win today. Instead, the tide turned and we suffered a real thrashing. Worse, I contributed to our loss.

I didn't get the start. Husk went with the Brakeman. Jack did not have his good stuff today, giving up five runs in four innings, so Cap'n Chance told me to warm up. Mike Kahoe, just up from Columbus, caught me, and Chance put us both in during the fifth. Things began to sour in the sixth. Billy Maloney, a light-hitting lefty, worked me for a base on balls—never a good way to start an inning. The next Brooklyn batter, shortstop Phil Lewis, sent a routine grounder out to our substitute shortstop, Billy Sweeney. Billy nabbed the ball fine, but threw wildly to first. Billy uses a strange, sidearm motion for his tosses—it's the weakest part of his game. He's been making a whole lot of errors lately, pressing too hard to avoid another trip south. Old Dog Ritter, their catcher, then made the first out, but Maloney scored on it. I was able to retire pitcher George Bell easily. So I could have eased out of this predicament if I got the next guy, their hefty second baseman Whitey Alperman. Could have, but I didn't. I tried to get fancy and fed Whitey a slow ball. He whacked it for a triple to left field, sending Lewis home. I got the next guy out, but the two runs put us deeper in the hole.

The seventh inning proved equally messy. Ed Reulbach had warned all Cubs pitchers about the next hitter, left-handed-hitting out-fielder Harry Lumley. The guy could kiss a ball farther than anybody in the league, including Frank Schulte. Reulbach said that Lumley hit "320-something last year but was drinking up a storm and putting on some weight lately." He remained a dangerous hitter. So I stayed low with him, but he managed to sneak a groundball through our infield. Then, sad to say, I allowed another free pass, walking Heinie Batch on four pitches. My normal body swing just did not feel smooth. The ball seemed to shoot out of my hand at the wrong point. Steiny then fielded a grounder at third, but Hofman couldn't handle the throw to first. The bases were loaded and no outs—every pitcher's nightmare. Billy Maloney came up again. I walked this guy the first time around and damned if I didn't do it again, forcing in another run. Upset and unable to concentrate, I laid one in for Lewis who nailed a clean single, bringing in another tally. Ritter then hit an easy fly ball to Sheckard in left field and, wouldn't you know it, Jimmy lost the ball in the sun. Two more runs scored. I held them after that, but those four runs nailed the coffin.

Husk had a heart-to-heart talk with me in the clubhouse. "Durbin," he said, "let me tell you a story about the great scientist Charles Darwin. He was tramping around some God-forsaken island, collecting insects. He'd already filled up his specimen boxes and, while heading back to his ship, he saw a rare beetle. He grabbed that beetle with his right hand and proceeded on his way. Ten steps later he sees another remarkable specimen, and he clutches it with his left hand. Another ten steps later, as luck would have it, he sees a third incredible insect that he simply must have. But without any convenient place to put it, he had to plop it into his mouth for safekeeping. Well, this critter thinks he's about to be eaten so he squirts some smelly shit into Darwin's craw. The stuff is so potent it knocks Darwin over and he loses all three insects. Now that's the end of the story and you're supposed to say to me, 'Thanks for the story, Cap'n, but what's it got to do with me?'"

So I say that to Husk and he explains. "You got a good fastball and a very good curve. But when you tried today to get fancy with the slowball, well, you saw what happened. For the time being you ought to stick with the two good pitches you got before you go testing out that third one, okay?"

I agreed. Probably good advice and it should make my life more simple.

Mother told me to always look for the silver lining. My efforts on the mound stunk. My curve jumped all over the place, resulting in five walks. Despite this, Charlie Dryden told me he wrote me up in his story as having "good speed and a baffling curveball." Thanks, Charlie! But the real silver lining here was my hitting. I batted three times and managed to get three hits! They weren't screaming line drives but in tomorrow's box score they won't look any different than the hard knockers.

A perfect night—temperature in the mid-seventies and no wind to blow Connie's hair about—found Durbin and Miss Dandridge meandering around the Loop. They ducked into the Monadnock Building from Van Buren Street. A long, mosaic tile hallway traversed the building, leading to an exit on Jackson Boulevard. Clear-globed electric lights in hallway ceiling fixtures and affixed to massive columns lit the way. Inside each globe, double-looped filaments gave off a warm, orange-tinged light. The couple window-shopped the stores on both sides of the hall, and then departed through the double wooden doors. They turned right onto Jackson, walking slowly toward Dearborn and the Majestic Theater to catch the Thurston Magic Show. Connie wore a blue taffeta shirtwaist with a white skirt while Durbin sported a twenty-five dollar blue serge Hart Schaffner & Marx suit he had purchased for the occasion. The most money he had ever spent on a suit of clothes. He was absolutely thrilled to be escorting Connie around the Loop.

"You know," Durbin started, "I didn't see the coppers hanging about the house earlier. Where were they hiding?"

"I meant to tell you. They're gone."

Worried, Durbin's grip on Connie's hand tightened. "What? You mean there isn't any protection on the premises?"

"We don't need it anymore. Mr. Wilen notified us of the death of Percy McGill."

Durbin's pace slowed. "I thought he had made good his escape."

"Mr. Wilen told us that he managed to get out of the military prison but that he drowned in New York Harbor. They recovered his body almost a week ago."

A weight lifted off of Durbin. The monster is dead, he thought. The threat to Connie is gone.

"My mother told me it's no good thing to be happy about a man's death," Durbin said, halting with Connie as he spoke. "But this is different. This man deserved to die like no other man I have known."

"I am certain it is God's work, Blaine. I can live my life without that lurking fear now."

A tall man with a smudged face and torn clothes, looking eerily like Percy McGill, approached the two as they resumed their stroll toward the theater. Momentarily startled, Blaine and Connie froze in their tracks. The man asked them for a nickel for supper. Connie smothered a nervous giggle. Durbin relaxed and fished out the coin. The couple then stopped to observe a small crowd gathered around an Italian organ grinder and his monkey. The small man wore colorful green and red clothes and he turned a crank on a barrel organ to produce a twangy tune. The monkey, noosed on a string, held out a tin cup for donations. Durbin asked the man the name of the animal.

"His name-a Jocko. Good-a boy, Jocko."

Durbin gave Connie a nickel for the monkey, and she gingerly placed it in the cup extended to her by Jocko. The monkey removed his hat and bowed at the gift, causing Connie to chuckle. She placed her arm across Durbin's back and whispered, "What a funny little creature." Durbin then related the less humorous story of Henry the Ape to Connie.

The marquee of the Majestic Theater loomed ahead, bold black letters on the brightly lit snow-white background spelling out "THE GREAT THURSTON: THE WONDER SHOW OF THE UNIVERSE." A small crowd of well-dressed men and women chatted outside the box-office window, the men puffing on large cigars and the women adjusting their hats. A small girl of about ten, in a dirty cotton dress, carried a tray of penny gum. At the sight of the child a matron pulled at her husband's sleeve and the man gave the girl a shiny quarter.

"Keep the gum, child," he said, as she gave him a small smile.

Durbin and Connie stood in a short line at the ticket window. Howard Thurston arranged for them to sit third row center. On their way, a teenaged usher provided them with handbills and led them to their seats. A middle-aged couple sat next to Connie, the woman wearing an expensive gown and a necklace of white pearls. Connie complimented the woman on the pearls just as the lights dimmed. A bright yellow spotlight focused on the red stage curtains. As they drew back, a man elegantly dressed in a stage tuxedo emerged. He wore a top hat and carried a thin black cane. Connie smiled at Thurston and he smiled back.

The show began with an act called "The Boy, the Girl, and the Donkey." An attractive girl of eighteen and a boy of the same age emerged from stage left and walked to the center with a donkey trailing behind them. The girl and boy wore sequined costumes that glittered in the stage lights. Thurston led the three to a large, blue-curtained cabinet, opened it, and motioned them to enter. They complied, and one of Thurston's female assistants took no more than two seconds to lock up the cabinet. The moment she secured the cabinet, Thurston fired a pistol toward the ceiling. At that very instant, from the rear of the theater, the girl, the boy, and the now reluctant donkey came noisily running toward the stage. The audience puzzled at the ability of the young couple and the donkey to "jump" from the locked cabinet to the rear of the theater in three seconds. They scrutinized the three but these were the same people and the same animal. A huge applause resounded throughout the building, with Connie and Durbin enthusiastically contributing to the din.

Thurston, as always, thrilled the audience that night. An astonished Connie gripped Durbin's arm when Thurston caused a gorgeous black stallion to vanish in a flash of smoke and spark.

"How did he do that?" she wondered aloud. "Has he told you?"

"No. Magicians never reveal their secrets."

Thurston placed a beautiful young assistant in an ornate golden box at front stage, her feet popping out of one end and her head sticking out of the other. After a short conversation with the girl—Thurston introduced her as Velma—the magician employed a large ostrich feather to tickle her toes, causing her to laugh uncontrollably. Thurston then displayed a large iron saw to the audience and invited five young men from the first row to come up and inspect the tool. They pronounced it genuine and returned to their seats.

Thurston snapped up the saw and brandished it like a weapon.

"Members of the audience," he began. "What you are about to see may disturb you greatly but I beseech you to remain seated. You must suspend belief from reality, do not trust what your own eyes will show you, for I promise you that the young woman in the box will not be harmed in any way."

He placed the giant saw carefully in a notch in the middle of the box. A new spotlight gleamed off the metal instrument, sending sharp reflections out in all directions.

"Are you feeling all right, Velma?" he inquired.

She replied "Yes."

He began to saw, forward and backward in long, broad theatrical strokes, the metal teeth cutting noisily through the wooden container. Sawdust smoked off the box and dropped to the ground. When the saw reached midway through the crate the woman gave off a blood-curdling scream, her feet and head jerked spasmodically, and she fell unconscious. Thurston paused, gazed at the audience as if, perhaps, something had gone amiss, and then plunged ahead, more rapidly, almost maniacally. A thick red pool of blood formed on the floor in front of the box, dripping out of the box and off the saw as Thurston continued to cut. As the pool grew larger an uncomfortable murmur swept the audience.

The saw cut through the final portion of the box and Thurston separated the two pieces, pulling them two feet apart but carefully angling the boxes away from the view of the audience. He walked between the two pieces, avoiding the pool of blood on the stage floor.

"The power of the mind is absolute," he called out. "You create the world, and you can right all wrongs with the power of positive belief! I will demonstrate!"

Thurston pushed the two boxes together again and, facing the audience from behind the wooden container, bent over it, laying his hands on it and mumbling, "Alianna, Alisanna, Talliana, Toom!"

The girl stirred. Her head turned, her eyes opened, and her feet moved.

"Velma, can you collect yourself now?" The audience tittered.

"Why, yes," she answered.

Thurston opened the back of the container and she climbed out, smiling broadly to the audience. Clearly relieved, they burst into huge applause.

While clapping, Durbin bent over and whispered to Connie.

"I hope that wasn't too intense for you."

"Not at all," she responded. "She came back from the dead. I know just how she feels."

Durbin chose a slow, horse-drawn cab to take Connie home. Connie went on and on about the show, and promised Durbin that she would soon learn the secrets of Thurston's tricks.

"He'll tell me, Blaine. I am sure of it."

As the cab grew close to the Murphy residence, Durbin remembered the advice from Mike Kahoe during the Practice Season, "Always do what you are afraid to do." He placed his arm around Connie. Careful not to disturb her hair (as Bates the Bigamist had recommended), he drew her toward him and kissed her gently on the lips. She pressed into him, and the kiss was long and sweet. He stopped for a breath, and pulled her toward him again as the taxicab came to a halt. The perfect silence of the moment and the electricity of their embrace capped the magic of the night.

June 19, 1907   Chicago, Illinois

The morning sports section had an item that instantly caught the attention of Frank Chance. During the Giants-Reds game yesterday, a pitch thrown by Cincinnati southpaw Andy Coakley struck Roger Bresnahan in the head. The headline screamed, "Rendered unconscious for thirty minutes." When Bresnahan regained his senses he asked for a priest. Ushers located a man of the cloth enjoying the ballgame in the grandstand. "Convenient," said one usher to the other. Delivered to the clubhouse where Bresnahan lay, the priest administered the last rites. Later, an ambulance transported the fallen Giant to the Seton Hospital. The *Courier* noted, "Should blood clots result from the impact, Mr. Bresnahan could die."

Chance shook his head, remembering the last time he had suffered a beaning and lost consciousness. When he came out of it Evers asked him whether he dreamed during the episode. Chance lied and said he didn't remember. But he did.

In Chance's dream he stood naked on a sun-drenched California beach, his legs firmly rooted, unmovable in the sand. He tried, without success, to lift his leg out of the sand. Then he began to sink, inch by inch, into the warm, gritty dune. All the while the tide pushed the ocean waves closer and closer to him. Finally, just his neck and head remained above the sand, and the cold Pacific water rolled past him, the salty liquid stinging his neck and cheeks and surrounding him. He gulped his last breath as the water covered him. The water rose only as high as his forehead. Just enough to drown him.

"They say baseball is a game of inches," mused the Cubs skipper. "So is life."

June 20, 1907 Chicago, Illinois

The Boston Doves, occupiers of fifth place in the National League, invaded the West Side for a four-game set, uniformed in the National League's first pinstripes. The Cubs grabbed two out of the first three games. Thursday afternoon's three o'clock finale featured Orvie Overall facing Gus Dorner, a moundsman who had somehow accomplished the loss of twenty-six games in 1906.

The Dovey brothers, owners of the Doves, and Cubs owner Charles Murphy negotiated the details of a trade all morning, first in the Doveys' suite at the Palmer House and later at the ballpark. At two o'clock they agreed to send Cubs rookies Newt Randall and Billy Sweeney to the Doves for Boston first baseman/outfielder Del Howard. Twenty-nine-year-old Howard, six feet tall and a native of Illinois, batted left-handed and earned a reputation as a decent stick man with a capable glove. Randall and Howard literally traded uniforms as each man was penciled into his new team's lineup with no time to spare before the first pitch. Thirty-year-old Herbie Larson, who ran up and down both foul lines with a megaphone to announce the lineups each day, informed the three thousand fans in attendance of the trade at the start of the game.

Overall showed some jitters in the first inning, loading the bases on a double and a couple of walks. But he escaped the jam and proceeded to shut out the Doves for the win. Newt Randall, wearing the Boston uniform for the first time, went hitless but chased down a Johnny Kling liner in the eighth, robbing his former teammate of a double. Del Howard, greeted cooly but civilly by his new teammates, singled once in his four at-bats.

The next day's *Tribune* headlined: "OVERALL BLANKS BEANY BOYS 4 TO 0" and "QUICK SWAP OF PLAYERS." Why did the Cubs make the deal with the Doves? Chance no longer trusted Sweeney's glove after the four-error effort earlier in the week, and President Murphy had long coveted Del Howard. Seven years earlier Murphy's brother Jim played with Howard on a minor league team in Illinois. Jim Murphy witnessed Howard sting three home runs in one game against Joe McGinnity in Matoon, Illinois. He hadn't forgotten it, and he related the story to Chubby Murphy on more than one occasion. With the announcement of the trade, Durbin looked around and realized that he was the last man standing. All the other rookies, every last one of them, were gone. Perdue, Seabaugh, Osborn, Sweeney, and Randall. All released or dealt away. *I'm here just by the grace of God and Mr. Barney Dreyfuss,* thought Durbin. And then he wondered how long he would remain. Randall and Sweeney had mixed feelings about the trade, knowing they would get more playing time with the Doves, but aware that they would lose out on the championship money the Cubs were bound to win. At the end of the day the slightly reconfigured Chicago Nationals rested comfortably in first place with a record of 41-12, seven games ahead of the Giants. The White Sox, the Cubs' nemesis of 1906, sat atop the American League by a two-game margin over the Cleveland Naps.

June 20, 1907 **New York City, New York**

McGill lay in a bed at Lebanon Hospital in a ward with eleven other male patients. Chemical smells—most frequently spirits of ammonia—wafted through the air. The small windows had iron bars and the hospital personnel referred to the patients as "inmates." *Not much differ-*

ent than my cell on the island, he thought. Every once in a while a patient moaned and a nurse or doctor would inspect or inject the man. Two patients died during this first week of Percy's stay. Hospital workers garbed in street clothes removed the bodies without ceremony.

"What was it that killed Mr. Mulaney?" Percy asked Nurse Donis. "You know, the ugly guy two beds over."

Nurse Donis, an attractive, statuesque blonde, did not reply.

"Did you go to school to become a nurse?"

"Yes. Three years at the St. Louis Baptist Hospital Training School for Nurses."

"What caused you to leave St. Louis for this hellhole?"

"My husband."

"He's a lucky man," said McGill, looking Nurse Donis over, up and down.

"I have told him that many times."

Movement meant pain, and it shot through McGill's midsection when he inhaled deeply, laughed, or sneezed. His left leg, immobilized in a large crane-like contraption, disturbed him more each day. The broken nose was a mere nuisance, interfering slightly with his breathing. As the night progressed, McGill grew more irritable, and the night nurse paid less attention to McGill than Nurse Donis.

"I need more medicine," Percy told the plump forty-year-old nurse, referring to the laudanum.

"No, you do not, Mr Crandall." He had given the hospital the name of his grade school teacher, Albert Crandall.

"What the fuck would you know of my suffering?" he lashed out. "Give me the medicine or get me the doctor!"

June 21–26 **Chicago, Illinois**

The schedule called for six games in six days against the cellar-dwelling St. Louis Cardinals. The Cards came into Chicago with a 15-42 record. They departed 15-48. While Cardinal manager John McCloskey pitched lefty Johnny Lush and former Cub Fred Beebe twice each in the series, Frank Chance elected to start six different Cubs slabmen—Brown, Lundgren, Reulbach, Overall, Fraser, and Taylor. Everything fell into place for the West Siders. Brown and Lundgren tossed shutouts and in three of the other four games the Cubs pitchers gave up only one run. For Brown it marked his tenth consecutive victory. Johnny Kling's right arm aided the pitching effort in game one, nailing four Cardinals who attempted to steal.

Chance experimented in two of the games, putting Kid Durbin in right field. With the Cubs suffering from injuries, Husk needed a fresh body. He knew Durbin went 3-3 last time out. The redhead told Chance he would give it his best. He went 1-7, made a couple of put outs and no errors. All in all, a credible performance. Newcomer Del Howard joined Durbin in the outfield and covered first base on occasion, contributing a good number of hits.

The series concluded with a doubleheader. The first game, a sloppy, back-and-forth affair marked by four Cubs errors, ended with the Cubs slipping by the Cards 7-6. Jack Taylor got the assignment in game two. With two outs in the bottom of the second, Johnny Evers stroked a clean single into right field off of Fred Beebe, a tall righty. The Cardinal pitcher had broken into the majors with the Cubs the year before, going 6-1 under Kling's tutelage before Husk traded him to the Cardinals in the deal that brought Jack Taylor back to the Cubs. Evers keenly remembered Beebe's slow windup and pickoff motion to first, so Johnny had no trouble stealing second off the Redbird hurler. As Evers slid into second safely, Chance yelled out proudly to his teammates, "Did you see that, boys? Johnny read Beebe's mail! They never had a shot at him!"

Then Kling singled, with Evers settling in at third. Kling, also very familiar with Beebe's slow delivery, stole second, bringing Jack Taylor to the plate. Chance didn't figure that Taylor would hit safely, and he discounted the defensive skills of Card backstop Pete Noonan, who had been a Cub very briefly in 1906. So Chance stood up and changed places with Jeff Overall on the bench—the signal to Evers to steal home. The little second baseman pounded down the line as the Cards pitcher began his delivery. At the same time, the entire Cubs bench let out a whoop. The racket and the speedy approach of Evers unnerved the Cardinal catcher, who let the ball dribble by him. Evers raced home without a slide, and Kling followed after, Noonan cussing at himself as the second Cub crossed the plate. Surprising everyone but himself, Taylor then cracked a single. He strutted about first base for a pitch or two before he raced to second in an ill-advised attempted theft. This time Noonan's peg beat the slow-footed Taylor, ending the inning. When the Brakeman returned to the dugout for a drink of water, Chance confronted him.

"I didn't give you the signal to steal."

"No, you didn't. That ain't stopped me before and it ain't gonna stop me in the future."

"Well, I'm gonna put a plaster on you that you'll remember, Brakeman. Fifty dollars! Maybe that'll stop you."

Unfazed, Taylor returned to the mound and allowed only six hits and one run, capping the Cubs' sweep of the series. Although the West-Siders rattled off six straight victories, the Chicago newspapers began to focus on a minor league prospect who the Cubs had scouted, Henry "Heinie" Zimmerman. Called the "Wilkes-Barre phenom," the Wednesday newspapers trumpeted that the twenty-year-old infielder had slammed six hits for Wilkes-Barre in the New York State League the day before. Chubby Murphy was negotiating with the minor league club.

Although he did not inform the press, Chance levied a fifty-dollar fine on Brakeman for running without permission. Knowing that Taylor would not voluntarily pay, Chance instructed Charlie Williams to deduct ten dollars from each of Taylor's next five paychecks.

At the request of Chance, the Cubs assembled for a team meeting in the clubhouse anteroom after dressing into their street clothes. No one except Kling and Chance knew the purpose of the meeting, although Rabbit Slagle voiced his prediction to Jimmy Sheckard.

"Aw, he's jes gonna tell us not to let up. Jes because we're runnin' ahead of the league by so much and all, he'll wanna make sure we still go 100 percent. You watch."

Chance bounded into the room, neatly dressed in his suit trousers, white shirt, and a blue bow tie. He had his folded suit coat over his arm and an unlit pipe in his scarred right hand.

"Gentleman, we have a proposition to play an exhibition game here in Chicago on Monday, September 9, an off-day. It's an unusual offer. Rather than splitting up half the gate receipts, we are being guaranteed $175 a man, paid two days before the game."

An enthusiastic murmur rumbled through the room. Most of the men smiled and started shaking their heads "yes" before Chance could continue.

Del Howard yelled out, "What's the catch? There's gotta be a catch to this one."

Chance proceeded. "There is indeed. The team that's making this offer is a local colored team. The Leland Giants is what they call themselves. Johnny Kling can tell you all about them if you want—he's seen 'em play. Because the money is good I'm not gonna tell you what to do. We'll talk some about it now and vote. If enough of you wanna play, we'll play. Not every man has to. Those that decide to play will get the money. And those that choose not to play will not be questioned."

Several Cubs asked Husk what he thought about the proposal.

"Gentlemen, this has gotta be your call, not mine."

Taylor stood up, rocking sideways as he spoke. "Boys, this would be a big mistake. Forget the money. No white man should do this. It's like a bribe to get us on the same field with a coon team. It's blood money, boys. Us playin' ball against the coon team gives them equal footing with us when we all know they're second rate. You don't wanna let things get outta hand. Why, if we let them play baseball against our champion team, who knows the next thing they'll want—maybe they'll be wanting to play in the National League. The white man's league! We gotta turn this down for the good of baseball now and for the future."

Slagle spoke next. "I dunno, Jack. We give these colored boys a good thrashing and we make a point. That they cain't play at our level. We make that point whiles we get $175 each to do so. Almost two hundred smackers for one lousy game. Shee-it, to me that sounds like a damn fine deal."

"And if they beat us?" Taylor responded. "Then what kinda point do we make, Shorty? We'd be the laughingstock of the nation."

"You jes said they's second rate so they ain't gonna beat us. We can stomp their black asses and get paid for doin' so. A country boy's dream, Jack."

"I think we ought to do it," said Johnny Kling. "I know a few of these boys and they play hard. They're strong and as tough as a pine nut. They got this pitcher, Rube Foster, he'll be a real challenge. I think we can beat them but it's no sweat if we don't. Other colored teams have played white teams before and nothin's come of it. It's not like it's the World's Championship Series. It's only one game. And $175 is nothing to sneeze at."

Harry Steinfeldt started to speak. "I once played some niggers in the Texas League. We beat 'em bad. It don't say nowhere you can't knock 'em around when you play, right? Hell, for $175 I'll play the devil! We should play 'em so long as we don't have to stay in a nigger hotel."

Steiny's teammates laughed at that.

"I think it does establish a poor precedent," said Johnny Evers, standing and looking around the room as he spoke, an unlit black cigar dangling in his left hand. "We are the National League Champions and we're on our way to being the World's Champions. It's one thing for a bunch of has-beens to play a colored team. It's different if we do. If we misstep here, we hurt the game. Some folks might get the wrong notion. I know I won't be able to take part. It just doesn't sit right with me."

Chick Fraser too had his doubts. "We hafta insist on a white umpire if we do it. We can't expect a colored ump to be fair. It ain't in their nature. And we oughta play here, on home turf."

"They already offered both of those things, Chick," said Chance. "Only reason Murphy would go along with this is because the club gets one thousand dollars rental fee for the Grounds."

"These guys ain't gonna be easy, you know," said Miner Brown.

"I don't know," Overall piped up. "They'll be playing before the biggest crowd they've ever seen. They'll be sweating nervous, gentlemen. We'll have a big edge. There's no reason we shouldn't take 'em up on it. If we lose we can always blame it on not having Johnny at second!"

The boys laughed.

Chance called for a vote and only Taylor, Evers, Fraser, and Pfiester voted no. Chance did not vote. The game was on.

From the Journal of Kid Durbin

June 30, 1907

These last few weeks have been exciting for me. Connie and I have grown very close. I kissed her in a hack after the Thurston show two weeks ago—our first kiss. I don't count the time I kissed her in the coffin at her funeral because she was dead then. At least we thought she was. By the way, since the night we saw Thurston perform there have been more kisses! We had an outing to Riverview, a swell amusement park way north on Western Avenue and Belmont. We rode the "Shoot the Chutes" two times, hugging each other as the boat slid down a two-hundred-foot incline and splashed into a pool of water. We strolled the Midway and enjoyed a wonderful evening.

Connie is the picture of health, robust and rosy, and her disposition is very positive. She says her turnaround is the result of a combination of things and I am at the top of the list of those things! A week ago she told me she wanted to work again and now I learn that she has a job already. With Thurston, as a stage assistant in his show. She is certainly pretty enough to be a performer. One of Thurston's assistants left the stage to get married and Connie asked him if she could take the job. The Murphys agreed and I too thought it would be good for her so Connie has already started. Thurston pays her twenty-five dollars a week, much more than she had received at the flower shop. And shorter hours too! There is an additional benefit—Connie will probably see how Mr. Thurston does his magic and I am hoping she will share these secrets with me.

We still lead the league by a large margin, but we have run into a bad stretch. In game one of today's doubleheader the Pirates' Sam Leever bested Orvie Overall. That made four losses in a row! Game two matched Jack Taylor against Vic Willis and we went twelve innings before the darkness ended the game. Jack pitched all the way and would still be throwing now if the sun had stayed up in the sky. With four losses and a tie in the last five games you can bet that Frank Chance has not been a happy man. Far from it. He and Taylor got into it after the game got called today. Jack started whining about how we only scored four runs in twelve innings and Husk said if Taylor hadn't gone and given up four runs we wouldn't have had any problem. One thing led to another and then they traded insults in the clubhouse, jaw to jaw. Taylor bit off more than he could chew because Husk whomped him real good in the face. One punch and Taylor fell down and out cold, just twitching behind the piano. The left side of Brakeman's mug swelled up like a winter melon and Husk walks away without a scratch. Yet wouldn't you know it that one hour later Taylor comes up to me outside the ballpark and says, "Did you see me stand up to the P.L.?"

"Looked to me more like you were lying down than standing up."

Jack walked away in a huff. "I'll get the last lick," he yelled.

I walked away from Taylor shaking my head. The poor fellow is only half a human being. He is missing a big part of what a person ought to be. Because of that he doesn't see things right. He's missing most of the signals life sends us. In a ballgame when you miss a signal it usually means a screw-up and that seems to be what's been happening to Jack. He doesn't feel what he ought to feel, when he ought to feel something. Only time I ever saw him show a hint of compassion was out on Lake Pontchartrain, in a drunk, and that was for a worm. The man also has enough hate in him for ten men. My guess is that the hate and the other deficiencies will someday be his undoing.

At the Biggio Brothers saloon following the game, Charlie Dryden, the Tribune sporting writer, bought me a couple of beers. I mentioned that Jimmy Slagle called out "It's a can of corn," before catching an easy fly ball today. While I have heard ballplayers use this expression many times, I never did understand where it came from. Dryden educated me. Most grocery stores, he told me, used to store their canned vegetables, like corn and peas, in tall piles stretching up out of reach. "Some stores still do this," he said. "So when you want a can of corn the proprietor of the store uses this long stick, that looks like a pool cue and sometimes is a pool cue, to push the top can off the pile. That can falls down into your grasp, an easy catch. A can of corn." That made a lot of sense to me.

Charlie is one of the guys who helped pull Chance and Taylor apart in the clubhouse today, so I asked him if he would write about the fight in tomorrow's "Tribune." He said, "No, it ain't news." I told him he could put a cartoon illustration of Jack Taylor's swollen face with the story and arouse quite a bit of interest.

"If I did that," said Dryden, "Jack Taylor'd probably beat me about the face till I looked like he does!"

Charlie is a decent and right smart fellow. This is his last day covering the Cubs. He switches over to do the White Sox for a while and his colleague at the "Tribune," Cy Sanborn, will be traveling with us. We will miss Charlie.

July 4, 1907 Chicago, Illinois

This being getaway day, most of the Cubs rose early to pack their bags—they wouldn't have time after the two scheduled games. The day's agenda called for a morning/afternoon doubleheader with the Cincinnati ballclub, after which the Cubs would grab a 5:30 train for New York. The July 4 doubleheader, as in most other big league cities, would feature a marching band, parades, and fireworks. Unlike other clubs, however, the Cubs festivities would also include the solemn raising of the National League pennant flag.

The West Side Grounds sported forty American flags and was draped in red, white, and blue bunting. The air dripped with humidity and the temperature edged up each hour, headed for the nineties. President Murphy and Secretary Williams carefully orchestrated the ceremonies preceding the morning game. At the stroke of ten, a uniformed marching band, one hundred men and boys strong, started playing as they strutted across the field from home plate to the center field clubhouse. In the shadow of the clubhouse the Cubs and the Reds formally joined the parade as it wheeled around to return to home plate where the home town crowd enthusiastically applauded last year's pennant winners. The athletes and the band then paraded back to the clubhouse area, removed their caps, and solemnly observed ace groundskeeper Charlie Kuhn pull the 1906 National League Pennant, a large blue and white banner, up the flagpole over the West Side Grounds.

As the pennant ran up the mast, all hell broke loose in the grandstands. Despite a prohibition, a good percentage of the crowd had brought fireworks and firearms into the park with them. The raising of the pennant providing the first excuse of the day for abandonment, the rockets began to fly. Small explosions erupted in the grandstands and on the field, the blasts echoing throughout the ballpark. Dozens of men drew pistols and fired them into the air. A stray bullet nicked the ample vest of ticket taker Jimmy Roach, leaving the young man shaken but unhurt. One teenaged fan went home that day with one finger less than when he arrived, the result of a large firecracker exploding in his hand. His buddies thereafter called him "Three Finger" Calhoun. Amid the commotion and confusion the players marched back to their benches and the game commenced.

In game one the Cubs only managed four hits off Reds twirler Charley Hall, but the big righty gave up six passes, allowing five Cubs runners to score. The first inning set the stage. Slagle worked Hall, who would turn twenty-two later in the month, for a base on balls to start the game. Jimmy Sheckard, in the number two slot, got nicked in the leg. Back from his "charley horse" injury, Frank Schulte sacrificed the runners to second and third. The Peerless Leader, in the clean-up spot, shot a tough groundball out to Huggins at second base. Huggins stopped the grounder but had only one play, to nip Chance at first, while Rabbit Slagle plated the first Cubs run. Meanwhile, Jimmy Sheckard thought he might catch the Reds by surprise and tried to score from second when Huggins threw to first, but first baseman John Ganzel pegged a rocket to the Reds catcher, nailing Sheckard at the plate. Still, the Cubs finagled a score without the benefit of a hit.

Miner Brown had little difficulty in taming the Reds this day. His famous curveball deftly arced across the plate all morning, stymieing any serious Reds challenge. In the sixth inning, with Hans Lobert on third base and one out, Lefty Davis lifted a fly ball to Slagle in center. Slagle caught the ball running full tilt toward the plate, and smoothly windmilled his throw home in the same motion. The perfect throw to Pat Moran in front of the plate stopped Lobert dead, neutralizing one more scoring threat. The Cubs ace did not give the Reds many more shots and the Cubs won 5-1.

The club had little time to grab lunch before the start of the second game. Many of the Cubs brought sandwiches with them to the ballpark while others paid Howie the mascot to fetch their food. Eager to oblige—and to earn their tips—Howie collected the money and composed a list of the players' orders. Roast beef sandwiches drew the most votes.

The second game began at three with the temperature soaring to ninety-two degrees. Jeff Overall worked on a shutout, stopping the Reds every time they tried to piece together a rally. He had pinpoint control this afternoon, able to place the ball exactly where Kling held his glove, and walked no Reds batters. Overall came off the mound after the seventh inning perspiring heavily and puffing, his uniform five pounds heavier, soaked with sweat. He lay down on the bench in the shade, sucking on shaved ice, while Durbin and Trainer Jack fanned him with damp towels. Chance asked him if he wanted to continue and he responded, "Hell, yes." Timely hits by Evers and Chance netted the Cubs two runs, enough for a 2-0 lead in the top of the ninth.

An animated crowd chanted, "Hold them down!" With one man retired in the ninth, Evers muffed a groundball and Ganzel laced a single through the infield, mounting the Reds' strongest threat of the day. Reds catcher Larry McLean, standing 6'5" tall, tapped his bat on the plate and waited for the next pitch. McLean had battled a vicious hangover early in the day. Manager Hanlon, figuring that McLean would have a problem in the morning, penciled him in just for the afternoon game. Overall took a few breaths as Kling signaled a pickoff play for first base. He pivoted and threw to first but Ganzel dove back safely. Overall then fed McLean a high fastball. "Stee-rike," called Umpire Hank O'Day. The next pitch missed by an inch outside. Overall then looked over to first before breaking off a sensational curve, which surprised the batter, O'Day yelling out "Stee-rike two!" The count stood 1-2. McLean swore at himself and rubbed a little spit and dirt on his hands before stepping back into the box. Overall got the sign from Kling and reared back to deliver a low fastball. McLean picked up the ball's trajectory but swung late, striking out.

"Shit!" he exclaimed, storming away from the batter's box.

Chunky third baseman Mike Mowrey presented the last hope for the Reds. Kling started off by calling for two inside fastballs, and Mowrey's feeble swings couldn't catch up to them. Half the fans in the park knew that the next pitch would be a curveball. Even Mowrey figured that out. Overall did throw a great, twisting curve that started off heading right for Mowrey's head and crossed the plate on the outside corner. Mowrey's knees buckled and he froze. By the time he realized the ball spun toward the strike zone, it was too late. The umpire's shout of "Strike three!" cut through the haze of Mowrey's bewilderment.

As the game concluded Chance jogged over and congratulated his pitcher. He firmly grasped Overall's hand and patted his left shoulder. Brown and Overall gave up but one run to the Reds in the twin bill. The second game concluding at 4:45 p.m., the Cubs rushed to shower, dress, and make their 5:30 sleeper to the east coast.

July 6, 1907 Brooklyn, New York

It was hate at first sight.

It happens, in the course of human affairs, that one man takes an instant dislike to another, for the flimsiest of reasons or for no reason at all. It is common in our species. This warm afternoon found Washington Park's grandstands and pavilion packed to the gills—and overflowing onto the field—with more than twenty thousand screaming fans of the Brooklyn Superbas, all bracing for a slated doubleheader. Across First Street, looking down on right-center field in the ballpark, loomed the

Guinea Flats apartment building, with six hundred sweaty bugs observing the game from fire escapes, opened windows, and the soft-tarred roof. Even the pungent sewage smells from the Gowanus Canal failed to deter the enthusiastic crowd.

Maybe it was the heat. Or maybe it was the density of the crowd. Whatever it was, two of these Brooklyn fans inside Washington Park got off to a bad start. Fan #1, a short, lumpy, unassuming fellow, maybe twenty years old with oily hair and no hat, sat in the first row down the first base line near the outfield wall. He came to the game alone, munched on a ham and cheese sandwich, and said nothing except for one catcall at a Cubs outfielder in thick Brooklynese: "Hey Schulte ya bum! We gonna moida ya today!" Fan #2 sat with a group of friends in the second row, directly behind fan #1. Twenty-two years old, tall and lean, fan #2 came dressed in a cheap gray suit, lavender shirt, pink tie, and straw hat. The trouble began just before the first pitch, when fan #1 turned about too quickly and jostled the bottle of beer held by fan #2, causing a small spill.

"Hey, watch it fatso," cried fan #2, to the delight of his two friends. Fan #1 ignored the remark. But the insults had just begun. Shortly after the Cubs pushed across two runs in the first inning, fan #2 issued another insult.

"You there, Mr. Plug-Ugly! You are blocking my view."

"Fan #1 said nothing, which fueled fan #2's desire to continue his harassment.

The aggressor turned to his friends and belittled fan #1 in a stage voice, designed to carry. "I do believe the man is inside-out today, his internal juices oozing out of him. It's dreadful, isn't it?"

Fan #1 feigned disinterest in the attacks, not reacting at all when called a donkey in the third inning and a horse's ass along the fourth. Nor did the stolid fan #1 flinch when labelled a Nancy-boy and a jerk around the seventh inning. With each new epithet the crowd surrounding these two guffawed a little more, further egging on fan #2. But the victim of the torrent of abuse did not respond or comment in any way.

As the Cubs took the field in the bottom of the eighth, fan #2 mounted another assault. "You, sir," the man started, "do resemble a lowly turtle. An unseemly large and lowly turtle."

The last jibe started a slight stirring in fan #1, a rippling tremor. He stood up slowly and turned to face his tormentor. "Did ya call me a toitle?"

Fan #2 smiled and stood tall to tower over the man he had been taunting. "I confess I did, sir, you have the aspect and smell of a slimy swamp turtle." The surrounding crowd heaved a nervous laugh.

Fan #1 began breathing swiftly, his face reddened, and sweat started to pour down from his hairline. He roared, "Ya can't call me a toitle!"

To which the other man replied, "I just did. The resemblance is uncanny. You are the spitting image of a turtle."

A dark look fell across the face of fan #1 while a deep-seated animation roiled to the surface. He began to slowly wave his stubby arms and bellow, "Nobody calls me a toitle!"

Fan #2 expelled a huge laugh but it did nothing to deter the "Turtle," as he would thereafter be known. The Turtle snapped, slugging fan #2 repeatedly on his nose, breaking it in two places, and knocking him down to his knees, where he pounded the poor fellow into an unconscious, bleeding heap. He would have continued to pummel the man had a cop and several fans not pulled him from the scene, still shrieking in a chilling screech, over and over, "Nobody calls me a toitle!"

The Cubs split the doubleheader with Mr. Ebbets' Superbas, allowing the partisan crowd to go home with a victory in game two, called on account of darkness in the eighth inning. As soon as umpires Carpenter and Emslie called the game, the Cubs scrambled for a train to Utica, to earn a few extra dollars in an exhibition game against the Utica minor league team on the Cubs' Sunday off-day.

July 8, 1907 Brooklyn, New York

Another hot and humid day in Brooklyn, with no breeze of any sort to cool the bugs in Washington Park. It was worse for the players, sweat soaking their uniforms and stinging their eyes. The pitchers stuck their heads in pails of shaved ice between innings. Save for a smattering of Cubs fans, the 4500 attendees had little to cheer about this afternoon. The Cubs led the entire way and at no point did the Superbas raise a legitimate challenge. Despite the ease of the contest, Frank Chance became embroiled in a series of squabbles with umpires Emslie and Carpenter. The crowd, having nothing to cheer about this day, grew increasingly irritated at the Cubs manager. They still buzzed with two outs in the bottom of the ninth and the Cubs leading 5-0 on the strength of Miner Brown's dominating performance.

The Gates of Hell opened up before the third out could be recorded.

It started with a string of catcalls and epithets. Several Brooklyn rooters down the first base line lashed out at Frank Chance.

"Hey, peerless asshole Chance," they shouted, "you cocksuckers ain't got no chance. You'll get your asses kicked in the Championship Series jest like you did last year!"

Husk ignored these words. He'd heard worse. One more out and it would be over. But the fans upped the ante. A group of drunken young men started throwing soda pop bottles, dozens of them showering down around Chance and Umpire Carpenter near first base. This wasn't the first time the Brooklyn bugs demonstrated their feelings by throwing bottles. They had a name for it—Flatbush confetti.

But when a large glass bottle narrowly missed Husk's head, he lost it. Without thinking, he grabbed a beer bottle at his feet and whipped it back into the maw of the mob. And then two more. The second missile thrown by the athlete's powerful right arm slammed into the leg of a small boy, knocking him over. Chance did not know that he had hit someone, let alone a child.

The Cubs manager's response enraged the crowd, which now launched a second, broader volley of pop bottles. This time the bottles rained down on Chance in dangerous numbers, and he backed away from his tormentors, toward second base. A few fans managed to squeeze onto the field and Chance picked up two bottles, ready to fight fire with fire. The throng crept toward him, but a taut wire fence prevented them from advancing. Joe Tinker grabbed Chance from behind, getting him to drop the bottles. With the Cubs providing a shield, a police detective then escorted Chance to the Superbas's clubhouse. Superbas owner Charles Ebbets raced onto the sideline, and with the help of police with drawn revolvers, calmed the rabid Brooklynites. Ebbets grabbed a megaphone and assured the roiled crowd that he would have Chance arrested. After a ten-minute delay, the game resumed for the final out, with Artie Hofman installed at first base for Chance.

Chance, along with three detectives, six police officers, Johnny Evers, and Harry Steinfeldt, sat in the clubhouse for three full hours. Captain Erasmus Maude told Chance that he would have arrested him if he'd seen him launch the pop bottle.

"You're right, Captain," Husk responded. "I did wrong to lose my temper and act the way I did. But it's hard to be cursed and made a target and not lose patience with a senseless crowd. They're just sore because we beat the home team."

Even though roving gangs of miscreants still lingered outside the ballpark, the cops expressed their belief that they could accompany Chance to the elevated train station one block away. Ebbets rejected that plan. He demanded that the police bring in an armored vehicle to cart Chance out of harm's way. Capt. Maude made a bargain with Chance. He would obtain the vehicle if Chance would not play the remaining two games of the series. Figuring his actions would result in a suspension anyway, Chance agreed. The "buzz wagon" arrived, and Ebbets accompanied Chance, Evers, and Steinfeldt to New York City.

July 15, 1907 **Philadelphia, Pennsylvania**

On July 9, the day after the pop bottle incident in Brooklyn, Chance walked into the New York City National League headquarters without an invitation, and asked to speak to League President Harry Pulliam. He explained the episode to Pulliam and apologized for losing control. Pulliam appreciated Chance's directness but suspended him indefinitely. He visited the Superbas ballpark a day later to review diagrams of the pop bottle trajectories. A few days later, keenly aware of the Cubs manager's spotless ten-year record, Pulliam announced that the suspension would last one week.

The Cubs took the field on July 15 bruised and exhausted. Kling's thumb was still swollen from a foul tip earlier in the week, necessitating Artie Hofman to play first, and Pat Moran took over the receiver duties. Carl Lundgren assumed the mound for the Chicagoans while thirty-two-year-old righty Tully Sparks, in the midst of his career-best season, would toil for the Phillies. Jimmy Sheckard continued to skipper the squad in the absence of Chance. Each day without Husk, at least one fan taunted the Cubs with "You guys don't gotta Chance today!"

Although the two teams had no inkling, the game was decided in the top of the first. Leadoff hitter Slagle grounded to third to start the game with an out. Jimmy Sheckard then poked a base hit through the infield. Frank Schulte mightily drove a ball to right for another single, with Sheckard taking third. From his perch on third base, Sheckard signaled the suicide squeeze bunt to Hofman at the plate. The first pitch, a fastball outside, was perfect for the squeeze, and gave Hofman his opportunity. He laid the bat out over the plate and pushed a decent bunt to the right of the pitcher. The Phillies hurler jumped off the mound and reached the ball quickly, fielded the squibbing bouncer, and pegged it to catcher Red Dooin as Sheckard bolted for the plate. Freckle-faced Dooin, a small man who had once been advised by Charles Comiskey to go home and return to his trade as a tailor, prided himself on his fearless defense. He blocked the plate perfectly this time, oblivious to the approaching spikes of Sheckard. The collision violently upended the tiny catcher, and the ball hopped away from his mitt like an insect from under a rock. Umpire Klem yelled "Safe!" in a loud ringing voice, and the Cubs had the first and only run of the day.

The Cubs only managed two more safeties in the game. The Phillies came to bat in the last frame with the score still 1-0. Fred Osborn pinch-hit for pitcher Sparks. The former Cub had delivered a key pinch hit for the Phillies two days earlier. This time he popped out. Lundgren outpitched Sparks, giving up only three hits and no runs while backed up by the Cubs errorless defense. As the fans streamed out of National League Park and the Cubs walked off the field, Kid Durbin thought back to the lone tally, squeezed home in the top of the first. *That was the break. We just didn't know it then.*

From the Journal of Kid Durbin

We took a sleeper train from Philly to Boston last night. The train left around six o'clock and pulled into the Boston depot at eight this morning. I played poker for three hours before I turned in. At the college boys table—that's what Brakeman called it. Big Ed Reulbach, Carl Lundgren, and Jeff Overall—all college grads. I call it the twirler's table. The stakes were low—twenty-five cents the maximum bet—and the discussion was lively. All of us had a few beers in us except Big Ed, who never drank. Ed's dark eyes shined brightly through his spectacles when he spoke about what he liked most about being a pitcher.

"The feel of the baseball as it flies out of my grip at the point of release—it's pure pleasure. I lay my fingers across the ridge of the ball, where the stitched seams give me gripping power and traction. As the ball leaves my hand, my fingers drag across that ridge and there's a sound, a kind of a 'whiff.' The pitch is like a child going out into the world—you can guide that child, but in the end it has a life of its own."

Carl Lundgren, a Midwest man like me, referred to the cat-and-mouse game between pitcher and hatter, and declared it important for righty pitchers to work off the first base side of the rubber when facing right-handed hitters and the third-base side for lefties. "That slab is twelve inches long," he said, holding his hands a foot apart. "You should use those twelve inches to your advantage." These guys devote a good deal of thought to the fine points of the game.

We grabbed hacks to the Copley Square Hotel, a massive, seven-storied stone building on Huntington Avenue. As we registered at the ornate front desk this morning, we couldn't help but notice some of the two hundred fifty black-suited Massachusetts undertakers who were attending their annual state convention. You would think these fellows would wear somber expressions and speak in low, even monotones, but that is not what we observed. These men were cutting loose, playing pranks on each other, and having a jolly good time. I guess it's a chance for them to get away from their serious routines, which do not permit these sort of high jinks. I mean, if the Cubs have a string of victories, we celebrate. If an undertaker gets six new corpses, he doesn't want to be seen dancing up and down for joy.

Today's game against the Doves marked Chance's return to the helm. He, as much as anyone, earned us a victory by recognizing that Jack Pfiester had withered by the eighth inning and bringing in Miner Brown to save the day. Pfiester sailed along with a 4–1 cushion in the eighth when the Doves manager, Fred Tenney, came to the plate with a man on and nobody out. Tenney is old school. He has this grim face, a thick black mustache, and he has been around a long time. In fact Johnny Evers told me in the locker room afterwards that Tenney is the guy who invented the 3-6-3 double play, ten years ago.

I made the mistake of razzing him about his age. I yelled, "That's Father Time catching up to you, Fred!" He dumped the next pitch into the right field bleachers in this sardine can of a ballpark for a two-run homer. While the blast couldn't have traveled more than 260 feet, it sailed far enough to bring the Doves to within one run of us.

Husk then brought in a new pitcher, the man Charlie Dryden likes to call "our fingerless phenom." Miner Brown pitched like he had twenty fingers! He struck out his first Dove and then retired five more to sew up the victory.

Those undertakers were whooping it up in a frolic by the time we made it back to the hotel. They invited us to share Parlor A with them and the kegs of beer flowed all night. A friendly mortician from Chelsea offered Jack Taylor a job in the off-months driving a hearse. Jack may take him up on this, although Jimmy Slagle told Jack if he did we'd have to call him "Gravedigger" instead of "Brakeman."

I had a few too many—free beer will do that to me—when I found myself talking to an undertaker from Salem, Massachusetts, a man by the name of Oscar Repogle. For some reason I let Oscar know about my recent experience at Connie's funeral. Oscar did not seem surprised to hear about the turn of events I described. He even told me of a similar incident in Salem some five years ago. A "dead" eleven-year-old boy, *in the presence of ninety people, jumped out of his open coffin during his wake. The boy ran to his mother, who fainted. He then collapsed at her feet, dead again. This time they didn't close the boy's coffin for a week. I asked Mr. Repogle if he blamed bad doctoring for these occurrences. His reply surprised me. "No, son. This isn't the work of men but rather the fickle hand of God."*

July 19, 1907 **New York City, New York**

The Cubs strutted into the Polo Grounds with confidence in-
stilled by an eleven-game lead over the second-place Giants. McGraw
started steaming again when he learned that Chance had saved Mordecai
Brown to open the series. Again Frank Chance sensed that Miner would
bolster his cadre and unnerve the opposition. He figured right.

Iron Man McGinnity toed the rubber for the Giants. The Cubs'
half of the first inning provided a not-so-subtle indication of how the
game would unfold. Slagle led off with a ringing triple, sliding into third
at the urging of Jack Taylor in the coacher's box. Sheckard walked on four
pitches, bringing hot-hitting Frank Schulte to the plate. The Cubs right
fielder slammed a double to right, scoring Slagle. Husk then lofted a fly
ball to center, deep enough to send Sheckard scuttling home from third.
Steinfeldt approached the plate, still hurting from the news from home
that somebody had poisoned his favorite fox terrier, Steiney. Harry socked
a single in memory of the pooch, scoring Schulte for the third tally of the
inning.

Brown did not overpower the Giants this day, but pitched well
enough to snatch another victory. The Cubs launched a terrible assault on
the Giants pitcher, punching out sixteen hits, culminating in a seven-run
ninth inning featuring Miner Brown's three-run homer into the right-field
bleachers. Every Cub collected at least one hit, while Schulte knocked out
three doubles and Steinfeldt managed three singles. A disgusted McGraw
sat silent on the bench, arms folded over his paunch, as the Cubs paraded
around the bases in the last frame. Muggsy refused to put McGinnity out
of his misery. While the Iron Man had won twenty-seven games last year,
McGraw now recognized that the thirty-six-year-old hurler would never
pitch like that again. *You cannot defeat Father Time*, thought McGraw.
Although he would never acknowledge it, deep in his gut something
screamed out that the Cubs of 1907 could not be stopped either.

※　　　　　　　　　　※　　　　　　　　　　※

Still recuperating in the hospital, Percy was no longer confined to
his bed. With the help of a wheelchair he could travel up and down the
second floor wards, and using the elevator, he managed to go wherever
he wanted in the hospital. Not that there were many destinations that he
cared to visit.

McGill frequently wheeled himself to the first-floor hospital pharmacy, where he cultivated a mutually beneficial relationship with assistant pharmacist Jimmy Corcoran. Corcoran had no compunction regarding the sale of laudanum to McGill for an appropriate gratuity. McGill's pain had subsided but by now he suffered a strong addiction to the narcotic. McGill preferred Sydenham's laudanum, a reddish-brown tincture, 12 percent alcohol, sold as *Tinctura Opii Crocata*. The taste, to Percy, resembled a delicious wine with a glorious saffron texture. But the flavor, in the end, did not matter. What mattered was the electricity that surged through McGill's veins and tingled in the base of his skull when he sipped the liquid. To augment the stingy doses granted him by his doctors, he purchased his own supply from Corcoran. The Italians provided the money to fund the habit.

Percy began with a small nightly dose to allow him to sleep. The dreams, spectacles in which he frequently starred, came as pure bonus. Later the laudanum brought peace and tranquility in the hot afternoons or even in the hectic mornings, when nurses and doctors scurried about. And there were times he used the tincture simply to make the dull day turn quickly into night.

One of the patients in McGill's ward, a small homely man known as Tannen, sat up in his bed reading the newspaper. He growled in Percy's direction.

"The fuckin' Cubs is in town. You wanted to know."

Percy peered out from the fuzzy confines of a pleasant daydream. "Ah, the Cubs have arrived. I thank you for the notice."

"You ain't no Cubs rooter, is you?" Tannen asked.

"No sir. You needn't worry about that. I have no fond feelings for that team. I hate the assholes, in fact."

"Good!" said Tannen. "Dem Cubs is stealin' da pennant from da Giants."

Percy's focus shifted to the Cubs and the red-haired pitcher named Durbin. The young punk got in the way, complicating things greatly. *I could wheel myself over to the Polo Grounds and shoot the fucker.* But in the next second Percy realized he had no powerful animosity toward the Cubs pitcher. *Just a stupid kid in the wrong place at the wrong time!* As he slipped back into the laudanum haze, he resolved not to kill Durbin unless he got in the way again.

Brakeman and the woman he had met the night before headed down to New York Harbor. Their destination: the Statue of Liberty. A warm breeze gently blew over them from the Atlantic, and the couple strolled along the beach, killing time before boarding the ferry. A rough sea had churned up a bounty of dead fish, driftwood, and seashells. Brakeman, as always the great admirer of the animal kingdom, came across a dead octopus, the first he'd ever seen. The lifeless sea creature lay sprawled on the sand, extending about eighteen inches.

Jack pointed to the dead sea creature on the beach and said, "Lookie here, Elaine, an octopus. These fellers got eight testicles!"

Elaine wisely chose not to challenge this observation.

July 25, 1907 Chicago, Illinois

The Doves of Boston, languishing in sixth place, occupied the visitors' dressing room at the West Side Grounds. The Cubs maintained an eleven-game lead over the Giants and the press anointed them National League champions although two months of the season remained to be played. During batting practice, after noticing that manager Chance was still in the clubhouse with a headache, Durbin sought out former teammates Newt Randall and Billy Sweeney. Durbin felt envious that these men now started for the Doves. They shook hands and wished each other well.

The Cubs exploded in the third inning. Evers tapped a single to center and stole second and third while Cubs pitcher Overall coaxed a walk out of Doves hurler Irving Young. Slagle also extracted a base on balls to load the bases for Sheckard, who rammed a base hit to right, scoring Johnny Evers. Frank Schulte then hit a low liner to center field. It dropped in front of outfielder Ginger Beaumont, and two more runs came in. Frank Chance, next up, swatted a mighty triple to the gap in left-center, and another two Cubs crossed home plate. Harry Steinfeldt added to the onslaught, cracking a base hit to score Chance with the sixth run of the inning. More than enough to ensure victory.

On the mound Jeff Overall scattered eight hits and walked none, pitching a complete game, 8-0 shutout.

After dinner several groups of Cubs headed for the Levee District. One foursome consisted of Slagle, Steinfeldt, Taylor, and Fraser. The boys started out with a few beers in a saloon on Dearborn. When they emerged from the smoky barroom at nine o'clock, Slagle pointed his little hand skyward, toward a full disk moon floating on the eastern horizon.

"We got us a full buck moon tonight, gents."

"And what the fuck is that?" asked Fraser.

"It's your full moon in July. About this time the buck deer have their new antlers poke out of their skulls like new shoots of asparagus. All covered with the velvet fur. It drives the other animals into a frenzy. Not a good night to be trampin' around the forest."

"There ain't never no good night to snoop around a forest," offered Steinfeldt.

"Aw shit," groaned Slagle, as they wandered south past 21st Street. "You gonna need to go out at night if you wanna bag you most any varmint."

Fraser piped up. "Well, Shorty, I'll certainly keep that in mind the next time I have a craving for varmint. By the way, I've always wanted to know. What in the hell is a varmint?"

"Shee-it, Chick. You truly are a city boy! There's a good many different varmints and you can even find 'em in the big city. Your ordinary squirrels and beavers is a varmint as is your rabbit and your possums. Any troublesome little critter is a varmint."

Steinfeldt got a big grin on his face as he turned toward the little outfielder. "Any troublesome little critter, huh? Don't that make you a varmint, Mr. Rabbit Slagle?"

From the Journal of Kid Durbin

We was licked bad today, the Boston Beaneaters beating up on Lundgren and Pfiester and carrying the day by a score of 9-7. I know they are calling themselves the Doves this time around but "Beaneaters" is a whole lot better name for these fellows. Especially for starters Billy Sweeney and Newt Randall.

Sitting in the stands today, in Mr. Murphy's box, was Miss Connie Dandridge. And while she didn't bring any luck to the team, she must have brought me some, because I got to make my first pitching appearance in a ballgame in a long time.

Husk had me warming up in the eighth. We went into the top of the ninth down 9-7 and Chance tells me to get in there and throw strikes. I answered, "I will," and that's what I did. I put everything out of my mind, including Connie, and concentrated on each batter like nothing else existed or mattered. Just me and the catcher. I got relaxed, threw mainly my fastball, and targeted the outside portions of the plate like there was no other place to throw the ball. The result proved a pure success—three up and three down. My father will be happy to hear about this! Chance did not comment about my performance after the game but I knew he appreciated me doing my job.

Connie, on the other hand, gushed about my pitching effort. Mr. Murphy came down into the clubhouse when I had showered and invited Connie and me to dinner with him and Mrs. Murphy. I took a little heat from some of the guys about this as most of them had never dined with the owner. Harry Steinfeldt's crack was typical: "You got real connections, Kid. Put in a good word for ole Harry with the cheapskate bossman. Maybe he'll raise me a hundred bucks next year."

Cap Anson attended today, with dozens of bugs flocking around him before the game. The Grand Old Man came down to the bench to greet the boys and seemed to be engaged in a heated argument with Harry

Steinfeldt and Jimmy Slagle. When things simmered down I mosied over to shake his hand and remind him about the luncheon invitation he extended to me.

When I mentioned that he says to me, "Do you intend to play against those colored boys?"

I said I did and he tells me, "I don't break bread with nigger-lovers."

He turned and walked away from me. Feeling my oats more than I should have, I called out, "We don't have to eat any bread!" Anson kept on walking and did not reply.

July 27, 1907 Zion, Illinois

Healing night in the City of God. A large crowd—more than two thousand souls—waited patiently in the huge Shiloh Tabernacle. Each man in a suit and tie and every woman with a collared dress no shorter than three inches above the ankles. Fitzgerald surveyed the large crowd, noticing about one-fifth to be African-American and a large number of children. A strange assortment of leg braces, eyeglasses, crutches, bandages, and walking sticks hung on the wall behind the podium, in full view, like awards on exhibit. Church members called this collection the "tools of the devil" and boasted how the healed had left these behind as they received their cure from the hands of the overseer and the spirit of the Lord.

"These are our trophies that we have captured from the enemy," a man told Fitzgerald.

The front row had a little paper sign: "For Cripples Only." Men, women, and children in wheelchairs and with crutches, and a blind man with dark glasses and a cane sat in hushed anticipation. Mike Fitzgerald sat in the fourth row alongside his coworkers from the lace factory. Mike hungered to witness the power of a healing hand, although he yearned for the mending of his soul rather than his body.

Overseer Wilbur Glenn Voliva, a portly thirty-seven-year-old sideburned man, entered the hall, wearing a black suit and tie. No clerical gown as his predecessor wore. The assembled grew quiet.

"Peace be to this house!" The greeting rang out loud and crisp.

"Peace to thee," responded the congregants.

"Almighty Lord," Voliva began,"we humbly gather here tonight to receive the blessings of your holy spirit. Your spirit can cure any disease, heal any illness, mend any fracture. Your love can restore sight to the blind and permit the crippled to walk again. There are, in our midst tonight, Lord, worshippers who desperately need your help. We beseech you Lord, this summer night in your city, to touch us with your healing power." Voliva stepped out from behind the podium and reached out his hands in a beckoning motion.

"Mr. Thomas L. Monand! Please advance to the stage."

A ramp had been constructed at the side of the stage. A boy pushed a man in a wheelchair up the ramp and turned him to face the audience. Forty-five years old with a full head of gray hair and silver-rimmed spectacles, the man folded his hands in his lap. Voliva went to his side and grasped his hand.

"Are you ready for a miracle, Mr. Monand?" Voliva shouted to the audience.

The man, dressed in a brown suit and a tan shirt, nodded. Voliva went around in back of Monand's wheelchair and placed his hands on the man's shoulders.

Shouting at the top of his lungs, Voliva asked, "Do you believe in the power of the Lord Jesus Christ?"

"I do," replied Monand in a firm voice.

Voliva placed one hand flat on the top of Monand's head. He swung the other in a great arc until it swooped down forcefully on the back of Monand's neck, with a great smack.

"Then rise and walk!" Voliva moved his hands to the sides of Monand's sweaty face, and violently jerked the man's head right and left.

Voliva yanked Monand up and out of the wheelchair, and the man took a small, shaky step forward toward the audience. And then another. And one more.

"Praise God!" screamed Voliva.

"Praise God!" the crowd replied.

August 1, 1907 **Chicago, Illinois**

The Cubs took three in a row from Brooklyn, and this final game between the two offered the Cubs another opportunity to beat up on a team down on its luck, a team ten games under .500. Evers, always early to the ballpark, arrived outside the park at eleven on a day with large black clouds bumping around the sky. Chomping on a stout cigar, he noticed two black boys, aged twelve and five, hanging around the players' gate with a bat and glove in hand, their small dog scurrying around them. The twelve-year-old recognized Johnny.

"Yer Johnny Evers, right?"

"Yeah. How ya doing?"

"Good. Can you show us how you hold the bat, sir?"

"Sure, let me see that lumber." Evers choked up on the bat, demonstrating his grip and a tight, level swing. "You gonna see the game today, boys?"

The little one answered "No suh. We ain't got no money."

Five minutes later Evers emerged from the park and slipped the moon-eyed grateful kids two tickets.

The menacing clouds finally burst just before game time, delaying the start of things for thirty-five minutes. When the storm passed, the two groundsmen removed the five canvas tarps, each about six-feet square, from the bases and the mound. They also applied liberal doses of sawdust to the basepaths, which were caked in mud. Umpire Klem mistakenly announced the Cubs starting pitcher as Pittsburgh hurler Lefty Leifield instead of Jack Pfiester. Once Klem rectified that, the Cubs rained down their own storm of hits, nailing the Superbas pitcher for three runs in the first and one in the second.

Umpire Klem ran out to first base after the completion of the second inning and removed the base from its anchor to inspect it. As he bent to replace it a bug called out, "Hey Klem, you lookin' for your eyeglasses under that sack?" Klem scowled as some fans within earshot applauded the remark.

While taking the field in the top of the third, Evers looked west, out over first base, and saw the ominous sky and the billowing clouds. His thoughts turned darker than the sky. While men of his age do not often think of death, Evers, a brooding fellow, frequently did just that. *Death is like that approaching storm*, he mused to himself. *You know it's on the way and will surely get here. But when? Will a stroke of lightning leap out of the first black cloud and claim me, or will I make it through this storm?* Emerging from his reverie, he glanced over at Tinker, who had already made two bad throws for errors. *That asshole,* he thought, *if there's a lightning bolt headed this way, I pray the good Lord has sufficient sense to direct it toward the shortstop position.* A boom of thunder cracked out of the west.

In the fourth inning the score stood 4-0, and the Cubs began to worry that another approaching storm would wash away the game before the four and a half innings needed to make it official. To expedite matters, Cubs that made it safely to first or second base attempted leisurely steals of second or third, only to be cut down by strong-armed Brooklyn catcher Bill Bergen. While such suicidal base running did speed the game along, it proved unnecessary as the drizzle subsided and the game went the full nine, the Cubs emerging with a 7-2 win.

August 2, 1907 **Washington, D.C.; The Debut**

The rookie was so green he smelled like grass. One month earlier he signed to play in the big leagues out of Idaho where he averaged more than fifteen strikeouts a game. His contract called for a $100 bonus, $350 a month, and, at his insistence, the promise of a ticket back west if he didn't make it. He had wavy brown hair and his name was Johnson. A prankster joked that the Johnson Hotel was named after him. The young man was startled, believing the assertion and not for a moment considering the possibility that someone would take pleasure in fooling him.

Gripping the ball deep in his palm, the nineteen-year-old righty walked onto a major league pitching mound for the first time in his life. He wore the uniform of the Washington Nationals, his arms hanging long out of the sleeves. His debut took place on a day the Nationals faced the league-leading Detroit Tigers. The young man kicked at the dirt around the hill and rubbed up the baseball like every other pitcher. But this hurler was different. When he cut loose with a sidearm fastball, it was near impossible for the batter to get around on it. He only had one pitch—the fastball—but that's all he needed. Ty Cobb, in his second full season with the Tigers, managed the first hit off the tall, lanky Kansan, a bunt. Cobb razzed the young twirler from first base.

"Hayseed, you're on the way back to the farm." From the bench two Tigers shouted "moooo." The Tiger manager, redheaded Hughie Jennings, kicked at the dirt in the third base coacher's box, screaming his trademark war cry, "Ee-yah!" He claimed it meant "watch out" in Hawaiian. When the young pitcher ignored his shrill shouts, Jennings pulled out a tin whistle and chirped away until the umpire ejected him from the game for this stunt, which earned him a ten-day suspension.

The kid did not falter. He pitched his heart out but lost 3-2. No matter. He developed into one of the finest pitchers in the history of baseball, winning more than four hundred games over the course of the next twenty years. He eventually acquired a curveball and a change-up, but for the most part he simply threw fastballs, one after another. Ring Lardner said, "He's got a gun concealed about his person. They can't tell me he throws them balls with his arm." Soon his teammates gave him the nickname "the Big Train" because his fastball screamed past the batter like a locomotive. Cobb later described his first encounter with the young pitcher: "I watched him take that easy windup and then something went past me that made me flinch. The thing just hissed with danger; every one of us knew we'd met the most powerful arm ever turned loose in a ballpark." Walter Johnson came to play.

August 2-6, 1907 **Chicago, Illinois**

Again the Giants visited the West Side Grounds, hoping to chip away at the twelve-and-a-half game lead that separated them from the

Cubs. McGraw had little hope that the Cubs could be overtaken, but he figured that if his Giants swept the five-game set it could begin to shift the momentum of the season.

During batting practice, the New Yorkers, including manager McGraw, paid their respects to former Giant Mike Donlin and his wife, actress Mabel Hite, who sat up front, next to the Giants' bench. Donlin's departure from the team for the vaudeville stage had clearly hurt the Giants, and McGraw used this chance to importune his return. But Donlin, who had hit .356 for McGraw in 1905, candidly told Muggsy that his current situation could not be better. McGraw let Donlin know that he would be welcomed back should circumstances change and then turned his attention to the game. Another matchup of aces Mathewson and Brown.

The Cubs faced a number of minor injuries and a suspension that weakened their lineup. Manager Chance, owing to a bruised finger, benched himself in favor of Artie Hofman, while Johnny Kling still had a couple days on a suspension for an on-field altercation. And Jimmy Slagle could not start due to a foot injury. Nevertheless, with Miner Brown on the mound the Cubs beamed with confidence.

Mathewson opened the game with a high inside fastball at lead-off hitter Hofman. Artie backed away, then dug in at the plate, ripping a clean single to left to start things off. The second batter, Jimmy Sheckard, sacrificed Circus Solly to second. Schulte fouled out to catcher Bresnahan, and when Del Howard bounced a routine ground ball to rookie second baseman Larry Doyle, things did not look promising. But Doyle, a gangly twenty-one-year-old whom the Giants had recently purchased from the Springfield, Illinois club for the then record sum of $4,500, fumbled the ball, and Sheckard came all the way around from second to score the first Cubs run. Newspapers around the country headlined the Cubs-Giants game the next day with variations on "Costly Rookie Makes Costly Error."

In the bottom of the third the score remained 1-0. Three Finger Brown took his cuts at the plate and fouled one straight back into the overflow crowd that sat on wooden planks twenty feet behind home plate. The ball shot like a rocket into a young man's face, knocking him out. Brown waited to resume his turn at bat until the bleeding man had been revived, and then struck out on the next Mathewson fastball, unnerved more by the fan's plight than the pitch.

By the bottom of the sixth the score remained the same. But Mathewson slipped up badly in this inning, allowing another hit to Hofman, and following it up with a free pass to Sheckard. Frank Schulte slammed a triple to the bleacher fence, and Del Howard knocked in Schulte with a base hit. When the Giants recorded the third out, four runs had crossed the plate and the score stood at 5-0.

Brown could not be touched. He coasted the rest of the way, another shutout victory over the Giants on a four-hitter. A bitter Mathewson walked off the field in a dejected silence as the Cubs fans hooted and sang.

The second game of the series, on a glorious Saturday afternoon, matched Orvie Overall against Hooks Wiltse. Frank Chance, the sore finger still ailing, put Del Howard at first, and the newest Cub responded with three hits. The Giants defense wobbled, with newcomer Larry Doyle making three more errors and shortstop Dahlen committing two. In the bottom of the ninth the game stood tied 2-2, with one out and the bases filled with Cubs. But Sheckard was due up, and Wiltse had easily retired the Cubs outfielder three times in a row. *Jimmy couldn't hit Wiltse with a handful of sand today*, Chance mused. The Cubs manager looked up and down his bench for a pinch hitter and realized he himself was the best man for the job. He removed his jacket and grabbed a bat, signaling Sheckard that his day was over. As he walked toward home plate the crowd recognized the Peerless Leader and let out a lusty cheer, while on the Giants bench McGraw shook his head and muttered a profanity.

Wiltse peered in and got the sign from Bresnahan. The brawny Giants catcher did not want anything inside because he knew Chance would not budge off the plate and a hit batsman now meant a Cubs run and the game. So he called for a fastball off the plate. Chance swung hard, nicking the bottom of the ball and sending it spinning back toward the upper deck for strike one. Wiltse's next delivery, an outside curve, hung over the plate, fat and hittable. Chance connected solidly and sent a line drive up the middle, maybe ten feet off the infield surface. Shortstop Bill Dahlen, thirty-seven years old and 5'9" tall, leaped for the ball but could not snag it, and the game was over. A younger man or a taller shortstop might have made the play. McGraw thought Dahlen should have caught the Chance liner, needling the infielder on the way to the dressing room. "Nice jump, Bad Bill! I couldn't have slud a dime between your spikes and the ground!"

The Sunday game took the same course and ended similarly, with

Big Ed Reulbach and Joe McGinnity toiling away in a 1-1 duel through twelve innings. This time number two catcher Pat Moran grabbed the hero honors for the Cubs. With one out and the bases empty, Moran jumped on a 1-2 pitch, sending a whistling liner toward center fielder Sammy Strang. As Strang prepared to field the ball on a hop, it jumped crazily over his head, bouncing all the way to the bleacher fence. Moran tore around first and second, but as he approached third base the aging Cub lost steam as the whole world seemed to slow down. But Jack Taylor, in the coacher's box, urged him to keep going as the ball winged its way to the cutoff man, Bill Dahlen. Moran rounded third as Dahlen waited for the relay. Dahlen's throw sailed toward home, but Moran crossed the plate two steps in front. The home run gave the Cubs their third win in a row over the reeling Giants.

In the fourth game of the series the Giants exploded in the first inning. Not against the Cubs, but against umpire Bill Klem. When the Cubs loaded the bases, Del Howard lashed a grounder to the shortstop, who threw home, forcing Slagle at the plate. But Klem called the Cubs runner safe. Every Giants infielder surrounded the man in blue, shouting their protests vehemently. McGraw then butted in, screaming at the top of his lungs.

"You lousy sonofabitch busher. How much did they pay you to do that? A quarter? You're either crooked or blind. Which is it?"

Klem threw Muggsy out of the game but the Giants manager would not depart. "You goddam cocksucking cur. You're a disgrace to this game."

"Mr. Manager, if you do not exit this ballpark now I will declare the game forfeited to the Chicago ballclub."

McGraw walked slowly toward the center field gate to the visitors' dressing room, but forty feet from the bleacher wall he laid down on the grass. At this point, Mathewson and reserve Danny Shay got on the ump, and after a heated exchange Klem ejected them from the game too. They took the same leisurely stroll out to where McGraw still sat. Knowing these antics greatly irritated the man in blue, the three Giants relaxed on the grass, their backs to the infield, ignoring the commands to leave the field. Finally, when Klem shouted for them to get up off their asses and leave or suffer a forfeit, the trio departed.

There was a method to McGraw's madness. His calculated mistreatment of umpires mirrored that of other managers, and originated a quarter-century earlier with Charles Comiskey in the American Association. "Commie" believed that the strategic use of "kicking," the art of vigorously disputing an umpire's decision, greatly enhanced the chances of gaining the *next* close call from the umpire. McGraw stated that a vigorous protest would "impress upon the umpire that the players are not going to let anything slip by them." He believed he could earn his team fifty runs a year by such bullying tactics. But not this day.

The game, once resumed, pitted Jack Taylor versus Red Ames, a curveball artist who had trouble controlling the pitch, leading to a lot of walks, wild pitches, and hit batsmen. Ames pitched in typical fashion this day, walking two, hitting one (Schulte in the back), and uncorking a wild pitch. Taylor, on the other hand, walked four and gave up eleven safeties, a subpar performance. The Cubs lost it in the ninth on a Bresnahan triple that drove in the Giants' fifth run. With the final out the Cubs found themselves on the short end of a 5-4 score. Chance's only comment after the game: "The Giants do considerably better when the maniac McGraw is not at the helm."

The final game of the five-game set, on Tuesday the sixth, found dark clouds still scudding across the sky. Joe Tinker located Husk on the field before the game, stretching and sprinting alone. Sweat rolled down Chance's brow. Tinker inspected the infield, still soggy from rains the previous night. The groundskeepers started to remove the canvas that covered the bases, the pitcher's mound, and home plate. Tinker complained to the Cubs manager of the difficulty in throwing to first from deep short off a wet infield surface.

Wiping his brow, Chance spoke. "I noticed that the other day, Joe. It got me to thinking. Next time you go deep to retrieve a ball on a slick infield, why not, when you peg it over to me, bounce the ball to me? One bounce, if it's not too close to me, would be simple for me to corral. And it should be a helluva lot easier on your arm."

Tinker thought about it for a second and replied, "Okay. I'll whip my throw low, about ten or twenty feet in front of first base and you can take it on the hop." Five minutes later they tried it out, nailing it after a few attempts.

The occasion did not arise that day to try out the new play, but Tinker and Chance later used this stratagem successfully dozens of times. Tinker sometimes used the play on sunny days, with dry field conditions, when the throw was long or difficult. Other infielders soon copied the maneuver.

Mordecai Brown threw for the Cubs and pitched a gem. Another shutout for the Cubs ace, this one a three-hitter. The Giants hurler, Dummy Taylor, pitched brilliantly, his "drop ball" fooling the Cubs all day. Taylor allowed only four hits, but his own wild throw to third base allowed two Cubs runs to cross the plate. Final score: Cubs 2, Giants 0.

"Four out of five ain't bad," Evers said to Chance. "The Giants slipped to third place. Life is good!"

Chance smiled, sitting on a bench by his locker. "Yeah. But just think if we'd taken all five."

August 8, 1907 New York City, New York

With the aid of the laudanum, McGill finally achieved a semblance of stability, a routine that allowed him to endure the hospital stay. He spent much of his waking time reviewing the strange series of events that led to his current situation. A chain of misfortunes, all starting with a woman named Connie Dandridge. He played back every detail that he had stored away regarding this woman. Nothing about her stood out. *Not a great beauty, not particularly intelligent, nor rich. An ordinary person—save for her extraordinary stubbornness. How had this average being managed to cause my fall? Since I ran across this bitch in Iowa, there's been nothing but trouble. I should have stuck her with the needle. Should have shot so much dope into her veins that she couldn't have moved. And then she would've begged to stay, for the dope. It's worked before.* The turn of events amused Percy. *The world turned topsy-turvy!* he thought. For evidently this woman now pursued a normal life while Percy danced to the tune of an opiate drug. *But what a melodious tune!*

The doctors removed the cast on Percy's leg to inspect the progress, but when they uncovered the final gauze coverings they discovered a serious infection on the lower shin. The unpleasant smell of the leg wafted into Percy's nostrils.

"Damn, that stinks," he said.

Doctor Landingham turned to Nurse Donis.

"Hasn't this patient complained of pain?"

"No, doctor. Not after we started the laudanum."

"Well, I want you to apply an antiseptic immediately. Make it carbolic spray and apply every three hours. And orally administer sodium of sulphite solution, two ounces every six hours."

"What's the problem, Doctor?" Percy asked.

"Your leg is infected. Septicemia. We need to treat the infection, both internally and with external applications."

Percy exhibited a twisted smile inappropriate for the moment. "Be my guest," he stated.

August 11, 1907 **Chicago, Illinois**

The hot, muggy weather contributed to the low scores in the Cubs-Phillies doubleheader. The ninety-three degree heat took such a toll on the players that after the first game both teams agreed to shorten the second contest to seven innings, and not a single bug squawked at that announcement. Cubs fans had good reason to cheer all day as their club took both ends of the twin-bill by the same score of 1-0.

The first game saw Jeff Overall throw a masterpiece for eight innings and then wilt in the ninth. Del Howard, the Cubs first baseman this day, produced the only run in the first game by driving home Frank Schulte with a long triple in the fourth inning. The Phillies managed only two hits in the first eight frames, but the overbearing heat got to Overall as he gave up three hits, loading the bases in the last frame. With the scoreboard showing two outs, Chance brought in his secret weapon, Mordecai Brown, to face left-handed hitter Ernie Courtney. Brown dispatched Courtney with ease, getting him to send a pop-up to Tinker, sewing up the victory.

The second game featured the cleverness of Johnny Evers and the fine pitching of Jack Pfiester. Early in the second contest Evers pulled off a decoy play—a play he claimed to have invented. Sherry Magee, the fine-hitting Phillies outfielder, led off the second inning with a base hit. The Phillies manager signaled for a hit and run. The batter, third baseman Courtney, slapped a fly ball out to Jimmy Slagle in center. On contact, base runner Magee had put his head down and started to sprint to second, not realizing the ball traveled in the air to center. To trap Magee, Evers pretended to be chasing after a groundball near second base. He bent down, scooped up some dirt, and shovelled it over to Tinker at the base. Fooled by this decoy, Magee kept running toward second base to try to break up the double play. The excited shouts of his Phillies teammates came too late, as Slagle pegged the ball over to Howard at first base for a double play.

Pfiester went the distance—seven innings—giving up only four singles. His teammates congratulated him in the clubhouse. The Cubs stood atop the National League with a record of 75-28.

From the Journal of Kid Durbin

We hopped on a sleeper to Philly after the doubleheader. We had sleeping cars nos. 3 and 4 reserved for us while the Phillies are up front. We've got four more games against them. Ed Reulbach, who I now consider a friend, did not travel with us, because his wife is seriously ill. We are all praying for her.

The praying did not prevent most of the boys from getting drunk as we sped across the country. My teammates are drinking hard because tomorrow is only an exhibition game against the Altoona, Pennsylvania, ballclub. Chance is playing poker with Fraser, Steinfeldt, Tinker, and the Tribune writer, Cy Sanborn. College boys Lundgren and Overall are writing letters all night—they tend to be wordy—while a few guys like Rabbit Slagle and Jack Taylor are making life miserable for everyone else with their pranks. Taylor keeps egging on some of the Phillies and I wouldn't be surprised if one of these guys pops him one. Taylor saw Freddy Osborn emerge from the john and started yelling "George Washington" at the top of his lungs. Very strange—even for Taylor. Osborn keeled over and started vomiting and had to be carried off to his berth. He must have had one too many.

I too drank a couple of beers, wrote in this journal, and re-read one of my favorite books, "Huckleberry Finn." When I took a break from reading I overheard Cy Sanborn give what he called a "history lesson" to the guys at his poker table. Cy explained how the Sun King, Louis XIV of France, married Maria Theresa, the daughter of the King of Spain, making Marie Theresa the Queen of France. Happened around 250 years ago. Later, a prince from Africa visited Louis and Marie Theresa and gave the Queen a gift, a Negro dwarf no bigger than the mascots on some baseball clubs now. The dwarf became her servant. About a year after she received the dwarf, Marie gave birth to a baby girl, black from head to toe. But the Queen had an explanation for the baby's color. She said it

THE BEST TEAM EVER

was caused by the dwarf scaring her during her pregnancy. All the boys laughed when they heard this except Steinfeldt.

"What's so funny about that?" Steiny asked. "I once knew a gal who gave birth to a dead baby 'cause she got hexed by a black cat! Them sort of things happen."

President Murphy announced some roster moves a few days ago. We released Mike Kahoe. The old warrior smelled it coming so he took it okay. He told me he was a cat with nine lives and still had one or two left. And he was right, as we learned today that Mike has already signed on with the Washington ballclub. Mike's a tough-skinned veteran and gives a team a solid backstop. We picked up a replacement catcher, Frank Olis, a babe in the woods from a semipro team called the Oak Leas in Chicago. Anyhow, the upshot of all this is that I am no longer the only yannigan on the squad! Compared to Olis, I am a veteran!

August 11, 1907 **Chicago, Illinois**

Mike Fitzgerald sported a new three-piece seventeen-dollar suit that he had purchased in Waukegan, the first new set of clothes he had bought in a decade or more. New shoes too, still needing more breaking in, chafed his inside arches. They made little squirting, fart-like sounds as he walked. But nothing could disturb the tranquility of this day for Michael Fitzgerald. He toiled six days a week in the laceworks, but Sundays could be spent in any manner he chose after the obligatory morning services. This Sunday he chose to travel back to the scene of his descent, the city of the devil, rough and tumble Chicago. To revisit the same streets on which he lived for all those years. The round-trip ticket cost fifty-five cents, and he soon found himself walking east in the Loop under darkened skies, on the same streets where he wasted the last twenty years of his life.

Numerous figures haunted these gloomy streets, reminding Fitzgerald of an ugly chapter in his life. Tramps and drunks sprawled on the sidewalk and retched on the curbs. One of these men approached him and asked for a nickel. Mike scanned the man's face carefully, but the dirty, unshaven man sparked no memory. When he deposited a shiny nickel in the man's scabbed palm, the pitiful creature scrambled off to his next drink, without even a token nod of thanks to his benefactor. Just then the sun broke through a gray cloudbank, and broad shafts of sunlight lit Jackson Boulevard. Mike felt the sun's heat as it soaked into the dark gray fabric of his clothing. Like the warmth he felt that morning, basking in the Light of the Lord.

The Workingman Exchange was the same as the last time he had seen it, a dingy, stinking dive. Fitzgerald entered the saloon and strode to his usual place at the bar. A bartender he had never seen asked him what he wanted.

"Coca-Cola," said Mike, as he slapped a nickel down on the moist bar.

Mike sipped the Coke slowly, enjoying the little dramas that played out before him like never before. The bartender equally cursed his help and the drunks that pushed him to pour. Two angry patrons gearing up for a fight. The reeking stink of the place, the smoke, the sawdust, the spitting, the din. *This is a hellish dive!* he thought, and calculated he must have wasted several thousand hours of his life in these very quarters.

A clamor arose outside the bar. The beating of a drum. And someone—a man— screaming at the top of his lungs. Five or six men moved to the door and the windows to observe the source of the racket.

"It's that Sunday bastard," someone shouted.

Rev. Billy Sunday, the street-preaching former ballplayer, stood outside the Workingman Exchange, accompanied only by a husky bass drummer and a young man in a black suit. Sunday himself wore black, but he sported a bright green tie and a mottled cardboard megaphone.

"Come out and renounce the devil!" he yelled. "Your lives are at stake, sinners. John Barleycorn will rob you of all you have. Come out here and shake my hand, boys. A few steps can take you down the right path. The choice is yours. Come out here and find Jesus Christ. Live your life for him."

The door swung open and a tall man emerged, wrinkling up his eyes as the sunlight momentarily blinded him. The man walked right up to Rev. Sunday.

"My name is Michael Fitzgerald, sir. I have heard about you. I would appreciate your help."

Sunday, lean and athletic, shot his arm out toward Fitzgerald to shake his hand and smiled and embraced him while saying, "God bless you!" And then the Rev. Sunday told Mike Fitzgerald something he would never forget, something he thought about years later, as he lay on his deathbed.

Sunday told him, "Michael, each and every breath of air you take in this world should be a prayer to God."

August 16, 1907 New York City. New York

Shortly after Percy started taking the sulphite medication, his hair began to fall out in large clumps. Nurse Donis reported this to Dr. Landingham, but he made no changes.

Percy was not alarmed. "It's just hair. It will grow back." After a week all the hair on his head was gone. "My mustache is still hale and hearty," he commented to the nurse. Percy did not care about his hair loss. The brown bottle with its precious liquid erased all concerns. Again confined to his bed, Percy increased his dosage of Sydenham's to the point where Nurse Donis became concerned. But Dr. Landingham ignored her comments because the patient responded in a reasonably coherent manner to the doctor's inquiries.

The doctor focused on the infection. Gangrene could set in.

He had an idea. Pulling up a chair next to Percy's bed, he said, "I want to propose an unorthodox treatment."

"Propose away," Percy replied. "I don't have to accept, right?"

"Correct, Mr. Crandall. The treatment is unusual because it involves using maggots. You know what maggots are?"

"Sure. Baby flies."

"Yes, the larval stage of houseflies. Well, during the Civil War army surgeons often found men with serious wounds. These men had lain unattended on battlefields, sometimes for three or four days. When the men arrived at the field hospitals, doctors found some of the wounds covered with maggots."

"Flies laid their eggs in these men's wounds?" asked Percy.

"Yes, and when the maggots and all other detritus were removed it was discovered, in every case, that these untreated wounds were clean and fresh, with no sign of infection or putrefaction. The literature I have read states that the maggots had accomplished this by devouring the diseased flesh while avoiding the healthy flesh."

"Very agreeable of them."

"That is correct. So my plan is—with your permission of course—to apply the maggots to your wound, which is not healing of its own, and let these unpleasant little creatures work their magic on you. I can write this up for the medical journals and make you famous. What say you to this plan, sir?"

Percy shifted uncomfortably in his bed. "Doctor, in one word I say no. I also say that you're the only maggot around here, you fucking quack. You and I are through. Get out and fetch me another doctor."

Dr. Landingham withdrew in a huff.

From the Journal of Kid Durbin

August 18, 1907

Eleven players, Secretary Williams, and Trainer Jack left New York City and traveled to Bridgeport, Connecticut, today for an off-day exhibition game against the local nine, at a little resort community called Steeple Chase Island. This place is like Bridgeport's Coney Island. I'm not sure it actually is an island, but we did have to take a short ferry ride to get there. Our squad consisted of four pitchers (Fraser, Lundgren, Overall, and me), Artie Hofman, Del Howard, Sheckard, Schulte, Steiny, Pat Moran, and the new guy, Frank Olis. We only got twenty dollars each for this game so most of the guys found excuses not to travel. Moran skippered the unit while I was slated to play center field. The game was being held in an old bicycle racing park, with a huge grandstand and bleachers area. The place filled up with about three thousand folks, most of them vacationers. It was as hot as a Texas cattle call in July but we prepared for the game as always. I shagged some fly balls in the outfield and took a few swings off Carl Lundgren in the batting practice. Every time I connected, Carl hollered, "I thought you were a pitcher!"

But fifteen minutes before the start of the game a great plume of smoke erupted from underneath the bleachers, quickly followed by screams and a sheet of flames. Chick Fraser, Steiny, and I raised a yell to the bugs up there, and soon a bunch of people came tearing down toward the field at full chisel. Now the wind started to blow the flames toward the rest of the structure, including the grandstand, and in a minute hundreds of people rushed down toward us.

A wire screen and a low railinged fence blocked their way to safety. So all the ballplayers—both teams—along with Charlie Williams, Trainer Jack, and a few writers began to tear that screen and fence apart. We ripped these down in about two minutes and this quick work enabled all the fans to escape the bleachers and the grandstand for the safety of the field. As far as I know, no one was hurt. It could have been a great disaster if we hadn't done what we did.

There was no stopping the flames, however. The whole place was consumed, as well as a small building next door. The bleachers and grandstands just crumbled down into an unrecognizable heap of burning rubble.

Believe it or not, the players, with the urging of the fans, decided to go ahead with an abbreviated five-inning contest. The fire still burned but we didn't let that stop us. The cranks just formed a huge ring, maybe six or seven deep, around the diamond and the outfield and we played the game. In centerfield the crowd hovered just in back of me—it's a good thing I didn't have to run deep to gather one in. So as the timbers of the bleachers and grandstand continued to burn, we played baseball fifty feet away. We lost three foul balls that burned to a crisp. I made a hit and three putouts. Chick Fraser threw well, allowing us to win the "hotly" fought contest 3–1. The grandstand still smoked and crackled as we left.

On our trip back to New York City there were lots of fire jokes. Several guys said that Chick really threw heat today, burning them in to the catcher, while Steiny said the hot corner seemed even hotter today. Then the boys broke into a spirited rendition of "It's a Hot Time in the Old Town Tonight," but I mainly dozed in my seat, dreaming of Connie.

Nurse Donis unwrapped Percy's bandage and had to stifle a gasp. The wound looked much worse than the last time, and an acrid smell cut through the air. She immediately summoned Percy's replacement doctor.

Dr. Landon measured the patient's blood pressure level and heart rate. He then examined the wound carefully, using a magnifying glass.

"It is what we feared, Mr. Crandall. It is gangrene. You understand what this means?"

"You want to cut my leg off?"

"It will save your life. If we do nothing you will die."

"What about Landingham's idea about maggots? Could that work?"

"That treatment will not help you now that gangrene has set in. I am sorry. We will be able to save your knee if we act promptly."

Percy slumped down on his bed, stupefied by the news and sweating profusely. "Do what you have to do," he said resignedly, with a bitter edge to his words. When the doctor and the nurse left he reached for the brown bottle of Sydenham's. Just holding the bottle in his hands, cupped against his chest, gave him a sense of well-being.

The Cubs prepared for a Wednesday afternoon contest at the Polo Grounds, the final joust of a four-game series. The Saturday opener had featured yet another Mathewson-Brown match-up, pumping up the crowd numbers, with more than twenty thousand fans stuffed into the stadium. After the umpire yelled "Play!" Matty pitched the first eight innings like the legend he was, the Cubs mustering only a bunt single against the Giants ace. Chance winced as the Giants hurler exhibited his legendary prowess. The Cubs manager knew Mathewson possessed everything a pitcher needed: velocity, movement, control, and confidence. He also knew that even the best pitcher makes mistakes. In this contest Big Six made the mistake of not yielding when he tired in the ninth. The Cubs pounced on him for two runs, enough to tie it up and send it to extra innings. Meanwhile, Jack Pfiester relieved Miner Brown. As Jack took the mound, McGraw directed his players not to attempt to swipe a base off of southpaw Pfiester.

"He'll hold you close to the bag and then Kling will nail you at second."

Jack the Giant Killer pitched flawlessly. In the top of the twelfth, Johnny Kling got around on a Mathewson fastball and slugged it over three hundred feet into a crowd of white-sleeved bleacher fans, putting the Cubs ahead to stay, 3-2. As the Cubs walked to the clubhouse, Chance commented, "Talk about driving the last nail into the coffin."

The New Yorkers came back to win the Monday match on the pitching of Dummy Taylor, while the Cubs secured a victory Tuesday with Jack "The Giant Killer" Pfiester again on the mound. Late in Tuesday's game the resourceful Evers figured out that McGraw was signaling for the steal by blowing his nose, but before he could take advantage of it the game concluded. The Crab alerted his teammates to look for it next time.

Frank Chance departed New York City a few hours prior to Wednesday's finale, taking Kid Durbin and new Cubs catcher Frank Olis with him. The three taxied to Penn Station to hop on the Twentieth Century Limited for an express ride to Chicago. Chance had been suffering from "the grippe"—a bad cold—for a week and could not shake it, while also complaining about "neuralgic teeth." A great believer in the healing powers of mineral baths, the Cubs manager intended to take to the waters in Mt. Clemens, Michigan, while scouting young prospects for the Cubs in the surrounding venues. Durbin and Olis would not be needed on the rest of the Cubs' eastern road trip.

Jimmy Sheckard was named to pilot the Cubs in the absence of the Peerless Leader. Jack Taylor pitched the fourth Cubs-Giants game and was awful. In the first inning alone, the Brakeman allowed seven hits and seven runs, including two homers and a double. On the day, he gave up sixteen hits and twelve runs. Frank Schulte popped five hits, including a four-bagger and a double, but the Giants easily won this contest 12-4. Taylor, stomping around the dressing room and beginning to fear for his job, imagined Chance reading the box score the next day and shaking his head. *Shit*, thought the Brakeman, *I wasn't that bad!*

August 22, 1907 New York City, New York

Four young orderlies in street clothes came for McGill at six o'clock in the morning. Still groggy from sleep and laudanum, McGill did not have a great deal of time to get nervous. But the lack of laudanum and the prospect of losing his leg soured his attitude. Placed on a cot for transportation, he was carried into the operating room and gingerly transferred to the metal operating table. Percy noticed the table slanted down into a small conduit at the bottom left and realized this was to allow the blood to drain off. He wondered if the hospital sold the blood like the packinghouses did. One of the orderlies, a scruffy-haired twenty-year-old, then washed down the leg, first with soap and then with carbolic acid. When the acid coursed into his wound Percy screamed out in an unexpected pain.

Three doctors and a nurse entered the room just as Percy screamed.

"Any problem here?" asked Dr. Landon.

"Just this asshole trying to kill me," responded Percy.

"Well, it was absolutely necessary. Won't hurt long."

"We need three or four people just to lop off a leg?"

"Standard procedure, Mr. Crandall." The doctors prepared their instruments. They wore simple, heavy white cotton gowns over their street clothes, although the men had removed their suit jackets. One of the doctors asked Dr. Landon if he thought it would rain that day and Landon replied, "I heard we're in for a gully-washer."

Percy grew agitated at the chitchat. "Let's get this fucking operation started already, for chrissakes! There will be time later to gossip and chat."

The anesthesia was administered earlier than necessary to quiet the unruly patient. A doctor positioned himself over Percy's head and began to let drops of liquid ether drip directly from a bottle into an Esmarch mask that had been strapped to Percy's face. The strong vapors wafted right into his nostrils and he immediately began to cough. But the coughing quickly subsided. McGill recognized the smell of ether at once, as he had used the substance frequently to subdue recalcitrant women like Connie Dandridge. He thought of her, briefly, until the drug wiped away all thoughts and swept him into a black unconsciousness.

The doctors wore no surgical masks or gloves. One of the doctors, a bearded fellow wearing spectacles, tightened an ancient leather bind around the leg, just above the knee, to restrict the flow of blood below it. Forceps were applied to the major arteries. As an electric saw made the initial deep rotational cuts three inches below the knee, crimson fluid splashed out of the limb. The lead surgeon followed with a curved hand-saw, swiftly cutting through the bone. The amputated portion of the leg and foot fell away, clanging loudly as it struck the polished iron table. The nurse, along with one of the surgeons, removed it, placing it in a wooden disposal barrel. Two doctors applied clamps to major blood vessels, while another doctor cleaned the cut with a different electric saw. Then that doctor smoothed the raw end of the bone with an electric grinding tool.

That completed, Dr. Landon cauterized the stump with an electrocauterizing instrument, the smell of burnt flesh and blood and a hazy smoke filling the operating room. The lead doctor had left several flaps of skin and muscle draped over the cut. They now sutured these to cover the stump. The last black suture thread was cut slightly less than two hours after the procedure began. The nurse sponged away all the blood and applied surgical dressings and bandages as the doctors prepared to depart.

The orderlies carried the patient, still dead to the world, back to his room around eight o'clock.

Percy did not wholly emerge from the anesthesia until ten o'clock. When he opened his eyes the first thing he thought of, even before he looked at his leg, was his bottle of Sydenham's. But as he took stock of his situation he realized that there was no need. An injection of morphine had done its work. Nothing mattered now, not the loss of his leg or his unfortunate predicament. The morphine carried him away to a calm refuge, a place of peace and complete pleasure. *Fuck the leg*, he thought.

From the Journal of Kid Durbin

You have to call this a strange twist of fate. I find myself alone with Frank Chance in Battle Creek, Michigan, while my teammates are battling the Doves in Boston. What happened was that Husk came down with a bad case of the grippe as well as a number of aching teeth on the left side of his jaw—what he called "the beanball side of my head." So Mr. Murphy suggested that the P.L. get himself out to Mt. Clemens, Michigan, where he could seek the water cure at the sulphur baths. Husk brought me and Frank Olis to keep him company and help scout three teams. But today we learned that Pat Moran's mother died, so Olis is on a train to Boston because with Moran gone Kling is the only catcher with the squad.

Husk and I are relaxing in the Hotel Medea in Mt. Clemens (the "Bath City of America") because it houses the Medea Bath House. The setup here is not unlike West Baden, but the water seems darker in color and, although it's hard to imagine, even smellier than the Sprudel Water from Spring No. 7. But Chance is a great believer in the restorative powers of this mineral water. He will soak in the heated porcelain tub for two hours, then get an expert massage and finally fall asleep underneath a large heated towel in the solarium. The price for all this is steep: one dollar for each of us, plus fifty cents for the attendant, and another fifty cents for the massage, for a total of TWO BUCKS! But the Cubs are footing the bills! We had a great dinner over at the Crocker House last night, also on the Cubs. Frank wants to take in a horse race tomorrow too. Being with the skipper has its benefits!

August 31, 1907 Cincinnati, Ohio

This game, a tough pitcher's duel between Jeff Overall and spit-baller Bob Ewing, came down to one play in the fifth inning. With two outs, Johnny Evers danced up and down at third base while Pat Moran clung to second base. Overall took his place in the batter's box. While Jeff had earlier knocked a single off of Ewing, Evers concluded that the odds did not favor Orvie again solving Ewing for a hit. He decided to take matters into his own hands. Or rather, his own feet.

As Ewing rocked back to deliver, the Crab launched himself from third. Ewing caught sight of Evers as he sped toward the plate and hurried a pitch to catcher Larry McLean. The toss went right where Ewing intended, low and on the third base side of the plate, and McLean grabbed it a split-second before Evers arrived. But Johnny would not be denied. He threw his body toward the pitcher's mound while dragging only the toe of his right foot across the corner of the plate as he slid by. The catcher swung around in a big arc to tag him, but missed by a mile, and the umpire, his arms outstretched, hollered "safe!" The deed was so outrageously daring that even the partisan Cincinnati crowd burst into applause. On the Cubs bench, just up from Wilkes-Barre, husky, strong-jawed Heinie Zimmerman pranced up and down singing, "When Johnny comes marching home again hurrah, hurrah!"

Evers' steal of home meant the difference, the Cubs snatching the victory 2-1.

September 9, 1907 Chicago, Illinois

For the Leland Giants, this game against the Cubs marked the crowning moment in their short history. A chance to play a white pro-fessional team, let alone the National League Champions, did not come along every day. It was an historic opportunity to demonstrate the high quality of black baseball. They could not squander this moment— they must make the most of it. None of Leland's players received a nickel for playing this game. In fact, Frank Leland wasn't sure the gate would cover the three thousand dollars he paid the Cubs for their share, the five hundred dollar rental fee for the West Side Grounds (which went to Al Spalding who still owned the stadium), and the five hundred dollar fee to Chubby Murphy.

But even if money was lost in the process, a match-up of the black Leland Giants versus the white National League Champions was a dream come true for Leland and manager/pitcher/outfielder Rube Foster. Foster was certain the Leland Giants could defeat the Cubs. "It will be a case of Greek meeting Greek," he declared. "We ain't got no reason to fear nuthin'."

The crowd, an unusual amalgam of black and white, numbered around nine thousand. Many black men brought their sons to witness this rare competition between the races, carefully pointing out the great stars of the Leland Giants to the wide-eyed waifs.

"That there is Rube Foster," one forty-year-old man said to his twelve year old. "The best twirler in the country! And that fellow over there is a 'markable ballplayer, catcher by the name of Pete Booker."

Three days prior to the game Frank Chance told his team that he would not be playing or managing. He did not explain his reasons, but he privately told Johnny Evers, who also sat out the contest, that "there's more at stake here than meets the eye." Chance selected Pat Moran to manage the Cubs that day. Both Evers and Chance attended the game, sitting with President Murphy in his box, well back from the playing field.

Moran briefly toyed with starting Miner Brown, but the Cubs ace had pitched the day before. Instead he chose Blaine "Kid" Durbin, an untested, fresh arm. Moran deliberately went with the yannigan. If the Cubs lost, it could all be pinned on Durbin's inexperience. But Moran did not think the Cubs would lose.

During batting practice Durbin recognized Giants pitcher Pat Dougherty picking up baseballs along the left field line. The same man he had met in the mists of West Baden Springs in March, and in May when he, Kling, and Big Ed attended the Giants game on Wentworth and 79th. He wandered over and greeted the tall black man.

Dougherty started. "Durbin, I understand you're on the slab today."

"That's right. For me it's a great opportunity. You're starting too?"

"Yeah. Big deal for me too. It would normally be Rube but his arm's been actin' up some on him. He's almost ready, and champin' at the bit to throw. But he wants me to go."

"Well, good luck to you, Pat. Just don't knock one of my fastballs, alright?"

"You got nothin' to worry about there, Kid. Just throw 'em outside as I cannot hit 'em out there."

"Thanks for the tip, Pat." As Kid walked away he wondered how accurate the "tip" was.

The Cubs had selected forty-four-year-old former Chicago White Stocking outfielder Jimmy "Pony" Ryan to umpire the game. A former teammate of Cap Anson and Billy Sunday, Ryan had a long and productive big league career, knocking out more than 2,500 hits over eighteen years. Frank Leland initially opposed the selection but the Cubs stood firm and Leland relented.

Ryan called out, "Play ball!"

Durbin toed the mound to begin the game and a strange hush came over the crowd. Moran set a simple game plan for Durbin.

"The toughest pitch to hit is knee-high and outside, so stay right there!"

Bobby Winston, the leadoff man for the Lelands, carried a white-taped fat black bat into the batter's box. He stood no taller than five feet seven inches and carried a reputation as a speed demon. Durbin, warned about Winston's bunting prowess, threw the first pitch high and outside to the right-handed hitter. Winston did not go for it. The second pitch, a curveball, provided an opportunity to lay down the bunt. He got the bat above the ball and pushed it down the third base line. Steiny ran in and gloved it, but Winston easily beat the throw to first. The crowd erupted with cheers. Many black spectators felt relief that the first Leland hitter had solved the white pitcher. The next batter, Nate Harris, another fleet-footed small man, played second base. A light-skinned, slight man, he leveled his bat across the plate while teammates shouted encouragement. Moran signaled for a low fastball and Durbin complied, but the ball came in too straight and higher than he wanted. Harris laid his scruffy bat flat over the plate and tapped the ball down toward Steiny. Another bunt! This time Steinfeldt grabbed the ball off the top of the turf midway between home and third base and whipped it underhand to Kling at first, nailing Harris by one step. As Steinfeldt threw, Moran, behind the plate, screamed his head off, pointing toward the left side of the infield. The base runner accelerated past second and dug toward third. Kling set up to throw, but thought better of it. Steiny lay on the ground and Tinker had not covered third. Winston motored into third without a play.

Durbin did not let it bother him. He scrutinized the next batter, Andrew "Jap" Payne. The muscular center fielder spit on his hands, rubbed in some dirt, and took his place in the batter's box, choking up on the bat six inches. He wore his collar up, like most of the Cubs. Durbin looked in for the sign and hurled a curveball that nicked the inside corner of the plate for a called strike. He tried the same pitch again and got strike two. Then Durbin missed with two fastballs. On the 2-2 count Durbin threw another curve and Payne lifted it to Jimmy Slagle in medium center. Winston had no problem making it home after the catch, the Giants taking a 1-0 lead, with half the crowd going absolutely wild. Durbin retired the next batter, shortstop George Wright, on a bounding grounder to Hofman at second, and the inning ended without further damage.

That's okay, Durbin said to himself, *we're gonna be fine.*

Pat Dougherty walked to the mound, and after warming up with eight tosses, laid his glove next to the rubber and hitched up his pants. He then picked up the glove, got the ball from the first baseman, and looked in for the first sign. Booker wanted a fast one, low and away. Rabbit Slagle dug in at the plate, his spikes scratching a foothold while he wagged the ash bat over the dish. Dougherty began a fluid windup and sidearmed the ball right down the middle. Slagle took the first pitch, wanting to get an idea of the slabman's stuff. The umpire yelled "Stee-rike!" Twice more Dougherty unloaded right down the tube but Slagle could not connect, almost jumping out of his shoes on strike three. Many of the fans screamed their approval.

The next batter, Jimmy Sheckard, checked his swing on the first pitch, a curveball that missed the plate by a wide margin. He swung at pitch number two and fouled the ball behind him. But the next two pitches eluded Jimmy, and he retreated to the bench, another strikeout victim. Frank Schulte, the next hitter, took his time at the plate, picking up some dirt and wiping it over both hands. *Let's slow this thing down,* he thought. Pounding his bat on the plate, he looked out at the mound, inviting the pitcher to throw. The first pitch came inside and Schulte inched back as the umpire called it a ball. The Cubs right fielder spit out a long stream of tobacco juice as the Giants pitcher looked in for the sign. The next pitch came in fast and low. Schulte swung hard but failed to make contact. He squibbed a foul ball on the next delivery, bringing the count to 1-2. The Leland infield came alive, razzing the batter with "Hey, batter, batter!" and "Swing, sucker, swing!" Dougherty went into his motion and pegged one on the outside corner. Schulte hesitated a fraction of a second, and by then it was too late. "Stee-rike three," called the umpire.

Three up and three down. Three strikeouts. The black fans applauded enthusiastically and screamed their appreciation. Many whites just shook their heads. But confidence leaped in the hearts of the Leland squad. Owner Frank Leland encouraged his players from the bench, telling them, "This game is ours!"

The second inning started with thirty-one-year-old Harry "Mike" Moore, the Giants first baseman, setting up in the batter's box. Moore, a dark-skinned man with large feet, rubbed his hands together rapidly and gripped the bat. Durbin took his time, and then threw two wide ones that the Leland firstbagger ignored. On the third pitch Durbin induced Moore to slap a groundball to Tinker at short. Tinker threw him out easily. Manager Rube Foster, not pitching today but playing right field, proceeded to the plate. The tall, burly man waved his bat across the heart of the strike zone, and Kid threw a nifty curveball that Umpire Ryan called a strike. The next two pitches, outside fastballs, missed the plate. Foster correctly guessed fastball on the 2-1 pitch, and sent a line drive screaming over Tinker's head into left field for a single. Foster hustled to first base and took three steps toward second, but Sheckard got the ball into the infield quickly.

The Lelands had a little mascot, a seven-year-old black boy, hovering around their bench by the bats. When the ball sailed past Tinker, the little fellow jumped up and down and scampered over to third base to shake hands with the coacher, one of the Leland reserves. The boy yelled out to Tinker, "You never got close!" Irritated, Tinker took a few steps toward the lad, glared, and spit out, "Get back to the bench, nigger!" The coacher, a thirty-year-old pitcher named Walter Ball, approached the Cubs shortstop.

"Mr. Tinker," Ball started, in a low, calm drawl, "that child that you just called a 'nigger,' he's my wife's baby."

Joe Tinker looked at the boy and Ball, who had addressed him with respect. He immediately regretted what he had said. He called for a time-out and extended his hand to the Leland pitcher.

"I am terribly sorry. I truly am. Please forgive me, sir."

Years later Tinker told this story about himself on more than one occasion, each time explaining how bad he felt about the incident.

The only other person who heard Tinker's remark, Harry Steinfeldt, flashed a look of disgust at Tinker. "Shee-it," said Steiny. "You ain't said nothin' that you needed to be sorry for."

The backstop, husky Pete Booker, approached the batter's box while Durbin peered over at Foster on first. Catcher Moran gave the sign for inside heat, and Durbin complied. The pitch sailed inside for a ball. But Booker could not resist the next delivery, a sinking fastball. He cracked a two-hopper to short. Tinker fielded the ball cleanly, flipped it to Hofman at second, who threw to first, completing the double play. Tinker to Hofman to Kling.

The bottom of the second inning began with a determined Harry Steinfeldt striding to the plate. As he entered the batter's box he gazed down at the Leland catcher, Pete Booker.

"Tell your boy he ain't gonna strike me out," Harry said.

"Tell him yourself," Booker replied.

Harry decided against trading another quip with Booker, maybe accusing the catcher of being uppity. *First things first*, he thought. *We need a hit.*

The initial pitch sailed a little wide and Harry let it go for a ball. But the second pitch came right down the pipe and Harry took a clean stroke at it, smacking it down the left field line, and strolled into second standing up. While Kling peered back to the bench from the plate, manager Moran signaled him and Harry at second for the sacrifice bunt. Kling leveled his bat over the plate and calmly pushed the first pitch toward the hot corner. The third baseman pounced on the bounding ball and heaved it to first for the out, while Steinfeldt took third. Harry asked the Leland third-sacker how he came to be called "Danger."

"Don't rightly know for sure, Mr. Harry, lest it's because my given name is 'Dangerfield.'"

"Yeah," deadpanned Steinfeldt, "that might explain it some."

Pitcher Dougherty took a deep breath and scrutinized the next hitter, Joe Tinker. The first pitch came inside and high at the Cubs shortstop, sending him a message: "You're crowding my plate." But Joe dodged it nimbly and resumed his at-bat in the same spot, the same distance from home plate. The message from Joe Tinker: "I won't be intimidated." From high in the stands, the unmistakable voice of Frank Chance bellowed to Tinker, "Attaboy Joe. Go after 'im!"

Tinker nibbled at the next pitch, but succeeded only in fouling it to the third row behind the plate. A fan recovered the ball, and gave it to an usher who threw it back onto the field. On the third pitch, Tinker shot a one-hopper to Danger Talbert, positioned five steps in at third, and Steinfeldt wisely retreated to the bag. Talbert threw out Tinker, and with two down the Cubs needed a safety from Artie Hofman to get Steinfeldt home. Hofman covered his hands with dirt and spit and stepped into the box. The fans started chanting, "Put him over, put him over!" and others yelled, "Hold 'em there, hold 'em there!" But Artie, a cool professional, paid no attention to the commotion in the grandstands.

Dougherty's first pitch streaked in low and outside, but nicked enough of the zone to be called a strike. Hofman thought it a ball, but said nothing. Dougherty looked in for a sign, and the catcher signaled a pick-off play at third. Dougherty obliged, but Steinfeldt made it back to the bag easily.

Harry shouted over to the pitcher, "You ain't gonna catch old Harry asleep at the switch!"

Dougherty came in with a slow curve that Hofman waited on, slapping it into right field for a hit. Steinfeldt waltzed home with the Cubs first run, and the score stood tied at 1-1.

Kid Durbin took the mound and faced off against the Lelands' third-sacker, right-handed hitter Danger Talbert. Durbin shook off a signal for a fastball and threw a curve, but it missed. Moran called for another curve and Talbert, expecting a juicy fastball, swung early for strike one. Moran then called for the lightning, but Talbert was guessing fastball and he timed his swing perfectly, smashing it toward the gap between third and short. But Steinfeldt dove, leaving his feet and snaring the liner for the first out. Durbin nodded to his teammate, and looked in to see pitcher Dougherty coming to the plate.

Durbin remembered their earlier conversation. *This guy tells me he can't hit the outside pitch. So that's probably where he wants me to throw. I'm goin' inside.* Moran wanted a fastball so Durbin delivered a sinking fastball on the inside corner. Dougherty smashed the ball down the left field line between Steinfeldt and the bag. The Giants pitcher strode out of the box and eight seconds later stood on second base. Durbin looked back at his adversary, shaking his head. Dougherty shouted, "I wasn't joshin' you." Durbin looked down at the rubber, thinking, *Shit, the one time some guy tells me his weakness and he's tellin' me the truth!*

The next batter, shortstop Winston, slowly ambled to the plate, swinging his lumber as he approached. Moran walked out to the mound to calm Durbin. He said they should go low and outside, and then cross up the hitter with high heat. Durbin followed those directions, and the count went to 2-2. Moran then called for a high, inside fastball. Winston swung but could not catch up to the pitch. So with two outs and a man on second the Giants second baseman, Harris, came to bat. Harry Steinfeldt razzed the batter, yelling a provocative, "Jigga, jigga, jiggaboo!" Harris took two outside pitches for balls, and creamed an outside fastball into the left-center field gap. The Cubs outfielders gave chase, but the runner came around to score. Harris loped into second with a double, putting the Lelands ahead 2-1.

Durbin cursed under his breath, but retired the next batter, and the Cubs jogged to their bench.

In the bottom of the ninth it was tied 4-4. Durbin gave up all four runs on six hits and a walk, pitching seven innings, at which point Moran used Carl Lundgren to nail down the eighth and ninth frames. Moran told himself he must do everything possible to win this game, and passed the word along to his teammates.

"Take 'em now, boys," Moran hollered. "We don't want this one to get away from us. We couldn't live it down."

Rube Foster had inserted himself as pitcher in the eighth when Dougherty showed signs of fatigue. The Giants manager pitched a perfect eighth inning and had to face three Germans in the ninth, Sheckard, Schulte, and Steinfeldt. Foster's first three pitches to Jimmy Sheckard missed the plate, but he came back with three untouchable fastballs that the Cubs right fielder flailed at, striking out. But Schulte would not be denied. He cracked a ball over the Giants center fielder and dashed to third. Tempted to try for a game-winning homer, Schulte pulled up, confident that Steinfeldt would knock him in. But Foster bore down and struck out Steinfeldt on three nasty curves.

The last curveball caused the Lelands pitcher to wince as a sharp pain knifed through his right shoulder. He knew he could not throw another pitch. With Johnny Kling sauntering to the plate, Foster asked for a timeout and, rubbing his shoulder, walked slowly toward the Giants bench behind first base. He had Big Bill Gatewood warming up down the sidelines, and Bill would need to come in to throw. But as Foster walked off, ball in hand, Frank Schulte took off from third toward the plate. Foster heard a commotion behind him and turned in time to see the runner three steps from the plate. *What the fuck?* he thought. *There's a timeout!* Schulte scored and the umpire signaled the game over. Foster charged at the umpire.

"I called time out, ump. You saw me!"

"You don't get to call time, boy. Only I can do that, and I didn't. It's over!"

"But Mr. Ryan…"

"There's nothin' more to discuss." Ryan turned his back on Foster and walked away. Foster stood frozen at home plate, looking down, still dazed by the turn of events. Johnny Kling, standing five feet away, looked into Foster's eyes and told him, "You guys got fucked. You got nothing to be ashamed of. The ump robbed you!"

Foster dipped his head to agree with the Cubs catcher and found himself in the middle of a swarm of white fans. Startled by the bizarre conclusion to the game, Cubs rooters leaped onto the field to congratulate their team. Most black fans sat stunned.

A small black boy turned to his father. "I don't understand!"

The father told his son, "Neither do I, Robert, but I will do my best to put you wise on the way home."

September 9, 1907;

An Original—Rube Waddell

In Boston's Huntington Avenue Grounds, across from Tufts Medical College, the Pilgrims faced the Philadelphia Athletics in a duel between two future Hall of Fame pitchers, a confrontation that rivaled the Mathewson-Brown battles in the National League. Cy Young versus Rube Waddell. The original flake, Rube earned his nickname for chasing women and firetrucks, and never refusing a drink. The *Sporting News* called the left-handed Waddell an "amazing sousepaw." Author Lee Allen described one year in the life of George Edward Waddell:

> *He began that year [1903] sleeping in a firehouse in Camden, New Jersey, and ended it tending bar in a saloon in Wheeling, West Virginia. In between those events he won 22 games for the Philadelphia Athletics, played left end for the Business Men's Rugby Football Club of Grand Rapids, Michigan, toured the nation in a melodrama called the Stain of Guilt, courted, married and became separated from May Wynne Skinner of Lynn, Massachusetts, saved a woman from drowning, accidentally shot a friend through the hand, and was bitten by a lion.*

A famous teammate from Waddell's minor league years, Sam Crawford, said Waddell would disappear from the team for three or four days after pitching. "He'd... go fishing or... be off playing ball with a bunch of twelve-year-olds in an empty lot somewhere. You couldn't control him because he was just a big kid himself." On more than one occasion opposing teams successfully distracted Waddell while he was on the mound by displaying shiny toys or puppies. The thirty-year-old pitcher's off-diamond antics would soon finish his career, but he still possessed the remarkable curveball that earned him twenty-seven victories two years earlier. His adversary, forty-year-old Cy Young, a living legend, was the polar opposite of Waddell. Married and an Ohio farmer in the off-season, Cy's hard work and straight living resulted in a long major league career.

Boston's "royal rooters," an elite group of fans bestowed with seats on the field in front of the main grandstand, cheered until they were hoarse, with little result. The two men pitched their hearts out, putting goose eggs up on the scoreboard for thirteen innings. Darkness forced the game to be called after the thirteenth inning, a scoreless tie. As the teams drifted out of the dugouts toward the dressing rooms, the huge sign stretching across the outfield fence proclaiming "Boyle Bros. World's Greatest Clothiers" faded into the night.

Cy Young retired four years later with 511 victories, a record that will never be broken. He won thirty or more games in a season five times, and tossed three no-hitters, including a perfect game against the A's in 1904. In fact, the opposing pitcher in the perfect game was none other than Rube Waddell. Years later Young reminisced about that game: "Funny thing about that one is that there wasn't even one hard chance— until Waddell came up for the final out. He hit a sizzler but it went right at an infielder." Cy Young lived until 1955, long enough to see his name venerated in the game of baseball. Waddell pitched only three more seasons. He would be dead in seven years.

From the Journal of Kid Durbin

I learned a powerful lesson from our game with the Leland Giants. The Giants put up just as good a fight as any of the teams in our league. They could do well in the National League—given the chance. That's the thing. They'll never be given the chance. Not with guys like Jack Taylor and Harry Steinfeldt around. I don't even think Husk or Mr. Murphy would give the coloreds a shot either.

Husk told me I did a fine job, but I have to believe that giving up four runs was not up to snuff. It sure as hell isn't gonna earn me a start in a regular game anytime soon. The way we won also disturbed me and some of my teammates. The umpire should not have allowed Frank to come home when Foster thought time was called. To win like that cheapens the game. In my mind it's almost like we cheated those boys, just because they're colored and we could get away with it. Kling feels the same way, as do the college boys, Lundgren, Overall, and Reulbach. But Taylor, Steinfeldt, and Slagle look at it different. Jack lectured me, "You guys almost ruined our reputation. Too much was at stake. It's a damn good thing somebody on that field had the balls to make sure the good guys won." Heinie Zimmerman, the new guy, put it in even cruder terms: "If you don't fuck with the niggers, who is you gonna fuck with?"

My girl Connie attended the game with Velma, a lady friend who also works for Thurston. Velma, a fine fleshy girl of eighteen, told Connie she was lucky to be stepping out with a handsome ballplayer like me. At least that's what Connie said. She also told me that it was a shame the game ended on a "sour note."

We had dinner with Howard Thurston and his wife tonight. It was a birthday celebration for me, as I turned 21 today. Howard bought us a great trout meal at Henrici's. Now that I am finally free, white, and twenty-one I cannot say I feel any different. But I appreciate the friendship of Howard Thurston and the affection Connie has shown me.

She has come a long way in the last few months. I truly believe her dark days are behind her. Thurston's hypnosis treatment helped her some, and working in his show has given her a new purpose that lifts her up. There's a steadiness to her life. We are both indebted to him. And I like to think that I have had something to do with Connie's improved health too.

September 13, 1907 New York City, New York

This was not the same Percy McGill of *Lila's* or Castle Williams. Events conspired to transform him. A little hair had grown on his head, a few gray patches framing his ears. The mustache was gone, a black hospital barber removing it at Percy's request one week after the lower leg amputation. The look of the man had changed. Numerous wrinkles lined his forehead and spilled away from his eyes in all directions. The vigorous, slick ramrod that stood on the stage of the Majestic Theater next to Blaine Durbin no longer existed. The loss of his leg and the laudanum dependence changed him inside too. Bitterness filled every sober moment, but the number of these moments soon decreased to almost zero. The drug melted away the anguish and soothed the torment of his existence. Only one thing remained unaltered—the desire to kill the woman who sent him down this path.

The thought of taking her life was McGill's only satisfaction outside of the brown bottle of Sydenham's. He did not dream of women as before, or relish the prospect of a drunken binge. These things no longer mattered. She who had wronged him must be paid back a hundred times what she had taken. Only her death could balance the ledger. Whether it was quick and painless or slow and tortured was irrelevant. *She must die if I am to live.*

He had learned to walk with crutches. And while the doctors encouraged him to be fitted for a wooden leg, he refused.

"I want to get the fuck out of this hellhole, the sooner the better."

Nurse Donis informed Percy that he could leave in one week. An hour later, he stole the clothes and one shoe of another patient and fled, bound for Chicago.

September 15, 1907 Chicago, Illinois

Jack Taylor seethed with anger for Frank Chance, who had just told the Brakeman that he would probably not start again for the Cubs.

"Why not? I can still throw! Let me throw against the Reds today and I'll prove it."

"You've been a pain in the ass all year, Jack. We need to let the main guys get their work in for the Series."

"Great. So you're not gonna let me pitch against the American Leaguers either?"

"It don't look like it's going to happen, Jack."

Taylor walked away from Chance swearing, but Husk did not hear the tirade due to his impaired left ear.

A number of Cubs filed into the clubhouse just before noon. Chance tossed Howie the batboy a quarter to get some chili from the joint on the corner of Polk and Wood streets. Howie jogged out of the clubhouse past Jack Taylor. Taylor deliberated whether to ask Howie to bring him back something, but then had another thought. He walked slowly to his locker, clutching his glove at his side.

Ten minutes later, Taylor stood outside the clubhouse, leaning against the wall next to the entrance. He spied Howie returning from the chili house carrying an eight-inch tin for the Peerless Leader.

Taylor approached the boy. "Husk wants you to collect the bats right now, Howie. I'll take that to him."

"What about the ten cents change?"

"He said you can keep it." Howie handed the tin to Taylor and shuffled toward the storage shack.

Taylor withdrew into a corner. He drew a wrinkled, brown bag out of his back pocket. The gray zaggeratin powder. He dug into the powder, which had congealed into little chunks, and pinched a small amount. Carefully removing the lid of the chili tin, Brakeman dropped several pinches of the powder into the cylinder. Using his index finger to stir the powder into the chili, he then carefully replaced the cover. Ten seconds later, Trainer Jack appeared, heading into the clubhouse to rub down Ed Reulbach.

"Husk is lookin' for this chili, Jack. Can you give it to him? I got a buddy out front waiting on me."

"Sure."

McCormick took the tin. He found Chance reading a newspaper.

Chance looked up at Trainer Jack. "Thanks, Jack. Anybody besides Sheckard turning up lame today?"

"No. I just gave Carl a rubdown. The arm is fine and dandy."

"Good." Chance grabbed the tin, found a spoon, and began to eat.

One and a half hours later the Cubs loitered on the field during batting practice. Frank Chance gripped his bat at the plate while Jack Pfiester lobbed pitches. Chance felt a wave of edginess overtake him, a strange, undulating tingle radiating up and down his limbs. At first he worried that another headache could be starting, but quickly realized it was something different. As a pitch from Pfiester twisted toward the plate, Chance saw colors spinning off the ball like a comet's tail. Hues of red and blue, following the ball into the catcher's mitt. Stunned by the beauty of the pitch, he didn't swing. He stepped out of the box and looked around. A Cerulean blue sky dazzled his eyes. Looking down, the grass beneath him shimmered and pulsated, as if alive with energy. Like it was a living, sentient creature, undulating beneath him. To Husk's amazement, the green color leaked into the air above the turf in little waves and luminous bubbles. Chance slowly walked to the bench and sat down to figure out what was happening to him. Joe Tinker noticed the befuddled gaze on Chance's face.

"You doin' alright, Husk?"

"I'm okay," answered Chance. He did not look at Tinker.

Collecting his thoughts, Chance considered the possibility that he was going mad. More waves of color swept across his field of vision, and the ordinary sounds of the ball coming off the bat and toe-plates digging into dirt became magnified and strangely beautiful. For a moment, Chance "saw" sounds and "heard" colors, a sensory confusion that amused and troubled him. He carefully picked up a tin cup filled with water. Sweating beads of condensation grew as he watched, each bead of water shining like a diamond. He sipped the water and delighted in the cold liquid sloshing around his mouth and trickling down his throat. Chance removed his cap and wiped his brow with the sleeve of his jersey. The touch of the flannel uniform to his forehead delighted him, a velvety caress that he repeated for sheer pleasure.

Chance resolved to accept what was happening to him as a gift rather than a curse. He would not fight the strange feelings and his unusual perceptions. He would attempt to go about his business as always. Maybe a little slower.

Chance noticed Jack Taylor on the other end of the bench, peering at him, a curious look on the Brakeman's face. Taylor's uniform was not wet with sweat like the other Cubs. He was dogging it again. The Cubs manager stood up and walked toward him. As he approached Taylor, and again when he eased down next to him, Husk scrutinized Jack's face. Little wrinkles spread out from the Brakeman's eyes. Looking deep into those vapid blue eyes, Frank perceived only bitterness and hatred.

Taylor studied Chance. "How you feelin', Cap'n?"

Chance paused before responding. "Good of you to ask, Jack. Any particular reason you're interested in the state of my health?"

"No. You just look a little pale, that's all."

"Well, I'm in real good shape, Jack. In fact, I have to tell you I am enjoying this day. It is… illuminating."

"Whaddaya mean?"

"I mean I am seeing things I have never seen before, and more clearly than ever. Crystal clear. I can see the true and the false of everything. You know I'm a Californian?"

"Yeah. So what?"

"When the fires swept San Francisco after the earthquake last year, soldiers and hospital workers had to kill some of the injured they tended. Too many to move and not enough time. So they shot 'em dead or injected them with enough drugs to kill 'em rather than let them burn to death from the approaching fires."

"What's that got to do with the price of tea in China?"

"I'll tell you, Jack. When I look at you now, I see nothing but trouble. A fucking trainload of sorrow. We gotta put you outta your misery, partner. We gotta let you go. End of the line."

"What the fuck? What's got into you? You been guzzling whiskey?"

"Whatever it is, Jack, it's tellin' me you're through. Empty out your locker now. I want you gone before the game begins."

"You're gonna regret this, you son of a bitch. I got another four or five years left in my wing. I'm gonna hook up with another outfit and come back to haunt you."

"Hell, Jack. You been haunting me and your teammates for over a year now. Good luck."

Taylor stomped away, his words and sounds creating broad black and orange ripples in the air around him. At least that's what Chance observed. Taylor was gone in forty minutes. No goodbyes to anyone except Harry Steinfeldt and Chick Fraser. He never pitched another inning in the majors.

With Taylor's departure, Chance gathered his strength and stood up in front of the bench, bathing in the warm sunshine and feasting on the sounds and smells of the ballpark. At that instant the sky opened like a blooming flower, the clouds parted, and the vast blue dissolved into nothingness. Frank Chance found himself peering into the endless depths of a wondrous and momentarily understandable universe. And he glimpsed God. A God that told him not to worry, that all was well and would always be that way. A God that said, "Enjoy the game," and dissolved into a golden mist when Johnny Evers yelled, "Where the fuck is the Brakeman?"

Chance never shared this moment, this experience, with anyone, but he cherished it the rest of his days. "I'm not a church-going man," he often said, "but I got religion."

From the Journal of Kid Durbin

On Wednesday, while Jeff Overall tossed a great game against the Reds, Husk tells me to head back to Chicago alone. My heart sank and I thought, Oh no! The hatchet's coming down on me so close to the World's Championship Series. But that's not what Husk had in mind. He wanted me to head back to Chicago early to rest up so I could pitch the second game of the Sunday doubleheader against the Doves in the Grounds! My first start in the big leagues! Rather than stick around in Cincinnati and twiddle my thumbs, I took him up on the offer. Sort of.

I figured I could make an adventure out of these few days so I purchased a ticket to Cleveland rather than Chicago. I wanted to see the ballplayer I worshipped as a kid, the same guy some of my teammates now told me might be the best hitter in the game— Napoleon Lajoie. They liked Lajoie so much in Cleveland that they named their team after him—the Cleveland Naps.

So I hopped on a train for Cleveland and on Thursday, the 19th, I made my way to League Park where the Naps were playing the St. Louis Browns. Nap Lajoie managed the Cleveland Americans and played a fine second base. This is a player who hit 426 percent six years back or so! And he struck fourteen home runs in that same year! One dollar bought me a fine box seat back of first base where I enjoyed watching the boys play and not caring a whit about who won the game. I witnessed a fine duel between slabmen Dusty Rhoads for the Naps and "Handsome" Harry Howell for the Browns.

The ballpark threw me for a curve. The left field wall lay 375 feet down the line and center field had to be more than 450 feet from the plate. But the right field fence was only 290 feet deep so the lefty batters were always trying to poke it out there. I carefully observed the two hurlers and the types of pitches they made in certain spots. Howell looked like he was throwing nothing but spitters. The ball dipped and dived like a worm on a fishing line. Not even Lajoie could tee off on Handsome Harry, although Nap did manage two hard-hit liners and played his position smoothly. Rhoads favored inside pitches early in the count and outside pitches once he had two strikes. Howell used the spitter in all spots but after the third inning he often tried to sneak a fastball by the hitter on the first pitch. He got away with it almost every time. Rhoads threw a decent game as well, but the righthander sulked to the clubhouse after nine, a 2-1 loser.

I also kept my eyes on the Naps first baseman, George Stovall, a big man with a big temper. All the newspapers recently printed a story of Stovall going berserk when Lajoie told him he would be lowering him a few pegs in the batting order because he wasn't hitting. Stovall grabbed a chair in a hotel lobby and brought it down on Lajoie's head! One of the papers said something like "Stovall Can't Hit Baseball So He Slugs Manager." An older fellow next to me told me Lajoie didn't discipline Stovall for the incident in any way and that Stovall felt horrible about the affair soon after. That's the thing about tempers—you usually regret your actions just when it's too late to fix what you messed up.

Anyhow, this older guy I was sitting next to turned out to be a doctor accompanied by his seventeen-year-old daughter, Dr. George Weiss and Alta Weiss. They lived in a small town a hundred miles south of Cleveland. The doctor, a bearded man who wore spectacles, seemed about fifty. Alta, a pretty girl with brown hair, did not talk a great deal. At least at first. Dr. Weiss knew his baseball and told me quite a bit about the Naps and Lajoie. He got very excited when I told him I pitched for the Cubs. At first he didn't seem to believe me but I just happened to be carrying a couple of articles from the Tribune that mentioned me. He asked me if I was going to stick around for the exhibition tomorrow, a game between two Ohio semiprofessional teams. I told him I didn't know about any exhibition.

Dr. Weiss said, "Son, this is a once-in-a-lifetime event. All of Cleveland has buzzed about the game for a week. A baseball contest that you will remember all your life because it features a newly discovered pitcher. A youngster who is a phenomenon."

"A fastball artist?" I asked.

"Indeed. This pitcher throws a remarkable fastball, as well as a befuddling knuckleball and an excruciating spitter."

I noticed Alta smiling as her father talked.

"What's so funny?" I asked.

"My father's description of the pitcher. He exaggerates."

Dr. Weiss then spilled the beans. "Mr. Durbin, you are looking at the pitcher."

I looked around but didn't see no pitcher so I asked him straight out. "Where?"

He pointed to Alta.

"Is Alta on a bloomer girls team?"

"No sir. Alta is on the Vermilion Independents. A men's semiprofessional club. She is their star pitcher who tomorrow will face off against Cleveland's Vacha All-Stars."

I looked at the girl. "You throw a spitball?"

"It's a little indelicate to talk about, but yes, I've thrown a wet one since I was fourteen."

I laughed a little and confessed I wanted to see this game. The doc told me half of Cleveland would be there, gave me a ticket, and invited me to dinner with him and the girl pitcher.

We had a swell evening. Alta showed me how she held the knuckler and we talked pitching for two hours. I showed her how Miner Brown educated me to throw a slowball. Alta recommends chewing gum for spitballs as it "increases the abundance of saliva." Right before I fell asleep that night the thought crossed my mind that the whole thing might be a disappointment like the Fish Man in the dime museum—maybe Alta's pitching might not live up to the description. After all, it was her father who was raving about her.

But I was not disappointed!

When Alta strode to the mound, 3,500 pairs of eyes were trained upon her. Yet she warmed up like she was alone in her own backyard. A cool cucumber! She wore a big skirt that came down to just above her ankle. She could maneuver around pretty good in it but it looked to me like it hurt her ability to run some. She opened the game with a barrage of sinking fastballs. She sure didn't throw like a girl. She was hurling heat at those boys, and she mowed down the first two Vacha All-Stars on strikes, sending the crowd into a frenzy. The third batter got around on a slower offering, maybe a knuckler, and grounded it to Alta's right. She pounced on that ball like a cat on a mouse, pivoted, and threw a strike to first base, nipping the runner. As she jogged off the field the crowd—which included more ladies than your usual ballcrowd—gave Alta a thunderous applause. She tipped her blue cap in acknowledgement.

Alta put on a wonderful show that afternoon. She pitched five innings, struck out seven men, and gave up only four hits and two runs. By changing the speed on her pitches she kept the batters off balance. Her control failed her in only one inning when she went too often to the knuckler and couldn't get it over the plate. But her squad--Vermilion--led when she moved over to first base in the seventh and they won the ballgame 7-6. Her fielding, both on the mound and at first, was excellent. Her only problem was hitting--while she only struck out once, she couldn't smack the ball too hard. The bugs ate it up, giving her a hand even when she grounded out to the secondbagger.

I congratulated Alta after the game. She threw hard and on target and she seemed to appreciate my telling her this. I told her and Dr. Weiss that if they came to Chicago I could get them free tickets to the World's Championship Series. After saying my goodbyes I hopped a cab to the train station to return to Chicago. I am writing this entry while I eat my dinner as the train is rolling through Indiana.

All my life I looked upon baseball as a man's game, played by white boys like the ones I grew up with—tough-talking, fun-seeking smart alecks like me. But now I have to re-think this notion. A few weeks ago I saw a colored team nearly beat the reigning National League champs. With a square umpire they might've walked out of the West Side Grounds with a victory. And today I witnessed the Girl Wonder–Alta Weiss—a lady pitcher who looks like she can throw a baseball as hard as me! My world is beginning to spin. For all I know there's a girl ballplayer in China who can hit a ball farther than Frank Schulte!

From the Journal of Kid Durbin

September 22, 1907

Just like he promised, the Peerless Leader finally gave me today what I have long hankered for. My first National League start! We had a doubleheader with the Doves and my assignment was game two, after we knocked off the Boston crew in game one for our one hundredth victory of the year.

When the man with the megaphone announced me as the starting pitcher, a loud round of applause sent a chill up and down my spine. A real tingler! Our new man, rookie Heinie Zimmerman, came over to me and said, "You ain't oughtta worry, Kid. 'The Great Zim's' in the lineup for this one." While I think Heinie was trying to pep me up, something about this guy rubs me the wrong way. Jimmy Sheckard told me that Zim was "dumber than a keg of nails."

I took the mound and roughed up the ball. The first Boston batter, an outfielder about my height named Izzy Hoffman, hit from the left side. I threw him three straight fastballs and he never came close. With that strikeout under my belt, I gained some confidence to face the next Dove, manager and first baseman Fred Tenney, another left-handed hitter. I got him into the hole, zero and two, but my sixth pitch of the game soaked him. I hit him square in the small of his back and he trotted down to first. I figured this was good a time as any to send a message to the Doves batters: "Back off. If I am willing to hit your manager and best player, I am willing to hit you too." So who's up next? My old buddy Billy Sweeney, who had earned himself a starting role with the Doves. Billy jumped into the box, anxious to get around on one of my tosses. He had his usual bat, a featherweight piece of wood that the boys used to ridicule. Billy hugged the plate, figuring I wouldn't plunk him, especially with a man on. He was right. But all he could do was ground an easy chance to Tinker. But when Joe threw the ball to first, Del Howard somehow managed to drop it, putting two Doves on with only one out.

Ginger Beaumont, their center fielder and another lefty, came up. He had a smirk on his face when he stepped into the box, but my first pitch, a heater inside and high, wiped away that grin. Johnny Evers razzed Beaumont with his real name, Clarence. The Crab probably found Ginger's moniker in "The Sporting Life," which Johnny reads religiously. I missed with the next pitch, and then Ginger sat on my fastball, smacking it between our outfielders and driving in both runners. My world began to crumble. I should have taken a couple of deep breaths to focus, but instead I plunged ahead. Switch-hitting second baseman Claude Ritchey sent my first curve of the game sailing into right field, scoring Beaumont from third. Already three runs in the top of the first! I was shaken, but I managed to stop them there.

We mounted an offensive in our half of the second inning, with Tinker, Sheckard, Howard, and me coming through with hits, pushing across two runs. But we couldn't do any more damage against the Boston twirler so that's as close as we got. I pitched seven innings and gave up one more run. For the day I only allowed five hits, but the problems in the opening frame doomed me. We lost, 4-2. Frank Chance consoled me in the clubhouse.

"We let you down, boy. We made five errors behind you. You deserved better."

Moments later Big Ed gave me some advice about wasting a pitch every once in a while, telling me it's better to waste one high than in the dirt, which I'd done a couple of times today. While Reulbach gave me the dope, Heinie Zimmerman, wearing only a towel, sat down next to us, whining and complaining about this and that.

"The Great Zim," as he likes to be called, then lowered his voice and said, "That goddam kike catcher is really something, ain't he? One day he's as smooth as silk and the next he can't do nothin'. I never played with no Jew boy before."

Reulbach gets this strange, serious look on his face and says, "You don't know how much good Kling has done for this team. Good pitching doesn't happen without a good catcher. We finished first last year—and we're doing the same this season—largely on account of Noisy John."

"Yeah, well, Jews and Eye-talians. Next thing you know it will be coons sitting in this clubhouse."

Reulbach paused a second and then tells Zim, "I guess you didn't know that I'm Jewish?"

"Hell no! Are you shittin' me?"

"Not at all. So now you're playing with two Jew boys. And neither of us wants to hear you calling anybody a kike. Okay?"

"Oh, take it easy, Big Ed. I didn't mean nothin' by it. Just blowing off steam after my first game. I'll keep your secret."

"It's no secret."

"Well, I can't wait to see you pitch the next time. We'll have an all-Jew battery. Never seen that before! We could maybe advertise it in the Yid papers."

A look of disgust on his face, Reulbach got up and left. Zimmerman looked all puzzled and says to me, "What did I say?" I didn't respond.

One thing I forgot to mention. Before the game, in fact before the batting practice, a photographer took our team picture. Right in the dugout. Everyone's in it 'cept of course the Brakeman, Gessler, Kahoe, and the rookies who we dealt away. Still, I will get me one of these photographs to keep forever. Twenty-one of us assembled in three rows, twenty ballplayers and Trainer Jack. The back row guys stood while the middle row sat on the bench. The man with the camera directed three "little" guys, me, Slagle, and Evers, to sit in front, on the dugout step. But Miner Brown shouted to the photographer, "Hold on, Mr. Tintype Man," and he scooted on down to sit right next to me, his right knee knocking up against mine. It was a small gesture but I appreciated it.

September 23, 1907 **Chicago, Illinois**

The fourth-place Phillies visited the Cubs on a miserable day, too wet and cold for a decent game of baseball. But the game had to be played. A Cubs victory would clinch the 1907 National League pennant. Furthermore, the game marked the annual Children's Day at the ballpark, all schoolkids getting free admission. Thousands showed up and management didn't want to disappoint them. While Mordecai Brown started, the game plan called for him to pitch just two innings, a tune-up in preparation for the Series. Reulbach would be ready to pitch after Brown got his workout.

In the bottom of the second with one down, Johnny Evers got around on Lew Richie's offering and sent a line drive down the right field line for a double. When Evers took a large lead from second, the Phillies catcher patted the back of his head, signaling the pitcher to wheel around to pick him off. But Evers saw the signal and retreated to the bag in time. The Crab soon scampered over to third base on a ground out by Tinker. With two gone and a man on third, Miner Brown was due up, but Chance called upon Kid Durbin to pinch hit. The little redhead approached the batter's box with orders from Chance to take the first two pitches. A minute earlier, while on second base, Evers noticed that Ritchie's wind-up was slow—slow enough to allow a steal of home. So as Ritchie rocked back to deliver the first pitch, Evers broke for the plate. Pitcher Ritchie fired a fastball down the middle as Durbin, batting lefty as usual, eased back from the plate. Evers dashed down the line in a blur and slid smoothly under the tag.

"Safe!" called Umpire Carpenter.

Durbin helped Evers up to his feet and exclaimed, "Sweet!"

By the top of the fifth the skies grew dark as the Cubs led 3-1. Knowing that they needed three outs to make the game official—and to secure the pennant—the Cubs bore down. The next batter, third baseman "Harvard" Eddie Grant, delayed a moment before stepping into the box. The freckled infielder's ears extended out from his head, occasionally earning him stares. On the first pitch he bounced a one-hopper to Reulbach on the mound. Big Ed grabbed it, but tossed hurriedly to Howard who bobbled the low throw, allowing Grant to reach safely. Shortstop Mickey Doolan then stroked a single into right field, further threatening the Cubs lead. First and second, no outs.

Now Catcher Red Dooin leveled his bat at the plate. He jumped on Big Ed's initial pitch, sending it streaking on a line to right. But first-sacker Del Howard dove to his right and picked the ball out of the air, six inches off the ground, before he fell to the dirt. Doolan, halfway to second, put on the brakes and retreated toward first, but Howard scrambled on hands and knees, tagging the bag with the ball for the second out. Howard then heard Evers shrieking on second base.

"Let me have it!" Evers yelled, for Eddie Grant, still retracing his steps, had rounded third before figuring out that Howard snagged the ball. Howard pegged the ball to Evers and the Cubs completed the triple play. As he trotted off the field, Howard realized he could have completed an unassisted triple play by tagging second base himself. *I had plenty of time,* he thought.

After seven and a half innings the umpires called the game, darkness claiming Chicago's West Side. The 4-1 victory clinched the Cubs' second consecutive pennant, and while it was not the custom of the times to celebrate, a palpable sense of satisfaction rippled through the clubhouse.

September 28, 1907 **Chicago, Illinois**

With the Cubs scheduled for a day off and the pennant clinched, the Peerless Leader cancelled the afternoon practice session and gave his players a well-deserved break. Most used the opportunity to sleep late and dine well, while a few drank themselves into a stupor. Durbin planned to see Connie's performance in the Thurston show at the Majestic, now in its final three weeks. The matinee would include Connie's first appearance in the "girl cut in two" trick, and the redheaded Cub arranged to observe the show from the stage wing. Connie and Kid enjoyed a Wiener schnitzel lunch at the Berghoff, and then walked the block to the theater.

Connie had gradually developed a strong attachment to Blaine Durbin. She enjoyed his company, his gentle manner, and the optimism he communicated. She felt safe in his presence and was sure he cared about her. As for Blaine, he had made up his mind that he would like to devote himself to this woman, to spend his life with her. On the verge of asking her to marry him, Durbin was waiting for the right moment, maybe after the season ended. He had already put aside some money for a diamond ring.

Inside the theater Connie raced back to her dressing room to change into her costume while Kid amused himself behind the curtains, studying the flurry of activity that preceded the performance. George White, Thurston's backstage assistant, readied a number of props. Durbin observed the great magician from a distance, not wanting to disturb his preparations. Thurston busily tested his devices and jumped about, shaking himself in a ritual religiously performed before each show to ease the nervous tension.

"I love my audience. I have the best job in the world. I am a happy man. I will entertain this audience." Thurston smiled.

Thurston started the show ten minutes later by asking the first three rows of the audience to select a volunteer.

"Please choose someone who is clearly not connected to the show, if you will," he requested. Audience members near the stage selected a portly banker of fifty, a prosperous man known to many of them, and he strode up the five wooden stairs on stage right. He wore a black pin-striped suit with a blue cravat and a high collar.

"How do you do, sir? Please tell the audience your name."

"Robert Hanover."

"And your occupation, Mr. Hanover?"

"I am a banker with the Harris Bank."

"Very well, sir. We are pleased to have you with us today. Please face the audience."

Thurston placed himself alongside Hanover and asked the man, "Did you launder clothes today, sir?"

While Hanover smiled slightly, shaking his head to say "no," Thurston slipped his hand inside the banker's vest and pulled out a wash line of women's clothes with nine or ten pieces of lingerie clothespinned to the line. The man gasped and the audience guffawed.

"Well, sir, I understand you played baseball earlier today, pitching and having a catch as you engaged in our great national pastime, correct?"

"Why, no, sir. That is not correct." As Hanover answered, Thurston dug his hands into the pants pockets of the banker, withdrew four official Spalding baseballs, juggled them for ten seconds, pulled a silver platter out of the astonished Hanover's suit coat, and caught all four balls on the platter. In the midst of boisterous applause, George White came onto the stage and collected the gleaming tray and baseballs from Thurston. Thurston guided Hanover forward, in front of White. Unknown to the audience, a knapsack on White's back contained a sur-prise in a cloth bag. Deftly, Thurston drew the bag from White's knap-sack and in one clean motion surreptitiously slipped it into Hanover's coat. After the quick transfer, as George ambled off the stage with the platter of baseballs, Thurston placed himself on Hanover's left.

While gesticulating with the hand visible to the audience, Thurston worked the other hand up into Hanover's ample coat from behind, tugged at a zipper device, and then eased away from the man. Two seconds later, a large white duck poked his head up from behind Hanover's coat collar, jolting the banker and the audience with a loud "quack." Hanover cried out, "Mother of God!" as the duck began to peck vigorously at the back of his head. He streaked toward his friends in the audience as the duck grew noisier and continued to peck. The audience reeled in laughter at the sight, thankful that they had not been chosen to participate in this demonstration. Back at his seat the banker's friends helped him to remove his coat—and the duck—and stepped back to watch the animal scurry back up the stairs to the stage and exit, stage right.

Off on the left wing of the stage, near where George White perched, Kid Durbin sat on a tall stool, dangling his feet and delighting in the performance. Connie approached from behind in a sparkling stage dress that revealed the wondrous curves of her body. Her act was next.

"Are you enjoying yourself?" she asked.

"Even more so now. You look gorgeous!"

George White began to push a long box onto the stage, while Thurston and Connie walked in front of it. Holding Connie's hand, he turned to the audience and began in a somber tone.

"What you are about to witness on this stage may trouble you greatly, but I beseech you to remain calm. Belief is not reality! Your eyes are about to fool you, to lead you away from what is so. I promise you that this beautiful young woman—Miss Connie—will not be harmed in any way."

Thurston opened the box from the top as Connie climbed up a few stairs and lay down in the contraption. The audience could not see the second woman already in the box, who poked her feet out of the two holes in the box toward stage left while Connie's head emerged from the other side of the container. The audience, of course, assumed those feet belonged to Miss Connie. Thurston then replaced the top of the wooden container, sealing Connie and the other woman within. Thurston walked around the box with a feather in his hand. He periodically tickled the dangling toes and Connie laughed, as did the audience. Connie's cue was her own name—every time Thurston uttered the name "Connie" it signaled her to laugh as if her toes were being tickled. Thurston retrieved the saw, and brought four members of the audience onstage to inspect it and verify its true character. That done, Thurston placed the giant instrument in a notch in the middle of the box and pronounced himself ready to proceed.

As he drew back the saw and began to cut into the box, Thurston could not see the man who had gingerly negotiated the stairs to the right of the stage and had reached the footlights. A one-legged man on crutches. A man carrying a knife in his right hand.

Percy McGill approached within fifteen feet of Connie when Durbin nearly jumped out of his skin with the realization that the devil

McGill was still alive. Durbin saw the knife and, in the same desperate moment, realized he stood too far away to stop the madman before he would reach Connie. The tray of baseballs from the last act lay on a box to his left. He grabbed one of the balls as McGill advanced on Connie, a cruel smile etched into his crazed features. Connie could not see the advancing madman. As McGill raised the knife into the air, Kid reared back and fired the stitched sphere with every ounce of strength he could muster. McGill never knew what hit him. Struck squarely above his left eye, the one-legged man collapsed senseless to the stage. The crutches splayed out from his sides while the knife dropped cleanly to the floor, sticking upright as a marker to McGill's folly.

Sometimes there is a fleeting interlude between life and death, a last dream in the gray interstice between the white of life and the black of death. McGill edged into this shadow place as he lay dying on the stage floor of the Majestic Theater. He dreamed of his father, angry and armed with a cane, looming over a terrified child and its weeping mother. Their pleas did not stop him. In the midst of his frenzy the face of the angry man froze like a stone, trapped in horrific rage. Suddenly the eyes liquified, pouring out of their sockets, as the face began to melt, particle by particle, only to transform into the face of the dying dreamer. A face not unlike his father's, also locked in a ghastly wrath. Then the dream dissolved as the life that nourished it slipped away.

George White immediately ordered the curtains closed, as Thurston quickly released Connie from the box. He also ordered the other girl—the feet in the box—out of the container. Durbin ran to Connie and whisked her off the stage.

In her dressing room, Durbin threw his arms around Connie in a blissful embrace. "Are you all right, my darling?"

"I'm fine, my love," Connie whispered quietly.

Durbin kissed her on the cheek and turned.

"I need to help Mr. Thurston…"

George White called the police while Durbin and Thurston stared down at McGill. Blood oozed from the forehead of the unmoving man. Thurston bent down and took his pulse.

"I think he's dead. How did you recognize him?" asked Thurston.

"The eyes, Howard, the eyes." It was the first time Durbin had addressed Thurston by his given name.

No doubt about it, Durbin mused to himself, *this is my One Day.*

All the Chicago newspapers and dailies as far away as the coasts carried stories about the attempt on Connie Dandridge's life by Castle Williams escapee Percy McGill, and the perfect strike by Kid Durbin of the Chicago Cubs. Connie and Kid gave interviews, and many of the stories featured the romantic link between the two. On the South Side of Chicago, Michael Fitzgerald read about his daughter in the *Tribune* and set the newspaper down alongside his cup of coffee.

He walked to the living room and picked up the telephone. Thirty minutes later he was still talking to Connie.

September 30, 1907 **Philadelphia, Pennsylvania**

The Columbia Avenue Grounds sat close to numerous small brewery houses in a section of North Philadelphia aptly called Brewerytown. The smell of hops and yeast permeated the ballpark, constantly irritating the teetotaler manager of the A's, Connie Mack. Mack, a courtly man who never employed profanity, stood over six feet tall but never weighed more than 150 pounds. "The Tall Tactician" managed the A's from the bench, always garbed in a dapper three-piece suit and high collar, whether the temperature was ninety or twenty. With few exceptions, he customarily addressed his players formally, as "Mr. Smith" or "Mr. Jones," and they reciprocated by calling him "Mr. Mack." That formality extended even to opposing players. For example, Mack wisely enjoined his players: "Never get Mr. Cobb angry."

The Tigers faced off against the Athletics in an important battle. Having dispatched the White Sox, the first-place Tigers maintained a mere one-and-a-half-game lead over the A's with seven games left in the season. The *New York Times* proclaimed this American League pennant race as "the greatest struggle in the history of baseball." Over twenty-four thousand fans crowded into Columbia Avenue Grounds, ten thousand more were turned away, and another five thousand rooftop partisans observed from buildings across the street. Still others devised ways to sneak into the ballpark, some by scaling the outfield walls with the help of confederates on the inside.

The Athletics came out swinging, pounding the Bengals' ace, Wild Bill Donovan, for seven runs in the first five innings. When the Athletics' starter faltered in the second, Mack pulled out all stops, bringing in his fabled lefty, Rube Waddell. Inserted with the bases loaded and one out, Rube methodically struck out the next two batters, extinguishing the rally. With each strikeout an explosion of joy and thunderous applause rocked the park.

Waddell still straddled the rubber in the bottom of the ninth, clinging to an 8-6 margin. Wahoo Sam Crawford, the great Tiger outfielder, stood outside the box, scowling at the pitcher. He then slapped Waddell's first pitch for a base hit, bringing the twenty-year-old firebrand Ty Cobb to the plate. Cobb slowly leveled his black bat over the plate and snarled at Waddell. Cobb had learned that a teammate of Waddell recently strangled Rube's pet mockingbird to shut it up. So Cobb shouted out to the mound, "Where's your cuckoo bird, bo?" The A's pitcher grew angry but restrained himself. Ordinarily he would have beaned Cobb, but he could not afford to do so in this situation. He bore down on the Georgia Peach, throwing a tough, inside fastball for strike one. Years later, Waddle insisted the next pitch was another fastball "in the same spot," but Cobb, in his autobiography, claimed it was a "big curve." Whatever the pitch, Cobb turned on the ball, smashing a deep fly that left the ballpark and bounced down 29th Street, tying the game. Connie Mack had a fit, and fell backwards off the bench into a pile of bats. A dismayed partisan crowd sank back in their seats while a jubilant Cobb circled the bases. Waddell kicked up a small cloud of dirt on the mound.

Forty-five-minutes later the sun hung low in back of the grandstands along the third-base line as the A's came to bat in the fourteenth inning. The score stood at 9-9 when the Athletics' first baseman, Harry Davis, sent a ball screaming into deep center field. Sam Crawford galloped back toward the ropes that held the fans, and leaped at the last second, right at the rope. He appeared to drop the ball into the crowd for an error, with Davis being awarded second base as with any ball hit into this section. But Crawford immediately argued that a cop sitting on a soda-pop box by the rope had jumped up and bumped him, causing him to drop the ball. A prolonged argument ensued, creating a hiatus that enabled much mischief to occur. Cobb took this opportunity to tell his teammate, Claude Rossman, that A's shortstop Monte Cross had just called Rossman a "Jew bastard." Rossman steamed over toward the A's bench and slugged Cross. Minutes later the police removed a still-enraged Rossman from the park. After much heated discussion, Umpire Silk O'Loughlin decided that the cop in center field had indeed interfered with Crawford, and ruled the batter out. The A's fans screamed obscenities at the umpire, calling him a "robber," while skirmishes between several groups of players erupted on the field. When the fans poured out of center field and advanced toward second base, the umpires almost called the game, but tensions soon subsided.

At the end of the seventeenth inning, with the game still tied at 9-9, darkness forced the umpires to end the protracted conflict. Wild Bill Donovan had pitched the full seventeen frames for the Tigers, making 231 pitches. While Philly could still overcome the deficit and challenge the Tigers, deep down inside the A's knew it was over. The Tigers sensed that this game had broken the back of Connie Mack's crew and looked forward to meeting the Chicago Cubs in the World Series.

Connie Mack, still stewing on the bench, then and there decided to dump Waddell at season's end. The eccentric twirler's declining skills no longer merited the effort required to manage him. Mack, normally gracious in defeat, confronted O'Loughlin in the umpires' dressing room to no avail, and then scurried to center field seeking affidavits from lingering fans. He would present these documents to the National Commission in an unsuccessful effort to protest the game. The A's manager remained bitter about this defeat all his life, never speaking another word to O'Loughlin. Forty years later, Ty Cobb described his ninth-inning homer this day as one of the most satisfying moments of his career.

From the Journal of Kid Durbin

October 2, 1907

It is hard to write about. Difficult for me to stitch my thoughts together so they make some sense, even though I waited til now to do so. Three days ago I killed a man. Percy McGill. In the same spot where I first crossed paths with him, on the stage of the Majestic Theater during a Howard Thurston show. I perched offstage on a stool sixty feet from Connie while she lay onstage in a box with Howard sawing her in two. I wouldn't say anything, but that box she was in made me think of Connie in her coffin earlier this year.

Having seen the act before, I knew something was wrong when I saw a ragged man lope across the stage towards Connie. I caught a flash of light off the knife in his hand and time froze for me. He came at her like a rabid dog, those mad eyes bulging out, and his mouth twisted up in a horrible leer. I nearly fell to the ground but caught myself, and providence handed me a baseball, inches from my throwing hand. Not stopping to think, I grasped the ball like on the mound, took my measure, and heaved my best lightning like the World's Championship Series depended on that pitch. Actually, my world did ride on that pitch. It sailed clean and hit him flush in the head, just before he reached Connie. A death pitch.

I believe he died the second that beanball cracked open his skull. Thurston told me I did the right thing right then and there, as did the police and Connie. Frank Chance said it took guts to do what I did. Heinie Zimmerman said I had earned a new nickname, "Sudden Death," but I told him that "Kid" suited me just fine. The papers blew the story up big and called me the "Young Hurling Hero of the Chicago Nationals." But I was no hero. Just a guy who can throw a strike two times out of three.

My conscience is telling me it's a terrible thing to take the life of a man, but deep in my heart I have no regrets. If ever a man needed dyin', he did. If I could have saved Connie some other way I might have done so, but there was no other way. I simply did what I had to do, and was

ALAN ALOP AND DOC NOEL 451

lucky enough not to mess it up.

We played our last regular game on home turf today before the World's Championship next week. The Giants put up no fight, McGraw and his crew just going through the motions. Their slabmen broke down and allowed us thirteen runs. We slipped ahead in the third inning and never looked back. Brownie pitched for us, but he couldn't get his head into the game, giving up seven runs before Husk asked me to pitch the eighth.

Husk didn't say it, but I knew he wondered if I'd be able to throw so soon after the events at the Majestic. But I figured no Giants batter would dare crowd the plate against me today, and I was right. Three up and three down, and I was eager to pitch the ninth when the game got called on account of darkness. I expected the Giants to razz me about putting down McGill but they laid off. When the umpire called the game, a gray-haired man walked toward me, near our bench, and our eyes met. Without slowing or stopping, he said, "Durbin, you got what it takes. On and off the field."

I was so surprised that the great John McGraw spoke to me, I plumb froze, and then he was gone.

Ty Cobb champed at the bit in anticipation of his first World Series. Still only twenty years old, 1907 marked his first season playing more than one hundred games for the Tigers. The Georgian's performance for the American League pennant winners was nothing short of phenomenal. He won the batting title with a .350 average and led the league in hits with 212. If baseball statisticians had publicized runs-batted-in then, they would have noted that Cobb led the league in RBIs with 119. For good measure Cobb stole fifty-three bases. Not a modest person, he predicted he would do well in the World Series. "I oughtta hit .800 against the National League," he told the press. Jimmy Sheckard, the Cubs outfielder, had made comparable boasts one year earlier, telling sportswriters he would sock the White Sox pitching for a .400 clip. He went 0-21 in the Series, one of the reasons the Cubs lost.

On the last two days of the regular season, the Cubs had two doubleheaders scheduled with the Cardinals in St. Louis at Robison Park. On both of these days, Frank Chance, accompanied by pitchers Overall and Pfiester, slipped away from the Cardinals ballpark and walked the four blocks to Sportsman's Park, where the St. Louis Browns faced the Detroit Tigers. The trio of Cubs purchased tickets like any other fans, not announcing their presence to their friends and associates on the field. Chance informed his two pitchers that they would be starting the first two games of the Series. Pitching ace Miner Brown was doubtful, his arm still painful from an August injury.

Chance, Pfiester, and Overall carefully studied the Tigers hitters taking their cuts against the Browns, jotting copious notes on what types of pitches each Tiger hit or missed. For example, Tigers outfielder Sam Crawford knocked curves on the outside corner for three opposite-field hits. But the three Cubs expressed disappointment that the Georgia Peach, whom they had never seen perform, did not appear in the games. They later learned that Cobb sat in the first row back at Robison Park, scouting the Cubs as a guest of the Cardinal management.

On Sunday, October 6, the season concluded. The Cubs won the National League pennant, finishing seventeen games ahead of the second-place Pirates. The Series started two days later on a cold Tuesday afternoon at West Side Grounds. President Murphy did not lay out any money to decorate the Cubs ballpark. No bunting, special flags, or pennants. He did, however, construct new bleacher seats along both foul lines to pack in extra paying fans. He also raised ticket prices for the occasion to $1.00 for general admission, $1.50 for grandstand, and $2.00 for a box seat. The chilly breeze did not deter the fans. More than twenty-four thousand showed up for the opener, the largest crowd ever at West Side Grounds. The Metropolitan Elevated train dropped off thousands of ticketholders at the Polk Street station, only a block from the park. The overflow fans were stowed behind ropes in the outfield and on the plank-covered ground along the foul lines. A new *Tribune* sign stretched from center to the right field foul line: "BASEBALL STORIES BY DRYDEN AND SY IN THE TRIBUNE THIS YEAR."

Outside the offices of the *Chicago Tribune*, the newspaper had erected a large scoreboard dubbed "Electrical Baseball Board." It charted the progress of the game with a schematic in the shape of a diamond. Crowds in the thousands gathered to "watch" the game there, and at less elaborate hand-operated scoreboards inside the Auditorium Theater as well as the turreted First Regiment Armory at Michigan and 16th Street. While tickets for the games in Chicago sold out immediately, the Tigers had plenty of seats available for the Detroit contests. The Grand Trunk Railroad advertised a special fare for Series fans: Chicago to Detroit roundtrip for $5.50.

The Cubs lost three games in the 1906 Series while dressed in their white home uniforms. Consequently, the intensely superstitious Frank Chance convinced the tight-fisted Cubs owner Charles Murphy to purchase crisp new gray uniforms for the team to wear in the Series. With a vertical green stripe down the left side of the pants, a "C" over the breast, and a "C" inside a diamond on each sleeve, the new grays were individually tailored for each player. But after the first game, Garry Hermann, president of the National Commission, commanded the Cubs to don their white uniforms for all remaining home games. The new gray uniforms, Hermann explained, were too similar to the Tigers' gray road wear.

Chance wanted to pitch Miner Brown in game one, but Brownie's right arm still bothered him, so Orvie Overall got the nod. Other than Brown, only Artie Hofman was unavailable due to injury, having wrenched his knee on the last day of the regular season.

Wild Bill Donovan, who led the American League with a 25-4 record in '07, took the mound for the Tigers. Donovan, a handsome fellow almost six feet tall, featured a nasty fastball that broke in on right-handed hitters at the last moment.

Overall took the mound and pitched his heart out, going into the eighth leading Wild Bill 1-0. Orvie suddenly struggled in the top of the eighth. A vicious liner to right field by "Wahoo" Sam Crawford scored two former Cubs, Germany Schaefer and Davy Jones. Crawford crossed home later, making it 3-1, and an uneasy quiet fell over the Grounds. Hundreds of fair weather fans began to leave. A drunken Cubs fan in the outfield called Cobb a "lousy kike," to which Cobb retorted, "The kike is on first base, you idiot," referring to his teammate Claude Rossman. The Cubs came to bat in the bottom of the ninth still trailing 3-1. Frank Chance stepped into the batter's box with a nasty snarl masking his fear of defeat. Determined to start something, the Cubs manager took a few balls before smashing a pitch from Donovan into right for a clean single. He then advanced to second when Steinfeldt walked on four pitches. Evers then sent a double-play grounder to the third baseman Coughlin, who muffed it, loading the bases for the Cubs with no outs.

An overeager Frank Schulte swung too hard at a Donovan offering, squibbing a ball near first. Tigers first baseman Rossman fielded the ball and tossed it to Wild Bill covering first for the out, as Chance scored. Del Howard then pinch-hit for Tinker and struck out on a low curveball. But an angel who was a Cubs fan caused the catcher, Charlie Schmidt, to miss the ball, allowing Steinfeldt to race home to tie the game. With Pat Moran batting for the pitcher, Evers took a calculated gamble and broke for home. Donovan cooly threw a strike to the catcher, and Evers was tagged out, sending the game into extra innings.

The Cubs almost won in the bottom of the tenth when, on another passed ball, Jimmy Slagle raced home to score, beating a throw from catcher Schmidt to Donovan covering the plate. But Harry Steinfeldt stupidly stuck his bat in front of Donovan on the play. The umpire ruled that Steinfeldt interfered with Schmidt's throw to Donovan so Slagle was called out. Chance waited a minute to calm himself before telling Steinfeldt, "Don't fuck up like that anymore, Harry."

Reulbach finished the game for the Cubs. He and Donovan pitched through the twelfth until darkness forced the umpires to call the game, the first tie in World Series history. Ty Cobb went hitless in five plate appearances. Frank Chance made a statement for the newspapers after the game:

"I am proud of the way the boys went in and tied up the score in the ninth inning. It showed their spirit… It was a hard fight and a hard one to see wasted. We are up against a splendid team but we will win."

In addition to two passed balls, one of which allowed the Cubs to tie the game in the ninth, Detroit's Charlie Schmidt allowed seven stolen bases. Cobb lashed out at him in the clubhouse. "Damn you. Why didn't you hang onto that pitch, you dumb fucker?" Tiger owner W.H.Yawkey also came down hard on the backstop: "I never saw Schmidt catch such a game as he did today. His work was far below his usual standard and if he had been in condition we would have won." Days after the series concluded, Schmidt disclosed that he played the entire series with a broken bone in his throwing hand.

October 9, 1907 Chicago, Illinois

The Cubs were not discouraged by the results of the first game. Instead, they felt proud of their comeback from the brink of disaster in the ninth and their ability to run at will on the Tigers catcher. They trotted onto the field for game two wearing their normal white home duds, still soiled and wrinkled from the regular season. A number of the Cubs told the press boys that they felt more comfortable in these uniforms than they had in the stiff brand-new apparel they wore in game one.

Jack Pfiester took the mound for the Chicagoans, facing off against "Wabash" George Mullin, who went twenty and twenty in the regular season, a typical year for him. While Pfiester's won-loss record of 14-9 did not impress, his remarkable ERA of 1.15 led the league. Warmer air descended on Chicago, loosening up both teams. The fans squatting on planks along first and third base were required to remove their hats to preserve the views of the box seat holders, so they wrapped the tops of their heads in handkerchiefs to ward off the sunshine.

An hour prior to game time Frank Chance told Howie the mascot to sneak over to the Tigers bench and steal Ty Cobb's fabled black bat. Chance offered Howie two dollars for the bat, which Cobb sincerely believed to possess magical powers. Chance figured that a distraught Cobb would not play his normal game. Howie, a real go-getter, made several efforts but soon learned that Cobb did not keep the bat with the other players' lumber. He always kept it with him or in his sight. The Tigers mascot also informed Howie that if anyone even placed a finger on Cobb's black bat, they were in for the beating of their life. Howie, who possessed good judgment for a child, slinked away, never to return to the Tigers bench.

In the Cubs' half of the first, Jimmy Slagle found himself on third base, only ninety feet short of scoring the Cubs first run. After Tigers third baseman Bill Coughlin conferred with Mullin on the mound, Slagle edged off third with a small lead. Coughlin, who set up close to the bag, took one step toward Slagle and swiped at him with his glove. He showed the ball to the umpire (who was standing behind the pitcher), and the ump called Slagle out. The hidden ball trick. First and only time ever used successfully in the World Series. The Cubs should have known better, because Mullin had often used this trick. Slagle swore mightily at Coughlin, hung his head, and trudged toward the bench where a stunned silence greeted him.

At the end of three innings the score stood tied 1-1. The portly Tigers pitcher took a long time time between pitches, strolling off the mound, adusting his cap, tightening and loosening his belt. It was all designed to upset the batter's hitting rhythm, which it did, while also slowing the game considerably. The slow game upset league officials, and after the game the National Commission ordered umpires O'Day and Sheridan to crack down on any delays in the remainder of the Series.

Joe Tinker led off the fourth by bouncing a hit off pitcher Mullin's fingertips. After Mullin cursed himself loud enough for both benches to hear, Pfiester sacrificed Tinker to second from where he stole third on the new Tigers catcher, light-hitting Fred Payne. Jimmy Slagle, still smarting from his bonehead victimization in the first, sent a grounder out to the shortstop, Chicago native Charley O'Leary. O'Leary's neighbors raised a cheer when he fumbled the ball, allowing Tinker to score. Slagle then stole second and scored when Jimmy Sheckard sent a screaming line drive past first.

In the middle of the game Ty Cobb stood on first base, eyeing second. When the pitcher called time to repair his glove, Cobb stood on the foul line kicking at the first base bag. Not a nervous habit, Ty did this often because the bag, held to the ground by a spike and straps, moved an inch or two closer to second base once Ty finished with it. Just that much closer to a stolen base. That small distance might also mean the difference on a close pickoff play at first. But Frank Chance understood Cobb's game. He strolled over and kicked the base back to the foul line. "I take care of the housekeeping around first base," said Chance. Cobb did not reply.

The three runs held up as the Cubs again ran rampant, stealing five more bases on the substitute Tigers backstop. Johnny Kling, on the other hand, showed the Tigers the difference a good catcher can make, throwing out three Tigers who tried to steal.

Ty Cobb again was not a factor, gaining one hit on the day and no stolen bases. Superstitious, Cobb continued to tag second base as he jogged in from the outfield after each inning. But it did not help. While Pfiester gave up ten hits, he spread them out, and good defense, including two double plays, helped to hold the Tigers down.

When it was all over, Chance praised Pfiester in the clubhouse, and, while downing a beer, hollered, "We got 'em on the run, boys. We got the fuckers on the run."

❖   ❖   ❖

Seasoned vets like Harry Steinfeldt often had no truck with rookies like Heinie Zimmerman, especially when the youngster, as in Zimmerman's case, gunned for the veteran's job. But Steinfeldt liked Zimmerman. They were two peas in a pod. Both men were born of German immigrant parents, neither was particularly bright, and both showed a little roughness around the edges. Except on the diamond, where they shone. Differences did exist. Steinfeldt wore a permanent smile, and affected a happy-go-lucky persona. Zimmerman had a sneer etched into his face, and his words often dripped with a caustic sarcasm. And no Cub could match the size of Zimmerman's huge feet—size 16 clodhoppers!

Steinfeldt asked the rookie whether he wanted to go with him to the theater that night.

"I ain't no highbrow, Harry. Didn't know you was."

"I ain't talkin about that kind of theater," Harry explained. "You like girls, don'tcha?"

"Yeah. At least seven days a week."

"Well then, you'll like this theater, my young friend."

Steinfeldt and Zimmerman had dinner in the Loop and then caught the show at the Park Theater. Dozens of women dancing the Midway Dance, an all-nude revue that had been banned in New York. After the show the theater had a "wine room" where the naked dancers could be hired to perform other acts for small sums of cash. Zimmerman couldn't have been happier.

October 10, 1907 **Chicago, Illinois**

Bookmakers favored the Cubs at 7-5 to win all the marbles. Hughie Jennings, the Tigers first-year manager, took his customary position in the third base coacher's box, a picture of enthusiasm and confidence. The grinning Irishman, a law school graduate and old friend of John McGraw, started to hop on one leg and yell "Ee-yah!" before the first pitch. His usual routine. Five times he gyrated, shouting "Ee-yah!" at the top of his lungs. If nothing else, these cries irritated Steinfeldt fifteen feet away at third base. Jennings bent over to pull a handful of grass out of the ground, and then kicked some dirt toward Steinfeldt. Harry kicked back twice as much. Only 13,100 fans turned out, a much smaller crowd than the first two games, probably because the original schedule called for this game to be played in Detroit. The tie in game one changed those plans.

Chance gave Ed Reulbach the nod to start the third game, but he let Miner Brown warm up before the contest to test his still doubtful arm. Early in the warm-up he uncorked a wild pitch that hit a small girl, sitting in the first row, in her eye. Brown quit his tosses and sat by the child's side, relieved to see she was not seriously hurt.

"It's a battle of the Eds today," Charles Dryden told his twelve-year-old nephew in the press section. "Big Ed Reulbach versus the Tigers' Ed Siever, an eighteen-game winner and a lefty. Siever is famous for his 'Lady Godiva' pitch. It's got nothing on it!" The kid didn't get it.

Down in the clubhouse, Frank Schulte wore a big smile and nothing else.

"Why are you grinning like that?" asked Evers.

"I found four hairpins by the entrance to the clubhouse," he replied.

Evers, who had carefully placed the hairpins where Schulte found them, flashed a warm smile back to the Cubs slugger.

"Then you oughtta get four hits today, right?"

"Yessir. Gonna be a fine hitting day for me."

Ed Reulbach came out throwing hard. Ty Cobb, whose picture graced the cover of the latest issue of *Sporting Life*, stood waiting to hit in the second inning, twirling three bats at once. Evers, who had never seen a batter do this, took notice. When Steinfeldt ridiculed the move, Evers disagreed.

"It's a smart idea," said the little secondbagger. "When he dumps two of them bats his lumber is gonna feel lighter and faster."

Cobb took his place in the batter's box, assuming a slight crouch with his feet close together. A left-handed hitter, he kept a space between his hands on the black bat, allowing him to slide his left hand up six inches or so to execute a bunt. But not this time. Reulbach painted the edge of the plate with a fastball for strike one. The second pitch, a curveball, dropped from the sky and caught the inside corner of the plate, belt-high. Cobb swung and missed. The third pitch was a carbon copy of the second one, only six inches lower. The young Tiger missed again, striking out amidst a rising tide of cheers from the West Side fans. Cobb walked away from the plate shaking his head, marveling at the pinpoint control of the Cubs hurler. Fifty years later, Cobb still seethed about this three-pitch strikeout in his autobiography.

The Tigers managed only one scratch hit off of Reulbach in the first four innings. In the second, two ground-rule doubles by Steinfeldt and Evers netted a run, but the Cubs mounted their best attack of the day in frame four. With one out, Kling singled to right. Evers then lined his second hit of the day, also to right field, and Kling lumbered into third. Frank Schulte, confident on a four-hairpin day, singled to center, scoring Kling, but Evers got tagged out in a rundown trying to take third. Then Joe Tinker walloped a ball over the head of left fielder Davy Jones, near where the ropes contained the outfield crowd. Jones nearly bagged the long fly, but it bounced off his fingertips. Schulte skipped home while Tinker chugged around to third. When Big Ed chipped in a base hit, the third run of the inning came in, giving the Cubs a 4-0 edge. Given the stuff Reulbach was throwing, an insurmountable lead.

Detroit manager Jennings grew solemn and quiet in the chalked confines of the coacher's box. Reulbach only allowed one run on six hits all day, pitching exactly in the manner that earned him a 17-4 record in the regular season. Toward the end of the contest, which the Cubs won 5-1, Chance whispered to Evers, "It's a thing of beauty, Johnny," while Evers nibbled at his fingernails.

October 11, 1907 Detroit, Michigan

The fourth game of the 1907 World Series took place in Detroit's Bennett Park, across from the police station and the creamery on the corner of Trumball and Michigan avenues. A large, roofed grandstand stretched behind the diamond, from seventy feet beyond first base to sixty feet beyond third base, and bleachers ran farther down each of the foul lines. No seats existed in the outfield areas where the park dimensions extended deep, about 380 feet to left and right and 470 feet to straightaway center. A small ballpark, it could hold little more than eleven thousand, even crammed with people as today. In the adjoining backyards outside the ballpark, beyond the left-field wall, neighborhood entrepreneurs constructed "wildcat bleachers," complete with staircases, railings, and large advertising signs. A few years later, the Tigers management erected obstructions to block the views from these wildcat seats, but for the time being this venue provided a cheap alternative for a large number of penurious fans.

The Cubs went back to the new gray uniforms created for the games. By now the Cubs exhibited a raw confidence regardless of their garb.

The match-up today mirrored that in game one, Wild Bill Donovan versus Orvie Overall. Wild Bill earned his nickname by walking a lot of batters early in his career. Six years earlier he had given free passes to 152 hitters while still amassing twenty-five victories. During those years, Donovan's reputation for wildness caused opposing batters to wait for a walk. At this stage of his career, however, he had developed excellent control, and when he threw an inside pitch to Frank Chance in the first inning, it hit his target precisely. But Chance, as usual, stood his ground, and the fastball hit him on his hand, bloodying and numbing a finger. The Peerless Leader had the finger wrapped by Trainer Jack, and stole second base two pitches later. In the Tigers half of the first, Cobb bounced a lazy grounder to Tinker at short. Attempting to beat the throw, Cobb slid into first with his spikes high, just missing Chance's bandaged finger. Chance did not let it pass.

"Who the fuck do you think you are?" yelled Chance.

Cobb's eyes flashed as he replied, "Somebody you'll think twice about!"

In the bottom of the third inning, still a scoreless game, Wild Bill laced a sinking liner to Schulte in right field. Schulte raced in and grabbed the ball on a bounce, and pegged it to Chance at first base. Husk snagged the throw a half second before the Tigers pitcher crossed the bag, completing the rare 9-3 assist and putout. A surprised Donovan sheepishly returned to the Tigers bench.

The Cubs could not score in the top of the fourth, so when Ty Cobb came to bat with two gone in the bottom half, the score remained 0-0. The Detroit fans stirred to encourage their young star, and he responded, lashing a ball out to right-center between Schulte and Slagle. Tearing around first base, Cobb saw Evers set up at second to take the throw, with Tinker ten steps behind Evers, backing him up. As Cobb approached second, Evers, focusing intently on the ball in flight, heard the shout, "Tag him!" Cobb, in full stride, stepped on second and sped toward third. Evers grabbed the throw and swiveled around to swipe at what he thought would be a sliding Cobb, only to find thin air. He hesitated a moment before he realized that Cobb—not Tinker—had yelled at him, and pegged the ball to Steinfeldt at third, too late to get the sliding Tiger. Many years later Cobb bragged about this stunt:

I knew that Evers couldn't see Tinker and that if I hollered

"Tag him!" he'd figure Tinker was yelling. Then, when no one was there, he was thinking of Tinker, wondering why Joe yelled at him. And the split second he took to think about it gave me time to make it into third. It just didn't dawn on him that the voice he heard was mine. Sometimes a little suggestion can go a long way.

The Tigers capitalized on Cobb's move when the next batter, Rossman, knocked him in with a base hit. But the Cubs pushed across two runs in the fifth and exploded for three more in the seventh, in an inning built around two bunt hits. Overall grew tougher with every inning, giving up only six safeties and one run in the contest. When shortstop O'Leary flied out for the final out, the Cubs claimed a 6-1 victory and led the World Series three games to none. A cakewalk. The Tigers, dejected and demoralized, walked slowly to their clubhouse, realizing that they would now need to win four games in a row to take the Series. For all intents and purposes it was over.

October 12, 1907 **Detroit, Michigan**

A raw, bitterly cold day dawned in Detroit, reducing the crowd for the fifth game to 7,370. Those fans that did show up were garbed in heavy overcoats and black gloves. Frank Chance's swollen middle finger prevented him from sleeping after the third Cubs win. An x-ray in the morning revealed the finger to be dislocated. Doctors re-set it and placed it in a splint, but Chance could not play this game.

For two days Mordecai Brown begged Chance to let him pitch the fifth game, but the Cubs skipper would not commit. In fact, Chance waited until after batting practice to give Brown the nod, at which point Miner thanked the skipper for the opportunity.

"The writers are saying the Tigers stand a good shot to win this game because we would rather win the championship in Chicago," Husk mentioned.

"To blazes with that," replied Brown. "I'll finish 'em off today."

The Tigers threw George Mullin, whom the Cubs thrashed in the second game. Mullin walked the first batter, Rabbit Slagle. After Jimmy Sheckard flied out, Slagle tested the arm of another Tigers catcher, Jimmy Archer, a twenty-four-year-old native of Ireland. Slagle made it safely to second. The Cubs razzed the rookie Tigers backstop relentlessly.

Two years later Archer reminded them of this abuse when he joined the Cubs for a nine-year stint. After Del Howard struck out, Harry Steinfeldt came through with a single to center, scoring Slagle.

The Cubs played aggressively in their half of the second, still winning 1-0. Evers reached first base safely on an error by first baseman Rossman. After Schulte popped out to the catcher on an attempted sacrifice bunt, Joe Tinker pumped a solid single into left field, Evers taking second. Chance signaled for a double steal and Archer's low throw to third base did not do the job. When the air cleared, Evers and Tinker commanded third and second with one out. A rattled Mullin then walked Miner Brown to load the bases. Jimmy Slagle, a big plug of tobacco filling his mouth, then rolled a slow grounder out to Germany Schaefer at second, bringing in Evers to score the Cubs second run of the day.

The Tigers' fourth started with Wahoo Sam Crawford at the plate, a muscular lefty with legs as thick as tree trunks and a wide stance. The sour-faced Tiger squinted towards the mound, his left eye squinting appreciably more than the right. Crawford then picked on a Brown fastball and knocked a double down the right field line, bringing up Cobb. The crowd clapped, encouraging their young star. Brown bore down and fed Cobb nothing but curves. Three great breaking balls, two low and one right down the middle, seemed to break Cobb's back, and he stalked away from the plate shaking his head in disbelief. Two hours later Brown said, "I knew then I had him at my mercy." Rossman then solved Brown for a single to right, but Schulte got to the ball quickly and Crawford had to hold at third. The next batter, Coughlin, popped the ball behind the plate where Kling, almost falling into the stands, snagged it for the second out. Archer then came up to face Brown, who fed him a high fastball that resulted in a can of corn, stranding the Tigers runner at third.

That set the pattern for the rest of the game. The Tigers threatened, but Brown rallied to stifle all challenges. Or Johnny Kling came to the rescue. In the bottom of the sixth, Cobb stood several paces off second base, lusting for third. Joe Tinker tried a recent ploy, screaming to Cobb, "Don't get too far from the bag or the Jew will nip you!" Cobb flashed a look of contempt at Tinker, allowing Evers to sneak up to second base from behind, while Johnny Kling snapped off a throw to the bag. The play did not work this time, as Cobb scrambled back, safe by a hair. Emboldened by his good fortune, Cobb made off for third in a great burst of speed on the next pitch. Kling threw a perfect strike to Steinfeldt to nail the Tigers phenom by two feet.

Charlie Schmidt pinch-hit for Archer with two out and one on in the bottom of the ninth. Desperate to make amends for his miserable Series, the Tigers backstop lunged at a Brown curveball but got under it, popping the ball to Joe Tinker for the final out. Celebrating their first World Series Championship, the Cubs leaped with joy and ran quickly to the sidelines, anxious to make their way to their dressing room. The Tigers sulked off the field while a sad pall descended on the ballpark, interrupted only by an occasional Cubs rooter. Frank Chance, carried away by the moment, violated his own rule against fraternization. He waylaid former Cubs Germany Schaefer and Davy Jones as well as Tigers manager Jennings to shake their hands. He was warmly received.

In Chicago, outside the *Tribune* offices at Madison and Dearborn, more than eight thousand Chicagoans mobbed the streets to view the giant electric scoreboard. Police on horses struggled for a while to keep the streetcar tracks clear, and then abandoned the effort. At the final out, the crowd heaved with excitement and then gradually dissolved into the Loop. Cubs fans all over the city poured into saloons to imbibe what *Tribune* writer Charlie Dryden called "bug-juice."

The Cubs triumph marked the first World Series in which the victors did not lose a game. Ty Cobb, foolish enough to boast before the Series that he would rip the Cubs pitching, ended up with a .200 average. The young Tigers outfielder, who had stolen more bases in the '07 season than any player except Wagner, stole no bases in the World Series, a tribute to Johnny Kling's right arm. Cobb wasn't talking after the finale, but years later he said, "[T]hey taught me as much baseball in a short, painful time as any opponent I ever met." The Cubs—not Cobb—ran the bases with abandon, stealing sixteen bases off three different Tigers catchers. Jimmy Slagle alone stole six. But the Tigers catchers didn't deserve all the blame for the Cubs' great running game. Right-handers Donovan and Mullin did not effectively hold Cubs runners close to the bags. When lefty hurlers Siever and Killian took the mound, the Cubs did not steal a base.

The Bengals made ten errors in the five games while the Cubs committed only five. And the Cubs outscored them 19-6. Harry Steinfeldt hit .471 and Johnny Evers stroked seven hits for .350. But like the regular season, fine pitching proved the key to the Cubs coast to victory. Cubs pitchers gave up only four earned runs in five games for a Series ERA of 0.75.

A jubilant Husk addressed his teammates: "Gentlemen, we no longer stand in the shadow of Cap Anson. We now cast our own shadow." While his teammates horsed around, tossing wadded-up wet towels around like fat baseballs, Chance sat alone on a bench in the shabby dressing room, still in his uniform. Joe Tinker, wearing just a towel, sat down next to him and patted him on the back.

"It was a long journey, Husk. I wasn't always sure we would get to this place."

"I never doubted it, Joe."

Chance savored the moment. He pulled his pipe out of the locker and lit up, a trail of smoke curling around his arm. The Cubs manager would not long dwell on this success. That was not how his mind worked. There were new worlds to conquer. Another season to plan, and a good steak dinner before heading back to Chicago.

Returning to their hotel, every Cub except Evers, Ed Reulbach, and Johnny Kling proceeded to get drunk. Johnny Evers telephoned his mother to inform her of the Cubs victory. When Steinfeldt begged Evers to have a drink, Evers resisted, relaying what his mother had warned him, "Wine has drowned more men than the sea." Steinfeldt countered, "We ain't drinking wine. How about a beer?" The Crab, cognizant of the six-month gap before the next official game, gave in and took him up on the offer. Evers later reported, "We were invited to drink a little toast by almost everybody we met, and by train time most of the boys were looking for trains that were not on the schedule."

From the Journal of Kid Durbin

October 16, 1907

I got it today—my check from the Cubs for my share of the World's Championship Series. It was made out to Blaine A. Durbin, like all my paychecks from the Cubs. Only this one was for $2,300, bigger than my entire salary for the year! I feel a little guilty to be getting the same amount as Chance, Kling, Tinker, Evers, Steiny, and the rest of them. But that's the rule and I can sure put the money to good use. There's a million different ways I can spend it, but it makes more sense to just hang onto it for a while. It might come in handy, especially if Connie and I get hitched.

All the guys have different plans for their money. Frank Schulte told us he already spent his share, purchasing a chestnut gelding by the name of Billy Jeffrey from a woman here on the West Side of Chicago. He's going to ship the horse back east to his home in Syracuse. Johnny Evers will be sinking the money into inventory for his shoe store, and he has an idea for a new sign there—a bear cub devouring a tiger! Pat Moran wants to fund a chicken-house and will need to buy an incubator. Jack Pfiester knows where his dough is going—he just had a new baby back in Cincinnati, while Rabbit Slagle says he is considering an addition on his flour mill. The Rabbit aspires to be a captain of industry.

It came as no surprise to me that I did not get to play in the World's Series. Even Carl Lundgren and Chick Fraser did not get to throw. The closest I came was game three on Thursday when the Tigers slated lefty Ed Siever to pitch. Husk asked me to throw the batting practice because I'm a left-hander and our guys could get better prepared for the Tiger southpaw. Husk directed me to "cut loose with the smoke" and to mix some curves in as well, to make sure our guys were ready. With the new guy Frank Olis as receiver, I threw about as hard as I can, but the fellows, especially our Peerless Leader, teed off on a lot of my pitches. Jimmy Slagle hit two liners and then refused to continue, afraid he'd "use up" all the hits in his bat. While I threw my best stuff, I avoided crowding them like I would for real. Last thing I wanted to do was to nail one of my teammates that day. Still, I'm sure glad I'm not facing our boys anytime soon. We got five runs off Siever so maybe I helped out some, and it sure was fun to throw off that mound before a championship game.

I had a crew of rooters cheering me on in the batting practice. My father and brother came in for game two and stayed on for game three. My father said he was "right proud" of me and Howard said he wanted to grow up and pitch for the Cardinals. I told him he should consider the Cubs as they are a first-rate organization. Connie was there too—she attended all the games in Chicago. And Dr. and Alta Weiss took me up on my offer of tickets, sending me a telegram last month. They came in for Thursday's game and Mr. Murphy seated them right next to Connie in his box. Mr. Murphy also arranged for Alta to be introduced to the crowd before the game, right after Cap Anson. Connie seems a shade jealous about Alta. Ever since my trip to Cleveland she has asked me many questions about the Girl Wonder—and very few about Dr. Weiss. Maybe I shouldn't have told Connie about Alta's wet one.

On Friday, before the fourth game, I took a good look at Ty Cobb during the batting practice. Pretending to shag some balls, I trotted out halfway between home plate and third while he took some swings in the box. But I must of got into his field of vision because he pointed that black bat at me and shouted in his high pitched Dixie drawl, "Get yo' ass outta heah, Doo-bin!" I jumped, and wondered how in the hell he knew my name. We knew he had been scouting the Cubs back in St. Louis on the final day of the regular season, so he must of learned something about me then. Especially because I'm a southpaw, him being a lefty. Our boys were mighty satisfied to hold Cobb to five hits in the five games, and we're proud of the job Johnny Kling did on him, preventing the Georgian from stealing any bases. Kling's got an arm like a rifle, and he nailed Cobb and his teammates almost every time they got greedy on the base paths. Ty and me are the same age, but he's already proved himself while I have a ways to go. Still, from what I've seen and heard about the Georgia Peach, I wouldn't want to change places with him. He's got a mean streak from here to Kokomo. It's like there's a permanent chip on his shoulder, and he's

always trying to prove he's a better man than you. Even his own team-
mates don't seem friendly to him.

The train ride from Detroit to Chicago after the final game of
the Championship Series was a drunken revelry. Even Johnny Evers
downed some beers while the rest of us cut loose. We didn't ever have to
pull out our wallets because every bug on the train was buying us drinks.
When we reached Chicago there were hugs all around before we staggered
out of the station.

One of the local papers ran a story about the seven bachelors on
the Cubs with a picture of each of us—me, Johnny Evers, Pat Moran,
Frank Schulte, Orvie Overall, Artie Hofman, and Heinie Zimmerman.
The caption said, in big letters, "HERE THEY ARE, GIRLS." Connie
thought this to be "amusing." At least that's what she said.

Strange as it may seem, our work did not end until today, as the
boys scheduled one final exhibition game. All the World's Champions—
that's us—made it out for this one except Johnny Kling, who is back
in Kansas. Our opponents were Jimmy Callahan's All Stars, a team
composed of some former major leaguers like Turkey Mike Donlin, Jake
Stahl, and some semipro players. Jimmy "Nixey" Callahan used to pitch
for the Cubs before the turn of the century. In fact, Frank Chance, still
a catcher for the West Siders then, served as a battery-mate of Callahan
in those days. When Nixey blew out his arm, he became a decent hitting
outfielder for the White Sox. Callahan and Husk talked about "the old
times" before the game, but Chance couldn't play on account of his finger
still ached. Burt Keeley, an Illinois boy who has never pitched in the big
leagues, matched off against Orvie Overall. Turkey Mike interested me
the most, because my teammates said he was a tough competitor against
us in years past. Mike wore his cap high on the back of his head so the
ladies could see his handsome face. He chewed on a big plug of tobacco
and Shorty Slagle told me the two-inch scar on Mike's right cheek was
the product of a knife fight. A woman was involved. McGraw has been
pressing Turkey Mike to return to the New York ballclub and the scuttle-
butt is that Mike will be back.

Since Jeff Overall pitched against an unknown, you can guess the
results. Overall blanked the All-Stars in a five inning game and we won

2-0. I hugged the bench for this one as I did most of the year, but I still enjoyed watching our well-oiled machine roll on once again.

Now that my first big league season is over, I have to be honest about the results. While we won the championship of the world, my contributions were small. I had some good outings, but only pitched sixteen innings and haven't earned my first victory. Still, I am only twenty-one years old and next year offers unlimited possibilities. I am optimistic that I will be able to prove myself in the coming campaign.

December 14, 1907   Chicago, Illinois; "Chicago Ain't No Sissy Town!"

There was good reason that the facade of the Chicago Coliseum looked like a turreted, medieval dungeon. Its walls of 200,000 hewed stones once constituted the front of Libby Prison in Richmond, Virginia, a notorious stockade for Union soldiers. The Coliseum could hold fifteen thousand people and occupied an entire city block on 15th Street and Wabash, very close to the Levee District. The immense structure housed national political conventions, farm machinery exhibitions, and many a circus. This night it served as the site of the Tenth Annual First Ward Ball, a bacchanal that would put fifty thousand dollars into the pockets of Hinky Dink Kenna and his portly partner, Bathhouse John Coughlin.

Tickets to the ball sold out early, as it promised—and delivered—sex and free-flowing booze under the protective auspices of the City of Chicago. Moreover, Alderman Kenna himself developed a quota system that required every crook, pimp, madame, whore, cop, thief, and saloon keeper in the First Ward to purchase tickets. While cops only had to purchase one ticket, saloon owners' quotas were tied to the size of their enterprise. Ward workers kept detailed lists of the buyers, lists that would be scrutinized later when favors were asked of the alderman. In addition to every local criminal, the ball attracted many city and state politicians, well-to-do Chicagoans, and other thrill-seekers. This would be the first time in seven years that Percy McGill would not be in attendance.

By nightfall, crowds of the curious mobbed the entrances to the Coliseum, straining for a look at those fortunate enough to possess a ticket. The ball was an ornate masquerade, allowing women to don provocative costumes that bared more than they covered. Over two thousand prostitutes wore exotic costumes, with Gypsy, Native American, Egyptian, or just plain erotic themes. Men wore their finest evening wear and a five-cent black mask. A cadre of police officers escorted each group of masked women from the Coliseum entrance to their private box or reserved table. Inside, a security force of three hundred bouncers, police, and ushers tended to the reveling crowds, occasionally dragging a pair of dueling drunks outside the gates where they could resume their hostilities.

Everything before midnight was simply a warm up, like batting practice at the ballpark. Two bands of musicians played while two hundred waiters served seventy thousand pints of beer and ten thousand chilled bottles of champagne. Hinky Dink and Coughlin paid bargain rates for the alcohol, but the partygoers paid premium prices to indulge. Festivities gradually built to a crescendo just before the stroke of midnight, when Ada and Minna Everleigh arrived in a carriage pulled by a team of matched bay horses. Escorted into the Coliseum by a uniformed retinue, the sister madams dazzled the expectant crowd in exquisite silken gowns and glittering jewelry saved for this occasion. A procession led them to the dance floor of the auditorium, where they linked up with Bathhouse John. The alderman, in his glory this night, sported lavender trousers, a white waistcoat brocaded with pink and red carnations, and a deep green swallowtail coat with forked tails. He accessorized with a dainty pair of pink gloves, footwear consisting of yellow pumps, a blazing red sash across his chest, and a silk top hat with a lime green hatband, perched precariously on his silver-gray pompadour. He linked arms with the Everleighs, one on each side, and with the help of a small battalion of police officers, the threesome pushed its way to the center of the dancefloor where Bathhouse John proclaimed, "On with the march!" as the band burst into a raucous rendition of "Hail, Hail, the Gang's All Here."

The "March" was a sight to be seen, and an encouragement for the crowd to cut loose. As the band shifted to a song written by Bathhouse John himself, "Dear Midnight of Love," two thousand of the most drunken or exhibitionist denizens of the Levee strutted, twenty abreast, around the auditorium floor, waving, gyrating, and staggering to the appreciative applause of the throngs surrounding them. Petty criminals, burglars, pickpockets, horse thieves, and blackmailers strolled proudly right behind Alderman Coughlin. Next came the madams, pimps, and a thousand prostitutes, some shedding their masks and garments as the cheers grew lustier. Dozens of female impersonators danced in the line. All marched arm-in-arm with a liberal sprinkling of police officers, state legislators, and state court judges. After a few minutes, Bathhouse John, arms raised above his head, pivoted and led the parade while marching backwards, the better to enjoy the delights of the procession.

Bathhouse John soon slipped out of the frenzied, smoke-filled Coliseum, as he always did after the march, but the party had just ignited into what the next day's *Chicago Record-Herald* called "a riot of unbridled license." The river of beer and champagne dissolved any remnants of civility and manners. The dancing grew wild and abandoned. Pushing and shoving escalated to fistfights and brawls such that the police had their hands full in removing the combatants. Dozens of women stripped naked and danced on tabletops, while some couples crawled under the tables or into the reserved boxes to have sex. Drag queens openly performed a variety of sex acts without interference from the police or the bouncers. Scores of women and a few men, fainting from the heat or the thick stench of tobacco smoke, were passed over the heads of the crowd, hand to hand, toward the exits. Liquored up ruffians literally ripped the clothes off some women whose screams simply melded with the madness in the hall. The waiters did not stop serving liquor until 3:00 a.m. when most of the remaining crowd lay passed out on the floor or in their chairs, some couples locked naked in each other's arms, dead to the world. Only the pickpockets remained alert and busy at this hour. The next day the *Tribune* editorialized: "If a great disaster had befallen the Coliseum last night, there would not have been a second-story worker, a dip or plug-ugly, porch climber, dope fiend or scarlet woman remaining in Chicago." When other reformers attacked the ball, Bathhouse John grew defiant: "All right, we'll compromise. We won't let parents bring their children." Hinky Dink, who left even before the Grand March, nevertheless vehemently defended the ball: "Chicago," said Alderman Hinky Dink Kenna, "ain't no sissy town!"

December 30, 1907 New York City, New York; "An American Dad"

It started as a long-running, friendly argument between A.G. Spalding and Harry Chadwick. It ended on December 30, 1907, with the issuance of the Mills Commission Report, and the establishment of an official myth—a fairy tale to explain the origins of the game of baseball.

A.G. Spalding possessed a magnificent baseball pedigree. A pioneer pitcher who once threw for Cap Anson and the Chicago White Stockings, he later purchased the team but finally realized that more money could be made in manufacturing sporting goods. Every National League baseball bore his name. Harry Chadwick was the dean of American sportswriters, a baseball historian, and influential in the development of American baseball after 1858. Born in England, Chadwick published an essay contending that the game of baseball had its roots in the English games of rounders and cricket, games he had played in London as a youth. The essay infuriated Spalding, who insisted that baseball had a pure American lineage. Or, as he wrote to another sportswriter, "Our good old American game of base ball must have an American Dad."

Spalding, in 1904, threw down a challenge to Chadwick. "Let us appoint a commission to search everywhere that it is possible and thus learn the real facts concerning the origin and development of the game," Spalding proposed. "I will abide by such a commission's findings regardless."

And so the Mills Commission came into being in 1905. Spalding wanted to make sure that the commission reached the "right" decision, so he carefully hand-picked each member of the body. He selected Abraham G. Mills, former president of the National League, to chair the commission, but only after he confirmed that Mills already believed in a solely American origin of baseball. Knowing the views of James Sullivan, an employee of Spalding, he designated him secretary of the body. Spalding also selected another sporting goods manufacturer, Al Reach, for membership on the commission, aware that Reach also believed that baseball originated in America. Soon after being named to the commission, Reach wrote a letter to a friend asking him to send Secretary Sullivan a missive: "[M]ake up something as strong as you can proving the game is of Am[erican] origin." Spalding carefully excluded certain persons from the commission. When he learned that pioneering ballplayer John Lowell put some stock in Chadwick's view, Lowell failed to gain a slot on the body.

The commission, mainly Sullivan, began its work. The members did not have the capacity or inclination to engage in their own research. Rather, they simply solicited information from the American public through a series of newspaper and sporting magazine articles. While this became a nationwide effort, no such inquiry took place in England.

In April of 1905, in response to one of the advertisements placed by the commission, Abner Graves, a frail seventy-one-year-old Denver mining engineer, directed a letter to the members. That correspondence changed forever the way people thought about the origin of baseball.

Graves declared how his schoolmate Abner Doubleday made refinements to the game of "town ball," transforming it into baseball. It all happened, according to Graves, in Cooperstown, New York, in 1839, after a marble game behind a tailor shop. Town ball, as Graves described it, had one player tossing a ball to another player who would hit it with a flat bat. More than twenty players, distributed haphazardly about the field, tried to catch the ball before the batter could reach a goal fifty feet from where he started. Doubleday, according to Graves, dramatically changed the rules. His first modification was the most important—he made it a team game, with two opposing squads. He then limited the number of players on each side to eleven, and placed the pitcher in a six-foot ring. Graves claimed that Doubleday also devised a diamond-shaped field with a base at each corner and named the game "base ball."

Spalding celebrated when he learned of the testimony of Abner Graves. "It certainly appeals to an American's pride," he wrote, "to have had the great national game of Base Ball created and named by a Major-General in the United States Army."

Neither Sullivan nor Mills nor any member of the commission

ever met with or corresponded with Abner Graves. No one investigated or tested Graves' claims in any way. Yet based entirely on this single source, with no corroborating evidence, the Mills Commission issued a report concluding that "the first scheme for playing [baseball], according to the best evidence obtainable to date, was devised by Abner Doubleday at Cooperstown, N.Y. in 1839." While Chadwick scorned the report, the American public accepted its conclusion unequivocally as a simple, popular resolution to the question of baseball's genesis.

It is now clear that the Mills Commission erred in accepting without question the recollections of Abner Graves. Graves described an event that allegedly took place sixty-six years earlier, when he would have been only five years old. Abner Doubleday, moreover, did not attend school in Cooperstown in 1839—in fact he never attended school there. Doubleday, who would later fire the Union Army's first shot at Fort Sumter, had just enrolled in West Point Military Academy where he spent 1839. In his memoirs, he discussed his early years but never once mentioned baseball. Doubleday died in 1893, after baseball had achieved a great popularity, and none of his friends or relatives ever related that the general claimed to have invented the national pastime. In fact, it developed that Mills himself served as a close confidant of General Doubleday for over thirty years, and the general never mentioned any association with baseball to Mills during that time, which included the years Mills served as the chief executive of the National League. Simply put, the Mills Commission's reliance on the addled memory of an old man constituted either gross ineptitude or an act of fraud.

Spalding, a manufacturer of baseballs, single-handedly manufactured a Great American Myth. A myth that is still believed in some quarters, and which resulted in baseball's Hall of Fame being placed in Cooperstown.

From the Journal of Kid Durbin

When I played my last professional baseball game in 1909, I stopped following baseball at the major league level. Not for any particular reason, it just worked out that way. I attended a few Cardinal games in St. Louis but nothing more than that. I turned to earning a living, and to my wife Connie and our son. But they are both gone now. I am alone, and my thoughts have turned back to the preoccupations of my youth. At the age of seventy-nine, it seemed like the right time to journey back. To see the game and the Cubs as they are today. All my teammates are dead now, except for Heinie Zimmerman, the one guy I could not stand. But the need bubbled up in me. There is something deeply satisfying about this game of ball. It was time to go back and watch the young men who are still called Cubs play the same game I enjoyed so many years ago.

On a warm Saturday morning I took a train from Indianapolis to Chicago's Union Station. I walked five or six blocks, boarded the subway in the Loop, and headed north toward Howard Street. A bent old man—actually he was younger than me—told me to get off at Addison Street. The train stayed underground for fifteen minutes and then emerged into the sunlight, the elevated train snaking just a few feet from the back windows and gray-painted porches of the North Side. They tore down the West Side Grounds long ago. For fifty years the Cubs have played in Wrigley Field, and that is where I traveled on this scorcher of a day. The Cubs no longer are the powerhouse of the National League. In fact, they are the doormat, finishing eighth out of ten last year, and this year they appear destined to do worse. But this made it easy for me to get a fine box seat near the Cub's dugout, close enough to the field for me to get a feel for the game. Only about six thousand folks attended, even though Wrigley holds thirty thousand or so. I sat there like any other bug, not telling anyone in the organization who I am (or was). Not that anyone would remember or believe me even if I told them. I sat there with a bottle of

Sprudel Water that I had to sneak in because glass bottles are no longer allowed inside the park.

This Wrigley Field is a beautiful ballpark, much nicer than the Grounds or any of the other places we played. I entered a main gate at Clark and Addison, finding myself in a dark, low ceilinged concourse. When I walked up the short flight of stairs from the darkness down below, the great expanse of green grass, blue sky, and white clouds grabbed a hold of me, taking my breath away. I had entered heaven. Then the crack of the bat brought me back, followed by the weird calls of the vendors ("cold beeeyarrr heeeyarr!"), and the rumblings of the fans. I bought an Oscar Mayer brand hot dog from a vendor named Irving who had only two teeth, squeezed some mustard on it from a little plastic sack, and sat in my fourth-row seat to observe the Cubs take the batting practice.

Since I never followed the Cubs or big league baseball much after I left the playing field, I did not recognize any of the ballplayers other than Ernie Banks, the Cubs big star of the fifties who was still around. Ernie looked like a utility infielder, slim and unremarkable in build. But in the batting practice I watched him drive three balls into the Wrigley Field bleachers and catwalk, all low line drives with a perfect little arc, sailing cleanly about 340 feet. Banks owns the quickest wrists I have ever seen, even faster than Frank Schulte! He uncoiled so fast that the ball shot into the bleachers, a perfectly patterned path for this ballpark. Ernie is a black man—the biggest and best change since my playing days. Twenty years ago the owners finally let black men compete in our national game.

The Cubs pitcher, a lefty named Dick Ellsworth, started out fine but weakened, and the Cardinals pounded him in the eighth inning. A Cards outfielder, Lou Brock, showed some speed, and poked a home run, too. This young fellow sitting next to me said Brock played for the Cubs 'til the "Cubs gave him away to the Cards a few years back."

I am puzzled how these Cubs can be doing so poorly because I saw some fine young talent. They have a third baseman, Ron Santo, who is a crisp fielder and looks solid at the plate. Then there is the right fielder, a young lefty by the name of Billy Williams, who smashed a home run. You have to see his splendid swing to appreciate its smooth stroke and perfect mechanics. The Cubs double-play combination, Don Kessinger and Glenn Beckert, while no Tinker and Evers, are still first-rate. To top it all off, a young right-hander, Ferguson Jenkins, a black man from Canada, came in to pitch late in the game. While he got nicked for a homer, he sure knew how to throw a fastball. If these Cubs could pick up some more pitching they might make a mark.

The game took twice as long as our games used to, mainly because the pitchers puttered around between pitches and both sides took a lot of time bringing in new twirlers every time one got in a jam. The delays in the game got on my nerves. In my day Husk would use a swingman like Miner Brown or Jack Pfiester maybe once a week. Now they call these fellows "relief pitchers," and they are a regular part of most games. When it was all over the Cubs ended up getting pounded 9-4.

I loafed around the ballpark for an hour before a blue-uniformed "Andy Frain" usher politely asked me to leave. When I got near the el train half a block from the field, one of the Cubs, a big outfielder by the name of George Altman, was signing an autograph for a twelve-year-old boy. As George turned to enter the station, he tumbled over a small kid behind him. As they fell, George took particular care to avoid injuring the boy. They both laughed, and George signed the child's program. It reminded me of a Charlie Chaplin bit. I boarded the train and sat down next to George for the ride back toward the Loop. Tall and muscular, he told me that he taught school during the off-season. A quiet man who lived on the South Side with his family, George was an All-Star for the Cubs a few years back but now his career was on the wane. He confessed to me he was exploring the possibility of playing ball in the Far East and laughed when I said, "New York?" He meant Japan. I wished him well when I got off at the Jackson stop. Nice guy.

From the Journal of Kid Durbin

May 11, 2004

Of course it was the Sprudel Water. Figured that out about seventy years ago. At 118 years of age, I am what Harry Steinfeldt used to call "a regular Mefoolsalot." The Sprudel Water kept me young and spry until 1996 when I finally ran out of the stuff. I had no difficulty getting the water until some goddam Jesuits bought the West Baden Springs Hotel in the nineteen-sixties. The first thing those idiots did was to remove the huge turrets from the hotel and pave over Spring No. 7. I don't care one way or the other about the turrets, but covering up Spring No. 7 with a ton of earth has got to be about the stupidest thing they could have done. The Jesuits said that the Lord didn't want people "wallowing in mineral waters and imbibing sulphurous liquids." Where in the hell does it say that in the Bible? These morons literally dried up my source of Sprudel Water, my fountain of youth! As soon as I used up my last crate I began to age.

When the Jesuits sold the hotel twenty years ago, I traveled back to West Baden to talk to the new owners, a well-meaning bunch of do-gooders intent on fixing up the hotel. I found a crew digging at Spring No. 7. But to no avail—Spring No. 7 could not be resurrected. The geologists could not find a trickle, so the magical waters were lost. The strange thing is, they call this part of Indiana the Valley of the Lost Rivers. Well, them priests lost another one! Sprudel Water, and an old competitor called Pluto Water, are still sold, but they don't come from Spring No. 7, and don't even taste the same. Believe me, I'm an expert! And they sure as hell don't keep you young like the real Sprudel Water did.

But I'm over it. As one of those Beatles said, "All things must pass," and that includes me. I had a long life, a loving wife, and a wonderful child. And through some amazing jest of fate, the Cubs paid me good money to play baseball for two years on the best team ever. Those two years I truly heard the music of the spheres. And the harmony of perfec-

482
THE BEST TEAM EVER

tion. And glory be to God, I was part of it! Frank Chance assembled this magnificent group of ballplayers, worked them into shape, and guided them to four pennants and two world championships. Maybe the Sprudel Water had something to do with it. The Cubs never again attained that kind of success.

I played another season with the Cubs, 1908, and what a wild ride that campaign was, what with Merkle's boner, a playoff for the pennant, and another great World Series triumph over the Tigers. While I hung on in the majors for a year and a half after '07, my left arm just sort of gradually petered out, so I couldn't whip the ball as fast as before. Husk figured this out in the spring of 1908, and I never again pitched in the big leagues. I played some outfield for the Cubs in 1908 and again sat on the bench for the Series. Just before the '09 season opened, I mouthed off to the press about not getting to play, so Mr. Murphy traded me to the Reds. I didn't see much action with them—just pinch-hitting four or five times. But in one of those at bats I faced up against the Cubs and—honest to God—Miner Brown! I gritted my teeth and went up swinging but his curveball made me look silly. Best I can say is that I didn't whiff. I managed to get a piece of the ball and squirted an easy grounder for an out. I flashed a little smile to Brownie running back to the dugout and he gave me a wink. Not long after that the Reds swapped me to the Pirates. The owner there, Barney Dreyfuss, always thought highly of me. While the Pirates of '09 went all the way, winning the World's Championship Series, I just hugged the bench for a month or so before they realized my arm was gone and dropped me. I caught on as an outfielder with the Omaha team back in the Western Association but in a few years my professional baseball career was over.

I have one fond memory of my brief service with the Pittsburgh Pirates, and that involves Honus Wagner, greatest shortstop in the history of the game and a wonderful human being. My first week with the Bucs, the Dutchman took me and our hotel elevator operator on a tour of Smoky City bars in his huge Jackson automobile, which had a squirrel tail hanging from the front lantern for good luck. The barkeeps in most of the places we went that night idolized Wagner, so we drank for free. Things was different then than now—there wasn't this wall of money between the players and the public. Wagner was a good example of this. One of the best players of the time, he was a man of the people, sharing a beer and telling his yarns to all that crossed his path.

I can't exactly say I tore up the league my last two years, riding the bench as I did. But if you look me up in a statistics book you'll see I went fourteen for fifty-one in my three years in the big time, a .275 batting average. Hell, some kids get millions of dollars nowadays for that kind of production! I tell you, it was great fun while it lasted.

Connie and me got hitched in 1908 and enjoyed a wonderful life together. In fact her father, Mike Fitzgerald, married us. Connie never did tell me the whole story about Mike, but I did learn that he disappeared out of her life when she was little and somehow re-appeared shortly before we wed. I do know that alcohol had taken him away from his family. But by 1908 he had forsaken the bottle and become a man of the cloth, a deacon working with Billy Sunday. He spent most of his days helping those who still suffered under the spell of John Barleycorn. When our son, Frank Robert Durbin, was born in 1911, Connie's father baptized him—with Billy Sunday himself assisting. Deacon Mike lived long enough to see Frank grow into a fine little pitcher in the fifth grade. We had every reason to be proud of our son. A kind, generous kid, he never gave us any real reason to worry. I became a baseball coach at a small college in St. Louis, and ultimately became the athletic director. The fact that I played ball for the World's Champion Chicago Cubs didn't hurt me none in these endeavors.

I insisted that Connie drink the Sprudel Water every day and it kept her young like me. Tried innumerable times to get my father to take the water also, but he flat-out refused. He passed in 1919, a victim of the cancer. Connie and I figured we would have some trouble explaining our youthful appearances to our friends and relatives as the years went by. But the water could not protect us from other perils. Connie lost her life in an automobile wreck in 1940 when she was fifty-three years old. The county coroner had a hard time accepting her birth certificate, saying she couldn't have been a day over thirty. But he finally relented. Grief paralyzed me for a long time. God, how I still miss her! But Connie and I had thirty-three wonderful years together. There were many heavenly *days—it'll be hard for God's heaven to beat those. Most folks don't get as lucky as I have been.*

My son Frank is gone too, killed in an aviation accident in the service in 1942. His commanding officer in the Army Air Corps told me Frank witnessed a plane crash and died while trying to pull someone out of the burning wreckage. After getting the news, I was blue as a white man can be—alone in the world and a nasty war raging. I got to thinking that my life was all about losing the people I loved the most. But I came to accept that's just the way of things. Saying goodbye is a big part of life. Ma used to say, "Life is like a never-ending party. You arrive in the arms of a woman but you leave alone. You'll meet lots of people at this party and come to love a good number of them. You'll have to say goodbye to some of these folks when they leave. And sooner or later it will come time for you to leave the festivities behind. The thing to remember is to enjoy the party."

In 1943, I started a new life by killing off Blaine "Kid" Durbin and taking a new name. Assuming a new identity in those days was a snap. I had resumed my friendship with my childhood buddy, Bucky Gunderson, by then the president of the Gunderson Funeral Home and Mortuary in Kirkwood, Missouri. I asked Bucky to pretend to bury me and he agreed, no questions asked. So you can visit my grave there, in St. Peter's Cemetery in Kirkwood, Missouri, as I have done on one occasion, but nobody lies beneath that hundred-dollar tombstone. I left St. Louis and settled into a new life in Indianapolis, where I started my own public relations firm, working for small savings and loan institutions. Mainly preparing press releases when the institution opened a new branch or when they celebrated their fiftieth year. Didn't get rich but I made a living.

I adopted a new name, Durbin Blaine. Just reversing my names like that wasn't too creative. In fact, that's what enabled those two writer fellows, Alop and Noel, to track me down. Alop said he found me on something called Google, and investigated just for the hell of it. Imagine his surprise when he located me alive after all these years. He nearly passed out when I answered the door—he recognized me right off the bat. I eventually spilled the beans to him about the Sprudel Water and all, a

secret I kept for almost a century. These two authors, real nice fellows al-
though a little too wild for my taste, asked my permission to publish parts
of my journal in the book they were writing about the 1907 Cubs. Their
timing was pretty good, because I had just read a science fiction paperback
novel about another world where the law required that a person be totally
forgotten when they died. Machines called "time scrubbers" removed all
record of the deceased's existence while social conventions and the law
did not permit any references to the life or deeds of the dead. History was
illegal. We don't live in a world like that, but we do let too much of our
history slip away. While lots of folks have heard the names Tinker, Evers,
and Chance, not one out of a hundred baseball fans could tell you a sliver
about the 1907 Cubs. So I figured the book might open a few eyes and
I gave the authors the go-ahead to use my journal. So far they have not
disappointed me. I sure hope that folks enjoy reading my part of this his-
tory. I always tried to set things down straight and true.

A couple weeks ago, these two author fellows took me out to the
place where the West Side Grounds stood back then. Polk Street, Wood,
Taylor Street, and Lincoln—although now Lincoln has been renamed
Wolcott in that area for some reason. All I could see as we approached the
former home of the Cubs was building after building, every one of them
occupied by the University of Illinois Hospital. No monument marks the
spot of the old Grounds. Folks walking in the area—mainly white-shirt-
ed doctors with pagers—have no idea that this site was the home of the
best team ever. But if you take a look, hidden behind all the structures,
there's a small, peaceful, and secluded courtyard, with grass and a few
little trees. By my reckoning, that open space just happens to include a
scrap of earth that used to be the diamond of the West Side Grounds. So I
found the spot where the pitcher's mound lay some hundred years ago and
stood there real quiet, peering straight up at the sky. For a brief instant
I was back in 1907, preparing to pitch to a ferocious batter with hammy
fists wrapped around a thick hunk of lumber. Then the moment passed.
Like it always does.

When I started a family, I did not have the time to spend on my
journal. One item that did not end up in my journal is that I stumbled
across Frank Chance in 1923, a year before he passed at the age of forty-

seven. I told him I named my son after him, and he invited me to have a drink. We downed a beer together in a restaurant in Los Angeles and he treated me as if I had been one of his star players. First thing he says to me is, "You haven't aged a day!" That was true, thanks to the Sprudel Water, but I just told him it came from clean living. That was my usual response. He introduced me to the restaurant's owner as "the man who threw a perfect strike when it really meant life or death."

We shot the shit for an hour, punctuated by bugs who came up and begged an autograph from Husk. He complied with friendly banter. At the end of our reminiscing, we walked together to catch our taxicabs, and he draped his arm across my shoulder. I told him I regretted that my contribution was so small, that I never developed to my full potential.

Chance said, "It's a team effort. Every man plays a role."

I said, "Husk, I was just along for the ride."

He looked me straight in the eye and said, "We're all just along for the ride, Kid."

EPILOGUE

The 1906 Cubs achieved the best winning percentage of any baseball team, but the White Sox humiliated them in the World Series. The 1908 Cubs barely beat the Giants, with a strange twist of fate and a playoff game getting them to the World Series. But the 1907 Cubs finished seventeen games ahead of runner-up Pittsburgh, and won the World Series easily. Largely due to a great pitching staff, this team was the best ever. Their opponents only scored 370 runs, eleven fewer than the 1906 Cubs allowed. The Earned Run Average (ERA) statistic was not widely used until the 1940s. When the baseball statisticians went back and calculated the team ERA for the 1907 Cubs, it came out at a phenomenal 1.73, the lowest team ERA in baseball history. Five out of the top six lowest individual ERAs in 1907 were by Cubs: Pfiester 1.15, Lundgren 1.17, Brown 1.39, Overall 1.68, and Reulbach 1.69. Of the career ERAs by pitchers with at least one hundred victories and one thousand innings pitched since 1900, three of the top twenty-eight all-time started for the 1907 Cubs:

> *No. 6 Brown*   *2.06*
> *No. 13 Overall* *2.23*
> *No. 16 Reulbach 2.28*

If Pfiester and Lundgren had won one hundred games, they too would have made this list, with career ERAs of 2.02 and 2.42. This remarkable stable of pitchers earned the Cubs another World Championship in 1908, and lays claim to the title of the most dominating staff ever—an accomplishment even more amazing given Frank Chance's refusal to sign spitballers. Between 1906 and 1910 the Cubs won the National League pennant every year except 1909, the year star catcher Johnny Kling held out for better pay, devoting himself instead to pool, and winning the pocket billiards championship of the world.

Four of the 1907 Cubs made the Hall of Fame (Brown, Evers, Tinker, and Chance), and a good argument can be made for the inclusion of three more—Reulbach, Kling, and Schulte.

So what ever happened to...

FRANK LEROY CHANCE

Frank "Husk" Chance often gave Johnny Evers the credit for "gluing" the team together, but it was the players' intense loyalty to the Peerless Leader that bound them into a solid unit. Once described as a "hulking genius with 10 broken fingers," the burly first baseman stuck with the Cubs until Charles Murphy fired him in 1912, charging that Husk let his players carouse and drink alcoholic beverages. Murphy, however, didn't complain about booze and broads when Frank led the Cubs to four pennants and two World Championships. Chance stole an amazing 401 bases in his career. In fact, from 1900 to 1909 only one legendary base path artist—Honus Wagner—stole more bases than the ever-battling Cubs player-manager. Husk developed an excellent glove at first base, and his career batting average was a fine .296. After leaving the Cubs he managed the New York Highlanders (Yankees) for two years and the Red Sox for one year before he died in 1924. When he realized he was dying, Chance asked both Tinker and Evers to come to the Pacific Coast to visit one last time. Husk's motivation in summoning his former double-play combo to California had as much to do with repairing their relationship as it did with making his farewells. They both made the trip, and it marked the first time Tinker and Evers had spoken off the diamond since 1905. Tinker, Evers and Chance—a "trio of bear Cubs"—were voted into the Hall of Fame as a unit in 1946.

Frank Schulte.

Frank "Wildfire" Schulte played most of his great career with the Cubs. One of the first free-swinging power hitters, he led the National League in home runs in 1910 and 1911. His sterling performance in 1911—twenty-one homers, 107 RBIs, and a .300 average—made him the first recipient of the Chalmers Award, the equivalent of the MVP. It also marked the first time in the twentieth century that a major leaguer broke the twenty home run mark. Schulte smashed four grand-slam home runs that season, and became the first man to reach at least twenty doubles, triples, homers, and stolen bases in one year. He performed well in four World Series, averaging .321. Schulte possessed all the skills of a superstar. In addition to his great hitting, he stole home plate twenty-two times in his career, and reportedly had the best outfield arm of the decade. A fine fielder, Schulte's .976 fielding average from 1900-1909 ranked first in the big leagues. In the spring of 1908, he acquired the nickname "Wildfire" after one of his horses, who Schulte had named in honor of a stageplay starring Lillian Russell, whom he adored. After his last year in the majors in 1918, Frank played minor league ball with Baltimore, Toronto, Binghamton, Syracuse, Atlanta, and Oakland until he retired in 1923 at age forty. He lived until 1949.

Jno. G. Kling.

Johnny Kling deserves to be in the Hall of Fame. He was regarded by his contemporaries (outside of New York City where Roger Bresnahan caught) as the best catcher in the major leagues between 1902 and 1908. Not so long ago, respected baseball historian Donald Honig wrote a book, *The Greatest Catchers of All Time*, and Kling was among the fifteen subjects chosen. Rifle-armed Kling proved a solid hitter, a great defensive catcher, a smart backstop who consistently outguessed hitters, and a remarkably effective receiver/mentor to the Cubs pitchers. When young pitchers like Overall, Pfiester, and Three Finger Brown joined the Cubs, two things happened: they won more games and their ERAs dropped. While the excellent Cubs defense contributed greatly, Johnny Kling's role cannot be disputed. Honus Wagner rated him the best catcher ever. Walter Johnson chose two best catchers of all time: Kling or Bill Dickey. Anti-Semitism may have played a role in keeping Kling out of the Hall of Fame. After his death, his wife Lillian (herself Jewish) denied that Johnny was Jewish in a futile effort to help his candidacy. Once she claimed he was a Baptist while years later she said he was a Lutheran.

In 1909, the year that Kling took off from the Cubs to pursue the billiard championship and other business interests, he organized a semipro baseball team in Kansas City, "Johnny Kling's All Stars." The All Stars traveled to Chicago in September 1909 to play a series of games, including one against the legendary black team, the Leland Giants. Chick Fraser on the mound and Kling nailing two would-be base stealers did not stop the Giants, who smashed the All Stars 6-1. Johnny turned from baseball to a number of business interests after the 1913 season. He purchased the American Association's Kansas City Blues in 1935, and immediately eliminated the segregated seating policy at the ballclub's Muehlebach Field. When he sold the club to the Yankees in 1937, that organization again segregated the park. Kling passed away in 1947 at age seventy-one, a millionaire.

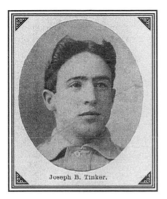

Joseph B. Tinker.

Joe Tinker played fifteen years in the big leagues, collecting 1,690 hits and stealing 336 bases. He hit in the clutch, batted .264 lifetime, and brought a sterling defense to the field. Tinker's mastery over Mathewson never faded. He hit .350 against the Giants legend over his career. In the winter of 1912/1913, when Johnny Evers replaced Frank Chance as manager, Tinker requested a trade. He became the player/manager of the Reds, the team finishing seventh, and Tinker batted .317. He later skippered the Chicago entry in the Federal League for two years and still later briefly took the helm of the Cubs. On Christmas day of 1923 Joe's wife Ruby, who suffered from depression, used a pistol to commit suicide. In 1938, the Cubs organization invited both Tinker and Evers to broadcast the Cubs World Series. After making and losing a fortune in Florida real estate, Joe Tinker spent his last years in poverty. His fourth wife left him not long after they married in 1942, and a series of illnesses took their toll, including the loss of his leg in 1947. He asked for and received financial help from old friend Johnny Kling during World War II. In the last year of Tinker's life he obtained public assistance from the State of Florida—thirty-eight dollars a month. Joe Tinker died on his sixty-eighth birthday in 1948.

Arthur Hofman.

Arthur "Circus Solly" Hofman played seven positions, often with distinction, but never pitched or caught. This master utility player stuck with the Cubs from 1904 to 1912, then came back for a reprise in his final season, 1916. Artie became the regular Cubs center fielder in 1909, and led the team with a .285 batting average. A good glove man, he also provided a consistent, steady bat, maintaining a career average of .271 with the Cubs.

Hofman starrred in the 1906 World Series, when he played every inning and hit .304. *Baseball Magazine* cracked that the lively Hofman was "serious only when he sleeps." Upon retirement from baseball Hofman opened a haberdashery in Chicago and ran a baseball clinic for youth on the site of the abandoned West Side Grounds. Later he became a high school baseball coach. Circus Solly died in St. Louis in 1956.

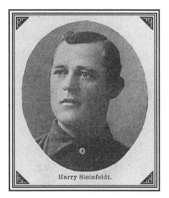

Harry Steinfeldt played third base as the best Cubs teams ever assembled won four pennants and two World Series from 1906-1910. Steiny earned a reputation as a great fielder, leading the league in fielding percentage for third-sackers in 1906 and 1907, finishing second in 1908 and 1909, and third in 1910. He led the Cubs in batting in 1906 with a .327 average, and in the '07 Series when he hit .471. An excellent run producer, in the decade from 1900-1909 Harry's RBI totals ranked eighth highest in the majors. After Harry went two for twenty in the 1910 Cubs-Athletics World Series, Chance traded the fading minstrel man to St. Paul in the American Association. When Harry got off to a good start in the 1911 season, St. Paul traded him to the Boston Nationals. Steinfeldt played nineteen games for the Boston club before he suffered a nervous breakdown. He tried yet another comeback with the Cardinals in 1912, but the Redbirds released him before the season started. Losing his job with the Cubs and falling out of the major leagues took a heavy toll on Steinfeldt. He lost his place in life. Unable to accept retirement at age thirty-four, he unsuccessfully attempted to hook on with minor league clubs in Louisville, Chattanooga, and Meridian. One commentator wrote that Steinfeldt "could not reconcile himself to Father Time's claim." He went home to Kentucky, climbed into bed, and died in 1914, only thirty-six years old.

Mordecai "Three Finger" Brown had a long and productive baseball career, winning 239 major league games with a magnificent career ERA of 2.06—the sixth best ever. His ERA of 1.04 in 1906 stands as the third best single-season ERA of all time. Brown won twenty or more games in each of the six seasons from 1906-1911. He threw fifty-seven shutouts in his career and won five World Series games. On twenty-four occasions he went up against the legendary Christy Mathewson, and

Mordecai Brown.

bettered Big Six in thirteen of them. There was no love lost between these two legendary hurlers, but Mathewson went out of his way to compliment his rival's agile fielding abilities, saying, "It is fatal to try and bunt against him." Brown's last game in the majors came in 1916, a staged and highly publicized match-up against Mathewson, then manager of the Reds. It was also Mathewson's final game, and both old war horses went the full nine in a sloppy donnybrook won by Cincinnati, 10-8. Brown later pitched in the minor leagues, ending his playing career with the Terre Haute Tots, sometimes called the "Hottentots," of the Three-I League in 1920. He and wife Sarah never had any children. For a long time the "Fingerless Phenom" worked for the Indiana Refining Company as a fire inspector, and later operated a successful Texaco gasoline station and adjacent parking lot in Terre Haute, Indiana, from 1935 to 1946. The Hall of Fame Veterans Committee voted Miner Brown into Cooperstown in 1949, one year after he died.

Carl L. Lundgren.

For Carl "The Human Icicle" Lundgren, 1907 was his last hurrah. He posted an 18-7 record with seven shutouts. He lost his fastball the next season, winning only six games, and the Cubs cut him early in 1909. Lundgren earned ninety-one victories in seven big league seasons, posting a 2.42 career ERA. Although a member of three Cubs World Series squads, he never appeared in a post-season game. His great second career as a college baseball coach included succeeding Branch Rickey at the University of Michigan and later piloting alma mater University of Illinois teams to many championships. Born in Marengo, Illinois, he died there when a heart attack struck him down at age fifty-three.

Johnny "The Crab" Evers, (he pronounced it "EE-vers" as in "beavers") so often a cantankerous, touchy bastard, also had a sweet, affectionate streak. In each of the Cubs team photos of 1906-1908, he is shown with his arm draped over the legs of two teammates, the only

Jno. J. Evers.

player in such a pose. A great base runner, he stole 324 bases in his career, including home plate six times in 1907 alone. A lifetime .270 hitter, he hit .341 in 1912. The Crab married in 1908, and soon was blessed with a daughter and a son. In 1910, his shoe store partner fled after gambling away their money. Evers suffered a nervous breakdown, which kept him out of action for most of the 1911 season. The Crab went through hell again in 1914. His three-year-old daughter, Helen, died of scarlet fever, and his wife left him, never to return. Nevertheless, he somehow managed to lead the Boston Braves to a World's Championship, winning the Chalmers Award as the National League's MVP, and hitting .438 in the Series as the Miracle Braves swept four straight from the A's. Evers later managed the Cubs and the White Sox. Johnny's post-baseball business pursuits did not succeed. He died from a cerebral hemorrhage at age sixty-five in 1947, six months after his election to the Hall of Fame.

Ed. M. Reulbach.

Edward Marvin "Big Ed" Reulbach won 185 games over a career that spanned from 1905 to 1917. His lifetime ERA of 2.28 is sixteenth best in the history of the game. He is the only major leaguer to ever pitch shutouts in both ends of a doubleheader, beating Brooklyn twice on a memorable September Saturday in 1908. Ed led the National League in winning percentage from 1906 to 1908, threw forty shutouts in his career, and hurled a one-hitter against the White Sox in the 1906 World Series. When he quit baseball he studied law at Columbia University and later became a businessman. Reulbach had to declare bankruptcy in 1931 after spending all of his savings to fight his son's terminal illness. A 1932 *Chicago Tribune* article described Big Ed as a "sad and lonely man." He died of a heart attack at age seventy-eight in 1961, on the same day as Ty Cobb.

Jimmy "Rabbit" Slagle spent ten years in the major leagues. Also known as "Shorty" and "The Human Mosquito," he peaked with the Cubs in 1902 with a .315 average and forty stolen bases. Renowned for

James F. Slagle.

his great throwing arm, he produced twenty-seven assists in 1905. With darting speed, the diminutive Cub stole 274 bases in his career. Proud of the six bases he stole in the 1907 Series, it proved to be the Rabbit's last moment in the spotlight. The Cubs dumped Slagle after the 1908 season, without allowing him a single at-bat in the '08 Series. He then caught on with the Baltimore Orioles, a minor league club in the Eastern League, for one last shot. Later, he and his wife ran a laundry on South Racine back in the Windy City. Slagle died in 1956 in Chicago, virtually forgotten by baseball. Somebody remembered Slagle in October 2007, when Worthville, Pennsylvania, Slagle's hometown, commemorated his career with a bronze plaque "dedicated to the memory of a country boy who made his mark on the world."

James T. Sheckard.

Jimmy Sheckard, one of the few Pennsylvania Dutch to play big league baseball, got more than two thousand hits in a seventeen-year major league career. His best years with the bat came with Brooklyn before he joined the Cubs, but he provided solid defense and clutch hitting for the West Siders. A magnificent outfielder, his 307 career assists ranks in the top ten all-time. His talent for drawing bases on balls set a record in 1911: 147 walks, a mark that stood until Eddie Stanky drew 148 passes in 1945. The low point of his career came in the 1906 World Series, when he went 0-21, never hitting the ball out of the infield. After baseball, Sheckard lost most of his money in the stock market crash of 1929. He worked in a series of menial jobs for the rest of his life. In 1947, while walking along a highway in Lancaster, Pennslyvania, on the way to his job as a gasoline station attendant, Sheckard was struck from behind by an automobile. Suffering fatal head injuries, he lingered for three days before he died. The city of Lancaster honored Sheckard with a monument in his memory in Buchanan Park.

Jack Pfiester's major league career lasted only nine years. Between 1903 and 1911 he started 128 games (123 with the Cubs), winning 70,

John Pfeister.

and losing 44. His 2.02 career ERA remains one of the lowest of all time. He deserved his nickname "Jack the Giant Killer" as the result of a 15-5 record against the New Yorkers. Arm trouble plagued him in 1910 and 1911, ending his career, although he tried a short-lived comeback in 1916 with Sioux City of the Western League. He died in 1953 of a blood ailment at his farm in Loveland, Ohio, leaving a widow and one son.

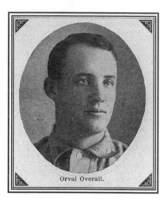
Orval Overall.

Orval "Jeff" Overall broke into the majors with the Reds in 1905 and lost twenty-three games. The next year he joined the Cubs, and with Kling's guidance and the solid Cubs defense behind him, he went 12-3 in 1906 and 23-7 in 1907. In a big league career spanning 1905 through 1913, he won 108 games with an ERA of 2.23. Big Jeff had a fine fastball and, after baseball, a good business sense. He became a banker, ultimately serving as the vice president and manager of the Fresno, California, branch of the Security Bank of Los Angeles. A heart attack killed him in 1947.

Jack "The Brakeman" Taylor recorded 187 consecutive complete games, a feat that will never be exceeded. He won 152 big league contests, and after the Cubs dropped him in the summer of 1907, he spent the next six years pitching for a string of minor league teams, including Columbus, Grand Rapids (for whom he tossed a no-hitter in 1909), Kansas City, Dayton, Evansville, and Chattanooga. He never made it back to the major leagues. When his playing days were over he worked as an ice deliveryman and a coal miner in Ohio. In 1917, Taylor ran into Miner Brown and Joe Tinker in Columbus, when Tinker was managing and Brown pitching for the Columbus Senators. Much to the relief of Three Finger Brown, former foes Taylor and Tinker embraced. Taylor died of cancer in Columbus in 1938, at age sixty-four.

Patrick J. Moran.

Pat Moran, the Cubs reserve catcher from 1906 to 1909, provided experienced back-up behind the plate. Somewhere along the line he acquired the moniker "Whiskey Face." In 1915 he became the manager of the Phillies, and after a series of trades and the implementation of new rules of discipline, Moran led them to the pennant in his first campaign. He repeated this success in his inaugural year at the helm of the Cincinnati Reds in 1919. The Reds proceeded to defeat the Chicago "Black Sox" in the World Series. He died of Bright's disease during spring training in 1924 in Orlando, Florida, only forty-eight years old. Johnny Evers, an old friend, visited Moran in his last days.

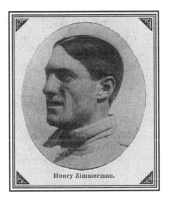

Henry Zimmerman.

Henry "Heinie" Zimmerman replaced Steinfeldt as the Cubs regular third baseman in 1912. Always a good hitter, the "Great Zim" stroked a league-leading .372 batting average that year. But his bizarre temperament affected his relationships with fellow players. In 1908 he got into an altercation with Jimmy Sheckard in the Cubs clubhouse. Zimmerman threw a bottle of ammonia at Sheckard during the brawl, which shattered on Sheckard's forehead, spilling it into Jimmy's eyes, almost blinding him. Chance and other Cubs then beat up Zim so badly that he had to be hospitalized. The Cubs traded Heinie to the Giants in 1916. John McGraw quietly drummed the Great Zim out of baseball in 1919 for trying to bribe several teammates to throw a game. Zimmerman became a plumber in New York City, and in 1929 Heinie partnered in a speakeasy with mobster and bootlegger Dutch Schultz. Six years later the government named Heinie as an unindicted co-conspirator in a tax evasion prosecution of Schultz, but the criminal case against Schultz ended with his gangland execution in a Newark restaurant. Zimmerman resumed his work as a tradesman, employed as a steamfitter for a construction company. He outlived all of his Cubs teammates (save Kid Durbin), dying of cancer in 1969.

Harry "Doc" Gessler played minor league ball after leaving the Cubs in 1907. But in 1908 he starred as the regular Red Sox right fielder, hitting a sparkling .308 and sporting the best on-base percentage in the American League. Gessler befriended a rookie on that Red Sox club by the name of Tris Speaker. His big league career ended with the Washington Senators in 1911, lolling in the outfield while Walter Johnson mowed down batters. Gessler, who batted lefty and threw righty, hit .280 in 880 major league games, capping his baseball career with a brief stint—eleven games—managing the Pittsburgh club in the Federal League in 1914. Physician Gessler died in the town where he was born, Greensburg, Pennsylvania, on Christmas Eve 1924, at age forty-four.

Mike Kahoe finished out his playing career with the Washington American League team in 1909, and then went to work for them as a scout. A weak hitter, Kahoe managed only a .212 batting average in his 410-game major league career. But he provided a solid defense as a receiver. In February 1909 Kahoe was fined $200 ($150 of which was suspended) for what the *Chicago Tribune* described as "playing against a Chicago outlaw team." Kahoe died in Akron, Ohio, at age seventy-five in 1949.

William "Billy" Sweeney played major league ball from 1907 through 1914. Three games with the Cubs in 1907, and 134 games with them in 1914, bracketed a career spent with the Boston Nationals. Playing mainly second or third base, he hit a respectable .272 and provided solid defense. He turned some heads in 1912, hitting .344 with one hundred RBI. The Kentucky native died at age sixty-two in Cambridge, Massachusetts, in 1948.

Charles Fraser.

Charles "Chick" Fraser contributed eight victories to the Cubs world championship in 1907, and another eleven to their repeat performance in 1908, before ending his big league career that year at age thirty-seven. While he won twenty games twice, he walked more batters than he struck out and still holds the record for the most hit batsmen in a career. Fraser pitched a no-hitter in 1903 against the Cubs. After leaving the major leagues, he pitched in the independent leagues for Los Angeles and Chicago and managed minor league ballclubs in Decatur and Pittsfield. From 1914 forward he earned a living as a scout for the Pirates, the Dodgers, and the Yankees. He died in Chicago in 1940.

Newton "Newt" Randall saw action in twenty-two games for the Cubs in 1907 before being traded to the Boston Doves with Billy Sweeney. The Canadian Randall did not shine with Boston, hitting only .213 in 258 at bats. After 1907 Randall never again played at the major league level, but he starred for the Milwaukee Brewers in the American Association. A minor league team, the Brewers bordered on big league quality, and Randall sparked them to two league championships in 1913 and 1914. In the latter year, the thirty-four-year-old hit .321 and stole a team-high twenty-nine bases. He died in Minnesota in 1955, age seventy-five.

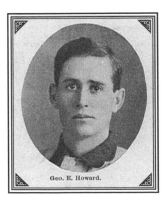

Geo. E. Howard.

George "Del" Howard, the Illinois native who joined the Cubs mid-stream in 1907, only played in the major leagues from 1905 to 1909. History-buff Howard covered outfield and first base for the Cubs on a spot basis for a few years after 1907 and then his baseball career ended. Born on Christmas Eve 1877, he died on Christmas Eve 1956.

Blaine A. Durbin.

Blaine "Kid" Durbin never pitched another inning in a major league game after the 1907 season, his arm going bad during the Practice Season of '08. He stuck with the Cubs during that year as a reserve outfielder, and spent much of the 1909 season with the Reds and Pirates. At the time of the publication of this book, he uses the name "Durbin Blaine." Residing in a small town in southern Indiana, he looks a lot younger than his 121 years. Mr. Blaine's last will and testament stipulates that if he ever does pass away, his resting place shall be marked with a new tombstone inscribed, "The good don't always die young."

The Cubs *averaged* 106 victories a year between 1906 and 1910. The team won 322 games from 1906 to 1908, more victories than any other team in history over a three-year span. Warren Brown, a Chicago sportswriter elected to the Hall of Fame in 1974, wrote that the Cubs of this period "will be recalled as long as baseball is played." But fame is a fleeting phenomenon. The 1907 Cubs team is now seldom acknowledged. Were it not for the renowned poem trumpeting the great trio of Tinker to Evers to Chance, or the memorable Three Finger Brown, it is doubtful that anyone but a baseball scholar would remember this remarkable team. Yet this club, built around speed, defense, and cunning, plus pitching, pitching, and more pitching, deserves to be remembered as The Best Team Ever.

THE END

Acknowledgements

Alan Alop wishes to acknowledge the help of many people in putting this book together. First, he is very indebted to the research and comments of his son, Jim Alop. He also wishes to thank David Shiner for his early edits and Wally Winter for his encouragement. John Peldyak, Barry Levinsky and Bill Wilen provided thoughtful comments, and Roger and Sharon Marth provided inspiration. Colleen Alop's constant support enabled the project to go forward. Last but not least, heartfelt thanks go to my co-author, Dr. David Noel, for a great collaboration.

Doc Noel acknowledges Ace (Alan) Alop, Susan Fournier, Roger and Sharon Marth, Barry Levinsky and Miriam Frank, Gary Johnson of the Chicago History Museum, Joe Holtz at Copy Central, John and Norma Peldyak, Joyce Griffith of Griffith Publishing, Paul Peldyak and Phyllis Wolf, Second Ward Alderman Robert Fioretti, David Gerholdt of The Holly Press, Dr. Charles Steinberg, Brian Degan, Karyn Evens, Renee Dulkin, Jack Rosenberg, Bob Pierson, Matt Stickney, Hunter and Audie Black, The Ananda Community, Ira Parker and Donna Katan, Inee Foreman, The Ho Ho Kams, The Chicago Cubs, everyone who helped at Mill City Press including Mark, Anna, Jenni, Chelsea and Rosey, and The Noels—Mary, Andrew, Adam and Allison Dawn.